I0688759

Free Time

More by Brooke Shaffer

The Timekeeper Chronicles

The Chivalrous Welshman
Time to Kill
Tick Tock
Windup
Stopwatch
Free Time
Leap Second (Summer 2021)

The Hands of Time
In the Hands of the Enemy (Fall 2020)

The Lone Wolf
Wolf Pack (Spring 2021)

Singles
Of Saints and Sinners

Free Time
Book Five of The Chivalrous Welshman
The Timekeeper Chronicles

Brooke Shaffer

Black Bear Publishing

Copyright © 2020 by Brooke Shaffer

All rights reserved. No portion of this book may be reproduced, stored in a retrieval system, or transmitted in any form by any means—electronic, mechanical, photocopy, recording, scanning, or other—except for brief quotations in critical reviews or articles, without the prior written consent of the publisher.

Published in Michigan by Black Bear Publishing.

This novel is a work of fiction. Names, characters, places, and incidents are either products of the author's imagination or used fictitiously. All characters are fictional, and any similarity to persons living or dead is purely coincidental.

ISBN:
Hardcover: 978-1-7336954-6-6
Softcover: 978-1-7336954-8-0
eBook: 978-1-7336954-7-3

Mzinhigan ndizhbiigetawaan Gneejawnisananik miinawaa
Tyvin kumá'ii káru
DℐSW ℒ WⱭℭ℧ ℎℴℽℰℑ.
Akututa tla lahiya tsihnte'i.

O h, good, you're here," Lisa sighed as Walter walked in the door of the emergency room.

"Did you think I wouldn't come?" Walter demanded testily. "Where is Tommen?"

"He's right this way."

Walter had been on duty when he got the call that Tommen had been taken to the hospital after a fight at school. Although, according to the principal and the teacher, it had been less of a fight and more of a gang beating.

Tommen had been made fun of and bullied since his first day of school. If it wasn't because of his accent and poor English, it was because of his low grades because of his poor English. Tommen was a bright kid and quick to learn when given his own time and space, but he still struggled to keep up in the streamlined academic world. He was in third grade, where the ages of the students ranged from nine to eleven. They shouldn't be beating up on each other like a bunch of street thugs.

But Walter knew which one of them had done it. Even at twelve years old, Tyler Freeman was a hateful son of a neo-Nazi, and he was always bragging about his black belts and state titles. Walter had no cause to doubt his claims as he'd been the primary bully over Tommen this year. It had started out just as menacing looks and threatening body language. When Tyler figured out just how poor Tommen's English was, it escalated into any number of profane insults.

The actual physical bullying hadn't started until a couple

weeks ago. A push, a shove, an "unintentional" trip. Tyler had been sent to the principal's office for a good scolding, given detention a couple times, threatened with suspension. Apparently it had little effect on the nasty little boy, or else Walter would not be walking through the emergency room now.

"He suffered a moderate concussion, broken nose, fractured cheekbones, and he lost a couple teeth. He also has broken ribs and a broken arm," Lisa was saying. "And he's pretty bruised otherwise. I don't think even the car did as bad a damage."

Walter let out a breath. "That's what I'm afraid of. Thanks, Lisa."

He opened the door and went in the room. She was right; he hadn't looked this bad even when he'd been hit by a car. There was no normal-colored skin left on his face. Everything was black, blue, yellow, red, and his left eye was swollen almost shut. He looked over when Walter walked in. He burst into tears as Walter gently tried to hug him.

"I'm sorry, Dad," he bawled. "I didn't mean to."

"No, no," Walter whispered. "It's not your fault."

"*Pam ydy nhw fy casau i yn fawr?*" (Why do they hate me so much?)

"Why do they hate you so much?" Walter sighed. "I don't know."

There were any number of reasons, not the least of which being that whole neo-Nazism thing, but what caused that kind of hateful ideology?

"I don't know," he repeated.

"*Gwnes i gerddio i ffwrdd a dim cwffas, ond talwn nhw ddim fy adawaf.*" (I tried to walk away and not fight, but they wouldn't let me.)

"I know. You tried to do the right thing, and it doesn't always work out."

Tommen sniffed hard and whimpered at the pain. "I want to hurt him."

"I know." *So do I.* "For right now, though, you just rest and get better. When you get out of here, then I'll try to teach you a few things, okay?"

Tommen nodded uncertainly. "Like police things?"

"No. Like Timekeeper things."

Chapter One
Summer Vacation

Tommen woke to a pounding headache, feeling like he hadn't slept at all. After a minute, he figured out that the pounding was actually his alarm going off. He rolled over and fumbled for a minute or two until he found the button to switch it off. Even when it was no longer screaming at him, he still didn't get up right away, instead rolling onto his back and staring up at the ceiling. It was the first week of June, and with the days getting longer, even with the mountains in the way, he still had pretty good natural light coming in through the window.

He couldn't recall any specifics of his dreams, only that they'd been equal parts terrifying and confusing. Maybe it was another nightmare about the warehouse, when he'd been kidnapped by the psycho mass-murderer Rifun Ndolo and been forced to watch his father (almost) die. Maybe it was some awful recount of his journey to a distant world in order to find one little miracle cure that would bring his dad back to life. Somewhere in there, he thought he remembered something about his godawful review, going before the Hands of Time in order to advance from probationary to Apprentice Timekeeper. He'd endured it, but for little gain as Rifun had, not two weeks later, launched a coup that resulted in the deaths of countless Time Agents from all parts of the universe, and enslaving countless more. His dad and one of his friends had been among those captured. They, too, would have been murdered if not for Micaiah's quick thinking and risk taking. After all, they'd been sentenced to death; what was the worst that could be done to them? Other than that whole clock-breaking deal, stripping them of their ability to even perceive Time.

Groaning, Tommen rolled over again, burying his face in his pillow, building a Fast Band in order to buy himself more time to wake up and get motivated for the day. Throughout the whole series of whatever dreams he'd had, he was fairly certain that there had been a white rabbit involved somehow. Or maybe it was some other kind of rabbit. Or some other kind of white animal. Now that he was awake, he really couldn't be sure.

After a minute or two of dreary contemplation, Tommen pulled himself out of bed and moseyed his way to the bathroom, dropping his Band as he did so. Some things didn't Band well: electronics, fire, air, water to an extent. So he still had to shower, keeping in mind that he couldn't just take all the sweet time he wanted. He could do that after he got out, which he did, taking his own sweet time to brush his teeth and shave. Since his man's beard had finally come in, he actually had to shave every day now.

His dad was already up and off to work. Glancing at the clock, he would have been at work about an hour and a half already. Used to be that he might not get home until eight or nine o'clock, but since the city started cutting budgets and micromanaging the police department, he was starting to get home around two or three, four at the latest.

Not that it mattered a whole lot, Tommen thought, grabbing some leftover pizza to toss in the microwave. He himself still had to work. Working at a bakery wasn't much to write home about, but being the manager of the bakery was. He'd been promoted after one of his bosses—Micaiah, the elder twin—had lost his leg escaping the Wheel and took some time off to deal with it. Micah couldn't run the store by himself, so Tommen got his promotion. Even after Micaiah had come back, he was still the manager.

Of course, he wasn't working today or tomorrow because of final exams. Two days ago, Wednesday, he'd taken his AP Physics exam. Yesterday had been his Law and Geometry exams. Today was History and Mechanical Drafting. After that, he was home free for the rest of the summer, sophomore no longer. He would still be working, true, but he would have more time to himself, more time to do what he wanted which included spending more time with his girlfriend Becky.

Oh, but that was for later. He still had to get through today. At least with it being the end of the school year, he didn't have to worry about packing his backpack and lugging it around with him; the most he would need were his pencils and a calculator. And, because it was the last day with only two exams, he didn't even need to pack a lunch because they would be getting out around lunchtime anyway. It was a win-win all around.

Except for that part where he had to get up early to open the store tomorrow. But at least with no having to work today, he would be able to get to bed on time. Considering he'd gotten almost no good sleep the night before, he should sleep good tonight. He rubbed his eyes, leaned on the counter, and yawned. But he still had to get through today.

He knew why he hadn't slept well, but that didn't mean he had to like it. Last weekend, Micaiah had led a revolt against Rifun and successfully ousted him. After some scrambling and deliberation, the remaining Time Agents in the universe had gotten together to elect a new Council of Hands, among other positions within the Time industry and the Wheel of Time. Last night had been the new inauguration. It had gone well this time, with no surprise coups or mass murders. The new Hands were ushered in, and everyone went their merry way.

Well, except Tommen. He'd gone off to investigate the new Coliseum—or the Amphitheater as he called it now—only to be cornered by Rifun. Except Rifun didn't look like Rifun; he'd worn a Disguise in order to walk right into the inauguration without being recognized. In any case, he threatened Tommen and reminded him of a deal they'd struck—well, Rifun forced him into it under duress—which he claimed Tommen still had to make good on. Given the power he wielded, Tommen wasn't able to just walk away from it by sheer willpower. So, to some extent, he was going to have to make good on his end of the bargain.

It wasn't a bad bargain, actually. He just had to attend some mystical trainings hosted by Rifun. But, Tommen thought that if he could get close enough, maybe he could finally murder the bastard and put an end to all the trouble. It might take more than one "training" to get that close, but as long as he kept his head on straight and didn't allow himself to get sucked into some cultish whackjob ideology, he would be okay. He'd even let his dad and the twins know about everything that transpired. They would know what he was doing, and they would help in any way they could, the twins especially.

Tommen still wasn't sold on this whole "Akari" business, but he always professed to be a "see it to believe it" kind of person, and, boy, had he seen some shit lately. He'd seen people don a Disguise that made them look and talk just like him and his dad; he'd seen the entire inside of the Wheel redecorated by just one man and turned into 1600's London; he'd seen—well, heard about—portals exploding from the inside out and completely sealing the Wheel off from the rest of the universe. And he was sure there was more that he hadn't seen, or hadn't seen yet. It was a little unnerving, especially when he considered his paltry parlor tricks. Being able to Band Time and make it go fast or slow suddenly didn't feel like such an awesome superpower.

But it still helped get him through his days, especially since the Suppression had been lifted and he could use Time again. Having to suffer through six months of school without the ability to Band...he wasn't even sure how he did it, managing to balance school and work and the school play and a girlfriend and homework. How did normal people do it? So, while he did have a distinct advantage over other students, he had a lot of respect—okay, a little more respect than he previously had—for those students who had similar obligations and no Time to help them out. Becky was one of those students, and not only had a job, but she owned her own business, so her load was even greater most days.

He yawned as he went out to the end of the driveway to wait for the bus. Fuck, but he still had to get through today. It was too bad he couldn't Band while unconscious, otherwise he would have just taken more time to sleep. As it was, he was just going to have to slog through his day and hope it ended quickly.

Becky was on the bus already, one of the rare people able to read a book in a moving vehicle. He collapsed beside her and tried to relax without going to sleep.

"You stay up all night or what?" she wondered, looking up at him. She was a dwarf, so she looked up at everyone. She was also a conniving little spitfire who could make anyone tremble and fall before her if she wanted to.

"No," Tommen replied lamely, fighting a yawn. "Just didn't sleep good."

"Sleep well."

"What?"

"Sorry, I have an English exam today. Trying to make sure I get everything right."

"Uh-huh."

"And I have a pre-Calc exam. What about you? What are your exams?"

"History and Mechanical Drafting."

"Well, the first one shouldn't be too difficult, right?"

"I'm not sure how I feel about your apparent lack of faith in me for my Mech. Draft exam."

"You're the one falling asleep. Knowledge can't speak if it isn't awake."

Problem was, she was right. He was so fucking exhausted. He was glad that his AP exam had already come and gone or he never would have made it. He couldn't even say why his sleep had been so terrible. Yeah, so he had bad dreams every so often, but why did it affect him so much today? Was it just because he'd only gotten maybe five or six hours instead of eight or nine?

Tommen figured he must have fallen asleep at some point, because the next thing he knew, Becky was shaking him awake and telling him to move it or lose it. Yawning, he stood and made his way into the aisle, halting traffic so Becky could get out ahead of him. Once they got in the school, he mussed her hair and went to his locker. She'd been pissed at him the first time he'd done that, but she had since come to accept it as a gesture of endearment of sorts.

Had he been any more tired, he might have passed right on by without noticing, but maybe he was just alert or something caught his attention, because as he headed for his locker, he walked by the hall of all the senior lockers, and saw Eric.

Eric used to be one of his best friends. Then he'd been accused of raping one of his classmates, which prompted him to move to all online classes for the remainder of the year. A short time later, he and Varad, another best friend who had since moved away, had been kidnapped by Rifun and exposed to Time. Now he knew that there was a much bigger universe than what the eye could see. He also knew that Tommen had been holding out on him. The circumstances of his exposure certainly didn't help, and he and Tommen hadn't really spoken since the beginning of the year. The only comfort Tommen got was that they were still friends online and occasionally chatted back and forth.

"Hey," Tommen said cautiously, turning and approaching slowly. "What are you doing here?"

Eric gave him a neutral regard. "Cleaning out my locker. Figured I better do it today since most of the seniors are excused from their last exams."

"Yeah, graduation is Sunday, isn't it?"

"Yup."

"How have you been doing?"

"All right. I mean, still working my ass off. I'm leaving two weeks from Monday to go to college."

"During the summer?"

"Yeah. Heading out to California. There's a course that meets during the summer. It's kind of like a night class. A little more expensive, but with the scheduling, there are more credit hours so I can get my degree faster."

"Oh." Tommen grinned. "Registered Dietitian?"

Even Eric managed a small smile and shook his head. "No. Professional chef."

"So, what's the class?"

"It's the restaurant that's owned by the school and run by the students. Like on-the-job training, except I pay for it the first time around. Then I go through regular college courses in the fall, winter, and spring semesters, and then next summer they'll be paying me to work there like a normal restaurant gig."

"Sounds like a great fit for you."

"It is." Eric closed his locker and tied off the trash bag. "So, what are you up to? I see your dad pulled through."

"Oh, yeah. He did."

"Did you have something to do with it?"

"A little."

"You're not going to say anything about it, are you?"

"Last time we spoke, you didn't want to hear anything about it. You just wanted to be able to control it and move on."

Eric shrugged. "Yeah. But I guess that since I've had time to think about it and process it a little more, and play around with what I can do, I might be a little more open to discussion. Not that I want to do what you do, but it's not so weird anymore, I think."

"Well, there's a lot that's been going on. Cassius is dead, but Rifun got away again."

"Again?"

"Long story. If you really want to hear about it, text me or hit me up online."

"Maybe I will."

Tommen sighed. "Have you heard from Varad at all?" Varad had not been quite so accepting of his new Banding abilities. He'd blocked Tommen on every front both online and off, so he had no clue what he was up to.

"Living the dream, apparently," Eric answered. "He wasn't too keen on the farming bit, but I guess his father is really supportive of him collecting all the local stories and traditions. As long as he's out doing that, he can get away from the farm. Guess he's really well-known in the local Hindu temples, too."

"By the priests or the prostitutes?"

Eric laughed. "Probably both." He let out a breath. "You know, I wish we could go back to a time before we found that body on the soccer fields. I mean, we just wanted to drink a little, smoke a little, get laid." He made a noise then that was something between a laugh, a cry, and a scoff. "Just...stupid teenagers doing stupid things." He shook his head. "But I guess it's too late for any apologies now." He hoisted the trash bag and started walking. "Maybe I'll hit you up online like you said. Don't weird me out or anything, just try to tell me what happened without sounding like a lunatic."

"I make no promises," Tommen told him honestly.

It was not lost on Tommen that Eric didn't invite him to his graduation party, even though the three of them, when they'd been best friends, had all promised to invite each other. At the same time, Varad was half a world away anyway, and Tommen counted himself lucky that Eric was willing to even speak to him at all after six months of silence. Maybe their friendship could be salvaged.

He headed to his locker, but really couldn't figure out why. He'd already cleaned it out, and he didn't have anything to put in it, not even a coat.

Tommen was just getting ready to close the door when suddenly his face met the back wall. His reflexive Banding was still sub-par in his opinion, and he felt every inch of the cold steel. After a second of dazed confusion, he straightened, and who should he find but Tyler Freeman.

"Happy last day of school," he sneered, folding his meaty arms and leaning against a locker a few down from Tommen's.

"What are you doing here?" Tommen wondered, suppressing

every urge to Band and beat him bloody. "Seniors are excused from exams and you got expelled."

"Seniors are, but sophomores still have to take them."

For a second, Tommen thought he meant it as a stalking confession. Then he remembered that Ricky, Tyler's younger brother, was also a sophomore. Tyler went on, "Brought my little bro in and then I thought, 'Gee. This is the last time I'm going to see this place. Maybe I'll take a walk through the halls one last time.' And who should I run into but my old buddy Tommen?"

Tommen shook his head and grinned. "With friends like you, who needs enemies?"

Then Tyler got a familiar sneer on his face, and he took a step closer. "As I said, it's the last day of school. What's Layman going to do? Expel me again?"

Tommen shrugged. "It's the last day of school. Either you're just blowing hot air, or else this is the only time we're going to fight. Why don't we see what Layman will do?"

For a good ten seconds, Tommen's blood pressure was through the roof even as his heart leapt into his throat and his stomach twisted. He was almost sure that Tyler was going to take a swing at him, or try to outright grab and throw him. At the last moment, Tyler seemed to recall Layman's threat of having him taken out in handcuffs, and he backed down. In the same way a lion might back down from a challenge. It wasn't a surrender; it was a promise to come back later. When they weren't in school with Layman around to intervene.

His demeanor was as much a threat as any spoken word, but Tyler still walked away, down the hall, disappearing out the door. Tommen let out a breath and leaned back against his locker, feeling dizzy. That could have ended very badly. He'd taken a gamble, and it had paid off, but just barely.

More to the point, today was already starting out weird. Just going by past experience, weird days never ended well. They usually ended in near-drownings, beatings, kidnappings, shootouts, cryptic messages, perilous journeys, military coups, and all manner of unpleasant and dangerous things. Given that not just one, but two weird things had happened back-to-back in the last ten minutes, Tommen had no desire to find out what terrible things awaited in his near future.

"Hey, are you okay?"

He looked down at Becky. "Huh?"

"You look like you've seen a ghost. And about ready to drop dead from exhaustion, but mostly the ghost part."

"It's nothing." He rubbed his face, trying to wake himself up. "Just ready to be done and out of here so I can go home and take a nap."

"All right. Well, if you're awake enough to comprehend what I'm saying, I was thinking..."

This could be his awful thing destined to happen right here. Still, he sighed and asked, "What?"

"Why don't we go to dinner tonight, after you've gotten your nap and are a little more lively? Or we can go to lunch right after, if you're not working."

Oh. Okay, so dinner with his girlfriend wasn't a bad thing. Yet. "Yeah, sounds good. Um, why don't we make it dinner? I don't know if I'm going to survive until lunch. Where did you have in mind?"

She told him, and he agreed. She finished with, "I'll even let you buy, if you want."

She'd said this on a couple different occasions when they went out places. Normally she bought her own food, her own tickets, whatever. He wasn't sure about her motives when she told him that he could buy if he wanted, but he dutifully picked up the tab on such occasions.

"Cool. I'll let my mom know."

"Okay."

"I'm going to head to my exam a little early. I'll see you later."

He watched her go. Despite his fatigue, Tommen managed to muster up enough motivation to mentally kick himself. He had to get his license. He would spend his summer looking for a car, then take his test in August. He had no other choice; he couldn't keep riding in the van with his girlfriend's mom. It was embarrassing, both as the boyfriend and as a man. It was time for him to grow up, get his act together, and start doing some real shit.

The bell rang, and he headed off to his first exam.

Mr. Morris was the only teacher he'd had for all three semesters, all different classes. He knew how his exams worked, and he'd kind of picked up on a pattern of the material Morris was likely to put on the exam. Now it was just a matter of sitting through his speech about how to take the exam, don't cheat, what to do when done, and so on. It was dull, and Tommen was tired enough as it was. Somehow he managed to stay awake through it and grudgingly accepted his packet of horrors as it got passed back.

The good news was that he was almost done with his social studies classes; the only one he had left was Government which he would take next year. Of course, next year his schedule was going to be composed entirely of required classes so that when he got to his senior year and dual-enrolled, he wouldn't be crunched for credits.

At some point during the exam, his brain came back to life, at least a little bit. Maybe it had to do with having to pay attention to the questions and arrange events chronologically. That was one nice thing about history, he thought, it always happened the same way, and in the same order. No matter what version of history you read, the American Revolution always came before the Civil War, and World War I always came before World War II. Go figure.

All the same, it could be tough to remember which battles happened when. Sometimes he wondered if the soldiers themselves could even keep it straight in their minds. Maybe the soldiers from the Civil War, when they had to march everywhere. These days, when you could be anywhere in the world in a matter of hours or maybe a day, war and conflict could be damn near continuous. Not a few times, Tommen walked past the military recruiters when they visited the school and wondered how much combat a twenty-five year old today would have seen compared to a twenty-five year old from the Revolution. And they still thought it was a good idea to fuck with the brain of an eighteen year old and mess him up for the rest of his life? No, thank you. His eighteenth birthday was only a little over a year away and he would spend it at home with his family, not in some godforsaken desert, thank you.

Tommen didn't know his actual birthday, but it was listed on his birth certificate as August 12th, the same day he arrived in the twenty-first century.

He finished his exam early, but sat for probably fifteen minutes before getting up and turning it in. He hated being the first one done. Not only did it attract attention to himself, but it made him doubt his work. Had he gone through and read too quickly? What if he'd missed something? What if it was something stupid? What if he'd picked the Spanish-American War instead of the Civil War? What if he'd mixed up Ulysses S. Grant and Robert E. Lee?

Well, there was nothing he could do about it now. Well, yes, actually there was. He could Band, go up, look in the teacher's answer key, and change his answers. Or he could just go back and give his test a second look. But he didn't. He just moseyed his way back to his seat. And sat. And waited. No phones were allowed on exam day. Since the Internet didn't Band well, his options were limited anyway.

Maybe he should have just waited until the very end of class to turn in his test. At least then he would have had a little reading material to keep him occupied. Maybe he should Band and go down to the library to pick something out quick.

He elected for a different option completely: napping. It came easily enough once he put his head down. He wasn't sure how long he napped, only that it wasn't long enough. But someone shook him awake, and he sleepily marched out of the room with the rest of them.

The time between exams was a little longer than the time between normal classes, enough to get a snack, chit chat a little, and "wiggle out the stress bugs" as Reisig had once said. Tommen did not see Becky during that time, but that was almost to be expected. She put as much stock in her grades as he didn't (except where it really mattered, like science).

So he trudged to Mechanical Drafting, telling himself that in less than two hours, he would be home free to spend the summer how he pleased, and hoping it was true. He had no illusions; the universe would demand payback for the weird and good things that had happened so far in the day.

Mechanical Drafting had its exam in two parts. Part one had been a final project that they'd been working on for the last week or so. The concept and design was completely up to them as long as it demonstrated things they'd learned in the class. Today was the day for the paper exam.

There weren't too many students in the class, an oddity since it counted as an alternative math credit, and there were even fewer today because most of the students were seniors. But it gave Tommen some breathing room as he found a spot at one of the large work tables and waited for Mr. Zak to hand out the tests.

Tommen had loathed the thought of Mechanical Drafting when he'd first seen it on his third semester schedule. Not only was it another course almost exclusive to seniors, but it was a math course. Sure, it was more of the algebraic math that he was good at, but he was already taking Geometry. Did he really have to do both at the same time? Once they'd gotten started, gotten going, he'd warmed up to it. There was a shit ton of math, true, but it was applied math. They could work on a concept, read about it, see the math behind it, but then they could experiment with it.

Not that it made him all that confident about the exam. It was still a course almost entirely exclusive to seniors, which meant that Tommen was working on formula memorization rather than application. He hadn't gotten around to Algebra II or pre-Calc or any of that. He was still working with the whole, not the pieces, and it was harder to manipulate a whole.

But he trudged through it like a good little student, working out the math and trying to apply it to the current story problem. Less than an hour now. What was the first thing he wanted to do when he got home? Nap. Definitely needed a nap. Okay, what about after that? Well, he was having dinner with Becky. And after that? He'd probably go to bed, and he had to open the bakery tomorrow. If he remembered right, they had him working a double to make up for the hours he was losing during exam week. Fucking hell, when was his summer vacation going to start vacationing?

"When you guys are done, you are free to leave if you are driving or getting picked up," Mr. Zak said as he collected the first test. "If you ride the bus, stay here."

Damn. He had to get his license. No more excuses or uncertainties; he needed his fucking license.

At the same time, it was a nice day out, and he was having dinner with Becky, not lunch. He could always just walk home. The fresh air might do him some good. And, if he Banded, he could get home mere minutes after he left the school, which would add time to his nap. Yes, that sounded like a very good idea.

He finished up his exam, took a minute to double-check his work, then stood and took his test up to the teacher. Mr. Zak gave it a quick once-over, then nodded. "You ride the bus, don't you?"

"Well, normally, yeah, but if I can leave early, I can walk home. It's not far."

"Don't let me hear you in the halls. Have a nice summer."

Tommen grinned and left the room. He was done. That was it. Home free for the summer. That meant he could have his music loud when his dad wasn't home, he could stay up until midnight and sleep in until noon. Well, except for those days when he had to be up early for work. But hey, summer break and being out of school had to count for something, right? No sitting through dull lectures, no homework, but most importantly, no Tyler Freeman or Mr. Layman. Even better, Tyler Freeman was now officially graduated and gone. Even if he did drop his brother off every morning and pick him up every afternoon, Tommen wouldn't have to watch out for him every time he roamed the halls. He wouldn't have to cringe in fear at lunchtime. He might even be able to have a conversation with Becky without worrying that Tyler was going to sneak up behind him and deck him.

Holy hell, but he was feeling good, almost good enough to bust out his Michael Jackson impression right there on the sidewalk. But...maybe later. He wasn't feeling that good. He was still tired, and he had to make it home yet. Maybe he would do it later to make Becky laugh. Hey, he only said it was an impression; he never said it was a good one. Still, he felt pretty light on his feet as he walked home.

As expected, the house was empty when he arrived. His dad wouldn't be off until two at the earliest, so he had about three hours to himself. He went to one of the cabinet drawers and pulled out a pen and sticky note.

" 'Exhausted. Napping. Please wake at 4' " he wrote, tearing the note off the pad and sticking it to the door that led to the garage. Hopefully his dad would see it.

His body seemed to understand what was going on, as every step he took to his room, his whole body felt like it got heavier and heavier, slogging through tar as it shut down before making it to the bed. Tommen pressed on, rubbing his eyes and shaking his head. He stopped once at the bathroom for a glass of water, then dragged himself into his bedroom, onto his bed, and he was out.

And, really, he seemed to be out. Outside, that is. He found himself in a forest. Looking around, it was mostly white pine, the sterile forests planted decades ago for loggers to harvest when they were ready. This one was in some kind of regrowth stage as ferns, bushes, and young maple saplings pushed their way through the thick pine needles toward the sunlight. Overhead, the sky was cloudy, and not in a friendly way; there was rain coming, he was sure of it.

A bush rustled. Tommen jumped as he tried to pinpoint the sound and assess for any threats. He didn't see anything, so it wasn't likely to be anything big like a bear or a mountain lion. Still, he couldn't seem to locate the source. Tommen closed his eyes, listened, tried to recall the things his pa taught him about tracking and hunting. *If an animal is making that much noise, it's either feeding or fleeing.* Or fucking, Tommen added silently. *Either way, you have to be patient. If it's feeding, it's distracted, which makes it prime for hunting. If it's fleeing, you might want to start running, too.*

The bush stopped rustling. He opened his eyes.

"You again?" he found himself saying.

It was the white rabbit. He knew he'd dreamed of it before. Once was just like any other dream. Twice was generally okay, too. Three or more times, something was fucked. Probably him.

"Yes," the white rabbit answered, sitting up on its hind legs. "Me. Again. You're catching on."

"What?" Tommen shook his head. "No. This is too weird. This has been such a strange fucking day. Get me the fuck out of here before some shit happens."

"It's too late for that. Things are already in motion. You must be prepared for them." The rabbit got down on all fours. "Follow me."

"Why?"

The rabbit turned to look at him. "When we first met, you followed without question. Why hesitate now?"

"Because the first time, I thought it was just a stupid dream. This is fucked up."

"Because you do not believe in God or Fate or anything of the sort."

"Exactly. Well, no, not really. I mean..."

"Then what do you have to fear?"

That I could be wrong. Tommen swallowed. "Um. Right. Okay. Lead the way, I guess."

He followed the rabbit, down the long rows of sterile forest until they emerged into real forest, where rocks and earth and trees and plant life all mixed together as one. The rabbit kept going, but it got harder and harder to follow it in the dense undergrowth.

They came to a clearing, moving as steadily as they had. There was maybe ten feet between Tommen and the white rabbit. The rabbit disappeared again into the undergrowth. Tommen was just about to go after it, when there was another voice.

"Welcome, Tommen."

He stopped and looked around. He heard rustling bushes, but the wind overhead made the source difficult to track. Then he turned around and found himself staring at an enormous wolf. Not just any wolf, though, but a white wolf. Because of course.

"The white rabbit—"

"Brought you to me," the wolf finished.

"Why?"

"Because you and I must speak."

"Okay. Well, I'm here."

"Yes, but we cannot speak here. You must search me out."

"But you're right here. Why can't we talk here?"

"It is unsafe. Not all who tread these lands are friends."

"What are these lands?"

"Call them what you will. The Dream Lands, another dimension, a figment of your imagination."

"Okay..." Where the hell had his mind come up with this dream? "How do I know you're a friend?"

"If I was not a friend, I would simply devour you. As the one who hunts you tried to do."

"You're talking about Rifun?"

The wolf took a step back and almost seemed to bow. "As I said, we cannot speak here. You must search me out."

Tommen rolled his eyes. "Okay, fine. Where do I find you?"

"Follow me."

Then the wolf turned and bolted into the undergrowth. Tommen, more accustomed to the easy pace of the rabbit, was caught off-guard and had to sprint to catch up, or at least get within sight of the wolf and its big bushy tail slapping through the bushes and ferns. Either the wolf started slowing down, or he started speeding up, because the gap between them closed until he was almost on the wolf's tail.

As they ran, the wolf started doing something strange. At first, Tommen couldn't identify it. Nevertheless, he slowed a step or two so neither one of them would get hurt. Then he saw the wolf's pelt turn yellow, then red. Suddenly he no longer had fur, but fire covering his body. All around him, everything he touched caught fire until the whole forest went up.

No longer caring about the wolf, Tommen skidded to a stop and looked around frantically for a way out, but found none. The smoke got thick and the fire burned hot. Not knowing what else to do, he simply got down as low as he could and covered his head with his arms, squeezing his eyes shut. Just when he thought he was going to burst into flames, it all went away. Cautiously, he opened his eyes.

It was dark, but he could see himself when he put his hands in front of his face. He didn't even appear to be burned. Then he looked up and saw only a single candle, burning there in the darkness.

Tommen jolted awake, startling his dad in the process. He fought a tangled mess of blankets and sheets and eventually got free, nearly landing on the floor.

"What? Huh?" He looked at his dad, standing in the doorway as if he wasn't quite sure what to do. "What happened?"

His dad raised a brow. "Your note said to wake you up at four. You might have warned me I was going to need a ten foot pole."

Tommen rubbed his eyes and glanced at the clock. Four-oh-one. "Yeah. Okay. Sorry. I'm up."

"I see that. Everything all right?"

"Yeah, just...I don't even know. Bad dream, I guess."

"Okay. Well, it's four o'clock. Did you have something planned for tonight?"

He got out of bed and stretched. "Yeah. I was going to walk down to Becky's house and we're going to dinner."

His dad nodded. "All right. Where are you going?" Tommen told him. "And when do you expect to be home?"

"I don't know. Eight, nine maybe."

"Okay. Just remember you have to work in the morning."

"I know."

His dad left the room, and Tommen got ready for dinner. Becky hadn't mentioned the formality, but given the restaurant she picked, it wasn't exactly a black-tie event. A nice shirt and pants would do. He hoped. Sometimes it was difficult to read her intentions.

He still couldn't get over how much the house had changed as he walked back out to the kitchen to grab his shoes. While he'd been down and out from his injuries, his dad had effectively remodeled the entire house, or contracted someone to do it for him. The 60's had finally been evicted, and the twenty-first century moved in. No more shag carpet, but hardwood floors. No more paisley and flower power, but solid colors and modern luxuries, such as a couch that didn't sag. Even the kitchen looked better with its new cabinetry. No amount of redecorating could make it bigger, but it looked nicer.

"You know the rules," he dad said before he walked out the door. "Have a good time."

"I know. I will."

And he was out the door. The rules were pretty simple: Don't have sex with her. Remember your table manners. Don't complain if you get back late and don't get enough sleep before work. Don't call me from jail because I'm not going to bail you out. Don't call me from the hospital unless you're truly dying or you have your story figured out.

He made it to Becky's house in good time, not that he was ever really worried about that. He was just about to turn up the walkway, when the garage door opened and Mrs. Polski backed the van out of the garage.

"Am I late?" he wondered.

"Not officially," she answered in her Hungarian-accented English, "but Becky's been pacing for the last ten minutes anyway."

Tommen nodded, went around to the passenger side, and waited for the side door to slide open. His gut was twisting and mind racing with a hundred possibilities, few of them good. His day had been too weird, too strange, for anything really good to happen. This was his dose of karma. Becky was probably going to break up with him. Knowing her, it wasn't going to be the "it's not you, it's me, but we can still be friends" routine. It was more likely to be "You're an idiot, and I don't want to be associated with you anymore in any way."

But then, why the dinner? Was it her attempt at softening the blow, a kind gesture knowing that she had no kind words? No, that wasn't right either. Could this really be just...dinner?

"Well, you look mighty perky now," Becky said as they backed out of the driveway and started off down the road.

Tommen froze and felt himself blush even as he Banded to check himself. No, his dull mood and low expectations for this date had effectively killed—oh. Right. Double-entente. She was good at those, better than he thought she should be for a good little Catholic Jew. He released the Band and tried to quell the embarrassment. "Yeah, I had a good nap."

"How did your exams go today, Tommen?" her mom asked.

"Good, I guess. " He shrugged. "Considering how tired I was." He looked at Becky. "What about yours?"

"Yeah, mine were good. I hate that it's going to take a month before everything gets reviewed and posted for the year."

"You were only there six months."

"I know."

"Are...you coming back next year?" Maybe that was it. It wasn't a breakup because of either of them, but maybe her family was moving again.

"Obviously. I have to graduate before I can start the genetics program at the university."

Back to the breakup scenario then.

Her mom dropped them off at the restaurant and told them to call when they were ready. It wasn't a bad place, more reminisce of the kind of place a family might eat at after church on Sunday morning. Polite staff, good lighting, good food, decent prices.

"So what's the occasion?" Tommen asked once they'd been seated.

Becky almost looked normal whenever they went out to eat, but it probably had something to do with the table hiding her short legs. Oddly enough, "normal" just didn't fit her, even when it came to size. She was never meant to be anything but a dwarf, of that Tommen was sure.

"Isn't the end of the school year and the start of summer break good enough?" she wondered. "We've had dinner before with no occasion."

"Yeah, but I was just wondering."

"Your voice gives you away. What's on your mind?"

Even as she said it, he could detect a change in her voice, and instantly he knew that this dinner was never about a breakup or any bad news. She was as afraid of him leaving her as her leaving him. Still, she could spot a liar across the room, and he reluctantly confessed his original fears.

"I don't want that," he finished, feeling rather embarrassed about the whole thing. "I still like you. A lot."

"Oh, good," she sighed, slumping back in her seat a little. "For a second I was thinking the same thing, except, you know, the opposite direction. And I do, too. Like you, that is."

Didn't make the next five minutes any less awkward, though, but they were saved by the waiter coming by to take their drink orders.

Other than the weird start—just one more tick on the weird list, which Tommen knew he was going to pay for eventually—dinner passed uneventfully. They talked; they laughed; they tried each other's food when it finally came; they argued over dessert whether they wanted to share a dish or get separate ones. Then they had a small argument over the bill. Becky argued for separate bills while Tommen pointed out her earlier comment about letting him pick up the tab. Eventually they settled on Becky paying for her own dinner entrée, but Tommen got her drink and dessert. He was pretty sure they confused and pissed off the waiter, but he didn't care. Ironic given he had a good idea how the guy felt about it. But hey, he was the customer this time around.

"We're going to have to figure something out over the summer since we won't see each other every day at school," Becky said as she texted her mom and they went to wait in the front entry.

"Oh, I'm sure we'll just randomly show up on each other's doorsteps from time to time," Tommen said. He meant it as a joke, but Becky did not appear to see it that way.

"That's great for you coming to my house, but you go elsewhere to work."

"So text beforehand. It'll at least give me time to get ready."

"Spend your summers in your birthday suit, huh?"

"Not exactly."

"Oh, and that reminds me. I wanted to give you something. Come here."

Tommen got down on one knew in front of her, meeting her at eye level while she dug in her purse.

"Okay, close your eyes," she ordered.

He did so, fully expecting her to give him a breath mint or some other sarcastic present. What she did give him, however, he couldn't even process for a second. He opened his eyes. She'd kissed him. On the cheek, true, but still. She kissed him. Where the hell had that come from? Her eyes glittered with amusement as she saw his expression.

"Just so you don't go getting any ideas about breaking up."

"Right."

Then the van pulled up to the curb, and they went out.

Tommen had kissed girls before, and it had been a hell of a lot more than just a little peck on the cheek. But this was Becky. She'd blackmailed him within two days of meeting him, and it had taken almost a month before she would let him even touch her for a hug. This whole kiss business was just startling. It meant something.

No, he didn't have any ideas about breaking up with her

anytime soon. This would certainly play into that.

Good things were happening today. He was going to pay for this big time.

Chapter Two
Time Scare

C ai. Wake up."

Micaiah rolled over and tried to bury his face in the pillows. They had a system going. Micah would open the store and do all the prep work and stuff, and he would show up a few hours later. Micah would leave a little early, he would leave a little late, and, depending on the day, Tommen would close. All of this only to point out the fact that he shouldn't have to wake up so dang early anymore. So why the hell was Kayla shaking him awake?

"What?" he finally asked irritably, turning his head to look at her.

He was annoyed by the wakeup, but he wasn't going to argue with the naked woman in his bed. Fifty years married, and she still had a sexy body. He relaxed a little.

"A message just arrived," she told him. "We're wanted in the Wheel."

Back to the pillows. He didn't want to go to the Wheel. They'd just been there for the inauguration of the new Hands; why did they have to go back? And why so fucking early?

"Come on, Cai," Kayla said, pushing him a little harder. "We have to go."

"We have to go now?" He looked at the clock. Five-forty-three. "Fucking hell."

"Meeting's at seven, but we have to pick up Micah, too. He's been requested as well."

"So text him and tell him to get there himself."

She sighed. "Fine. I just thought it might be easier since you have to be to work at eight anyway, maybe go in a little early. For goodness' sake, Cai, you used to go in every day at four-thirty for eleven years. One day at seven won't kill you."

"All right, all right." He stretched as best he could. "I'll go."

She stretched out beside him and rubbed his back. "Yes, but first, you're going to come."

Damn, but he loved her word play. Almost as much as he loved her smooth, dark skin, tight stomach, and full breasts. How in the world did he manage to score a woman like her? Beautiful, smart, talented, and one hell of a warrior with gun, sword, and battle ax. Better to be with her than against her. Best of all was being both with her and against her.

If not for Banding, by the time they were done, they would have been scrambling to get ready. Actually, they were both trying to cut down on Banding, but until they were completely off the Time grid, they couldn't forsake it completely. Time messed with the body, slowing down aging and messing with metabolic processes. In women, this included their regular cycles; Kayla hadn't had one in fifty years. While neither of them was complaining about that bit, they both knew that if they wanted children, that was going to have to come back. In order to do that, they had to give up Time and let their bodies reset themselves. That alone could take years. It was still up in the air whether the Akari had the same effect, but for safety's sake, they were cutting back on everything.

By the time Micaiah got out of the shower, Kayla had breakfast ready and was calling him out to the dining room.

"Be right there!" he called back, sitting on the edge of the bed and reaching for his prosthetic leg. He'd become accustomed to his new morning routine, his new leg, but that didn't mean he had to like it. The last thing he remembered was collapsing a portal and then to his knee as Walter tied off the tourniquet above the spear-like weapon that had pierced his right calf and blown it to shit. Then he woke up in the hospital, and his right leg below the knee was gone.

He'd loathed the prosthetic at first, had mental temper tantrums like a toddler because he wanted his real leg, not this fake one. But he'd come to terms with it since then. And he figured that if he still had qualms about it, he only had to remember that he'd successfully gone into battle with it and come out alive. Well, not this specific one. He'd actually gone in with his running leg. His regular walking leg was just as pristine as ever.

Breakfast was hurried, and soon they were on their way to the bakery, riding on Micaiah's motorcycle. It was a custom-built 2013 Honda with a custom paint job and passenger seat for just such an occasion. They reached the bakery in good time and entered through the back door.

"You're early," Micah observed as he put a pan of something in the oven. He glanced at Kayla. "Morning."

"We have to go to the Wheel," Micaiah told him blandly. "We've been summoned."

"Really? Funny, I don't remember receiving any summons."

"One size fits all," Kayla said, handing him the message rod.

Micah opened the rod and read the message over a couple times. His expression went from curious to sullen acceptance. "I guess some things really don't change. How likely are we to die this time?"

"Not likely, I should think. Depends on if they are going to consider us heroes and reward our efforts, or condemn us as traitors and kill us."

"Your enthusiasm never ceases to amaze," Micah told Kayla sarcastically as he handed her back the rod. "Do you have any sisters?"

"Oh, I thought I heard the door open."

They turned as Tommen walked back to the kitchen.

"We're going to the Wheel," Micaiah said.

"Am I going, too?" the teenager wondered warily. He'd seen way too much excitement lately.

"No, you're not going. But when we get back..." Micaiah sighed. "The three of us are going to have a chat."

The boy went pale, but there was no time to dwell on that future conversation, not while impending doom had been thrust over their heads. Again.

Making sure they were out of sight of the dining room, the twins opened a portal to the Wheel of Time. It was nice that multiple portal rooms had been created in this new iteration of the Wheel. It turned a veritable marathon into a pleasant walk in the park, to get from their portal to the translator dispenser.

Speaking of walking in the park, that was about what the Wheel had become. No longer was it gray walls and hard steel; now it was a fucked up version of 1600's London, from city streets to royal gardens. It was a little unnerving.

But, as they made their way to the Amphitheater, the new iteration of the Coliseum, they also noticed that life was getting back to normal. A few Merchants had set up shop and sold Time Capsules to the few customers that meandered through the marketplaces. It was skittish and questioning, the difference between a fair maiden on her wedding night and the orgy of shady sales that had gone on before. But, Micaiah figured, it was a start. It was only a matter of time before the customers started really returning, which would bring the Merchants, and that would bring the Harvesters.

"I don't know," Micah said, looking around. "Somehow, I never imagined the largest industry in the universe as being filled with gardens and cobblestone streets."

"Maybe you can bring up your concerns to the new Hands," Kayla said, a hint of sarcasm in her voice. "A measly little human has a problem with the new decor."

"That would be funny, except I'm not the only one."

"Maybe it will be brought up," Micaiah said seriously. "We won't know until we get there."

Not to say he didn't secretly agree. It was beautiful and very well done to be sure, but not only was it reminisce of the man who'd designed it, but it was sorely out of place with the nature of the industry. Still, they made their way through the twisting, winding maze that was the Wheel, eventually making a right turn and landing in Imperial French Madagascar, or rather, the Amphitheater as designed by Rifun Ndolo.

The decor was still severely out of place, but Micaiah liked the new system in general. Maybe it was because of the incident of the first Inauguration Day, but he hadn't really liked the Coliseum, how enclosed it had been. Even though there was still only one way in and one way out, having everything laid out in an open landscape helped to relax his paranoia and claustrophobia.

"Masters," the secretary greeted as they approached the direction desk. It gave only a cursory glance at Kayla. "The Hands are waiting for you."

"That's never a good sign," Micah murmured.

They were given directions and started out, Micaiah feeling very much like he should see little cookfires and children running around playing stickball or whatever games children played in African villages. Instead he found aliens of all shapes and sizes wandering in and out of oversized huts made from vegetable fibers and red clay.

Eventually they found the hut they needed to be at, that only because they were flagged down by one of the new Hand Assistants. Micaiah wasn't sure what to call it or compare it to as far as visual appearance, but the creature only introduced itself as the Slide. So was it a rule that the Assistants be given new, vague names like Popes would change their names, or was it just a trend that the Bat and the Day had started?

They entered the hut, and again there was a distinct change of scenery. This was more like the old Wheel, where everything was cold steel and precision planning, hi-tech abounding everywhere. Micaiah might have mistaken it as being the war room on some heavy artillery spaceship or something.

"Ah, Masters, come in," the Zero Hour said, hardly looking at them.

It was a huge relief that they'd gotten rid of the cloaks and shrouds. The replacement was actually an attachment to the translator that each Hand wore, tailored specifically for that species. Supposedly, it was no longer a matter of just walking into the Wheel and having it automatically attached, but it was a physical object the Hands had to keep on their person. If they walked into the Wheel without it, they had no governing authority. As a backup, though, it was linked to the Hand's DNA, so the device couldn't be stolen and used. There were, theoretically, other safety features designed to keep any other "rogue Hands" from doing as Cassius had done, but Micaiah was not aware of all of them.

The three of them moved forward to take their place around the table. Micaiah wasn't sure what to expect now that everyone could see and be seen, and it was disquieting.

"Welcome, Masters," the Zero Hour said, now looking at them. "Please, introduce yourselves."

So they did, the only slipup coming when Micaiah started to introduce himself as a Lieutenant, then had to correct himself and restate that he was only a Lieutenant-trained Master. Courtesy of Regina DeBitch, ahem, DeWitt. He didn't say that part out loud.

The Hands then introduced themselves in turn, but only briefly, stating only their name and title.

"The formalities of old took far too long," the Zero Hour explained. "But they are still a necessity with certain merits."

"Um. Right," Micaiah said, unsure how to respond. Before, when everything was bloated and corrupt, he knew how to play the game, at least well enough to survive. Now the rules had changed. He'd helped to change the rules. Now he wasn't sure he knew how to play anymore. "Why have we been summoned here?"

"There are many reasons. First, you were the ones who instigated the revolt against Cassius and Rifun. Second, you were the ones who slew the Bat. Third, it has come to the attention of the Council that you are all identified members of the cult known as the Akarin."

"Hardly a cult." Micaiah folded his arms. "What about it?"

"Because of your unprecedented actions and unique insights, we want to understand things from your point of view, how things happened, why they happened the way they did, and what we may learn from it so we can better protect the Wheel and Time itself from this sort of catastrophe in the future."

It was the polite way of saying that the three of them were under heavy suspicion for treason. Cassius and Rifun were part of the Cult of the Akari. Micaiah, Micah, and Kayla were of the Akarin. Apparently, the Hands saw no difference between the two. And they were apparently suspicious of how their plan had worked so well. How had just the three of them managed to fool Cassius and Rifun so well? How had they gotten through the dampening field not only by themselves, but with an army? How had they figured out that Doug wasn't really Doug? Was Cassius really Cassius? Was he really dead? How had they defeated the Bat? Most importantly, though, how had Rifun gotten away, where did he go, and how much of a threat was he likely to be going forward?

Really, they were all very valid questions. Had their positions been reversed, Micaiah would probably be asking them himself. But there was something about being on the receiving end of that suspicion that grated his nerves. He might have been able to understand the suspicion that they'd helped Rifun escape. He might have even bought that he'd let them go in the first place in order to concoct such a ruse. Except for the part where he'd lost his fucking leg. Okay, if he was relying on someone to help him make an escape, he wasn't going to maim that person and then wait for them to recover. It would be an excellent ruse, but far too risky for any sane person to attempt. Rifun wasn't right in the head to be sure, but he sure knew what the hell he was doing.

Micaiah felt a rock settle in his stomach. He didn't need to go to jail again. At the same time, however, this was the game he knew, the one where he had to tread carefully, watch his words, watch his back, and always assume that anything he said could and would be used against him in a Time court of law. And here, he had no right to a jury of peers, so if he got canned, he was screwed.

"Glad to hear we're on the same page," Kayla said stiffly. "We also want to prevent another catastrophe from happening. How can we assist?"

"Tell us about your escape from the Wheel after Cassius took over."

Well, that brought back some memories Micaiah would have preferred to keep buried. It was a story told in three parts. First, Kayla, who hadn't even been in the Wheel when it happened. She didn't know about the coup at all until word slowly made its way around. Then she packed up everything she could carry and booked it to Charleston, waiting for Micaiah to come out of his pity party and rejoin the world. Then Micah told his story of escape and what a fight that had been, slipping past guards and Grandfathers.

Micaiah gave his testimony last, detailing the lockdown of the Coliseum, the Judgment Wing, being locked in prison. He was less than enthusiastic about talking about the escape. He remembered being taken out of the Judgment Wing and herded toward the Coliseum like a flock of sheep. To an extent, he remembered collapsing the portals, cutting off the Coliseum and the Judgment Wing from the rest of the Wheel, and making a break for the portal room.

"What happened next?" one Hand inquired, looking particularly enthralled by the tale.

"There, my memory becomes hazy," Micaiah admitted. He took a few steps back and Micah followed, and he showed the Hands his prosthetic leg. "One of the guards wounded me, but we made it to the portal room. I remember standing, somehow, and collapsing the portal, cutting off the portal room as well. Micah had modified a translator to act as a beacon when we were ready to return home. He is the one who managed to open the portal, but there my memory ends as I passed out. When I woke up, my leg was gone."

A few of the Hands murmured to each other. Were they starting to follow the logic that Micaiah didn't willingly give up his leg just so Rifun could go free? He'd been on his way to die. He'd risked everything to escape. Then he'd turned around and launched a coup to depose Rifun. If he'd wanted Rifun in power, he wouldn't have had to do that last bit. And he would still have his leg.

"Is it difficult for your species to adapt to artificial limbs?" another Hand asked.

They didn't believe him! For fuck's sake...

"That depends on many factors," Micaiah replied stiffly. He felt Kayla's hand brush his. He elected to be a little more diplomatic. "But it is easier than it was a hundred years ago. I count myself very lucky that I survived the Time Trial, never mind the battle that ensued, but even so, my recovery is ongoing."

"Those who follow the Akari in any fashion," another Hand began diplomatically, "believe that their god called the Author watches over them and writes them either a good or bad ending depending upon their actions." Put simply. "Do you believe the Author favors you?"

Micaiah folded his arms. "I'd like to think so."

"What happened in the six months between your escape and the trial?" the Zero Hour asked.

"I recovered. I spent a while by myself, trying to cope with the loss of my leg. Then I began to plan my revenge on the man who took it."

"Why did you choose a Time Trial as your method of revenge? It seems a strange thing to do."

"Because I knew it was one thing that Cassius and Rifun wouldn't be able to resist, as bloodthirsty as they were. It was a gamble, but it paid off."

"What if they hadn't accepted your offer?"

"Then I imagine I would have been carted off to be executed, or to prison. Either way, there was still a chance for escape."

"And how is that?" the Zero Hour inquired. "How did you not only manage to escape, but break back in? Furthermore, how were you and your comrades able to summon an army through the dampening field? What Time abilities do you possess that allow such a thing?"

That's when Micaiah knew where the conversation was going. On the one hand, he could evade the question, but it would only increase their suspicion, and they could go to another Akarin who wasn't such a staunch, stubborn asshole for answers. Or he could answer honestly, and attempt to control the situation.

"I did not use Time for such things. I used the Akari."

"A myth!" someone said.

"Then *you* explain what he did," Micah shot back.

"A madman who worshiped the Akari overthrew the established government of Time," the Zero Hour interrupted before a fight could ensue. "Another man who follows the Akari sought vengeance against the madman. In both cases, Time was discarded like little more than scraps to the animals." Beat. "Regardless of any of our personal feelings or beliefs, we must recognize that what transpired happened because the weapon used was left unchecked."

"It's not a weapon—" Kayla began hotly.

"Time is a universal industry," the Zero Hour cut in, fixing her in a stare. "It had its flaws, true, but it services everyone if they so choose. We can't have it disrupted by myths and fantasies, regardless of how real they may seem. If it is Time-related, then the industry will suffer from the fear, and it will never recover. If it is not Time-related, then the industry will suffer from the fear that there is more out there."

"But there is more out there," Micaiah protested.

"They can't know that."

"Who can't? And why not? Why wouldn't you want others to know that there is more?"

"Because there is no governing body to control it. The people want control. They want to know that everything is secure again. The customers want to know that they can come to buy Time and other trinkets freely without worrying about another coup. The Merchants want to know that they can set up shop to sell Time. The Harvesters want to know that they can continue to Harvest and sell and make a profit. People want security. They want to go back to the way things were, but better. It does no one any good to introduce something so wild and unknown, especially when it is the thing they believe just destroyed their old lives, murdered their friends, and threw everything into chaos.

"As long as it remains a Time issue, the Time issue has been resolved. There are scores of Timekeepers and Scouts looking for Rifun. They will find him, and they will execute him. If it becomes something other than Time, then they begin to wonder if there are others."

"But—"

"As far as anyone will know, Cassius, Rifun, and everyone else involved, was part of the Cult of the Akari, a deranged group who worshiped a myth and acted upon false beliefs. They are all dead now. The cult is gone, and all is put to rights."

"What about us?" Micah asked. "What are we, chopped liver?"

"No mention will be made of the Akarin," another Hand said. "If anyone asks, you are simply Lieutenant-trained Masters with exceptional skill. After the coup, you worked in the privacy of your home planet to train and strengthen yourselves, enough to be able to break through the dampening field and bring others with you. That is all. Nothing less, but nothing more."

"We're not the only Akarin," Kayla pointed out. "You can't keep everyone quiet."

"As a matter of fact, we can," someone else said calmly. "All known members of the Akarin were sent a notice to remain silent on the matter and wait for your signal to convene and discuss. We expect you to relay our orders at such time."

"And if we don't? Or if we tell them to tell others?"

"Then it is a good thing that we have a list of all known Akarin members," the Zero Hour told them.

It was the closest thing to a threat Micaiah had heard all day. He sighed internally. In revealing themselves, they had revealed themselves. Now the Hands knew of their existence and probably had a fairly accurate count of their members, fighting numbers, and a host of other important information. They were out in the open now, but only inasmuch as the Hands were going to stuff them back in a box and hide away for themselves, like a child's most precious toy. They'd gone from being a harmless little club to a real threat to the very ones they'd just helped put in power. How fitting.

"So then what do you expect to do with us, once we're all good and quiet and sitting politely in the corner?" Micaiah questioned.

"As long as you stay quiet and go about your regular Time duties, you are free to act as you see fit among yourselves," the Zero Hour answered. "But no mention of the Akari, the Akarin, or any other group or cult will be permitted anywhere in the Wheel or where the Laws of Time prevail. If there is such a mention, then you — or those responsible or implicated — will also be doing a thorough investigation of the new setup of the Judgment Wing and the Grandfathers."

No, no, that might have been closer to an explicit threat than the last veiled threat.

As much as Micaiah would have loved to have gone into a full-blown pissing match and give every single one of the Hands a piece of his mind, he was hardly in any position to do so. He was not the one in charge here, and he had no backup to call on this time.

"Is anything about this unclear, or do you have questions?" the Zero Hour prompted.

Yeah, I wonder how fast I would have to be to clear the table, strangle you, and then escape, hopefully without losing my other leg. Does anyone here know? No? Anyone want to time me?

"Perfectly clear," Kayla answered for him, though sounding no less pissed.

"Excellent. I expect we shall have no further trouble as we continue on and rebuild the Time industry."

It was a dismissal, one they took gratefully before one or all of them ended up in prison for murdering a Hand or two. Or fifty. Kayla was the first to move, whirling around and pushing her way out of the room. Micah followed, and Micaiah brought up the rear.

"Well, that was just fucking lovely!" Kayla snarled once they were all out in the open air again. "Bunch of fucking ingrates! For fuck's sake, you lost your leg, and we all risked our lives to get Rifun out of power so they could get into power. They didn't even say so much as 'thank you, now get out.' "

Micaiah took her gently by the shoulders until she took a breath and calmed down a little. "I know. I don't like it either. But the good news is that now we know what cards we have. We just have to step back for a minute and learn how to play those cards."

She shook her head. "They are the opposite of Rifun, but just as bad. Rifun wanted to control Time using the Akari; the Hands want to control Time without it."

"Rifun wasn't using the Akari, though he thought he was."

"Then what was he using? Because it looked an awful lot like the Akari."

"I don't know, but our ability to discover that information seems to have diminished considerably all of a sudden."

"So what do we do now?" Micah wondered. "The Hands already sent a message out to everyone else saying that we want to meet them and make an important announcement. What are we going to tell them?"

"We're going to tell them exactly what happened here, just like they want. There is no reason to keep everyone in the dark about that. The Hands hate us; the others deserve to know that. As for what comes after, I don't know. I'm still working on that one."

Kayla sighed. "Well, maybe a little food in our stomachs will calm us down and give us an idea."

"I'm up for that," Micah quipped.

Micaiah agreed and they left the Amphitheater. All the important things such as the Amphitheater, the Judgment Wing, and so on, those were all conveniently found in the town square. The Food

Court they had to go hunting for a bit. As expected, it, too, had been given the Shakespearean treatment, looking something like an outdoor family reunion potluck meets classic sixteenth century outdoor stage theater. It was a shameful thought, but Micaiah wondered who Rifun had expected to find to perform at this dinner theater. At the moment, the stage was woefully empty.

"I miss this," Kayla said as they got their plates and found a spot to sit on the grass. "Not only good food, but free food."

"Amen, sister," Micah said, stabbing into his salad. He looked at Micaiah. "So, boss, what do we do?"

"I don't know," Micaiah admitted. "I haven't eaten yet. But even then, I still don't know. I haven't even heard who's been appointed to Doug's position. I have no clue who to contact."

"Guess we'll find out when you contact everyone else."

Kayla shook her head. "No matter what, the meeting is going to be terrible. Cassius running around as Doug? The cleanup is going to be a nightmare."

"Agreed." Micah nodded. "Guess that's one good thing about the Hands staying out of our business now."

"The Hands aren't going to stay out of our business," Micaiah warned him severely. "They're just going to be less public about it."

"But they told us—"

"They told us to stay quiet and sit in the corner. They'll leave the cleanup to us, make us deal with the fallout from Cassius' treachery. But as soon as we're back on track, they're going to pull that noose tighter and tighter. We're no longer a cute little religious club; we're a real threat with real power. Old Hands or new Hands—especially new Hands—they are going to treat us like every other threat out there."

Micah let out a breath. "Fantastic." He took another bite of salad.

Micaiah had never expected that the Akarin would be some enormous, highly-influential group in the Time industry. His hopes only went as far as a casual knowledge of their existence and general apathy. To be told now that he wasn't allowed even that? It boiled his blood, though he'd learned in recent weeks to let the rage simmer a while before blowing his top.

They finished their meal in silence, Micah confused, Kayla brooding, Micaiah planning. There had to be a way to salvage the situation, a way to fix the mess Cassius caused in the Akarin ranks and still retain autonomy apart from the Hands and the Time industry. They couldn't let the Hands win again.

"So, what's the plan for when we get back?" Kayla wondered.

"Do you have to work today?" Micaiah wondered.

Kayla did interior design consultation and planning. Before finally moving in with them, she'd had her own place outside the city on the east side. She catered to rich jerks who wanted the most exquisite penthouse in the city limits, and rich jerks who wanted the most luxurustic getaway cabin high in the mountains.

She shrugged. "I have phone calls to make, research and planning to do, but as far as I know, I'm not scheduled to be anywhere. Do I need to be somewhere?"

"Where was Doug living?"

Even as he spoke, he saw the light come on and a mischievous glint sparkle in her dark eyes. "Up the coast, I think. You want me to check out his house?"

"If you think you can do it."

"I am a battle ax wielding bad ass. I think I can handle one little breaking and entering."

"That's what I thought."

Micaiah kissed his wife, even as he saw Micah in his peripheral vision, rolling his eyes. Well, let him be jealous. If he wanted a girl, he'd have to go out and get his own.

"Gee, dear, is there anything I can do?" Micah said, elbowing him in the ribs as he kissed Kayla again.

"You can stop being a pain in the ass and interrupting us," Micaiah told him, elbowing him back.

"Hey, it's my house, too, and a guy's gotta sleep."

"You're such a dolt."

"Careful with your language, or I'm going to tell."

Micaiah raised a brow. "Tell who?"

Micah shrugged. "I don't know. Someone." Suddenly he bowled into Micaiah's chest. "Or I'll just have to kick your ass myself."

Micaiah let himself get driven to the ground, careful to protect his leg. "Oh, jeez, and who was just complaining about my use of language?"

They tussled for a moment, but eventually Micaiah won, as he always did, sitting on Micah's chest until he cried uncle. After a second of consideration, Micaiah got up and offered his brother a hand up.

"Do you ever lose?" Micah asked breathlessly, dusting himself off.

"Not for a while, but I don't intend on pushing my luck anytime soon."

"Okay, boys, recess is over," Kayla said, walking over. "Time to go back to the real world."

"But mom," the twins said simultaneously in the same whiny voice. Micaiah broke first, laughing then sighing dramatically. "Okay."

They left the Food Court, each in his own thoughts. Where did they go from here? How could they rebuild a trustworthy leadership when one of their best leaders—not the most well-liked, necessarily, but their best mind and tactician—had become, not just corrupted, but perfectly impersonated? What should they say? What could they say? Who could they trust? Were there others who weren't who they appeared to be? Would they know? Could they root them out? Too many variables and not enough time to investigate them all. Reflexes demanded instant paranoia and suspicion of everyone and everything. Micaiah told himself to keep a level head, but with the added threat from the Hands as well as new threats that hadn't even made themselves known yet, they didn't have time to waste on slow, cautious proceedings.

Then there was that matter of having to call everyone together. Likely it would just be a game of telephone, passing the message along from person to person to person. If that was the case, they would have to set the meeting date a little ways in the future to get as many in attendance as possible. Let's see...this was the beginning of June, so...July, maybe? After the Fourth would be ideal since the bakery was so swamped, Micaiah knew he would inevitably lose track of time and miss any meeting he was supposed to go to. At the same time, doing it beforehand would be a weight off his shoulders before the Fourth, too. Hopefully he could pass it off to someone else. Oh, why did this have to be so fucking hard? Just once, he wished the answer could be easy, nice and spelled out for them. A road map to follow, X marks the spot.

They returned to the portal room and dropped off their translators. Sometimes Micaiah wondered what would happen if he took a couple back with him and passed them off as his own inventions. Would he be hailed as the greatest interpreter since Rosetta Stone and Google Translate? If someone opened it up to search for the linguistic database, would it lead them to the Wheel? What sort of adventure would that take them on? Would it open up Earth as an Engaged civilization?

Knowing humans a little too well, Micaiah figure that Earth would inevitably become a Reserved or Engaged Privilege civilization, those where the use of Time was limited to those who were allowed to have it. Most likely, on Earth, those would be the leaders, governors, and all their special friends. Instead of gun control debates, there would instead be Time control debates, an irony in its own right.

"You look deep in thought," Kayla observed as they made their way down one of the rows of portals to the one that would take them home. "Something you want to talk about?"

"Not until I know what I want to say," Micaiah mused.

As expected, the bakery was just as they had left it, all the ovens working at full capacity, half a dozen bowls of doughs and batters in various stages of completion, the sink already amassing an impressive collection of dirty dishes. Even Tommen was still standing there, pale, guilty, clearly expecting some awful news. Worst part was, awful news was coming and he didn't even deserve it.

"You guys okay?" Tommen asked as the trio landed in the kitchen, a little disoriented from the trip but no worse for wear.

"Fine," Micaiah told him, straightening and getting his balance.

"Should I wait in the office?"

"No. We have some things to take care of first. Carry on like normal. Looks like someone is on their way in now."

Indeed, just after he spoke, the bell above the door jingled, and Tommen went to the front to take care of the customer. After a few more seconds of recuperation, Kayla spoke.

"So, you want me to check out Doug's house. Where did he live?"

It was strange to think of Doug in the past tense, even more so since it was more past tense than it initially seemed. No one had ever particularly liked the man, but it was just weird to think that he was dead. No more ego and narcissism, true, but also no more brilliant plans and strategies. Micaiah was forced to wonder just how it was that Cassius and Rifun managed to outmaneuver him.

Still, he went into the office and dug around until he found Doug's address. As he handed it to Kayla, he asked, "So, what were you planning on taking to get up there?"

She shrugged. "Well, I can either take your bike, Micah's car, a blind portal, or I'll hop a bus if I have to."

Micaiah sighed. "You still remember how to ride?"

"Of course."

She held out her hand and he reluctantly dug out his key. He'd been the only one to drive his bike since he got it. So far, Kayla had only been a passenger. She was a good driver, to be sure, but still...his bike, man. He didn't want to give that over to just anyone, even if that person was his own wife.

"I promise I won't get a scratch on her," she said, apparently reading his thoughts. "If you want, I'll even wash and wax it before I bring it back."

"Oh really?" He raised a brow.

"Provided I get one from you when I get back."

"You certainly know how to drive a hard bargain."

She grinned. "Come on. You know who you married."

"I know. That's the problem. Just be careful."

"I will. As much as I hate to say it, but I'll be Banding there and back anyway, so anything that happens in my own fault."

Micaiah shook his head. "Don't Band. Not for this. It's not worth it. Take your time; do it normally. I'll have Micah or Walt take me home."

"Are you sure?"

He stood and put his hands on her shoulders. "Doug's house is not worth more than our future. Okay?"

She nodded. "Agreed. But I'm not saying I won't Band long enough to get me out of the city."

"Fair enough. I don't want you getting hurt either. Wear your helmet."

"Yes, Dad."

She kissed him and left the office. He followed her at least to the back door, where she handed him his helmet, put on her own, then started the bike and moved slowly around until she got in a position to leave. Then he approached and kissed her again.

"You can be such a sap sometimes," she told him.

"You know who you married."

"And that's the problem. I'll see you in a few days."

"Call and tell me if you find anything."

Her brows furrowed and she ran her tongue over her teeth. "Actually, I was thinking about keeping it all to myself and leaving the rest of you in terrible suspense." She noted his expression and shook her head, sighing. "Of course I'll call and tell you. Sheesh. All right, I'll see you later."

A third kiss, and no sooner had he stepped back than she was gone. Literally, she was gone, the wake of a Band the only indication that she'd been there at all.

"Holy shit, he does live," Micah said when he walked back inside.

"What?" Micaiah asked.

"Took you long enough."

"Did the store burn down while I was away?"

"No, but it could have."

"Ha ha, very funny." He rolled his eyes.

"So, we having that meeting with Tommen now?"

"No, not yet. I have some scheduling and phone calls to make first."

Micah just shrugged and carried on with his work while Micaiah returned to the office and closed the door, not missing the worried, sideways glance that Tommen gave him from the counter. One thing at a time.

Doug was dead, but there were still others he could contact. It was a list of the known Akarin in the District, and also the hit list that Lily had been given before the elections. Sleep with him and kill him, kill Micah, then hit everyone on the list. Actually, everyone on the list would have died if she hadn't had an attack of conscience and come forward with the plan. As it was, only one of the people on the list had died. Time to pick up the phone and start calling.

On a normal day, Micaiah made calls all day long for the bakery. Catering, advertising, billing, stock ordering, all sorts of things. Sometimes he made calls for Time investigations and inquiries. Any of those, he was perfectly fine with. His mission now, he was not fine with. Maybe it was because someone had told him to do it, and not just told him, but ordered him, almost with a gun to his head. So he hesitated for just a second before actually picking up the phone and dialing the first number.

"Hello?" came the voice on the other end.

"Amy Rowlings?"

"Yes?"

"It's Micaiah Durvin."

"Oh, yes, of course. I should have recognized your accent. Tell me, did you actually send this message or what's going on?"

"I wish I knew, but either way, there needs to be a meeting."

She sighed. "Yes, there does. We heard about Doug. He was a prick, but all of this...it's just too hard to believe."

"Agreed, and we need to get it cleaned up and figured out as soon as possible."

"When are we meeting?"

Well, that was the question, wasn't it? When were they meeting? On the one hand, he had to give it enough time for word to get around so everyone could plan for it. On the other hand, they had to meet soon enough that shit could get resolved before things descended into chaos. At the same time, give it a little time and the panic and fear would wear off on their own. Once people realized the sky wasn't falling, they would be a little more reasonable and easier to deal with.

"June 28th," he decided finally. "I'll let you know a specific time once we get closer to the day."

"Three weeks? That long?"

"I need to get some things figured out. Let's just say that the meeting with the Hands did not go well."

"Ah."

"If you could help pass the word around, that would be huge."

"Sure."

"I'm going to call the others in the District and let them know, too."

"All right. Guess I'll hear from you at some point in the next three weeks."

Micaiah ended the call and leaned back in his chair. The fuck was he thinking, three weeks? Any number of terrible things could happen in three weeks. The Hands could launch a hostile takeover. Although, if they had wanted to do that, they could have done so without speaking to Micaiah and the others. But, by doing it this way, they would be getting everyone in one place. It could be a ploy for another massacre. And by forcing them to keep quiet, no one would ever know.

He shook his head. For as ruthless as the new Hands appeared, he was fairly certain that everyone was tired of the bloodshed. If they did launch a hostile takeover, it would be political in nature.

That didn't mean bad things couldn't happen. They still hadn't figured out who had originally contracted Lily to kill him and the others before the elections. It was likely to have been the Cult of the Akari or the Grandfathers, but there was no shortage of Akari-based groups within the Time industry. Some were passive, others humanitarian. Still some were a little more active and politically charged, such as the Akarin. But then there were the heretical groups like Rifun's group, those who did not follow the Akari however much they professed to do so. So even if it wasn't the Cult, there were still others who would love to move against the Akarin and take advantage of their confused state to do so.

After a minute or two, he dialed another number.

"Greg Fields," a husky male voice answered gruffly.

"It's Micaiah Durvin."

"The fuck do you want?"

Time or Akari, Harvesters were still Harvesters.

"I'm calling about a meeting." Micaiah forced his voice to remain level.

"Yeah, I got your summons or whatever you call them. Said something about a meeting with the Hands and some changes that were going to be coming down and to ask you about them. Well, all right. I'm asking."

"There's going to be a meeting June 28th."

"That's a long fucking time. Shit could change between now and then."

"If it's bad enough, then no amount of talking would have

prevented it anyway," Micaiah informed him. "That's when the meeting is; I'll let you know the exact time as we get closer."

"All right, fine. Guess three weeks isn't all that bad. Gives me enough time to get off work. Some of us do work, you know. We have day jobs."

"Good-bye, Greg."

Click.

Was it just some unwritten rule that all Harvesters had to be assholes? Couldn't he, just once, talk to a Harvester without coming away feeling like he'd been bound, gagged, beaten, and left for dead? Was it really too much to ask?

He called the rest of the people on the list, then moved on to a secondary list. The first list was one of those people who were Akarin members, but also active within the Time industry. The second list consisted of those who were Akarin and inactive in the Time industry, or considered Runners. Kayla was on that list because, although she was a Master Timekeeper, she was also considered a Runner, or she had been. It was tough to judge where things stood now with the Runners.

That list was considerably longer; few who were part of the Akarin wanted much to do with the Time industry. They preferred to keep to themselves, go about their daily lives in peace and meet with other Akarin without being interrupted by the Hands or anyone else. Most had some form of training in one discipline or another, but it wasn't worth much. The Akari, not Time, was where they drew their power from.

They were also considerably friendlier, at least once he explained who he was. Some had already heard from Amy or another person, but it was still a pleasant conversation to have. He updated his list, making notes of those who had died, gone missing, or forsaken the group entirely.

The whole thing took him probably two hours, a lot longer than he'd intended to spend. At the same time, now that it was done, it was done. He could sit back, relax, and take a small break to plan the next move. He still had to figure out what he was going to tell them, figure out a plan that didn't involve them rolling over like whipped hounds. And he had to figure out how to do it tactfully.

At least now, though, he had a little time. The initial announcement was out there, and that took a huge weight off his shoulders.

He rubbed absently at his knee for a minute before sitting up and taking a second to actually look at it. He'd healed well since getting back from the Time Trial and the battle that ensued, but maybe there was still something there, a sore spot that was still rubbing a little. Probably he should let his knee relax a few more days.

Now was the hard part. He'd already had to pull out part of his teeth today, so why stop there? Grudgingly, he fished through the filing cabinet and pulled out some paperwork. Once he was satisfied he had everything in order, he stood, stretched, and went to the door.

Chapter Three
New Experiences

Manager or not, Tommen hated running the front counter. Okay, so hate was a strong word. He extremely disliked it, especially during the summer. If it wasn't the mundane boredom from customer after customer after customer in an endless drone of orders and handling cash and doing chores, it was the mundane excitement of the occasional angry customer who was intent on causing a scene, trying to embarrass Tommen and make the store look bad.

There was one lady who had become a regular customer lately. Her first visit to the store, the kitchen had caught on fire. That should have been the first clue. She was one of those with special dietary needs. Those didn't bother Tommen too much, really; the twins were very understanding and did their best to make ingredient lists available, mark the trays whose baked goods might contain allergens, and try to keep a clean kitchen. That just was not good enough for this lady. Even though she came in at least once every two weeks and had found a few things she could have, she always insisted on having the ingredients read to her for almost everything in the case. She didn't even say what her dietary needs were, only that they were very specific and she needed to know the ingredients and the ingredients of the ingredients.

True to form, she had come in a couple weeks ago, and they went through their usual routine of going through the ingredient lists. At the very least, Tommen had most of the items down pat by now and could recite them without having to go back to the kitchen and look around for the box or bag of product. So they'd been going and going, back and forth as usual, and the line had been steadily getting longer, and Tommen could see that some of the customers behind the lady were getting impatient. As politely as he could, he tried to suggest that the lady step aside, consider her options, and let some people pass.

She refused, instead looking rather insulted that Tommen told her to step aside at all. So they continued for another minute or two. The person in line behind her finally asked her to stand aside so he could get in and get out. Well, that certainly didn't help her disposition any, and another three minutes were wasted on them arguing, and Tommen trying to stop them from arguing. The second customer ended up leaving in a huff, and the lady still would not budge.

A few of the remaining customers were looking almost ready to leave, but Tommen got fed up. The next time the lady asked for an ingredients list, he simply asked the next customer to step forward and place his order. The lady protested venomously, but Tommen had eight customers out the door in less time than it would have taken him to give her another ingredient list. By the time he got back to her, she was fuming.

She fumed and huffed and sputtered complaints and curses and carried on for quite a while. Tommen simply listened to her for a minute before asking if he could also take her order, politely inquiring if she had made up her mind yet. Well, that sent her over the edge, and she just exploded on him, laying out every tragedy of her life for the last forty years, saying things about humble upbringings and glass ceilings and hard-won earnings and all she wanted was a cookie and why was it so difficult and so on and so forth. Again, Tommen let her go, listened patiently, then went to the case, grabbed her one of the cookies he knew she could have, and rang it up for her.

Of course, she was irate that he was still going to make her pay for the thing after everything he'd put her through. He'd simply pointed out that he still charged the other customers for their orders, despite what she had put them through. That didn't help her disposition, but it did get her out of the store, muttering the whole way that she was going to call her lawyer and sue the place for emotional distress and a whole host of other things.

That was probably what the meeting was going to be about. She had sued the bakery, probably exaggerated her story, and now he was going to be fired. It wasn't because the twins disliked him, but it was what was expected of them following such an offense, a customer being abused at the hands of one of their employees. If he was lucky, they would wait a little while until the whole thing blew over and then hire him back, but that could take months; he would have to find something else to do until then. He would have to get another job. He wasn't even sure how to do that, really; he'd only ever known the bakery. He barely knew what a resume was, never mind how to make one or what to include.

He glanced at the office door, still closed. The blinds were down, but the slats wide so he could see Micaiah on the phone. Judging by his expression, Tommen guessed that the nature of the call didn't have anything to do with the bakery. Or if it did, it was far from good news. Maybe it was that lady's lawyer. Maybe he was talking with his lawyer, trying to figure out what to do about the whole thing. Was there a way to keep Tommen on and still appease Her Grouchiness?

The hands on the clock ticked by slowly, and still Micaiah was on the phone with one person or another. Tommen kept an eye on him between customers, which got harder and harder to do as the day wore on. During the week, they were busy right from opening because of everyone heading to work early. On weekends, they built up to their busy time as people slept in, got a later start, and usually weren't in as big a hurry to be anywhere in particular.

Or maybe they would keep him on, but keep him in the back, out of sight of Her Grouchiness. It was where he normally was anyway, whenever Kyle or Jenna worked. Actually, looking at the clock, Kyle was due in any minute now, so he would take the counter, and Tommen would go back to help Micah.

Even as he thought it, he heard the back door open. Giving a quick check of the dining room and the sidewalk outside to be sure no customers were about, he went back. As expected, it was Kyle.

"Hey, guys," the Runner greeted. "How are things going?"

"Great," Micah replied, even as Tommen said, "Busy."

"Sounds good. Guess I'll head up front, then."

Kyle was a good worker, too, Tommen thought. The only thing that really bothered him was Jenna, but when she wasn't around, he was an ideal worker: on time, easy to work with, good with customers. He never really let anything get to him. He probably would have handled Her Grouchiness better than Tommen had. If it did end up that Tommen was fired because of that incident, he could see Kyle stepping into the managerial role.

Tommen took a breath and tried to compose himself. They hadn't even had the meeting yet. No use getting all worked up over something that could exist only in his mind. He glanced toward the office where Micaiah was still on the phone.

"Who's he been on the phone with all day?" Tommen asked, hoping to sound conversational and curious rather than fearful and paranoid. He went to the production list, found the next item up, and set to searching for the appropriate pans and product.

"The other members of the Akarin," Micah answered, scraping out the last of the batter from a bowl into a large pan. "Let's just say that the meeting with the Hands didn't go as planned."

Tommen suddenly felt foolish for worrying. If all of this was about something that happened Time-side, then his Earth-side job was not at stake. Well, that only only ninety-nine percent likely. Either way, it meant that he probably wasn't going to have to answer for his last encounter with Her Grouchiness. He let out a sigh of relief, hoping it didn't sound too obvious.

"So, not all is well in the Wheel?" he wondered.

"Depends on who you ask," Micah replied diplomatically. "For the majority of Time Agents, everything is great. Couldn't be better. For the Akarin and Akari-bearers everywhere, well, that's a different story."

It was still worrying, but not as much as potentially losing his job to Her Grouchiness. So when Micaiah finally emerged from the office, Tommen was decidedly less afraid of having his head chopped off.

"Micah. Tommen," was all Micaiah said as he poked his head in the kitchen.

The two of them followed him dutifully into the office and took a seat, though Tommen noticed how Micah pulled up beside his brother. If this was regarding Time in general, they would be sitting in more of a circle, Knights of the Round Table and all that. But with both twins facing him, this was more of a disciplinary matter, a breach of hierarchy or code of conduct. Maybe this was about Her Grouchiness. Tommen felt his heart rate skyrocket.

Micaiah spoke first, leaning back and putting his right, erm, ankle on his left knee. "Tommen, do you remember that lady from a couple months ago who got all upset because she ordered one tart but got another and all the rugs were flipped up and she could have tripped and the sidewalk was icy and so on?"

"Vaguely. She wanted to see cameras and get a free tart or something. Why? Is she actually suing the store for a free tart?"

"No. If you want my opinion, what she's done is much worse, immoral and unethical."

"What happened?"

"She went to OSHA to file a complaint—or a 'concern' I think is what they called it. You remember the surprise inspection?"

"Yeah. I thought it was weird, but what about it?"

"I don't know how it came about, but she orchestrated it. You may know that OSHA also looks at employee files, makes sure we're complying with overtime, FMLA, and all the other regulations. Unfortunately, the guy had an issue with your work history. Specifically, he found a problem with a sixteen year old working as a manager, the work load and the hours. He said it was a violation of your rights as a minor, and whatever." Micaiah waved a hand dismissively. "Point is, he gave us thirty days to remove you from your position. That was almost four weeks ago."

"Am I...being fired?" Tommen was at a loss.

"Not fired," Micah assured him, "but you can't stay on as manager."

"Believe me, Tommen, I looked for a way to get around it," Micaiah sighed. "A loophole, a law, something that would let you stay. I had our lawyer look into it, too, but he came up with the same answer. He said that while, yes, it is known to happen, especially in the state of West Virginia, it's usually overlooked. But, once someone files a complaint about it, we must comply, no questions asked."

"But that's bullshit!"

Micaiah nodded sympathetically. "You're going to keep the raise; there's no law saying we have to take that away or can't give you a normal employee pay raise. If you want, you can even keep the hours, opening, closing, you're pretty flexible during the summer. But we can't have you doing office work, stock orders, or any of that. We also can't give you managerial final say in matters such as cranky customers."

"But it's not fair!"

"We know," Micah said calmly. "We like having you as manager, and in a little over a year, when you turn eighteen, we'll be glad to hire you back as manager. But until then...no go." He shrugged helplessly.

So that was it? Some bitch didn't like that he was a manager, so she set out to ruin his career and his life? What kind of sorry shit was she that she was so upset over a teenager being a manager? He thought he was finally advancing, finally getting somewhere, doing something other than going to a shitty entry-level job after school. What the fuck? Seriously, could nothing ever go right just for its own sake?

"So," Micaiah went on distastefully, gathering up a couple papers, "you might remember the paperwork Micah had you sign when you got promoted. These are similar papers, detailing your change in position. Like I said, no change in pay or hours, only title.

I've listed the reason as extenuating circumstances. If and when you get another job, I am personally giving you permission to list your last rank as Manager. If they ask, you may tell them, briefly, of what transpired. It was not a situation of your own doing. You understand?"

Tommen nodded sullenly. "Yeah, I get it."

He silently took the papers and signed them, feeling like he was signing his own detention slips. It wasn't fair. It just wasn't fucking fair. He did a good job; the twins always told him so, and Kyle and Jenna didn't have any problems with him (that he knew of). All this really came down to was one spiteful bitch who didn't get what she wanted, and rather than going the traditional route of filing a straight lawsuit, she called in a few favors and got her revenge the roundabout way. Well, given the circumstances, she probably worked for the government. That alone explained pretty much everything. Still...spiteful bitch.

Sighing, he handed the papers back to Micaiah who filed them away in his personnel folder. And just like that, he was no longer the manager. He was just another grunt in the kitchen. An average person, plodding away at his entry-level job.

"Who's going to be manager now?" he dared ask.

"For the time being, no one," Micah answered. "I'll step into the role, but we won't have any official manager right away. With the time crunch, we had to do this. But we'll still try to figure out a way around the rules. If you're interested, that is. If you're not worried about it—"

"No, I'm worried about it," Tommen cut in hotly. "Fuck the government. I don't like being bullied, and I want my job back."

"Fair enough," Micaiah said. "We'll see if there is anything we can do."

Tommen let out a breath and slumped in his seat. "Thanks." He shook his head. "So what was up with the meeting, if you don't mind my asking?"

"Less than three days into the new Council of Hands and

they're already making a power play. Mostly it's done out of fear, but fear and the power that comes with this move are not easily given up or reasoned with."

"Are you guys in trouble for something?"

"Not yet, but that seems to be the answer to all the questions these days. At any rate, it's not anything you need to worry about."

"Is it about your Akari group or whatever?"

"The Akarin? Yes. But it's not limited just to us. I would explain it, but there are more politics involved than I want to bore you with right now, and it wouldn't matter if shit goes south anyway. Once we get everything cleared up, then we'll introduce you to the guys as it were."

"Oh. Okay."

"Don't worry about it," Micah repeated. "You already have enough on your plate. Now, why don't you head back to the kitchen, and I'll be there in a minute?"

Tommen nodded reluctantly, hauled himself to his feet, and left the office. It wasn't fair. Why was he being punished for the grouchy, snobby, self-righteousness of some spiteful government employee bitch? Would it have made a difference if he had been a female on the counter? Maybe. After all, even at sixteen, he was totally dedicated to reaffirming the white male patriarchy in society, and totally not focusing on saving up for college, a car, an apartment, and trying to advance his working career through integrity and good work ethic.

Well, fuck them anyway. Fuck them all. Fuck the bitch for being a bitch and hiring someone else to destroy his livelihood at work. Fuck society that told him he was worthless for any number of reasons that he couldn't control. And then fuck society again for telling him that he had to go to college and lead a conveyor belt life. Okay, so having his own car and his own place did have some merit, but fuck college anyway. He would go as long as he was interested and had the means, but it wasn't the only path to a career, and he had more opportunities than most. He had the ability to try anything, do anything, go anywhere, and he had access to the means of forging whatever paperwork was necessary to achieve such things. And he had the time to do it, whole lifetimes in fact.

He could travel the world if he so chose. Provided that he advanced in his Timekeeping career, his salary ought to be enough to sustain him for a while. He could visit big cities and rolling countrysides, go on mainstream, commercial cruises and secretive treks through mountains where only the well-seasoned traveler could go. Given enough time, he could learn dozens of languages. He could become an interpreter, a guide, immersing himself in a foreign culture that most people only saw in *National Geographic* magazines.

And why should he stop there? Why limit himself only to Earth? He had the means to travel throughout the universe, so why shouldn't he? Even as a Timekeeper, he could figure out the worlds where it was safe for aliens to tread, and tread he would. He would see things no human had seen before, things most people could only dream about. He could take pictures and send them back to his dad like postcards. *Hey, Dad, I'm twelve million lightyears from home. Wish you were here. Selfie time!*

Or he could take it one step further and become a Scout. Then he would go where no one had gone before, explore parts of the universe untouched by man, untouched even by Time. He would be the first to meet alien peoples and civilizations. He would be the first to observe their customs and rituals. He would be the first to decipher their languages. He would be the first to walk their worlds and see awesome geological formations of all types, including some he probably wouldn't have names for. He would be the first to observe alien animals of all shapes and sizes. He would be the first to do everything.

He was jerked from his thoughts by the clatter of metal on metal. He startled and looked around to see Micah cleaning up some metal spoons that had fallen on the floor, grudgingly carrying them to the sink and dropping them off in the water.

"Sorry," he apologized weakly. "I was trying to be quiet."

"Why?" Tommen wondered.

"You looked deep in thought, and I didn't want to disturb you."

"Oh."

"So, now that I have your attention, what's on your mind?"

Tommen was silent for a minute, running his tongue over his teeth. Somehow he'd made a mental leap from the unfairness of losing his position to being the first to explore alien worlds as a Scout. Now that he thought about it, it seemed rather silly. Sure, entry-level Baker's Assistant wasn't anything to write home about, but neither was being the manager of the same bakery. He still did the same work, just with the added responsibility of stock and paperwork. It wasn't like he could brag about owning the place. He was still sixteen, still in high school. No one would take him seriously until he was in college, and even then, that was a dubious thing these days.

He would still love to be a Scout—that had never been a question—but it wasn't really considered a noble position for a Time Agent. Some saw it as cheating, a way to use Time without as much responsibility. Others saw it as a suicide mission. Alien cultures were just as likely to be man-eating headhunters as technologically sound and civilized. The casualty rate among Scouts was astronomical, so high in fact that just surviving for three to five years made someone a veteran. Or so he had heard.

"Nothing much," he said finally, answering Micah's question. "Just thinking about stuff."

"Would that stuff be something along the lines of 'It's not fair, I want my job back'?"

"Well, it's not. Why should it matter that I'm only sixteen? Why can't I be manager?"

"Because that's what the government says. They place more emphasis on you going through their government-run daycare than going out, getting a real job, and making it on your own without their assistance." He chuckled dryly. "After all, we didn't build this, right?"

Tommen couldn't decide if Micah was expressing his own

political views or just mirroring his frustration. Either way, he didn't contradict him.

"Besides, you're not going to work here forever," Micah went on after a minute. "As much as I know you love us and just love running off the bus into the bakery, you will, one day, hand us your two-week notice and inform us that you are moving on to greener pastures. Or you'll do something really stupid and we'll have to fire you. Or you'll outlast us anyway, and we'll have to tell you that you're fired because we're closing up shop."

"I'm not sure how I feel about that second one, about being fired for doing something stupid."

"Well, unless you're planning on doing something stupid and getting fired, I don't think you have much to worry about. Do you?"

"Guess not."

"Good. If you're done with that scale, can you slide it this way?"

Tommen did as he was asked, sliding the scale down the table before taking his brownie pan to the oven, swapping out a pan of scones which he delivered to the front case. Then he went back and retrieved the pan of brownies, baked thoroughly thanks to the magic of technology and Banding.

"How's it going up here?" he asked Kyle who was just finishing up with a customer.

"Great. Do we have any cinnamon rolls coming, or are those done?"

Tommen glanced at the clock, almost noon. "I think we're about done with those, unless someone wants a full pan of them."

"Roger that."

Then he returned to the kitchen where Micah was just taking a cake out of the oven. He handed it to Tommen for decoration, then moved on to his next project.

Tommen had just gotten done decorating and was preparing to take it out to the front cooler when Kyle meandered back.

"Hey, it's pretty dead out there...you mind if I take lunch?"

His question was actually directed at Tommen. Guess he hadn't yet been informed that Tommen no longer had the authority to grant him his lunch break. Still, he didn't hear Micah chiming in, so he just nodded. "I'll cover the front."

"Cool, thanks. I'm going to go out and get something, if that's okay, but I'll come back here in case you need me."

"That's fine." Tommen's voice was strained. He didn't want to break down and actually tell Kyle that he wasn't manager anymore, but not doing so felt like a lie. Still, Micah was standing right there doing his thing, and he wasn't saying anything. Either he was totally in the zone in his own work, or he was totally good with Tommen carrying on like he was.

Either way, Kyle headed out to get lunch, and Tommen delivered his cake to the cooler, taking up his position on the counter and looking around the dining room. A couple people sat at a booth, chatting amiably. A few more people sat at the barstools looking out the windows toward the parking lot and the street beyond. One person sat at a barstool at the counter, watching whatever channel was on the TV. Outside, a group of teenage girls exited the clothing store kiddie-corner from the bakery and went out to a nice convertible.

After a minute or two of people-watching, Tommen went around the room, checking trashes, refilling napkins, and finding small chores to do, returning to the counter when a young woman entered the store and went straight for the display case.

"You guys don't have any cinnamon rolls, do you?" she mused. "Too late in the day?"

"Afraid so," Tommen told her. "Unless you want to buy a pan of them."

"How many are in a pan?"

"Sixteen."

"Oh, that would be perfect. If you could. How long would it take?"

"Not long. Ten minutes, maybe fifteen."

"I can wait that long. Hey, can I ask a question?"

"I think you just did, but go ahead."

She grinned. "Yeah, so I see you have your, like, community bulletin board down there on the wall."

Tommen nodded. "Maximum five business cards, and all flyers and posters have to be dated."

"Do you guys allow, like, job postings? I mean, it's kind of a last minute thing, and it'll only be up for a week, max."

He raised a brow and shifted his stance. "What's it for?"

"Well, I'm the co-director of a summer camp up in Wellspring. Yesterday, one of our counselor assistants dropped out unexpectedly, and we really need a replacement. Like I said, it's super last minute, and we're just trying to get the listing out there, everywhere we can."

Normally the twins could be pretty finicky when it came to job postings in their own store. If it was for something along the lines of restaurants, fast food, or anything entry-level, it was a no-go. No competition. If it was for something like manufacturing, technology, truck driving, that they might allow conditionally.

"Um, I'll ask just to double-check," Tommen decided. "Do you have the ad with you?"

"I do, out in the car. I'll go get it while you're asking."

They parted ways.

"What's up?" Micah asked, not looking up from where he was icing some cupcakes.

"First, we need a pan of cinnamon rolls," Tommen told him. "Second, how do we feel about a job posting for a counselor's assistant for a summer camp? Lady says it's last-minute and it'll only be up for like a week or something."

Micah paused in his work and looked thoughtful. "Does she have the ad?"

"She's going out to get it."

"I'll come look."

She just walked in the door when they reached the counter. She handed it to Micah who looked it over, Tommen peering over his shoulder.

"It'll only be up for a week; we're just trying to get it out there," she repeated.

Micah let out a breath, and for a second, Tommen was sure he was going to say no. At the last second, he nodded. "All right. One week. We're taking it down next Saturday if you don't do it beforehand."

The woman let out a sigh of relief. "Thank you so much. We had a hard enough time the first time around; I don't even know that we'll get anyone in such short notice. Yeah, yeah, so a week. Totally good. Do you mind if I...? Or do you...?"

"Go ahead." Micah handed the flyer back to her. "Your cinnamon rolls will be out shortly."

He returned to the kitchen, but Tommen followed the woman to the board and leaned against the wall, arms folded. "So, uh, what's the job entail, exactly?"

The woman raised a brow as she fished for a few thumb tacks. "You know someone who might be interested? Or are you using company time to search for a different job?"

"Hey, my two weeks are coming up anyway." It was a blatant lie. Tommen had no real reason to leave the bakery other than he was pissed about the whole being demoted business. At the same time, five grand for twelve weeks' worth of work was nothing to sneeze at, seeing how he would only make a fraction of that at the bakery.

The woman didn't seemed convinced, but she answered anyway. "It's a counselor's assistant. This person stays in the cabin with the counselor and the campers, attends all the meetings, helps do planning and set-up for the activities, but final authority goes to the counselor. It's like being a counselor, but more...entry-level. Good for high school kids who want to do this sort of thing, who maybe don't have the qualifications or experience for the lead counselor position."

Her tone was decidedly less than friendly now, as if she was accusing him of somehow betraying Micah and Micaiah. She turned as if to leave, but only went to one of the tables and sat down, bringing out her phone. "I'm heading to a meeting with the director and counselors, hence the cinnamon roles. I'll be sure to let them know that you might know of someone who might be interested."

Her tone was dismissive, and Tommen found that he didn't really appreciate it. She had no idea what had just transpired not two hours ago. This morning, he'd woken up the manager of the bakery, someone who was in charge and had authority. He probably could have gotten away with accepting or rejecting her flyer if he had so chosen. Now she was dismissing him as some loser entry-level Baker's Assistant who was still in high school and barely knew what a resume was. Problem was, he was a loser entry-level Baker's Assistant who was still in high school and barely knew what a resume was. But this morning, he'd been the fucking manager. He'd been someone. Then the government told him—well, told Micaiah to tell him—that he wasn't allowed to be someone. He wasn't allowed to be in charge, to advance in his position. He had to sit right where he was.

Tommen took a moment to Band and write down the contact information before heading back to the kitchen and retrieving the pan of cinnamon rolls. The woman went back to all smiles and happiness as she paid for the pan and left. Tommen couldn't decide if she was a bitch or not. It wasn't polite to throw the term around haphazardly, but he couldn't stand the thought of being looked down upon just because he was young and still in school. If only she knew the things he had seen and done.

But she didn't. Ninety-nine percent of the world had no clue about the things he'd seen and done. So they would treat him only as they saw him: young, dumb, ignorant, and weak.

His mood did not particularly improve over the course of his shift, but by the time he left, he was more thoughtful than brooding. Maybe he should apply for the job. Maybe what he really needed was a change of pace, something other than seeing the same people and doing the same thing day in and day out. It wasn't like it was a permanent thing, either. He could get out of the bakery for the summer, work at the summer camp, make a shit ton of money, then return to the bakery just in time for the new school year to start. He would have his fun, get the wanderlust out of his system for a while, then everything would go back to normal.

Yeah, because that ever happened.

Still, when he got home, he took the time to studiously research how to make a nice resume, downloading what he thought was a decent template and filling in the information. Of course, compared to some of the examples he found, his was pretty sparse. He'd only ever attended South Charleston High School and wouldn't be dual-enrolling until his senior year. He'd only ever had one job—well, could he list his agreement with the sporting goods store, where he supplied them with furs? Why not? Anything to eat up some of the white space on the page. And, hey, outdoor summer camp, maybe it would win him some brownie points.

He heard his dad walk in the door sometime after five, a late day for him considering how early he'd been getting home lately.

"You get a good one?" Tommen asked as his dad walked down the hall to his bedroom to change out of his blues.

"Huh?" he wondered.

"You're late."

"Didn't realize I had a curfew there, Dad."

"That's why I asked, you got a body?"

"We did, but it wasn't homicide."

"Ouch. Suicide?"

"Yup. Twenty year old male. Been to his house before to talk him down, but...today he got smart. Waited until after his girlfriend left for work before doing anything."

"That couldn't have been fun for her to come home to."

"No, I don't think it was."

Curious, Tommen got up from his desk and went to stand in the doorway of his dad's room.

"What?" his dad wondered, looking up from his socks.

"Are you okay?" Tommen asked.

"Why wouldn't I be?"

"I don't know, maybe because you just went on a suicide run today?"

Walter gave him a look. "I'm fine. It's not really anything out of the ordinary. I appreciate the concern, but I'm fine."

Stubborn pride and determination was as genetic as color-blindness it seemed, and Tommen did not push the issue. Truth be told, he wasn't all that worried about his dad. His dad could face bloody suicides, gruesome homicides, probably run into a mass-casualty bombing scene and not bat an eye. Stick him in a dark room for more than three seconds, though, and watch him crumble.

"What are you working on?" his dad asked, standing. "Summer homework?"

"Um, no. Not exactly."

No way out of it now. Tommen returned to his room, his dad following.

"Nice little resume," he mused. "Why make it, though? Something happen at work I should know about?"

"It's not what you think."

"Oh? Then what is it?"

So Tommen recounted the tale of the cranky government employee who had gone out of her way to make sure he lost his position as manager. He did not, however, mention the lady with the flyer and the camp counselor job. Counselor's assistant, but who's counting, right?

When he was done with his story, his dad shook his head in disbelief. "The lengths some people will go to in order to make other people miserable for their own suffering. Misery loves company, I suppose."

Tommen scoffed. "Yeah. Micaiah said I'm allowed to tell other employers that I left as a manager, in the event that I don't make it to my eighteenth birthday there. Guess this is just me venting my frustration."

"Better than fighting, I suppose. Actually, I'm very proud of you for sticking with them for so long. How many of your classmates—or maybe the senior class would be more likely—how many of them change jobs every season?"

He shrugged. "I don't know. I mean, Eric's had the same job for years. Some of them I think just work summers..."

"The point is," his dad cut in, "is that you are committed. I'm not saying you should work there for the rest of your life, but it's good to see that you don't give up when things get tough." He put his hand on Tommen's shoulder. "I'm living proof of that."

"Thanks, Dad."

"Well, I suppose that since you're sixteen, this summer we'll make it in your room by ten, lights out your call. How about that? If you lose sleep and can't function at work, that's your own fault."

"Works for me."

"Just keep in mind that us old folks need our beauty rest, so keep it down."

"Got it."

"I'm going to make me some hot dogs. You want any?"

"Sure. Three or four. I'll be out when I'm done with this."

His dad nodded and wandered off to the kitchen. Tommen looked over his resume, feeling like there should be more that he could add. He couldn't exactly add his Timekeeper training, but still...it looked so pathetic. One school, one job, his only notable talents being his fur trapping and fluency in three languages. Well, the lady did say that the job was good for high school kids. Or maybe she was just saying that to bait him, see if he would actually apply—use company time to look for a new job as it were—only to turn him down and give him a lecture on the way out.

Well, the worst they could do was say no. Tommen fished out the paper with the contact information, copying the email address into the recipient line, and having a blasted time trying to get his resume to attach. The application requirements had asked for an informal cover letter. He'd found plenty of examples of formal cover letters, but no one seemed to be able to tell him what an informal one was. So, he did what he did best: improvise. It would probably bite him in the ass, but once again, the worst they could do was tell him no, right?

And away it went, disappearing into the depths of cyberspace and the Internet. With a sinking feeling in his stomach, like he'd somehow betrayed the twins and nothing good was going to come from this job if he did get it, he shut down the computer and headed out to the kitchen to claim his hot dogs.

Chapter Four
The Interview

Sunday was Tommen's day off, but he still found himself getting up obnoxiously early. Oh, the things he did for love. Sometimes it was Saturdays at the synagogue, but most of the time it was Sundays at the cathedral. Well, not really a cathedral, but it was Catholic nonetheless.

He figured he couldn't complain too much; Becky only asked for once or twice a month. And he reluctantly agreed. He figured that the only thing he was losing was a little sleep; according to most of the people in the parish, his soul was already long gone, anyway.

His dad was already up and off to work, leaving Tommen to get ready alone and walk down to Becky's house where she, her mom, and an assortment of young grandchildren were already piling into the van. Becky couldn't ride in the front seat because air bags and dwarfism didn't mix, and since her dad didn't go to Mass because he was Jewish, he ended up riding shotgun.

Tommen had never been to church before his trip to the twenty-first century, but he still remembered his pa had a moderate disdain for Catholics. He was always grumbling about the "self-righteous modern Pharisees" who used flair and fanfare to cover up the darker souls residing secretly in their darker bodies. Tommen wasn't sure he would quite go that far, at least not with all of them. For his general misgivings about religion, a few of the people were actually very nice, Becky and her mom included.

That wasn't to say he wasn't grateful for his phone ringing just as they were walking across the parking lot of the church. Becky gave him a look, but Tommen shrugged and said, "Must be God's calling me direct this week."

"Tommen…"

"I'll be in, just give me a few seconds. Trust me, I could stand a block away and still hear the music." He swiped the answer key on his phone. "Hello?"

"Hi, is this Tommen Forbes?"

"Depends on who's asking."

"My name is Jerry Wilson; I'm the director of Eagle Eye Youth Summer Camp."

"Oh, hi. Yeah."

"Is now a good time to talk?"

"Yeah, it's great."

"I'm calling because you applied for the assistant counselor position, correct?"

"Yes. I saw it on a flyer."

"What made you want to apply for the job? I see on your resume that you're the manager of a bakery."

Not anymore, but Micaiah said I could say that. But Tommen gave him a brief description of events, not mentioning any dates in hopes that the man wouldn't ask and figure out that this was more of a reflexive temper tantrum than a calculated job opportunity. Oh well, at least the job was only temporary; that would give Tommen enough time to quit his job, start his new job, regret quitting his old job, think about quitting his new job, and about the time he got around the actually quitting the new job, summer would be over, and he would be free to return to his old job.

The director asked him a few more questions about his schooling, his responsibilities at work, and so on. Tommen had never actually interviewed for a job before; he'd just started helping out around the bakery and was one day added onto the payroll. Talking on the phone with Mr. Wilson, he wasn't sure if he was doing the interview thing well or not. He could be answering honestly and professionally, or he could be whining and blathering on like there was no tomorrow.

"Well, it's been good talking with you, Tommen," Mr. Wilson said. Tommen felt his hopes plummet. "I'm sorry this was such short notice, but I was hoping to chat a little and get a feel for you, if you'd be good for the position. If you are free this week sometime, I'd like to meet with you in my office so we can have a more formal discussion and go over some of the finer points of the job."

Tommen blinked in surprise. "Oh, yeah, sure. I mean, that'd be great."

"Excellent. Are you free tomorrow around, say, one o'clock?"

"Well, I'm working at that time. If it was later..."

"Hm...how about Tuesday?"

"I've got Tuesday off."

"What do you say to eleven o'clock on Tuesday, then?"

"Sounds great."

Mr. Wilson gave him the address and directions and wished him a good day before hanging up. Tommen couldn't suppress a small happy dance as he put his phone away and headed into the church, easily picking out Becky in the mass—ha ha, Mass, mass? No?—throng of people.

"You look pretty happy," Becky observed quietly. "God finally wash away your sins?"

"No, but He might have gotten me a summer job." When she raised a brow, he simply shook his head and said, "Tell you later."

His mind was too active to pay much attention to the sermon—something about Job or Jonah, he couldn't recall which. He'd just applied last night and already got a call back. Now, he'd never had any other job, nor had to go through the interview and hiring process, but he'd heard enough conversations from customers in the dining room to know that such a quick turnaround was at least a good start. If they were as desperate as the lady claimed, he might just have a shot.

Although, thinking about it, he wasn't sure that made him feel better about himself in the position. They were desperate; chances were, they would hire anyone who was still breathing and not a pedophile. What if someone else applied between now and Tuesday, someone who was more mature and had camp experience? He'd be out of the running instantly.

Not like that was a bad thing, really. He did still have his job at the bakery. If things did fall through, the twins would never need to know that he'd gone behind their backs.

But what if they hired him? How was he going to tell Micah and Micaiah—especially Micaiah, holy fuck—that he was just packing up and leaving them for twelve weeks? He'd just kind of assumed that they'd be cool with it, but what if they weren't? What if they refused to give him his job back at the end of the summer? He'd be gaining five grand and losing the rest, losing his steady paycheck during the school year.

Well, that's what you get, dumbass, for letting your emotions lead you on. You got pissed about something that happened at work—something that wasn't your fault and the twins didn't like but were forced to comply with—and now your emotional reaction could throw everything you do have down the toilet. It wasn't even anything really bad. You got stripped of your title, sure, but they seem pretty chill about letting you keep some of your management powers. And, even better, they let you keep the raise. More money, less responsibility. Why are you having such a problem with this?

He really wasn't sure. At the same time, maybe a change of pace would be good for him. Yeah, he'd only been on the books for two, almost three years, but he'd been helping out around the bakery since he was ten. That was like seven years, man. He had to get out of there.

Becky was less confident about it, citing dependability and commitment in times of adversity, and he struggled to maintain his optimism as he walked into the store Monday morning. The twins hadn't taken away his keys, either, allowing him to open and close the store when they weren't around. Could he really turn his back on them over something they had no control over? Over something they were forced to comply with even as they had explicitly stated that they would still look for a way to get around the rules? The more he thought about it, the worse he felt.

"Morning," Micah greeted as he walked in the door. "Hope your day off didn't get you too relaxed because we are going to have a busy day today. We've got at least three parties coming in, all different types. Got a birthday party, a retirement party, and a baby shower, God help us."

"Oh. Sounds...busy. All at the same time?"

"Thankfully no, though the birthday party and the baby shower could overlap, depending on how things go."

"That's good."

He could feel Micah's stare. "You okay? You didn't suddenly become a bachelor over the weekend, did you?"

"No, it's not that."

"Then what is it?"

Tommen shuffled his feet guiltily. "You remember that lady who came in Saturday, the one with the flyer?"

"Yeah...?"

"Well, I kind of applied for the job. The director called me yesterday with a phone interview, and he wants me to go in tomorrow for an interview at his office."

Micah folded his arms and leaned against the table. "Okay...?"

"Well, that's just it. I mean, it was kind of an...emotional...reflexive response to the whole being demoted thing. I realize it now of course, but I don't know what to do."

"What makes you say that?" Micah's tone was difficult to judge.

"On the one hand, it's reflexive, and I know that. I mean, it's not like you guys had any legal control over what happened, and you're not being dicks about it to me. You let me keep my raise, my keys, the whole bit, so it's not like I can cite any of that as a valid reason for leaving."

"But...?"

"But..." Tommen sighed and let his arms flop down to his sides. "I've been here for seven years. I finally got something good going for me. It got taken away. Now I just feel like...I've got to get out of here. There has to be something more. Even if it's just something temporary, like a temporary summer camp counselor job."

Micah nodded slowly. "You sound like Micaiah, you know that?"

"All the more reason to get out of here."

The younger twin grinned at that. "Well, we'll talk more once Cai gets here, but I'll give you my two cents. First, yes, this is a very emotional, reflexive response. It's the working class equivalent of a temper tantrum. But, you seem to recognize it, which is a good thing. You've done a lot of growing up in the last year. To that end, I understand that you're frustrated. Regardless of this whole manager-not-manager fiasco, being stuck at an entry-level restaurant job is no one's idea of glamorous, regardless of pay or title. Seriously, if you worked at any of the fast food chains as long as you have here, you could open up your own store about now. Even Cai. Maybe you've noticed, maybe not, but he's getting restless himself, and he's owned this business for twelve years."

"What are you saying? You think I should take the job?"

"I'm not saying you shouldn't, although the short notice is decidedly less than professional, though admittedly not too uncommon in restaurants. And it's a summer job. Ten, twelve weeks, a chance to get out and see the world beyond the bakery."

"So...I would be able to come back here to work during the school year, when I'm all done there?"

"I see no reason why not. We don't hate you, and you've done nothing to get yourself in trouble or blacklisted or fired. Like I said, we'll talk to Micaiah when he gets here."

That was what Tommen was afraid of. He liked Micaiah, he really did, but he'd been on the receiving end of the elder twin's righteous anger before, and it was a scary thing to behold.

Micaiah walked in the back door around ten o'clock, just as the retirement party walked in the front door. It was a crazy twenty minutes as everyone tried to figure themselves out, who ordered what, who needed what, what was going on, and, oh, right, there were the regular walk-in customers, too. It was closer to eleven when Tommen followed Micah into the office.

"Good things never come from you two walking into the office like this," Micaiah said, spinning around in his chair; he didn't wear his prosthetic today, and his crutches were tucked up against the desk. "What happened?"

So Tommen gave Micaiah about the same speech he'd given Micah earlier that morning. He still felt guilty, like a child having to tell the principal about the fight out on the playground and admit that it was his fault. Micaiah listened patiently, not interrupting, but not in as dark a mood as Tommen might normally expect from him. Was it because he was, as Micah said, restless himself, so he was more sympathetic to Tommen's plight?

Micah also threw in his two cents, recounting what he'd told Tommen, finishing with, "I don't appreciate the short notice, especially if they need him as fast as the lady was implying, but we have the coverage with Kyle and Jenna, and it's only a temporary thing."

"It sounds like you two have already made up your minds, and you're just waiting for Uncle Micaiah to give you permission," Micaiah said, his tone somewhere between humor and irritation. He shifted in his seat. "Like Micah said, Tommen, you've grown up a lot in the last year. So, here's my bit. I'm not going to give you permission. If you want it, you're going to have to square your shoulders and make the decision yourself. Either you're staying here for the summer, or you're going there. I'm not your dad signing your permission slip and sending you off to summer camp. You are an employee here who is either going to act professionally and give us notice of your last day, or else drop it entirely. Like an adult."

"So...I wouldn't be allowed to come back at the start of the new school year?" Tommen wondered lamely.

"Are you asking for permission like a child, or expressing a professional desire?"

Tommen took a slow, deliberate breath. "Sir, if Mr. Wilson offers me the job for the camp counselor, I would like to take it. It's twelve weeks, and I would like to be able to return to my job here at the end of that job which should be the start of the new school year. If you'll have me back."

"That's better." Micaiah leaned back in his chair and nodded slowly.

"I'm inclined to say yes," Micah commented.

"So am I. On one condition."

"What's that?" Tommen asked warily.

"You do this, you lose your management raise — unless we can find a way to reinstate you as manager. If we can't, you lose that raise." Micaiah went on before he could speak. "As you yourself have said, this was a temper tantrum reflex, and you're giving us less than two weeks' notice. On top of that, you are leaving for more than sixty days for something non-emergent or non-essential. You want to keep your raise, you stay. You go, it goes."

Tommen didn't need to Band to run the math in his head. He was still going to make more at the camp over the twelve weeks than he would keeping his dollar raise here. Still...he'd worked hard to get that raise. He nodded. "Okay. Fair enough. If I go, I lose the raise."

"You said your interview is tomorrow?"

"Yes, it is."

"Did he say how long before you would know if you got the job?"

"No, but I don't think it would be too long if they're as desperate as they claim."

"Well, as soon as you know, let us know, because we're going to have to shuffle some things around. If there's nothing else, I have work to do."

Micaiah returned to his paperwork. Micah stayed in the office as well, while Tommen returned to the front counter just as a customer approached.

Holy shit, had that actually happened? They were totally good with this? Well, not totally, but they were willing to go along with it? That was less painful than he thought it would be, though that was nothing compared to how he expected his dad to react when he found out. If Tommen got the job.

His dad always liked to remind him that he was going to leave home someday, but sometimes Tommen suspected that he was really reminding himself. The man had spent the better part of his adult life searching and waiting for Tommen, taking him in and raising him as his own for his brother, Tommen's pa. Well, that time was quickly coming to a close as Tommen finished up high school and was set to advance in his Timekeeping—well, not exactly; he was a little behind in his studies thanks to Rifun's little coup which cut everyone off from the Wheel, including the Arena. But still, their time together as live-together father and son was ending. Walter had already overstayed his welcome; he would have to go dark pretty quick after Tommen left for college.

With this job, assuming he got it, he would be gone for something like twelve weeks. He'd never been away from home that long before. It would be an exciting experience for him, but he found himself wondering how his dad would take it. Would he be good with it, chill and supportive? Or would it remind him too much of the time Tommen had been kidnapped and under Rifun's power for two weeks? Would he get out and do stuff because he wanted to do it without worrying about his son at home, or would he simply busy himself at work with no real social life to speak of? Either was possible, though the latter more likely.

These thoughts he batted back and forth as he walked along the sidewalk toward Mr. Wilson's office for the interview. He did not Band, instead taking time to enjoy the warmth and the sunshine and the activity of the city—well, okay, so he could have done just fine without the bustling city life, but it was just something he'd grown accustomed to.

The address he'd been given was in, as might be expected, the business district. It was in a building complex that Tommen had never been in, but passed by on several occasions. He also knew that most of the offices were not permanent offices, but temporary, rented for a day or a week, up to a month at a time. At first, Tommen had been a little dismayed by it, until he considered that the camp itself was in Wellspring. They probably had an office up there, but it would be hell asking anyone to drive there just for an interview, especially if the position was intended for high school kids who might not have their license yet.

And that wasn't to say that the offices, though rented, weren't nice. They weren't exactly upscale New York bank executive kind of nice, but for a quick office setup, it still had the air of professionalism, perfect for a startup business. Or a temporary location for an out of area business in the city just long enough to hire someone and get out.

Tommen had taken his time preparing for the interview, unsure how formal he wanted to be. He skipped the full suit and tie; he wasn't going to interview for a bank or the Secret Service. At the same time, if he was going to interview for the counselor of a summer camp, was it better to go business casual to honor the interview itself, or in full hiking and camping gear to let the person know that he was ready to go out and start this afternoon? For safety's sake, he went with business casual.

Somehow, Tommen had always imagined that, when renting office space, the higher the floor, the higher the rent. It might be reasonable to assume that all the space on the first floor had already been rented, but when the guy's office ended up being on the fifth floor, Tommen found himself questioning his motives, especially if he was only going to be sticking around for a week or two. Although, if Tommen was getting paid five grand just as a counselor's assistant, it was also reasonable to expect that the counselors and everyone above him made just a little bit more. Good grief, how much did this camp cost?

An awful thought hit him then: this was going to be an outdoorsy camp for snobby rich kids who had no concept of camping. These were going to be entitled losers who wanted to go canoeing, but without actually having to paddle the canoe. They would want fresh fish for dinner, but had no interest in actually catching or cleaning the fish. Dread lodged itself in Tommen's gut as he punched the number on the elevator. Maybe he wouldn't be leaving the bakery after all.

He took a breath and shook his head. He couldn't go making wild assumptions yet. More than once, the way he perceived things and the way things actually were, were two very different things. He had to wait until he had the whole picture before making a judgment. And, as Micah had pointed out after their conversation with Micaiah, he was under no obligation to take the job even if they did offer it to him. He was only obligated once he signed the paperwork, and even then it was only a moral obligation. He wouldn't be hauled off to jail if he didn't show up.

The elevator stopped once to let more people on, then continued to the fifth floor where Tommen departed, feeling very conspicuous and inadequate. He was probably the least formally dressed in the entire building. Everyone else seemed to follow the whole "dress for success" axiom, while he was dressed for a mediocre existence as a middle manager. Hey, what a coincidence, that was exactly the position he'd just gotten fired from. Would it have made a difference for Her Grouchiness if he'd come to work in a suit and tie and waited on her like that?

Tommen turned and headed down the hall, hoping he looked purposeful and confident, hoping his deodorant worked as well as it advertised. The building wasn't large, just large enough to keep him guessing. The office number he'd been given was 504. When he got there, however, he discovered that there wasn't just a plain old 504. There was 504A and 504B. Did Mr. Wilson rent both of them? Were they connected? Would anyone really notice if he walked in the wrong one?

Well, the receptionist would, obviously, as he walked into 504A and inquired after Mr. Wilson. He felt less bad, however, when she sighed and said something about "not again." So apparently, Tommen was not the first one to walk in their office and ask for their neighbor. Still, he tried to be polite and thank her before leaving and, with burning ears and cheeks, walking into 504B. He paused for just a moment, just inside the door, trying to calm his nerves and not look like a dolt who'd just gotten caught with his hand in the cookie jar. Or, you know, in the wrong office suite.

Walking past the main reception desk which was empty, Tommen saw that this office only had two rooms, a reception office and a manager's office. He could also see how this office, despite being on the fifth floor, might have constituted a little cheaper rent: there was zero view from the windows. Trees grew thick in front of them for most of the length of the windows, and what wasn't tree was rock, a bit like the view from the kitchen in Micah and Micaiah's house.

Gingerly, he approached the manager's office, where the man he assumed to be Jerry Wilson sat at a small desk, currently on the phone. He dutifully took notes, not looking up until he was done. Then he grinned hugely and waved Tommen in.

"Good morning, you must be Tommen Forbes," he said, standing and shaking Tommen's hand in a bone-crushing squeeze. He wasn't even that big of a guy, mid-forties, five-ten, one hundred and eighty pounds, maybe. "I'm Jerry Wilson."

"Nice to meet you in person," Tommen told him, hoping it was the right thing to say.

"I'm glad I caught you in time; believe it or not, I'm really trying to pack up and get out of here. I have to be back in Wellspring tomorrow to get things ready ahead of the counselors and staff." He nodded as if his mind had already wandered off to a thousand different things he needed to do in Wellspring. "Anyway, so we spoke on the phone briefly on Sunday. Since you've had a little time to digest the information, I want to start out by asking if you have any questions for me about the camp or the job. The reason I do it this way, starting out with this rather than at the end, is I want to make sure that you understand what the job is before I seriously consider you for the position. If you're going to back out, now is the time to do it."

Well, that gave a pretty good clue about what happened to the last guy, Tommen thought.

Still, before he could ask anything, Mr. Wilson continued speaking. "So, let me tell you a little about the camp itself. There are actually two camps, one for younger kids, ages seven to eleven maybe twelve depending on maturity and special needs considerations, and another camp for older kids, ages twelve to fifteen, again give or take depending. The younger camp runs from June 20th all the way through July 18th, four full weeks. Then, all the staff gets a week to go home, rest, relax, and regain their sanity before coming back on July 26th. The older camp runs from July 28th through August 22nd, again just shy of four full weeks.

"On top of that, starting this Saturday, all of the counselors and staff, myself included, will be going to camp ahead of the campers to get the camp ready: clean out the cabins, dust off the furniture, all that stuff. That's when staff camping begins. Similarly, there is another cleanup at the end of the camp, but that doesn't take nearly as long. Depending on when your school starts, you might be able to leave early; that's not uncommon for our high school employees."

Mr. Wilson leaned back in his chair. "All right, sorry I interrupted. I got a little ahead of myself. Any questions about the camp? I noticed you started to squirm a little."

"Well, being an extended camp, I assume there will be calls home?" Tommen asked lamely.

"Of course, and this is especially important for the younger kids. The camp has electricity and running water; there are showers, toilets, and laundry. This might be an outdoors camp, but we don't need to look and smell like we've been stranded in the wilderness for four weeks, fending off hungry bears and mountain lions." He paused. "Although, phone time will be decidedly limited with all the activities going on."

"No, it's not that." Well, not only that. Reluctantly, he turned and pulled down his ear so Mr. Wilson could see his hearing aid. "I have hearing aids, and they need to charge overnight."

"Absolutely. No, there is electricity in all the cabins. And if you're really worried, you can leave them with the camp nurse to charge." He grinned as Tommen relaxed. "Well, if I haven't sent running out the door screaming yet, let me ask you a little about yourself."

Tommen had done a little research on how to interview well for jobs. Problem was, most of those techniques could only be applied to corporate jobs. How to negotiate your salary and benefits, for example. Well, his salary was a flat five grand for ten or eleven weeks of work. His benefits included sleeping indoors, electricity and running water, and making it out alive with his sanity in tact. Other examples, such as negotiating a schedule, inquiring as to working conditions and office environment, customer interacting and handling, and so on, were also out of the question. Everything else seemed to be pretty straightforward, or else he was terribly misreading the purpose of the questions, the answers he was supposed to give versus the answers he was actually giving.

At the same time, he couldn't have been doing too bad. Mr. Wilson remained politely interested, listening to his bumbling answers and always having the next question ready to fire. Eventually, it turned into something of a regular conversation, and Tommen found himself much more at ease than he had been walking in. Was it a good thing, when an interview went this long? Well, as Mr. Wilson had said, Tommen hadn't run out the door screaming. Similarly, Mr. Wilson hadn't cut the interview short and given him the "don't call us, we'll call you" speech.

"Okay, Tommen," he said at last, "I know that went a little longer than intended, but, now that we've chatted a little and you have a better idea of what's going on, do you have any more questions for me?"

"If the older camp is for ages twelve to fifteen, why hire high school kids for the assistant counselor position?" Tommen wondered.

"Good question, and the answers is as simple as familiarity.

We get a lot of kids with a lot of problems. Our counselors have to be at least twenty-three years old, but for a lot of kids, that's still an 'adult' in their mind. By having younger counselor assistants, sometimes they'll be more willing to talk. For older kids, it's chatting with someone they view as a peer. For younger kids, it might be that you act as an older brother, someone they can talk to without it being a grown-up.

"And, in order to cut down on mischievous shenanigans, we only hire those high school kids who have demonstrated responsibility and the ability to take the job seriously. Yeah, talk to the kids and make friends with them, get them to open up, but don't join them if they're planning to go egg the girls' cabins. That you would have to stop and report."

"Makes sense."

At the same time, Tommen felt his hopes plummet again. Most jobs did a criminal background check; working with kids, that was all but guaranteed. Mr. Wilson wanted to cut down on shenanigans, but if he researched Tommen, he was going to find a record, just a small one when Ryan forced him to go out and do a little graffiti. If Mr. Wilson didn't dig into it a little and find the "duress" notes in there, he might assume that Tommen was going to start more shenanigans and skip over him entirely.

"A few last comments," Mr. Wilson said, wrapping up. "This job is dealing with kids. Can you deal with kids?"

"Yes," Tommen answered, willing it to be true.

"Since you are dealing with kids, we conduct very thorough background checks. This interview is very short notice, I realize, and you would be starting the position before the checks came back. To avoid wasting my time or yours, would I find anything on you that might cause me to consider sending you home? Charleston is a pretty decent drive from Wellspring."

Tommen felt his cheeks burn as he gave an honest answer, making sure to emphasize the part where it was technically in limbo because of the "duress" clause. Mr. Wilson's expression turned severe.

"If you want a reference or need to actually get in the file, my dad's a cop with CPD," Tommen finished guiltily. "Walter Forbes. He can probably get it for you."

Mr. Wilson nodded. "I appreciate your honesty. To an extent, I also appreciate your embarrassment and self-consciousness over the whole thing. A record of the past does not always guarantee a pattern for the future, and everyone does stupid things at some time in their life, especially when they're young. However..." He dug around in a drawer and pulled out a sheet of paper. "I will need you to sign this, authorizing me to conduct a formal background check."

Tommen took the paper and signed where indicated. Mr. Wilson filed it away. "Excellent. Now then, if we decide to hire you, I will give you a call tomorrow or Thursday at the latest. You'll do the rest of your tax paperwork when you come out Saturday for camp prep, and we'll go from there. How does that sound?"

"Sounds good, sir," Tommen answered, trying to stay optimistic.

"Wonderful." Mr. Wilson stood and Tommen followed suit, trying not to flinch in pain at the second bone-crushing handshake. "It's been nice meeting you, Tommen. Enjoy the rest of your day."

At that point, he just wanted to get out of there. He'd probably embarrassed himself enough that he wouldn't even be out the door before Mr. Wilson lost it and started laughing, calling all of his friends to tell them about the idiot teenager who'd just walked into his office and interviewed for the job. *What a loser. You can definitely tell this one's never interviewed for a job before, boys. What are they teaching them in schools these days?*

He remained silent on the elevator, determined not to stare at the fine men and women in their luxury suits. Even as he felt intimidated by them, there was also the fact that they were wearing thousand-dollar suits just to go to work in a rented office. Were they just here on temporary business and every bit the wealthy snob they portrayed, or were they as much a fraud as he was and better at hiding it?

Tommen's mind went to the Disguises that Micaiah, Kayla, and the others had used. They'd said it was as much a modification of DNA as just a trick of the eye. Changing the DNA made them appear as other people, where the trick of the eye reconciled egregious differences—height and weight differences for example—as well as appropriate clothing. Was it possible to use a Disguise but without the physical changes? Could he learn to use it strictly for clothing purposes?

Then he thought of something else. If he went away to this summer camp, how was he going to get any of his training done in the Arena? He was already behind because of the coup, six months behind to be precise. Summer camp would put him nine months behind in his training. He'd had to wait six years to move from probationary to Apprentice; he had no desire to add any more years between Apprentice and Journeyman status.

By the time he hit the street, the summer camp job was seeming less and less likely, both because of how he'd made a fool of himself and how much he was losing by leaving home. He shook his head. This had been a stupid idea from the start, born of rage and emotion and all the other stupid things that got teenagers in trouble.

Fuck. He was sixteen, almost seventeen, and he was still giving in to reflexive, emotional reactions? He shook his head. He needed to get a hold of himself. So far, he'd managed to stop fighting with Tyler Freeman, and he was able to keep himself under control and not insist on sleeping with Becky, even if he felt like that was an overdue thing this far into their relationship. But he did keep himself under control in that area; he'd even managed to be good on the Internet lately. Well, better anyway; with the sheer number of ads out there these days, he couldn't avoid everything.

But still, it was time for him to step up and be a man. He should have done that a long time ago, really. It was time for him to take everything seriously, from his job to his relationships, to his education—college education, that is. Fuck high school—to his Timekeeper training. He had to stop relying on everyone else to do everything for him and remind him of everything like he was some stupid, forgetful, petulant teeny-bopper.

As far as school went, he was out for the summer. But he still had two years left, his most important years. Junior year was characterized by endless testing, and it was the year that colleges paid the most attention to when considering admissions. That meant he was going to have to give at least half a fuck about his work and his grades.

His Timekeeper training was even more important than that because that he would be taking with him through however many lives he went through. It was time to start really training and stop relying on sheer dumb luck to awaken new abilities in him. Predict and External Banding were products of adrenaline, but he needed to calm down, think logically, and hone them properly, plus learn more as an Apprentice.

But if he was going to do that, he was probably going to have to give up on the whole summer camp counselor idea. He couldn't afford to waste more time on frivolous pursuits caused by hormonal reactions. That meant he was going to have to go back to work at the bakery, and just suck it up that he'd been demoted. He didn't like it, but the twins couldn't do anything about it. It was just a fact of life. And they were willing to let him keep his raise and reinstate him once he turned eighteen, which was only a little over a year away. Was there anything really bad about the situation?

He made it home in good time, wondering if he wanted to call Mr. Wilson now and tell him he wasn't interested anymore, or just wait and see if they even wanted him for the job. If his application had been shredded the minute he walked out of the office, then there was no need to worry.

He changed out of his nice clothes into something more appropriate for summer, then went to the kitchen to make himself some lunch. At the same time, it would be kind of nice to have a purpose this summer, something more than just sitting around the house and occasionally going to work or hanging out with Becky when she wasn't zipping away on her sewing machine. And the money wasn't that bad either.

Chapter Five
Packing

S o, how did the interview go?" Micah asked when Tommen walked in the door the following morning.

"Um, good, I guess," Tommen answered, shrugging, punching in and grabbing an apron.

"You don't sound too confident."

"I've never actually interviewed for a job before. This is the only place I've worked, and here I just started helping out until I got old enough that you had to put me on payroll." Micah laughed and nodded. Tommen dropped his hands to his sides. "I'm serious! I made a fool of myself, I know it."

"Tommen, you're sixteen. The position is targeted for sixteen year olds; they are fully expecting that you've never had a job before; the fact that you do is only a bonus. It's probably why you're going to get the job."

"Yeah."

"You don't sound too excited about it."

"I just feel guilty about it, leaving you guys and the whole thing that led up to this. And the conspiracy theorist in me says that this was awfully convenient, too. Way too coincidental timing."

"Maybe, but what are we going to do about it? The timing, I mean. And as for the events leading up to this, we already went over that. It's done, it's over, the terms are set."

"I know, I know. But then I had another thought. What about my Apprentice training? If I'm gone to summer camp, I won't be able to go to the Arena to train."

Micah nodded. "This is very true. At the same time, if your

dad is having to drive you out there, I'm thinking one of us might be able to go with him, and then we can figure out a way to open a portal there so you can get in the Wheel to train. If you were interested in that sort of thing. But I think you're going to find that working for a summer camp is a lot different than participating as a camper."

"Oh, that much I know. But, I mean, if there was a way we could work it out that you could come and get me to go train, that would be cool."

"We'll see. First you have to get the job."

They worked in silence for a bit until Tommen headed up front to prep the dining room and unlock the doors. He served a couple early bird customers, then returned to the kitchen where Micah was just setting out more trays for the display case.

"So, what do you think?" Tommen asked.

Micah did not look up from his work. "About what?"

"Do you really think I should take the job? I mean, I still feel bad about going behind you guys' backs with the whole thing, and then there's my training—"

"Tommen. You're not going to work here forever. That's my first point. My second point is that, yes, I'm sure you feel like you've fallen behind in your training, but it's not going anywhere. This job is a chance for you to get out for a little while. It's camping, away from us, away from your dad, away from city life, a time for you to be you and see what you're made of. Okay, if you want my biased opinion, then yes, I do think you should take the job." He paused. "But, once again, it comes back to the asking permission versus expressing a desire. You're only a boy for so long; eventually, you have to take the reins and be your own man."

Tommen nodded, but before he could say more, the bell over the door jingled, and he went to attend some customers.

It was certainly a different way of thinking about it. Ten weeks without his dad or the twins. Ten weeks where he would be working in conjunction with a camp counselor to wrangle children. Yes, he would still be under the counselor and have to defer to them in some situations, but it would be different than being under his dad or the twins. This would be a strictly professional relationship, not parent-child, not officer-underling. He would be expected to conduct himself professionally by his own merits with no one to gently remind him of things. Discipline, being able to control himself and his actions and inspire the same in others.

Did he do that? Could he do that? Well, he'd been manager of the bakery with relatively few problems, and that took some measure of discipline, right? Of course, there was a difference between disciplining himself and functioning adults, and trying to discipline children.

But as the day wore on, his hopes of getting the job grew dim. He wasn't expecting the call first thing at six o'clock in the morning, but when the morning rush passed by, then lunch, and his out time got closer, he became increasingly convinced that the whole thing was a no go.

"Sorry it didn't work out," Micah told him as he reluctantly punched out. "But, we'll see you in the morning."

Tommen nodded. "Yeah. See you tomorrow."

His dad had the day off, but Tommen usually preferred to walk home during the summer. It was a way to get in some fresh air and get out of any chores he had waiting for him at home, or at least put them off a little longer. Plus, this summer he had a girl he could visit, too.

He had just crossed the bridge when he phone rang.

"Hello?" he wondered.

"Tommen, it's Jerry Wilson, the camp director. How are you doing this afternoon?"

"No worse for wear."

"Excellent. Well, I've finished all the interviews and, going back through all my reports and candidates, are you still up for ten weeks at summer camp?"

"What? Huh, oh, yeah! Yeah, I am. So, wait, you're actually, like, hiring me?"

Mr. Wilson laughed. "That's what I'm saying."

"Yeah. That's great. I mean, when and where?"

"So, I have your email, and I'll send over all the forms and information for you to print and fill out. If you can scan them and send them back, that's fine. If not, just bring them with you. I'm going to have you come out Saturday morning; any time before noon is fine. I'll also email you a map and directions using Charleston as the base. Sound good?"

"Absolutely."

"Excellent. We'll see you Saturday."

The call ended and Tommen couldn't help but do a small happy dance. He did it; he got it. He got the job and he was going to summer camp. The thought was awesome and terrifying at the same time, and by the time he reached Becky's house, he was pretty well ready for a nap.

"You look like you're in a good mood," Becky observed as he followed her up to her room. "I take it you got the job?"

"Yes. He literally just called me."

"Cool." She went and sat on her bed, startling a long-haired gray cat that ran under the bed.

"Where'd the cat come from?" Tommen wondered.

"Oh, it's my sister's cat. One of her kids has apparently developed a cat allergy, so she had to get rid of him, but she didn't want to take him to the pound. She asked if I wanted him, so I said yes. His name is Mr. Snuffles."

"Uh...huh."

"Don't worry; he'll make a good replacement for you while you're gone."

Her tone was difficult to judge, if she was seriously pissed that he was leaving, or if it was all sarcasm. Nevertheless, he knew her well enough to meet snark for snark as he answered, "Well, I hope I don't have to worry about you two being naughty, because I am a jealous boyfriend."

"Don't worry; he's fixed. No kittens here."

Tommen's first thought went back to the time he'd visited Sifura's world and witnessed the harvesting of their little fruity kitten bundles, grown in trees no less. His second thought mused over Becky's comment. Her mom was Catholic, dad Jewish, and she was certainly a little spitfire for both, yet she was also no stranger to dirty jokes and innuendos that would make Micaiah proud. Some days he wondered just how innocent she really was, and what it might take to actually get in bed with her.

"So, now that you got the job, what are you going to do?" Becky asked, jerking him from his thoughts.

"Um, well...the director said he was going to email me all the tax paperwork and stuff, and directions to the camp. So I have to fill that out. I definitely need to text the twins to let them know. And I'll have to tell my dad. And I guess I need to pack."

"You got a suitcase?"

"Yeah, I do."

"Is it any good?"

He rolled his eyes. "Yes, Mom, it's fine."

She grinned. "You think you could smuggle me out there?"

"Suitcase isn't that big."

"Neither am I."

"Bigger than the suitcase."

She sighed. "Okay, fine. But you have to text me at least four times a week to tell me what you're up to. I can get along fine in my workshop without you, but I still want details of all the shenanigans you're getting into. Putting a bunch of boys together in a cabin for four weeks, something is bound to happen and I want to hear about it."

"I don't know...putting a bunch of boys together in a cabin for four weeks, some of those things could be weird."

"You're not much of a speaker, but I think you can report things as tastefully as possible, with a little tact. I learned that in my English class."

"Right. And how many answers did you write in Hungarian or Hebrew or Polish?"

"Not as many as you do in Spanish class with Welsh or Irish."

Okay, so she had him there.

He spent a little time there, spending part of it trying to coax Mr. Snuffles out from under the bed, but to no avail. Eventually, though, he knew he had to get home. It was time to break the news to his dad that his son would be going away for ten weeks. Starting in approximately three days.

So he walked the last quarter mile back to his house, walking in the door just as his dad put away the last of the dishes.

"How was work?" Walter inquired conversationally.

"Okay," Tommen answered. "Work."

Habit told him to drop off his backpack. Reality reminded him he had no backpack. So he stopped at the threshold between kitchen and living room and leaned awkwardly on the counter. "Um, Dad, there's something I have to tell you."

"As long as you're not telling me your girlfriend's pregnant."

"What? No. Nothing like that." Where the fuck had—okay, Tommen knew exactly where that came from. Still...really? That was his first thought when Tommen said he had to tell him something?

"Okay, shoot."

"Well, there was kind of an incident at work."

Now his dad paused in his work to face him, raising a brow suspiciously. "Incident?"

Tommen described the incident as he understood it, based on what Micaiah told him. "So, they had to basically demote me from my manager position."

He saw his dad relax a little. "Well, that's the government for you, and I'm sorry it happened."

"That's not all."

"What do you mean?"

"Well, I got a little pissed about the whole thing, and I ended up applying for another job. I went back and told the twins about it, and we had a little discussion, and they think I should take it. And just today, when I walked home, the guy called me, said he wanted me to take the job, and I did."

"What's the job?"

"Um...a summer camp counselor. Counselor's assistant. And it's up in Wellspring. For twelve weeks. Like, six weeks at a time with one week to come home and stuff in the middle, but...yeah. That's what it is."

His dad was not a difficult man to read; he wore his heart on his sleeve. Actually, he wore it on both sleeves and both pant legs, too, probably. His expression was severe, thoughtful, confused, a little hurt, but also a little awe in there, too, if Tommen read him right. Finally he nodded and tossed the hand towel back in the sink. "All right, so I guess you're going to need a ride up there."

"Yeah."

"When?"

"Saturday."

Now he took a breath and let it out. "Saturday. This Saturday?"

"Yeah. It was all kind of short notice."

"I'll say. You said the twins know?"

"Yes, they do. I texted them today, and my last day is Friday morning."

"Does Becky know?"

"I told her, too."

His dad sighed but nodded. "All right. You know where this place is at?"

"The guy emailed me directions; I'll print them out."

Tommen followed his dad to his bedroom. "You're...not mad?"

"Why would I be mad?"

"Because I did this without telling you."

His dad chuckled. "That you did. But at the same time, you are making your own choices now, and now you're going to see how your choices affect the consequences. I'm not always going to be around to steer you like you're a little boy. I can give you advice—such as how I think you should have gotten your license first so you could drive yourself up there—but you are at the threshold of manhood, and you are going to have to learn to make your own decisions."

"Oh." Tommen was at a loss. So...his dad totally trusted him in this?

"Will you be back in time to take your road test?"

"Yeah, it's right after everyone gets back."

"So there you go."

His dad moved past him back to the living room. Tommen still followed. "Um, Micah said something about either him or Cai going with us up there, that way they can figure out how to open a portal so I can still go to the Arena for training since I'm so far behind."

His dad chuckled again and shook his head. "You are going to be so busy with camp, the last thing you're going to want to do is train. I know you feel like you are so far behind you can never catch up, but you have to remember that I was in my forties when I was an Apprentice and Journeyman. Twelve weeks isn't going to irrevocably screw up your training, no more than Rifun's coup did."

"But—"

"Have fun, Tommen. For your sake, and for mine. On top of your training, I also have to catch up on continuing Jenna's training as a Journeyman. The twins are doing what they can for her, but according to them, she's not the easiest to deal with."

"That's putting it mildly."

"I highly doubt you'll be doing any Timekeeper training while you're at camp."

"Oh. Okay."

"And if you really do get bored, you can always text me and ask to go to the Wheel, to the Arena for a couple hours. But I doubt you will."

"Okay. Thanks, Dad."

"For letting you take a job?"

"For understanding, and letting me be an adult."

"You may be an adult, but you're still my son. I can still boss you around if I feel like it."

"Yeah, but still. Just, thank you."

Tommen returned to his room and set to work, downloading the forms, printing them off, and filling them out. It seemed like forever since he'd done this for the bakery, and he went out to the living room several times to ask for help. For fuck's sake, how difficult did it have to be just to take his damn money? If people got taxed too much or too little, it wasn't for lack of paperwork, that was for sure. Still, he got it done and filed it away to be taken to camp, seeing how he didn't have a scanner. Then he printed out the directions to the camp and set them aside as well.

Then, feeling like he'd gotten a good amount of work done already, he headed out to the kitchen to make dinner.

The next day was Thursday, and while Tommen worked the closer, he went in early anyway.

"You're early," Micah observed when he walked in the door. "Trying to pack in as many hours as possible at your high-paying day job before you leave?"

"No, just want to make sure everything's cool and taken care of," Tommen explained. "Wellspring is a long ways away."

"That it is. Cai's probably got your paperwork in the office."

"He's not here?" Tommen followed Micah to the office which was surprisingly empty.

"No, not yet. He's got other stuff to take care of. He'll be in later." Micah picked up a small stack of papers. "Here we are." He handed it to Tommen, along with a pen. "We're not officially taking you off the payroll; as far as anyone is concerned, you're just going on an extended vacation. Leave of absence. Keeps you in good standing, and it's less headache and paperwork for us when you come back. Sound fair?"

"Is this paid vacation time?"

"That depends on how well you do at the summer camp, but I have no control over that."

"Ha ha, very funny."

"When you're done, just put it back on the desk; I'm sure Cai will get to it when he gets in. Then you can grab an apron and come back to help me."

"Are you guys going to appoint a new manager while I'm gone?"

"Haven't decided yet."

His tone was sharp and dismissive; that was a business decision that Tommen need not concern himself with, and that was that. Still, he finished the paperwork, double-checking the dates and lamenting the decrease in pay once he got back. But all the same, five grand from the camp was probably going to be more than what he would make from the bakery all summer, so it seemed to be a good trade-off. Plus, if he was reinstated as manager when he turned eighteen, he'd get that raise back, so it would all work out in the end.

He hoped. There was nothing like something going inexplicably right for there not to be something horrible waiting for him at the finish line.

When he was done, he set the papers back on the desk and checked the calendar. His last day would be tomorrow, Friday, working the opener. That would give him more than enough time to pack before Saturday morning, as if he totally couldn't just Band and make more time for himself.

Micaiah came in later than expected, and he and Micah disappeared into the office for a good three hours. Tommen couldn't even watch them from the counter and try to guess at their conversation because the blinds were down. Even when Micah came out, Tommen didn't want to ask outright, hoping that a hopeful, curious look would prompt an answer from the unspoken question. Micah caught his gesture, but only shook his head and returned to the kitchen.

The twins hadn't spoken a whole lot about Time-side affairs since their unexpected jaunt to the Wheel, and they were careful not to give anything away either by word or gesture or casual reference. Tommen had asked them about it once, but the only answer he got was that things were not going well. The Time industry was functioning fine, almost too fine. Now that things had changed and everyone was of a mind, the beast had reared its ugly head, come out of hibernation, and it was famished. When Tommen had inquired about the Akari and what that was all about, he'd only gotten a severe look, a warning to watch his back, and they would call him once things had calmed down.

As far as Time went, he wasn't feeling too good about himself. He was supposed to be training, learning new things, doing new stuff, maybe even learning a little more about the Akari from people who weren't psycho cultists, and he was still stuck as an Apprentice, spinning his wheels. Nothing was happening, or so it seemed. Maybe one day he would look back and think of how easy it all seemed at the time, but in the moment, he was bored. Like, really fucking bored.

Maybe this whole summer camp thing was a bad idea. He was finally getting out of the house, true, but look at everything he would be missing. He would be missing out on training, he would be leaving his dad alone, and he was leaving Becky, too. At the same time...it was his chance to get out and be a man without everyone hovering over him. Yes, his dad and the twins didn't treat him like a totally helpless kid, but to them, he was still that eight year old boy who tripped through a Time Portal. With the new people at camp, he would be starting fresh, in their eyes. It was a chance to be more than Tommen Forbes, the kid who got in fights at school, the weird kid who was dating a weirder girl, the Chivalrous Welshman. He would be more than that.

"So, are you excited to be going to camp?" Micaiah asked later on. It was just before closing, and they were the only two in the store. Tommen manned the front while Micaiah had crawled out of his den to clean up and close up the kitchen.

"Yeah, I guess. It'll be a good experience, anyway," Tommen answered, trying to sound optimistic. He paused. "Hey, uh, so I've been meaning to ask you..."

"Yes?"

"I mean, is there really anything to that, I don't know, Akari training you were talking about? Or something like that? Is everything okay in that department, or...what?"

"I would just as soon put it off a little while, at least until you get back from camp," Micaiah told him. "It's a lot to digest and try to wrap your mind around. Not exactly something you can just teach in one or two sittings like a normal classroom."

"Oh. Okay. There's nothing you can give me to kind of chew on while I'm at camp, something to think about, consider, come back with questions for a launching point?"

The elder twin paused in his work, rinsing the dish in his hand and setting it aside before shifting his stance and becoming thoughtful. Finally he nodded. "All right. Here's something. The Akari is known—by different names—throughout the universe. Some treat it lovingly, others disdain it. In the Time industry, the Akari is considered a threat, and all groups, from cult to church, are forbidden to speak of it. Given the power of the Hands, the Grandfathers, the sheer behemoth of the thing which is the Time industry, what would instill such fear as to make them ban it?" He went on before Tommen could speak. "Don't answer now. Answer me when you get back."

Tommen nodded. "Rifun gave me a riddle, too."

"Oh?"

"In order for a man to wield Time, Time must be given to him. In order for a man to wield the Akari, the Akari must be within him. What am I?"

Micaiah's expression turned into a grim mask. "That...the thing he speaks of is not the Akari, though he would like to believe it is. Maybe he honestly thinks it is. But it's not."

"Then what is it?"

"I don't know exactly. That's what I'm trying to find out."

"Oh."

"Don't worry about it. Only worry about the tidbit I gave you. Then when you get back, we'll have a nice, long chat. And you'll see what the Akari is, and not Rifun's convoluted version of it."

"That would be good, actually."

They closed up the store a few minutes early; the sky was still light, but the streets were unusually empty for a Thursday night. Tommen walked home from work and went straight to bed once he got home. Tomorrow he had to be up early, and he knew he would be too excited to sleep unless he was already exhausted.

He was almost too awake to sleep that night, and he arrived at work the next morning feeling both tired and confused. This was his last day of work before going to camp. He wouldn't be walking in the back door tomorrow, or the next day, or at all next week or the week after or the week after, not for three months almost. He didn't feel too sentimental about it, but it was just a strange thing to comprehend. Seven years in the bakery, and come Monday, he would be at summer camp hanging out with a bunch of teeny-boppers.

"You're not going to cry on us, are you?" Jenna had asked when she walked in around nine.

"No, I don't think that's the issue," Tommen said blankly.

"If he does, it's going to be tears of joy," Micah informed her, smirking at Tommen. "Got all your stuff packed yet?"

"Um, no, not really. Honestly, I haven't even gotten my suitcase out."

"Well, you might want to do that. Wellspring is a long ways away for your dad just to run you out your toothbrush."

"Oh, please. Wellspring is small, but they do have a convenience store. More than that, even the camp has a small store for just such emergencies."

"There's a price you pay for convenience, Tommen. Just make sure you have everything packed."

Tommen sighed. "Yes, Dad."

"We went over this. I'm not your dad; I'm your crazy uncle. Micaiah is your cranky uncle. Get it right; you have no excuse anymore to get us mixed up, either."

But whether it was the crazy uncle or the cranky uncle, both of them wished him well at the end of his shift. Had they been in the office, Tommen might have expected Micaiah to pull him into a full hug, as he was randomly wont to do. Since they were in the kitchen, however, and able to be seen by others, namely Kyle and Jenna, they elected for simple bro hugs and modest well wishes.

Originally, his dad had offered to pick him up from work to minimize time lost for packing, but he elected to Band and walk home instead. Or rather, he Banded about nine-tenths of the way home, then dropped it when he got close to Becky's house.

It took her a minute to come to the door, and she looked a little frazzled.

"Oh, it's you," she said. "Come in; I only have a minute."

"Something wrong?" he wondered.

"Well, I have a client coming over for a fitting. I thought you were her getting here early, and I'm not exactly what you might call ready." She spoke over her shoulder as she hurried back up to her room. Her hurry was considerably less than Tommen's hurry, but she made it and no worse for wear, moving Mr. Snuffles off the pile of fabric on her sewing table to the window seat, then taking her place at her machine, flipping it on, and zipping her work under the needle with scary precision.

"He seems like he's settled in," Tommen observed.

"Oh, he's made himself right at home. He's part of the reason I'm behind."

"Having second thoughts about having pets?"

"Not really; I'll just have to learn to work around him."

"Okay. Well, actually I came over to say goodbye before I leave for camp tomorrow."

"Is that tomorrow?" Becky leaned back in her seat, took off her glasses, and rubbed her eyes. "I am so messed up right now."

"Is everything okay? I mean, you're not normally this...frazzled. Seems like you got caught off-guard or something, and that's not like you."

"Yeah, no, just...this client wasn't supposed to come over until Monday. Then she called and asked if she could move up the fitting, and, stupidly, I said yes, I'd have everything ready for her."

"Oh. I guess I'll leave you to your work, then."

He stood, but before he could take two steps, she'd grabbed her glasses and followed him out of her bedroom. "Come here, you. Regardless of how busy I am, do you think I was really going to just let you walk out the door without a proper goodbye?"

The upstairs landing was plush carpet, which made it easy to kneel to give her a hug. Then she shocked him a second time by kissing him on the cheek.

"Just in case you thought the first one was fake, or a one-time deal," she told him.

"Ah. Well, just in case you thought I was...unappreciative..."

He did something bold, then. He kissed her. On the lips. It wasn't anything forceful or lingering, but it happened. The look on Becky's face resembled shock at first, probably how he'd looked when she first kissed him. Then it twisted into something where he was half-afraid she was going to slap him, then throw him off the landing to break his neck on the wood floors below. Finally it settled into something contemplative.

"Well," she said. "That was unexpected."

"Was it unwanted?"

"I haven't decided. It'll give me something to think about while you're gone."

"At least you won't forget me."

"Forget you? How in the world am I going to forget you? I mean, good grief, you're awkward and annoying...but you're also weird and sweet and very huggable."

"I'm not sure how to take that, so I'll just say thank you and move on."

"Good idea. You're learning. Okay." She hugged him again briefly. "Remember. Text me at least four times a week. And make sure to have fun. But not too much fun. I don't want to hear that you're having too much fun without me, or else I'll be afraid that you won't come back."

"The camp is only twelve weeks; I'll have to come back at the end anyway."

"Whatever. Still, not too much fun without me. Got it?"

"Whatever you say."

"You catch on quick."

He saw himself out the door and made it home in good time. Now was the time to start packing, which meant he first had to find his suitcase and hope it hadn't been destroyed by mice. True, he'd only had to use it six months ago when he stayed with the twins briefly, but mice were quick and deadly; they could have easily destroyed it in that time period.

But when he found it in his closet, it appeared no worse for wear. A little dusty, still one sock tucked in the front compartment, but otherwise intact.

Four weeks. Had to pack for four weeks. Well, not a full four weeks, maybe more like ten days. There was laundry on-site, two separate bays: one for the campers and one for the staff. So it wouldn't be all bad. It wouldn't be as bad as the time he'd gone with Sifura and traipsed around the desert and the jungle and gotten all sweaty and smelly. All while completely naked.

Of course, he did have to factor in weather and the activities they would be doing. Swimming, definitely, so he had to find his swim trunks buried at the bottom of his sock drawer. Campfires, probably, so he would need long pants for the cold outside the fire as well as the mosquitoes. Hiking, most likely, which meant he would need shorts, socks, and hiking boots. But with swimming, he wanted sandals. But for day-to-day activities, he would want regular tennis shoes. Not everything was going to fit in his suitcase, which meant he needed another bag.

Well, this was four weeks of camp at a time, so he shouldn't have been too surprised. And like the twins said, Wellspring was a long ways away for his dad to bring anything out to him, and the cost of convenience would be high.

Wait, did they expect him to bring his own laundry soap? He

paused in his packing and thought a minute. No, that would be impractical. And rude. He shook his head and carried on. Even if he did end up having to buy laundry soap, in four weeks, he might only do laundry two or three times. Plus he might make a few friends who would be willing to "loan" him some soap to offset the cost, in exchange for something else, a favor or something. It would all work out, he was sure.

He heard his dad walk in the house around four-thirty.

"How goes the packing?" he asked, poking his head in as he unbuttoned his shirt.

"Good, I think," Tommen answered.

"You got everything you need? Toothbrush, toothpaste, shampoo, all that?"

"Well, I can't pack that stuff until tomorrow before I leave."

"Bug spray?"

Tommen Banded and went out to the garage to rummage around for some bug spray, then returned to his room. "Yes."

"Sunscreen?"

Another Band and a trip to the garage. "Of course."

"Got enough clothes to last you?"

"Yeah, but there's laundry there, so I'll be okay anyway."

"What about your hearing aid charger? I don't think those will be available at the local convenience store."

"Once again, can't pack it until tomorrow."

"I know. I'm just getting you thinking about the stuff you'll need." He turned as if to go into his bedroom, then paused and looked back in. "I saw those Bands by the way."

Tommen shrugged. "Yeah, I figured."

"You hungry? How about one last pot of chicken chili before you go?"

"Sounds great!"

Yeah, it was summer finally, and the weather was getting warmer, but they hadn't had chicken chili in a long time, or so it seemed. And his dad made the best chili; supposedly it was the one good and decent thing he remembered from his childhood, his mother's recipe, slightly modified to twenty-first century foods and standards, and it had won more than one precinct chili cook-off. Fuck, Tommen was going to miss that, too.

Oh well. He just told himself that he couldn't have everything. This would be good for him, a chance to get out of the house and be his own man. In the future, he would be faced with the college decision, and he couldn't give up his education for a minimum-wage job and a chili cook-off at his dad's workplace. It was time to grow up, set his priorities, and make his own choices. That wasn't to say all his choices were good, but he thought he was getting better about them.

He wandered out of his room about an hour later, when the aroma of chicken chili permeated every room in the house. His dad was just turning off the stove when he walked in the kitchen.

"Grab your bowl," Walter said, setting the pot on the tiny kitchen table; Tommen could have sworn it wobbled under the weight of the chili.

Still, he found himself and bowl and spoon and ladled out a generous helping of chili. It wasn't a super spicy chili—that is, spicy for its own sake rather than any kind of meaning flavor—but it was a flavorful, wholesome chili, the kind where one bowl could fill a man, and he would never tire of the taste no matter how many days in a row he was forced to eat it.

"Do you want to take some with you?" his dad asked as they took their places in the living room and found a movie to watch.

"I'd love to, but what would I do with the bowl?"

"Mm, you might have a point there."

"But if you could save enough for me to have it for breakfast, that would be nice."

"Well, when you put it like that, I guess it'll keep me from eating more than I should."

Tommen shifted in his seat. "So, you're suddenly worried about your weight and you've been getting home late recently...Is there a lady friend involved?"

"Is this an interrogation?" Walter asked, quickly taking a bite of chili.

"No, I'm just wondering."

"And what if there was?"

Now Tommen paused. What if his dad was interested in a woman, only in its preliminary stages seeing how he hadn't introduced him to her, but what if? It seemed cute and foolish, and Tommen was happy for them, but...what if? First question, why now? Was it because he, Tommen, was grown up and his dad now had time for such things? Was it because his dad felt lonely, felt the impending doom of him going off to college and parts unknown?

Walter had raised Tommen by himself, a feat he was respected for, although not envied. But for eight years, it had been just Tommen and Walter, Walter and Tommen, father and son and no one else. Well, there were the twins, but as far as family and home life, it was just them. No mother, no sisters, nothing. And Tommen's girlfriends didn't count either. That was high school. But adults...they usually seemed to have a better grasp on things, or Walter did anyway. He wasn't a desperate bachelor; if he'd found someone, it was because he'd given it some thought and consideration.

"Your expression and your silence gives you away," his dad said finally, jerking him from his thoughts. "You don't have to worry about anything yet; we've just had coffee a few times."

"Do I know her? Is she in the precinct?"

"No and no. Actually, she's a paramedic, new in the area in the last six months, but she's been on the job for twenty years. We've worked together on a few scenes."

"Oh. Cool."

"Like I said, no worries yet. I'll tell you when you have to worry."

"Is she a Time Agent?"

Walter sighed. "No."

So it probably wouldn't pan out anyway. "What's her name?"

"Laura."

Tommen nodded. "Cool." He finished off his chili and stood. "I need to finish packing, make sure I haven't forgotten anything."

His dad merely nodded, but did not look at him.

Well, that was certainly a bombshell he could have done without, especially since he was leaving tomorrow. At the same time, it was partly his fault for prying. His dad had probably thought to send him off to summer camp blissfully ignorant, then tell him once he got back. Now he was going to spend the whole twelve weeks wondering and worrying.

Did the twins know about this? What did they think? Had they met this mysterious Laura person? Fuck, this was too much to take in on such short notice.

Tommen checked his bags and brought out his sleeping bag, but he couldn't remember if he'd gotten anything else done. His dad was seeing someone. Didn't matter if it was just coffee after work, he was seeing someone. He had someone else in his life, more than just a friend. And now Tommen was about to go off to summer camp for twelve weeks and leave them alone. Briefly, he was amused at the irony of it all.

He lay awake in bed for at least half the night, excited and uncertain. Maybe he was just overreacting. The woman wasn't even a Time Agent. This was probably just his dad feeling lonely and looking for a little friendship. It wouldn't last.

It couldn't.

Tommen figured he must have slept at some point, but as soon as his alarm went off, he knew it hadn't been enough. He'd spent too much time worrying and agonizing over his dad's choice of friends, as well as the camp which suddenly seemed like even more of an obstacle to the things he really wanted to do and see. He couldn't just leave his dad alone with some woman he didn't know.

But he'd already told the camp he was going to be there and made the commitment. He had to see it through. Reluctantly, he slapped off his alarm and rolled out of bed.

Even with Banding, he still felt like he went at a snail's pace, going through everything and making sure everything was packed and ready. Had to grab his shampoo, toothbrush, razor, all the little things he would need that he didn't feel like buying once he got there. He checked his suitcase again, just in case his clothes had decided to magically get up, walk out, and put themselves back in his dresser. Then he had to pack his hearing aid charger, wrapping it in one of his shirts so it didn't get knocked around too much and damaged, not that it could with how full his suitcase had become. Most of the vacations he'd been on had been a week, ten days at most. Four weeks was a lot longer and required a lot more stuff.

He headed down the hall to the kitchen, flicking on the light over the oven and fishing for the bowl of leftover chili for breakfast. His dad had asked not to be disturbed until he was ready to leave.

And how had he slept? Had he stayed awake half the night, questioning his life choices and whether or not he should have admitted to seeing someone just before his son left for twelve weeks?

Tommen glanced outside where the sky was already light with color, but the sun had not yet shone its face. Mr. Wilson had said any time before noon was good, but Tommen had elected to aim for eleven, just in case they got lost and had to call for directions, or any other assorted catastrophe arose.

He waited until the last possible minute before lugging his suitcase and stuff out to the car, then went and pushed open the door to his dad's room. As always, his dad had no curtains in order to let in as much light as possible, plus the night light in the corner. But the man seemed to be sleeping peacefully.

"Dad," Tommen said, standing back as far as he could while he poked his dad. The man slept peacefully most nights, but that didn't mean he wasn't still having nightmares and wouldn't come flying at him in a semi-conscious stupor, still fighting whatever demon had plagued him half the night.

Thankfully, this was a peaceful, if grumpy, wakeup call.

"What time is it?" he asked.

"Almost eight."

"What?" He started coming up out of bed, alarmed and confused.

"Whoa, hey, it's okay," Tommen said, putting his hands up. "You got the day off so you could take me to camp."

It took a second, but his dad seemed to remember, and he calmed down.

"Right, I traded shifts." He nodded and sighed. "All right. Wait for me in the kitchen."

Tommen left the room while his dad got up and around. He got to the kitchen just as he heard the shower turn on. It ran for about ten minutes. Not sixty seconds after it turned off, his dad was pulling his shoes on.

"Okay, let's get you to camp."

By that he meant, "You're driving and I'm going to finish sleeping." Not that his nap lasted very long, seeing as he got up every morning between four and four-thirty, and he'd already slept in quite a while.

"Okay, we're on 79," Tommen said once he'd woken up and adjusted his seat. "What's the exit I'm looking for?"

His dad flipped through the papers in the folder until he found the directions. "Exit...for Elkins."

So they had a ways to go.

It wasn't a bad drive. Most people, when they lived in an area a long time, grew accustomed to and even bored with their surroundings, grimacing every time some tourist gushed about how beautiful everything was. Tommen never felt that way with these mountains; he always loved looking at them, their majesty outlined against the sky, whether blue and sunny or black and stormy. There were mysteries and stories hidden in those peaks, some of which would never be told by the living.

Some days, when Tommen was in a particularly sour mood, he always imagined just walking through the mountains, exploration for its own sake. Want to see what's over that rise? Go do it. Want to climb that hill and look out over the valley? By all means. Want to go explore that cave and look for old treasure? Well, he'd wised up a little on that one. But still, to just go and do and explore, without worrying about trespassing or angry neighbors or having to share a trail with bright-eyed tourists...just him and the mountains...that was a dream.

"So...do you pick up Laura at her house or do you just meet up?" Tommen asked.

His dad raised a brow. "We meet up, usually after I get off."

"Oh, good. That way she doesn't have to be seen in this thing. It would probably embarrass her right out."

"Emb—what? No, she knows what I drive."

"Holy shit, and she still has coffee with you? Sounds serious."

"Tommen..." Walter shook his head. "You don't have your license, and Becky still dates you."

Ouch. Okay, so that was a fair shot, and Tommen couldn't retaliate because Becky wasn't here to defend herself if he pointed out that she couldn't drive anyway, which was something she had no control over. So it was a moot point.

"What's she drive?"

"She drives an '01 F250."

"Ooh, tough girl."

"Say that to her face and find out how tough she is."

"Right, and you're still just meeting for coffee."

"I don't see what the sudden obsession is." His dad shifted in his seat. "Do you feel threatened by her somehow?"

"What? No, not at all. I mean, I've never met her. You're just going out to have coffee with a friend."

His dad sighed. "Tommen, it's nothing serious. Even if it was—somehow—she's not going to come between us any more than Becky does. You're my son, and I'm your dad, no matter who else comes into our lives."

It was his tone as much as his words that told Tommen that Laura wasn't just a coffee buddy. Or maybe his dad was just sentimental. They were both faced with changes in their lives, and neither was sure how to deal with them. Tommen was growing up, moving on, moving out. He had his life ahead of him, and Walter had his life without him.

They spoke very little after that, except for the part where the directions got messed up and they got lost. There was quite a bit of backtracking and frustration, but eventually they got back on the right path.

Wellspring was not a big town; it hardly registered on most maps as little more than a post office, a gas station, a convenience store, and a myriad of struggling mom 'n' pop tourist shops that survived on the tourist boom that came only a couple months out of the year, six or eight weeks in the summer, and six or eight weeks in the winter. Otherwise, the place would be a ghost town.

"I think we've got some time," Walter said, looking at the clock and then back at the map. "Why don't we get something to eat before you go?"

They stopped at a sleepy diner, the kind where there was one cook, one waitress, and one empty dining room, where one would be hard-pressed to imagine that the place had ever been the most popular stop in town, however much the staff and old-timers proclaimed it so. One such old-timer sat at the bar with a steaming cup of coffee, but otherwise, the place seemed to be devoid of life.

"Sit wherever you want!" someone called.

They picked a window seat and sat down just as the waitress approached them, handing out menus that had seen better days and silverware that looked like it might have been licked clean by Dishwasher Dog in the back.

"So, where you folks coming from?" she asked when she brought their drinks.

"Charleston," Walter answered. "He's heading to work up at Eagle Eye Summer Camp. Is that close by?"

"Oh, sure, about ten miles outside of town." She gave them directions that more or less matched the ones they already had. "My daughter's going to be up there, actually; she's a camper." Because Tommen would have been frightened if she would have been old enough to be a staff member. "It's a nice place, really, probably the nicest thing about Wellspring. Probably the only thing that keeps people coming through here at all. Town's dead now, but in a week, when the campers start coming, you won't be able to find a table here. Kids come from all over the state just to go to that place."

"I've never heard of it before now."

"Well, in the city, it's not likely you would. The camp is open to everyone, but it's primarily for kids from poor Appalachian families, and for the kids from the Indian reservations, get them out doing something fun away from home, you know?"

So, basically, the campers were going to be the sons and daughters of poor coal miners, poor farmers, poor Indians, poor alcoholics and drug addicts, and poor unemployed loafers. That meant that the level of discipline was either going to be excellent, that sense of duty and right and wrong that came with the need to survive, or nonexistent as inattentive parents let their kids do whatever the hell they wanted with no consequence.

Nevertheless, lunch was decent, if expensive, and soon they were on the road again, following the directions the waitress had given. Wellspring was pretty much a one-road town, and they followed that road east until they came to the little side road that took them north, higher into the mountains, turning into a dirt road about halfway up. Their only saving grace was the sign that announced Eagle Eye Summer Camp, 3.5 miles.

"I think you're going to have to take this car to a mechanic when you get back," Tommen said as they bounced along the rutted road.

"I think you might be right," his dad agreed, grunting as they hit a pothole that might have been more like a small bomb crater.

It was a rough three and a half miles that took a lot longer than Tommen thought it should have. He was almost surprised when the dirt suddenly ended and they were back on smooth blacktop. It went on for about a quarter of a mile before opening up into what initially looked like a five-star luxury resort.

There was an enormous building right up front, and the only clue Tommen had that it was built from real logs instead of fake log siding was the huge windows that let him look inside without even trying. Even from a distance, it must have been sixty by eighty and thirty feet at the peak; the windows in front were probably a good twenty feet wide and ran the full height of the building. Inside looked like a common room, a gym or other multipurpose area.

East of that building was another building of similar construction quality, though considerably smaller. A couple vending machines sat along one wall, and from an angle, Tommen could make out the red cross and a sign reading "Camp Nurse." There might have been something else on the other side of the building, but he couldn't tell what it was.

West of the main building was the one that looked most promising. It was still log-built, but it faced the parking lot with a sign that said, "Offices."

"I'd say that's your best bet," Walter mused.

The parking lot itself was not very big, enough for maybe fifty cars, and most of the spots were already taken. Still uncertain, Tommen picked a spot, turned off the car, and got out. Should he take his stuff in with him? Should he just go in and say hi? Did his dad have to go with him to sign some release form or something?

"Why don't you check the offices?" his dad said, sensing his uncertainty. He handed him the folder with all the paperwork. "Take this with you. If you need me, I'll be right here. I won't take off on you."

Tommen was more frustrated at himself that he needed that kind of reassurance, but he took the folder and headed for the offices. What if the door was locked? He couldn't just stand there like an idiot. As he got closer and could see around the back of the buildings, he noticed there were a few other people out milling around. What if they saw him get locked out of the offices? They would laugh at him.

He Banded quickly and looked around. In the mountains, there was very little level ground to be found, so most building sites had to undergo some pretty serious excavation. So it came as no surprise that the landscape behind the three buildings at the parking lot was less of a nice rolling slope and more of a steep drop. Not steep as in, double black diamond open face ski run kind of steep, but steep enough that part of the hill had been landscaped for tiered retaining walls—think Machu Pichu—and the other side looked like dirt had been trucked in to level it out enough so that it wasn't a fight for balance with each step.

Taking a breath, he released the Band and went up to the office door. It was unlocked. He went inside and looked around.

"Hello?" he wondered cautiously.

He expected Mr. Wilson to greet him, but instead got a middle-aged woman. "Oh, good morning. You must be Tommen."

"That's me." He handed her the folder with the paperwork. "Mr. Wilson said to bring this with me."

"Yes, this must be your tax paperwork. I'll get this filed away."

"Um, my dad is here with me. I know I'm under eighteen, so does he have to sign any, like, waivers or release forms or anything?"

"Yes, please, if he's here."

Tommen nodded and returned to the car where his dad poked away on his phone.

"Their wifi is surprisingly decent," Walter said. "What's up?"

"Um, you need to come in and sign a few forms."

His dad nodded, and they went back to the office.

"Mr. Forbes, I presume?" the woman asked.

"Walter. You have some paperwork for me to sign?"

She brought out what looked like a small book of papers. "This is the general release form for the camp itself, all activities we'll be doing here under our own direction with our own equipment, including swimming, hiking, outdoor activities, indoor activities, all that. This one is for the ziplining we'll be doing."

"Ziplining?" Tommen wondered.

"Mm-hm." She nodded. "We'll be taking buses to another location to do that. This form is for the rock climbing, and this one is for the horseback riding. Then we have this one which is for the off-site hiking and camping we'll be doing. And the rafting."

Holy shit, this place was sounding better and better by the minute. Why had he ever had reservations about coming to work for this place? New question, why hadn't he found this place sooner?

"This is a lot of stuff," Walter commented. "We had lunch down in Wellspring, and the waitress told us that this camp was primarily for poorer kids. How do you do all of this?"

"Well, okay, that's a little misleading. This camp is for poorer kids, make no mistake. But the buildings and the facilities are all funded by the local Indian tribes. The agreement is that they'll fund and supply everything we need on the condition that their kids come for free and our primary focus is poor Appalachian families and not rich snobby kids." She went on before Walter could continue. "Take it how you will, but that's the agreement. The idea is to give poor kids a retreat from whatever home life they have. So that's what we try to accomplish."

And that was how they could afford to pay the counselor assistants five grand, to say nothing of what the rest of the staff probably made in just three months.

"What's this paper?" Walter wondered, finally coming to the last sheet.

"That's the one that says we can throw your son into slavery if he misbehaves."

She said it lightly, but given certain past events, both Tommen and Walter had a hard time mustering up the willpower to even fake a laugh. The woman seemed to recognize this as she said, "No, I'm kidding. Actually, that one is for both of you. It just states that you—" She looked at Tommen. "—will follow the rules of the camp, behave in an appropriate manner, and so on. And if you don't, then you—" Now she looked at Walter. "—are responsible for picking him up or making other arrangements."

They both signed the paper and handed it over.

"Excellent. Now—"

"Is Mr. Wilson here?" Tommen wondered.

She shrugged. "He's here, he's there, he's everywhere. Blink and he's gone. Don't worry, though, everything's been taken care of."

"So what do I do now?"

"Well, you can go ahead and take your stuff to the main hall there." She pointed to the huge building with the glass wall. "Everyone is going to be meeting there in about...twenty minutes or so. That's when everyone will be introduced, you'll get your cabin assignments, and you can ask any questions you still have. Okay? Does that sound good?"

Well, it wasn't like he could say no. They thanked her and left the office, making for the car.

"That wasn't so bad," his dad commented. "Sounds like you're going to be having more fun than I am this summer. Are you sure there aren't any other positions open here that an old guy like me can take?"

"You're going to go ziplining and horseback riding?" Tommen raised a brow.

His dad considered that for a minute. "All right, you might have a point there. The horseback riding I might be able to stomach, but I'll skip the ziplining."

"Whatever."

Tommen shook his head as he dug his things out of the backseat. Suitcase, bag of extra shoes, sleeping bag.

"You're sure you have everything?" his dad asked seriously. "Toothbrush, toothpaste, and all that?"

"Yes, Dad."

"Hearing aid charger?"

"Got it."

"Clean underwear?"

"Dad!"

"All right, all right." He put his hands up in mock surrender. "Do you want help carrying your things up there, or are you too much of a man to be seen with your old man?"

Tommen huffed. "You can carry my sleeping bag, if you really want."

So he did. As they crossed the parking lot, Tommen got a snarky thought in his head. "Now, are you sure I can trust you and Laura alone while I'm gone?"

His dad gave him a look. "Are you sure I can trust you with some of the young women here?"

He nodded toward a young woman, who couldn't have been old enough to drink, just walking out of the main hall. She wore a tight spaghetti-strap tank top, short shorts, and sandals showing off pink-painted toenails. Tommen felt his ears grow warm, and he was unprepared for Walter's Band.

"You remember your promise?"

"I'm not going to Band and rape them," Tommen said, insulted that his dad would suggest such a thing.

"I'm not talking about that. You have a girlfriend at home."

"I know. What are you saying?"

"You're not likely to see these girls again when you leave here. Don't do any stupid summer flings."

"I won't. Dad..." Tommen sighed. "Please, just trust me."

"I never trust a sixteen year old with his own cock."

"How old were you when you first did a girl?"

"Younger than you."

The straightforwardness of the answer shut him up, and Walter dropped the Band so they could continue on. Younger than him? Okay, Tommen was almost seventeen, and Walter barely let him look at girls. But he'd fucked a girl when he was even younger? Yeah, he'd told Tommen all about his drinking and fighting and stealing, but never once had he mentioned girls. Or maybe it wasn't really relationship material, more brothel excursion. But still...he had a hard enough time reconciling the man he knew with the man he claimed to have been. It just wasn't possible. Was it? Could a man really change that much? Well, in over a century, he supposed anything was possible. It was still mind-boggling.

There was more gear than people sitting in the main hall. Tommen found a corner to drop his stuff where he was fairly confident it wouldn't walk away, then he followed his dad back out to the car.

"Well, this is going to an odd three months," his dad said. "House is going to be pretty quiet."

Tommen nodded. "It will."

"Well, you enjoy yourself with whatever antics and shenanigans you get into. As long as I don't hear about them in a bad way. All right?"

"I make no promises."

"Knowing you, I believe it."

They said their goodbyes, then Walter started the car and drove away, leaving Tommen standing there in the parking lot. That was it. He was gone. Twelve weeks—well, technically only five or six weeks—until they saw each other again. He was on his own now. He was his own man, making his own decisions and the only one responsible for them. Any shit he got into was his fault alone. It was as terrifying as it was exhilarating.

After a minute, he turned and went back to the main hall. Everyone else milling about and walking around were probably camp veterans; they already knew which cabins they wanted, which bunks were the best, how everything worked. He knew nothing. So, if they were all meeting in the main hall, that was probably the safest place to start, just wait for everyone to mosey their way in.

The main hall was more than just one giant room; there were other rooms as well, including an enormous, fully functional kitchen. A couple of the cooks caught him staring.

"Hey, lunch will be ready in a bit, but if you want, I might be able to get you a snack," one woman said, grinning and approaching the window. "What's your fancy?"

"Oh, um, I'm not hungry. Just looking."

"Yeah? I don't think I've seen you before. You're too old and too early to be a camper. Are you the new counselor's assistant?"

"Yeah, I am."

"Cool. Well, I'm Pam. I kind of run this kitchen. That's Mark, Wallace, and Shireen." They waved or nodded briefly in turn. "What's your name?"

"Tommen."

"Nice to meet you, Tommen. Is this your first time here?"

"Yeah. I never even knew this place existed."

"No problem. Well, I can't speak for the rest of the camp and the staff, but as far as the kitchen goes, there's usually always someone here, from before you get up until after you go to bed. If you need something, don't be afraid to ask. The kids get food at mealtime only, and snacks at snacktime only. But, for counselors and staff, come by anytime. You guys work your asses off, and your meals will probably end up being shorter than the campers'. If you don't know what I mean, you will before the first day is out."

He didn't like the sound of that, actually.

"We're also the go-to place for all your s'mores needs," Pam went on. "And you will need a lot. Also, if there's ever anything you particularly want for a meal, let us know a couple days ahead of time, and we'll see if we can't do something for you. You got all that?"

"Uh, I think so."

"Great. Sure you're not hungry? We've got snacks to tide you over until lunch."

"I'm good, thanks."

"Suit yourself."

With that, she turned and went back to whatever she had been doing. If the set-up was any indication, Tommen guessed lunch would be some sort of taco bar.

He meandered his way away from the kitchen and went exploring down a hall that contained classroom-style rooms, with boxes stuffed with things for all manner of different activities, from arts and crafts to board games to movies. This was probably the inclement weather activity room.

After a while, he made his way back to the main room of the main hall, momentarily stunned by how many people seemed to have wandered in in just the last five minutes or so. There had to be fifty people in the room. Just how many campers were coming to this summer camp?

He carefully picked his way back to the corner where his stuff lay, untouched. He sat down, hoping that if he didn't move, no one would see him.

"Hey, you're new here."

Too late.

The man who approached him was about in his thirties and looked like he'd probably been the starting quarterback all four years of high school, plus got a college scholarship on it.

"Are you Joe's replacement?"

"Uh, I'm a counselor's assistant," Tommen replied.

"Yeah, you're here for Joe. Cool. My name is Rick."

"Tommen."

They shook hands.

"Who is Joe? I mean, everyone seems to know him."

"Everyone knows everyone here. By the end of the summer, everyone will know you, too. And Joe was with us for almost ten years."

"What happened to him?"

"Family emergency. Had to pack up quick and go to Houston."

"Oh." Tommen looked around. "So who is everyone here? How many campers are going to be here?"

Rick laughed. "Oh, this isn't just counselors. This is everyone. You've got Michelle the nurse there. That's Dave and Andrew; they run the camp shop. Those guys there aren't actually with the camp. They're the activity and safety instructors for some of the things we'll be doing like the horseback riding, the ziplining and so on."

"Why are they here?"

"They always come for orientation day. They want to know the faces of the counselors, get some numbers, and get a feel for things. Plus, some of them, like the kayaking and canoeing guides want to inspect our stuff. They supply the river, and we supply the equipment, and they want to make sure it's safe. I guess."

"Oh. Cool." Made sense, he supposed. "How many campers are there going to be?"

"I don't know officially; we'll get that number today, or at least the preliminary number. It shrinks as the camp goes on, for various reasons."

"What's the average?"

"About a hundred to a hundred and twenty."

"Wow. That's...a lot."

"We get kids from all over the state, even some from out of state; I'm surprised there aren't more, actually."

Tommen could agree to that, though he didn't say it out loud.

"So, where are you from, Tommen?"

"Charleston."

"Okay. Right on. I grew up about fifty miles northeast of there. I actually live in Pennsylvania now, but I still come down here every summer to work and camp out and have a good time." He nodded. "Brothers or sisters?"

"No. Just me and my dad."

"Mom?" Tommen shook his head. "I'm sorry."

"Doesn't matter. It was a long time ago. How do I know which counselor I'm supposed to be assisting?"

"We'll be getting our assignments today, just as soon as Jerry arrives. He's a little scattered. He's been the director for only three years, but he took over quite a mess from the last director. He's been working hard to rebuild the camp and bring it back to its former glory. Believe me, five years ago, you would not have believed what this place looked like."

Tommen nodded, but he'd lost interest. He was in way over his head. He took out his phone and texted Becky. "Made it to camp alive."

A minute later, she texted back. "Day One."

Yeah. Day one.

"All right, everyone!" Mr. Wilson's voice rang out over the din of the crowd. "Let's quiet down; can I have your attention, please?" Everyone quieted and looked at him. "Welcome to camp!" Some cheers. "So, this is going to be a great year; we've got some new activities we'll be doing, got some new staff. If anyone doesn't know me, I am Jerry Wilson; I am the director of this camp. It's been operating for the last forty years; some of the staff here now are the children of the original staff, which is pretty cool, I think. Ask any of them, this place has undergone quite a few changes over the years, especially the last five to ten years."

"That's an understatement," Rick murmured.

"So, to start off, I'm going to introduce some of the staff so you have an idea of who's who. You all know me, Jerry. When you came in, you probably met with Heather." The lady from the office waved. "Hopefully, none of you will have to see our camp nurse, Michelle

Trout." The woman in the short shorts and tank top. She was a nurse? Had she even graduated high school? "We also have our wonderful kitchen crew here, headed by Pam." Cheers from the assembled crowd. "And then we have our headmaster and headmistress for the boys' and girls' cabins, Shawn White Cloud and Casey Waterman."

"What does that mean?" Tommen hissed.

"Means they're in charge of the counselors if something goes wrong between us, or between us and our campers," Rick answered. "Jerry's the only one above them."

"We also have our partners in crime," Mr. Wilson went on, introducing a row of people. "These are the guys and gals responsible for our safety during some of our planned activities like the kayaking and the horseback riding. If you can, help them out and make their jobs easier, because it will make our jobs easier when we get to those activities. Thanks.

"Now then, our counselors for this year. I know most of you know each other, but I'll introduce them anyway for the benefit of the new people."

There were five female counselors and six male counselors. Some had been there twenty years or better, others this was only their second or third year.

"All right, now I'm going to read off the assignments for the counselors and counselor assistants. But first, I know that most all of you knew Joe Wicke; he's been with us for a lot of years. If you've spoken to him at all in the last five years, you'll know that his mother has been in poor health. Unfortunately, he is not able to be with us this year because her health recently took a severe downturn, and I got word this morning that she has passed." Murmurs of sorrow and well wishes. "So, keep Joe in your thoughts and prayers; we'll be sending a card around. Some of you have his phone number, so if you get a minute, send him a text or call him and wish him the best."

Well, that escalated quickly, Tommen thought, leaning against the wall.

"Jeremiah Wayne, you'll be with Rick Montgomery," Mr.

Wilson announced.

"That's me," Rick said as he put his hand up and looked around the room until he spotted the Jeremiah person.

"What cabin are you guys in?" Tommen asked as Mr. Wilson went on.

"Well, that's the fun part. See, once we're dismissed here, prep week is kind of like summer camp for the counselors. The first game we play is called first dibs. Basically, it's a way of claiming your cabin."

Adult summer camp. This could get interesting.

"Tommen Forbes," Mr. Wilson called, pointing at him with his pen. "You're going to be paired with Saul Wolf."

Because nothing bad ever came from guys with creepy names. Still, Tommen put his hand up and looked around for the other hand. He saw only the hand and part of a coat sleeve, but with the crowd, he was happy to spot that. Then they were moving on.

"So, uh, what can you tell me about Saul?" Tommen asked Rick.

Rick chuckled. "Well, as long as you've got a flexible sense of humor, you should get along great."

"What do you mean?"

"He's a bit strange. He tends to get assigned the weird kids, the outcasts, the troubled kids, things like that."

Oh, wonderful, just who I want to associate with, a bunch of misfits and outcasts. It's not even because I think I'm above them; it's because I know I'm one of them. Was this an intentional assignment? Did Mr. Wilson take one look at me and think, Yup. He's a weird one all right. Better put him with Saul and keep the weirdness contained so it doesn't spread; that shit could be contagious.

On the other hand, maybe Saul really was like Tommen, an outcast among his own, but not a bad guy once you got to know him. Maybe he'd once been the kid who got in fights and had a minor record, and now he was set to be the example to other kids on that same path. Tommen took a breath and told himself he had to be optimistic until proven otherwise, else this was going to be a miserable twelve weeks.

"Are the assignments the same for both camps, or do we change when the older kids get here?"

"Nope; you and Saul are going to be together all summer." Rick said it with a certain sarcastic smirk.

Tommen elected to stay silent after that and just wait and see what happened. Mr. Wilson finished up the girls' assignments and looked out over the crowd.

"This is prep week, where we get everything ready for the campers before they arrive. Well, in the interest of everyone's sanity, I try to make it fun for you guys as well. So, for those of you who have been here in years past, you know what comes next. Now is the time when you all get to claim your cabins, but it's not going to be just a leisurely walk outside, walk around, and pick a cabin. This is going to be like an adult scavenger hunt. But the first thing you need to do is get paired with your counselor or counselor assistant."

Given that he was in the corner, Tommen elected to remain where he was and let Saul come to him, which he did.

Rick was right. Saul was weird. Or he dressed that way, anyway. It was true that summer in the mountains didn't get as hot as the rest of the country, but the man still insisted on wearing black jeans, a white shirt, and a black leather trenchcoat with matching hat in a fedora style. He couldn't have been older than thirty-five, but he had unusual gold eyes that seemed to pop against dark skin and long black hair pulled back in a ponytail.

"Tommen Forbes?" he asked.

"Last I checked," Tommen answered. "I assume you're Saul Wolf."

"That I am."

Standing beside him, Tommen estimated him to be about six-two, maybe six-one or six foot if his cowboy boots were taken away. He had a longish nose and a chin that was just pronounced without getting into that ugly length. And while he tried to act calm and collected, ready for a good time, there was something about him that just screamed military, that he could go from care less to bad ass in two-point-four seconds or less. Maybe it was the way his gaze swept around the room, identifying people, exits, looking for threats. Maybe it was the way his hand kept fishing around his belt as if looking for a gun that wasn't there. Maybe his weirdness wasn't just from being weird, but from being damaged, scarred in some way.

Maybe he and Saul were more alike than he realized. Was it just coincidence that they'd been assigned to work together this summer, or had Mr. Wilson done it for more serious reasons?

Tommen took a breath and told himself to stop being paranoid. This was summer camp, and the week before the campers arrived was adult summer camp. This was a time for the adults to have fun, and he was determined to have some fun, regardless if his counselor he was assigned to was a weirdo or not. He couldn't be concerned about everyone's welfare.

"All right, this is how the game is going to work," Mr. Wilson continued once all the pairs had gotten together. "Counselors, when you arrived, you were given an envelope and told not to open it. There should be five for the girls and six for the boys. Inside is a paper marked with a number. You are to solve the riddles and go to the specified locations where there will be a pack or a box or a chest of items. Take the one with your number. When you get all of the items, you will be piecing together a particular item which is missing from each of the cabins. Find the cabin missing your piece, and that is your cabin. Begin!"

"Different than last year," Saul mused as he took a piece of paper from his pocket and unfolded it, Tommen glancing over his shoulder as he read. " 'Rainbow, Silver, Brook.' "

"Those are all fish. Is there a river around here?" Tommen wondered.

Saul shook his head. "Not just fish. Trout. The nurse's office."

So he'd done this before, Tommen figured, following him out of the main hall toward the nurse's office where the door was open and the nurse was busy organizing her things. She looked up as they entered and went to an unsuspecting box on a table in the middle of the floor.

"What's your number?" she asked.

"Two," Saul told her.

She fished out a brown package marked with a giant number 2 and handed it to him. "Good luck."

They moved off to the side and unwrapped the paper. It was a flat piece of wood in an indeterminate shape, stained white, with a hole in the center as if for a screw. Another envelope fell out from the packaging, and Tommen bent to retrieve it.

" 'Rain, Meteor, Baby' " he read. "Baby?"

Even Saul seemed puzzled for a moment. Then he nodded. "The showers."

Right. Rain shower, meteor shower, baby shower. Because everyone could just pull that off the top of their head.

They almost ran into another group on their way out of the nurse's office, but were on their way soon enough, Tommen with the paper, Saul with the piece of wood. The showers weren't located far from the nurse's office, but the chest of goodies ended up being hidden in one of the six lockers in the common room on the boys' side. Saul rummaged through it until he found a bag with a dozen screws and another envelope.

" 'Jackson, Worth, Knox' "

Tommen blinked and shook his head. "Those are all forts. So what does that mean?"

"Means we're going to go on a little hiking trip." Saul was already halfway out the door. "Problem is, there are two possible locations. If we follow the trail north, we end up on a hill overlooking the valley. There used to be a small fort structure there until a storm took it out. Or we can head south where a new fort was built."

"Well, all the forts listed are still active today," Tommen reasoned. "Might as well try south first."

"South it is."

Tommen didn't know jack shit about the camp or where anything was beyond what he could see, so he trailed dutifully along after Saul who seemed to have no shortage of energy. Thankfully, the fort wasn't too far away, though the steep climb was less than beginner friendly.

"You don't get out much, do you?" Saul observed as they entered the fort, ducking under the kid-sized arch to the inside.

"Not as much as I'd like," Tommen answered diplomatically.

"This camp is going to kill you. You know that, right?"

"Well, if I don't, I have no shortage of enemies who'd like to."

Saul raised a brow but said nothing as he found the box and opened it up. Tommen peered over his shoulder, and he brought out a screwdriver and another envelope.

" 'Nile —' "

"River?"

Saul gave him a look. " 'Nile, Malaria, Ebola' "

"Well, that escalated quickly. Definitely an adult game." Tommen folded his arms and leaned against the wall as Saul stood and seemed contemplative.

"All deadly diseases," he mused.

"They're all mosquito-borne pathogens," Tommen offered. "Is there a swamp around here somewhere?"

Saul nodded. "There will be. There's a seasonal river that runs not far from here, but this time of year it'll be slow to the point of non-existent, and all that will remain is a nasty swampy area."

"Lovely."

"Hope you brought bug spray."

Tommen still didn't relish the idea of trekking through a nasty, swampy area. Even before they reached the swamp proper, they were assaulted by mosquitoes and all manner of nasty, annoying, biting insects. Tommen futilely swatted them away, but Saul appeared completely unfazed, slogging his way through the mush toward a tree with a box attached, a big number 2 on the side. He reached in and pulled out a flat package which, when unwrapped, proved to be a wooden sign, stained white, with "WOLF" in large black letters painted on it. He reached inside the box again and grabbed another envelope.

" 'Fever' " he said simply.

"What else?" Tommen asked.

"That's it. But seriously, take a guess."

"I don't know." Tommen swatted at another mosquito.

"The cabins. Cabin fever?"

"Great. Let's go." *Let's get out of here.*

He was more than happy to leave the swamp and get back to the main camp clearing, this time heading for the cabins. The girls' cabins were on the west side of the camp, the boys' cabins on the east side of the camp. Up close, Tommen could see that they were all built similarly, but, as promised, each one was missing something different. One was missing a bell, another a little outdoor table, a third the door itself.

The cabin they approached seemed normal, until Tommen started considering the smaller details of each cabin. Each one had a large animal print wood carving on the door; one had a bear paw, another a bird track, and so on. Their cabin was missing its animal track.

"Let's get what we have installed, then look for the rest," Saul decided, digging out the screwdriver and bag of screws.

The WOLF sign attached first to the heel of the paw which then attached to the door. There were more holes in the door corresponding to what Tommen assumed to be toes.

"The toes will be in or around the cabin. I'll check outside."

Tommen got the impression that Saul was accustomed to working alone, or else he just didn't like working with Tommen. Either way, he wandered off to one side of the cabin, and Tommen slunk inside to start looking around, unsure if the toes were going to be individual or one solid piece. He found out quickly enough when he found one toe stuffed under mattresses, and another under a loose floorboard.

"I got two," he reported, meeting back up with Saul outside the cabin.

"I found the other two. One under the porch, another in the eaves."

They attached the toes, and their cabin was fixed, their mission complete.

"Well, that's that," Saul said decisively. "Let's go get our stuff."

Tommen had little trouble finding his things, but Saul's stuff had gotten kicked around and scattered, and he seemed none too pleased for it. But they returned to their cabin no worse for wear.

"So, if you don't mind me asking," Tommen said, unrolling his sleeping bag. "What was it? Army? Marines? You just look like a guy who's...seen a thing or two. Knows a few things."

Saul did not look at him. "Six years in the Marines. Busted up my back pretty good, so I got out on medical discharge." Could have fooled Tommen. "That's why they put the troubled kids with me, because they hope I can instill some discipline in them. Because no other counselor will take them. Joe and I had a system going; we understood each other. We knew how to work with each other, work with the kids."

"Sorry to cramp your style."

"I'm telling you now so you're aware. No other counselor assistant wants to be with me, so don't bother asking Jerry if you can trade. Quite frankly, I don't know what possessed him to hire a kid like you for this job."

"Are you saying I can't do it?"

"I don't know. I don't know you well enough. But I do know that if you can't help with these kids and you're going to wuss out on me, quit now and save everyone the trouble. I would rather work alone than have a useless assistant dragging at my heels."

So, basically, he was going to have to be Mr. Layman. He could do that. Tommen shook his head. "No. You can't get rid of me that easily."

"Suit yourself," Saul said, shrugging. "But if you're really intent, let me give you a word of advice. Michelle, the nurse? She has a few extra lockboxes that she uses for the kids' medications. Get one of them from her, and put everything you value in it. That means phone, keys, wallet, and especially your hearing aids and whatever you have with them. These troubled kids aren't troubled just because they tug on girls' pigtails and push each other on the playground."

Chapter Seven
Welcome Week

To say that Tommen was less than encouraged by Saul's warning would be an understatement, but he didn't really feel threatened by it. Maybe it had to do with the fact that he'd seen and done so much shit in the last year—shit that actually had life-and-death consequences—that he could only look upon petty school fights with pity. Maybe it was because he'd once been one of those troubled kids. He'd gotten into fights, done stupid stuff, had a record (even if it was still technically in limbo). He knew what went on in these kids' heads, and his recent experiences had made him immune to it. He no longer took everything personally—unless you count that time he got demoted over stupid government regulations and quit his job shortly thereafter—and he could only look back on all his antics and sigh with resignation. Those shenanigans would stay with him, but at least he had the presence of mind now to move beyond them.

Once they were settled, they returned to the main hall for lunch, where tables had been set up in long rows, and where Tommen learned just how wonderful camp food could be. Pam and her team had a real gift.

"All right, everyone," Mr. Wilson said, moving down the rows of tables and handing out stacks of papers. "What I'm handing out is the schedule of events for this week, as well as the tentative schedule for our first run of campers. As always, everything is subject to change due to the weather."

Each pair of counselors and assistants got the lists. Saul put his papers between them so they could both look and try not to spill taco sauce on them.

133

"Wait, so, basically, we're going to be doing all the off-site activities before the kids?" Tommen wondered. "The horseback riding, the ziplining, all of that?"

"Yup," Saul said. "You remember what I told you earlier about quitting and saving everyone the trouble of a wimpy counselor? Yeah, I probably should have told you to at least get through this week, and then quit."

"I'm not quitting," Tommen informed him sharply.

"All right." Saul shrugged. "Don't say I didn't give you the chance."

"Stop trying to scare the poor kid," one of the female counselors said, sitting across from them. She looked at Tommen. "He'd have you believe that the kids in your cabin are going to be arriving in some prison work detail van. They're not. Yeah, they have problems, but they're not little ax murderers."

"Not yet." She rolled her eyes, but Saul went on. "Then tell me why no one else will take these kids, hm? And why can't they find a tough as nails female counselor for troubled female campers, hm? Easy for you to say when you don't have to deal with them."

"They're not going to burn down the camp, or do anything that a mischievous group of boys wouldn't normally do."

"Mischievous little boys have started more than one wildfire out here."

She ignored him and looked at Tommen. "Saul can be a little cranky. He's not much of a people person, and he's upset that Joe's gone this year. It's nothing personal. But don't let him talk you into thinking that you're going to be running the prison cabin."

Saul scoffed and shook his head.

In a way, Tommen was torn. There was every chance that Saul was exaggerating a little and making the troubled campers out to be more troubled than they actually were. On the other hand, if what he said was true and no other counselor would take these boys, their actions were probably a little more serious than simple mischief.

"So, what's on the agenda for tonight?" he asked, hoping to

get away from what appeared to be Saul's bone of contention.

"Cabin cleaning, mostly," Saul said, glaring at the female counselor for a moment longer before looking down at the schedule. "Unless you prefer shacking up with the mice?"

"Not really."

"Didn't think so. Yeah, pretty much cabin cleaning, grounds cleanup, that sort of thing. Get things running and operating again."

Apparently, that meant going beyond sweeping floors, washing windows, and changing light bulbs, and actually getting into the electrical and plumbing of the place. It did not appear to be a new thing as Saul removed the cover plate of one of the outlets, then removed a larger panel that allowed him access into the wall to get to a spot in the wiring where mice had chewed through and made a nest.

Saul did the work with all the grudging determination of a Marine whose career got cut short, but Tommen found the experience enlightening and even enjoyable. He knew a few things about electric work and wiring, but he'd never done any real work, like in a house or cabin, and he'd certainly never learned how to fix it when things went wrong, at least in the sense of mice chewing through the wires.

Plumbing was a little different story, one Tommen was decidedly less enthused about. He usually didn't mind cleaning the bathroom at home, but there was something just awful and disgusting about cleaning and fixing the facilities of a public bathroom and shower, especially when it hadn't been used in almost a year. That was hardcore scrubbing and cleaning of molds and mildew, plunging up dead animal carcasses from the toilets—okay, Tommen might understand a mouse in the toilet, but a squirrel?!—and, only slightly less traumatic, cleaning the air vents.

Saul and Tommen weren't the only ones working with the wiring and plumbing, but certainly not everyone was involved.

"So, are you like a master electrician or plumber, or what? Like, why not get a team of professionals in here to fix some of these things?" Tommen asked when they finally got done cleaning and repairing the showers and then used them to wash off all the grunge and grime.

"We would, if there was anything really major that was wrong," Saul told him, brushing out his long hair. "But what we did today pretty much amounted to general maintenance, things that could be accomplished by basic wiring knowledge, basic household plumbing knowledge, and a little elbow grease from a housekeeping staff. No pipes were burst, and no one reported a particularly dangerous electrical situation. Therefore, we can do it ourselves."

During the day, Saul had kept his hair in a tight, neat braid, but now he tied it back in a loose ponytail that fell almost to his waist. They grabbed their things and headed back to their cabin. Over the course of the afternoon, Saul seemed to have warmed up to Tommen a little, once he saw that he wasn't just a stupid, lazy teenager who didn't know shit about anything.

"What about the others?" Tommen looked around at some of the other counselors who were not busy with wiring or plumbing.

"Well, not everyone knows wiring and plumbing." It was difficult to judge his tone. "Personally, I would just as soon clean the showers as help anyone else with their cabin wiring. And the other counselors are happy to have it that way."

"You don't like the other counselors?"

"Some are okay."

His answer was evasive, and yet dismissive, some silent undertone telling Tommen not to push his luck too far. They'd only just met, so don't expect him to start divulging his life sob story. Tommen sighed internally. *If only you knew.*

Camp maintenance took up pretty much the entire afternoon and evening. Once everyone was done or close to done, the call came down for dinner. The staff was decidedly less enthusiastic as they shuffled their way into the main hall, but it was like the sigh of fatigue at the end of a long day of hard labor and satisfying work. Well, hard labor anyway. There was nothing satisfying about plunging a half-rotted squirrel out of a toilet. Tommen couldn't speak for anyone else's experience that day.

Dinner ended up being a spaghetti bar with endless garlic bread, and Tommen loaded up, picking out several different types of noodles, a different sauce for each, and then covering it all in cheese.

"Don't eat too much," Rick said, sitting down on his other side. "We've still got the campfire and s'mores to do yet."

Tommen sighed and rubbed his eyes. "I am so tired right now."

Saul chuckled and shook his head, but said nothing.

"Well, you're going to have to pay extra attention at the campfire," Jeremiah told him. "That's where we learn all the campfire songs that we have to do with the campers. The s'mores are just the sugar to keep you awake and upright."

At least he was honest, and it turned out to be largely true. Tommen scarfed down probably half a dozen gooey s'mores, but he still couldn't remember any of the campfire songs when they were finally dismissed and allowed to slog off to bed. As he finally crawled into his sleeping bag, he caught Saul smirking at him.

"What?"

Saul shook his head. "This camp is going to kick your ass."

"Whatever, man."

Tommen removed his hearing aids and set them on the charger, still debating whether he should get a lockbox like Saul had suggested and leave his hearing aids with the nurse as Mr. Wilson had suggested. Had that been just concern for his staff, or had that been the first hint of the awfulness to come? Should Tommen have taken this job? In the end, he couldn't remember what he decided, because he was already out.

After that, the camp prep week turned into something of a routine. Mornings were spent in back-breaking labor of one form or another—from taking axes and saws and clearing out the walking trails around the camp, to repairing the leaky roof of one of the cabins—and then after lunch came the fun stuff, the ziplining, the horseback riding, kayaking, the whole bit.

Saul was still a somewhat prickly bastard, but he seemed to

have warmed up to Tommen a little. According to all the other counselors, just surviving the summer with him would be about the equivalent of friendship. Mulling it over a little, Tommen wasn't sure how he felt about such a statement, and decided to rule it as just a little new counselor initiation or something similar.

When he texted Becky about his exploits, she very nearly dropped her work right there to run out to the camp. Horseback riding might be a little tough, but she could do the swimming and the kayaking. Heck, she could do the hiking, even. If a four-foot teeny-bopper could do it, she could do it, too.

Tommen talked her out of it, telling her that she had clients that needed tending to.

"Oh, yeah, because tending to 'I need it right away but can't make any of the fitting appointments' is just the highlight of my summer," she responded.

"If you hate the job, why do you do it?"

"I don't hate the job. I love my job. I hate the clients."

"You wouldn't have a job without clients."

"I could launch my own clothing line with standard sizes and leave it up to people to buy this season's latest fashion."

"Or you could do that. Why don't you do that?"

"Because I don't have time. During the summer I do, but not during the school year. And anyway, it's really just more of a hobby, something to make money so I can save up for college. Genetics is not a cheap career path."

"Yeah, well, neither is traveling."

"So, where do you plan on traveling first?"

Tommen leaned back against his pillow on the wall and thought for a minute. Really, he wanted to go out into the universe, visit different worlds and meet new aliens, not just new people. He wanted to see a culture that had no bearing on or resemblance to his own. Well, rephrase, he wanted to visit new worlds without it being a life and death situation. He'd already done the traveling and seen a new culture, but it was less of an exchange student experience and more of a tool to get the cure for his dying father's illness.

"I don't know," he replied finally. "Maybe somewhere in Asia. Or Africa. South America."

"Anywhere but home?"

"Pretty much."

"You know, Germany has a pretty nice genetics course in Berlin. Go there, and maybe I can come with you."

"Maybe. We could tour Europe or something."

"Official genetics research, you know."

"Absolutely."

After a minute or two, they ended the conversation, and Tommen started putting his things away. He'd ended up getting a lockbox. Even if he didn't need it as insurance against their troubled campers, it was sealed and waterproof anyway, which would be good for the kayaking and other water activities.

"Texting your girl?" Saul asked, walking in the door and hauling himself into his bunk.

"Yeah," Tommen admitted. "Her name is Becky."

Saul did not reply, simply rummaged around in his bag for something. Whether he was actually looking for something or using it to stall was anyone's guess.

"You got a girl?" Tommen asked finally. "Girlfriend, wife?"

"No. The only women in my life are my sister and my mother."

"Oh. Any brothers?"

"Two. One older, one younger."

"Cool." Tommen was determined not to let this die as a one-sided conversation. "Yeah, it's just me and my dad for the last nine years."

"No mom?"

"No. Actually, my dad is my uncle. My family died. Carbon monoxide poisoning. I ran away that night because I was mad, got home, and found everyone dead. So...yeah."

Saul gave him a look he couldn't interpret. Then, "Damn.

That's gotta be rough."

"Doesn't matter anymore. It was a long time ago."

"Of course it fucking matters. It will always matter. How much it matters is dependent on the situation. The things you've done in your life, some of them, can probably be traced back to that. How you interact with the campers this summer, you think that event won't have any bearing whatsoever on it?"

"Well..." He'd never thought of it that way before. Well, he had, but more in passing thoughts that he didn't want to stop to dwell on. It was made even worse when he considered the real story behind everything. His family was dead, yes, but they'd been dead for over a century. He'd abandoned them, albeit unwittingly, and only recently had he found out that his dad was his uncle, his last living relative from that era.

Saul got himself positioned and leaned back so he could read a bit, as he had every night so far. Some detective novel or other.

"For a guy who busted up his back, you seem to move around and get around pretty well," Tommen observed casually. "Mind if I ask what happened?"

"I do, actually." Saul did not look up from his book. "All you need to know is that you don't know the strength you have until you're faced with your own certain death."

I know that better than you think. The words were there on the tip of his tongue, but Tommen bit it back. He had no desire to try and fudge the truth, nor explain it. And he was pretty sure that, as a Marine, Saul definitely won that contest, whatever his story was.

"So how did you start as a counselor here?" he asked instead.

"Fuck if I remember. I guess I must have seen some advertisement for the position—newspaper or online or something. I wasn't out of the Marines long, still recovering from my injuries, trying to get get back into civilian life. Some part of me thought that it might be an easy job, do some fun things, hang out with the kids, that sort of thing. Another part of me thought that maybe it would be a nice transition from military life to civilian life—I was more fucked up on drugs back then; there's no other way to explain that sort of shitty logic. You know, early mornings, late nights, set schedule, me in charge, others below me.

"Camp is not like that. Yes, it's early mornings and late nights, but pretty much the 'set schedule' is more relative than I would prefer. Kids are not soldiers; you can't just order them to do something and expect them to do it."

"What about the troubled kids?"

"My first year, I had a group of regular campers. Nothing too difficult there, really, but I didn't really know what to do with them, and I think they were a little afraid of me. Anyway, one of the other counselors had a group of difficult campers. Not the troubled kids cabin necessarily, but that type. And they'd been beating up on the poor guy all summer.

"One day, I decided that I couldn't stand to watch them beat him up and take advantage of him anymore. So I intervened, spoke my mind, and got them set to rights. Or more right, anyway. I ended up switching places with that counselor, and there were no more problems from that group for the remainder of their time in camp, which was only about a week anyway. After that, those are just the kids I've gotten."

"Do you enjoy it?"

Saul hesitated and looked up briefly from his book. "There's no good way to answer that. If I say no, then I wonder why the hell I still do it. If I say yes, then I just sound like a sadistic asshole who enjoys yelling at kids like this is bootcamp because I can't adjust to normal life. So I really don't know."

"Oh."

"I think I heard somewhere that your dad's a cop?"

"Yeah, he is. Twenty years."

"How adjusted is he to life at home?"

"Um, good, I guess." *Sleeps with a night light, has nightmares that'll wake up the entire neighborhood, questions himself constantly, worries about me obsessively...* "I mean, I know he has some problems sleeping, but he still does his job."

"What's he do? Twenty years, he must have some sort of rank."

"Well, officially he's a Captain, but he works homicide."

"Homicide? Huh. He ever sustain any injuries? Debilitating ones, ones that might require surgery or anything?"

Tommen studied him. "Yeah. He was shot."

"Oh, even better. He get painkillers?"

"Yes."

"Is he off the painkillers?"

"I know where this is going. He told me to watch him and monitor him, to be his accountability. I disposed of the script bottles myself just to be sure."

Saul dipped his head. "Good. Just be sure to keep him honest. And I'm not talking dirty cop level. Whether you're in the Marines or on the streets as a cop, you see things. And they change you. Keep an eye on him."

"What's that supposed to mean?"

"Furthermore, keep an eye on yourself. Chivalry and bravado is great and all, but never forget to look after yourself."

"Chivalry?" Tommen shook his head. "Wait, who the fuck are you to know that?"

"Well, shit, I knew I'd been out of school a while, but I didn't realize that they've stopped teaching even the concept of chivalry. But hey, not really a surprise, I guess."

Tommen flopped back on his sleeping bag and let out a breath. *Stop being paranoid. You're the Chivalrous Welshman, but it's not like it's a unique title. Other people have been called chivalrous, too. Old ladies lament that chivalry is dead. It's just a coincidence.*

Yeah, because anything in my life is a coincidence.

"Well," Saul said after a while, placing his bookmark, "I guess we should try to get some sleep. Tomorrow's the big day, when all the little campers start arriving. Tons of fun, if you enjoy chaos. Otherwise, I think Pam starts the coffee about six."

Tommen wordlessly agreed as he wiggled into his sleeping bag. He'd honestly thought that, given enough time, maybe he and Saul would get to know each other and summer camp would be awesome. Except the other counselors had it right all along; he was weird. Good at what he did, keeping the troublesome kids in line, but he was not well-adjusted. Whether it was from his time as a Marine or just a shitty personality, Tommen wasn't a hundred percent sure.

Either way, he was right about needing sleep. From all the stories he'd heard, prep week was hard on sleep, but the actual camping was even worse. Given all the fun they'd had so far and all the work they'd done, it was easy to forget that they had little teeny-boppers coming in.

But it all came back in a rush when the first car pulled into the parking lot. It looked like a brother and sister team, older brother possibly ready to move out of the younger camp and into the older camp next year, younger sister looking like it would be her first time away from home for so long. He looked ecstatic; she looked terrified.

"So, are you going to point out the troubled campers to me, or do I have to guess?" Tommen asked, taking a drink of coffee and watching the parents try to get everything together for their kids.

Saul chuckled as he stirred in another creamer. "Oh, believe me. You'll know them."

It was not a comforting thought, but it was a precise one. At least Tommen figured he wouldn't have to watch every camper and try to guess. He ruled out the girls immediately, for obvious reasons. As for the boys, well, he figured that as long as they didn't come out of the car with fists flying, it couldn't be too bad.

The plan was to funnel all the kids to the nurse's office to check for lice first, then set them free in the main field area for games until about noon when they would assemble for lunch and cabin assignments. That was the plan. According to everyone, rarely did anything go according to plan.

"Here comes one of the little devils," Saul said after a while. It was about eleven o'clock, and the campers were coming in at a fairly steady flow. The vehicle Saul pointed to was a beat up old truck with only one headlight and a piece of plywood for a tailgate, spray paint covering most of it in obscene words and pictures. Well, it would make sense, Tommen figured.

"So, who is he?" he dared ask.

"Randall McLeod. Ten years old with such a mouth on him, he could make a sailor blush. He's probably the least vicious of the group; he's mostly bark but with very little bite."

Tommen watched the kid get out of the truck. He also appeared to have hit puberty early with no concept of deodorant or regular bathing. At his apparently repulsed look, Saul grinned and added, "We also have to make sure he takes a shower every night. At least, we have to get him in the water; getting him to use soap is just a bonus."

Oh, God, by the end of the summer, their cabin was going to smell wretched. Fuck.

"Oh, and here comes his partner in crime."

The vehicle in question was at least a decent-looking midsize SUV, and the boy looked like he knew what soap was.

"Carson Wilhall. He's actually Randall's cousin, but the family has moved into the twenty-first century and uses soap. He's eleven, getting ready to move into the big kids' camp next year, but the way he acts, he thinks he's the director. He's very bossy, but the worst part is, he knows how to get others to follow him. Don't take anything he says lightly and dismiss it as cute child's play. If you hear that he's going to set fire to the camp, always make sure to keep matches away from him. If he says he's going to hang you, don't let him get anywhere near rope."

"He's threatened to hang someone?"

"First year he was here, he tied a noose and hung it from one of the bunks so when the kid on the bottom bunk got up—all tired and not paying attention—he walked right into it. He was tall enough that it didn't actually hang him, but he hasn't come back. Carson got kicked out that year and suspended for two years, managed to smooth talk his way back in after one. Last year he talked about starting a fire in the woods, but never actually did anything. But just in case, don't let him out of your sight."

Oh, this just kept getting better and better.

"I know we're not in charge of them, but are there any girls we should be watching out for? Just as a precaution?"

Saul mulled it over, ran his tongue over his teeth. Finally, he shrugged. "Not really. I mean, at this age, this camp, boys and girls still have cooties. If the girls are mean, it's generally toward each other. The biggest threat you'll probably face from them is the vegetarian cabin."

"Vegetarian cabin?"

"Yup. One cabin of girls comprised entirely of vegetarians, or so they'd like to believe. I imagine that at least once this summer you're going to get a lecture about the cruelty of harming animals and butchering them for food."

"I thought this was supposed to be a poor kids' camp? Sorry, but it seems like the phrase 'beggars can't be choosers' applies here."

Saul shrugged again. "I'm not their dad. And this camp is targeted toward poor kids, but it's open to anyone."

Tommen scoffed. "Must be nice to live in a time and place where their pithy dietary choices and frugalities—" Was that a word? "—can be catered to on a whim. Lock them out of the kitchen for a few days, see what they do." He shook his head. "Their ancestors would be ashamed."

"Preaching to the choir, sir. Thankfully, we don't have to deal with them. Oh, and here's another one of ours. James Calder. Little Jimmy, eight years old."

"Eight years old and he's in the troubled kids cabin?"

"Yes sir. His older brother is a runaway, joined a gang in Charleston. Well, apparently, Jimmy's fixing to follow him. He's not really troubled; his mom is just trying to prevent him from following in his brother's footsteps, or so the story goes."

"And putting him in with troubled kids—one of whom you

already stated is good at getting kids to follow him—is going to help how?"

"Beats me." Saul finished off his coffee and threw the cup in the trash. "But I don't make the assignments. Come on. It's about time to start rounding them up."

"So, we just call them in or what?" Tommen asked, following him.

"Well, for the rest of the kids, yes. As for us, well, let's go make sure they haven't picked the lock on the cabin door yet."

"Picked the—? What? Wait!"

True to his word, they found Carson and Randall busy trying to jimmy the lock on the cabin door, but with little success.

"Atten-tion!" Saul barked with all the force and authority of a Marine Drill Sargent.

Both boys startled; Carson jumped upright, and Randall went face-first to the ground but scrambled to pick himself up.

"We thought maybe you was fucking a whore or something, locking the fucking door," Randall said, every bit the slimy little cretin Tommen had seen from the main hall. And just as nasty with his words.

"Stop talking!" Saul ordered sharply. "If any damage has been done to this door, you're going to be repairing it. For right now, get yourselves back to the main hall!"

The boys rolled their eyes, but obeyed nonetheless, dropping their makeshift lock-picking tools and running off toward the main hall. Saul inspected the doorknob, but found no apparent damage.

"That's how you do that," he said finally, sitting on the porch in a heap.

"Didn't realize I'd signed up for bootcamp," Tommen said, trying to bring humor into the situation. It fell flat.

"Hey, you know where the exit is. If you don't think you can handle these kids, best advice is to walk out now, or they will eat you alive."

"No, I'm staying."

"Well, you're going to have to convince yourself before you convince me, because you look like you want to run out of here screaming. All right, these guys are just the little kids. They still listen to us. To me, anyway. Wait until we get in the teeny-boppers. Those guys don't listen. Believe me, fire, police, EMS, they all know this place real well."

Tommen was silent for a moment, watching Saul. If he had to hazard a guess, from his years of people-watching at the bakery, the man was dying for a cigarette, but he wasn't allowed to have any in camp. Finally, Tommen shifted his stance and said, "Let me ask you something. When this Joe person announced he wasn't going to be around this year, and knowing which cabin he helped run, why replace him? You said it yourself that you could and would like to run this cabin by yourself. Was it because all cabins are required to have two counselors? Or is it something else? Because I've seen a lot of summer camps where they have only one counselor and a lot more kids than this."

"It's not required for there to be two counselors, in the event of an emergency like this, but it's nice to have two. The Powers That Be might not have put out the help wanted, except for this cabin. They thought I would need help." Saul stood. "At this point, I don't know if I want the help they sent me."

He made to move past Tommen, but Tommen held his arm out to stop him. "You know, I don't appreciate being written off as some dumb teenager who doesn't give a crap about anything or anyone but himself and goes whining to Daddy whenever something doesn't go my way."

Saul met him head on. "Then stop acting like it. You probably took this job because you thought it would be a great opportunity to get out and be your own man. Because you've never been on your own before; you've never been your own man. Well, newsflash, you've got from now until cabin assignments to man up. All right, they look like kids, and at times, they'll play like kids, but our cabin...isn't like the other cabins. The sooner you realize that, the easier it'll be."

And he shouldered his way past, heading for the main hall. Tommen watched him go, stalking off like, well, a wolf. What the fuck was his problem? Okay, so they had to watch their boys a little more closely, so what? Camp according to Saul sounded more like prison.

After a minute, Tommen followed the crowd to the main hall. He didn't want to look for Saul or be anywhere near him, but he figured it was the right thing to do when the assignments came down. He found the counselor in the same corner where Tommen had set his stuff when he first walked into camp.

"Still haven't run out the door screaming," Saul mused.

"Nope. And I'm not going to," Tommen informed him.

"We'll see."

Tommen gritted his teeth and forced himself to change the subject. "So, what happens now?"

"Well, once Jerry gets his act together, he'll come out and do his little welcome speech. We do a little song and dance. He does the cabin assignments. We get lunch. Then everyone goes to their respective cabins to do a little unpacking, a few leisurely get to know you games. Then there'll be a bigger game of some form in the middle of the camp. Then it's dinnertime, a little free time, then campfire time, then lights out. That's just the quick rundown of things."

And that was exactly how it went. After a few minutes, Mr. Wilson walked into the room with a clipboard and a box full of stuff. He welcomed all the campers, new campers, returning campers, counselors, staff, everyone just short of the Academy. Then the counselors had to do just one of the many campfire songs they would be repeating endlessly for the next four weeks as a way of loosening everyone up and getting everyone excited for camp. Tommen had learned the songs well enough, but he was so preoccupied with keeping an eye out for his troubled campers that he missed or mixed up several lines, which the other counselors assured him was totally fine; he'd get it eventually.

"All right, now that we're all acquainted," Mr. Wilson went on, "we're going to get everyone broken up into their cabins and introduce you to your counselors. So, I'm going to have all the counselors go to that side of the room, and all the campers go to that side of the room; take your things with you, please."

Thus began ten minutes of awkward shuffling, pushing, maneuvering, and "Who took my stuff?!"

When they were all settled, Mr. Wilson began assigning each pair of counselors and assistants to different tables. Saul leaned close to Tommen and whispered, "Stay here. A couple of our boys decided to escape in the confusion. I'm going to go round them up. Just play along and make sure no one else goes wandering off."

"Roger that."

Tommen went to his table as assigned and waited patiently. The girls' cabins were called first, and Saul returned with the missing boys before long.

"You sure you want to do this?" Saul asked. "Once these boys are assigned to us, there's no going back."

"I'm sure," Tommen replied, trying to keep his voice level.

"Boys with Saul and Tommen!" Mr. Wilson called. "James Calder, Tanner Dickson, Louis Faltrow, Peter Harrison, Eric Jameson, Randall McLeod, Carson Wilhall."

Tommen didn't miss the sympathetic looks the other counselors gave them as the named boys grabbed their things and made for their table. He nearly vomited as Randall McLives-in-his-own-filth decided to sit right next to him, which apparently amused Saul who smirked, even as he himself looked ready to choke.

"So, what the fuck are we doing tonight?" Randall asked obnoxiously.

Saul looked at Tommen, a silent challenge.

"Well," Tommen said, appearing to be amiable. "First we're going to have lunch. Then we'll go back to the cabin, get unpacked, play a few games. After that I think is dinner, then a little free time before campfires. After the campfire, we're all going to go and take showers, and we're going to wash your mouth out with soap, followed by the rest of you."

Saul raised a brow, but said nothing as he was distracted by something else from one of the other boys. Randall, meanwhile, just gave Tommen a weird look as he asked, "The fuck are you? My fucking grandma?"

Now he had a smart reply. "No. Your grandma will threaten to wash your mouth out with soap. She might even do it just a little. But think of me as more like your big brother. I will not only wash your mouth out with soap, but I'll make you eat the bar."

"And he's just the new guy," Saul informed him, returning to the conversation. "Remember what I told you I'd do with that bar of soap?"

Apparently, it put enough fear in the boy that he shook his head vigorously and didn't say another word the rest of the time as they got up and got lunch. The kids went up first, Tommen and Saul following a step or two behind.

"How was that?" Tommen asked lowly.

"Interesting," Saul said. "Not a bad start. But this is only your first interaction, the first time you've ever even exchanged words. They're feeling you out right now. Don't give them any cause to think you have a chink in your armor, because they will exploit it in any way they can."

So he was sixteen, working as the counselor of a summer camp cabin, and he was still having to defend himself from bullies. And those bullies were the eight year old boys in his own fucking cabin! What—the—fuck? Could he find no respite anywhere? Was there anywhere in the world where he could be in charge and just be in charge? Or just not have to worry about bullies; that would be good, too, and he wouldn't even ask to be in charge if that was the case.

The good thing was that lunch seemed to be uneventful for the simple fact that the boys were too busy catching up with each other to be much concerned with either Tommen or Saul. They talked about their schools, their homes, their families. In their complaining, Tommen caught on to a lot of their woes and what made them troubled. All of them came from a household of either a single parent, or, if there were two adults in the house, one or both was an addict of some form. Some of them had brothers and sisters who were just as bad, but not at the camp because they were too young, too old, a runaway, an addict, in jail, or some other form of absence.

Tommen suddenly felt very much like his dad, looking at these boys and wondering, hoping, praying that his son didn't turn out so horrible. He also had the revelation that this is what he probably would have become if he'd been the victor in his fights with Tyler Freeman. This is what he would have become if he'd allowed Ryan—his foster brother from hell—to seduce him and get him to join his street gang.

In a way, he was both proud of himself for staying on the straight and narrow—okay, so maybe the slightly wavy and a little wider than narrow—but he was also a little humbled to hear the stories of those who had nothing and would probably never amount to anything without intervention. They were seven, eight, nine years old or so, and even now he could tell that every single one of them was going to be in jail before he was fourteen. The only one who might have had a chance was Jimmy Calder, but that chance would be gone if he stayed in this sort of company. Maybe he was being irrational. The kid could be just as much a little demon as the rest of them. After all, it was always the quiet ones, wasn't it?

Thankfully, even for his hypervigilance as they entered the cabin, the boys did not immediately trash the place or set it on fire. There was the first and foremost war of the bunkbeds. Everyone had to have a top bunk. Tommen wanted to intervene and show some authority and assign beds, but he followed Saul's lead to simply stand back and let them sort it out themselves. He fully expected there to be fisticuffs involved, but the worst came only from Randall's mouth as he cussed out everyone who took "his" bed.

Eventually, they got themselves sorted out and started unpacking. Sleeping bags, pillows, blankets, flashlights, comic books, action figures, cell phones—which were confiscated per camp rules—the whole works, until each boy was successfully back in his own room.

"Okay, guys, are we settled in?" Saul asked after maybe twenty or thirty minutes of mayhem. His words were friendly, but his tone left no room for questioning his authority.

"Do we have to play those stupid games?" Carson whined. "We already know each other."

"Except him," Randall said, pointing to Tommen. "Who the fuck are you, asshole?"

"There will be no name-calling," Saul told him sharply. "There will be no foul language of any kind while you are here, regardless if we're in the main hall with everyone or alone in our own cabin. His name is Tommen, and he is taking Joe's place this year."

"He looks kinda wimpy," Tanner observed casually. "I thought teenagers were supposed to be hyped up on steroids and shit."

"Not me. I win my battles the old-fashioned way," Tommen answered. *Old-fashioned cheating, that is.*

"Yeah? You wanna go?"

"The only place we're going," Saul cut in, "is to the open field for some game time. Remember that today is only day one. Some of your parents haven't even made it home yet. Don't make me have to call them and make them turn around."

"What game are we playing?" Jimmy wondered.

"I don't know. Mr. Wilson will tell us when we get out there. So, let's go."

Of course, whether or not the children were little demons, there was no going anywhere faster, except to mealtime. They spent probably five minutes of "Can I bring this?" and "Are we going to have time for that?" and so on. Strangely, though, they were not the last ones onto the field.

"Typical girls," Randall said. "Always taking so fucking long."

"Randall, remember what I said about the language," Saul cut in sharply.

"Whatever. They're taking too long."

Tommen was instantly reminded of Becky. She didn't wear makeup usually. Maybe for church or synagogue or on special occasions, but most days, she really couldn't be bothered. Her hair she simply gathered in a ponytail, and she didn't typically bother too much with wearing fashionable clothes because her orthopedic shoes looked tacky with everything.

They ended up playing a modified game of kickball. To no one's surprise, the boys of the Wolf Cabin, when they weren't cheating and getting kicked out, were usually aiming for specific people to kick the ball at. The worst part was that their aim was pretty deadly. Anything they aimed at, they managed to hit, or at least go in the direction they wanted.

"Sounds pretty rough," Becky texted later when he got ten seconds to be alone, that is, the bathroom, waiting for all the boys in the showers. "Are you sure you can handle it for four weeks?"

"Of course. It's just the first day, and they're excited to see each other again. It's no big deal. We can handle it."

"Do you really think so, or are you just playing the tough guy?"

"Yes, Mom, I can do this by myself."

"Ha ha ha. Jerk."

"Well, that's mild compared to what they've already called me so far today. Holy shit, I never knew an eight year old could swear like a trucker."

"That's absentee parenting for you."

"I guess."

"So...I've been thinking..."

This could be bad, Tommen thought. "About what?"

"About that kiss. Before you left."

Tommen let out a breath, preparing for the worst. "And........?"

"I liked it." He could imagine her decisive nod. "I did. I do. When you get home, we might have to see what happens when we mutually decide to do it."

His mind went a hundred different directions at once, but he forced himself to keep his thoughts relegated to the kiss only. "Oh. Cool. I mean, that's great. Good. Yeah. We should do it again. I think that's what I want to say."

"English never was your best talent."

"Dw i eisiau ulw dy cusanu rŵan. A pethau cilydd." (I totally want to kiss you right now. Among other things.)

After a minute. *"Wyt ti'n amgyffredu beth gallu i fo taro i Google Translate?"* (You do realize that I can pop that over into Google Translate?)

He didn't need to hit the translate button on his phone as he read the message and blushed. "Right. Fuck. Sorry. I guess...I mean...Sorry? I think?"

She texted back something, but Tommen heard one of the showers turn off, and he put his phone away before any of the boys caught him. God knew what they would have to say about the things he was texting about. Thankfully, it was only Saul.

"Go ahead and get in," he said, tossing his towel in the laundry bin. "I'll watch your stuff."

It was a camp rule that during cabin showers, only one counselor could be in the showers at a time; the other had to stand watch over the stuff to make sure nothing got stolen.

Only two of the boys were out by the time Tommen was done. Still wet, he went back and pounded on the walls next to the curtains.

"Come on, boys, time's up! Let's go!"

After a minute, a couple of the showers turned off. Tommen went back through again, yet three of the showers were still running.

"Carson?" he wondered.

There was no answer. Come to think of it, there was no sound at all beyond the water. No shuffling or movement, no singing or talking or taunting or anything at all. Curious now, Tommen Banded and pulled back the shower curtain.

Empty.

All three of them were empty.

"We have to go," Tommen said, moving swiftly to the locker room.

"Why? Who's missing?" Saul did a quick head count. "Not surprised, but how did they get past us?"

He said "us" but Tommen heard the subtle, accusatory "you." He was on guard when the boys got in the shower. And, unbeknownst to Saul, he'd been texting his girlfriend. He wasn't about to admit to it, but he'd been distracted.

They hurried back to the cabin where the door was left wide open. Once inside, it took Tommen a second to realize what was going on, but when he did, he somehow managed to pull out some kind of internal Drill Sargent because he almost set the boys through the roof with his voice.

"All right! Everyone stop! Put everything down! Step away from my stuff! Put it down now! Back away!"

He crossed the room to where his hearing aid charger had been confiscated and mutilated as Carson, Randall, and Tanner attempted to jerry-rig it into a drone battery charger. Tommen picked it up and turned on them. "Do you know what this is?!"

"It's a charger," Carson replied, trying to act tough, but looking ready to piss himself.

"Yes! It's the charger for my hearing aids! I need these! Why did you think it was okay to go through my stuff?!"

"We needed a charger for Tanner's drone that he brought," Randall explained, no profane word to be found when he was in trouble and he knew it.

"I didn't ask what you needed; I asked why you thought it was okay to go through my stuff."

"Why isn't it okay?"

"Answer me first. How would you like it if I went through your stuff and just started cutting and tearing and ripping into whatever I found? How would you like it if I took your drone and mutilated it because I needed something off it?"

By now, the boys seemed paralyzed with fear. Even the rest of the boys were hiding behind Saul who stood in the doorway. After a second, he stepped in the room.

"We're going to have a talk with Mr. Wilson." He looked at Tommen. "You should be able to handle the rest of them on your own. Just get them to bed."

Tommen nodded wearily, almost ready to cry. How was he going to call his dad and tell him that he needed a new charger? It was the first fucking day of camp. Maybe he should have taken Saul's offer to leave.

Said counselor returned after a little while with the three boys in tow. The rest of the campers were asleep. Once the three troublemakers went quietly to bed, Saul motioned for Tommen outside.

"Well, I have to say, you scared even me," he said.

"Don't patronize me," Tommen told him.

"No, I'm being honest. That's a little more of what they need. Actions, consequences. Anyway, Tanner is being sent home in the morning. I think all three of them had an in on it, but he's taking the fall, especially since he brought a drone when the signup clearly said no electronics."

Tommen sighed. "I don't know. I guess it's something."

Saul studied him. "Does the charger still work? I see you don't have your hearing aids in."

"Yeah, it works. As long as no one else touches it for the duration of this camp. I called my dad and he'll call the audiologist in the morning. I can get a new one when we go home between camps."

"That's good. So, you're still sticking around?"

Tommen gave him a look. "I've been bullied since I was eight years old. I'm not about to be bullied by eight year olds."

He pushed past him and made a beeline for his sleeping bag.

Chapter Eight
Coffee

Walter rolled into the parking lot, turned off the car, and tried to relax. Oh, what a long day. What a long night. And he was ready for it to be over. He didn't know why, since he would just be back tomorrow doing the exact same thing. But at least tomorrow would be his Friday, so it wasn't all bad. And today couldn't get much worse. Well, there were a thousand ways it could get worse, but he tried to remain optimistic as he got out of the car and headed into the precinct, more than ready to finish his paperwork and punch out.

Since December, they'd hired in half a dozen new officers, five of them fresh out of the Academy, one a transplant from some little podunk town where their biggest threat was the occasional rabid moonshiner and maybe a bear or a mountain lion. All six of them had a lot to learn, and the whole place still felt severely understaffed, both from lack of staff and everyone's hours being cut.

"Welcome back, Walt," Jim Standish greeted amiably, leaning against the fragile fabric wall of his cubicle.

"Please don't tell me we've got something," Walter said, trying not to sound as exhausted as he felt.

"No, not that anyone's told me. How's life with Tommen gone to summer camp?"

"Well, yesterday was his first day, and he's already got trouble." Walter collapsed in his chair and spread out his paperwork.

"Is he beating up on the other kids? Or sleeping with the female counselors?"

"No, actually the kids beat up on him pretty bad, sounds like. Guess they decided to turn his hearing aid charger into a drone launch station or something."

"Aw, damn. Does it still work, I mean...?"

"According to him, it does work, as long as no one disturbs it. I talked to the audiologist this morning, and he'll have one in for him when they get released between camps."

"Oh, good." Standish shook his head. "Probably not helping his self-esteem any, is it? I mean, you said he was just starting to get comfortable with them, and now this happens. That thing breaks, he's SOL."

"Well, I offered to come and get him—doesn't sound like anything is going right so far—but he's determined to stick it out."

"Good for him. See, he didn't turn out all bad."

"He only didn't turn out like me, and that's all I asked for."

"Yeah? You think so? What's this I hear about you and one of the paramedics?"

Walter sighed, leaned back in his chair, and rubbed his eyes. "We just have coffee sometimes."

Standish gave him a look. "Mm-hm. You seem to be going out for coffee a lot lately. Last week, the week before, twice the week before that." He chuckled. "Today."

"How do you know about that?"

"Oh, please, my sister-in-law is a nurse in the ER. She and Laura talk. Guess they've been talking about you."

"Yeah? What do they say?"

"Well, I'm assuming you don't really care about Rachel's opinion; you want to know what Laura thinks."

"Come on, Jim."

Standish grinned like a cheeky bastard. "All right, all right. Rumor is, Laura really digs you. You'll have to ask her for the details, but I believe the words, 'handsome,' 'witty,' and 'charming' were passed around."

"Damn. There goes the 'ruggedly handsome lumberjack' angle I was going for."

"And?"

"And what?"

"Do you like her?"

Walter folded his arms. "Are you asking because you care, or are you asking so you can tell your wife who's going to tell her sister who's going to tell Laura?"

"Do I have to answer?"

"Answer enough." He went back to his paperwork.

"Come on, Walt. It's a simple question."

"Well..." He moved back a bit. "She's nice, funny, down-to-earth, very engaging in conversation."

"You sound almost as dodgy and embarrassed as Tommen any time you try to get answers out of him about a girl he likes. How long did it take him to tell you about his current girlfriend?"

"Less than a week."

"Oh. Well, still."

"Still what?"

"You're evading the questions." Walter scoffed, and Jim pressed further. "You're evading the questions, countering them any chance you get, giving vague answers. If I didn't know better, I'd say you like her. What's the word I'm looking for?"

"Annoyed?"

"Twitterpated."

"Oh, for goodness' sake, Jim, we're not four years old."

"Exactly. You are forty years old. Older, actually. It's not like Tommen's going to be around a whole lot longer, and you're not exactly in your prime either."

"What do you want me to do, ask her to marry me when we see each other today?"

"No. It's just something to consider. You're not an idiot teenager, Walt. Trust your gut."

"My gut says it's hungry, and I need to get this finished so I can go out and get something to eat."

"Fine. Then I'll tell you what my gut says. Actually, I'll tell you what my eyes and ears say. They say that you haven't looked and felt this good in a long time. And it shows, in your work, probably at home, too. Walt. You're happy."

"I don't know that I'd go that far."

"Well, say what you will, I can see it, and so can everyone else here at the office. Does Tommen know?"

Walter let out a breath. "Well, he's a perceptive kid. He figured it out without me telling him."

"How'd he take it?"

"He figured it out right before he left for camp. He hasn't said anything about it, so I figure to just let him think about it a little while he's at camp."

Jim shrugged. "I guess that's all you can do. Anyway, I'll see you tomorrow. I'm heading out."

"I have this paperwork to do yet."

"And 'coffee' with Laura."

"Yes, and then coffee with Laura." Walter shook his head. "See ya, Jim."

Well, if anyone in the precinct didn't know about him and Laura, they would now; Jim hadn't exactly been whispering. That and the fact that rumors at the precinct flew almost as fast as they did at a high school. There were probably already rumors out about him and Laura, ranging everywhere from just having coffee to getting married next week. Well, maybe not quite that extreme. Maybe.

There had been several times in his life when Walter at least looked at women, even if he didn't pursue them in the end. Part of it was because they weren't Time Agents, and he didn't want to lead her on, only to dump her when he had to go dark. Part of it came from the fear of his own past; if he and someone ever got serious and started to divulge dirty laundry, well, his was a little dirtier than most. He couldn't just ignore it, either, because it always seemed to find him. To that end, what if he had been pursuing a woman and Tommen had shown up, speaking of a time before 2005? He couldn't have managed both at the same time. And after Tommen had come into his life, well, forget about it; he'd had no time for himself, never mind anyone else.

But now...well, maybe it was time to seriously consider retiring from Time and settling down. Chances were, it wouldn't be Laura. But seeing her made him feel normal again, feel human. For just a few hours each week, he was just a police officer, and he was doing something normal. Not fighting bad guys, chasing Runners across the universe, thwarting evil schemes to take over a corrupt industry, trying to outwit and outmaneuver those who would like to see him and his son dead.

He finished filling out his paperwork, and began the equally mundane task of filing it appropriately. That did not take quite as long, however, and soon he was on his way. He crossed the parking lot but did not get in his car right away. Instead, he took a minute to just look at it. It was old, a little beat up, a small dent testifying to Tommen's misjudgment as he "bumped" the mailbox. The brakes still needed work, and he was pretty sure the transmission was starting to slip. It had been a faithful little car, but maybe it was time for something new, something that Tommen might actually want to drive when he finally got his license. Something that Walter could look at him and say, "No. This car is mine. Maybe you should get one of your own if you want to drive that bad."

Ah, the evil little musings of fatherhood.

Another thought entered his mind then, as he started the car and backed out of his spot. What if he raised another child? Surely Tommen couldn't be the only child who ever got exposed to Time accidentally. There had to be others, and maybe one of them would need a home. Maybe he would adopt a girl this time, see how it compared, and finally be able to raise a daughter, the right way this time.

He shook his head. Boy or girl, kids were hard work. He didn't have the energy to go through all that again. And if he wasn't going to do that, then he was probably going to retire. He'd fulfilled his mission, kept his promise, done his good deed, lived his life. There was just...it was time for him to be done.

It would be easy to dismiss it all as sentiment, a mid-life crisis or maybe the impending doom of becoming an empty-nester. But, in Walter's mind, maybe there was a reason God installed time limits on human beings. It was good to enjoy Earth and all its pleasures for a time, but in the end, he just needed to rest. Maybe it was different because he'd come into his later in the game; maybe his past life had something to do with it. Maybe things were different for those like the twins, trapped in their late twenties, early thirties, still in their physical prime with an almost invincible attitude to match. And Micaiah? Damn that boy for keeping secrets. How the hell did a guy hide his wife for over a decade? That just made no logical sense.

Well, no use dwelling on it now. According to Micah, Micaiah was very happy now, and much more agreeable to live and work with. Walter had witnessed this as well, almost stunned at the change.

Was that how his coworkers saw him? Did they see a man who was exhausted, on the verge of burning out, suddenly come alive again? Did they see a man who was now more agreeable and easier to work with, someone they didn't mind walking in the door? And if that was the case, and they'd all seen it for a while, what had taken Tommen so long to notice?

Well, that answer was easy. At home, he didn't have to pretend that half his life didn't exist. At home, he didn't have to pretend that he was going to the bakery only to get a pastry and shoot the breeze with the twins. Home...well, home kind of served only as a reminder of the other half of his life, if he really wanted to be honest. Everywhere he looked, he saw the touch of Time. Even Tommen...Every time he looked at Tommen, Walter saw his younger brother, Tommen's father. There was no escaping the resemblance, the relationship; it was all there, serving only as a reminder.

Maybe that was why Laura made him so happy. He still had to stuff his Time life in a back pocket, but everything else was completely natural.

He let out a breath as he navigated city streets and pulled into the parking lot of the little cafe where they were to meet. He didn't see her vehicle, and it was hard to miss a huge silver F-150 with the tailgate covered in bumper stickers and the back window covered in some paramedic decal.

It was a nice little cafe, really, old-school, for the older generation who remembered lunch as being an interpersonal affair with no Internet needed.

Walter had deliberately been avoiding the bakery as a coffee venue. He didn't want to start any unnecessary rumors, and he didn't want to get the twins' input on it. He was a big boy; he could go on a date by himself.

Had he just called it a date?

Furthermore, he avoided the bakery because he hadn't wanted to tell Tommen just yet. He could have asked the twins to keep a secret, and he knew they would have, but better to minimize the risk and the interference.

Of course, now that Tommen knew and everyone in the precinct knew, there was no good reason not to meet at the bakery. Maybe next time they could go there, and get a light lunch or something. Laura wasn't exactly a kale and spinach kind of woman, so it wasn't like she would balk at the thought of a few carbs. Although, speaking of which, he probably should consider his diet. Not a diet-diet, like a fad diet, but his general nutrition diet. He didn't metabolize the same way normal people did, so he had to be more conscious of his eating habits.

Bah. This coming from the man who gets a pastry every morning. One quick lunch isn't going to mess you up forever. Besides, with Tommen gone for a few weeks, maybe you can have her over for a proper home-cooked meal. Show her what the "ruggedly handsome lumberjack" is capable of in the culinary world.

Walter rubbed his eyes. Maybe it was his fault for not marrying before adopting Tommen. Because right now he couldn't decide if these thoughts were stemming from honest, understandable loneliness, or his desire to retire from Time. Maybe a little of both. And how did he reconcile the two, make them fit together? On the one hand, if he retired from Time, it would take a while for the slowed-aging effects to wear off, so he would still have a good chunk of time left on this earth. But in the end, he was resigning himself to death. He had no doubt the Good Lord had been looking out for him over the last century or so, but how far did His coverage extend? Somehow, he couldn't shake the fear that Hell would be going back to Beaumaris Gaol, but with no release date, no execution, and no hope of escape. Good deeds meant little and less, but could mercy really cover up his crimes? Did he get no extra credit for fulfilling his promise to his brother and raising Tommen? Furthermore, in resigning himself to death, would Tommen feel betrayed, like he was abandoning him?

It was all too much to think about, even worse that he was supposed to meet Laura for coffee in about five minutes. He really needed to stop having existential crises in the middle of good days. The last thing he wanted to do was go to lunch and be the silent grouch, so focused on his problems that he inadvertently projected the illusion that he was mad at the one person who might care enough to help him work through his problems.

Jeez, Walt, you're only going out for coffee. This isn't like therapy or anything. It's not like you're married, where she knows you inside and out and knows how to help. It's not like she can comprehend the things that go on in your head. If she knew even a fraction of the things you've done, even if you kept everything within a reasonable timeline, she'd be running out that door screaming.

He sighed. *That's what I'm afraid of.*

As he moved to get out of the car, he felt a pain shoot down his leg, twisting around the scar tissue in his thigh. He gritted his teeth and tried to power through it. *Don't do it. It's just a trick of the mind. Tommen already tossed your script bottle. That's all done now.*

Oh, but it hurt. He had to do something. He didn't need Laura driving up and think he was having a heart attack or some other medical emergency—at his age, that was a real concern.

No. Your script bottle is gone.

Yes, but I'm a Timekeeper who knows where the evidence is stored.

Before he knew it, he'd dug out the little bag he kept stashed in an inside pocket and popped a pill. His leg relaxed, but the rest of him felt disgusting.

You're an addict. Worse, you're an addict and a thief. You need to get help and stop this now.

He elected to go inside and wait. Maybe being among people would help calm his nerves a little. He got about halfway to the door when he heard an engine he'd come to recognize. He turned around to see Laura pulling into the lot and parking next to his car. Debating for just half a second, he turned around and went to meet her.

"Were you worried I was going to be late?" she asked.

"Well, the A/C in the car is a little sketchy," he said, shrugging. Not entirely a lie, just one more thing that had to be fixed.

"Yeah, I don't need to break any windows today, or do any work when I'm not at work. So, good call on your part."

"Shall we?"

"I daresay we shall."

Tommen had taken a girl to a dance in seventh grade. First they got dinner, then went to the dance, all the while Walter drove them around. The whole time, Tommen had been too scared to hold the girl's hand or even look at her half the time. Walter had thought it all very cute and picked on him about it for weeks afterwards. Now, walking with Laura into the cafe, he was starting to get an idea of just what that felt like.

Walter could honestly say he'd never really properly dated a woman. Paige had found him, and she'd done her damnedest to take him from some Welsh country boy to a proper British banker. Most of the effort had been on her, educating him in the proper speech, the proper etiquette; he'd been more of a pet than a suitor, or even a husband. So when it came to a real relationship, he was at a total loss. He wasn't really sure about proper physical contact—well, other than the obvious—so he didn't really do any of it. Everything he knew came from 19th century London.

"Good afternoon, what can I get for the two of you today?" the man at the counter inquired.

"I'll have a small coffee and one of your Italian subs," Laura said.

"Will this be together or separate?"

Laura answered "separate" at the same time Walter said "together."

She looked at him and he nodded once. "I'll get it."

Her uncertainty gave him enough time to order his own coffee and a sandwich, and he handed over the twenty dollar bill before she could protest. Then they went to the end of the counter to get their food and drinks and dress them up a little before heading to a window seat.

"So, what was that all about?" Laura asked.

"What was what all about?"

"You bought my lunch."

"Was I not supposed to or not allowed?"

"No, it's just...it's nice. Not that I expect it or anything, but..."

"As a show of friendship," Walter finished.

"Yeah. Something like that."

They started in on their sandwiches, both of them a little too self-conscious to jump on that line of thought. After a moment, though, Walter leaned back and sighed. "Although, my son seems to know me better than I thought he did."

"Ah. Went home singing the other day?"

"No, but he managed a good guess all the same. Still, he hasn't said anything about it."

"He's a sixteen year old boy. How likely do you think it is that he would say anything?"

Walter shook his head and took a drink of coffee. "I couldn't say."

"What about you when you were sixteen?"

Oh, God, he didn't even want to think about that. "I don't think my experiences apply here."

"Well, when my kids were sixteen, they didn't tell me

anything. I mean, we had a good relationship then, like we do now, but they were trying to be their own people, live their own lives. I couldn't expect them to tell me everything that went through their minds."

"Ha. Yeah. Speaking of being his own man and living his own life, Tommen's away at summer camp for twelve weeks working as a counselor. He called me last night to tell me that a couple of the boys got a hold of his hearing aid charger and destroyed it, trying to make it work for their drone or something."

"Oh, that's terrible."

"It still works, which is good. Otherwise, they're coming home for a week between the different camps, so he can pick up a new one then."

"Well, that's good."

Walter hesitated. "Actually, that was kind of when I was planning on telling him. Before he guessed. About us."

"About us," Laura echoed. "Is there an us?"

Well, that was the question, wasn't it? Even if they were just dating, it was still a commitment. It was an unspoken promise to be available for the other person, emotionally, physically. It was an honest appreciation for the other person, and a desire to get to know them more, to see if...it might go beyond that. Walter enjoyed Laura's company, enjoyed their coffee time together, and he did want to know her better, find out who she was, about her life, all of it.

It was said that all men fear commitment, and maybe Walter more than most. It stemmed from a filthy past, a failed marriage, and his Timekeeping duties. The first two, he'd seen several of the guys at the precinct work through so they could have a happy, healthy marriage and their own happily ever after. It was that third part that he struggled with, not the least of which came from the slowed aging. Even if he stopped Timekeeping right that very second, he could still very well live for a few more decades. Was there a way to undo that? Was there a way to jumpstart his biological clock, get it ticking normally again?

He hated to say yes and attempt to pursue a relationship, knowing that he would outlive her by so long. And he had no intentions of leading her on, dating her for a little while, then dumping her when it became convenient or inconvenient; it was rude. Even if he knew and understood the reasons, it wouldn't make him feel any less rotten. So here he was, stuck between a rock and a hard place with nowhere to turn.

"I don't know," he said at last. "Is there an us? Do you want there to be an us?"

"Well, I mean, my kids are grown. Your son is almost grown. Neither of us is getting any younger."

He grinned. "So I'm your backup plan."

"No, of course not." She chuckled nervously. "No. I mean, I do...I like you. You're funny and sweet, and you love your son. I've dated guys who were real smooth-talkers, but had virtually no relationship with their kids. You and Tommen seem to have a really good relationship."

"I'd like to think we do. But, like you said, he doesn't tell me everything, I'm sure."

"How do you think he'll react?"

"I don't know. I really don't. I think that, to our faces, he'll be polite but generally indifferent. As for what goes on in his mind, I'm afraid I would have to ask other sources."

"Like what?"

"His girlfriend. His bosses. His teachers." He paused and drummed his fingers on the table. "What about your kids? Have you told them?"

Laura nodded, then shrugged. "I only told them I was seeing someone and I would let them know more if anything else happened. After ten years, well, I keep them in the loop generally, but I don't get their hopes up."

"So they want you to find someone."

"They seem to think I'm too lonely, that I need someone to cook me dinner and let me vent about my bad days at work."

"Oh, so that's how it is. Do you need a foot massage, too?"

"Depends. You offering?"

"Well, that's a line of thought that I'm not going down just yet." Walter may have been single for over a century, but he was still a man, after all.

"Good answer, on more than one level."

"What's that supposed to mean?"

She grinned and shook her head as she laughed. "Don't worry about it."

"Now you have me worried."

"No, no, don't worry about it. Really." She took a nervous drink of coffee. "Just my own evil mind trying to get me in trouble again."

"Paramedic humor?"

"Not quite."

They spent the better part of an hour at the cafe. On the one hand, it was strange not having to get home to keep an eye on Tommen, or rush to pick him up from work. At the same time, even if that were the case, Tommen was growing up and should be able to fend for himself and make his own decisions, within reason. And anyway, it was kind of nice to have some time to himself, to spend in the company of a wonderful woman. His woman. His...girlfriend, by all accounts.

So there was an us. Apparently, this was what qualified as a first official date in the 21st century. Now, instead of just Walter, it was Walter and Laura. If one went to a formal event, they were obligated to invite the other or obligated to attend if possible. Maybe not always, but that was kind of an unwritten rule. They were dating, so they ought to consider bringing the other person into their lives, get to know them in a variety of circumstances. Damn, that sounded cold and impersonal. Walter mulled it over for a minute before deciding to let it go. Love was not just an impersonal chemical process, but an interpersonal emotion. It had no explanation. Really, it needed no explanation.

Not that he considered this love per se, but maybe, in time, they could grow to truly appreciate one another, rely on each other, depend on each other, and then they might call it love. He'd do it the right way this time. Mutually. And without the drinking or the violence.

Yes, but what about the narcotics? More than that, what about the narcotics you stole? Shit happens and you get caught, you not only lose your job, but you go to jail and lose everything.

I can stop.

How many guys have you hauled in who say the same thing but never actually follow through?

I can. I will. This is me stopping. Right here. Right now. Done.

Well, you better hope so, because she's a paramedic. She knows exactly what to look for. You took one before you walked in, so your pupils are probably still pretty tiny at this point.

I said I'm done. It's over. No more pills. No more anything.

We'll see.

"Well," Laura said at last, "I suppose I should be getting home, get a few things done before my shift. Seventy-two hours at a time. I swear, they'd work us to death."

"They couldn't do that," Walter told her. "If something happened to you on the job because of the job, they wouldn't be able to charge you for the ambulance ride, and they'd have to pay workman's comp. They won't work you death, but right up to it."

She laughed. "Ain't that the truth? All right."

They got up, tossed whatever trash they had left, and exited the cafe.

"So, is this part of the us?" Laura asked as he walked her out to her truck.

"It is if there is an us," Walter told her.

She thought a minute, then nodded. "Yeah. There's an us."

"Seventy-two hours, so you're not off until Thursday."

"That's right. Why, you already had something in mind?"

"I might. I'll let you know."

"I'd like that. I'll see you then."

He got out of the way as she got in her truck and drove off. He watched after her for a moment before turning back to his beat up old Cadillac. Yes, it was probably time to cut his losses and trade it in while it still had some value. Or he could keep it and gift it to Tommen when he got back from camp; after all, he'd trained in it for his road test, and he still talked about getting his own car. Oh, the evil little things he could come up with.

In the end, he simply headed home. Had he been Tommen's age, he'd be rushing home to update his Facebook status and let the whole world know that he was seeing someone. As it was, Walter did not use social media, for obvious reasons, and anyway, the rumor mill would make sure everyone knew soon enough. It would probably start with Laura talking to Jim's sister-in-law who would tell his wife who would tell Jim who would tell everyone in the precinct, and it all went downhill from there.

At the same time, it wasn't like Walter was embarrassed about it. Well, about "it" itself, the news getting around, but he wasn't embarrassed about Laura. For those who knew them and suspected something was up, they were good together. Personality-wise, anyway. Inevitably, there were jokes about the things that could happen when a cop and a paramedic got in a fight, or when they weren't fighting and were instead on the more, ahem, intimate end of the spectrum. It left many things to the imagination.

Was this really what it was like to date someone as an older person? Was it really just as uncertain and embarrassing as a couple of young people? Or was Walter overthinking things due to the garbage in his past? Maybe he could somehow discreetly ask around for a little advice, get a feel for how things proceeded from here. Damn, that sounded cold and impersonal, too. Was it that obvious he was a cop? He knew he'd managed to steel himself against a lot of things, but could he learn to un-steel himself a little bit? Was that possible? Was un-steel even a word? Wow, now he sounded like Tommen.

Speaking of which, how would he take the news? Did Walter

want to text him the minute he got home, tell him now and let him think about it while he was at camp? Would that only cause a simmering resentment? Did he wait until Tommen got home so they could speak face-to-face? Personally, he preferred to do it that way, but with Tommen gone for another month or so, it seemed a little dishonest. Tommen would come home from summer camp and surprise! I've been dating Laura for the last month while you were gone! Cat's away and all that. Well, it sounded petty in his head, but he knew what he meant. It really seemed like there was no good option. Maybe he could wait a week, give himself time to process it before springing it on his son.

He pulled in the driveway, but hesitated on going all the way into the garage. Maybe he should wash the car, take a few pictures, and try to sell it. Well, he could wash it anyway; it would give him something to do.

Mrs. Lawson next door was out in her garden along the fence, weeding and carrying on. She stood and stretched as Walter got out of the car.

"Afternoon, Walt," she greeted.

"Stacy," he acknowledged, then paused and went over to the fence. "Mind if I ask you a question?"

"Sure. Everything all right with Tommen?"

"Oh, yeah, he's at summer camp right now. Actually, I wanted to ask you something else."

"Well, if it's about Hank burning his trash and tires again, I have photo and video evidence, as well as sworn statements from all the neighbors."

"Interesting. Nope, not about that either."

She folded her arms. "This is unusual. All right, shoot."

"You and David got married a little later, didn't you? When you were both over forty?"

"Yes."

"How did that go? And what I mean is, I assume that you both at least dated before that. How did it make a difference when you got older?"

She thought for a moment, shifting her stance. "Well, it became more and less practical, and more and less about love. On the one hand, we were both self-sustaining, both had our own house, our own car, the whole bit. So it's not like we were college kids where our combined income might get us some run-down apartment. At the same time, our combined income would allow us to get a better house, a better car, nice vacations, and so forth. But, being seasoned adults, we had the practical economic sense to know how to make it happen without drowning ourselves in debt.

"But to that end, since we were already pretty secure and had our heads on straight, we were able to marry for love, too. Though I think that aspect was harder at an older age. We took care of ourselves just fine, and we were pretty set in our ways. So there were a lot of fights about money in the sense of, 'Well, you did just fine on your own, why do you need my money now?' It was hard to go from independence to interdependence. Unlike younger couples where they marry for love just fine, but have a hard time with the finances overall."

"And neither of you had kids, did you?" Walter asked.

"Nope." She noted Walter's sigh as he shifted his stance and looked away. "Why are you asking me this? Are you getting sentimental, or is there something more?" She grinned. "Are you seeing someone?"

Well, there goes the rumor mill, off to a running start. "I don't know how to tell Tommen. He's already figured out that I was seeing someone on an infrequent basis, but now, we decided to...step it up, I guess you might say. Regular dating, I guess. He's going to be gone for the next month. Do I tell him now, or wait until he comes home?"

"Hm. That is a good question, because it's always been just you and him, and he's getting to an age where he wants to be his own man."

"Exactly."

"Does she have kids?"

"Three, but they're all grown up and moved out of the house, last one just last year."

"Okay. Well, I wish I had an easy answer for you, Walt, but I don't."

"I was afraid you'd say that."

"For what it's worth, from an outsider's perspective, you and Tommen seem to have a good relationship. You know him better than anyone. If you told him now, is he likely—or even able—to keep a burning grudge or resentment against you for the next month, if you told him today? And if you waited, is he likely to get upset that you waited a month to tell him?"

"At least if he got upset here, we would be able to speak face-to-face."

"There is that, too. And, really, you don't have to tell him today, right this minute. Only kids operate on such immediate terms. Old people like us, well, we can wait a day or two. Think about it, sleep on it, figure out what you even want to say. He won't know or care if you told him today or tomorrow."

Walter nodded. "I suppose you're right."

She grinned. "You learn quick."

"Thanks, Stacy." He started walking away.

"Anytime. But, hey." He turned back. "Do I at least get to know her name?"

He sighed dramatically. "Laura."

"All right. Well, let me know how it goes if you do decide to tell him."

He did not reply to that as he went in the house. At the very least, the perspective helped to calm his nerves. He poured himself a glass of root beer. She was right; Tommen wouldn't know if it was today or tomorrow that they'd made it "official." He had time to consider his words, what he wanted to say and how he wanted to say it.

At the same time, it still didn't solve his Timekeeper dilemma. If Tommen had any advantage in this, any reason to stay calm, it was because he knew it wasn't likely to last. On the one hand, he didn't consider them anywhere near really serious, so he figured he wouldn't have to give up his Banding just yet. But, considering the time it took for the effects to wear off, even if he stopped now, it wouldn't make much of a difference, not for quite a few decades, maybe even a century. Was there any way to get around this problem, or was this relationship failed from its very inception?

Chapter Nine
First Day

The alarm going off may as well have been an air raid siren telling everyone that bombers were coming and everyone should take shelter immediately. Tommen startled awake, then settled down once Saul found the off button. It was way too early for this shit. He looked at his own phone. Seven o'clock. Well, not horrible, he supposed. An hour to get ready, an hour for breakfast, the day starting at nine o'clock sharp. Still, when bedtime came at midnight—at the earliest—and it took probably another half hour to get the kids to sleep, plus another half hour for him to get to sleep, six hours of sleep was not a lot of time. Ten weeks of this shit. Fuck. What the fuck had he agreed to? Why had he agreed to it? Why was there no way to Band while he was asleep, or somehow set up a Band to give him a full night's rest and then dissipate? There had to be some trick like that.

"Wake up, sleepyhead," Saul said, shaking him.

"I am awake," Tommen grumbled, grudgingly fighting his way to a sitting position and swinging his legs over the edge of the bed. He looked at his stuff; well, his hearing aids were still there, and the base said they were charged. Although, after the events of last night, he wasn't so sure he could trust it. Nevertheless, he grabbed his things and headed for the bathroom with the rest of the boys, all as sleepy as him. Only Saul seemed any kind of awake and alert.

Probably the only relief came from the fact that Randall cleaned up nice when he could be bothered to clean up at all; the cabin didn't smell like trash and dirt and the shit of the six dogs he apparently had at home. Now if they could just keep it up for the next four or five weeks, they would be golden.

The bathrooms were already swarming with girls as they lined up for their showers, but the boys' bathroom was quiet and empty. Thankfully, with all the boys so sleepy still, it made the morning routine go much smoother. Tommen was able to wash his face and brush his teeth without drowning or getting the toothbrush shoved down his throat. Then he and Saul herded their group back to the cabin so they could grab clothes and go over the itinerary for the day.

"So, today is kind of a stay-at-camp day," Saul said, bringing out the schedule. "This morning, we have open free time between breakfast and lunch. Games in the yard, arts and crafts in the main hall. No campers are to be in their cabins without a counselor. After lunch, there will be a basketball tournament, soccer tournament, and hide-and-seek in the camp and surrounding area. Then we'll have dinner and about another hour of free time, then a campfire. Any questions?"

"What if we fucking don't wanna do that fucking shit?" Randall asked.

"Then you can sit in here with a bar of soap in your mouth, while I watch you," Tommen threatened.

Saul raised a brow at him, but answered, "Well, it's open free time. What do you want to do?"

"I wanna go rock climbing."

"Well, I don't know about rock climbing, but we can certainly go on a hike if you want, around the camp."

"I don't want to go hiking," Peter said. "I want to be in the soccer tournament." Louis and Jimmy agreed.

"Fortunately for you, we have two counselors. So, I can lead the hike if Tommen can stay here and keep an eye on the rest of you."

Saul looked at Tommen who nodded. "Sure. Who's up for soccer?"

At least if Randall and Carson went on a hike, it might make life easier for Tommen back at camp. With any luck, Saul would take them and hike them right over the edge of a cliff. Then they might get some peace and quiet around here.

Once everyone was dressed and ready, they headed to the main hall for breakfast. They were one of the first to arrive, so it made finding a seat easy, but waiting for breakfast hard. Coffee, orange juice, and other drinks were already set out, so they made do with that while the other cabins meandered their way in. Not surprisingly, the girls' cabins were the last to arrive.

"Why the fuck do they take so fucking long?" Randall sneered. "Are they, like, using vibrators and masturbating and shit?"

Saul was a bit like Micaiah, difficult to read and fearsome when angry, mostly because theirs was a quiet anger. Saul had never given any indication that he was exasperated with having to put up with Randall and his constant swearing and inappropriate jokes, but when Randall spoke those words, he simply stood and used one finger to motion him to follow. Randall kept grinning cheekily, but all color had drained from his skin. He was trying to act the tough guy in front of his friends, but he was afraid of what Saul was going to say or do to him. Truthfully, while Tommen was curious, he was afraid of what Saul would say or do to him.

Breakfast proved to be pancakes. Everyone was supposedly limited to three, though Saul, when he returned with Randall in tow, informed Tommen that counselors could go back for seconds. Not that it mattered since there was an endless buffet of cereal and fruit along one wall for him to graze from as well.

"Why do boys eat so much?" one girl asked as Tommen poured milk over his cereal which sat between his pancakes and eggs and a banana.

"I don't know. Maybe because we're bigger," Tommen offered.

"Do you eat a lot because you're bigger or are you bigger because you eat a lot?" She lowered her voice. "Seriously, Jessica, in our cabin, is huge. She eats so much. I was just wondering if it's her fault."

Tommen raised a brow, trying to hide his repulsion. This girl was all of, what, ten? Why the hell was she concerned about this at all? Finally he knelt and said, "You know, I don't know. But I do know that everyone has their own version of healthy. Maybe she has problems, or maybe she just looks a little different than all the ideal models you see all the time on TV."

The girl stared at him for a minute, then returned to her table, her tray consisting of one pancake and an apple. Looking around at her cabin group, he guessed he could pick out Jessica. She wasn't the teeny tiny little girl like the rest of them, but she didn't look fat and unhealthy.

He shook his head, took his tray, and returned to his seat. How had he even gotten mixed up in that conversation? Why did he feel the need to defend the girl, Jessica? Was it because her cabin mate was so rude? Probably. Just him being the Chivalrous Welshman, most likely. Maybe because defending Jessica made it feel like he was defending Becky. Becky wasn't an hourglass model, but she wasn't a slob. She just had a few health problems that she had to pay close attention to. That was all. Nothing sinister, no secret midnight ice cream binges or anything like that. It was her version of healthy.

Mr. Wilson appeared about halfway through breakfast to snag a few leftovers and scarf them down before addressing the group at large. It was basically a reiteration of what Saul had said earlier that morning. Today was a stay-at-camp day. Morning would be open free time for the kids to do whatever they wanted. Games, arts and crafts, and so on. For anyone interested, there would be beading instruction starting once breakfast was over, and a soap making class after that.

"Doesn't soap involve lye?" Tommen hissed to Saul.

He shrugged. "You can buy lye-free soap kits at craft stores. Half the work is already done, so the rest is easy-peasy and kid-friendly. I think in the older kids' camp, they do actual soap making with actual lye, but I don't know for sure on that."

Had Tommen not been stuck in the prison cabin, he might have been interested. As it was, he almost wondered if it wouldn't have been smarter to sign up as a camper rather than a counselor.

Could he do that? Could he resign as a counselor, go back and sign up for the older kids' camp? Was there an age limit? Would they reject him?

As expected, none of the boys were interested in beading or soap making, so they headed out to play some yard games. A couple went to start a game of pick-up basketball in preparation for the tournament that afternoon. A few did the same with soccer. Tommen ended up playing life-size chess with Jimmy.

"So, how did you get in our cabin?" Tommen wondered innocently.

Jimmy shrugged. "That's where they put me."

"You do understand kind of what our cabin is, who's in it?"

"The losers, the rejects, kids with a record and no parents, who aren't accepted anywhere else. The only reason they're allowed here is because Saul has the balls to deal with them. You I'm not sure about yet."

Well, at least the kid is honest. "So why are you here? I mean, you haven't done anything wrong so far; you don't talk dirty, or, really, at all; you just keep your head down and go with the flow. You should be in another cabin."

"My mom told them to put me in with the others. I'm bad."

"Why? What did you do?"

"I don't know."

The whole conversation, Jimmy hadn't even looked him in the eye. He'd moved his pieces and effectively checkmated Tommen, but nothing about the kid tipped him off as being troubled. If there was any problem with this kid, it came from home, most likely his mother.

Tommen was ready to say more as they reset their pieces when Saul approached, Tanner in tow.

"Keep an eye on the others," he said. "Tanner's mom is here."

Tommen just nodded and watched them head toward the main office. So there went the kid, one of them, who decided to destroy his hearing aid base because he had no concept of personal space, boundaries, respect for privacy, or anything at all beyond what he wanted or needed. He'd be in jail or have some run-in with the law before he hit high school, Tommen was sure.

Saul had not returned by the time he and Jimmy finished up their next quick game, so they were forced to move on to the basketball and soccer fields, alternating in order to keep an eye on the other boys. In both games, there were inevitably fouls and illegalities, which inevitably led to accusations, denial, frustration, and a little pushing and shoving. While the boys from Tommen's cabin were the cause of most of the problems, they were by no means the only ones who got in trouble.

"Oh, good, they didn't burn the camp down while I was away," Saul said when he returned.

"I don't know how I feel about such a distinct lack of faith in me," Tommen commented, not looking at him.

"I wasn't sure, seeing how you kept on with your chess game before coming to check on them."

"It was a good game."

"Jimmy kicked your butt."

"Yeah, I know he did. Why is he in our cabin anyway?"

Saul wore an expression that was difficult to interpret. "Last year was his first year, and his mom told everyone to keep an eye on him because he was a bad boy and needed to be watched. Naturally, he got placed in our cabin."

"Is he a bad kid?"

"No. Any trouble he causes is because he's too submissive for his own good."

Tommen shifted his stance. "My dad's a cop, and he used to work Missing Persons, especially for children. I mean, maybe it's just me, but it sounds like—"

"Abuse?" Saul nodded. "Oh, undoubtedly. I expect you saw the bruising on his ribs last night." Actually, Tommen hadn't, but he remained silent. "Protective Services were the ones to pick him up last year. I don't know what's going on at home, but it can't be anything good. But the most any of us can do is either take the law into our own hands, which never ends well, or tell those who have the power to make a difference."

Immediately, Tommen's mind went to Ryan, his foster brother from Hell. No good had come from having him in the house, and one was forced to wonder just how effective foster care had been for him. If he hadn't been bounced around from home to home, would he have still been so evil? Sometimes Tommen wondered whatever happened to him, then decided the most likely outcome was either prison or death by cop, if not himself.

"So. Day one." Saul looked at him. "You really think you can do this for four more weeks?"

"No," Tommen said. He met Saul's gaze. "But I've been put through a lot of sh...tuff where I couldn't back down no matter how much I wanted to. I'm not going to let myself get bullied by eight year old kids."

"Excellent. Then you will have no trouble going to all my meetings for me."

"Meetings?"

"Yes. The counselors go to meetings while the kids are distracted. Go to them for me. There's one right now in the main office. Now then, off you go."

Saul made a little shooing motion while Tommen obliged, if for unknown reasons. He headed to the main office and cautiously opened the door. The main reception desk was empty, but another door was open and he could hear Mr. Wilson and a couple other counselors. As he entered the room, they looked up.

"And the Wolf Cabin is here," Mr. Wilson said.

"Even if the wolf himself is nowhere to be seen," one of the female counselors, Julie, snickered.

"Well, that's to be expected. Come, Tommen, sit down. Don't worry; we don't bite too hard."

"Certainly no more than Saul," Rick told him.

There were pleasantries and a little small talk before finally getting down to business. In a way, it made Tommen feel important, that he was actually getting to sit in on this instead of being told to wait outside like a good little boy while the grown ups had their talk.

"All right, so, we've already had one camper sent home," Mr. Wilson sighed. "Otherwise, how is everyone holding up?"

While the others murmured positive assent, Tommen remained silent, though he got called out on it.

"Something you want to add?"

"No. I mean, I'm new, I'm just trying to figure out how this all works."

It was plausible, but he could see the sympathy from the rest of the group. None of them had wanted his job, which was why they'd had to go out and hire someone. Any of the other cabins could be managed by one counselor, but no one had wanted to switch and be the second man in the Wolf Cabin.

"This week is kind of our rest week, as most of you know," Mr. Wilson said, moving on from pleasantries to real business. "Our focus this week is the basketball tournament, the soccer tournament, things to do around camp." He started passing out papers. "Here is our schedule of events for this week, subject to change with weather.

"Next week is our outdoor activity adventure, which includes the ziplining, the horseback riding, all that sort of stuff. It will also include some short indoor activity classes on the rocks, plants, and animals in the area. Here is a tentative schedule for those events. If we have to, we can move around the large events with the open free time and such. We'll get it figured out.

"After that is our water adventure week, so that's going to be the kayaking, canoeing, swimming, and so forth. I know we don't have a lot of water up here, so our bus trips are going to be a little longer than the others to the stables and such.

"Finally, our finale is the three-day hiking trip. We're going to take a bus to a nearby trailhead and hike to our campground. We're going to show the kids how to pitch tents, start fires, fish in the streams, prepare the fish, gather herbs and berries, all sorts of things. And these are the schedules for those weeks. Any questions as of this moment?"

Rick raised his hand. "So when do we get to learn how to pitch tents and catch fish?"

Chuckles around the room.

Tommen raised his hand. "Will there be any electricity at all while we're hiking? At the campsite and whatnot?"

"There will not be electricity at the campsite itself, but we have ways of charging phones. I assume you are referencing your hearing aids."

"Yes." *Assuming the charger lasts that long anyway.*

"Don't worry about it; there will be electricity you can tap into."

Tommen didn't want to be reassured; he wanted to know, dammit. But he accepted the answer and plodded along through the rest of the meeting, which didn't actually last very long. He found himself wondering whether Saul skipped the meeting because the boys really needed that much supervision, or if he used the boys as an excuse to skip a mundane meeting.

Didn't matter, he supposed. The meeting was over soon enough, and he met up with Saul at the soccer game where most of the boys had migrated to.

"So, did they manage to keep it under ten pages?" he asked sarcastically.

"Nine," Tommen answered, meeting his sarcasm. "Your absence was noted."

"I'm sure it was. And I'm sure they wept over it."

"Hardly."

Saul grinned and folded his arms. "Honestly, I don't think they like me."

Tommen raised a brow and shifted his stance. "Gee, what would give you that impression? I mean, what's not to like about being constantly insulted or mocked with crude and sarcastic humor?"

"I don't know, but you're not too bad at it yourself when you want to be."

Was this an example of reverse psychology? Tommen was pretty sure it was. He didn't like it. He didn't know how to respond to it. Damn it. Now he'd waited too long and any snappy comeback would look like some Johnny-come-lately weak ass comeback. Saul grinned as he realized his victory. "Don't worry. A couple years with me and you'll be half as good as I am."

"Only half?"

"Well I can't teach you all my tricks."

"And what makes you think I'm going to come back in the future? What happens if Joe decides he wants his job back next year?"

Saul shrugged. "Then Joe gets his job back. What happens if he doesn't want it? You think a revolving door of counselors is going to help these boys at all? Some of them have already experienced that enough with their families. And after all, this camp is supposed to be a respite from family life." He said it with half a sneer.

"If anyone thinks a month-long camp is actually going to impact these kids that much in their lives..."

"The sad thing is, it will. Did you never go to summer camp?"

"Well, my dad sent me to VBS a few times, but that's about it."

"I won't ask your religious beliefs, but how did the camp itself impact you?"

"It didn't, really. I was usually left out because I couldn't speak English well at the time. I was 'that kid' because I had special dietary needs—"

"So you hate camp. Maybe not with a wrathful vengeance, but you hate camp. It's boring and exclusive. Now, between your dad being a cop, doing good for all mankind, and you wanting to be your own man, you're hoping that life on the other side of the bunk will be better, that maybe this time around you'll have some measure of control and you'll be able to have fun and maybe, as a little bonus, you can inspire a few young minds yourself. And, somewhere deep down, you're wondering just how much you can get away with yourself, see if you can't be a camper yourself so you can do all the things you wanted to do at other camps but couldn't for one reason or another, while still exercising control over the other boys. Do I have that about right?"

His silence was probably enough of an answer. Was it really that obvious? Was he really so easy to read? How did he obtain psychological superpowers like that?

Thankfully, the morning seemed to go pretty smoothly with no more fighting, and soon enough, they were heading to lunch. Just as breakfast had an open cold bar for cereal and fruit, lunch appeared to boast an open salad bar, though the salads were pre-made, probably so lettuce and cheese didn't get flung everywhere by the kids.

Lunch itself was a pretty light fare, more of a snack bar. Cheese and crackers, fruit and vegetables, and various sandwiches. Tommen got some of everything, including a bowl of soup which Pam informed him was only for the counselors. She laughed when she said it, citing the fact that he was clearly a starving teenage boy and to come back if he wanted a second or third bowl.

"So, when they get to the culinary classes, am I going to lose you?" Saul asked when Tommen did in fact go back for a third bowl of soup and a second salad.

"Probably not. I like eating more than I like cooking, and I'd say I'm pretty good at cooking anyway."

"Oh, so you're going to teach the class."

"What? No way, man. I can't teach."

"Too bad."

Before either of them could say more, they were distracted by a ruckus near the open salad bar. One of the boys from their cabin, Peter, had picked a fight with a boy from a different cabin. Apparently the other boy had committed the ultimate sin of taking the last salad which Peter wanted. However the fight had started, it had quickly devolved into intimidation—which didn't work well seeing how Peter was the smaller of the boys—and everything that Tommen knew about fighting—which was quite a bit—said that fists were going to start flying pretty soon.

The other boy was not about to give up his salad and just wanted to walk away back to his table, but Peter kept blocking him and challenging him. The more Tommen watched, the more he realized that it was about how he and Tyler must have looked when they got into fights.

Saul stood and approached, but only the other boy saw it. He shrank back, which Peter apparently took as submission. He was just getting ready to throw himself into the other boy, beat him up, and take his salad, when Saul scooped him up and put him firmly behind himself.

"Enough!" he barked. "What's the problem here?"

"He took the last salad!" Peter whined. "I wanted it!"

"Then you should have been faster." Saul looked at the other boy. "Go back to your table."

The boy took the out and hurried back to his table. His counselor stopped him momentarily and whispered something in his ear before letting him sit down.

Saul looked at Peter, now an amusing conflict of wanting to fume and wanting to whine and cry and throw a temper tantrum. Whatever Saul said, Tommen was too far away to hear. Among the rest of the boys, Randall and Carson especially, there were whispers and snickers. After a few minutes, Saul and Peter returned, Saul as stoic as ever, Peter like a whipped puppy.

"Everything okay?" Tommen dared ask.

"I expect so," Saul answered.

"Dude, are you in trouble?" Randall asked bluntly, grinning.

Peter shrugged but gave him a look which Tommen sometimes got from Becky. It was one that said something like, "Duh, loser. The fuck do you think, he promised me ice cream and cake for dessert?" The look was fearsome coming from Becky, but on these eight year old boys, it was hilarious.

"So, what are we doing after lunch?" Louis asked eagerly.

"Round one of the basketball and soccer tournaments. You

each pick the one you want to participate in, but it can only be one and you either stick with that through the whole tournament or forfeit the whole thing," Saul explained. "If you don't want to do either one, then it's open free time. I think there's a hide-and-seek mini-tournament going on, too."

Tommen was afraid what would happen if one of them didn't want to do basketball or soccer, and he loathed what could happen if any of them opted for the hide-and-seek. The trouble they could get into while "hiding" was beyond what he felt like trying to comprehend.

Thankfully, all of them picked either one tournament or the other.

"So, how do we know who wins the tournament if the cabins are mixed on the teams?" Tommen asked.

"It's only like that until the quarterfinals. I don't know, Jerry has some kind of funky point system he uses to determine who goes where and what rank they are. I'm not too concerned about it as long as these guys are playing fair and don't turn soccer into tackle football."

"Who, us?" Carson asked innocently.

"We would never do such a thing," Randall said.

"Yeah, and pigs might fly," Saul told them.

Soon enough, Mr. Wilson went to the front of the room and basically reiterated everything Saul had just said, though giving a little more insight as to the "funky point system" he used to determine cabin ranks even as the teams were mixed groups to begin with. Tommen tried to pay attention and take notes, but if there was any real order to the system, it was lost on him. Maybe there was a system, or maybe Mr. Wilson just ranked the cabins according to goals, good sportsmanship, and whoever did the most sweet talking to him on the sidelines.

But, as Saul said, it wasn't their business to know. Their job was to make sure their boys played fair, didn't cheat, and didn't turn either of the games into tackle football or boxing. Tommen would intervene if he had to, but he was honestly afraid that if he had to, the adrenaline would kick in and his instincts would take over and he might start whaling on these kids like he was fighting Tyler Freeman. He only had to scare the kids and shape them up a little, not send them to the hospital and go to jail himself for child abuse.

After lunch, they made their way to the fields. Saul elected to take the basketball boys — probably because Randall and Carson were in that group — and Tommen took the soccer kids. He watched them kick a ball around for a little bit until Mr. Wilson finally emerged to make the teams and figure out who was playing whom.

Tommen and the other counselors were given whistles to use when they spotted a foul or other illegality, as well as to keep for all other activities during camp. He watched as the kids were taken out onto the field and given a quick rundown of how a proper soccer match worked, the different positions and a few basic techniques. Even just watching from the sidelines, Tommen could tell that, with exception of the goalie, all of the instruction would be for naught. The kids were going to rush the ball like a pack of hyenas, running, kicking, crashing, pushing, and shoving. There would be no order here, no positions or captains or anything at all, just the kids, the ball, and the goals they scored.

Or didn't score. Tommen had to admit that for as evil and disobedient as his kids seemed to be, they appeared to have some talent when it came to soccer, and they appeared to be the ones carrying the team. They knew how to dribble and pass, and even the uneven playing field didn't seem to deter them as they raced back and forth. Actually, without the Wolf Cabin boys, the whole game would have been a wash, an easy victory for the other team. As it was, the two teams stayed tied or close to tied for the duration of the game.

But, of course, it was too much to hope that the game would go smoothly the whole time. In the last sixty seconds, the Wolf Cabin team had the lead, but the other team — the Bear Cabin boys comprising most of it — had the ball. As expected, the boys didn't give much of a damn about proper field positions other than the goalie, and the entire herd was centered around the little black and white ball as it moved down the field.

If the Wolf Cabin team had any weakness, it was their goalie who came from the Coon Cabin. He was big, but had slow reflexes. More often than not, any goals that did get deflected had more to do with the other kids on the team intercepting the ball. But the kid who had the ball now was quickly outpacing the rest of the boys, with exception of Jimmy. The kid was a small fry, but he could run. Tommen saw him make several attempts at stealing the ball, but to no avail.

Twenty seconds on the clock and the Bear Cabin boy was gearing up for his kick, which would have forced the game into overtime and a tiebreaker goal. Jimmy was still keeping pace, still trying to steal the ball. At the last possible second, the Bear Cabin boy suddenly tripped, just as he was getting ready to kick the ball and score the goal. He went down and the ball bounced harmlessly past the goal.

Several whistles blew, but Tommen and the Bear Cabin counselor assistant ran onto the field. Thankfully, the Bear Cabin boy did not appear to be hurt as he got to his feet. But he didn't stop with just standing; he went straight into vengeance mode, going after Jimmy who ducked and dodged with the precision of a snake. Tommen and the other counselor got the boys separated.

"He tripped me!" the boy shouted, as it it would make his point.

"You tripped yourself!" Jimmy shouted back.

"Enough!" the Bear Cabin counselor snapped. When the boys in question and the boys in the crowd had quieted, he went on, speaking to the player who had been tripped up. "I saw no evidence of foul play. Jimmy made a legal move to try and steal the ball. You tripped yourself. If you could be bothered to tie your shoes once in a while, you might not have stepped on them."

"But—"

"No. That's it. We're done. They won. We can talk about it

later in the cabin. For now, line up, and we'll tell each other how nice it was to compete against them."

The boy huffed and folded his arms. He got in the line, but did not put his hand out to wish the other team good game. Jimmy, however, was suddenly the star of the whole team, though the poor kid looked terrified of the honor, as if he didn't know what to do with it.

They cleared the field so the girls' teams could play and went to the basketball court where fouls appeared to be much more rampant, mostly thanks to two particular Wolf Cabin boys. The boys claimed a few seats, but Tommen did not join them right away.

"You think you boys can behave for five minutes?" he asked.

They gave him the "sure, sure" spiel, and Tommen uncertainly went off to find Mr. Wilson who was mildly refereeing the basketball game.

"Hey, I saw your team win the soccer game," he said. "That was great!"

"Yeah, it is," Tommen acknowledged. "But I have a question."

"Don't worry, I know which team is advancing and how the cabins work."

"No, it's not that."

"Then what is it?"

"Why is Jimmy in our cabin? He seems to be the only one who isn't misbehaving like the others. I mean, he's a boy, but he's nowhere near as bad as Carson and Randall."

Mr. Wilson nodded. "I know. And next you're going to tell me of your suspicions of abuse at home. That much has been proven."

"So what's the holdup?"

"He won't go. He firmly believes that he belongs in Wolf Cabin."

"He's eight! Maybe. He doesn't get to call the shots. Okay, that's called Stockholm Syndrome, I'm pretty sure. He needs help, which means removing him from the current environment."

Mr. Wilson sighed. "Tommen, the woman who dropped him

off won't be the same one picking him up. Even as we speak, back home, his things are being packed up—what little he does have—and he'll be going home with foster parents who live quite a ways away. He probably won't be coming back. He has problems at home. Yes, it's not right that he's in with your boys, but he needs some familiarity right now before it all gets taken away."

"He doesn't know that he's going into foster care."

"No, he doesn't."

Tommen looked away for a second. "Well, take it from a foster kid that the longer you stay in Hell, and the more people tell you that you deserve to be there, the harder it is to leave. And even if someone does rescue you, sometimes you never really leave."

In all reality, Tommen was citing his dad's experience in the asylum more than his experience in foster care. His foster experience had been mild compared to some. Ninety percent of his time had been spent with Walter. There had been one point where they tried to move him to another "normal" family with two parents and other children, but he would have none of it, and they moved him back.

He returned to the basketball court where his boys had been the little angels they promised to be, except for the part where they had moved and stacked the chairs and were now doing a very dangerous rendition of King of the Hill. Tommen got them back to solid ground just as the basketball game ended and the players came off the court. They were sweaty and grouchy, and Randall was back to his usual, potent self. Tommen had to turn away and Band so the kids didn't see him gag.

"So, how did it go?" he asked, trying to sound pleasant.

"Well, we lost," Saul reported, completely unsurprised. "But, had it been a wrestling tournament, we would have had a victory worthy of the Olympics."

"The stupid fucking fucker fucking pushed me!" Randall protested.

It was enough to make an old lady keel over with a heart attack, the way he swore, but Tommen just found it amusing. Still,

Saul wasn't known for his idle threats, and he left Tommen in charge of the gang while he took Randall away for a good soapy scrub down.

Between the game and dinner, Tommen kept the boys amused with hide-and-seek. They came in at the end of the mini-tournament, but he wasn't sure what else to do with them; they weren't exactly the artsy-craftsy type. Eventually, Saul returned with Randall who grudgingly joined the game.

"Heard the soccer match went well," Saul said.

"Yeah. Jimmy was our star player," Tommen replied. "He'll at least keep us from being too much of an embarrassment."

"That's all we can hope for."

Tommen did a few quick stretches, feeling almost as worn out as the kids just from watching them. Then, conversationally, he asked, "So, where are you from?"

Saul gave him a sideways glance. "I live on the reservation not far from here."

"Oh, so Wolf isn't just a coy word play?"

"No. My family was one of the ones who helped build this camp. I remember running around as a child, gathering this or that for the adults as they built the Wolf Cabin."

"I thought this camp has been around for forty years? You don't seem that old."

Saul gave him a look he wasn't sure how to interpret, but he answered, "And you thought they just pulled a huge main hall and ten cabins out of their asses the first time around? This place used to be part of a Shawnee reservation, pure, untouched, virgin ground. Then the government got greedy and took it away, then tried to sell it back to the tribe under a land contract. Long story short, the tribe managed to turn the deal in their favor. The first summer the camp was open, there was one small building for the kids to crowd into in case it rained. The cabins and everything else came slowly." He smirked. "But the one thing that hasn't changed is that the tribal kids get in for free and the white kids have to pay."

"Oh."

So was that why Saul was so uptight about everything? Or was he just a naturally cranky person and such social circumstances only exacerbated the problem in his own mind? Personally, Tommen didn't see what the problem was or how it could be so bad, but that wasn't his realm of expertise. It was only a place to camp. If the tribe owned it, they had the right to do what they wanted with it, but punishing the kids for the sins of their fathers and their government hardly seemed fair, especially when most of the kids were from poor families.

Tommen startled when Saul started laughing. When he calmed down, he was more frightened by the laugh itself, like a creaky wheel that didn't get used often.

"You actually believe that?" Saul said.

"I...didn't have any reason to not believe it?" Tommen offered.

Saul shook his head. "Only stories. Stories and the lies we tell ourselves and others."

His words were eerily reminisce of a particular Time Agent whom Tommen had encountered multiple times, none of them on friendly terms. Tadashi had been Rifun's companion before going off the deep end, but his one consistent mantra was that everything was a lie, a story to tell the world, and nothing and no one could be trusted.

Tommen's first thought that was Saul was secretly Rifun using a Disguise. Was there a way to break a Disguise? Was it like breaking a Band? Or, if Disguises were purely Akari, how did he tap into that in order to use it and break the Disguise?

Cautiously, Tommen used Time instead, feeling out Saul's place in it and moving around him. He had no clue what made a Disguise work, and would probably never know what a Disguise felt like even if he did find it. Overall, Saul felt as normal as any of the kids playing in the field and the woods.

He kept his suspicions to himself as dinner came around followed by free time and then campfire time with songs and s'mores and everything else. He thought he might have even forgotten about his suspicions until it came to ghost story time.

All just stories and the lies we tell ourselves and others.

"I have a question," Tommen texted Micaiah that night.

"I have lots of questions. What's yours?" Micaiah replied.

"Is there a way to see or feel or somehow detect a Disguise?"

"Well, Disguises fall in the realm of the Akari. For anyone not trained in the Akari, they can be almost impossible to detect and even harder to break. Why, you got something?"

"I don't know; I'm not sure." He relayed the events of the day and his suspicions surrounding Saul.

"Has he said anything to you or made any threats?"

"No, just that one statement. I don't know, maybe I'm being paranoid."

"Your paranoia has saved you more than once. Listen, as long as he hasn't threatened you or done anything more than say weird things, don't say or do anything. If he is Disguised, you don't want to tip him off. I'll grab Kayla and Micah and a few others, and we'll see if we can dig up anything. And if he does try something, get yourself to safety and call one of us."

"Will do."

Tommen turned off his phone and lay back on his pillow. Why? He'd come out to this camp as much to get away from Time as anything else. Was he cursed? Was he just doomed to have this thing following him everywhere? Even more than that, why did it have to be the Akari? Ever since he'd first heard it uttered, it had been causing him nothing but trouble. He was kidnapped because of it. He was attacked by the world's ugliest cat and bear-slash-komodo-dragon because of it. His dad had been held prisoner by nutcases who worshiped it. The only good the Akari had done was help Micaiah and the others free the Wheel from those nutcases. So, really, this whole thing turned into a what—the—fuck? If the Akari was supposed to be some sort of living thing, as Micaiah had implied, was it good or evil? Because right now, the only thing he could figure was that it was a leech of some form.

Grudgingly, he picked his phone back up and texted Becky,

not sure if she would even answer for as late as it was.

"Are you still up?" he asked.

"Barely," was her reply. "Still working, but that's the magic of not having school tomorrow. What's up? How was your first full day of camp?"

Was it only the first day? It felt like he'd been through the first week at least already. He was ready to go home.

"Good," he answered. "We won the first round of the soccer tournament."

"Cool."

"Lost the first round of the basketball tournament. How's life at home?"

"Boring. If not for Mr. Snuffles, I think I wouldn't even leave my room most days."

"Well, you have to eat sometime."

"Yes, and I do. But my summer workload is always huge. It's when I make probably eighty percent of my yearly revenue."

"Don't work yourself too hard. How long has it been since you left the house?"

"How long have you been gone?"

They chatted back and forth for probably half an hour before Tommen decided he should get at least a little sleep. At this rate, he would be lucky to get five hours tonight. Still, he wished Becky well, turned off his phone, rolled over, and closed his eyes.

Chapter Ten
Pyrrhic Victory

Mornings came too soon. Sometimes, despite only getting four to six hours a night, the boys were still awake before the alarm went off. Then it was a fight for everyone to grab their clothes, get to the showers, and then take a shower in a timely manner. The biggest victory there, if it could be counted as such, was that they managed to get Randall to take a shower four out of the six days. Although, with the heat and the games they played and the campfires at night, Tommen sometimes wondered if it wouldn't have been better to make him shower two or even three times per day. At least his language had cleaned up some, though Saul refused to say what he'd done to get Randall to stop cussing every other word.

Mealtime was probably Tommen's favorite part of the day. He'd never been much of a coffee person; sometimes he'd swipe a cup from the bakery before having to dump an old pot and brew a new batch, but otherwise it wasn't his thing. With camp the way it was, he'd learned to bite his tongue and swallow the bitter taste. He tried everything he could think of to make it more palatable, but there was no disguising the awful flavor. Still, it helped him get ready for the day. He'd even gone to the camp store and bought himself a camp thermos.

As for the food, well, Pam was certainly more than they deserved. She could take anything at hand—even if the ingredients were as far from each other as no chef would dare to combine—and turn it into a gourmet meal. Tommen later learned that she had been professional chef once with her own restaurant that was acclaimed far and wide, even internationally; unfortunately, her business partner ended up stabbing her in the back and took everything for herself. Pam was ousted, and the restaurant ultimately failed a couple years later. How or why she ended up being a cook at a children's camp instead of opening up another fabulous restaurant was beyond him.

At any rate, the food was wonderful. Even better that counselors usually had a secondary option for food at mealtime—in order to sustain the starving teenage boys, as Pam liked to joke, referring to him—and they often had snack options throughout the day, too, when they could get a few minutes to themselves to grab a snack. The snacks themselves were more like tiny meals; Pam did not do small or simple.

The food was probably what made the rest of the day more bearable. Tommen had learned how to handle the boys and navigate their treacherous ways, from Randall's language, to Peter's ability to hide in places a mouse couldn't fit, to Carson's ability to speak and have anyone within earshot listen to and follow him. The way Tommen figured it, Carson was the reason the Lord's Prayer ended with "lead us not into temptation." Wherever Carson was, there were sure to be others. They would all be in trouble, but all of the followers would be dumbfounded by it because their fearless leader had made it sound so wonderful they couldn't even think about being in trouble.

But in dealing with their antics, Saul had eased up a little on him, no longer breathing down his neck about every little thing. Tommen figured that maybe, since he, a newbie, was more comfortable and able to handle these boys, that maybe it wasn't so bad after all. Maybe the years of running the prison cabin with Joe had only exaggerated the problem in his mind, making mountains out of mole hills. Maybe getting a new person in the cabin, a pair of fresh eyes, was exactly what the doctor ordered.

Of course, Tommen also hadn't forgotten Saul's cryptic words from the other day, and now he was watching Saul like a hawk, taking note of his every word, his every move, looking for any sign of a Disguise—namely, that Rifun wasn't quite as "fled" as reported by Micaiah and others. But, as Kayla had pointed out, other than a

Disguise being almost impossible for him to detect because he wasn't trained in the Akari, Disguises were only ten percent appearance and ninety percent mannerisms; that was how Cassius had fooled them for so long as he ran around Disguised as Doug. Doug was someone they inherently trusted and knew well, so they didn't think to look for a Disguise in the first place, and Cassius played him so well that the question never came up. Although, reportedly, they were starting to rethink some of their security measures.

Micaiah hadn't gotten back to him yet with any information on Saul, and Tommen tried to tell himself that no news was good news. Maybe Saul was exactly who he said he was and the whole thing was a coincidence, his statement as more of a byproduct from being in the Marines and not because of Time. Yeah, because there were any harmless coincidences in his life. Fucking hell. But, when asked, Micaiah only said that he was looking into it and to focus more on the present. If Saul was Rifun in Disguise, best not to let on that he was suspicious. This time, Tommen had more to think about than himself; he was charged with a bunch of kids. They, and everyone at camp, would be defenseless if Rifun tried something. Think of it as hostage negotiation and put the safety of the hostages first.

Camp was just wonderful, wasn't it?

Becky still expressed her jealousy, though she claimed she was saving the majority of her jealousy for the weeks when they started doing the stuff that she wanted to do, such as the ziplining, horseback riding, and so on. Basketball and soccer, yeah, cool, whatever, but they could keep that to themselves for the most part.

"Hey, so I left my room today," she texted late Friday night, or maybe it was Saturday morning. It was hard to tell anymore.

"Holy cow," Tomment replied.

"More than that, I left the house."

"Hey now, girl, you're going too fast."

"Now, I mean, maybe it's nothing, but has your dad ever said anything to you about seeing someone?"

Tommen paused for a minute. Actually, he'd pretty much

forgotten about the whole thing. Finally he answered, "Well, I kind of worked it out for myself, and he admitted to it. He said they were just having coffee and it was nothing serious."

"Oh. Okay."

"Why?"

"Well, when I went out, I went by your house and there was a vehicle I didn't recognize. Then your dad walked out with a woman and they were talking and laughing and carrying on. Then they got in their vehicles and went somewhere for I don't know how long."

"Oh."

So she had been over to their house? His dad never said anything, and that was a pretty big jump from just having coffee to having her over for dinner, plus whatever they'd done afterwards. Had it all been a ploy? Had they been waiting for him to leave so they could do stuff without him around?

Tommen shook his head. His dad was a grown man and didn't need Tommen's permission to go places and do stuff with people. But at the same time, maybe a consultation...or even just a heads-up would have been nice. A "hey, Laura's coming over for dinner tonight, then we're going to see movie" or something. He looked down as his phone jingled again.

"Sorry," Becky said. "Maybe I shouldn't have said anything."

"No, it's okay," Tommen told her. "He's a big boy and he can make his own decisions, go where he wants, do what he wants, with whoever he wants. He doesn't need my permission."

"And you're just a perfectly reasonable hormonal teenage boy who's never known anything but just him and his dad."

He rolled his eyes even though she couldn't see. She was right, damn her, but he wasn't going to admit to it.

"Well, I have to sleep at some point tonight, and so do you," she said. "Good night."

He sighed. "Yeah. Love you. Good night."

He turned his phone off, but the realization hit him a second later. Love you? Had he really just said that? As in I—love—you?

Where had that come from? Was it just emotion and sentiment stemming from his thoughts about his dad seeing someone, or did he actually love Becky? What did that look like, anyway? What did love look like in a relationship? He'd seen other people talk about it, or the lack thereof, especially when his classmates referenced their parents or other relatives. He'd heard it said a thousand times in the halls between couples who would inevitably break up the next week. But, as Becky said, it was just him and his dad. He didn't know what love looked like.

At the same time, he knew that was a lie. He knew what love was; he just had to go back more than a few years to find it. It came in the dead of winter when they were all trapped inside the cabin in a snowstorm with only a few candles and some busywork to keep them occupied. It came in the heat of summer when they had only each other's strength to rely on as they built and repaired everything on the farm, knowing there was no Home Depot or Tractor Supply to run to in order to grab whatever they needed. It came in the coolness of fall as all the neighbors far and wide banded together to bring in the harvest. It came in the wetness of spring as baby animals were born and it was as much a fight to keep them alive and growing healthy as the human children. Love came in the songs his ma used to sing and the Bible his pa used to read. It came in the times when Tommen, frightened by a storm or noises outside, would go running to his parents' bed, snuggling down between them, safe and sound.

Even now, love came in the times when his dad came to his side after another fight with Tyler Freeman. It came when his dad gave him the keys to the car, effectively saying, "I trust you." It came when his dad faced down a horde of mercenaries and cult zealots, taking three bullets to rescue him. It came when he crossed the universe and started a civil war just to save his dad.

And love came when he defended the honor of a girl who had no fault of her own for being different, when he willingly got down on one knee to hug her and damn what other people thought of it.

So, did he love Becky?

Honestly, he couldn't say for sure. But he thought he might.

As usual, morning came too soon and the morning routine was too slow. Breakfast was too loud and too pushy, and the food itself was too good. Worse, the day wasn't going to get any better because today was the finals of the basketball and soccer tournaments.

Wolf Cabin had long ago forfeited any hope of taking home the basketball champion title. Between the cheating, the yelling, the fighting, and the arguing, they'd been kicked out in the second match, and Carson and Randall were banned from the soccer match as well. That left just Jimmy, Louis, Peter, and Eric to carry the team through the soccer tournament, which they had with ease, advancing to the finals. They had to borrow a couple boys from the Beaver Cabin to make a full team, so even if they won, they would be sharing the victory, but according to Saul, it was more than they'd ever been able to boast about.

Morning activities, for the competing finalists anyway, were centered around practice and honing skills. For professional athletes, this probably would have meant fine-tuning down to the millimeter or the millisecond. For a bunch of little kids, this meant being able to properly dribble the ball without tripping over it, among other basic necessities of soccer.

"So, are you ready for this shit to be over?" Saul asked, moving to stand beside him.

"Well, it hasn't been as bad as I thought it would be, so I'm not desperate for it to end," Tommen answered. "At the same time, it'll be kind of nice to move on to something else."

"You like outdoor activities and stuff?"

"Ziplining, heck yeah, man. I could do that all day."

"So you're not afraid of heights. That's good."

Actually, Tommen was deathly afraid of heights, but the thought of being suspended from a cable over hill and dale was exhilarating. "Yeah."

"You good around horses? You seemed to know what you

were doing during the counselors' week."

"It's been a few years since I've ridden, but yeah. You?"

"Oh please, I've worked with dogs the size of small horses."

"Great Danes, or what do you mean?"

Before Saul could answer, Mr. Wilson called for everyone's attention. All kids were shooed off the fields as the grand championship matches in soccer and basketball were announced, including the teams, the players, a reminder of the rules, and a whole bunch of other things which Tommen thought were both boring and unnecessary. If the kids didn't understand the rules by now—such as no touching the ball with their hands for soccer—then they probably had very little hope of victory.

Eventually, the kids were set where they needed to be. The first matches had been half an hour long, adding time for time outs and fouls and other assorted things that came up in a game. The actual tournament matches—quarter-finals, semi-finals, and so on—had been forty-five minutes. The grand championship would be an hour long, plus all the extra stuff.

"I don't see why we can't play," Randall said, pouting. "Then we wouldn't have to share with those losers."

"You're right," Saul told him. "But your conduct in basketball told us that if you can't play by the rules, then you don't get to play. Simple as that."

"Well that's dumb," Carson said. "Just because we bend the rules a little and don't always follow them word for word shouldn't get us kicked out like that."

"That's the way things are, and those are the rules we're playing by here. Stop complaining."

The boys assented but made it clear that they weren't happy about it. Well, they didn't have to be happy; they just had to be quiet and sit still long enough for them to win the championship. Regardless of the circumstances, how they got there or who they had to share with, it would be a rare victory for the Wolf Cabin, one that Tommen was sure they would celebrate.

It proved to be a tough match, Wolf-Beaver Cabin versus the Crow Cabin. According to Saul, Crow Cabin were the soccer champions for the last four years, and they didn't seem like they were ready to give up that title now, especially not to Wolf Cabin.

By the end of the first quarter, the teams were tied at two. It wasn't that either team had a particularly spectacular offense or defense; rather, just the opposite. Offense was as likely to hit a spectator as the goal, and defense ran into the oncoming team as often as they actually stole the ball.

There was only one injury, at least in the first half. A boy from Crow Cabin twisted his ankle. Whether this was the case or if he just wanted out of the game because he hated soccer—as the counselor suggested could be the case—was difficult to determine on the field. Still, the boy was helped off the field to the nurse's office.

The remainder of the game was played straight through. Unless there was another catastrophe like an injury or an earthquake, or a fairly called timeout, there would be no stopping the clock. By the end of third quarter, Wolf-Beaver Cabin was ahead, six to five. After a brief timeout where the boys were given a rousing pep talk, they went back out for the final quarter.

"Winning team gets a special cake for dessert tonight," Saul said as the ball was dropped into play. "Losing team has to serve it to them."

"Ouch," Tommen commented.

"Humility is a wonderful thing to learn."

"Humility, yeah, but that just sounds like torture. Talk about rubbing salt in the wound."

"More like frosting, but I get your point."

Saul's sense of humor could be difficult to judge sometimes, even more since Tommen was analyzing every word that came out of his mouth, looking for some evidence that he was not who he said he was. But, as Micaiah had pointed out, the Disguise was in the nuance. Someone close to Saul might be able to tell he was acting weird, but not someone who'd never met him. Problem one, however, none of the other counselors had said anything about him acting weird, and problem two, no one seemed to be able to get that close to him to find out what normal even was.

So it was a standoff. Tommen still watched and observed, but he tried to do it discreetly. It was difficult to do when there was little else to do, but it became a little easier when there was more activity going on around them, such as a first-time victory in a soccer match.

True, it was one of the Beaver Cabin boys who actually scored the winning goal, but the Wolf-Beaver Cabin team took home the victory. As expected, everyone celebrated, even Randall and Carson who'd had no part in it at all.

They spent a good amount of time cheering and yelling and screaming and carrying on before finally settling down long enough to tell a very sad, very cranky, very reluctant Crow Cabin good game. Then they resumed cheering and running around the camp like a pack of wild banshees. The counselors let them go for a few minutes, hoping to use up some of the boys' energy, which they did. Eventually, they all came plodding back, exhausted but still ecstatic.

Saul checked his watch. "Well, guys, we've got about twenty minutes until dinner. Why don't we all get washed up with a fresh change of clothes, and then head to the hall?"

Tommen ended up leading the way while Saul spoke with the other counselors for a minute or two. It didn't take long for the stench of prepubescent teeny-boppers to stink up the whole cabin, and Tommen opened a few windows while the boys dug out shirts and shorts that weren't sweaty and dirty and nasty. God help him when the older kids got to camp, where they'd break out in sweat just at the sight of a girl, never mind playing sports or doing anything else. Hopefully by then they would have learned about the magic of deodorant at least.

Tommen would never claim to know the boys half as well as Saul seemed to, but if he was any judge of children as a whole, he figured they would be in for a pretty quiet night, maybe an early retirement from the campfire later. They'd run and played their butts off that day, and already they looked like they were dragging. Once they got some food in them, they'd perk up a little initially, but then they'd be dead out. Saul had mentioned once that the weeks were designed like that so that Sunday and sometimes Monday could be sleep-in days, which was perfectly fine with him.

They made their way to the main hall, one of the first groups to arrive. The basketball tournament was just wrapping up, which meant the groups would be going back to their cabins to get a fresh change of clothes and relax for a minute, which meant it would be a few minutes before dinner was actually served. Tommen stretched for a minute or two before sitting down, acutely aware that falling asleep in his food was a very real possibility at that point. And he hadn't even been one of the players. Just watching them had been exhausting enough.

"I think we're all going to sleep pretty good tonight," Saul observed, sitting down. He seemed to be the only one in the group who wasn't completely pooped.

"Speak for yourself," Randall said. "I could stay up all night." Even as he spoke, he yawned hugely.

"Right. You're going to be out first, I'll bet."

"How are you not tired?" Tommen wondered.

Saul shrugged. "I didn't play. I watched. Why are you tired? A little too exciting for you?"

"Apparently."

"Don't worry." Saul slapped him on the back. "Only six more hours until bed."

That was the last thing Tommen wanted to hear, especially since he knew he couldn't Slow Band his way through. That was the thing about camp; with exception of a few very small, very weak Bands in order to dodge flying objects or uncover some prank the boys were trying to pull on him, he had to do everything in Base Time with the rest of them. It was almost as bad as being Suppressed, except this time around, he had his abilities but couldn't use them.

Instead, he went up to the counter and topped off his coffee thermos. He figured he was well on his way to becoming a normal American.

Pretty soon, the rest of the groups filtered in, either screaming in joy at winning the tournament or screaming in frustration at losing, and soon the main hall was the noisy, pushy, riotous, mess Tommen had come to expect. It was in moments like this that he appreciated the "quiet" mode on his hearing aids, the ability to flip a switch and the sound would be taken down to about twenty percent. Then, when it got quiet again, he could flip the switch back and it would go back to his preferred settings. He did this now, switching to quiet mode as all the kids filed in, switching back when Mr. Wilson walked in and got everyone's attention.

"Congratulations, campers!" he began. "Everyone here, regardless if you won or lost, you all worked hard. You gave it all you had, played hard, had some good memories, good laughs, and a lot of good sportsmanship. You developed your skills and your teamwork, and everyone had a good time." Tommen could see where a couple of the kids were still crying over their losses. "Now, to announce our official winners. Winner of the boys basketball, congratulations, Coon Cabin!" Polite applause, mostly from the counselors and staff. "Winner of the boys soccer, congratulations Wolf and Beaver Cabin, a deadly combination if there ever was one." Nice save. "Winner of the girls basketball, congratulations Trout Cabin. And last but certainly not least, winner of the girls soccer, congratulations, Dragonfly Cabin."

"Why do the girls' cabins have such gay names?" Carson wondered aloud, though not loud enough for it to get far past their table.

"To make sure you don't go in there," Tommen told him smartly, just a moment before Saul told him something else.

"Now then," Mr. Wilson went on, "as most of you know, the winners of these tournaments get a special cake just for them, and the second place team is obligated to serve them that cake. Miss Pamela, if you would please."

"Dessert before dinner," Saul said. "The only way to do it."

Tommen thought the whole thing was a little fishy. No matter how well-mannered the children seemed to be, he couldn't believe that every single one of them would just willingly and wordlessly serve cake to the team they just lost against. Maybe in an adult tournament, he could give the benefit of the doubt, but not with kids. There was no way.

And yet, there they went, the losing cabins going up and grabbing a piece of cake, kids and counselors. Then, with almost scary synchronization, they all approached a target. Kids went to kids, counselor assistants went to counselor assistants, and counselors to counselors.

"Congratulations, winners," Mr. Wilson said. His cheeky grin was enough to alert Tommen that something was indeed fishy about this ritual. "But here's to knowing that you can't have your cake and eat it, too."

If not for his Banding giving him "quick reflexes" Tommen probably would have gotten a face full of chocolate cake with multi-colored icing. As it was, he managed to get his hand up around his ear so that when he couldn't quite get out of the way, his hand got the cake that would have otherwise been smooshed in his ear and, subsequently, his hearing aid.

There was laughing and cheering and applause. Despite his initial dodge, the Crow Cabin assistant still got enough cake to go for a second attempt, which he somewhat managed to accomplish.

The whole thing started a small food fight which the staff allowed to continue—and even participated in a little—for a few minutes until the real dinner was set out and paper towels and spoons were given to the poor victims of the cake assault.

"I don't know where they get the idea that we can't have our cake and eat it, too," Saul commented as he licked his fingers clean, as carefree as Tommen had ever seen him. Saul looked at him as he wiped his face clean. "If you're really worried, there will be more cake after dinner."

Tommen just nodded. Normally he wouldn't have minded except who knew what germs were on the cake now that it had been flung around by kids who already had dirty hands; chances were pretty good that the cake had been scooped up off the floor as a plate prior to being thrown. Maybe he would just wait this one out until after dinner.

When did you become a germophobe? You braved poisonous plants in a jungle halfway across the universe, drank water which could have killed you on the spot, and you're worried about a little cake from a little food fight?

One look at Randall quickly put that line of thought to rest.

The winners were afforded first rights to the dinner line. As usual, Tommen loaded his plate as much as he was allowed, always promising to come back for more. Pam just shook her head and said something about being a starving teenage boy before moving on to the next person in line.

It was probably the first time that their table felt normal, like any other table in the hall. It didn't feel like the special needs table, the outcast table, especially not the prison table. They talked and laughed and joked and carried on. Even Saul seemed more at ease than normal. Maybe one small victory was really what this group needed, Tommen thought. A way to bring them all together in a way that wasn't getting into trouble. After a minute, Saul excused himself to refill his drink.

But when one minute turned into two, then five, Tommen began to worry. It shouldn't take that long to fill a cup of soda. He looked around and just spotted Saul entering the main hall, his expression an even grimmer mask than normal. Mr. Wilson followed him, but only as far as the main area, preferring to stay back just out of sight.

"Aaron, can you watch our table for a second?" Saul asked the Crow Cabin counselor. Even before he agreed, Saul looked at Tommen, then at Jimmy. "Tommen. Jimmy. Come here."

Tommen was no stranger to being called to the principal's office, but he was pretty sure he hadn't gotten in any fights with the little boy who followed behind him as small and as quiet as a mouse, still holding his fork. They trailed after Saul who followed Mr. Wilson to the main office where a woman in a familiar dark suit waited for them.

"This is not a discussion," Mr. Wilson began, looking just a little too long at Tommen. "This is simply an informative meeting."

"Am I going away?" Jimmy asked.

Tommen might have expected the boy to break down in tears and cry and beg not to go. When he didn't, that was when he knew that this was nothing new to him, not anymore. He'd been going through this circus for a while now, long enough that when he was told to pack his bags, he did so without asking.

"Yes, you are, Jimmy," Mr. Wilson said sadly.

"Your aunt in North Dakota has agreed to take you in," the social services woman said, looking a little too cheery about the whole thing.

"Why can't he finish out camp?" Tommen wondered. "I mean, we've got three weeks left. Horseback riding, ziplining, swimming, tons of fun stuff. He just led the cabin to victory in the soccer tournament." Not entirely true, but she didn't need to know that.

"Jerry asked the same thing." Her expression was neutral, but hardly saddened even as she sighed. "Let's just say the news didn't go over well with everyone involved. He's being moved for his own safety. Once his aunt takes custody, she'll probably be moving, too."

So Jimmy's mom was less than thrilled and they were worried that she might try to kidnap him from the camp or do something else stupid.

"Is he leaving now?" Saul asked, as cold and impassive as ever. The perfect Marine.

The woman nodded. "I'm afraid so. I was personally hoping to put it off until, like you said, after camp, but that was considered too risky. When I tried for something like tomorrow morning, a fresh start, that got shut down as well. He has to go now. He's got a plane to catch."

"All right. Come on, Jimmy, let's go get your stuff."

"I'll take him," Tommen offered. "You go watch the other boys."

Saul eyed him suspiciously for a second, but ultimately agreed. The five of them left the office, Saul, Mr. Wilson, and the woman to the main hall, Tommen and Jimmy to the cabin.

It wasn't right. Well, that might not be true. If Jimmy's mom was hurting him and threatening to do stupid shit, it might be right, but that didn't mean it was fair. Didn't he have a dad? Maybe not. But why the roller coaster? Why put the kid through so much hell that he never so much as flinched when someone from Protective Services came walking up to the door? Tommen had heard numerous stories from his dad from his time in Missing Persons about kids who would cry if they just saw anyone in a suit within fifty feet of them, no matter if they were Protective Services or some rich and famous company CEO.

"So, you're going to live with your aunt," Tommen said when they reached the cabin.

"Yeah," Jimmy said simply, making a beeline for his bunk and packing his suitcase with the deft efficiency of someone whose every worldly possession lay within it.

"Is she nice?"

"I don't know. I never met her. Mama says she's a witch, though."

And if she's the witch, what's your mom like? "She can't be too bad, if that's where the nice lady out there is sending you."

Jimmy just shrugged. "We can be bad together, I guess. Like Mama says."

Now he'd had enough. Tommen knelt down and turned Jimmy toward him. "Listen to me very carefully, Jimmy. You are not a bad kid. You are smart and very nice. I don't know that you could ever hurt a fly. I don't think you were able to kill that spider that was on your suitcase the other day. Okay? You are not bad. You are good. Very, very good. And I'm sure your aunt is a nice lady, too. She'll treat you right. You understand me? You deserve the best because you are a good kid."

"If you say so."

"I do say so. I know so. You deserve respect as much as anyone else. Okay?"

The boy still shrugged, but this time he nodded. "Okay."

"All right. Do you have everything packed?"

"No. You interrupted me."

"Right." Tommen stood. "Sorry. Carry on."

It didn't take long; Jimmy's worldly wealth was comparatively small. As they were crossing the open yard back toward the main hall, they ran into Mr. Wilson and the woman who were just coming to meet them.

"Okay, Jimmy, are you ready to go?" the woman asked.

Again, Jimmy shrugged. "I guess."

"All right. How about I take your suitcase? You can have a few minutes to say goodbye to your friends, then we need to go."

Surprisingly, Jimmy shook his head. "I don't have any friends. I'm ready to go."

Tommen found himself surprisingly hurt by the boy's comment. First he hurt because Jimmy thought he had no friends. He'd probably never been in one place long enough to make any lasting friends. But secondly, he hurt because he'd really tried to befriend him, to go out of his way and make sure that Jimmy wasn't seen as just another kid from the prison, er, Wolf Cabin. Whether that had any impact on everyone else's perceptions no longer seemed to matter since it didn't seem to have affected Jimmy at all. It was just one more stepping stone on his way to wherever, tossed here and there by the whims of the government and whatever abuse and instability he had at home. Tommen let out a breath. It might be right, but that didn't mean it was fair.

"I know what you're thinking," Mr. Wilson said as they watched the woman take Jimmy to the car and drive off. "And I'll tell you now, there is nothing you or I could have done. We have zero legal say in this. Once she produced papers detailing who she was and what the courts had ordered, our jurisdiction ended."

"Does this happen often?" Tommen asked.

"This camp...it's not targeted to the rich snobs who turn up their noses because they already have a pool and a camper and a stable full of purebred horses at home. It's for the poor and destitute who may never get to do these things again in their lives. The courts won't touch any of the Native kids, for obvious reasons, but the rest...well, as much as I hate to admit it, they're fair game, depending on what's going on at home."

"It's not fair."

"No. But there is nothing we can do about it."

Well, there was, but then it would put him on the same plane as Jimmy's mom and carried multiple felony charges.

They headed back to the main hall which suddenly seemed too lively for Tommen's mood. He'd helped to bring down a tyrannical regime that would have enslaved the universe, but he could do nothing for an eight year old boy who'd been tossed around in the system so much he didn't even notice it anymore. Where was the justice in that? He wanted to talk to Becky about it, but texting left much to be desired, he couldn't call, and he was just exhausted from the whole day. First the soccer tournament and now this. He just needed to sleep it off.

He finished his dinner, more surprised that it had been left untouched, and simply looked at everything going on around him. Did anyone else know what had just happened? Would there be a meeting of the counselors? What would the other boys say when they noticed Jimmy missing? What sort of malicious rumors would start going around? Oh, he had no desire to try and quell the tide of the teeny-bopper rumor mill.

He took his stuff back to the kitchen, declining a second course. Pam gave him an incredulous look but did not ask questions. She seemed to be a perceptive person. Tommen appreciated it and her discretion in the matter, but it also made him wonder just what else she knew about the camp. How many campers had she watched disappear over the years? He returned to the table and plopped down.

"No campfire tonight," Saul told him. "Everyone's too tired, and Jerry wants to give everyone as much sleep as possible before we start on our outdoor adventure week."

At the moment, there was no better news in the world. There would be a little free time between dinner and bed, but they wouldn't have to stay up until midnight or later with s'mores, candy, songs, and stories. He leaned back in his seat as far as he dared and dared to hope there was a God and He was showing just a little mercy. Though Tommen wished He could have poured out a little more mercy on Jimmy, but, whatever. He'd take what he could get at this point.

"A couple of the boys want to go stomping around by the swamp and creek," Saul went on. "I'll take them if you want to take the others, get showered, get ready and go to bed."

Just looking around at the table, Tommen could see which boys were practically asleep already. He nodded. "Works for me if it's okay with you."

"Better than trying to force you to stay awake and having something happen."

Well, there was no denying that. After a few more minutes so the boys could finish up the last of their food and take their plates to the kitchen, Tommen and Saul split the group. Saul, Randall, Carson, and Peter headed off to the swampy area while Tommen and his tired ducklings dragged themselves back to the cabin.

"Do we have to take showers?" Louis whined.

"Yes, you do," Tommen told them, as much as he just wanted to collapse into bed himself. "At least get in the water and rinse yourself off."

That much they would compromise. Showers didn't last long, and soon they were slogging their way back to the cabin where Saul and his gang were just getting ready to head to the showers themselves.

"How was the swamp?" Tommen asked.

"Full of mosquitoes," Randall whined, scratching at a bite on his arm, then on his leg, then on his neck.

"I told them, but they didn't believe me," Saul said, shrugging. "Anyway, we'll be right behind you as far as bed goes."

Tommen put up his hands. "Hey, whatever. If I'm still awake enough to notice you coming back..."

The problem was, he was awake enough to notice them coming back. He lay there in the dark, staring at the ceiling, all alone until the door opened and the group of four came back. Even Randall seemed too tired for some sarcastic remark as he climbed in bed and was soon snoring. About ten minutes after everything was quiet, the door opened once more and Tommen saw Saul's silhouette in the moonlight; the man was pulling on his long trenchcoat and hat.

Tommen closed his eyes. *Go to bed, Tommen. You don't need to get involved. You don't want to get involved. Maybe he's got a pack of cigarettes hiding in his coat and he's going out for a smoke. Or, knowing him, maybe he's got some weed in there. God knows he could stand to mellow out a little.*

But when five minutes went by, then ten, then half an hour, and still no sign, Tommen began to worry. He worried first because the longer he waited and worried, the more awake he became over it because of his damn paranoia telling him the camp was about to burn down and Saul had something to do with it. Only once he got that worry quelled was he about to worry about Saul being gone for so long. Even if he had just been out for an innocent smoke or late-night stroll, he could have easily gotten hurt out there, whether from a fall or maybe some wild animal.

Don't do it. Just stay put. Close your eyes and go to sleep.

He managed to convince himself of that for about another half hour—estimation only—but finally his curiosity won out. Experience had taught him to be cautious, but there was no way he could just ignore Saul's disappearance. Besides, what if morning came and they found out that something had happened and Tommen knew that he could have stopped that tragic something if only he'd just gotten over his fear of the dark and gone looking?

Of course, it wasn't his fear of the dark that paralyzed him. His dad was afraid of the dark. Tommen was afraid of what lived in the dark.

Carefully, he got down and pulled on his shoes, debating whether he should grab his hearing aids. If something was out there, he would be at a distinct disadvantage. In the end, perhaps foolishly, he decided against it. He would just go out, take a quick look around, and come back in. Saul was a big boy and could take care of himself; he still had to look after the boys in the cabin. Like Micaiah said, treat it as a hostage situation where the boys would have no ability to defend themselves. And wouldn't it be perfect for Rifun, Disguised as someone Tommen didn't know well enough to call out, to lure him out into the dark forest to kill him?

Because paranoia never hurt anyone.

He stepped lightly as he crossed the cabin, but when he opened the door, his breath caught in his throat. Saul stood in the doorway, hand halfway to the handle.

"Where the hell have you been?" Tommen hissed.

"Out," Saul told him. "I wasn't tired, and you're not my mom. I don't need your permission."

"No, but you could have told me."

"Sorry, I thought you were asleep, and I thought it would be rude to wake you up just to say, 'Hey, I'm going out.'"

Tommen rubbed his eyes. "Fine, you have a point. But still. What if something happened to you?"

"Then I feel sorry for you, getting stuck with these kids all by yourself, never mind the older kids when they come."

"Whatever. Just...go to bed."

"Yes, Mom."

Saul pushed past him, removing his hat and coat and getting into bed no worse for wear, as if their exchange hadn't just happened. Tommen stood there for a second or two longer before closing the door and returning to his own bed. Could he have imagined the whole thing? His dad had said once that the darkness played tricks on people, and skewing of time was certainly a common thing. Had he only imagined that Saul had been gone for an hour? What if he'd only been gone fifteen minutes?

No, he'd been gone at least an hour, and Tommen suspected that it wasn't just some late-night stroll because he had insomnia.

Chapter Eleven
Hideaway

The Wheel of Time wasn't the only hub of activity in the universe, whatever the Hands thought. They just had the monopoly on channeling the power needed to open the portals across the middle dimension. If it took eighty percent concentration to open a portal to the Wheel, then it took a hundred and sixty percent concentration to go anywhere but the Wheel, and where the ride to the Wheel was less than invigorating, the ride anywhere else was even worse.

Micaiah dropped through his portal like a sack of potatoes into water, slapping the surface with all the comfort of a brick wall and still sinking, no air in his lungs, strength in his limbs, or sanity in his mind. Once the nausea cleared, he was able to lift his head and look around, not even realizing he was moving until he was going down again. He managed to catch himself on his hands, bringing everything into focus enough that he got his feet under him and could stand. He turned and helped Kayla up as she swayed and seemed uncertain about the whole thing.

"We should have stolen some of the Wheel's technology while we had the chance," she said, leaning against him. "I don't particularly enjoy going to the Wheel, but it's a much better experience than that."

"I know, but fixing the doors around here isn't exactly on the high priority list right now," he told her. After a minute, he added, "Come on, might as well get this over with."

The Wheel of Time was always built to attract attention to itself, whether through general decor or just the wow factor of being able to manipulate physics and fuck with the average mind. This was even more evident now with Rifun's remodel of the Wheel and his desire to bring some Shakespearean culture to the universe.

The Akarin fortress was far removed from all of that. In fact, it was probably more "sci-fi looking," as Tommen would put it, than the Wheel, more appropriate to the scene and workings at hand. Everything was metal, the floor, walls, ceiling. It wasn't the high-tech silver or white sort of metal either, but the more dark and depressing dark gray and black metal. Where the Wheel was like walking through Shakespeare meets *Relativity*, the hideaway was more like a secret military bunker. Like the Wheel, light seemed to come from nowhere, and pipes and other mechanical or engineering-looking things carried out daily operations to keep the place running.

Also like the Wheel, the corridors were built to accommodate some of the largest alien species. Unlike the Wheel, they were hardly packed wall to wall. Actually, as he and Kayla went along, they saw only about a dozen others in the corridors.

Unlike the Wheel, the hideaway was a single, three-dimensional unit, a regular building versus a sickening conglomeration of individual rooms thrown together haphazardly and connected via portals. There were a few rooms like that, but it wasn't the whole layout of the place.

The portal room was located on the bottom floor. Unlike the Wheel, it was not a endless series of rows of portals. The portals here did not stay open once the opener walked through and close when they returned. Portals had to be opened manually as they closed automatically. To that end, that also meant that there were no layered dimensions as in the Wheel, where it might appear that Time back home simply stopped. Every second that went by in the hideaway also ticked by at home, which meant that Micaiah was taking some serious time out of his day to be here.

From a strictly architectural point of view, once out of the portal room and in the main fortress at large, the place was laid out like an old medieval castle or citadel; supposedly it was modeled after some famous citadel on Iurinta, Parsec Five, Sector Nine, System

Thirty-One, Planet Twenty-Six. The Iuri were flying aliens, like what might happen if a mouse, a manta ray, a bat, and a jellyfish all got together and had a kid, and the supposed citadel replica reflected that.

Just starting from the stairs, the first set of which were just off the portal room, the rooms were wide open, allowing any flying creature unrestricted access to any floor, even as grounded aliens, such as humans, were forced to walk up a massive flight of spiral stairs. The larger rooms, meant to accommodate larger aliens, were also ideal for flying creatures, and there were perches everywhere for them to land on, a bit like how birds would fly around in the rafters in greenhouses and the walled-in landscaping department in big box stores.

"It's been a long time since I was here," Micaiah said as they trudged their way up the stairs. Some parts were actual stairs and other parts were more of a ramp or gradual slope, but none of it was easy. Climbing one flight of stairs here was like climbing three or four on Earth.

"You remember where you're going?" Kayla wondered, less affected by the long climb, but then, she didn't have a prosthetic to deal with. At least, that was what Micaiah told himself.

"Of course I remember," he told her. "How could I not remember?"

"After all the times you got called for discipline?"

Yeah, yeah, and this time felt no better, that was for sure. He was the one delivering the news, and he still felt like he was the one being punished. Maybe it was because of all the fucking work he'd put into freeing the Wheel, and look at how he'd been repaid. All of them, really. The fortress had never been as packed as the Wheel, but there should have been a lot more aliens roaming the corridors. How many had died to bring peace to the universe? How many of them had died in vain?

So they trudged up the steps to the third floor. There were eight floors in all. The first floor contained the portal room, cafeteria, recreational areas, and other things generally not considered essential. Each floor, if need be, could be sealed off from every other floor. The theory was that if they were invaded, the bottom floor could be sealed off with minimal loss. The second floor was what might be considered the barracks, with a comfortable capacity of ten thousand, maximum capacity of fifty-thousand give or take depending on the aliens, able to be evacuated and sealed off in under ten minutes.

The third floor, where they were going, was comprised largely of meeting rooms and offices, the first floor to contain any kind of sensitive information, though certainly not anything too damning. All of that paperwork was on the fifth floor, between the fourth floor which was something like officer barracks, and the sixth floor which was small and personal weaponry. The seventh floor contained the food stores, and the eighth floor held the big guns and what would be appropriately classified as weapons of mass destruction. In a pinch, the entire compound could be rigged to self-destruct, and there was a secondary emergency exit portal room that could be used as a means for escape.

"I am not looking forward to this," Micaiah sighed when they reached the third floor.

"I know," Kayla said. "Neither am I. Do you know what you're going to say?"

"No. But I expect the Author will tell me what to say, and we'll see where things go from there."

That didn't bring him much comfort, however, as they began their long trek through and around the third floor, looking for the meeting room they were supposed to be meeting in. Looking at the citadel from above, it would appear to be square in shape with four massive towers which were the staircases. The floors themselves were a mess of rooms and corridors that seemed to make little and less sense as far as the layout went.

They might have wandered around for half an hour trying to find the room by chance or just taken half an hour to reach their destination; there was no good way to tell. Nevertheless, they reached their destination no worse for wear, ready for the lynch mob that would no doubt form before they were ready to leave.

Actually, the meeting room was very simple, sort of a Knights of the Round Table getup, but without King Arthur, Excalibur, any of the knights, or any chairs for that matter. It was just a round table with approximately seventy to a hundred different aliens milling around, talking, chatting, whispering, and doing whatever it was a particular alien species did.

One thing set the Akarin fortress apart from the Wheel, set it above the Wheel even. That difference was that the fortress did not require translators. Somehow, someway, probably a gift from the Author, everyone was mutually understandable in his own language. Micaiah could speak Irish to them, and they would all understand him in their own language. They could speak their own language to him, and he would understand them in Irish.

So it was that he made his way to the table and said loudly, "All right! I'm here! Let's get this show on the road!"

It took a minute for everyone to quiet down, look around, and realize who had spoken. Most of them stopped talking out of sheer curiosity of, not who had spoken, but who had disrespected them and spoken to them like a bunch of children to be corralled and led somewhere. It was one reason why Doug had always been such a good leader; his Narcissism was right up there with the best of them.

"And who are you?" someone asked once they'd all more or less assembled around the table.

"Micaiah Durvin," Micaiah answered, and gave the universal coordinates for Earth. "I believe most of you have heard my name by now or else you wouldn't be here."

"You're the one who called the Time Trial and launched the coup against Cassius and Rifun," someone else said.

"I am."

"And you're the one whom the Hands wanted to speak with afterwards. They sent word to us that you would have something to say to all of us."

"That is correct."

Before he could say anything, however, another leader butted in. "But who are you that you should speak here? Why would the Hands of Time want to speak to you? Or is this a continuation of Cassius' deception?"

There was some murmuring.

That was another thing that set the Akarin apart from Time. There was a different hierarchy here. Those just learning about the Akari were Novices. Tommen would be considered a Novice. Then there were the Generals, though it referred more to the general population. They were split into three groups: the Core, who were dedicated Akari-bearers and had the chance to advance in rank; the Whispers, those who had the knowledge, maybe some power, but were considered inactive or just fleeting; and the Wanderers, the Akarin version of the Scouts who went to the ends of the universe to seek out more Akari-bearers.

Core Akari-Bearers, once they'd been active for so long, had the opportunity to become Captains. It wasn't an officer rank, more of a sub-officer rank, like what Micah had done with Tommen when he and Walter had been captured by Cassius and Rifun. Captains were kind of the over-seers of Akari-bearers of a planet, like Gatekeepers. Captains would shadow the officers and after a length of training would decide whether to become and officer or remain simply a Core Akari-bearer, like how Micaiah was technically considered a Lieutenant-trained Master. He had the training, but not the title.

Among the Generals and the three main groups, there were dozens of unofficial sub-groups of clubs and committees and whatever else. It helped, in that someone could almost always find a group to belong to, but it also hurt, in that sometimes group rivalry sometimes went from friendly to ruinous.

As far as the officers went, there were only three real ranks: Lieutenant, Commander, and Admiral. Most of those in attendance were Lieutenants and Commanders, and they would take the information presented today to the various Captains who would distribute it to the Generals.

Micaiah himself was officially a Captain-trained Core member, though Doug had often threatened him with changing his status to a Whisper, seeing how he'd gone over a decade with little progress. Micaiah had often retorted by saying he was watching out for his little brother and should be considered a Wanderer instead.

Regardless, he was not an officer, and the officers in the room knew it.

"That is what we are here to discuss," Micaiah said finally, answering the accusation. "Among other things." Once the crowd had quieted, he went on, "We cannot allow paranoia to get the best of us."

"Prove that you are who you say you are," the same officer challenged.

"And how would you know if he told the truth?" a new voice snapped. Micaiah turned to see the newcomer who spoke as he walked, faithful companion at his side. "You don't know him well enough to make a judgment one way or the other."

"The Akari will show us."

"Yes, but that was your second choice, considered only when I called you out." He grinned and shook his head. "Is it any wonder that Cassius was able to dupe us? Is it any wonder he and Rifun were able to do what they did? In our name? In the name of the Akari?! My God, we've all become so lax. So dependent on ourselves and caught up in our own power while cowering in the shadow of the Time Industry.

"But, back to the issue at hand. Unlike the lot of you, I did Test Micaiah with the Akari, and he is who he says he is, his wife as well." He tipped his fedora-like hat at her and she nodded graciously. "I also happen to know him, and he is very much Micaiah Durvin."

"And who are you to make judgments against us and upon him?" someone else asked.

"Enough!" Micaiah barked. He looked at the man. "Thank you, Saul."

Saul Wolf dipped his head. His companion, a massive white

wolf the size of a small horse sat obediently at his side. "Of course. Please, continue."

"As I said, we cannot allow paranoia to get the best of us. My wife Kayla went to Doug's house to do some investigating, see if she could tell when it was that Cassius switched places with him."

"At the inauguration coup," someone suggested.

Micaiah shook his head. "No. Long before that. Based on the evidence she found, she estimated that Cassius killed Doug at least two maybe three months, about sixty to ninety Base Days, prior to the inauguration." *Around the time of the first woman's murder when he would have emerged from Forbes Cave a second time looking for Julianna's journal,* but Micaiah did not say this out loud. "He had ample time to learn how to pass as Doug both in regular life and here, and he would have had a good enough understanding of the Akarin to fool us as well."

"But if he had such knowledge, why did he not try to wipe us out?"

"He did try, but he underestimated us. When I proposed my plan to him, thinking he was Doug, he collaborated with Rifun on how to trap everyone in the Pit to be slaughtered, but he was unprepared for our strength and the power of the Author to save us."

"So we have nothing to worry about."

"Do you think we are immune to pain and suffering because of the Author?" Saul said hotly. "Become a Whisper and see how well that works for you. Go join any of the other factions claiming to tout the Akari and the favor of the Author and see how that works for you. What we have to do now is prepare ourselves for another assault. Cassius is dead, but Rifun is still out there somewhere, and he may still have friends. With all the information he has, we have to be ready."

"How do you suggest we do that? And who are you, anyway? What is your rank?"

"Does my rank matter when I speak the truth? To answer the only valid question in your speech, our first goal should be education. You can't fight an enemy you know nothing about, or else we end up fighting shadows and ghosts. As far as anyone out there, outside the Akarin is aware, some nutjob touting the Akari just tried to wipe out ninety percent of Time Agents. We have to make sure, first, that they know he was not an Akari-bearer, and second, that they understand what the Akari is. As much as I hate to admit it, but that may mean making nice with the Hands of Time, setting aside our feud for a little while."

Micaiah shook his head and cut him off before he could say more. "We can't do that."

"And why not?"

"Because that is what they called us in to talk about." He sighed and looked around at those gathered. "The Hands of Time have decreed that in light of recent events, there is no be no further discussion or even mention of the Akari in any fashion, whether it comes from the Akarin or the Cult of the Akari. We are free to govern ourselves, but any and all mention of the Akari is not to leave these walls 'wherever the Laws of Time prevail' I believe was the exact phrase. If so much as a whisper gets back to the Hands about the Akari, we'll be inspecting the new Judgment Wing and getting to know the new Grandfathers really well."

Immediately there was outrage as everyone began shouting his opinion, all striving to be heard, as if it would make a difference in the grand scheme of things. Micaiah let it go for a minute or two before fighting to get them to quiet down again, but even then it was Saul who spoke.

"Then how are we supposed to clear our name and bring the Akari out of the mud?"

"We're not," Micaiah told him sharply. "The Hands expect all of us to take the fall for what happened. They're using it as an excuse to be rid of all Akari factions, regardless of their merits or demerits. Once they wipe us out, they have no competition for the power of Time and their Time Agents. And this time around, they are united in such a way that we can no longer simply tiptoe around them and try to play off their petty Narcissism and little lordling mindset. I fear that this time the threat is real. Furthermore, I don't think they'll just stop there. Paranoia will get the best of them. They force us out of the public, but they worry about what we do in private. Eventually, they will come for us, even here."

"We can seal off the first floor and the main portal," someone said.

"And how long do you think they're going to wait?" Saul asked. "They'll be the ones on the outside with all the resources, and secret back door portals in and out of here will only work for so long."

"As much as I don't want to, that will have to be a discussion for a later time," Micaiah said.

"Cai, it wasn't raining when Noah built the ark."

"No, but that's the long-term project which we should all consider in our own time. That thought process takes time, more time than we have here. I'd be willing to bet that Noah still had to farm to feed himself and his family, and that was, comparatively, much more short-term thinking, which is where we need to be right now. What do we need to do right now? The Wheel of Time and the Hands are putting themselves back together, but there is still enough residual chaos that we might be able to get away with a few more magic tricks before having to vanish completely."

"What do you suggest?" someone asked grudgingly.

"I don't know. That's why I'm here asking you."

Actually, he was just stroking their egos a little bit in order to get them thinking up plans and trying to figure a way through or out of this whole mess.

"What if we went to the other factions?" someone suggested. "The Hands know we're greatly divided, and they may be playing off that as much as we played off their divisions in the past. If we stand together, they wouldn't be able to stop us."

"What other factions are you referring to?"

"Akari Clan, the United Akari-Bearers, the Tribe of the Akari, the Wanderers, the Patient Akari, any of them."

"Why should we go to them? Some of them are heretical

groups who would be better off wiped out by the Hands' power play."

"Because the Hands are making no distinctions. If everyone is a target, we should all get to safety and resume our petty fights later."

"Petty fights? So you would have us ally ourselves with the Cult of the Akari, too? They started this whole mess!"

"Most of the Cult is dead or fled, and they ought to know better than to show their faces around here anytime soon. We can do just as well without them. But I agree that we may have to reach out to other factions, other groups, and form a temporary alliance."

"So are we preparing to go into battle again? We won, but we suffered heavy losses. Many are not ready to fight again, nor should they be forced to."

"If we fight, we only prove the words of the Hands true, that we are violent and cannot be trusted! That is not who we are!"

At some point, Micaiah simply tuned them out and took a step back. Who needed feuds between the factions when the feuds within a single faction was enough drama for ten soap operas? In all honesty, very little was likely to get done either at this meeting or the next or the next. Time would pass and the Hands would close whatever little chaotic loopholes were currently open, and they would be left in the dark.

"Perhaps now is the time we ought to reinvent ourselves," someone said. "As the Time industry has undergone a change, perhaps so must we."

"Such thinking is how we got so many different factions," someone else pointed out. "Even just little changes, those who support it dissent from those who don't. The last thing we need is more division. We must unite based on what we agree on. So we have little in common with the 'Patient Akari,' but we have more in common with the United Akari-Bearers. We could ally with them."

"Even if we did ally ourselves, who would lead us? Who would be in command? Whose system would we use? We are already having difficulty filling the holes that have opened up because of the fight in the Wheel."

"Doug was dead long before the coup, and Cassius obtained much information through him. Maybe we ought to fill his spot with the one who saw through it and defeated him."

The conversation had taken a decidedly unexpected turn as all eyes turned to Micaiah.

"What are you saying?" he wondered uncertainly, even as he knew exactly what they were implying.

"If we are to proceed, we must have internal strength as well as external strength. Will you fill the hole that Doug created? You are Captain-trained."

That was the nice thing about being an Akari-bearer; there was no pressure to become a leader when a position opened up.

The problem was, it was one of the few things they were absolutely right about. They couldn't hope to ally themselves in any way with anyone if they had weak or missing leadership. The former, Micaiah could do nothing about. But as for the latter...that meant a huge commitment. That was like stepping into Mi Chin's shoes as a Gatekeeper. He didn't want the responsibility, not now, not when he was supposed to be going dark here pretty soon and living peacefully with his wife. Even as he glanced at Kayla, he could see the uncertainty. It was like Walter being promoted to Chief of Police just before retiring.

"But...why?" was the best thing he could come up with.

"You are trained, and a natural-born leader. You led the uprising against Rifun, exposed and killed Cassius, and stand here among us now though you are not an officer."

"You wanted to lynch me ten seconds into my speech. And I'm supposed to be going dark soon."

"Yes, and it will prove advantageous in that you can dedicate more time to us, to the rebuilding of the Akarin and saving us politically in the Time industry." He didn't miss how they evaded the first accusation.

Micaiah let out a breath a little louder than he wanted. "I am going to defer my decision for now. Regardless whether I am made a Leader, we still don't have a plan."

Thankfully, it was enough to set them back on each other, shouting plans and arguments and counterarguments, each wanting to be the one who came up with the plan. Micaiah stepped back next to Kayla.

"That was unexpected," Kayla murmured.

"Not really, but it came up sooner than I was anticipating."

"You want to be a Leader?"

"I never denied the ambition, but it just...not right now. Right now, I just want to settle down into a quiet life with you. For once."

"I agree. Before we leave, I'll grab the paperwork for going dark."

"Get it to go. I'll get the same from the Wheel at a later date, once I've cooled down a little from this circus act."

She chuckled. "Some days, I think some of the other factions might be a little more appealing, at least the smaller ones."

"You spend too much time at home base. Our little neck of the woods isn't so terrible."

"I know, and that's probably my own fault. If we do go dark like we want, we'll only have each other. That might be just what we need."

"Each other, and kiddos." He kissed the top of her head and pulled her against him.

"There is that, yes, but not while we're in the middle of a meeting."

He stifled a laugh and instead pretended to be more interested in the meeting which was locked in a predictable stalemate.

After a time, someone got smart and proposed a short break, long enough for everyone to go out, stretch legs and other appendages, get something to eat, and cool off a little. Micaiah and Kayla went down to the first floor to the cafeteria.

The Akarin cafeteria wasn't like the Food Court in the Wheel. It was more like the mess tent on an Army base in the middle of the desert: rations with little variety. Every so often, there was something different, something interesting. Dessert was typically pretty good, but the actual meals were designed and created more for nutritional needs rather than personal taste. Still, they grabbed their food and found a spot to sit and eat.

"So, I contacted a few people in District One and District Nine," Kayla said, "just to get a feel of the area, as far as Time goes. I told them our intentions, and they said there shouldn't be any problems. Assim Foyez is the Captain of District One now, and he feels a particular debt to you, so he should be okay to deal with."

"Regina kept him on as Captain?"

Kayla shrugged. "Keep your friends close and enemies closer?"

"Then how do you explain Micah and I being demoted?"

"Personal grudge? She hates you and doesn't want you near any sort of power?"

"Makes as much sense as anything else, I guess."

After a moment, she said, "Would you do it?"

"Do what?"

"Would you be a Leader if they asked you to?"

"If they'd asked me a year ago, very likely. But now, with things the way they are, both between us and Time, and with me and you set to leave? Unless everything imploded right now and I was the only choice for any sort of leader, I mean, yeah, then I'd do it. But not now." He paused. "Or do you think I should?"

"Honestly, I don't want you to."

"Then I won't."

"I don't want you to," she repeated, "but you have to do what you think is right."

He hesitated, choosing his words carefully. "Going forward, getting bigger, and obtaining power is not always the right thing, even among the Akarin. It's certainly not the way of the Akari, not always. Sometimes, the right thing to do is back down and focus on the self, and by that I mean me and you and our future family."

She smiled and kissed him. "It means a lot to hear you say that." She finished her food and stood. "I'm going to go see about that paperwork."

"I'll catch up after the meeting."

He watched her go, in no hurry himself to return to the meeting and its inherent chaos. He shifted positions and almost startled as Saul and his giant wolf sat next to him.

"You, sir, are one lucky son of a bitch."

"Don't have to tell me that," Micaiah said.

"So, I could be as cocky as all those bastards upstairs and say something like, 'Hey, buddy, thanks for inviting me to the meeting so I could call them out and back you up.' Or I could mention that I know that's why you didn't really tell me to be here today. Or tonight, as the occasion demands. And, since I have three more weeks of continuous work and very little sleep to look forward to, and losing more every minute I'm here, I'll ask: Why am I here?"

"When I asked you to keep an eye on Tommen and watch out for Rifun, I asked you to do it discreetly."

"I am the master of discretion."

"Apparently not. He texted me the other day and mentioned that you said something in particular about the stories and lies we tell ourselves and the world. Normally it wouldn't mean much, but that is a very Time-esque phrase, one that is often repeated by the Cult of the Akari, Runners, and Whispers."

Saul shrugged, unconcerned, and tossed his hound a piece of meat. "Just a subtle clue that he may have friends where he least expects them and when he may need them most."

"Well, you know what they say about the road to Hell. Now he's all paranoid that you are Rifun in Disguise and you're going to kill him or threaten him or do something terrible. Worse, he thinks he's all alone, and he knows he is woefully unprepared to handle anything that comes up."

"Then let me tell him. Let me train him, for God's sake. He's not going to the Arena, clearly, so he's just dangling there at the end of his line, looking more and more like bait rather than some fearsome Time Agent or Akari-bearer."

"He wanted to go to camp to be his own man."

"Well, dead men tell no tales. And if Rifun is lurking around somewhere and strikes yet again, how many more times are you going to tell Tommen to just sit in the corner and let the adults fight? How much longer are you going to tell him 'we'll train later'? His dad almost died. You almost died. Eventually, you guys are going to start actually dying, and then there will be no one left to train him. Except Rifun.

"And let me tell you something else about that. Rifun tried to kill his dad using what he says is the Akari. You almost died in spite of the Akari. Tommen doesn't know the difference, only that this thing brings death and destruction wherever it goes. If he isn't brought in and trained to see and discern and make his own judgments, we'll lose him forever."

"I know. Believe me, I know. But how good will it look for him to come in and see the same squabbling leaders here as in the Time industry? What's the real difference between us and them?"

"The Time industry is selfish, motivated by Time and greed, their fear of death. Every Akari faction proclaims to have the power of the Akari, and most do, to varying degrees. But not every faction has the power of the Author. Whatever goes on upstairs on the third floor, doesn't matter, because it is the Author's decision. Even this conversation right here."

Micaiah rubbed his eyes. "Stop being philosophical, please, you're making my brain hurt."

"You know it's true."

"Yes, I know it's true, but just..." He shook his head and stood. "I should probably get back to that meeting, make sure they're not about to seal off the third floor just by their arguing."

"An excellent idea." Saul stood and started following him. "Well, I'm going to hit the head before rejoining the rest of you. All the excitement really gets me going, you know? Do me a favor and take

Yawi with you."

Micaiah didn't care one way or the other, and he wasn't sure if the wolf actually understood to go with him. Micaiah figured that if it followed, it followed, and if not, well, that was Saul's problem. He should learn to keep his pet on a leash if he didn't want it to run off. But either way, once they parted ways, the wolf, Yawi, started following him, padding up the steps, almost silent except for the clicking of his claws and heavy panting that sounded like it belonged more to a bear than a wolf.

They made it to the third floor and started down the corridor. As they neared the end of the first corridor, Yawi moved ahead of him and headed right, while Micaiah turned left. He paused and turned.

"Yawi," he said, unsure if he should whistle like he was calling a Labrador. "No, Yawi, we have to go this way. Yawi!"

He stayed there for a second, watching the wolf walk away. Micaiah battled internally. He should just let it be Saul's problem. Let him go after his dog and give him a lecture later on about leash laws.

Finally he turned around and started after the beast. Given the choices, he would rather go chasing after wolves than venture into the nest of vipers that the meeting room was likely to become. He did not have his running leg on, so the best he could do was a slow, awkward hop-jog, enough to close the distance between them a little bit, at least until the wolf turned right down another corridor, ears pricked, evidently attracted to something or another.

When Micaiah made the turn, the corridor was not empty, but the wolf was nowhere to be seen. He might have breathed a curse, turned back, and headed to the meeting, except for the sight of the only other person in the vicinity.

"Chandler."

The man stood there in the middle of the corridor, leather bag slung over one shoulder. He looked the same as Micaiah remembered him last when he and Micah were trying to break into the Judgment Wing, black hair, dark skin, clothes that hadn't been in fashion for well over two centuries.

"Micaiah," Chandler greeted.

"What are you doing here? Wait, are you even here? Can others see you? Or am I talking to thin air?"

Chandler looked around. "Do you see anyone else here who could judge you even if I were an apparition?"

"Fair enough, but, what are you doing here?"

"The same thing I have done since we first met."

"Light a match or a candle, speak in riddles, maybe make more candles, then blow out the flames and leave me in the dark?"

Reflexively, he caught an object that Chandler tossed at him. It was a candle, to no one's surprise. When he held it up, he saw the wick was lit, a tiny flame bouncing at the end. From somewhere he did not know, a small breeze came and snuffed it out, leaving nothing but a thin tendril of smoke.

"I love metaphors," Micaiah said, staring at the candle. "I like object lessons. You know what I like even more? When they're explained to me." He looked at Chandler. "Do I get that benefit? I'll even take a parable."

"War is coming," Chandler told him.

Micaiah took a dramatic, startled step backwards. "Holy shit, he is capable of speaking directly." He composed himself. "What kind of war? We just got out of a war. I fought in that war."

"You fought in a battle. A single battle of a larger war. This is not over yet."

"And you're here to tell me...that I'm going to be snuffed out in this war?"

"I did say that your time would not end at the Time Trial."

Even as he spoke, Micaiah saw that the light around him was fading, the walls and ceiling and floor of the corridor giving way to darkness. Before it could go away completely, however, there was a brilliant light as a thousand candles began flickering. Chandler hadn't moved, and Micaiah's candle was still out.

"Who are you?" Micaiah asked.

"War is coming," Chandler repeated. "A war of light and dark.

You see these candles. Some will be blown out. Some will be tipped over so they die in their own wax. Others will burn out in their own time. Some will be crushed and destroyed so there is nothing left to burn." As he said these things, the candles started going out, first one at a time, then by the dozen.

"And the darkness will win."

"Have you heard nothing I have said? A thousand candles are a brilliant sight, to be sure, but it takes only one to ward off the darkness. Ten thousand men may besiege a fortress and be turned away. But one man may slip through the gates and set fire to the city. But that one man cannot work while war is consuming the ten thousand. He must act alone after all else has failed."

"Okay, so we've moved back into the riddle part. What does this mean for me? If war is coming, and I'll grant that it certainly looks like a possibility, we need to be ready." Micaiah looked behind him, where he knew the corridor should be, back toward the meeting room. "Maybe I should take Doug's place. Is that what you're telling me?"

But when he looked back, all was as it should be in the corridor. In his hand, he held up the candle, where a tiny flame bounced around at the end of the wick. After a second of staring, mesmerized, into the flame, he blew it out and shoved the candle in his pocket. Then he turned and headed back toward the meeting room, hearing the arguing long before he reached the room itself.

Chandler was getting annoying with his riddles and parables and non-answers, but Micaiah found that he really couldn't just dismiss him. Lately, he only seemed to appear right before something really bad happened, or maybe it was just a coincidence seeing how the only things to happen lately were really bad things.

But what was he talking about, a war coming? All right, dumb question. He was probably referring to the Hands "declaring war" on the Akari-bearers of all stripes. Would it be a literal war, like the revolution they'd just gone through, or would this be more of a cold war, spies, secret assassinations, underground operations, KGB, and so on? If it was to be a literal war, was Chandler saying that they would all be wiped out except maybe a select few, a remnant of sorts? If it was a figurative war based on spies and underground ops, was he saying that most of them would turn away and betray their own? Could it be a combination of the two?

Truthfully, he didn't want to think about it. He didn't want to be here, in this meeting. And why should he be? He'd been involuntarily dragged before them in order to deliver the message from the Hands, but that was all. He wasn't an officer, and not showing up might drive home the point that he wasn't interested in taking Doug's place as a Leader either.

He found himself in the meeting room, just inside the doorway, about thirty seconds after thinking that. The arguing was still continuing, with no one acknowledging his presence, except Saul who backed up a step or two to step quietly.

"Maybe my wolf should have led you here," he said, amusement glinting in his eye. "Get lost?"

"Had to talk to someone." Micaiah was suddenly aware of the candle in his pocket. "Anything good here?"

"Nah." Saul shook his head and left the room, his wolf following. No one in the meeting raised an alarm or said anything at all about their departure. "Just one argument after another. I don't even think they know what they're arguing about at this point."

"Agreed."

Saul chuckled and shook his head. "I don't know, man, it's just weird. I mean, y'all look like me, or I look like you, but it still stuns me to be on Earth year after year at that camp."

"One little excursion turned into a bigger mess than you wanted?"

"Something like that. Anyway, we've got a big day tomorrow at camp. This whole week, actually. Ziplining, horseback riding, you know how it is."

"Yeah, I can tell you're suffering."

"Absolutely."

"Just be careful about what you say and do around Tommen. You're meant to be there as an encouragement, a backup. You don't need to make him think you're out to get him. Can you do that?"

"I make no promises. I only do what I do."

"Of course, just like the rest of your people."

They said their farewells, Saul heading for the first floor, Micaiah heading off to find his wife who was just heading toward the meeting room when he intercepted her.

"I got the paperwork," she said, showing him the Great American Novel that passed for New Life paperwork.

"All right. I'm ready when you are," he told her.

"You're not staying for the meeting?"

"No point. And anyway, staying would only make me a bigger part of it. If we're leaving, we're leaving. I did my duty, so now we can go home and focus on this nightmare." He indicated the papers.

Kayla nodded and led the way to the portal room where they opened a portal into the bedroom. It wasn't too late; the bakery would be open for another hour or so, but Micaiah wasn't going to go back in for one hour. He would tell Micah everything in the morning.

"I'm going to make me something to eat," Kayla said, opening the door and heading down the hall. "You want anything?"

"No, I'm fine." He didn't move.

"You sure?" She looked back at him.

"Yeah, just a little frustrated from the meeting."

"Okay. If you're sure."

"I am."

She went into the kitchen, and Micaiah went around the bed where he couldn't be seen from the hall. He dug the candle out of his pocket, set it on the nightstand, and lit it.

Chapter Twelve
Counseling the Counselor

It was as if Jimmy had never existed, the way he ghosted out of everyone's memories. The other kids in camp hardly knew such a person existed; the other boys in the cabin barely acknowledged his presence, never mind his absence; Saul seemed relatively unconcerned and once asked Tommen if he was planning on adopting Jimmy as his kid if he was so worried about him.

Tommen still had his suspicions about the night Saul went out "for a stroll" but he wasn't about to voice them. He'd contacted Micaiah to report it, but the reply had been that Saul checked out and could be trusted. For the time being, just don't say anything. He was there to work and have a good time, not engage in any Time fiascoes. For once, did he think he could manage that?

"I suppose," Tommen replied reluctantly. "But they seem to find me. I'm like a magnet."

"You'll be fine," Micaiah told him.

"How are things in the Wheel?"

"Still chaotic, but thing are getting back to normal, of sorts."

The thing about texts and emails was that tone was difficult to judge. "What do you mean? And don't tell me not to worry about it or that we'll talk later, because I really want to know. I want to be kept in the loop."

For a long ten minutes, Micaiah did not reply. Given how late it was, he was either hesitating, taking a minute to collect his thoughts, had fallen asleep, decided to take a minute to fuck his wife, or was typing up a super long reply. Finally, just as Tommen was about to send a poke text, he replied, "The Hands have banned all use or mention of the Akari or its related groups."

"What? Why? You guys were the ones who restored balance to the Force."

"According to the Hands, regardless if it's the Akarin or Cult of the Akari, we're all, for lack of better term, terrorists. But they can't say that, given all the work we did. So instead, we're free to govern our own affairs, but we're not allowed anywhere within the bounds of Time. As far as using the Akari and such. I can still go wherever I want on official Time business, not that I have much of that anymore after being demoted."

Tommen rubbed his eyes. After a minute, Micaiah texted again. "I'm only giving you the basic information. Like I said, don't worry about the details. You're at camp, you're working. More to the point, aren't you supposed to be sleeping?"

"I'm getting there."

But it was hard to sleep when he was still so uncertain about Saul. Even if Micaiah said he was good, Tommen just had a feeling that there was more to him than met the eye.

Of course, there was little time to really dwell on this during the day. He'd thought the first week of camp had been hectic. That was nothing. That was practice. The second week was what was going to kill him, he was sure.

Day one was ziplining at the camp. It was a short hike to the lines which the camp owned and operated; they were shorter and much closer to the ground than the ones they would be visiting during the week. These were just to get accustomed to the lines, the safety rules, how it felt, all that fun stuff. Tommen didn't remember ever using them during the counselor week, so it was all new to him, too. Actually, it was rather fun, and he found himself jealous that he was a counselor and not a camper.

Day two was also ziplining, but for real. That was the day when they had to get all the kids around, prepared, and on the bus to the actual ziplining site. The girls went in the morning, and the boys went in the afternoon. So while the girls just had to be ready from the get-go, that meant that the boys had to be entertained for the morning, then told to stop what they were doing, clean up, get ready, get on the bus, and a whole list of chores that Tommen did not think they should have had to do. But, do them they did.

Day three, Tuesday, was rock climbing. This time, boys went in the morning and girls in the afternoon, back to the same place where they had gone ziplining. Same instructor, too. As always, one instructor went first, then the boys, then the counselors, then the second instructor. As they tried out the various difficulties in climbing, including L2—standing for Level 2 as a mockery of K2—Tommen was determined to conquer every wall this time, even if no one could appreciate what it meant to him personally. He did manage to conquer every wall, including L2. The instructors chalked it up to his height, that he could reach more holds than the kids. Still, it was a victory for him.

Wednesday was dune buggy and two-tracking in Jeeps, crawling up and down all manner of steep, rocky, muddy, rutted trails in steel cages. The rules for those was one professional driver, one counselor in the front, and two kids in the back, which meant Tommen actually got to out multiple times on different trails, which he was totally cool with.

Thursday was horseback riding. According to Saul, the second time around with the older campers was a lot better because the kids got real horses and rode on some decent trails. This first time with the younger campers was spent mostly on safety and basic riding skills, and all the boys were stuck on little ponies and mini horses. Truthfully, Tommen was pretty okay with that. He hadn't ridden a horse in years and needed a little brushing up.

Their time with the horses went great, but supposedly there was an injury among the girls. One girl, who was one of the rich snobs around the camp, bragged about how her family had horses and she knew what she was doing. Another girl, who, according to the counselor, was desperate to fit in, being one of the only poor kids in the cabin, tried to keep up with the rest of them. Most all of them were rich, but only the one was bragging. The girl wasn't sure what she was trying to do, only that she was trying to imitate the others. Long story short, she fell off the horse and broke a few ribs. It wasn't anything bad and she probably could have stayed at camp if she had wanted, but she'd had enough of the intimidation by the rich girls, and she went home.

Day six was a ropes course. It was an all-day, all-camp event. Boys got the high ropes course first in the morning, while the girls took the low ropes course. It wasn't a really difficult thing, not like the rock climbing, but it was a way to start winding down and relax, catch their breath before gearing up to week three of insanity, which would be the water adventure.

Day seven, Saturday, was another camp day, mostly open free time, a chance to relax and unwind.

As for the boys themselves, they seemed to get in more trouble than the boys from the other cabins, but Tommen didn't see that their mischief was any worse. They didn't try to kill anyone, didn't cut the cable on the ziplines or the rock climbing gear or anything like that. They didn't try to set the cabin on fire—though Carson did manage to find a box of matches, which was spooky; maybe it was just Tommen. But at any rate, he wasn't quite seeing the need for the heightened security.

Still, he wasn't going to comment on it, because any time he did that—made any observation of how good things were going—things inevitably started going very, very bad. The last thing he needed was for the camp to burn down or wash away or get swept up in a tornado. No, he was going to try and take Micaiah's suggestion and have fun. He was at camp, doing a lot of fun things, chasing after some naughty boys, making friends with the other counselors, and life was good.

Well, except for that whole not getting more than six hours of sleep a night thing. He figured he'd gotten pretty used to it over the course of the week, plus last week, but it was the Saturday nights that killed him, when they went to bed earlier and were allowed a little more time to sleep in and relax. Then his body wanted to revert back to eight to ten hours of sleep, and he had to force himself to remain on high alert.

Of course, that seemed to go both ways as his plan this Saturday seemed to backfire. He lay awake, long after everyone else had gone to sleep. Saul did not go out again, nor had he done anything particularly sinister, no more than his questionable sense of humor anyway. The boys had been decent while they had been out, but perhaps that was because they were in unfamiliar territory and being watched like a couple of rodents in a lab experiment. Once they were back in camp, they were back at it again.

First, Carson had managed to not only find, but catch and contain, half a dozen mice which he intentionally released into the kitchen. Pam royally freaked out and turned into the female version of Gordon Ramsay as she started shouting orders to kill the mice and get them out of the kitchen and find out where they were coming from. She'd all but strangled Carson who did not seem to understand the concept of running and hiding, but stood outside the door, laughing hysterically.

That had delayed lunch which put everyone in a bad mood.

Not long after, Randall had done a similar thing, but by releasing snakes in the girls' cabins. There was quite a bit of screaming. One girl got bit, but the snake in her cabin wasn't poisonous. It was only sheer luck that the one poisonous snake hadn't bitten anyone—including Randall himself—but it was still masterfully caught, contained, and taken away to be released far from camp.

As for Louis, Peter, and Eric, when they weren't helping Carson and Randall with their schemes, they were making mischief of their own, mixing up mud as a substitute for spray paint and using it for graffiti, or climbing trees and throwing acorns and small rocks at anyone unlucky enough to walk within striking range.

With only five boys left, it was tempting to think that it would be easy enough for one counselor to keep an eye on them, but nothing could be further from the truth. Even with two, it was a chore. It was a tiring chore, but apparently not tiring enough as Tommen lay awake, pretty sure it was well past midnight, and his chance to get a good night's sleep for the week was quickly passing him by.

After a while, he sat up and quietly got out of bed, pausing only once as he considered inserting his hearing aids, but deciding against it. He was just going to go outside, go to the bathroom, take a quick look around, and come back.

Because anything in his life was ever that simple.

Still, he made it to the bathroom unmolested. As he was just about to head up the steps onto the tiny porch, something caught his eye. He looked around, but with his hearing diminished, it was difficult to tell where anything was. Just as he was considering Banding in order to rush inside and grab his hearing aids, if not wake Saul, he saw another flash of movement. He turned, watching the rustle of leaves.

There! For just a moment, he saw a flash of white fur. White? Now what kind of animal out here was white? Albino deer, maybe? The leaves rustled again, but he did not see it, only heard it. Well, his fatigue had gone, only to be replaced by sheer adrenaline, so there was no point in trying to just forget about it and go back to sleep.

He pushed his way into the trees, watching for disturbances in the leaves and undergrowth, looking down, hoping for tracks but unable to see that well in the darkness. But every time he thought he'd lost the animal and considered giving up, he would see it again. Or rather, he would see a flash of white. Once he thought he might have spotted a leg or a shoulder, but without a tail or, more helpfully, a head, it was still impossible to say what it was.

He hadn't gotten very far when he did hear something, and it had nothing to do with leaves or wind or any kind of nature. Well, that was a lie. The more he listened, the more he figured it was nature all right, but the kind of nature lesson that the kids didn't need to see, hence the need for secrecy.

Every part of him wanted to find it and watch. The more he thought about it, the harder he got. He almost did go watch, too, except for a brief moment when two things happened. First, he had a memory of being dream-raped by a white Borelian, and toyed with by a white Borelian a second time. Second, he got an image of Becky in his mind, and some stray thought from his pa about respecting girls. It didn't make his present dilemma any easier as far as the physical side went, but he managed to force himself to turn away and head in a different direction, hoping to catch up to the white animal again.

He never did, and he found himself at the little fort just outside of the camp on the south end, overlooking the valley the best it could as the trees started to crowd the view. The moon wasn't quite gone, but enough that it was still difficult to see. Without all the activity down below, the camp seemed almost spooky, haunted even. Maybe the white animal had actually been a ghost of some form, maybe the ghost of one of the English soldiers or Native American warriors who had once fought on this land, or so the story went. Wouldn't that be something?

Whatever the case, animal or ghost or some other phenomena, Tommen stayed there for a minute longer, looking over, looking out, looking beyond the camp to the valley, a new valley he'd never explored before. His inner sense of childhood curiosity rose in him, and he wanted nothing more than to race down the hill through the trees, ready to just explore wherever he felt like.

But that wasn't likely to happen. The world was no longer as carefree and wild as it used to be. These days it was full of No Trespassing signs and federal regulations and a whole host of other fun-killing things. Sure, there needed to be some measures taken to preserve the land, but man was part of the land. Let him explore and enjoy what was his.

Well, it was all a little too philosophical for his taste. And anyway, maybe he should be getting back and try to get some sleep in at some point tonight.

He was just starting to turn, when he heard a voice.

"Nice night, isn't it?"

It was Mr. Wilson, walking up the trail in plaid Mickey Mouse pajamas, hands in his pockets. Immediately, Tommen's thoughts went to fear, fight or flight. He'd pegged the wrong person as being in a Disguise. He'd thought it was Saul when it was Mr. Wilson all along. Now Rifun would kill him and no one would be the wiser.

But Mr. Wilson did not shed any sort of Disguise to reveal himself to be Rifun. He just went up to the wall next to Tommen and leaned on it, looking out across the valley.

"The moon isn't much, but the clouds are gone and the stars are out," he went on conversationally.

"Yeah. It's kind of nice, actually," Tommen said, returning to his resting position on the wall, suddenly overcome by fatigue. He never should have come out. He should have gone straight to the bathroom and straight back to the cabin, none of this gallivanting through the forest at midnight business.

"You may find this hard to believe, but I used to be camper here, back when this place first opened. Back then, there were four cabins—two boys, two girls—no bathrooms, no showers, no office, not even any electricity. The main hall was a small brick building for storage with a pavilion where we would eat after cooking our meals on the grill. The food we either had to catch ourselves, or it had to be brought in fresh every single day. Of course, back then, camp was only three to five days long."

"What did you do all day?"

"Things children used to be able to do, used to be allowed to do. We played. We had a few soccer balls, a football. We'd play in the woods here, down in the creek if it was in season. One summer we built a pretty impressive stick fort up here which was later converted to the fort on the north side of camp which was lamentably destroyed. Of course, when we built the fort, we made do with what we had, and it was a little forest fort. When this thing was built, they had to clear the surrounding area, which made for a nice view which is slowly being taken away, little by little, year after year."

"It's a nice camp now," Tommen offered.

"Oh, of course it is. Modern amenities, better sanitation, and tons of stuff to do. And four weeks! My God, if you would have told me as a kid that I'd be here for four weeks, I'd be equal parts excited and terrified. Four weeks without my parents to do whatever I wanted. A week in, I'd probably be bored out of my mind. These days, we have to pick and choose and arrange our activities because there isn't enough time." Mr. Wilson shook his head. "Fickle thing, time. You never have as much as you want, but only as much as you need."

"Need for what?"

"I don't know. It's different for all of us, I imagine. Some of us here in this pool of life will make a huge splash. Fame, fortune, winning souls to one cause or another, a household name as they fly around the world meeting with dignitaries and diplomats. But others of us, most of us, the most we'll do is make a small ripple. We'll never be appreciated at work, never travel beyond our own borders. And even if we do, we do it for ourselves, not because it will really help anyone."

"You don't know that," Tommen said. "A kind word or a compliment from a stranger might turn someone away from suicide. Having pity on someone at the store and covering part of their bill might stave off another fight at home which can ease tension and turn things around."

Mr. Wilson chuckled. "Always the optimist, aren't you? Always ready to see the good in things and believe in others, am I right?"

Actually, I am a very notorious pessimist who can't even decide if there's a God out there somewhere.

"Sure," Tommen said finally. "I guess you could say that."

"Well then, if that's the case—" Mr. Wilson turned around to lean back against the wall. "—then tell me something. Why are you out here?"

"I took the job."

"No, I mean, why are you up here on the top of the hill at one in the morning?"

"Why are you?"

"I was heading to the bathroom when I saw you heading back to your cabin. Then I saw you stop and start off into the woods. I got curious."

"Well, if you're curious about anything, let me tell you about—"

"Oh, believe me, I found them. Don't worry about that. Their discipline will be swift and severe. But unless you were looking to join them, I don't think that's why you took the detour."

Tommen shook his head. "I was following an animal."

"Deer aren't uncommon around here, among other large animals. You've no doubt seen the tracks around your cabin in the morning."

"I've seen the deer tracks, but I've also seen other tracks. Dog. Huge dog tracks, like the size of my hand. No, bigger." He sighed when Mr. Wilson grinned and shook his head. "Anyway, I thought I saw something. I couldn't sleep, so I decided to check it out. I got turned around, and when I got back on a path, I was already pretty much here, so I decided why not?"

"Why not indeed. As for your observations of the dog tracks, those have been known to pop up now and again, always around Wolf Cabin, and only since Saul started working here. He says it's the wolf spirit from his people, come to protect and guide him. Up to you whether you believe it, and part of me has a hard time taking him seriously with his usual dry humor and sarcasm. But still, I won't rip on his beliefs, whatever they are. If he thinks it's the spirit wolf, then by all means, we've got a spirit wolf hanging around camp. Up until the day I catch the son of a bitch threatening these kids or the counselors, spirit wolf can visit as much as he damn well pleases, and we'll all get a good ghost story out of it some time."

"So you've never actually seen a white animal hanging around here?"

"White? Well, any animal can be albino. And, hey, why wouldn't spirit wolf be white, hm? Like I said, until it starts threatening us, as far as I'm concerned, he can stay. I don't know why you're all so shook up about it. Just a story."

Tommen shrugged. "I don't know. Saul's a little weird in the first place, but then, so am I. But I don't really understand him or how to handle or interact with him. It's his moods and behaviors and some of the things he says. Like, we'll be chatting just fine, and then he'll just pull something from way out of left field, and I have no idea how to respond. Or he'll deal with the boys one way, but when I deal with them, it's a fifty-fifty shot whether I'm doing it 'correctly' or not."

Mr. Wilson shrugged and sighed. "Well, that's just Saul for you. Your dad's a cop, right?"

"Yeah."

"From the city, I'll bet he's seen and witnessed a few things that shouldn't be repeated out loud, right?"

Like aliens from distant worlds, his son being held hostage, a military coup, being locked up in a prison made of his worst nightmares... "Yeah, he's seen a thing or two."

"You think that some of those things don't follow him and change him a little?"

"Oh, I know they do."

"Same goes for Saul. He ever tell you the story of how he screwed up his back?"

"No. How do you know?"

"Because he and I had a similar chat his first summer here, about the same time, too, a couple weeks into the first camp. He wasn't nearly in as good a shape as you see now. He was in pain, and you could tell, every waking second of every day."

"Do I get to hear the story or no?"

Mr. Wilson shook his head. "It's not my story to tell."

"Oh."

"Which is good for you because then you know that your story is safe with me."

"My story?"

"What's bothering you? What really sent you up here tonight?"

Oh. That story. Well, it was better than his life story, he supposed. Mr. Wilson might not believe that one. He let out a breath. "I don't know if I can do this. And I don't just mean the sleep—everyone suffers together in that one. But, looking at the boys in the cabin, I see...I don't know."

"You see yourself," Mr. Wilson finished.

"Something like that. I was a foster kid. I lost my family. So to see Jimmy being carted away and punted back and forth according to the whims of the system, it didn't seem fair to me. Even if it's totally right and totally warranted, it's not fair. Because the circumstances of me being taken weren't right or fair."

"What happened?"

"I ran away when I was eight because I was mad for some stupid reason. When I got home the next morning, they were all dead. My ma and pa, brother, sisters, all of them. Carbon monoxide poisoning."

"Aw, damn. I'm so sorry."

"My dad is my uncle, and he's the only family I have left. I don't have a mom. A lot of times, I was left to my own devices. A couple years later, I had a foster brother, but he was ten times worse than anything these kids can come up with, and I tagged along sometimes. He moved on, and certain incidents afterwards forced me to shape up. And that's exactly what I see in these boys. I see what I was, what I used to be. The trouble and lack of discipline. Going into the older camp, I'm going to be looking at my old foster brother and what he was, but also who I would be if I hadn't shaped up like my dad wanted me to."

"Age is the mirror of the soul," Mr. Wilson said, turning back around. "You look back and see only what you were. But it's never a good idea to look too long lest the souls come up from the River Styx and drag you back down with them. The best you can do is look ahead and move forward, away from it."

"Yeah? What happens when those souls turn out to be demons intent on chasing you down and ripping you apart?"

"Are you a spiritual person?"

"Not particularly. My girlfriend's a Catholic Jew, or so she claims."

Mr. Wilson raised a brow but did not comment on that, instead saying, "If you have no shield, you have no defense. If you have no sword, you have no way to attack. I'm not particularly spiritual either, but I was raised Catholic. My mother was always dead-set that everything was possessed. She would always talk about how the demons laughed at the common man because the common man had no defense against them. She argued that the first defense was knowledge, just knowing that they were there. The second defense was physical objects—holy water, crucifix, you get the idea—things that demons hated to see and hated the power within them. The third defense was a protection prayer, to keep yourself and your loved ones safe—unless one of your loved ones was possessed, but I digress. Finally, the fourth defense was the offense, a prayer of attack, where legions of angels would come down and defeat the demons and Satan and every other evil thing in the world."

"Obviously enough people aren't praying, or they're not doing it right because there is still a lot of evil in the world."

"Indeed there is. As I said, that was my mother's faith. But I believe it still works in principle. Whatever demons are chasing you, do you know what they are? If they are physical threats, do you have a physical defense? If they are mental or psychological threats, do you have a mental or psychological defense? And finally, how are you going to defeat them?"

Tommen shook his head. "I don't know, but this is way more philosophical than I wanted to get tonight."

Mr. Wilson chuckled. "Strange things happen in the late hours of the night, or early hours of the morning, depending on how one looks at it. We ponder our existence and life's big questions. Is there a God? Which God is it? Who really has the right of things? The Christians, the Jews, the Muslims, the Hindus, the Ancient Egyptians, someone else entirely? What is our place in the universe?"

Quadrant One, Parsec Eleven, Sector Five, System Four, Planet Thirty-Eight, Tommen thought sarcastically. Out loud he said, "I don't know, and it still doesn't help me solve my dilemma of the camp going on right now on our little speck of space dust."

"Very true," Mr. Wilson conceded. "What good is looking at one's soul, confronting demons, and clearing one's conscience anyway? I'm sure we can all don another layer of fallacy and anonymity before the week is out."

"So you're saying I should leave because my judgment is too cloudy? That I'm incapable of looking past myself to see the campers and not myself?"

"I'm asking if you are capable of such a thing. I guess I didn't understand the extent of your story, or else I would have looked at someone else for a counselor assistant. It's not your fault, but it's the job at hand. No one else wants it, so I can't transfer you, and the boys already know you. And I know Saul well enough to know that he would rather work alone than—"

"—with a useless assistant dragging at his heels," Tommen finished. "I know. He told me."

"Exactly. And it's a fair assessment. You've worked with the boys long enough to know them, know how they operate. They're pretty docile this year, considering some of the shenanigans we've had in the past, but the five of them are still a bigger handful than some of the other cabins that have eight or ten kids."

"What do you suggest? I...really don't want to quit. It's not what I do."

"I can respect that. So I'll propose a compromise. Same one I gave to Saul years ago."

"I'm listening."

"Finish out this camp, the younger kids' camp. We've got two weeks left, lots of exciting things to do on the water and on the hike, tons of fun. Sleep deprivation aside, you look like you're having a lot of fun out there. Then we've got the week between camps. The Friday before the second camp, you call me and tell me whether you're coming back. If you come, you're here. Four weeks isn't a lot to ask. But if you decide it's not right for you, I won't hold it against you. Saul will just have to work with the older kids by himself. Whether or not he holds it against you isn't the point because you'll probably never see each other again anyway.

"As far as payment goes, for half the camp time, you'll get half the pay, twenty-five hundred, straight up the middle. No hard feelings, every goes home happy. How does that sound?"

It sounded fair and more than generous, but it still sounded like quitting. If Tommen was anything, he was not a quitter. He would fight Tyler Freeman until he was unconscious, bleeding on the floor. He would cross the universe and brave unspeakable dangers to save his dad. If he could do those things, there should be no reason why he couldn't do a little time at a kids summer camp. But, as Mr. Wilson had said, age is a mirror to the soul. Between exhausting activities, sleep deprivation, and having to be a warden of the prison cabin, he was giving it his all and it still didn't feel like enough, as if working here with these boys would somehow validate himself, that he wasn't as bad as them, that he could be a lot worse but wasn't. He wasn't even sure why he needed to justify that to himself.

"Sounds fair," he said finally. "I'll finish out this camp, and I'll do my best to come back for the next one. But I make no promises about next year."

"Nobody does, Tommen. Nobody does. As for the next camp, don't do it to impress me, and especially don't do it to impress Saul. You can't impress him; it's impossible. Whatever decision you make, do it for yourself. You're either helping these kids by coming, or saving your sanity by staying home. There is no shame in looking out for yourself from time to time. Sometimes you have to save yourself before you can save others. You're no use to anyone as a vegetable. You understand me?"

"I understand."

"Good. Now then, I think we've already forfeited any chance we had of catching up on all the sleep we've lost since we've been out here, so I think it's high time we attempted to salvage what little more sleep we can wring out of this night. What do you say?"

"Sounds good to me."

Even as he said it, Tommen yawned. Finally, fatigue was catching back up with him. Now it just needed to last all the way back to the cabin without getting distracted, disturbed, or scared away. No more animals or weird sights or sounds, just him heading back to his bunk and hoping to get maybe five or six hours of sleep.

"Other than that, is your cabin all right? Is your hearing aid charger still functioning?"

"Yeah, it works still. If it didn't, I probably wouldn't be wearing them."

That was a lie. Hearing aid charger was one thing, but his dad would probably murder him if something happened to the hearing aids themselves.

"That's good," Mr. Wilson said. "Well, if you need anything, just let me know."

They parted ways at the bathrooms, Mr. Wilson into said bathrooms, Tommen toward his cabin. Well, it hadn't been quite how he'd wanted to spend his night, but there was something refreshing about talking to someone and being a little philosophical. He did that with Becky sometimes, but with her personality, it was more ideal for the head-on debate, bulls locking horns. With Mr. Wilson, it had been a casual pondering of life, each lost in his own thoughts, his own beliefs, trying to make sense of it all.

Becky hadn't quite talked him into believing in God yet—as in Jehovah God or, per her dad, Yahweh—but she had him at a Great Big Something, whatever that was, whatever shape it took, something out there that saw all and knew all because it created all. Or some variation thereof.

He'd just put his hand on the door when a flash of white caught his eye. He closed his eyes, determined not to look. *Just go inside and go to bed,* he told himself. *Don't look, don't ask, don't even think. Just go in and go to sleep.*

But look he did. He didn't see anything at first, until he looked down at the ground where he thought the thing might have stood. There, perfectly preserved in a small spot of mud, was an enormous dog print, just like the ones that had been appearing almost every morning so far.

Just Saul and his spirit wolf beliefs, Tommen told himself, opening the door and stepping inside, mindful of a few squeaky boards as he crossed the room and got back in bed. No one seemed to have noticed his absence, or if they did, they weren't going to confront him about it right now. Actually, his biggest fear was that Saul would pull him aside in the morning and ask him about it. Maybe he was just being paranoid. But then, like good things and coincidences, such things didn't exist in his life without awful things following. If his paranoia alarm was going off now, shit was about to happen; he just knew it.

Nothing happened, at least not right away. He got back in his sleeping bag and even managed to get to sleep. He knew this only because when he opened his eyes, he found himself in a forest that looked oddly familiar. After a minute or two, he realized that it was the camp, or what the land looked like before the camp moved in. The clearing was considerably smaller, a rotting oak crossing the future soccer field. All around, ancient forest and new forest mixed, trees hundreds of years old guarding the lives of the young saplings as they competed for resources in a silent battle that only nature could hear. He stood about where he figured Wolf Cabin to be, between two huge hickory trees.

"It's beautiful here," he found himself saying.

"It is nice."

Tommen about jumped through the canopy as he whirled around. He did not have to go far to find the voice, but it brought him little comfort. It belonged to an enormous white wolf, sitting about fifteen feet away, about what the size would have to be to make the enormous paw prints outside the cabin each morning.

"Are you Saul's wolf spirit or spirit wolf?" Tommen

wondered.

The wolf looked thoughtful, or maybe he was imagining things. Finally, "I suppose I could be called such, though I am very real in both worlds, when I travel. I hunt, I eat, I sleep, as any normal wolf does."

"But you're not a normal wolf."

"You are a clever one."

Tommen couldn't help but spit a laugh which he tried to cover up. Badly. "Yes, you are Saul's wolf all right. You even sound like him. Or are you Saul as my subconscious imagines him?"

"If I were, then how could you have already dreamed of me previously when you hadn't even met Saul yet? As I recall, the white rabbit brought you to me first."

Suddenly he recalled his dream from forever ago, about the rabbit and the wolf, especially the part about the wolf catching on fire and burning the forest down.

"As I recall, that dream didn't have a very happy ending," Tommen said.

"No, it did not."

"So what is this about? Why do I dream of forest creatures?"

"The mind is a strange thing," the wolf mused. "It is capable of great feats of architecture and treachery. It can conceive of the greatest loves that know no bounds and the greatest loathing that eats away at the very soul of humanity. It is even capable of rejecting that which it sees plainly but does not wish to see."

"I hate riddles. Can you just answer my question?"

"You are not dreaming of forest creatures; you are being summoned."

"Summoned? By who? Wait, hold on a minute. No, this is a dream. I can't be summoned in dreams. They're my dreams. Okay, interactions of nerves and cells in the brain, REM sleep, that's all this is."

The wolf sighed and may have even growled a little. "Again, the mind rejecting what it does not wish to see. The Author has made you a difficult one indeed." The wolf stood. "But my job is not to convince you. I am here only to deliver the summons and a warning."

"Oh, I love warnings that come in dreams. Are the Redcoats coming?"

"War is coming. From all sides, both Time and Akari. The Hands have declared war on the Akari and all who call themselves Akari-bearers. In the end, you must choose a side."

"Okay, now I know it's a dream. See, Micaiah already texted me similar information. So you are my subconscious impression of Saul manifesting itself as his wolf spirit giving me information that I already got from Micaiah. Okay, so dreams aren't all dumb; they can be helpful in sorting out information that I already know, but—"

"Stay back!" the wolf suddenly snapped.

It lunged toward him. Tommen gasped, but was paralyzed with fear as it came right at him. He braced himself, preparing to be swept off his feet. Instead, it looked and felt as though the wolf passed right through him. It landed behind him with a thud and a hiss. A hiss?

He turned to see the wolf had landed squarely on a very large—like, Amazonian kind of large—snake, probably a poisonous one.

"Oh, shit," he breathed.

The wolf delivered the killing blow and looked at him, fire in its eyes. "War is coming, and you are personally being hunted. You are being warned and summoned."

Tommen rolled his eyes. "Okay, I'll bite. Who is summoning me?"

"The one Micaiah calls the Chandler."

"And how do I find this Chandler?"

The wolf took a few steps back, and the snake seemed to vanish. "He will find you. When you have chosen a side."

"Because that's really helpful."

"Such are the words I was given. And such are the words you will hear. Your choice to listen. As I said before, the mind often rejects what it does not wish to see."

"Fine, whatever. Does Saul's wolf spirit have a name?"

"Yawi."

"Yawi?"

"Indeed it is." The wolf, Yawi, turned, then paused. "I expect we will see each other again. Perhaps in the flesh. Then you may know."

Yawi disappeared into the undergrowth. This time, the forest did not catch on fire, and Tommen was left staring after him, confused and frustrated, until he woke up.

Chapter Thirteen
Water Week

Tommen could really only blame himself for what little sleep he got that night, but he woke up feeling better than he figured he would have if he hadn't spoken to Mr. Wilson. Something about talking and refreshing the soul and whatever. At any rate, it was a short-lived relief as the boys got up, got around, and got excited.

Living in the mountains, water tended to be a seasonal thing. Those living along the Kanahwa River in Charleston or any of its tributaries elsewhere along the way had water pretty much year-round. And Tommen was sure there were other year-round rivers scattered throughout West Virginia. But for the most part, rivers were seasonal, fed by the snowmelt each spring, dried up over summer, filling again with autumn rains before freezing during winter. It wasn't like the coastal states where anyone could just walk down to the ocean at a whim and go swimming. Here, they had to plan for it and make sure everything and everyone was accounted for.

The thing about the water adventures was that they were all-day excursions. They wouldn't be returning to camp to get their meals; Pam and the others would bring their meals to them. The only thing they were doing at camp was sleeping. All of this, of course, was in preparation for the three-day hiking trip next week.

It was small relief, however, when one of the boys forgot his swim shoes or his towel, or his favorite snorkel that he brought with him just for this week, or his extra swim trunks in case he ripped his, or any of a number of things Tommen thought were either unnecessary or too-bad-so-sad. Mostly he and Saul went with the "too bad, so sad" approach for the frivolous items, but when it came to

259

things like sunscreen, well, there was something to be said for safety, so they obliged, borrowing from the other cabins as needed.

"Damn, you sure know how to burn," Saul observed once when he and Tommen were out of the water and merely watching the children.

The first day they spent at a lake that had no right to be called a lake, but more of a wide river. It was a free swim day at a small park, and there were any number of beach games to play and a few small trails to explore.

"Yeah, I've never been very good at tanning," Tommen said, giving himself a once-over, seeing how pink he'd become.

"I know I've seen you put sunscreen on at least twice, but here." Saul tossed him a bottle.

"Well, not everyone can be blessed with Native blood, or even just sun- or burn-resistant skin. That's what I get for being Welsh, I guess."

"I thought it was somewhere over there, given your accent, though, personally, I would have pegged you more for Scotland."

"Nope, not quite. Wales."

Somewhere, someone blew a whistle and called for a buddy check. Every twenty to thirty minutes, they had to do a buddy check, but Tommen was pretty sure they were doing it more often than that. The first few times, he was perfectly okay with it. It was a safety measure in order to check on all the kids and make sure no one was drowning. After about the first two hours, in which they'd called buddy check at least ten times, he was ready to murder whoever blew their fucking whistle. He hadn't even called a buddy check yet and it was getting on his nerves.

Thankfully, that only happened on free swim days. Every other day, they pretty much had to keep an eye on everyone at all times, and the activities were more organized.

For example, Monday was a gentle canoeing day, which meant everyone had to be in the canoe. If they weren't in the canoe, then something obviously wrong.

It wasn't a bad day, really; Tommen had no problem with it, but he could see where the boys might find it boring—unless, of course, they were trying to do canoe jousting with other cabins. That escapade was quickly ended. It also quickly established a need for teamwork and coordination, neither of which Wolf Cabin possessed.

First, Saul was a Type A personality and a Marine. He was not only accustomed to being in charge, but taking charge when things weren't going right. If he thought the canoe was going even a little smidge off course and might go to the banks, he sometimes had a propensity to jump in and correct course himself, versus instructing the boys on how to do so.

Second, Carson was faced with the reality that for as smooth-talking as he could be, not everyone would follow him so readily, especially on such a boring adventure like canoeing. So he was yelling at the others almost as much as Saul was. Difference was, the boys would listen to Saul, or they were more inclined to listen to Saul. They didn't listen to Carson, which only made him upset, and then it all went downhill from there.

Third, the boys as a whole were more interested in raiding the other canoes and throwing things at them as they went by. This earned them another stern talking to from Saul.

Fourth, on the rare occasion that they could get the boys to settle down, pay attention, and row, they lacked the coordination to both go straight and go straight quickly. If Saul sat in the back to steer, they had to put Tommen and Randall on opposite sides in order to balance out not only the weight, but the power. Randall had quite a bit of power when he cared to use it, but it only came in short bursts, and on his timing.

So canoeing was pretty much a bust. Even other cabins reported boredom and frustration. Kayaking on Tuesday, however, proved to be much faster, and much more fun. Or it was, until the mean old counselors had to break up the kayak jousting and keep all the kids moving down the river. It also proved to be more difficult to control the boys since they were each in their own kayak. If two or more decided to go and raid the girls' kayaks or otherwise cause some mischief, Saul and Tommen got separated, and it was hell both trying to maneuver among the other campers, dodge common river obstacles like logs and rocks, corral the troublesome boys, and then get them back to the general group in some semblance of order.

And then there was the part where the boys would randomly head to shore so they could poop in the grass. Most of them admitted to peeing in their kayaks — making Tommen almost throw up — or in the water, but pooping they had to do on shore. Tommen would concede the point that there weren't exactly luxury public bathrooms — or even portajohns — around every bend in the river, and yet, he had to explain to them that they couldn't just poop in the tall grass. At the very least, go inland a little more and find a tree. It was just public decency, especially with the girls present.

As would be the norm for the week, they reached their landing destination where Pam and the others were just finishing up dinner. Shireen set out paper plates and plastic utensils while Wallace set out the free-for-all cold dinner items, salad and so forth. Pam and Mark huddled conspiratorially over the grill, turning this and that, everything wrapped in tin foil.

The landing did thankfully have running water and restrooms so no one had to pee or poop in the bushes, and they could all wash their hands with real soap instead of just hand sanitizer. Tommen still remembered life in the little cabin, how dirty it could be, and the lengths they went to in order to keep clean, or what passed as clean for the time period. He was always thankful for the invention of plumbing, toilets, and soap.

"I think today went well," Saul observed mildly as he pulled on his shirt. "At least no one got smacked in the face with a paddle."

"Another horror story from years past?" Tommen wondered.

"Something like that."

"So why am I hearing all these horror stories from years past, and yet not seeing much evidence of it? I mean, you keep saying that this is a really tame year. I'm beginning to wonder if you're just bull—pulling my leg and trying to scare me."

"No, not at all. Stuff happens, and this really is a tame year. With two of us and only five campers, it hasn't been too bad. Normally we have eight or ten campers like everyone else. Then things get fun. Just wait until the older kids show up."

At the beginning of the camp, Tommen might have felt uneasy about his statement. Now, though, he was starting to question whether Saul really was bullshitting him. There was a difference of opinion when it came to a Drill Sargent and the average American. There was Tommen's version of clean when it came to his room, and there was his dad's version of clean. Maybe this was the same difference of opinion. Saul, a Marine, accustomed to having things, if not his way, then *the* way. There was an order and a rule and a regimen to be followed. Kids did not follow orders or rules or regimens unless they were screamed at. Tommen was a little more flexible and willing to let a little mischief happen, provided it was in good taste and no one got hurt.

But then again, he had seen some pretty wily antics from their boys that none of the other cabins seemed to engage in, like the attempt at a food fight at dinner. But whether that warranted the title of "prison cabin" he wasn't really convinced. If they were running the prison cabin, he would have expected to see theft, assault, attempted murder, attempted rape...was it really that obvious his dad was a cop? Fuck, these were eight year old boys, not tiny gangsters.

Although, they could be. Tommen still couldn't shake the feeling that he was looking at himself in a way, and that when the older kids came, it might be too much.

Was that how his dad felt whenever he went on a call for a domestic? When he saw the drunk asshole and his black and blue wife, was he truly, objectively removed from the situation, or did he see only his past life? Did he think that by stopping these assaults that he was somehow atoning for his own crimes, saving someone's wife as no one had saved his, or did he somehow wish that someone had been there to stop him way back when? What went through his mind when he was reminded of his past?

"You dig your hole any deeper, you'll be thinking in China," Pam said when he went back for seconds.

"What?" Tommen wondered, snapping back to reality.

"You always seem deep in thought. Dig that hole a little deeper, you'll be in China."

"Oh. No, I think I have a little ways to go before I get there."

"Good to hear. So what are you thinking about? Can't be anything good if it bothers you at every meal."

"Nothing. Just...stuff."

"Nothing and something are two very different things. You don't have to tell me if you don't want, but if your deep thoughts are food-related, well, if you leave the table hungry, it's your own dang fault."

Tommen grinned. "That much I know. You're too good to us."

She just shrugged. "I know. You heathens don't deserve such luxuries." She grinned as she said it. "Now go on, and make sure those boys don't cause too much of a ruckus. I don't need any more mice in my kitchen."

That much was for certain. The boys could go out and spend hours trying to catch mice, snakes, grasshoppers, anything they could get their grubby little hands on. Try to get them to help put the kayaks and other water gear away? Forget it. Might as well enter the greased pig competition; he'd have an easier and better time catching the pig.

The ride back to camp was quiet, or maybe he just fell asleep. Either way, they made it back without incident.

"Wake up, Sunshine," Saul said, shaking him awake.

Tommen jolted awake, initially confused. Beside him, Saul was reading his book. Elsewhere in the bus, the kids were slowly being woken up by the counselors which started a chain reaction as the kids then woke each other up. Tommen yawned and tried to stretch, his range being sorely limited by the bus seats.

"How are you not exhausted?" Tommen wondered, twisting

another way to stretch.

Saul did not look up from his book. "Why would I be?"

Right. Marine. He could probably stay up for two days straight and only be a little sleepy. Tommen yawned again and looked around to see if any kids still needed waking. As the group came alive and the noise level increased, Saul bookmarked his page and stuffed his book back in his waterproof bag.

"Good book?" Tommen asked.

"Decent."

They rolled into camp and the kids swarmed off the bus. Those that could be caught got wrangled into helping put some of the stuff away, mostly just the kayaks and paddles themselves. The rest of the water gear would be needed for the rest of the week, so that was left where it was, just spaced out a little so it would dry.

"All right!" Mr. Wilson called. "Head back to your cabins, get changed and cleaned up a little, then we're going to have our campfire!"

Because what better thing to do than give kids a nap, then an exciting activity, then more sugar, right before sending them to bed? Of course, they'd been doing the same thing for the last two and a half weeks, and the kids went to bed pretty well. It was the counselors that probably shouldn't have the sugar, and Tommen began to question the wisdom of his nap.

Tommen enjoyed the campfires, actually. He might have enjoyed them more if it could be a more peaceful endeavor—calmly walking around the fire instead of running; patiently waiting for the graham cracker, chocolate, and marshmallow, rather than pushing, shoving, and yelling; telling ghost stories with good English and without the laughter, interruptions, and weird interpretations; singing the campfire songs as they were meant to be sung, without yelling, improvised verses, and interpretive dance which Tommen suspected would only get raunchier when the older kids arrived.

As it was, however, it was just camp life. He still questioned whether it was possible for him to drop out of the counselor role into the camper role, but decided that even if he could, he wouldn't. Everyone here would know him, and they would probably think him a selfish coward. When he expressed his thoughts to Becky later on—awake still only because of his nap—she agreed.

"Yes, that would make you a selfish coward," she said. "But why aren't you sure you can do the second camp? It sounds like you're having a ton of fun. I want to come up and be a camper now. You should be proud of my self-control to not break in there right now."

"That could be interpreted multiple ways," he replied smartly.

"Ha ha, very funny. Answer the question."

"I don't know, it's just...I feel like I'd be looking at myself, what I would have been if I hadn't straightened up."

"You mean from Ryan."

"Yeah."

"Well, I guess I can see how you might feel that way, but I would have to wonder...why? I mean, you're not that way. You could have been, but you're not. Don't dwell on the things that might have been, especially if things have turned out for the better. In all reality, would you rather have me beside you, or some jail inmate who's going to rape you in your sleep?"

If I had the choice, I'd rather be raped by you. Or, you know, the sort of roleplay pretend rape. Not interested in actually being raped. Even for a guy, that's...disturbing. "You want the real answer?"

"I can guess. Humor me."

"You. Obviously."

"That's what I thought. Among other things."

"What other things?"

"Oh, nothing. Hey, so, you should call your dad."

"I text him from time to time. Why, is Laura moving in or something?"

"I don't know about that, but I heard he was in an accident."

"What do you mean?"

"I don't know; I don't really talk to him. There was something in the news, and then your dad's been home ever since. I saw him the other day; he was going to get the mail, but he was on crutches."

Well, fuck. On the other hand, if his dad hadn't called him, or if the twins hadn't come to get him, it probably wasn't anything really serious.

"He's probably asleep by now," Tommen said finally. "I'll call him in the morning before we leave."

"What's tomorrow's big adventure?"

"Tubing and boating. Thursday is sailing."

"Sounds like fun. Make sure to give a loud yo ho ho for me."

"Uh-huh. Sure thing."

"I'm serious."

"Good night, Becky."

He could almost hear her sigh. "Good night, Tommen. If I was there, I'd kiss you."

"I could say something to that, but I won't."

"Like what? If I was there, we'd be doing a lot more than kissing?"

"Bad Catholic Jew! Bad Catholic Jew!"

"Ha ha. Good night."

Her coyness, coupled with her absence and his overactive imagination made for some interesting dreams and even more interesting questions. For example, if her brand of dwarfism was disproportionate, did that affect only her limbs, or were other things affected, too? How careful would he have to be if he did end up sleeping with her?

His thoughts were broken by the chaos of the morning routine as the kids came alive and ready for the day. He and Saul herded them to the showers where Tommen stopped.

"Can you watch them for a second? I have to call my dad."

He fully expected some snide remark from Saul, but the man just shrugged and stepped in the shower room. Tommen called his dad, unsure if he would even be awake this early, given that he was apparently off work.

"Detective Forbes," came the sleepy reply; he probably hadn't even looked at the caller ID.

"Dad?"

"Hey, Tommen. How's camp?"

"Camp is fine. How are you?"

"Is Becky your girlfriend or your spy?"

"Does it matter? She said you were in an accident and on crutches. When did this happen? Why didn't you tell me?"

"What were you planning on doing? It's not serious." Tommen could hear him adjusting position, probably sitting up in bed. "It was a high-speed pursuit. I was heading toward the staging area, lights and sirens. I approach an intersection, slow down a little to make sure everyone sees me and stops. In the traffic, it looked like they had, but someone somewhere got impatient and slipped the line. I couldn't hit the brakes in time and ended up T-boning him in the intersection. It was just lucky that it happened to be our suspect."

"So you're not really hurt, or what?"

"Busted up my knee pretty good, a few cuts and bruises, but that's about it. I'm out of work for a couple weeks, but I can go back in limited capacity once I start physical therapy."

"I bet the department insurance guy loves you."

"Absolutely."

"So...is Laura helping at all? Like, I don't know, driving or whatever?"

"She's a paramedic, not an in-home nurse. She has the sense of humor and bedside manner of a paramedic. Suck it up, buttercup." Tommen laughed and his dad went on, "So, what's on the agenda for today?"

They talked for a few more minutes, at least until the showers opened up and Tommen had to jump in real quick while Saul took the boys to breakfast.

Okay, so his dad wasn't hurt that bad. Out for a couple weeks, then back again. Not good, but good enough. No evil plots or schemes or anything within the realm of Time, just a bad guy trying to outrun the cops and gets T-boned by a cop. Open and shut case.

"Everything all right?" Saul asked coolly when Tommen finally joined them at the table. He briefly explained the phone call and the accident. Saul just nodded. "That's good. Glad he's all right."

"Your dad's a cop?" Carson said, mouth hanging open.

"That's right, he is," Tommen told him. "He's a homicide detective."

"Whoa. That's so cool."

"I wanna be a cop when I grow up," Eric said very matter-of-fact.

"You're too stupid to be a cop," Randall laughed. "And you're in our cabin. Our cabin is practically jail. You can't be a cop if you've been in jail."

Tommen let Saul rebuke him, figuring it best to just keep his mouth shut lest he make some slip of the tongue. His dad was a cop, yes, but he'd also once been on the executioner's block, sent instead to rot in a dungeon. He'd spent his entire youth and teenage years in and out of jail for one thing or another. He'd beaten his wife and child, then murdered the man who killed them.

Some days, Tommen still couldn't wrap his head around it. His dad, his uncle, had been married once and had a child. What would he have been like if he'd stayed on that straight and narrow? What would life be like if he and Laura really did get any kind of serious? What if she did end up moving in at some point?

His thoughts lasted only through breakfast before the chaos began again. At least with the same routine every morning, they'd gotten pretty good at making sure the boys had everything and were ready to go in good time.

It was Wednesday, tubing day. It was one of the few days when the boys were allowed to be a little rowdy as they tried to push each other off the tube even as the driver of the boat, none other than Mr. Wilson, tried to fling them off with wild, sharp maneuvers.

"It gets better next time around," Saul promised him. "The older kids get the option of water skiing or wakeboarding instruction, too. Which includes counselors. If you're interested."

Tommen figured he had a healthy fear of death and other great bodily harm. The ironic part came when he considered all the things he'd done so far in his life; water skiing and wakeboarding seemed like pretty small potatoes, comparatively speaking. At the same time, when was he ever going to get another chance to go water skiing and wakeboarding and not have to pay for it out of his own pocket? Although, when he considered the answer, he wasn't sure he wanted to dwell on it.

He still had every intention of becoming a Scout, but that dream seemed to be slipping further and further away the more his training was delayed. Here he was, almost seven months—seven months!—into his Apprenticeship and he didn't even know what the inside of the Arena looked like. Giving some slack for the coup and the time that the Wheel was sealed off, it was only like a month, but in Base Time, it was seven months!

Although, really, part of it was his own fault. If he hadn't taken this job and dedicated three months of his life to the camp, he probably would have been to the Arena already. His dad had even agreed to take him, but only if he really wanted and wasn't already completely exhausted from camp. Problem was, camp was exhausting. Supposedly, training in the Arena was somehow even more exhausting.

His thoughts were interrupted as the boys began chanting for him and Saul to get on the tube. Saul pleaded his back and was excused. Judging by the long scar that ran from his upper back to his lower back, the greatest among all the scars on his back, Tommen could understand how there might be a little lingering pain associated with his injury. But as for Tommen, he had no real excuse why he couldn't go. He removed his hearing aids and entrusted them to Saul as he got in the water and swam out to the tube.

Truth be told, Tommen had never actually been tubing. He'd seen it from a distance, watched the boys now, but he himself had never been on a tube. This was West Virginia for goodness' sake.

These were the Appalachian Mountains, not the Great Lakes.

He had no idea what to expect, and he gripped the handholds as tight as he dared, determined not to be thrown off before they even got up to speed. Although the initial jolt was shocking enough that he almost let go anyway. Thank God for the magic of Time.

If the whole point had been just the ride and the speed, Tommen would have been totally cool with it. The speed, the wind, the spray of the water, it was fun and exhilarating, a thrilling sense of freedom and life. The sense of *life*, however, was only exemplified when Mr. Wilson got going really fast and started making the wild, sharp turns. The first time, Tommen managed to hold on only because his Predict kicked in and he could see, not only his projected path, but how that path changed depending on what little motions and maneuvers he did, shifting his weight and so forth.

The second turn was what got him. He saw his projected path, but there was no way he was getting out of this alive. Okay, literally, yes, he would live, but every projected path depicted a flip. Tommen took a breath and braced himself for it, feeling the tube hit the wake and go airborne, then upside down. He slipped into a Fast Band so he could view the flip more conscientiously and let go at a point where he wouldn't break both his legs as he hit the water.

When he went under, however, he was suddenly overwhelmed by a terrifying sense of déjà vu, and his mind went immediately to the night of the break-in when he'd pursued Rifun and Cassius and been thrown into freezing water, forced to swim for his life to shore. The water swirled around him and, for a moment, he wasn't sure which way was up. Panic clamped down on him even as he told himself to remain calm; this day was not that day. He was fine and no one was out to kill him.

Already his lungs were burning, but he managed to right himself just in time to see the hull of a boat bearing down on him, propeller on full. Real, legitimate fear coursing through him, he pushed and pulled and kicked himself out of the way, finally relaxing enough to stop fighting the lifejacket and let it simply carry him upwards to the surface.

His head broke the water, and he gasped for air. He looked around for the boat and started swimming toward it. As he got within ten feet, he could hear the boys talking and laughing excitedly, frequently pointing at him. He could also hear Saul yelling and griping about the other boat coming too close to where Tommen had just gone in the water.

"You didn't want to go again?" Mr. Wilson asked as Tommen hauled himself into the boat and took off the jacket.

"No, I'm good for now," Tommen said.

He'd had enough water excitement for one day, thank you. The ride itself had been great. The flipping and the going underwater and the flashback and the almost getting creamed by another boat, no, he'd had quite enough excitement for his first time out tubing.

After a few minutes, they did manage to talk Saul into getting on the tube, but with the stipulation that it would be slow and easy with no attempts at throwing him off; he would ride the rest of the way back, thank you very much. So he did. And they returned to the dock where the next group was waiting to go out.

"There, that wasn't so bad, was it?" Saul said, hiking out of the water.

"What are you talking about, you didn't even go!" Peter exclaimed. "You just did a pussy ride."

And so followed another foul language punishment from Saul. Then he sent the boys to the playground.

"So, what is it? Direct impact or what?" Tommen wondered as Saul pulled his shirt back on.

"Yes."

They headed to a pavilion adjacent the playground where water and lemonade had been made up and set out. "What exactly happened? I mean, I don't need to know details, but still. I won't lie, I'm curious."

"Everyone is curious about something." Saul got himself a cup of lemonade. He raised a brow when Tommen kept staring. "If I could tell you in three words, will you stop pestering me about it?"

"Sure."

Saul bunched a fist and raised a finger with each syllable. "I—E—D. Fuck off." Three fingers turned into one at the end of the last phrase.

"All I wanted to know," Tommen said, trying to sound nonthreatening.

"I doubt it. The Marines giveth, and the enemy taketh away. The trick is figuring out who your enemy is. Piece of advice: if you don't know who the enemy is, don't go into the fight."

"Do you regret going into the Marines?"

"I don't regret being a Marine. I regret the circumstances that led up to me joining, and I regret the circumstances that led to my injury, but I don't regret being a Marine."

"Oh."

Before either could say more, they were alerted to the presence of a playground fight as Carson and Randall tried to bully a couple other kids off some spinning merry-go-round object, Louis and Peter tried to force their way onto a couple swings, and Eric refused to let other kids go down the slide. Whether they coordinated all of this or whether it was just a huge coincidence was beyond Tommen. At any rate, it took a few minutes to get all the boys wrangled and out of the playground.

They'd no sooner done that than the clouds turned dark and it began to rain. There were whines and cries of protest as everyone ran to the pavilion.

Well, such was the weather in the mountains. Without looking at a current radar, sometimes it did happen just that fast as the mountains obscured the view of the distant sky.

"It's just a little water," Randall scoffed, walking toward the playground. "We've been in water all day. You guys are such a bunch of babies."

"You ran here just as fast as anyone else!" Carson informed him.

"Enough!" Saul cut in before they could start arguing. "Randall, come back here. We're going to wait for Mr. Wilson to return and figure it out from here if this rain doesn't clear up."

At the beginning of the camp, Randall probably would have said 'make me' and made Saul work for it. Two and a half weeks in, however, Randall was more inclined to obey Saul, seeing how he wasn't exactly a pushover.

Tommen, however, was not so respected or feared. If he tried to pull that, there was about a 70/30 chance favoring Randall saying 'make me' and then making Tommen work for it. The only reason Tommen would be able to pull it off would be his use of Time, and that was divided equally between Randall's perpetual smell and the fact that he was no lightweight. Tommen could move him, but only when he wasn't putting up a fight; the only way he could (legally) ensure that was by using Time.

Mr. Wilson and his current group of girls returned, all of them whining that they hadn't gotten to go tubing and they wanted to go, it wasn't fair, and so on and so forth.

"Okay, guys, we're going to have to cut this one short," he reported reluctantly. "Other boaters have told me that there's a bigger system coming this way, and we all spotted lightning out there, so it's a no-go. Everyone needs to help pick up; the faster we can get everything packed up, the faster we can get going back to camp where we'll have open free time until dinner."

The thought of cleaning up everything in the rain was less than appealing, but it had to be done. In order to keep everyone motivated, the buses were locked until everything was picked up, that way no one could sneak on and hide and shirk responsibility. Didn't help anyone's mood, however, when they finally got on, soaked more from the rain than the water in the lake.

"So what are we supposed to do when we get back to camp?" Randall whined.

"It's open free time," Saul told him. "What do you want to do?"

"Is it raining at camp?" Louis wondered.

"I don't know; we'll find out when we get there."

Indeed, when they returned to camp, they found it was raining even harder than it had been at the lake, and the thunder and lightning seemed to be constant. Such storms usually passed quickly as they broke around the mountains, but that didn't make it any less of a nuisance in the present moment.

There was a lot of yelling and screaming as the campers and counselors made mad dashes to their respective cabins, dragging all their gear from the day with them. Anyone who had gotten dry on the ride back soon found themselves soaked again.

"Everyone got their stuff?" Saul asked once he got the door closed after losing it once to a wind that ripped it out of his hand.

Everyone looked around at their stuff and murmured assent.

"Well this is dumb," Randall said. Tommen was growing weary of hearing his voice, especially on the occasions that the little boy thought that by speaking loud that he was being tough. "What kind of stuff are we supposed to do now? We can't even go outside."

"There's the main hall," Tommen suggested. "If we move quick and are the first ones there, we can move tables and use part of it as a basketball court or something."

"I hate basketball."

"It's not just about what you want," Saul informed him. "Does anyone else want to play basketball?"

After a minute or uncertain silence, Eric spoke up. "I don't really want to play basketball, but I don't want to sit here in the cabin, either."

That comment got a consensus vote. Still, they waited a few minutes to see if the rain would let up at all. Once it got to what they thought was the lowest point, or the eye of the storm, they made for the main hall where most of the other cabins had already set up camp.

"I'm going to get something to eat," Tommen mentioned, breaking off from the group and heading for the kitchen where Pam and the others were busy rushing around, doing this and that.

Apparently, the campers and counselors weren't the only ones thrown off by the turn of events.

"Oh, Tommen, hi," Pam said, hardly looking at him. "What can I do for you?"

"I was just wondering if you had anything to snack on."

"Are you picky?" Her tone suggested hope that he wasn't. He shook his head. Relieved, she went to a cupboard and tossed him a snack packet of cheese snacks. "Will that work? We're a little behind on dinner."

"It's fine. Thank you."

Thing was, snacks were usually intended for children, a quick thing to toss in their lunch for school. On top of that, all foodstuffs were getting smaller in size and portion. So Tommen was able to upend the little snack packet and chomp all of the little squares down in about two bites before returning to the group.

"What's the verdict?" he wondered, sitting at the table across from Saul, noting that the only boy at the table was Louis who was waiting for Saul who was shuffling a deck of cards.

"Go Fish. Want to play?" Saul answered, fingers moving deftly like a magician to cut the deck and flip them back together.

"Where are the others?" Did he want to know the answer to that question?

"Playing Twister over there with some of the others, if you want to watch or join."

It was the last thing Tommen felt like doing. Mercifully, he was saved by the appearance of Mr. Wilson who summoned the counselors. Tommen had learned early on that when the counselors were summoned, he went in Saul's place. They met just inside the door of the main hall where the kids couldn't see them well.

"So, for all our studious tracking of the weather thus far, it looks like the system that's moving through is going to be dumping on us for the next couple days, which means that all the sailing and other outdoor activities for the rest of water week are canceled," Mr. Wilson reported. "We will still go to the nature center on Friday since that is an indoor activity."

"Do we have any sort of alternative for water week?" one counselor asked. "An afternoon is one thing, but a couple days?"

"I'm looking, believe me, but a lot of places want reservations for a group this size. I'm checking into other options, trust me. You guys are doing awesome in going with the flow and keeping things tight around here. I just need you to hold down the fort for this afternoon and evening, and hopefully, I'll have an answer tonight at the campfire or in the morning."

Well, there was no getting around it; rain was rain, and they hadn't planned for more than an afternoon or a day at the most. A couple days would drive everyone insane, looking for ways to entertain themselves and keep the kids out of trouble. Tommen returned to the table and waited for the card game to end before telling Saul the good news. As expected, he didn't see the news as good, but there was little he could do about it.

Becky gave him little sympathy about it either.

"Aw, you mean you don't get to go out in the warmth and sunshine and play in the water with tubes and water skis and pool noodles and all manner of fun water games without a care in the world? Aw, poor baby."

"Ha ha," he replied sarcastically. "Fun is only fun if it's fun. I have to keep an eye on five rowdy, mischievous boys. Believe me, that's not always fun."

"Believe me, I know. My parents are going out to dinner for their anniversary on Friday, so I get stuck with all my bratty little nieces and nephews."

"All of them?"

"Well, six of them anyway, between four and eleven years old. It's going to be a nightmare. They don't listen to me even when others are home to make them listen; they're not going to listen any more now because no one is around to make them listen. I don't know. I'm thinking about just locking the front door so they can't get out, and locking myself in my room. Let them do whatever they want. I don't care. As long as I don't have to call an ambulance or anything."

"Now, now, don't go burning down your parents' new house."

"Okay, ambulance or fire department. Or the cops. I just don't want them here, and I especially don't want to babysit them."

"Are you at least getting paid?"

"Are you kidding? It's family. The only currency we deal in is favors, maybe an occasional trade. No, the most I'm going to get out of this is an IOU."

"That sucks."

"Tell me about it. Oh, hey, I saw your dad today. He looked a lot better. Off the crutches, using a cane now. Guess his accident wasn't that bad."

"I called him this morning. Didn't sound that bad."

And, really, it hadn't sounded too bad. The kicker came when he knew his dad was Band-healing himself, speeding up and condensing the Time that his body needed to heal itself. He was probably doing it slowly, in stages, so no one would get too suspicious, and they just brush it off as, "Oh, it probably wasn't that bad, then. Just a little bed rest and staying off the injured knee and all is well."

"Well, I know you've probably mastered staying up into the wee hours and getting up just as early, but I need to get some sleep," Becky said finally.

"You overestimate my abilities," Tommen replied. "But thank you. Good night."

"Good night, my love."

They were still kind of tiptoeing around that whole love thing, each trying to feel out the other without the benefit of tone, expressions, or body language. Maybe when he went home for a week between camps, then they would be able to better express themselves and figure out what was going on, where they stood, and where they were going, if they were going anywhere. It would be a wild week, that was for sure.

That was also assuming that he planned on coming back for the second camp. It seemed less and less likely with each passing day. He was exhausted; the boys were manageable at best; Saul seemed to hate him more every day with a growing passion. The activities were fun, yes, but they weren't meant for him. It sounded terrible, but he was a selfish person, and he wanted to do the things without being responsible for anyone but himself.

Am I my brother's keeper?

All around him, the cabin was dark and quiet as Saul and the boys slept. It was the only time of day when he felt any kind of relaxation or peace, and even that was hesitant as he was sure he could hear something walking around outside the cabin, whether it was Saul's spirit wolf, a bear, or any other creature, he didn't know and he wasn't about to go looking to find out.

Well, he'd made it past the halfway point, and there was only a week and a half left. Ten days. He could do this. He had no choice.

Chapter Fourteen
Peanut Butter

For all his optimism, and certainly not for lack of trying, Mr. Wilson was unable to come up with anything on such short notice to replace the sailing that was supposed to happen the next day, Thursday. The only good news he had was that the rain was supposed to clear up late Friday morning. That meant that they had to fill three more sessions with fun and excitement, but they only had one common building and a scattering of individual cabins with which to do it.

For some, this was easy, as a handful of counselors took it upon themselves to host short "classes" in one of four little side classrooms in the main hall, using whatever they had on hand or could scrounge up, from beading and sewing, to various paper crafts and origami. One counselor gave singing and voice lessons, another acting lessons.

It was great. For the other cabins, comprised mostly of girls. As for the rest of them, specifically Wolf Cabin, they had to be a little more creative. Once, Saul managed to talk the boys into going down to the swampy area and seeing if the river was back flowing again, which it was. They observed a bit of wildlife, but for the most part, it was just wet and rainy and muddy.

Tommen managed to squeeze a compliment out of Saul Thursday night when he suggested that the cabins have a fort-building competition. Each cabin had to use anything and everything in their own cabins to construct a fort that started where the door swung open. Forts were judged based on beauty—for the girls' sake—fortitude and attack resistance, interior layout, interior design, and overall creativity, with extra prizes awarded for most clever use of beds, most clever use of sleeping bags, and most clever use of some miscellaneous item. It was great fun, and Tommen at least had a good time. Up until they had to tear down the fort.

"But we built the fort; why can't we sleep in it?" Eric wondered, echoing pretty much everyone's thoughts.

"What are you going to sleep in or on?" Saul pointed out. "We already used the sleeping bags, mattresses, and pillows. Do you really want to sleep on this hard floor?" He knocked on the wood floor. "I don't."

He had a point, but it didn't make the work any more fun as they slowly began taking everything apart. Pillows were redistributed and sleeping bags sorted. Suitcases were moved and found their way back to the original owner. Finally, the beds and mattresses that went with them slid back into place against the walls of the cabin. By the time they got everything back the way it was, everyone was good and tired and ready to go to bed.

"Good idea," Saul said as the boys got all tucked in and snuggled in their sleeping bags, dropping out like flies into sleep.

"Huh?" Tommen turned to look at him as he removed his hearing aids. The charger was still holding up, but he wasn't sure how long it was going to last; hopefully it would make it to the end of camp.

Sighing, Saul got out of bed and approached so he didn't have to yell. "I said it was a good idea."

"Oh. Yeah, I mean, just trying...to help, I guess. Are you complimenting me?"

"Let's just say an outside source suggested that I not strangle you while you're here."

"Oh. Um, right. I...appreciate that. I think." Tommen paused, but spoke before Saul could say anything. "Why do you not like me? Is it because I asked about your back?"

"About that, because you're a pest."

"Okay. I mean, that's all you had to say about it. And I'm

sorry. I'm curious, I can't help it. And if it's something that's bad enough to make you—" Tommen looked around at the boys who all appeared to be sleeping. He lowered his voice anyway. "If it's bad enough to make you an asshole to everyone around you, I want to know what it is, what the story is."

Saul grinned, and for just a moment, Tommen was put in mind of, indeed, a wolf. "I was an asshole before I became a Marine. It's why I became a Marine. My people didn't particularly enjoy my company, but the Marines were glad to have me."

"Is that part of the circumstances that you regret for why you became a Marine?"

"Could be. Not like you'll ever know." Saul turned to leave.

Tommen shook his head. "God, you sound like my girlfriend."

Saul turned back in a cutesy pose and batted his eyelashes. "Aw, are you asking me out?"

"Not even close."

"Good. Because then I would actually have to strangle you."

He returned to his bed, slipped into his sleeping bag, and didn't say a word the rest of the night.

Meanwhile, Tommen was left alone to stare at the ceiling. He figured he must have slept at some point, because the next thing he knew, the alarm was going off. His first thought was that they had to hurry up and get ready so they could get going, but as his feet hit the floor, lightning flashed and everything came rushing back to him. Nope, no need to hurry today. Hell, the only reason they still had the alarm was so they could get to the showers before breakfast. Given the rain, was that even necessary at this point? Could they just take showers in the rain? Barring that, if they were just having free time, could they take showers after breakfast so they had that much less time to putter around?

Well, it didn't matter, he supposed. They were awake and heading for the showers anyway, then on to breakfast. Tommen still hadn't gotten over how great Pam's food was. Even on the rare occasion that he had to pilfer a peanut butter and jelly sandwich from her for a snack, he was amazed. Maybe it was just him, his mind playing tricks on him. Maybe it was just proof of the fact that all food tasted better when he didn't have to cook it himself. Either way, he picked up three good-sized pancakes, several sausage links, a large scoop of scrambled eggs, a small bowl of oatmeal, and a bit of fruit.

"You eat enough for three people in the third world, you know that?" Saul said. His tone made it difficult to judge his seriousness or sarcasm. "Two in the first world."

"Only three in the third, but two in the first?" Tommen wondered.

"First world or third world, we're all human. We're not so different."

It was the way he said it that got Tommen's attention, because it wasn't a predictable reaction. He didn't sound like the narrator for some poverty relief agency, trying to evoke awful emotions that could only be quelled by sending nineteen dollars a month. He didn't sound like the actual humanitarian workers who dealt with the tragedies of starvation but also the joy of bringing food and medicine. He didn't sound like some uncaring asshole who believed that industrialization and so-called progress would somehow raise the impoverished to the upper crust of the first world.

No, Saul's tone was more...childish, if Tommen had to pick a word. He sounded like a child who was taking a real issue and turning it into a game, something along the lines of, "I know something you don't know, and I'll never ever ever never tell." It was both infuriating—both in the sense of that he would do such a thing in the first place, and also that he would pick such a topic—and yet alarming; Tommen could feel his paranoia alarms going off.

Whatever Micaiah said about Saul, there was still something off about him. Come to think of it, how had Cai cleared him without meeting him? Maybe the real Saul was a totally great guy—or a total asshole anyway, seeing how that appeared to be nothing new—but this Saul right here really was Rifun in Disguise.

Tommen took a bite of eggs before his mind did something stupid, like make him voice his suspicions aloud without the consent of his better judgment. He was getting better at that, keeping his mouth shut on certain occasions. Maybe it came from having Becky as a girlfriend.

This whole line of thought had taken hardly two seconds. Once he swallowed, Tommen simply shrugged and said, "Well, my dad commented once about how me being gone has cut the grocery bill in half."

"I'll bet it has."

Actually, his dad estimated that Tommen's appetite made up for roughly seventy percent of the grocery bill, and threatened to make Tommen buy his own food from now on, once he got home. Tommen replied that his dad need only to take him to the Food Court in the Wheel, and they wouldn't have to worry about a thing.

But that was neither here nor there. It was still raining outside, though it was forecast to clear up before lunch, which meant he and Saul only had to entertain the boys by themselves for one more session. After lunch, they would be heading to a nature and conservation center for an afternoon of educational fun, then return for dinner and a campfire, assuming they could get one going with how wet everything was. Personally, Tommen was just happy to finally be leaving camp at all, and going to the center was just a bonus, something that was planned where someone else would be doing the entertaining.

"So, who wants to do what this morning?" Saul asked, sounding about as excited as Tommen felt at the prospect of another open free time session.

"Let's build a fort!" Peter suggested immediately. "We have to use sticks and leaves and stuff, and we have to make it water tight."

"That's a shelter, idiot, not a fort," Randall said, Carson backing him up with a serious nod.

"Either way, it's an idea," Tommen said calmly. "Does anyone else have any suggestions?"

"Well, we—"

"Stacy? Stacy!"

Everyone looked around until their gaze settled on one of the girls' tables where one girl was gasping for air but finding little, and quickly turning blue. Her lips and face were puffy and her chin and throat looked almost like she had a small melon stuck there. Her counselor, Sarah, rushed around to her, catching the girl before she fell out of her seat onto the floor.

"Get Michelle!" Sarah shouted. "Call an ambulance!"

Even as she said it, she was rummaging around in the girl's pocket until she found an epi-pen. She stuck it in Stacy's leg. A second later, the girl began to breathe, but just barely.

Unsure if someone had already gone, Tommen took off out of the hall toward the nurse's office, using his long legs and a little bit of Time to shave seconds off his sprint. Even as he made for the door, Mark, one of the cooks, was on his way out, Michelle following closely behind.

"Sarah just gave her an epi-pen," Tommen reported, feeling awkward and useless.

"That's good," Michelle said wistfully. "Mark says Pam already called an ambulance."

When they returned to the main hall, the whole place was caught in a stunned, raptured silence. Tommen stopped at the edge of the ring of onlookers, unsure if he should go in and help. Aside from Sarah and the girl Stacy, Pam was there, phone in hand. Michelle was there, small medical bag at the ready, with Mark as her nurse. Saul was also among those gathered, springing into action like a true Marine and having probably not a little experience with field medicine—true field medicine, as in, using sticks and leaves and animal venom for wounds and ailments. Elsewhere, Mr. Wilson was off to the side door, on the phone, probably with the girl's parents.

The epi-pen did not last long, but Michelle had two more in her bag, and she stuck the girl just as soon as she showed signs of deterioration. Problem was, if Tommen could hear them correctly—which wasn't difficult, given how quiet everyone had become—she couldn't administer more than one, for a total of two, before the ambulance got there. If she was an adult, sure, but not in an eight year old child.

Mr. Wilson got off the phone and seemed to come to himself, quietly passing a word along that translated into, "Stop staring, and get the kids out of here."

It was the fault of all the counselors, really, for letting the kids stay and watch as long as they did. It was as much a spectacle to them as the kids; it was unusual and interesting and fascinating, and they wanted to see it, too. In the center, Tommen watched Saul stand and approach Jeremiah who nodded at something he said, albeit grudgingly. As Tommen gathered his boys, all looking on with open mouths, Jeremiah approached him.

"Saul wants you in there to help."

"Me?" Tommen asked dumbly.

"Just what he said. I'll take your boys."

He didn't say it as a kindly grandpa offering to give mom and dad a date night. He said it as the reluctant babysitter who had that one client who had kids who only saw discipline once a week when the babysitter came by, which was a fairly accurate assessment of the situation.

Still, Tommen did not argue, and he approached the group. Stacy was pale and shaking; even with the epi-pen, she still had significant swelling around her mouth and throat.

"What did you need me for?" Tommen hissed to Saul.

"Just in case we need an extra hand. Let Michelle direct, but do whatever you can to help."

Saul gave him a look then, and for a moment, Tommen was almost sure he saw Rifun staring back at him. At the same time, his words were as much a code to help as anything else. Tommen had no medical license, and his training amounted to whatever he found interesting when he perused his dad's EMR books. But he had other training that could help; it was the same training he'd used when he held his dad in his arms as he died.

"Stacy, your parents are going to meet you at the hospital, okay?" Mr. Wilson said, kneeling beside the girl and trying to appear nonthreatening. "The ambulance is almost here and they'll get you fixed up right."

The girl could barely breathe, much less nod, and she didn't say a word or give any indication that his words had the desired, comforting effect he'd hoped for.

Then the epi ran out a second time, and Tommen was quick to jump in with a Slow Band, pulling it tight around Stacy like a cocoon, making sure it was as Slow as he could possibly get it in order to minimize the time between her throat swelling shut and when help arrived.

"Tommen, go out and meet the ambulance," Mr. Wilson ordered.

He hesitated for half a second, but Saul just nodded. "I got it from here."

Tommen had good experience with taking over control and handing off control of Bands because of the bakery, but that was only when he and the other person were mutually experienced and ready for them. How did he hand one off to someone he didn't even know was a Timekeeper? Could he keep it going even as he walked away? He had virtually no experience with that.

Another thought entered his mind. What if Saul wasn't Rifun in Disguise? What if he wasn't a Timekeeper at all, or involved in Time in any way? What if he was just another guy, an asshole, true, but just another guy who did what most everyone did, just plodded through life trying to do the best he could? What if, by walking away, Tommen was condemning Stacy to death?

All of this crossed his mind in about the space of a second before he did as he was told, standing and going out to wait for the ambulance. He paced back and forth in front of the main hall, looking in occasionally to see if his Slow Band was holding. It didn't look like it, but neither did it look like Stacy was moving at all, struggling to breathe or otherwise.

He whirled around as the sound of sirens reached his ears. A moment later, a large white box pulled into the parking lot. He flagged them down and they pulled right up to the curb. Three medics jumped out. One grabbed a large bag, another started on the cot, and the third demanded to know who he was and the what the situation with the girl was.

"Second epi just ran out," Tommen reported.

"What is 'just'?" the medic demanded. "How long have you been out here? Three seconds, three minutes? I need specifics." It was like dealing with Saul, except as a medical professional. Even when they walked in the room, he was snapping at people. "Who are all these people? What are you doing here? If you are not essential and don't have a medical license, get out. Is this my patient?"

"Hi, Tony," Michelle sighed. "This is Stacy. Sarah tells me she has a severe allergy to peanut products."

They continued speaking, but Mr. Wilson took all the "unlicensed, non-essential people," which included Tommen, and shooed them out of the room. Looking back, Tommen couldn't see any evidence of any Band of any form, not that he would know what to look for beyond the standard Fast and Slow Bands from Time.

"Oh my God," Pam was saying. "Oh my God. I knew she had a peanut allergy, and I didn't think we put anything out this morning. I mean...I just..." Tears were streaming down her face.

"It's not your fault, Pam," Mr. Wilson told her, though the words sounded hollow. No one believed for a second that she would have done anything on purpose, but there was still the guilt of knowing that something happened under her charge, and it wasn't something simple like not putting enough salt on the potatoes.

Several agonizing minutes later, the medics emerged from the main hall. Stacy lay on the cot, able to breathe for the moment. Michelle accompanied them with all the comfort and ease of someone who probably worked with them on a regular basis during the rest of the year. Saul brought up the rear like the pack mule, carrying the bags and clipboards and whatever else, but doing so like a proper Marine, bending his back, digging in his heels, and moving with purpose, with no thoughts of whining or complaining.

"I called her parents," Mr. Wilson said, speaking to one of the medics who wasn't a dick. "They're going to meet you at the hospital." He handed them a folder. "These are her release forms and medical history that were provided to us."

The medic took the folder and briefly scanned through the papers. "All right, we'll get these to the hospital, too." He opened the side door and handed them to the asshole medic, then turned back to Mr. Wilson. "If there is nothing else you can give us, we'll be on our way."

"Wait! Here!" Sarah said, running up from the direction of her cabin. She had something in her hand that proved to be a stuffed dog. "She'll want this."

"We're moving!" Dick-medic said from inside the bus.

The non-dick medic took the stuffed dog, thanked Sarah, wished the rest of them well, then hopped in the driver's seat. Hardly three seconds later, the ambulance was pulling away. As soon as they passed the threshold between the parking lot and the road, lights came on and sirens were wailing.

The rest of the group just stood there in the rain, looking on like a bunch of idiots. After a minute, they wordlessly made a collective decision to move back into the main hall which was eerily empty.

"Okay," Mr. Wilson said quietly. "So, we're going to treat this like any other situation for any other emergency involving an ambulance or other emergency services. Counselor assistants will watch over their kids, keep them in the cabins, keep them calm, find something to do. Counselors and other staff are going to have a meeting. This time, there is no negotiating or substitutions." He looked at Saul when he said it. "My office, ten minutes."

Reluctantly, they went their separate ways, Mr. Wilson toward his office, Michelle to her office, Pam and Mark to the kitchen as Pam tried to stifle more sobs, Saul and Tommen to the cabin.

"What should I tell them?" Tommen wondered.

"Your dad's a cop, isn't he?" Saul said, still in Marine mode. "You were just on a traumatic scene where someone could have died, and now you have to address the bystanders and possibly the media and public at large. What do you tell them?"

Everything and nothing, Tommen thought ruefully. No details, no speculations, no theories, no what ifs, none of that. All the fluff and no substance. For the general public, it bordered on infuriating. For a bunch of little kids, it was imperative. Tough wannabe gangsters and future criminals or not, they were still eight year old boys who had probably pissed their pants a little at the sight of someone suffocating in front of them.

Saul went off to talk to the other counselors while Tommen just retrieved the boys and marched them silently back to their cabin. Even Carson and Randall looked a little shaken, pale and slightly unsteady on their feet, like some people got at the sight of blood. When they got back to the cabin, Tommen had them take a pillow and sit on the floor in a circle.

"Is she going to be okay?"

"What happened?"

"Did she die?"

Tommen took a level breath. "She didn't die. She was breathing when she went away in the ambulance, and they have the drugs and the tools and the technology to make sure she'll recover." He hoped he sounded reassuring.

"What happened?" Eric wondered.

"Well, from what I understand, she has a peanut allergy. Somehow, a peanut product got mixed in with her food, and she had an allergic reaction."

"What's an allergy?" Louis wondered innocently.

"Well..." He knew basically what an allergy was, but he didn't understand the technical terms of it. Actually, he had no idea how they worked. He shifted position and said finally, "You know how sometimes you get sick with a cold and you might stay out of school for a few days? Your nose gets runny, your throat gets sore, and you just feel really crummy?" Nods. "Well, colds are caused by germs, foreign bodies which can hurt you. But your body has a defense against the germs called antibodies. When you get sick, your body is working to fight off the germs, and that's when you get sick." He was pretty sure only about half of this was actually true, even in a mild sense. "Stacy's body treats peanuts the same way. It thinks peanuts are foreign germs come to harm her, so it attacks. Just like a cold where your nose runs and your throat hurts, allergies cause her throat to swell up."

That was a bad explanation and he knew it. Fortunately, he was only trying to explain it to eight year olds and not some medical professional or med student or something, someone who would be able to call bullshit.

"So a cold is like an allergy to germs?" Carson said.

"Yeah, you might say that."

"My mom says that you can't get the same cold twice," Peter chimed in. "But allergies don't go away, do they?"

"Are the peanuts in the peanut butter here the same as the peanuts in the peanut butter at the grocery store right now?" His argument was slipping, but his fudge worked. He shifted position again. "The point is, she is alive and in good hands, on her way to the hospital and some good doctors. They'll get her fixed up. Now then, Mr. Wilson wants us to stay in our cabins for the time being. So, what do we want to do?"

Thankfully, the counselor and staff meeting didn't take very long, and Tommen was saved from having to keep the kids entertained all afternoon. Still, he told the boys to be good for a few minutes while he followed Saul's prompting to step outside.

"What's the verdict?" he asked.

"Got a call from Stacy's mom. She's doing well, or better anyway. She won't be coming back to camp," Saul reported.

"That's good, though, that she's all right."

"Yeah, well, Daddy Dearest is threatening to sue the camp and whatnot for unsafe conditions and call the Health Department and all this other bullshit. Anyway, their problem, not mine."

"Is Pam sticking around?"

"Hard to say. Jerry wants her to stay, but she's going to be the next one in an ambulance if she gives herself an aneurysm with all her fretting. Once again, not my problem."

"Then what is your problem, or our problem? What do we do now?"

"Well, we're going to have lunch. Jerry is going to talk to the kids, give a little speech, give some reassurances, that sort of thing. Then we're going to head off to the nature center just like we planned, but maybe a little late." Saul shrugged. "The show must go on. Just like when Tanner got sent home and Jimmy got sent off, it's a terrible thing, but we got eighty more kids that we have to all deal with and do something with. We can't just sit around in a pool of our own tears. Cry a river, build a bridge, and move on."

"I think the phrase you're looking for is 'get over it,'" Tommen mentioned. "All right, so we're heading to lunch right now?"

"No, we still have a few hours of open free time. But we can let the boys out of the cabin if they want."

By this time, the rain had let up to a light mist, and the sun had managed to poke through the clouds a time or two. Of course that only served to illuminate the wet, muddy mess that the camp had become. The grass was soaked, and where there wasn't grass, there was mud, lots of it. One wrong step, and anyone would be soaked at least to their ankle; the smaller kids to their knees probably.

Tommen couldn't remember what they did to pass the time, and he pretty well tuned out Mr. Wilson as he gave the kids the nice speech. Stacy was fine. She'd had an allergic reaction. They should all be very safety conscious, even when it came to food, and never take allergies as a joke or as someone being stubborn or lame. Now they were going to eat lunch and head to the nature center to continue having fun. Just remember to be safe, and always know that the rules are in place for their protection. They didn't want to have to call an ambulance for anyone else for the rest of camp.

Pam was conspicuously absent from the kitchen, and the only thing the others would say was that she would be taking the rest of the day off. She lived not far from the camp, so she was going to go home to rest a while and gather herself. Tommen had his suspicions, but even if he did voice them, there was nothing he could do. Accidents happened, but that wouldn't help the guilt any, the thought that she'd screwed up and let something slip by that shouldn't have slipped by. Who knew what was going through her mind right now?

He took his tray back to the table.

Despite the counselors' best efforts at heading off the rumors and trying to keep the kids on track, as well as Mr. Wilson's official narrative of events, the incident at breakfast was the talk of the bus the whole way to the center, and the telephone game inevitably ensued. By the time they got off the bus, Stacy had been beaten up, held down, forced to eat peanut butter, then puffed up like a marshmallow and had to be forcibly stuffed in the ambulance. Where and how the story got so twisted was beyond Tommen. He did his best not to snicker at it; he found it funny and knew enough not to take it seriously, but laughing openly would only encourage the rumors, and it would be in otherwise bad taste.

They entered the nature center where a hostess greeted them. Mr. Wilson apologized for the delay and being late. She assured them there was no harm done—what else was she going to do? Berate them?—and began the tour.

The center was part traditional museum, part interactive museum, and part kids museum, which was where they ended up, and the kids were let go to run and play and touch and explore with little concern as to things breaking or, knowing this group, going missing. They talked about the overall environment, the trees and plant life of the Appalachians and specifically West Virginia. They talked about the insects and their benefits, much to the disgust of many of the girls. Saul and Tommen had to intervene frequently to hush the boys before they could make snide remarks. The group learned about the animals that abounded in the area, some that were endangered, and others that were extinct, both recently and eons ago. They learned about food chains and food webs, and the ubiquitous evil humans who destroyed everything they looked at. Well, more specifically—more politically correct, in Tommen's opinion—the evil colonial European and modern American humans who destroyed everything they looked at. Whatever.

They paused briefly for snacks before heading out on the nature trails that twisted and turned through vast acres surrounding the nature center.

"Just remember," Mr. Wilson said as a couple of the kids started complaining about being tired and other things, "next week is our hiking and camping week. So you better get used to it now."

His words did not help much, though Tommen noticed Carson was unusually quiet and lagging behind, not leading the pack with his cousin Randall. Tommen dropped back in the group to walk beside the boy who seemed much smaller than he remembered.

"Something wrong?" Tommen asked genially. "You've been looking forward to the hiking trip the last couple weeks. I'd think you'd be excited to be out and about now."

Carson shrugged. "I guess. I just..."

"What?"

"I don't feel good."

"Feel sick or what? Do we need to go back to the center to the bathroom?"

"No. I don't know. I'm okay."

"If you're sure, because we can turn back. I don't want you getting sick out here on the trail. We've already had one to deal with today, but it's a lot harder to get help out here."

"I'm fine."

"All right."

Tommen wasn't convinced. He slipped back into the main group and stood next to Saul at their next stop.

"Carson says he's not feeling good, but he doesn't want to go back to the center," he reported. "Just thought you should know."

"Duly noted," Saul acknowledged. "Personally, I'm not feeling too good myself, but I'd just as soon blame the food here. Damn vegans anyway."

Tommen snickered and turned his attention back to the host. Boys and girls had been split into teams in order to more effectively get through the trails. It was hard enough getting through with forty-three boys, never mind the counselors and Mr. Wilson.

Actually, Tommen rather enjoyed himself. He would have preferred to just be out on his own exploring and seeing what's up, but going in a group wasn't bad either. The host was knowledgeable and engaging, which was certainly a plus. Tommen had been on many a field trip where the host was bored, disinterested, and had no idea what they were even supposed to be talking about, never mind getting it correct.

The group got started late, so they ended late, and subsequently left the center late and got back to the camp—late. The cooks were more than happy for their late arrival since they weren't quite finished with dinner yet. Without Pam, they were scrambling to stay in order and get things ready and put out.

To buy time, they headed back to the cabin to offload anything they didn't need, then headed to the bathrooms to wash up. Carson still looked pretty pale, and he was certainly less talkative, despite Randall's repeated efforts at getting him to laugh and get into some mischief or other. Even when they finally got in the dinner line, he took almost no food.

"All right, Carson, what's up?" Tommen asked, taking the boy aside.

"Um, I don't feel so good," Carson said after a minute of shuffling his feet. "Can I just go back to the cabin and sleep?"

"Take your tray to the kitchen, then I'll take you back. And we'll make a stop at the bathrooms, too, just in case. All right?"

The boy nodded. As he took his tray back to the kitchen,

Tommen found Saul and explained things. Saul simply agreed and went back to his dinner.

"Do you feel like you need to throw up, or poop, or what?" Tommen inquired once he and Carson were out of the main hall.

"I have a headache and my belly hurts," the child reported.

"All right. Well, let's make a quick stop at the bathrooms."

They did. They stayed there for probably five minutes. All Tommen could think about during that time was that his stomach hurt, too, but from hunger. Carson needed to hurry up or else he was going to miss out on dinner.

Nothing happened, and soon they were on their way to the cabin, neither saying a word. Tommen opened the door and watched the eight year old scuttle in like a mouse and make for his bed. Once he was all settled in, Tommen made to leave and get the nurse, but Carson spoke first.

"You know that really icky feeling you get when you've done something wrong?"

Tommen was surprised the boy even knew what that sort of icky, guilty feeling felt like, considering some of his antics thus far. Still he nodded and said, "Yes, I do. Why?"

"I think that's why my tummy is upset."

"What do you mean?"

"I did it."

"Did what?"

Personally, Tommen was expecting him to say he wet the bed or soiled his pants; it was entirely feasible that he might be punished for it at home, given the way things stood for most of the boys in Wolf Cabin. What he wasn't expecting was, "I put peanut butter in her food."

"Carson, what are you saying?"

Instantly, the boy burst into tears. "I did it! I did it!"

Tommen wasn't sure if he should hug the boy or let him cry. Eventually, he just knelt and put a hand on his head. "Carson, what are you talking about? Carson, breathe. Just breathe. Calm down.

Now talk to me. What did you do?"

It took a minute for Carson to gather himself. Even when he did find his voice, he still spoke haltingly, voice ragged and coming in sobbing gasps.

"Randall—Randall said—he said that he was—tired of the other kids—picking on him—and calling him fat. He said that—the girls did it most. But he said—he knew how to—get back at them. He said he was going to—make one of them fat like him. I asked how because—he had no candy or sugar. He said that one of the girls—had an allergy to peanuts, and if we gave her some peanuts—then she would puff up—and get fat. Then she'd see how much—she liked it—being fat."

"Aw, shit," Tommen hissed, hardly caring that his audience was a child.

Carson went on, his words becoming harder and harder to understand as he blubbered his way through his confession. "Randall said—since Jimmy—was gone—I was the—next smallest person—so I had—to be the one—to do it. So I went—into the—kitchen—and—I—took—some—peanut butter. Then—at lunch—I put some—in—her food. I was—really—sneaky." He sniffed hard. "I—didn't—know—it—would—actually—hurt—her. I thought—it would be like—Randall said—that she would just—puff up—and be fat."

He burst into tears anew. It lasted only a second before he did finally get sick. Only Tommen's acute sense of Time saved him as he Banded and slipped out of the way.

"I didn't mean to!" Carson wailed. "It was supposed to—be—a—prank. To—to get—them—to stop—making fun of him. I didn't want—anyone—to get hurt!"

Tommen patted his head. "I know. I believe you. But someone did get hurt. Do you understand what you did?"

The boy sniffed and nodded. "I understand. Are you going to tell Mr. Wilson?"

"Carson, I have to. Because it's the right thing to do."

"But she's gonna—get better. I don't wanna leave camp!"

Tommen sighed and mulled over his words. "Carson, if we—and by 'we' I mean 'you'—don't tell the truth, Pam is going to be in a lot of trouble, because everyone thinks she's the one who put peanut butter in Stacy's food." Lie, but whatever. "She already blames herself. Do you want Pam to get in trouble for what you did?"

Carson looked away and mumbled, "No."

"Good. And before anything, I want to tell you that I am proud of you for telling the truth. Okay? Now then, you stay here, and I'll go get Mr. Wilson. Then you can tell him what you just told me. All right?"

The only thing Tommen could think as he headed first to the main hall, then to Mr. Wilson's office, was fuck, fuck, fuck, fuck, fuck. Oh, fuck. On the one hand, he was glad to hear that Pam wasn't at fault for letting something slip through her kitchen that wasn't supposed to. On the other hand, he was horrified by the prank that the boys had come up with. He wasn't even really angry at Carson, but Randall. Had Randall understood the real consequences of his idea? If he had, was he really that malicious? And how was it that he'd been so calm and cool about it for the rest of the day? Was he truly a serial killer in the making? A future hired hitman?

"Mr. Wilson?" Tommen asked, knocking on the door of his office.

"Yes, Tommen, come in," Mr. Wilson said, motioning him in. "I heard something about Carson not feeling well. How is he?"

"Well, that's what I want to talk to you about. Actually, maybe he should tell you himself."

Mr. Wilson raised a brow, but, seeing he would get no more from Tommen, followed him out of his office and toward Wolf Cabin. Carson was still in his sleeping bag, absently fiddling with some strings.

"Carson?" Mr. Wilson said, kneeling beside him. "Tommen says you have something to tell me."

Too exhausted to cry anymore, Carson simply mumbled his

way through the story again. Mr. Wilson listened patiently, not saying a word, though his expression became serious, even grave. Even after Carson was finished, tears streaming down his cheeks once more, Mr. Wilson said nothing for a long minute.

"I didn't know it would happen like that," Carson whimpered. "I promise I didn't want her to get hurt. I just did what Randall told me."

Mr. Wilson shifted position and looked at Tommen. "Get Saul to bring Randall here."

Tommen left the cabin and walked toward the main hall on numb legs. He went to Saul first, put a hand on his shoulder, leaned in and whispered, "Bring Randall to the cabin. Mr. Wilson wants to talk to him. See if you can't engage him in a little conversation about the incident this morning. Don't bring the others."

Saul just nodded but did not move immediately when Tommen turned and left. When he was halfway across the yard, he could hear Randall's obnoxious voice behind him, followed by the gentler murmur of Saul. Still, he did not give any indication that anything was amiss as he entered the cabin and went to stand beside Mr. Wilson who had dutifully cleaned up Carson's mess. A minute later, Saul and Randall entered the cabin.

"What's all this about?" Saul asked, cutting off whatever conversation he'd been having previously.

"I did it!" Carson blurted again. "I did it. I put the peanut butter in Stacy's food. But Randall told me to do it."

"You little—" Randall began, then checked himself. "No, I didn't!" He looked at Mr. Wilson. "Don't believe him!"

Mr. Wilson folded his arms. "Well, here's the thing. I do believe him. You know why? Because I know you two. You are our inseparable pair of partners in crime. I've even seen you fight before, but you've never ratted each other out like this. And he gains nothing by implicating you, because he's going home regardless, and in pointing a finger at you, I imagine he's about to lose a good friend. Therefore, I can only conclude that he's telling the truth."

"He's not! I never told him to do that!" Randall protested.

"So, we're stuck at a he-said, he-said," Saul mused. "Due to the nature of the incident, I'm inclined to send them both home regardless and let them fight it out there."

Mr. Wilson nodded. "Agreed." He looked at the boys. "I'll be calling your parents, and if possible, I'm going to have them come get you tonight. Pack your things and be ready to leave."

And that was that. Mr. Wilson left the cabin. Now it was Saul's turn to address the boys. "You heard him. I want your things packed and ready to go in ten minutes."

He left no room for argument, and the boys set to work. Saul looked at Tommen and gave a wordless motion to meet him outside. They stood on the porch.

"Started out with eight campers, now we're down to three. Is this normal?" Tommen wondered.

Saul shrugged. "More normal than you think, but very abnormal considering it's Randall and Carson who are at odds. But that's cabin and camper politics, which I'm not too concerned with."

"So, what do we do now?"

"Now we send those two home and hope we don't lose the last three before camp is over. I might ask Jerry if we can combine cabins with someone. Two counselors for three kids is a little excessive. Maybe you can finally get your transfer to another cabin."

Before either could say more, they heard a thump from inside, then wailing. Saul might have kicked in the door except it was dubious at best, and in doing so, they might be left without one for the rest of camp. So he settled for a violent shove, then all but launched himself at Randall who was pummeling a helpless Carson, using his sheer weight as leverage to keep the small boy down. Faster than what Tommen could comprehend all at once, Saul had Randall in a handcuff position and was sitting on him.

"Take Carson to Michelle," Saul ordered. "I'm going to deliver this one to Jerry. Their things can wait until their parents get here." He winced and paused as he tried to stand and something in his back caught or started to bother him. "I might join you in a minute."

As Tommen got Carson to his feet, he was struck by the similarity of the whole situation. Once upon a time, he was the little skinny kid getting beaten up and scraped off the floor, escorted to the nurse's office by a teacher or teacher's aide, heading to the principal's office after that. In those instances, he'd always thought the whole thing cruel and unusual and very unfair. Most often, they had been. He'd done nothing to ask for Tyler's cruelty. But now, maybe he was beginning to understand a little more of the situation from the other side of things, from the Good Samaritan's perspective.

He was forced to wonder, did the Good Samaritan ever get tired of scraping people out of ditches, or had he been "good" only that one time? Was his being "good" enough penance for his sin of being a Samaritan?

Chapter Fifteen
Strangers in the Shadows

Most people didn't give a rip one way or the other about her name or its irony. They just heard that she was Inuit, heard that her name was "Aklaq" but if they wanted they could call her Kayla, and left it at that. Anyone who saw her sign her name as Aklaq White Bear usually just assumed that the latter was the translation of the former, when in fact, it wasn't. "Aklaq" actually meant "grizzly bear." It actually came from how big and hairy she had been when she was born, or so her mother had liked to joke.

The "White Bear" part of her name came from her introduction into the Akari. The missionary who had come to their village had been very respectful of her culture and their traditions and beliefs. He said that God spoke through the things a person already knows in order to draw them closer to Him. To that end, if she wanted to find God, maybe she ought to follow the white bear and see where it leads. When she asked why follow the polar bear instead of the grizzly, as was her namesake, he simply smiled and explained that white was the color of purity and holiness. You can't find cleanliness by rooting around in the mud.

Well, she only said he was respectful of their beliefs. That didn't mean he fully understood them. Polar bears could be just as ferocious as grizzlies.

Long story short, it turned out that they were both right. She thought he'd simply been linguistically mistaken when he referenced a white bear instead of the polar bear specifically. What she ended up finding was an albino grizzly. That grizzly led her to Time, which in turn led her to Micaiah, which led them to the Akari and the Author.

Was that the same as finding God? She didn't know.

Ever since then, she'd seen the white bear only sporadically, sometimes going years or even decades between sightings. Her albino grizzly didn't follow her around like Saul's wolf did. But then, wolves were pack. Grizzlies were decidedly more solitary.

So she walked alone through the Akarin fortress. It had become both more and less busy since the battle in the Wheel. Less busy, because their numbers had dwindled considerably with the number of those who had died. More busy, because after six months of being told to stay put in such uncertain times and circumstances—some of whom had long since overstayed their welcome in their various areas and really needed to leave—everyone was ready to get going again with normal operations.

But "normal" around the Akarin fortress was less of a straight line and more like a fault line, winding and twisting and turning and ready to shift at a moment's notice. That's what happened when a person became hunted; he had to adapt and maneuver and change and, sometimes, just go with the flow of things.

No one had been pleased with the Hands' ruling that all practice and even mention of the Akari was to be banned, and differing opinions were boisterously voiced, or not so boisterously. Some thought they ought to take up arms again and launch their own coup, remind the Hands who had freed them and show just how powerful they really were. Others thought they should just meekly obey and wait for the storm to blow over; once the Hands saw that they were reasonably compliant and not trying to force the issue, they would calm down and let them walk freely again. Still some thought they should just ignore the Hands and carry on like normal, not provoking anything, but if they were apprehended or accosted, then unleash their power.

There were arguments back and forth on all sides, and there were variations of all opinions. Reportedly, things were no better in other Akari factions either, as some members slipped from one faction to another.

The problem that Kayla saw was that because of the extreme nature of the order, it had the potential to divide the factions to a point where every group would be considered an extreme. Before, every faction had its fighters, had its caregivers, had its pacifists, had its whatever. But as everyone came to a different "right" solution to their current predicament, they would seek out others who were of a mind until there was one single group of fighters, one single group of pacifists, and so on. There would be no middle ground to be found, an no unity among the Akari factions; they might as well have been completely separate groups and drop the facade that they were all acting under the same guidance of the Akari. After all, how could a group of militants be under the same banner as the pacifists? It would only destroy their credibility.

But there was a secondary problem to that. The Akari was not partial to any particular person or group; it operated under right and wrong and bringing everything together for good. So the fighters might have the right of way in one instance and use the Akari, but the pacifists might have the right of way in another situation. The Akari was as much a living thing as a vague concept, and it would choose when and how it would be used.

However, as the Cult of the Akari proved, even if they didn't realize it, the Akari wasn't the only player in town. It was the most powerful by far, but there were imitators out there. So even if the militants found that they couldn't use the Akari, they could certainly find something out there to bend to their will and advance their own agenda. Those who knew only Time wouldn't know the difference between the Akari and an impostor, which was why the Akari had been banned in the first place, because the Hands didn't realize that Rifun and Cassius were invoking an impostor, whatever they themselves seemed to believe.

Kayla finished her food and started for the stairs, always wishing that she could fly like the Iuri and float from floor to floor instead of having to climb up these blasted stairs. Portals wouldn't be bad either, but they didn't have that luxury. Portals acted like homing devices. As long as a portal was open, it could be traveled through, and not all travelers were kindly peddlers and merchants. If anyone had the strength and willpower, he could open a portal within a portal and walk into any part of the Wheel he wanted. Or he could just open a portal anywhere period. For the sake of privacy and security, the Akarin fortress only used portals to get in and out, but not within.

Well, just as well that she sometimes worked out alongside Micaiah. It had only been a recent thing, true, but now she found herself grateful for it. The trip up to the fifth floor was excruciating and, well, there were no overweight Akarin, put it that way. At least, none who were Generals and Cores, who routinely made trips to the Akarin fortress. There was no possible way a person could walk up and down these monstrous stairs and not lose at least some weight.

The fifth floor was where they kept the sensitive paperwork and information, such as current life files. Unlike the Time industry which allowed pretty much anyone to peruse someone's file and gain their present information, the Akarin restricted such information to officers only, and even then, they needed a good reason to go snooping. Kayla was not an officer. Like Micaiah, she was a Captain-trained Core.

The good news was that she was not after any records but hers and Micaiah's, which he had given her permission to do. More specifically, she was after information about their information, the new lives they were attempting to conjure up.

The paperwork was the hardest part because it was fairly generic paperwork that was meant to be used by a variety of species from a variety of cultures with a variety of values. Some of it they had skipped right over, while others they'd spent hours agonizing over. The hard part wasn't constructing the life they wanted to live, but the life they were saying that they had already lived. Micaiah could probably get away with saying he'd been the owner of a bakery for the last twelve years, but only if he wanted to say he was in his mid-thirties. If he wanted to say he was younger, he'd have to come up with something different. More than that, it would have to be plausibly verifiable. They had to pick a high school to graduate from for example, and then some gopher down in what was lovingly called the Hole would have to research said school, figure out what the diploma looked like for that school, and casually insert a few fake records into the system, if necessary, to make it look like they'd actually attended that school.

And that was just one tiny part of it. They also had to come up with a history of residence, credit history, job history, education, marriage records. It was exhausting, no matter how many times they'd already done it. The world was constantly changing, and they had to change with it. Gone were the days when an honest face and a piece of paper could get a man a job and a house. Now he had to prove who he was, where he was from, whose kid he was, and that his first-born child was really his.

"What's the wait time currently?" Kayla asked, turning in the stack of paperwork to the attendant.

"Due to the mess in the Wheel, both the coup and the subsequent ban, we're backed up pretty bad. You don't want to know the exact time," the attendant told her.

"Um, yes, I do. I may not like it, but I want to know."

"Two years."

"T-two years?" The normal wait time was two to six months.

"It is what it is. And the more complex the new life, the longer it's going to take. We're asking anyone who is able to stay where they are, to do just that."

Kayla shook her head. "No, we're long overdue for a change. Micaiah especially; he has to get out."

"Well, you can always stay in the fortress for a while, if the need is that great. Or, if you have the ability, we have the short form for places and cultures that don't require such extensive backgrounds and information."

Those worked well for places where computers and modern technology hadn't invaded yet, hardly effective in a world with the Internet in the palm of everyone's hand. At the same time, it might not hurt to look through it and see if they couldn't get away with it, at least for a short time. She took the paperwork, still a small novella compared to the Great American Novel that was the standard paperwork.

"What's the wait time on the short form?" she asked.

"Nine months to a year," the attendant replied.

Well, it was still an obscenely long time. Typically it was six to twelve weeks, used on Earth in case of emergency. But it was better than nothing. Before she could say anything, the attendant went on. "We do ask, especially in this backup, that you only submit one file so it doesn't get confused. Would you like this back?"

Kayla sighed. Two years was a long time to wait. Eventually she nodded and took back the previous paperwork, the stack that must have weighed ten pounds.

She got out into the hall and sat down, her paperwork sitting next to her, frustrated and exhausted. They didn't have time for this. As much as he wasn't about to admit it, Micaiah was too stressed, too exhausted, and too conspicuous to stay in Charleston. Running the bakery had been fine in its season, but things had changed too much. With the coup and the Time Trial and the loss of his leg, he could no longer put his heart in his work. According to all reports, he was much easier to deal with since they'd gotten back together, but she could see that it was largely short-lived.

The other day he'd come home from work — only about a ten-hour shift, easy compared to the fourteen or more hours he used to pull — and he'd been cranky, exhausted, and a little confused. He couldn't even say that anything had gone wrong really, just that it all felt so overwhelming suddenly. It didn't help that his stump had become agitated and swollen, but having her rub soothing cream on it had calmed him down some. Really, he just needed to get out from under everything. Whether that was more like a submarine surfacing and breaking the water, or a gopher burrowing its way deeper underground to safety, she couldn't be sure. All she knew was that they had to leave, and quickly.

Micaiah even knew what he'd wanted to do: he wanted to be a motorcycle mechanic who had his own shop and specialized in custom orders. He had the tools and the knowledge; the only thing he needed was official certification and a shop to work from.

Kayla had been less prepared for her new life and what she wanted to do. Her current run of interior designer and consultant had been an on-the-fly decision made years ago, driven as much by Micaiah's encouragement as both their naivete that thought that all it took was an eye for color and watching a lot of HGTV. What neither of them realized was that it also took a considerable amount of people skills, something she did not lack, but did not have in abundance either. Still, she'd gotten past the hump and the learning curve and did well for herself.

After twelve years, one might think she would have had all sorts of fantasies about what she wanted to do, but she'd discovered long ago that those fantasies were often the subject of daydreamers who worked for other people, or people generally unhappy with their lives. While she would like to get out of interior design, it wasn't a bad job, and she already worked for herself. She had no illusions about how great life would be if she called all the shots, and she didn't pine after some greener grass job on the other side of the fence. She simply did her job, paid the bills, and went on her merry way.

Well, she figured, if they did end up having kids, maybe she could just get some inconsequential interim job for a while until a pregnancy actually happened, then quit and be a stay-at-home mom. At the same time, how likely was that? Stay-at-home mom she could do, but there was no way she could just plod along at some dead-end job waiting for something to happen. She was extremely competitive, and a bit of a perfectionist. She couldn't just sit at some desk or on some counter, trying to keep her head down and stay right where she was. She would be a competitor, for hours, for wages, for good reviews, always looking on the up-and-up. If she was going to work, she was going to be the best darn worker any boss had ever seen. If she was going to stay at home, well, she wouldn't be sitting on the couch eating bonbons all day.

She smiled to herself. That attitude was much in evidence around the house now. She'd taken quite a bit of time while the twins were away to clean the house, get it organized, put everything back in its place, and start swapping out old, tired things for new things, everything from dishes to furniture. And, God help her, she was going to do something about that godawful paint job in the living room before they left.

The nice thing about the smaller stack of paperwork was that it didn't take as much to fill out, and she already had all the answers in the larger stack of paperwork. Didn't mean it didn't take a hell of a long time to fill out, certainly no less than an hour. Even when she was done, she didn't run back into the office and turn it in to the attendant. Today or tomorrow, it wouldn't make that big of a difference in the long run, and she still wanted to talk it over with Cai. The more detailed life was safer, but the shorter stack would see them out faster.

Of course, then she was faced with the daunting task of lugging all twenty pounds of paperwork back down the stairs. Well, she figured, she needed the workout anyway. Interior design had made her soft.

With the Akarin portals closing upon entry, and the fact that time passed normally in the fortress, portals had to be opened with some discretion. And, it seemed, with the new ban, she had to be even more careful. It wasn't like she could just open a portal in the middle of a crowded room and no one would notice because when she got back, it was like no time had passed at all.

So she chose to open a portal into the bedroom she and Micaiah shared. She stayed there just long enough to drop off the paperwork, then she opened a return portal and headed back into the fortress. This time she did not ascend an ungodly number of stairs, but remained on the first floor and headed to the recreational areas.

"Recreation" was actually a very broad term to describe the area. It was kind of like the Arena in the Wheel, where there were separate areas and each one was a controlled environment. That meant that, while each area was fully capable of being turned into, say, a soccer field, it was also useful for training and honing abilities without disturbing others outside the area.

But perhaps the most stunning feature of the recreational areas was that it was one place where the "creation" part of "recreation" was just a thought away. It was one of the places where the Akari flowed freely and was more easily manipulated. It still had a mind of its own, to be sure, but the rules were a little more pliable here.

Kayla did not even have to speak before the Akari reacted to her thoughts and the scenery began to change from a dull gray concrete box into open air and blue skies. She looked out across open tundra, ice spreading out in front of her as she left the last tree behind her. From here on out, there was only openness. She knew she should be shivering, succumbing to the cold in only a matter of minutes, but here she did not have to feel the cold if she did not want to.

She walked to the edge of the ice and looked out as a whale surfaced, spewing water everywhere from its *supuqtaġvik*, its blowhole, then retreating beneath the waves.

Aklaq came here sometimes when she get homesick. Part of her loved it, that she had only to think and she could see her home. Part of her hated it, because it was only home as she remembered it. And, ultimately, it was only an illusion anyway. She didn't have to feel the cold if she didn't want to. She could make it so the snow did not melt in her hands if she didn't want it to. At a whim, she could change anything and everything. Trees could grow to the edge of the ice, or all the ice could break apart into tiny islands.

The recreation area was simultaneously a wonderful and dangerous place to be. The power of creation was a treacherous thing. More than once, the topic had been brought up whether the recreation areas should be fixed, finite things. Some argued against that power of creation; others argued that it was the Akari which granted such power. Taking away the recreational areas would presume that they no longer trusted the Akari to act according to its own will. It had been known to refuse certain people or certain creations; it was an entity beyond them, and they shouldn't mess with it.

Times like this, standing on the ice, Aklaq was torn between the two. She loved seeing home. She hated being homesick.

"You humans are too emotional."

She turned. "I was hoping you would come."

The albino grizzly snorted indignantly. "I thought so."

"What happens now? What do we do?"

"Which 'we' are you referring to?"

"Micaiah and myself. What do we do? The wait list is excruciatingly long, and he has to get out soon."

"Why?"

"Because he's been in for too long. People will start to notice that he's not aging, assuming they haven't already. And the work and the wear is getting to be too much."

"Not bad enough, I think, if he's still there."

"So, you're saying we should stay?"

"Has he done any consulting lately?"

"He's mentioned something or someone called the Chandler who said something about war and candles and light and dark, but nothing about a course of action."

The white bear grunted. "Why do you humans always want everything mapped out for you? Do you not trust your instincts?"

"What do you mean?"

"The Author is all-powerful, but she gave you a sense of intuition to know generally what to do. For example, I don't need to consult the Author about when it's time to go into hibernation. I just know."

"So, you're saying we should just go with our gut?"

The bear sighed and rubbed at his muzzle with a huge paw, like a human pinching the bridge of his nose in exasperation. "I'm saying that you already know what to do. You just don't want to do it, so you pass it off as uncertainty or this or that."

Aklaq let out a breath. "Cai doesn't want to leave his brother."

"Something you already knew and didn't have to wake a sleeping grizzly to figure out."

She smiled and put her arms around him as far as she could, burying herself in his thick, white fur. "But you came anyway. And I'm glad."

The white bear grunted but did not immediately pull away. Even when he did, all he had to do was flex his shoulders a little and she slid off. "If you are quite done being sentimental, I have a den to return to."

She watched him walk across the ice and disappear into the trees. Once, a long time ago, he'd promised that he would always be there for her. It had been a grudging promise, probably saying it aloud only because the Author told him to. It wasn't that he wouldn't watch out for her, but that he wasn't, as he put it, as sentimental as a human. He was a bit like Micaiah in that regard; he would do his job with no pretense or emotional obsession. At the end of the day, a "thank you" would be sufficient, and that was the end of it.

She looked around at the ice again, the frigid water lapping at the edge of the ice and the floating pack ice beyond, the trees a good distance away behind her, and the open tundra that separated them. She was not cold, because this was not real. It was all an illusion. But perhaps, it was a message, too. A sort of meditative message.

Kayla clung to that hope as she allowed the vision to vanish and give way to the dull, concrete box. As the last of the ice faded, a calm, chilly breeze buffeted her face. She took a calming breath and nodded.

"Okay," she said aloud. "Okay. I get it. I'll just have to explain it to him and hope he understands."

She returned home again and grabbed the short form paperwork, but when she returned to the fifth floor, she did not turn it in. Rather, she requested a new stack, claiming she had made a mistake on the first. The attendant's expression was unreadable as he handed over a fresh stack of papers. Then she went back outside the office, found a good place to sit, and filled out the novella once more.

It was tiring work, even though she already had all the information, and her hand quickly cramped. It took her probably twice as long as the last stack of papers because of that, but what was a couple more hours compared to the year wait that inevitably followed?

"Are you certain these are the papers you want to turn in?" the attendant inquired when she handed them over. "With the backup, we're asking everyone to turn in the papers only once."

"I understand," Kayla told him. "Yes, I'm sure these are the papers I want to turn in."

"Very good. Current wait times are projected to be nine months to a year long. It may be shorter or longer, but you will be notified when everything is ready for you."

Kayla thanked him and left the office, suddenly assaulted by the all-too-familiar feeling of uncertainty. Had she filled out everything? Absolutely everything? Had she spelled everything correctly? What if something got misspelled? What if the researcher misread something and messed something up? What if technology changed and everything they received would become irrelevant anyway?

Well, there was nothing she could do about it now. The best she could do was square her shoulders and head back to the recreational area. Maybe this time she would actually do training of some form, get in her workout before Cai got home.

She closed the door to the area she claimed and looked around the dull concrete box. Well, better get to it, then, before her mind started to wander and the box reacted. Who knew what would happen then?

She'd no sooner considered this than something grabbed her from behind, one massive arm wrapping firmly around her, pinching her arms and crushing her chest. An enormous hand clamped down over her mouth, and might have broken some teeth out if she hadn't turned her head just a little so it rested in the cup of the hand.

Whether it was her stunned mind, her attacker playing some sick game, or the Akari itself lending a hand, she didn't know as a mirror appeared in front of her. Her assailant, if human, was a giant. He must have been eight feet tall and probably pushing five hundred pounds of sheer muscle.

"Be still," he hissed.

Kayla hadn't moved a muscle since he grabbed her.

"You were one of the ones who killed Cassius and the Bat and forced Rifun out of power."

If this was someone's idea of a joke, well, they had another thing coming. And yet, Kayla had a sinking feeling that this was not some weird, culturally-removed way of saying thank you.

"You got lucky once, but it will be a short-lived victory. As the Hands of Time bear down upon you, so will we."

Oddly enough, Kayla actually relaxed a little once the threats had been delivered. Things were much simpler when the lines were clear-cut. His grip on her mouth relaxed just enough that she could wiggle her head out to speak.

"And who is 'we'?" she asked predictably. "Are you part of the Cult?"

"Does it matter? Do I look like I'll tell? Putting a name to an assailant only unifies a cause against it. Keeping the killer in the shadows promotes fear."

"Terrorists, then. Are you human? Or trying to be? Because you're pretty big by human standards."

"I am a human, but not one of your puny species," the giant sneered.

"Okay. So, human, but a colonist human. Obviously, one of the giants. But the neat thing about a giant human is that he might have his strength, but he's not without his—"

Before she finished the sentence, Kayla lifted one leg and drove her heel as hard as she could back into the giant's knee. She felt the joint crack, break, fall backwards out of place. His whole body relaxed as he roared in pain, curling to grab and coddle his wounded joint. Kayla took the opportunity to wriggle from his grasp and turn on him, landing a solid uppercut to his jaw, snapping his head back.

She followed this with a swift double roundhouse. Or she tried, anyway. She got one kick in, but as she went for the second, he caught her foot.

She didn't wait to see what terrible thing he could or would do to her; it would have been nothing for him to have tightened his grasp when she blew out his knee and crushed her like a toothpick, but her gamble paid off. Now, though, with the element of surprise gone, she had only her skills, both physical and Akari.

She Akari-Banded before his grip got too tight around her ankle, then reached out to feel his body. Yes, he was human, no Disguise here. Were she a Borelian, she could have done any number of horrendous physical and mental tortures to him, keep him in suffering agony or kill him in a dozen different heinous ways. As it was, she did have the power to reach inside his body like that, to a very limited extent, though it was ethically questionable to engage in such things. But what she did have freely was the ability to manipulate everything outside his body. She did that now, creating a special type of Band and invoking Thermodynamics, raising the temperature, exciting the air molecules, sucking in the heat from the whole room.

Once his hands were good and sweaty, she was able to slip her foot free of his grasp, giving him another, much smaller kick as she released both Bands.

The giant stumbled back and fell hard to the ground, still roaring in pain, but nursing his wounded knee. Kayla walked over to him, giving him an equally hard kick to the ribs when he made another grab for her. When he still didn't learn, she landed a shot squarely on his bicep, making him howl. That was the wonderful thing about giants and bodybuilders, their muscles were bigger which meant the nerves were closer to the skin and easier to manipulate and send screaming. As she stood over him now, poised to deliver a secondary blow to his knee, she could see the surrender in his eyes.

" —weakness," she said. "Now then, let's try that again. Hi, I'm Aklaq White Bear."

"Tomos Cedarhand."

"Where are you from Tomos Cedarhand?"

"Sakaria II. Quadrant Three, Parsec Nine, Sector Two, System Twenty-Three, Planet Eleven."

"A colony planet."

"Yes."

"What faction are you with?"

"Soldiers of the Akari."

Kayla folded her arms. "Never heard of them."

When he did not answer immediately, she only had to threaten him with another blow to his knee and he spoke, saying, "A splinter group of the Cult, dedicated mercenaries to carry out the dirty deeds no one else wants to do, at the behest and in honor of Calis Cutthroat."

"Which allows Rifun to carry out subtler missions, but he can wash his hands of you at any time if he needed to," Kayla finished.

"That's right."

"Must not be very disciplined these days, if you're spilling your guts to me after such a superficial wound, comparatively speaking. I've seen men take their stories and secrets to the grave, even as they still kicked and screamed. And Rifun's big thing was never divulging his plans or anything that might come back to bite him."

"You Akarin threw everything into chaos," Tomos growled, glaring at her. "Rifun was a fool, but he kept everything together at least."

"So you're acting alone, is it? What, are you trying to win back some sort of favor by threatening me? What's the endgame here?"

For a minute, it appeared as though the giant wasn't going to answer. Then, "There is a power vacuum among the Soldiers, now that Cassius is dead. He who brings the best prize takes command. I was hoping to find your husband, but then I saw you. You were one of those who ruined everything, making you just as valuable, but if I took you, maybe I'd get a two-for-one."

Kayla forced herself not to react. "How did you get in here?"

The giant snorted. "Did you think Cassius kept all the information he gathered to himself? He showed hundreds, thousands, the tricks to getting into your little hideout here."

She took a breath, but could not hold her composure completely. "Eight months ago, there was an influx of new recruits. Some came from Doug, some came from other sources, most all of them from higher-ups." Her chest tightened. "But they were all spies."

Tomos shrugged. "All, most, some, doesn't matter really. What does matter is now, you people are training your own murderers in how to kill you. Isn't that wonderful?" When she did not react, he went on. "Who could they be? Is every new recruit a spy? What happens if you accuse someone who isn't a spy? You could be starting a whole new wave of paranoia. But you can't just let the spies run wild and learn all your deepest, darkest secrets. Oh, but who to trust? Were the higher-ups in on it? Were they duped? Were they double-agents? Are they Disguised, or true turncoats? How to tell?"

As he laughed, she kicked him in the face. It was more out of sheer anxiety than any show of intimidation.

"Next question," she said. "How do I know you're telling the truth and not out to just scare people and cause unnecessary paranoia?"

He was still reeling from the kick, but the smirk remained. "I'll leave that up to you. All you have on me is that I'm a colonist giant who attacked you in your own home. My motivation is all up to you. What remains to be seen is what you will do with me now that you have me."

That was an easy thing to do, regardless if the entire governing system of the Akarin fortress was corrupt. She simply took him to prison.

The prison wasn't normally talked about as it was a touchy subject. Some thought it was offensive and went against everything the Akari represented and what the Akarin stood for. Others thought it was a necessary evil, a way to deal with those who would not be persuaded by conventional means. On other days, it served well for those who attacked the Akarin outright.

The prison was located on a sub-floor, one of three. Actually, the second of three. The sub-floors were not easily gotten to, accessible only to those who knew of their existence and specially shown how to access them. It did not look like the Judgment Wing in the Wheel, but its effects on the individual were similar. It was dark, it was creepy, and there was a lingering odor of despair clinging to everything that stayed more than three minutes.

Kayla kept Tomos close, uncaring of his knee and other injuries. The warden studied them as they got closer. Kayla identified herself, then indicated Tomos.

"Calls himself Tomos Cedarhand," she reported and gave his celestial coordinates. "He assaulted me in the recreation area."

"Very good," the warden said. "How is this being handled?"

"Hold him for now. I have to discuss a few things with the Powers That Be."

"As you wish."

Unlike American courts where someone could be held for only a few days without being charged, prisoners of the Akarin could be held for over a year.

"And one more thing," Tomos said as the warden moved to take custody of him. "I believe one of Rifun and Cassius' favorite phrases, there at the end, was something along the lines of 'dropping like flies.' They used it often, usually in the same sentence as you and your dear husband."

The warden glanced at Kayla. She just nodded once, saying, "I'll be back for him. Eventually."

As soon as they disappeared, she turned and headed back down the corridor, found a quiet spot, and sat down against the wall to breathe.

Fuck. As much as she had grown to not like Tomos, what if he was telling the truth? He certainly had no good reason to lie. Cassius' deception was enough to ring the bells of paranoia, adding in all this would do nothing there. Except it might ruin any future recruiting, if every prospect was treated as a spy. More than that, were there other leaders who had been replaced by Rifun's minions in Disguise? Could there be real turncoats among them? Was there any way to analyze this logically without going down the Red Scare Road?

After a short time, forcing herself to just breathe and not think, she stood again and returned to the first floor. Well, she'd certainly gotten her workout, just not in the way she'd planned.

She returned home and collapsed onto the bed, burying her face in Micaiah's pillow. Oh, was it really too much to ask for a normal day anymore? He goes to work, she goes to work, they get home, have a nice meal at the dinner table, watch a movie, have sex, and go to bed? Sure, they'd had a few days like that, but there would never be enough of them as far as she was concerned.

God, they needed to get out of here. A year felt like an eternity.

"Kayla?"

She jerked awake and rolled over to see Micaiah standing in the doorway looking concerned.

"Are you okay?" he asked cautiously, moving to sit on the bed so he could remove his prosthetic, slipping it off easily, then laying down beside her.

Kayla sighed and shifted position. "Tell me about your day first."

He raised a brow, but obliged. "Well, not a whole lot happened, or nothing unusual anyway. Orders, customers, Kyle and Jenna fighting incessantly. If Tommen wasn't gone, I'd fire both of them."

"You could always fire both of them anyway and hire me."

"You already have a job, and we need full-time workers."

"You're looking to get out of baking, and I'm looking to get out of interior design. At least one of us wins."

He shook his head. "Nope. Can't do it."

"Well, you're no fun."

"Sorry, honey." He kissed her. "Love you, though. It was a

nice thought."

She laughed and grinned. "You have more sap in you than a maple tree."

"Must be my winning personality." She punched him in the shoulder. "Hey, now, watch it! Okay, okay, uncle. You win."

"Huh. Second time today. Although the giant put up more of a fight."

"Giant? You're not going around picking fights again, are you?"

"Not this time. This time, he found me."

As she explained the incident in the recreation area, she watched his expression and body language get darker and darker, as the desire to kill whoever had threatened his mate bubbled to the surface. This murderous rage was quelled slightly as she detailed how she'd gotten the better of the man who'd easily been two or three times her size.

"He said his name was Tomos Cedarhand, from Sakaria II," she said.

Micaiah frowned. "Heard of it, never looked into it. Sounds like a colony planet for giants and other weirdos."

"It is. But that's not the point. What is the point is what he told me once I finally got him down."

Chapter Sixteen
Ghosts of the Past

And Little Tony was never heard from again," Jeremiah finished, face sinister in the flickering firelight.

Eighty campers and staff members sat, rooted to their seats, staring at him as he finished up his ghost story, a tale of a young camper named Tony who'd begged to go exploring in the Deep Woods just down the valley. No one would let him, so he finally went off alone. It started out well as he found all sorts of things. But then things started to go wrong until he was dragged away by the ghosts that lived in Deep Woods. That was the short of it, anyway.

Tommen hadn't been scared by the story, but Jeremiah was a good storyteller, and no matter how weird or lame, Tommen could feel a few chills creeping down his spine.

"Okay, who's next?" Jeremiah said, finally breaking the stunned silence. He held up the Story-mallow—really it was some stuffed toy that looked like a marshmallow with a head and antennae—and faked out a few kids and campers before tossing it opposite the direction he was looking. Saul, who had been moderately passive thus far, jumped to life as the Story-mallow landed in his lap.

"Shit, now we're in for it," Tommen heard Wallace whisper to Pam somewhere behind him. She snickered.

"So, Saul, what spooky stories do you have for us?" Mr. Wilson prompted quizzically, though the look on his face mirrored what all the counselors were thinking. *Please don't scare the kids shitless.*

"I don't know," Saul said softly, sitting up and leaning on his elbows on his knees. "Have I ever told you guys the story of my wolf spirit, Yawi?"

"Ah, so he does have a name," Tommen said, prompting him to go on.

"Yawi is not a male. But neither is it a female. However, in the interest of story-telling and using pronouns, I will call Yawi a 'he.'" With that little morsel of information capturing everyone's attention, Saul shifted position to something he evidently perceived as being more comfortable.

"Most of you know I live on a reservation with my people. My tribe is called Krydik. We are not a large tribe; I don't think any of you have even heard of us. No matter, though.

"My people, like most Indians, love to tell stories, and there is one story that stands out here tonight. Now, whether you are atheist, Christian, Taoist, I don't care. But this is actually the creation story of my people, how man came to be, and it is not as nice as looking and seeing that all was good. It goes like this:

"In those days, the earth was empty, devoid of all people. The birds ruled the sky and the beasts ruled the land and the fish ruled the sea. But there were no people. Often it was the birds who warred with the beasts. Birds ruled the air, but they still needed trees to sleep in. The beasts thought them greedy and so fought to keep them away from their domain. One day, as Owl sat in his tree and looked over the land, Snake slithered up to the base of the tree and called for him. Owl turned and was ready to attack, but Snake said, 'Wait. Stop. I have not come to fight. Rather, I have come to make an offer. A bargain.'

" 'What bargain could you, Snake, a beast, make, that I would be interested in?' Owl asked.

" 'Birds and beasts have warred for generations,' Snake said. 'I propose a way to end the fighting.'

" 'And how is this?' Owl wondered, intrigued at the idea and certain the birds would win.

"Snake said, 'Let the birds make for themselves a warrior. And let the beasts make for themselves a warrior. They must be of the same type, beasts, as both birds and beasts share the land. But they cannot be animals as you or I. Let us have one year to form our warriors. Then they will fight. And whoever wins shall win, and be declared master of the land.' "

" 'How shall we fashion these warriors, to ensure they are equal but either is capable of winning?' Owl asked.

" 'Use your great wisdom, O Owl, and I will use my cunning,' Snake told him. 'When the time comes to fight, we shall each pick one to oversee the fight and ensure its fairness.' "

"Owl liked the sound of that, and he agreed, swooping out from the tree to tell all the birds of the forest and have them tell more birds until all birds of the world knew of the challenge. And so work began to form this new warrior, one who was strong, powerful, in a way that could not be matched. The beasts did the same.

"On the day the fight was to be held, the birds and beasts chose their mediators. Eagle stood for the birds, his keen eyes and discerning mind an asset to him and all the birds. For the beasts stood Wolf. His strength and calm demeanor were envied by the beasts.

"The birds and beasts had fashioned a warrior whom they called Man. However, only the beasts called their warrior Man. The birds took a different route and called their warrior Woman. Woman had dark skin and dark hair and blended well with the surrounding forest. Man had white skin and light hair as bright as the noon sun. But they were well-matched. When the mediators were satisfied that the conditions of the warriors had been met, the fight began.

"Man was strong and intelligent. He knew how to take the branches of trees and carve them into spears and bows with arrows, using rocks for tips, or grasses which he could light on fire. The beasts who had made him had given him the power from the land to use.

"Woman was swift and cunning. She could easily dodge the spears and arrows of Man, and knew how to turn his fire against him. But she had one distinct advantage, and that was the knowledge of the birds. See, the beasts only knew the land from below. They saw only what they saw in front of them. The birds, however, saw the land from above. They understood its nuances and intricacies, and they gave her the power of the land, the understanding of sky and earth, of plant and animal.

"The fight lasted six days and six nights. And on the seventh morning, Man ensnared Woman in a trap. The fight was supposed to end then, but the beasts had fashioned Man and so made him a beast as well. He was going to kill Woman and declare absolute victory for the beasts.

"At the last moment, however, Wolf stepped in. He defied his own kind, the beasts, and tore Man away from Woman so she could escape. Together, they chased Man out of the forest to the sea where he made a boat from wood and departed."

Saul paused for effect, looking around at the campers. It wasn't a ghost story per se, but it was still enthralling. He went on. "The beasts had created Man to dominate the land and all that dwelt upon it. The birds had created Woman to be part of the land and rule it lovingly. Seeing from above and using their wisdom, the birds had invoked a powerful force that dwelt within beasts, particularly in Wolf. Pack. Family. Wolf's instincts were to protect the pack, and the only way to ensure pack safety and survival is to protect the female, and so he did, even though that meant betraying his own kind.

"Wolf was shunned by the beasts for turning on them, but the birds wanted nothing to do with him either, for he was obviously not a bird, despite helping them to win the fight. So he went to Woman and vowed to protect her. He called her Krydik, Mother Leader, as in a wolf pack. In return, she gave him the name Yawi, Defender. And so it was that from that point on, all descendants of Yawi are sworn to protect the descendants of Krydik, of which I am one."

He leaned back and chuckled. "Sometimes, as the campers in my cabin know, when you go out in the early morning, you will find wolf tracks around our cabin. This is only Yawi, watching over me. You have no need to fear him, unless, of course, you try to threaten me. I have no control over what he does to you then."

With that, he tossed the Story-mallow to someone else.

"Holy shit, that was some story," Tommen said later once the boys were in bed and they stood on the cabin porch. "Like you said, definitely not looking out and saying everything was good." He looked at Saul. "Is that really what your people say?"

Saul shrugged. "Does it matter? If I can admit to it without you mocking me, then yes."

Ouch. Tommen flinched at that one. Still, he continued. "I've never heard of the Krydik."

"No, I wouldn't expect so. You might say we're not exactly a federally-recognized tribe."

"So it's a District Nine sort of thing."

There were two ways his comment could go. On the one hand, Saul might simply take it as a reference to the movie by the same name. Or, if he was part of Time, he might recognize it as the unofficial, unrecognized District designation for the Native American tribes in North America. Tommen had never heard of it until Kayla spoke of its existence, but if Saul was Native, he would probably know of it, assuming he was a Time Agent.

But Saul just shrugged. "I suppose."

Damn it. It was impossible to tell with a shitty reaction like that. Knowing Saul, he could have been acknowledging either aspect of the comment.

"If you don't mind my asking," Tommen went on, "what happened to Man after he was chased across the sea?"

Saul raised a brow, as if questioning his motives, but finally answered, "When Man arrived on the far shore, he was met by Snake. Snake did not take kindly to losing, especially when it was one of his own who had betrayed them. He instilled cold, murderous thoughts in Man, telling him that he was easily superior and should have won. Part of this came from his obvious physical superiority to Woman, that he was bigger, stronger, more intelligent, more able. Part of this came from his appearance. The challenge had been to create a warrior that was separate from the beasts and birds. Her dark skin had made her one of them, where his white skin was supposed to be noticed by all and help him stand apart.

"Generations passed. Woman, Krydik, had many children, and they spread far and wide over the land. They started their own families and their own tribes. Some remained loyal to Krydik and Yawi, while others fell away. Some even dared to cross the sea to find new lands. All who came from Krydik had dark skin and dark hair, and they respected the land.

"Man also had children, and they, too, spread far and wide over the land. But they were deceitful and self-righteous. They did not live with the land, but off it, and they forced others to work the land for them. They were driven especially by a burning hatred for Krydik and her kin. Most did not even know the origin of their hate, only that it was justified in their own eyes.

"One day, Man decided that he'd amassed enough of an army to go back and defeat Krydik once and for all, to claim his title as conqueror of the world, its land and beasts and especially the birds."

"Was this man's name Columbus?" Tommen interrupted.

Saul paused and shrugged again. "Stories are built upon stories. When Columbus and other explorers arrived from Europe, my people saw it as the return of Man, from a story we already knew. Up until that point, white-skinned men were the stuff of legend, and Man lived far across the sea, chased there by Krydik and Yawi. But here they were, and they were just as vicious as the stories said. Coincidence? I think not."

Tommen shifted position. "Let me ask you something else. Was everything you just said true? Or were you BSing everyone?"

"There are variations of the story, yes, but they are built around the same core truth."

"And what truth is that? White men are evil?"

Saul gave him a look. "Your greatest enemy is yourself. Man, Woman, two sides of the same coin. You've probably heard the same tired story about the Native elder telling his grandson about the two wolves."

"One is good, one is evil, and the one you feed is the one that wins?"

"Yeah, that one. Same basic principle." He looked out into the forest. "Man was created to be too powerful, capable of unspeakable atrocities. So he was set against himself, whether it is Man against Woman, or Man against himself. As long as he is divided, his evil can be controlled."

"You do know that there's a war or five going on, right? Nuclear war threats, suicide bombers, things like that?"

"And if Man, in all his imperfect glory, were to come together as a unified race, what do you think would happen? Would he be content to stay here on this lonely world? Or would he seek to go, conquer, kill, destroy? If, on some off chance, he found more life in the universe, do you think he would readily create an ethnologue and seek an alliance? Or would he capture and enslave, take them in for testing and experiments that are banned on animals? Be honest, Tommen, what do you think?"

We'd become just like the Borelians, Tommen thought ruefully. Out loud, he said, "I think the Marines weren't good to you."

"The Marines were great. It was the war that killed me."

"Ah. Saving that story for another night when you need to really scare the shit out of the kids?"

"Something like that, I suppose." He straightened, wincing in pain, and rolled his neck and shoulders. "At any rate, I think it's about time to go to bed, though at this point, I think sleep is optional."

He said it with resignation, as if he fully expected to not get sleep. Checking the time, Tommen saw that they still had the chance for about six hours. Before either of them could reach the door, however, Tommen said, "One more question. If Woman is the Krydik and other Native peoples, and Man is Columbus come with an army to subdue her, what do your people say about what happened next?"

Saul gave him a look that was impossible to read. "Some fought valiantly, either to death or enslavement. I don't need to remind you of that history. Some surrendered and were taken away anyway. Others fled to a spot where no man would touch, where they hoped they could live peacefully. Man and his armies pursued them there and conquered them, but found the land undesirable. So a compromise was reached. The Krydik could have their spit of land, and today it is the reservation. But if any of them stepped off that land, they would be treated the same as any other Native American." He paused. "Five centuries ago, that could mean death, rape, slavery, imprisonment. Today, well, things have improved a little. But the general sentiment remains."

"What general sentiment?"

"That we won. We found a place where we could survive and they couldn't. Man can't stand it."

Tommen had nothing to say to that, so he just followed Saul. As he reached for the doorknob, however, the damn thing fell off in his hand. Quick reflexes saved his toes, but the fact remained that the doorknob to the cabin had just fallen off. The door began to creep open with a chilly squeak. Saul sighed and pinched the bridge of his nose.

"The ghosts of the past just can't leave anything to rest."

"What's that supposed to mean?" Tommen wondered.

"Speaking of past wrongs stirs the ghosts to vengeance. Both Woman and Man are buried in this area, and I've disturbed them." He sighed as he bent to pick up the doorknob. "Keep an eye out for any more mischief in the coming days. The worse the wrong, the angrier the spirits become. And genocide is a pretty big wrong."

Saul managed to jerryrig the doorknob enough that the cabin door stayed closed, then he collapsed into his bed and fell asleep quickly. Tommen, meanwhile, lay awake—again—pondering everything he'd heard that night. Normally he couldn't care less about the ghost stories, and Native mythology was always interesting to listen to, a different take on the world. But he'd never actually met someone who believed in that mythology the same way someone might believe in Christianity or Islam. None of it was scientific, and it was barely historical, yet Saul still appeared to believe it, and not in a cultural aspect, but in a truly personal way. Maybe it was his way of coping with the horrors of war, returning to a time, even mythological, when things were simple and made sense. But even that didn't sound right, because he carried it deeper than that; it was part of him.

After a short time, Tommen heard Saul get up, saw his outline in the door as he went outside, finagling the doorknob so it wouldn't fall out again. But just before the door closed, Tommen saw something else. There, coming out of the woods, was a massive white wolf. It walked up to the cabin porch, its chin hovering over the railing. Saul walked fearlessly up to it, and, just before the door closed, he reached out and touched it.

By the next morning, Tommen had dismissed the whole encounter as a dream. They'd simply had their weird little chat, gone in, and went to bed. He knew for darn sure that Saul had been dead out as soon as he hit his sleeping bag. He himself had probably fallen asleep, but his active mind had dreamt up a continuation of his being awake, then conjured up some weird part about Saul going out to meet a white wolf. It all sounded very logical, up until the next morning when he looked over the porch railing and found massive pawprints leading right up to the porch, exactly as he'd seen the wolf do.

"Are you afraid?" Saul asked, apparently back to his chipper, sarcastic, graveyard sense of humor self. "As I said before, Yawi only attacks those who attack me."

"Right," Tommen said, moving off the porch toward the showers.

He might have thought on it more, but he had no time. It was the final week of camp, which meant it was the extended hiking trip. For the younger kids, it was only three days long, Tuesday, Wednesday, and Thursday, all projected to be excellent weather. Sunday and Monday, then, would be spent preparing the kids for that trip. They would learn how to set up a tent, how to hang their food so the bears didn't get it, how to fish, how to set traps, which berries were edible, all the fun stuff.

Truthfully, this was what Tommen had been looking forward

to the entire time at camp, a chance to get back to his own frontier roots—tents, sleeping bags, and small generators notwithstanding. He was even put in charge of showing the kids how to set up traps and snares. The kids were all excited for it, up until a few of them realized that it also meant killing the animal they trapped. Naturally, this sent the vegetarian cabin into a full-blown protest, but Tommen was having none of it.

"Fine," he said. "You don't want to eat meat? Then don't. I won't force you. But think of it this way: if any of your ancestors would have behaved the same way, they would have starved. You only get to be picky because modern life allows you to be both picky and wasteful. Quite frankly, I think your ancestors would be ashamed of you if they could see you today."

His last comment earned him a death glare from both the kids and their counselors, and a short scolding from Mr. Wilson. It was mostly for show, though, as the man secretly agreed with Tommen on principle, though he could have delivered the sentence with a little more tact, he said.

"It's a true thing," Saul said later on, when Tommen told him of the exchange. "Society enables such snobbery. Is it possible to live in the wild only on edible plants with no meat? It's possible, but more trouble than it's worth. A handful of berries is a handful of berries, and the bushes will be empty soon enough; a good elk will feed a man for weeks if he knows how to preserve and prepare it, every part of it."

"Vegetarian, old Indian word for bad hunter?" Tommen guessed.

"Something like that."

Before either could say more, someone started calling for Saul. The man turned and started off, Tommen trailing curiously behind.

The problem, as it happened, was that none of the buses or other camp vehicles were working. All of them decided to take a dump at the exact same time, or so it seemed.

"We've got a mechanic on the way," Mr. Wilson said, "but I

was hoping you might be able to take a quick look at them and see if it's just something simple."

Saul huffed a sigh and muttered something not in English. Probably blaming his vengeful spirits again, Tommen thought. Still, the Marine lifted the hoods on every vehicle and started his inspection. Once it became clear that it wasn't going to be a quick fix, Tommen crept away to go make sure the rest of the boys hadn't burned down the cabin.

Despite having three campers for two counselors, that was how things stayed. No more boys were brought in from other cabins, and Tommen was not transferred out to another cabin. But without Carson and Randall, theirs was no longer the prison cabin. Eric, Louis, and Peter were very well-behaved, within reason, and camp life went on with no real problems. So far, the last week of camp was shaping up to be the best week so far. Maybe he could make it through and come back for the second round.

He joined the group down at the campfire pit where they were learning about fire safety. More than just Smokey the Bear, Tommen could appreciate this instruction. Rather than telling the kids not to touch the fire or anything having to do with fire, the instructor was telling them how to do things correctly, how to correctly build the initial stick tepee, how to correctly start the fire, how to correctly move the sticks around in the fire, how to correctly add logs, how to correctly put out the fire, and so on.

"And you're probably going to tell us how to correctly roast the flesh of innocent animals, right?" one girl from the vegetarian cabin sneered at him.

"Well, as a matter of fact, yes," Tommen said calmly, saving the instructor. "Since you seem curious to know how it's done and recognize that it's smart for humans to cook their food prior to eating."

So, with the instructor's permission, Tommen did give a short lesson about cooking meat and fish over an open fire, how to secure the meat so it didn't fall in, how to tell when it was fully cooked, and how to add herbs and spices to make it more flavorful. By the time he was done, he was more than ready to go camping; he wasn't sure about anyone else, but he'd just made himself excited.

"Sounds like we have our own chef here with us," Saul observed dryly, walking up just as the group moved on to something else. His clothes had grease stains, but he was otherwise clean. "At least we won't have to worry about you wandering alone out there. Unless a bear finds you or something; then we might have to worry. But maybe not. You're pretty slim pickings."

"If we even get going," Tommen said. "Are the buses and things working now?"

Saul nodded. "They are."

"Undoing the mischief of your spirits?"

"Don't insult what you don't understand."

"Fine, fine. But let me ask you something. Why ask you to help if they had a mechanic on the way?"

For a moment, it looked like Saul wasn't going to answer. Then, "I was a mechanic in the Marines. Anything from small engines to diesel engines, I could repair it all. These things here are nothing."

"Oh. Sweet."

"It was a job. Come on, let's get the boys rounded up and washed up before dinner. No campfire tonight, that way everyone can be rested up for the early morning tomorrow."

"Makes sense."

"So, where are the boys?"

They found the three rascals in the class about poisonous plants, what they looked like, how to avoid them, and what to do in the event that someone came into contact with them — which basically amounted to, tell a grownup. Saul and Tommen waited patiently in the back of the room and watched as the instructor wrapped things up.

"Okay, boys, let's get all washed up before dinner," Saul told them as the kids jumped out of their seats. "Then we want to get to bed early so we're not dragging tomorrow morning. We don't want to be the last ones on the bus."

At the beginning of camp, the biggest taboo was being the last cabin on the bus. It meant they were slow, unprepared, and a bunch of other nasty things which the counselors had to quell before the name-calling got too extreme and hurtful. Now, though, at the end of camp, even the most adamant of campers didn't seem to care whether they were first or last on the bus. By this time, they were excited to go on the hike, but ready to go home, too.

They got the boys up to the bathrooms to wash their hands and get cleaned up. They were just preparing to leave when Mr. Wilson appeared and motioned for the two counselors.

"Everything all right?" Tommen wondered, afraid to know the answer.

"Dinner is going to be delayed a little bit," Mr. Wilson informed them levelly. "Some of the burners stopped working mysteriously, so Pam and her crew can't get everything cooking like they want. I asked them how long, and they think it'll be about another half hour to an hour before they're ready. If you want, you can hang out outside, get in some free time, or you can grab some of the cold plates they have set out; it's up to you."

Saul thanked him, and he moved on to the next group.

"More spirits?" Tommen wondered. When Saul glared at him, he added quickly, "It seems less like supernatural and more like a saboteur, at least to me."

"We're down to three campers. If someone was going to sabotage something, I'd think they might do it while they could still potentially blame Carson or Randall. So if it is a human saboteur, who do you think it would be?"

There were a number of answers Tommen might have put to that, but there were none that he could feasibly voice. Finally he shrugged. "I don't know. Maybe it isn't sabotage or your spirits, but just a huge coincidence that everything is taking a dump at the same time."

"I find that highly unlikely. And improbable."

"Considering some of the things I've seen and done, I can

agree. But maybe not all the way."

Saul grunted.

When the boys were finished washing up for dinner, Tommen and Saul took them to the main hall for some quiet table play, board games, cards, things that could be easily packed up, even if everyone protested when the call came to do so. Games were finished, winners were cheated their victory, all the usual complaints. Nevertheless, things got cleaned up and the campers and counselors settled down for dinner.

It would have been easy to just order pizza and have it delivered, but Pam the Master Chef came through once again. Apparently the biggest delay had been some of the toppings; they'd had to be slightly pre-cooked, but the burners weren't working, so everything got set back.

Not that Tommen cared. He took probably six different slices and devoured them all with just as much enthusiasm.

"You're going to fit right in next camp," Saul commented. "Pam told me once that we go through four times as much food in the older kids' camp as this one."

"I believe it. My dad told me that the grocery bill at home is decidedly lower since I've been here."

"What are we doing after dinner?" Eric interrupted.

"Well," Saul said thoughtfully, "I believe we're going to play a quick game, then head off to bed. No campfire tonight because we have to be up really early tomorrow."

"Oh. Do you know what the game is?"

"I think it's supposed to be a glow scavenger hunt."

The major difference between a glow scavenger hunt and regular scavenger hunt was that a glow hunt was done in the dark, and all the kids wore glowstick bracelets, necklaces, and whatever other concoctions they would come up with for the little things. Thankfully, being July, it wouldn't actually get completely dark. Darker, yes, because of the mountains, but not pitch black.

"What time are we leaving tomorrow?" Tommen wondered,

returning from a trip to the kitchen for seconds.

"Supposedly, seven o'clock." Tommen could hear the *yeah, right* in his voice. "We'll arrive at the trailhead around nine or so, and then we should be at the campsite by noon, just in time for lunch."

On a normal day, such a prospect would have sounded thrilling. Up early to go do some hiking through the mountains he loved? Yes, please. Up early, trying to wrangle a whole mess of children for a long bus ride and an even longer hiking trip? Oh, please, God, kill him now. He could put up with the kids for the short rides to the river, to the stables, that was fine. But five hours of riding and hiking, listening to them complain about how hungry they were, how tired, what was this, what was that, he could just as well up and leave right now and save himself the headache.

He said as much to Saul later on when they sent the boys out hunting. It was meant to be a group effort among the campers, with no help from the counselors who stood at key points along a boundary, turning the kids back if they wandered too far.

"Believe me, I share your sentiment," Saul told him. "I question myself every day of this camp."

"Then why keep coming back?" Tommen wondered. "So what if they don't have a counselor for troubled kids? I don't think the camp would suffer if they couldn't come, seeing how they just seem to keep getting sent home."

"True. You want to know why I come here? Because I need to remind myself that there are worse places to be than home."

"You don't like living on the reservation? Why not move? Or is it different for you? With your tribe and all, I mean."

"I know what you mean. No, it has more to do with internal politics. Problem is, due to the nature of the politics, I'm put in a position where I can't leave, except for little excursions like this."

"Oh. Are you, like, an elder?"

Saul raised a brow but merely answered, "I'm not, but my older brother is on the council, and family is everything."

"Oh. Makes sense. What's your older brother's name?"

"Logan. Sister Natalie. Younger brother Blake."

"Regular wolf pack, huh?"

Tommen tried to grin and bring humor to the situation, but all he got was a murderous look from Saul. He cleared his throat awkwardly and looked away. "So I guess it would be too much to ask about the politics that you seem to hate so much."

"The tribe isn't overly fond of disclosing its problems to outsiders," Saul told him. Then he relented. "But then, that's also half the battle. Let's just say that there are differing opinions on how 'modern' the tribe has become."

"Ah. Another small tribe losing its heritage and culture, right?"

The look he got then honestly made Tommen fear that Saul was either going to deck him right there or he was going to be dragged out of his bed and fed to the wolf later that night. Either way, he felt his whole face and neck burn with embarrassment.

He was mercifully saved by a sudden swarm of boys, all saying very resolutely that the things they were scavenging for weren't where they were supposed to be. Tommen and Saul quizzed them on the supposed item and its location, which the boys got correct. Figuring they just hadn't looked hard enough, they left their post to follow the boys to the hollow tree stump where such an item was supposed to be.

But to their surprise, when they looked inside, the stump was, in fact, empty.

"Do we have the right stump?" Tommen wondered, looking around.

"Three stony guardians for a hollow wooden throne," Saul recited. "There's the three rocks, and this is the stump."

"Maybe a squirrel took off with it."

"One, maybe. But not all of them. Jerry was setting this up during dinner, so they couldn't have all been taken by squirrels. And I don't see any evidence of anything larger."

"This spot, too?" Deborah said, walking up with her group.

Saul stood and faced her. "What do you mean, 'too'?"

"Everything is missing," Jeremiah said, also walking up. "The hanging basket, the swamp, now apparently the stump. All the items and clues are gone."

"Did Jerry forget to set up the hunt?" Tommen offered weakly.

Deborah shook her head. "No, I saw him out with the stuff during dinner. There should be no reason anything is missing."

"So what do we do?"

Jeremiah shrugged. "Head back to the cabins, get ready for bed."

The kids groaned and protested, but they returned to the open area anyway, dispersing to their individual cabins with Jeremiah heading off to report to Mr. Wilson. After all, it was a little difficult to have a scavenger hunt with no clues and no prizes, and it was getting late enough that it was pointless to try and start a new game if the whole idea was to get enough sleep to be able to get up early. Bed wasn't a fun option at the moment, but it was logical, and the only one they had.

"Your spirits ruin our game because I asked about your tribe?" Tommen asked Saul as they got ready for bed.

Saul gave him a nasty look, and if Tommen didn't know better, he might have even suspected that Saul Banded the two of them just so he could say, "Keep running that lip of yours and you might find it split open one of these days."

It probably wasn't a good thing to say in the prison cabin, but, as Becky pointed out, he would have deserved it anyway.

"Why do you feel the need to belittle people's beliefs?" she asked.

"Because they're dumb," Tommen replied. "And anyway, I thought you would agree with me on this."

"I agree they're hokey and incorrect, but that doesn't mean I'm going to offend them at every turn."

"No, you would just destroy their idols and burn their temples."

"Wrong again. I wouldn't do it; I'd wait until they saw the light and took them down themselves or converted them properly."

"And put up crucifixes everywhere? Or the Star of David? Tell me, which one is right, anyway? I mean, they can't both be right."

"What do you care? As far as you're concerned, they're both wrong."

"And as far as they're concerned, they're right and the other is wrong. More to the point, they're right and everything else is wrong. How do you know? Why isn't Buddhism right? Or how do we know the Ancient Egyptians didn't have the right way of things? We can't know."

"And you know all things to be able to say we can't know. In that, you're implying that we can know that we can't know, but we can't know what we don't know. However, we also don't know what we can't know, but we do know that we can know."

Tommen mulled that over for a second, trying to keep it all straight in his mind. Finally, "I'm confused."

"You say we can't know what's on the other side of a black hole. But you would have to know all possible ways in the vast universe that can be done to reach the other side of a black hole (and live to tell the tale) and know that all those ways won't work so we can't know what's on the other side. So you're implying that we can know that we can't know, but we can't know what we don't know, that is, all possible ways to reach the other side. Does that imply that we can't know what's on the other side? We don't know that we can't know, because we don't know what we can't know, because we can't know all the ways to reach the other side. But because we see galaxies and asteroids and even light get swallowed up by black holes, we do know that there is a possibility that we can know what's on the other side. We just haven't found it yet."

For a minute, he was still confused as he tried to keep everything straight. Once he figured he got it as sorted as he was going to get it, he answered, "Okay, fine, you may have a point. But how do we know which way will work? If only one way works—or even a couple ways—how do we know which one or ones that is if the ones that fail result in death?"

"Then you figure out what you can do while you're still alive which means examining the work and research of others who are alive or have gone before. You're a budding scientist, you should know that."

He sighed and rubbed his eyes. "Yeah, well, I'm tired and don't want to do that right now."

"Then why are you still talking to me? Afraid of Saul's vengeful spirits?"

"I don't think they're spirits. At least, not the way he sees them."

"Extra-terrestrial beings from another dimension?"

"Maybe."

"Hm. Good luck with that one. I don't do much fighting."

"What if they came in peace? What if they caused all this mayhem just because they were curious, not malicious?"

"Because you're there and involved. Things tend to go wrong around you."

Tommen was taken aback. "I'm not sure how I feel about that. We are still dating, right?"

"Yes. Jeez, have a sense of humor."

Oh, how he wish he could tell her about all the shit that had happened to him. She might realize how spot-on her assessment really was.

"At any rate," she went on, "I have a lot of work to do, and at some point, I still have to sleep."

"Yeah, I guess I should get some sleep, too. Just don't get mad if I can't text you for a few days; I make no guarantee of signal where we're going."

"Duly noted. Then you might stop distracting me."

"You're the one who keeps replying."

"Conversation is a two-way street. Okay, I'll talk to you later. Good night. Love you."

"Love you."

It still felt strange to say or type out. Neither of them was quite sure whether it was the appropriate thing to say, but they'd been dating for six months and it felt right. She said it freely, and he hadn't gotten any nasty calls from either of their fathers. Either that meant her dad was okay with it--which was highly unlikely, knowing him-- or she hadn't told him.

Tommen put his phone away and tried to relax and get comfortable. Oddly enough, he'd actually been able to sleep better at the start of camp, once he'd gotten more accustomed to having less time to do so. He figured his troubles now stemmed largely from there only being five of them in a cabin that could accommodate twenty-five. The room felt huge and open and empty. He knew he should have been a little grateful, since other cabins reported being roasted alive at night from all the body heat and all the stuff crammed in with them, but he would have much preferred that over the emptiness and the cold.

Tommen sat on the floor. It looked like hard-packed earth, but the texture wasn't right. All around him were only shadows, and the only light came from three candles before him. He thought he might be playing a game, like the cup game, three cups, follow the ball. Across from him, a man sat, though his features were difficult to make out. He may have had darker skin, or it could have been the shadows. He could have had long hair, or it could have been the shadows. Actually, Tommen's first thought was that he looked a bit like Saul, if Saul had a kinder demeanor.

He wasn't sure how he got there necessarily, but he felt only that he had to be there, in that spot, wherever "there" was.

"What do you see here, Tommen?" the man asked.

"Three candles," Tommen said, shrugging.

"What do you notice about the candles?"

"Um...they're lit?"

"And what would happen if all these candles were snuffed out?"

"Then we would be in, probably, total darkness."

The man nodded graciously once. "If that were to happen, what would you have to do in order to make your way in the darkness?"

"Relight the candles."

"What if the candles had burned down? What if the wax and the wick had all burned away to nothing? What if there was nothing left to light?"

Tommen had been looking at the mystery man's face, or what

he could see of it, but when the light suddenly became dim, his gaze snapped back to the candles. At the start, they'd all been burning at the same speed and they'd all been the same height. Now, though, one had burned down and was out. As for the two remaining, one was tall and appeared to be burning slowly while the other was about half the size and burning quickly, a huge flame on its wick.

"What happens when these candles burn out?" the man asked again.

"Then it gets dark," Tommen repeated.

"And how do you make your way through the darkness then?"

"I don't know. I guess I'd have to figure a way out, use the time to scope out my surroundings and be very careful."

"What happens when the landscape is constantly shifting and you find yourself surrounded by a great chasm? Luck will only take you so far."

So far, he'd mostly been humoring the man, curious to see where things led, but now he was growing irritated. He sighed. "I don't know. Okay? What do I do? Obviously my subconscious is trying to tell me something, and my paranoia is fucking with me."

The man studied him thoughtfully. Then, "You would leave your survival to mere chance and a few witty remarks?"

"You haven't given me enough information about the situation to say otherwise. Where am I? What I doing in the dark?"

"Then you are curious to find out this information."

Tommen shrugged. "I don't know. Are you going to tell me, or are we going to play a few more guessing games?"

The man stood. "If you wish to know the answers, you must seek me out."

"Oh, this again?" Tommen scoffed and got his legs under him, standing slowly. "Seek and ye shall find, am I right?"

But the man appeared unfazed. Rather, he smirked and said, "There is a difference between trying to force a stubborn ass to move, and letting it get to its destination on its own. We will meet again,

Tommen Forbes. All that remains to be seen is how you will find me."

Then he turned and walked away, the darkness swallowing him whole.

Tommen may have had more dreams, but he couldn't remember much about them as they were chased away too soon by the alarm going off.

On normal days, the boys were like coiled springs, ready and waiting and all too happy to leap out of bed to start the day. Well, that was a relative description; objectively speaking, they were about as enthusiastic as the rest of them. But no matter what, they always seemed to go faster than Tommen.

Today, however, they were all moving about the same pace. This was immensely unhelpful given the fact that they were supposed to be moving quickly today, getting their sleeping bags and toiletries packed, running to the main hall for a quick breakfast, then piling onto the buses which had hopefully gotten fixed sometime in the night.

"Up and at 'em, Sunshine," Saul said, shaking Tommen in his bed. He sounded the most awake out of all of them, but then, he always did. Fucking Marine.

"All right, all right," Tommen grumbled, pushing back his covers and sliding out of the relative warmth and comfort of his sleeping bag onto the cold floor below. He grabbed his hearing aids and started rolling up his bag and rummaging around for his toothbrush.

The five of them—or four of them anyway—slowly came awake on the way to the bathrooms, the boys decidedly faster than Tommen.

"What'd you do, stay up half the night texting your girlfriend?" Saul asked when they got to the showers.

"Something like that," Tommen admitted cautiously.

"Well then, it's your own fault, and you get no pity from me."

"Would I have gotten any pity anyway if I had said no, I just slept like crap?"

Saul paused a moment, then, "No."

Tommen shook his head and chose his shower.

The dream about the man and the candles still stuck in his mind for reasons he couldn't comprehend. Clearly his subconscious was trying to tell him something. From the way he'd been having these dreams—which were not only recurring but progressively building on top of each other—it was most likely something important.

So, not that he particularly believed in the spiritual aspect of dream, he did figure that there was something to be said for interpreting basic elements. Light and dark, the color white, and the number three were all very basic, easily recognizable principles. For shits and giggles, he might even throw in a little spiritual aspect with the rabbit and the wolf; maybe he'd ask Saul about those, what they meant to his people. Ha!

Light and dark, generally associated with good and evil, or intelligence and ignorance. The color white, pretty universal in its interpretation of goodness or purity. So then, if the white wolf was leading him to the old man with the candles...but was that true? Or could it be that the wolf was trying to lead him away from the old man because of his association with darkness, snuffing out the candles?

Tommen shook his head. Objective only. Logic only. Science only.

Problem was, it was impossible to objectively, logically, scientifically dissect religion. Make all the excuses and all the arguments, quote all the quotes, but in the end, there was still that one element of faith that could not be explained, the reason incredibly learned men did a complete turnaround from staunch atheism to true fundamentalism.

Now Tommen had a serious gut feeling, maybe even a fear, that he was going to be staring into a similar maw. He'd been raised religious and subsequently abandoned it for higher reasoning. He'd been standing at the mouth of the cave he'd been kept in and laughed at the people still inside, or that's how he'd always seen it. What if it was the other way around? What if he'd gone into the cave, and now something was trying to pull him back out?

He grunted and squeezed his eyes shut as soap slid down his forehead and into his eyes. Mother*fucker*, that burned. When he finally got his eyes clear, he felt like he'd come back to real life. Well, everyone had certain philosophical dilemmas every once in a while, no matter how deeply-rooted in their individual beliefs they proclaimed to be.

As he stepped out of the shower, he figured he'd had his doubts for the day, but now reason had come back to him. His dream may not have been just a simple dream, but it was a subconscious message to himself, a warning maybe, but certainly not a message from God or whomever.

He got dressed and waited in the locker area with Saul while the boys plodded along, still in their own showers.

"Do you believe in God?" Tommen asked.

Saul looked up. "What do you mean?"

What did he mean? How much simpler a question could he get? "I mean, do you buy in to some all-knowing, all-powerful, all-wise creator of the universe?"

Tommen watched Saul size him up, trying to determine if the question was serious or bait for mockery. Then, "I believe in a Creator, yes. One who existed at the formation of the world, who exists today, and who will continue to exist long after the earth is but dust again in space."

"Where do your beliefs come from? What I mean is, Christians have the Bible, Muslims have the Qu'ran, and so on. What do you have?"

Saul spread his arms out before him where the door was open to let out the steam. "This. The religions you just named have dusty texts which they read and interpret and fight over constantly. I, my people, and to an extent all Native peoples, we bypass all of that and go straight to the Creator himself, in the rocks and the mountains and the water and the trees." He leaned back as best he could and put one leg over the other. "It would be folly to think creation created itself. Prove that you created your own mother; that is an easier task."

Tommen was silent as he mulled over Saul's words. He didn't get to ponder them long before the boys returned from their showers, looking about as bright and happy as any other day. Then it was a quick roundup of things which they dropped off at the cabin before heading over to the main hall.

Breakfast was quick, but that did not mean it was sparse. Cereal, oatmeal, fruit, cinnamon rolls, biscuits, bagels, muffins, for a moment it was almost like Tommen had been transported back to the bakery. Shameful to say, though, he much preferred Pam's baking to the twins'. Maybe it came from eating nothing but the twins' baking that it had become bland and tasteless to him, however tasty customers said it was.

"Okay, campers!" Mr. Wilson called once everyone or most everyone was seated and eating. They all turned to listen to him. "We're are supposed to leave here in about forty-five minutes, which means that is when we are rolling out of the parking lot, not when we are just getting on the bus. Please make sure you have everything you need because it is a long drive and we won't be coming back for a few days. This means sleeping bag, toothbrush, toothpaste, clothes, clean underwear. If you need help, your counselor will help you."

They hurried up and scarfed down breakfast, Tommen still working on a cinnamon roll as they headed back to the cabin, the boys racing to see who could get there first.

"Relax," Saul told him and they walked leisurely. "He said forty-five minutes, but he's probably planned for an hour to an hour and a half."

"True, but I don't want to be the first ones on the bus and have to wait forty-five minutes for everyone else to get ready."

"Mm...you may have a point there. I suppose I'm not accustomed to being the first ones on the bus. In this case, though, with just three of them, we might just get that honor. Which means choice seating."

For Saul, that meant a window seat so he could mimic banging his head against it when the noise and activity started getting to him.

For the rest of them, that meant as far back in the back of the bus near all the gear and equipment—the tents, fishing poles and tackle, traps, and so on. Add in the gear that each of them brought, and it was a pretty tight squeeze. Naturally, there was some arguing over seats and complaints of loss or theft of items, and several times someone had to run back to their cabin to grab something they forgot. Mr. Wilson had decreed forty-five minutes, but Saul had predicted correctly at about an hour and fifteen minutes before they were actually pulling out of the parking lot.

At first, things were pretty mellow. With having to get up early and eat a pretty filling breakfast, most people were ready to take a quick morning nap while they had the chance. Tommen certainly felt like taking the opportunity, up until they got on the road and started bouncing around through the ruts in the dirt and potholes in the pavement. Then it all went downhill from there, no pun intended.

"Everyone hold onto your stuff!" Mr. Wilson said obviously as they were jostled around and loose items went flying.

"Just like Afghanistan," Saul said with a wry smile.

"How long did you say this ride was?" Tommen asked, feeling his teeth click together uncomfortably and a headache start somewhere in his brain.

"A couple hours. Then we'll have snack time, then it's a short hike to the campsite where we'll have lunch."

A couple hours might as well have been forever. Tommen might have considered Banding his way through the whole thing up until the point where the kids started whining and complaining about the ride, then getting into fights as things went flying and got lost and picked up by other kids. There were more accusations of theft, more whining, and more complaining.

"Where are we going, anyway?" Tommen wondered. "This isn't the same road we've taken to get anywhere else."

"That's because all those roads have taken us west. Now we're going south," Saul informed him. "We'll end up about eighty miles south of the camp, plus a few more miles to the campsite."

Some years ago, when Tommen was first officially adopted, Walter had decided to help him make the transition into modern life by taking him camping. But they didn't just go to anywhere local, no, they headed out west to Yellowstone. Tommen had thought the Appalachians were big, but they were anthills compared to the Rockies.

They'd driven a fair distance into the park before stopping. Walter announced that they were going to hike and climb the rest of the way; Tommen ought to be very familiar with that, right? He had been, to be sure. He was more than happy to hike and climb and explore, but he'd been rather disheartened when he was told that he had to stay on the trails. He'd protested, saying that the trails were places that people had already discovered; he wanted to go where no one had gone before, to discover and see things no one had yet seen. Walter sympathized, but they had to follow the rules. That wasn't to say he didn't afford him some leniency once they'd reached the campsite.

Looking back, the camping had probably helped him more than he could understand at the time. It was one of the few true bonding moments he and his dad had shared when he was younger. He tried to recall whether they'd spent more time speaking English or Welsh, then mentally scolded himself for not connecting the dots earlier and realizing that Walter was his uncle, or some part of the family at least.

Tommen figured he must have dozed a little because a sharp crunch into a pothole jerked him back to wakefulness. He sat up and looked around. Well, they weren't on a highway or anything, but it appeared to be a main road of sorts, decently maintained as the potholes were decidedly less of a problem.

Around him on the bus, some of the campers and counselors had found sleep while the rest talked quietly, playing car games or trying to write in books and journals. Beside him, Saul had brought out a novel, one he'd been able to read only sporadically since the start of camp.

"How can you read while riding?" Tommen wondered, yawning.

"Well, it's safer than reading while driving," Saul told him, not looking up. "But as to your implied question, no, I don't get carsick, at least, not easily."

"Lucky you."

"It's a learned skill, believe me."

"So, how is the older camp different from the younger camp, other than the number of days gone?"

Saul ran his tongue over his teeth, and for a minute, Tommen wasn't sure he would answer. Finally, he sighed and closed his book. "The older kids do a lot more work around the camp. They'll chop wood for the fires, clean the fish and game we catch. They do a lot more stuff with the sharp things, let me say it that way. As for these kids, they'll catch the fish, but we'll clean them—show the kids how to clean them, I should say. They'll set the traps, but we'll skin and dress, that sort of thing. Otherwise, they're pretty similar, except for the number of days gone."

"So, why go to this particular campsite so far away? I mean, there's plenty of them around."

"Part of the reason is to teach the kids responsibility. We won't be going back for anything they forgot, so it's on them to remember what they need. Part of the reason is because the tribe says so."

"The camp is on Indian land?"

"What, you thought the Game Warden would let a hundred people loose on the forest to go fishing and trapping at will? Yeah, they make exceptions for kids, sometimes groups and camps, and they'd probably understand that we're trying to teach them responsibility and respect for the land, but sometimes it's just easier and less hassle to sidestep the issue."

"This is your reservation, then?"

Saul shook his head. "No. If I remember correctly, this is Shawnee land." He went on before Tommen could speak. "And before you ask, yeah, the tribes have a history of animosity and war, but these days, it goes more along the lines of, 'The enemy of my enemy is my friend.'"

"Oh." Tommen shifted uncomfortably. "Do you...not like white people?"

The man shrugged and returned to his book. "I'm equal opportunity. I hate everyone equally. I just have a little more respect for my people and a little more disdain for everyone else. But believe me, it's a very small margin on both accounts."

Tommen was silent after that, unsure how to respond. On the one hand, it was easy to see why the man had no friends. Tommen thought about mentioning Kayla, that she was married to a white man, and she seemed to have no problem with others and no one seemed to have a problem with her. He refrained, however, because he could almost hear a dozen different snide remarks, everything from "Good for her" to "That's because Canada has more respect for their First Nations" to "No one wants their frozen wasteland, so they have nothing to worry about." So he kept his mouth shut.

"Okay, boys and girl, we'll be arriving at the trailhead in about fifteen minutes!" Mr. Wilson said suddenly, making Tommen jump. "Make sure you grab all your stuff! I want nothing left on this bus because you won't see it again for three days!"

Soon enough, everyone was moving, shifting, groaning, reaching, pushing, pulling, and rummaging through everyone else's things trying to find their own stuff. A few counselors grabbed a handful of stuff and started passing them out as they were claimed. Tommen ensured he had all of his stuff in a neat pile before getting up and drunkenly moving about the bus with the other counselors, gathering loose items from under and on top of the seats, sorting them and handing them out.

"What's the hike like?" Tommen wondered when he finally got to sit back down.

"Look out the window and see for yourself," Saul said irritably.

They were just pulling into a small dirt lot barely big enough for one bus, never mind three. If Tommen hadn't been told that this was the trailhead, he might have mistaken it for some roadside pulloff. He couldn't even really see the trail. Looking around at the surrounding scenery, he figured the trail could either be a treacherous feat heading straight up the side of the mountain, or a pleasant trek down along the ridge into the valley. It was a tough call, but he figured Mr. Wilson was a little more amiable than Saul and wouldn't force the kids to go commando and scale the side of a cliff. So they were probably going down into the valley.

"Please make sure you take everything with you!" Mr. Wilson called again as the doors opened and they began filing out like a clown car. Occasionally the counselors had to keep things moving so the kids didn't pile up around the bus doors, but mostly they were occupied with the kids who were ready to go and almost running off into the woods on their own.

As they were gathering together and counting heads, a van pulled into the lot with them, and Pam and her crew got out. Immediately they went into work mode, opening up every door and pulling out tables and boxes of food. As soon as one kid spotted them, word spread, and soon they were swarming the tables. Eventually the counselors got them in some semblance of order, and they all went through to grab crackers, some cheese, fruit, a bit of chocolate, and a drink.

There were no chairs or benches, so the cabins just gathered to sit around on the ground or on their things, eating and waiting for the next set of instructions.

"Last year we got a really low spot and when it rained, our tent got wet," Eric was saying. "We need to be the first ones there so we can get the high spot this time."

"Well, if we all stick together and keep moving, I'm sure we can make it," Tommen said, nodding. "With only five of us, we should move pretty quickly."

They finished off their snacks and took another inventory of their things, making sure one last time that they had everything they needed because there would be no coming back.

"All right, everyone, let's finish up our snacks and get ready to get moving!" Mr. Wilson announced.

There was a small frenzy as everyone tried to stuff as much food as possible in their mouths and still grab more to go. Then there was more shuffling and moving and pushing and shoving as bags were checked and hefted onto backs and rearranged, everyone trying to find the most comfortable position for hiking.

"Okay, so it looks like most of you are ready to go," Mr. Wilson went on. "Now, many of you have hiked this trail before. You know where we're going and what to expect. For those of you who haven't been on the trail or maybe need a reminder, there are a few things to consider. You remember all that rain we got last week? Well, that can wash out trails and make them rutted and tough to navigate. Please be careful and always keep an eye out for dangerous situations. I want everyone here to find a buddy, someone you're going to watch out for on the trail, help them up when they fall down."

There were a number of other little rules and things that he went over, too, plus a small spiel about the nature and wildlife they might see: deer, eagles, wildflowers, and so on. Tommen had little doubt that the wildflowers would quickly be decimated by the girls picking bouquets, and all the wildlife within ten miles would be frightened off by all the noise they made. But still, it was a nice sentiment, something to occupy the kids' time rather than having to listen to them complain.

Once he was done speaking, the group started moving out. Mr. Wilson and Coon Cabin led the way, ducking under some low branches and pushing through some bushes to get to the main trail.

At first, the trail started off very wide and manageable, and they were able to walk three or four across in some spots. As Tommen suspected, they headed down into the valley on a gentle slope, safe from the wind but overshadowed by enormous peaks that blotted out the sun and its direct warmth. With cold air settling into low places, a fair July day turned into a chilly October evening, and they stopped multiple times to grab coats and sweatshirts.

Seeing how there were five in their cabin, Tommen buddied up with Eric when Peter and Louis buddied up. Officially, Saul was their buddy. Also officially, he didn't much care to be the third part of that group, and he simply claimed that Yawi was his buddy and would watch out for him. He didn't say this in a mean way, of course, but Tommen figured he knew him a little better than that by now to think his real thoughts were a little more on the indifferent, even hostile side. Tommen didn't think Saul actively wanted the boys to die, maybe more that he was hoping the mountain would suddenly crumble and crush him under the rocks. More suicidal than homicidal.

"So, what are you boys looking forward to the most at the campsite?" Tommen asked conversationally.

"I wanna catch some fish!" Eric declared.

"That's what I was gonna say," Peter whined.

"Well you can both fish," Tommen said. "I want to go fishing, too."

Tommen did considerably less fishing than he thought he ought to. Mostly he did trapping, small game, bringing home the meat for dinner and selling the pelts to Becky for her to use in her sewing. Now that he thought about it, though, fresh fish didn't sound all that bad. It wouldn't even be very difficult seeing how he could Band and scoop the fish right out of the water, no fishing pole needed.

"I wanna do some trapping," Louis decided after a moment of consideration. "You know what I want to catch most?"

"No, what?"

"I want to catch a bear."

"Oh." Tommen nodded slowly. "Well, that would certainly be something to see, catching a bear in the tiny traps we've showed you how to set."

"Oh, I know how to set larger traps. My uncle takes me out sometimes. He takes the bear meat and makes steaks and sausages out of it. They're really good."

"I know. My pa did right with bear meat, too. And my ma." Tommen forced himself not to choke.

"Yes. I think bear would be good." Louis nodded, clearly satisfied with himself.

"How about," Saul interrupted, "for the safety of everyone in the camp, we don't go intentionally calling or luring in any bears, hm?"

"We won't need to. They'll be curious enough about us that they'll come right in by themselves."

"And if they do, let's not provoke them. We taught you guys what to do if you see a bear."

"Yeah, yeah," Eric said dismissively. "But what if the bear attacks?"

"The bear won't attack because you're not going to go off on your own to be bear bait. You're going to stay with the group, or at least with your buddy. It's not fall yet, and there is plenty of other game in the forest, so the bear won't be that desperate to eat a scrawny little thing like you."

"Hey, I resemble that statement!"

"I think the word you're looking for is 'resent,' " Tommen snickered.

Eric huffed grouchily and ended the conversation.

Traveling with a bunch of kids was about as productive and exciting as Tommen figured it would be, that is, not very. Had he been hiking alone, or even with a group of peers or adults, they probably would have made it to the campsite in half the time, and they would have had far more interesting and productive conversations. Video games were okay to talk about as a small part of the conversation, but how the kids could discuss it for more than twenty minutes was a mystery to Tommen. Personally, he would have rathered hike with Eric and Varad and talked about girls or going on a small binge. Fuck, that felt like so long ago.

He managed to sneak a glance at his phone once. As expected, no reception whatsoever. He'd warned Becky that the chances of his having signal out here were nil and not to get mad when he didn't text her as often as she wanted.

"Miss your girlfriend already?" Saul asked. "Or your daddy?"

"Just checking the time," Tommen lied.

"You're on Indian land now. Means you run on Indian time. You're either here or there, and the time in between is flexible. There is day and night, sunrise and sunset. There is no eight o'clock or three o'clock or eleven-thirty or a quarter after five. All time is relative here."

Tommen wasn't sure how to take his words. Saul apparently got a kick out of his uncertainty because he chuckled and said, "In English, that means put your phone away because it will do you no good out here."

That's what I'm afraid of, Tommen thought silently. He watched Saul for a moment longer before the grouchy man saw a widening of the path and took advantage of it, slipping their group up a couple spots to they could be one of the first to reach the campsite.

After a short time, the excitement that had driven the kids onto the trail started to dwindle. Chatter and laughing and jokes and games turned into sullen silence. It wasn't even very warm, but the path was, as foretold, rutted and rocky and difficult to navigate in some spots, and the group started to get worn out. Then the complaints started coming in. I'm hot. I'm hungry. I'm thirsty. I'm tired. My feet hurt. I wanna sit down. Are we there yet?

Mr. Wilson and his campfire songs did wonders to keep them occupied, but it didn't help the overall mood much. Tommen tried to keep up a good attitude, though. He could stand to eat and get a drink, but he wasn't desperate. He didn't really hurt at all in feet or knees or elsewhere. His biggest complaint was the kids and their complaining.

Eventually, someone must have recognized something because

they started moving faster up the hill. Complaints turned into challenges, and before he knew it, Tommen was fighting to keep up with Saul and the boys who were apparently racing Bear Cabin to be the first to the campsite. He had no idea where they were going, and the trail had become little better than a single-file footpath by this point. Still, he followed, acutely aware that some of the other groups wanted in on this, too.

He heard the whining a split-second before pushing past a couple low-hanging branches and breaking into a large forest clearing. He only narrowly avoided tripping over a Bear Cabin boy who was on the ground crying. Instead he fell to the side, rolled, and picked himself up.

"Wait, what?" Tommen said. "What happened?"

"He pushed me!" the Bear Cabin boy wailed, pointing at Eric.

"I did not!" Eric protested. "You tripped by yourself!"

More kids could be heard just down the trail.

"Why don't we get you out of the way before more people trip over you?" the counselor suggested, picking the boy up under his arms and moving him to a nearby stump.

"He pushed me! I know he did!" the boy proclaimed.

The counselor knelt in front of him. "Jonathon, Eric was in front of you. He couldn't have pushed you."

"He did! I felt him do it!"

"Does anything hurt?"

The boy, Jonathon, sniffed hard and nodded. "My knee."

"Which knee?"

"This one." He pointed to his right knee.

"All right. Why don't we get Nurse Michelle over here and she can take a look, okay?"

"Can we call Eric's parents and send him home, too? Why are they here, anyway? They cause nothing but trouble."

"Hey now," the counselor warned severely. "There will be no more of that."

"Do you need anything from me?" Tommen wondered.

The counselor looked up at him and shook his head, giving him a small, exasperated eye roll. "No, you're fine. Go back to your boys."

Tommen was still unsure, but he did as he was told, meeting up with Saul and the boys at what he presumed to be "the high spot" given that it overlooked the entire campsite. Saul was merely sitting on another tree stump, probably had been since he arrived, staking out his territory and completely unconcerned for the welfare of the child who tripped. Although, all things considering, Jonathon was probably making it bigger than it needed to be.

"Is he going to live?" Saul asked sarcastically.

"I expect so," Tommen replied. "It was touch and go there for a while, but he should be good in time to go home."

"I didn't push him!" Eric said.

"No one thinks you did. He just tripped is all."

After a moment of silence, Saul looked around and said, "Okay, boys, we got the high ground. Let's start pitching our tent."

Other cabins that still had their ten or more kids had two tents; the counselor would stay in one tent with half the group, and the counselor assistant would stay in the other tent with the other half of the group. For Wolf Cabin, though, they only needed one tent. That in itself was a relief given how much of a pain the tent was to pitch, never mind trying to get the boys to help. If they weren't messing with the poles and pretending to joust with them, they were walking all over the tent itself, pulling it off the poles and getting dirt everywhere. And when they weren't doing that, they were wandering off to bother other groups or do some freelance exploring.

Basically, it ended up being just Tommen and Saul working on the tent, which seemed to work just fine for both of them. At least then they knew it would get done correctly.

"Ready to go home yet?" Saul asked when they'd finally finished and were busy throwing all the bags inside the tent, rolling out their sleeping bags to claim their spots.

"I think so." Tommen took a back corner while Saul favored

sleeping by the exit flap. "I'm just exhausted from always going, going, going. It never ends."

"Ha! Has it made you reconsider any plans you had about having kids of your own?"

Tommen paused in his work. Then, "I don't know. Guess I never really considered that point. Why do you ask?"

"Because this job destroyed any illusions I had about it."

"Do you have kids?"

"Nah. My older brother does. My sister's engaged, so I imagine there will be nieces and nephews from her, too, eventually. You might have guessed, but they don't ask me to babysit."

"I'm told it's different when they're your own."

"Maybe so, but why take the chance? Because if it's not true, you're still stuck with them."

Tommen didn't usually give much thought to having kids. Part of it stemmed from the fact that he was only seventeen—okay, in a month—and had so much of his life left to live. The other part, feeding off of that, was the fact that his Timekeeping would keep him young for quite a while. That not only gave him time to do all the things he wanted to do without having to choose this or that based on his age and physical abilities, but it gave him time to find a woman who was either already in Time and so would stay young with him, or who was wonderful enough that he would deliberately expose her in order to bring her into Time so they could stay young together forever.

A thought occurred to him then, and Tommen looked around to make sure the boys were out of earshot when he said it. "So, I've heard that Natives don't believe in contraception, traditionally, I mean. You seem pretty traditional. Does that mean you don't get laid?"

Saul gave him an odd, mischievous look. "This coming from the sixteen year old virgin?"

Tommen blushed hard and he hated himself for it. Saul laughed. "Please. Women take either finesse or alcohol, neither of which I suspect you possess."

It was true, but he wasn't about to admit it. He was saved, thankfully, by the return of the boys. They came diving into the tent looking for their stuff, unpacking everything like they were camping for the next three weeks and throwing things everywhere.

"What are you doing?" Saul asked, catching a shirt as it went flying through the air.

"Louis brought binoculars," Peter said. "Mr. Wilson says there's an eagle nest that you can see across the valley as long as you have binoculars."

"So if Louis brought the binoculars, why are you all throwing all of your stuff around?"

If the logic made it through to the boys at all, they didn't show it and they never slowed. After a minute or two of the chaotic rummaging, Louis brought out his binoculars and led the charge out of the tent. If there had ever been any sense of order to the tent and the campers' belongings before, it was all gone now.

"Okay," Tommen said, letting out a breath, "what's the next step?"

"Lunch," Saul told him. "Pam and the others are coming up, too. They'll cook lunch, then carry on to their own camping spot farther along the trail. It's kind of like a mini-vacation for them, a little perk of being the kitchen crew. After lunch, our food is all up to us. We'll set some traps, then we'll divide into groups for foraging and another for fishing. Which would you prefer?"

"I'm partial to fishing." Mostly because Tommen figured the girls were less likely to want to deal with slimy fish and instead want to go looking for berries and flowers and pretty things.

"Guess I'll go foraging, then," Saul said. He hardly sounded heartbroken by it. If Tommen's suspicions were correct, he would be taking every opportunity he could to slip away and be alone, doing his own thing. Riding his wolf into battle or something, he didn't know.

"Okay, so, this is Indian land, right?" Tommen confirmed.

"And you're Indian, but not part of this tribe. What happens if they catch you, like, if you're out walking alone or something?"

"Then I imagine they'll say hi, we'll exchange pleasantries, they'll ask what I'm doing here, and I'll tell them I'm with the group. If they ask why I'm not with the group and I'm out alone, well, that will be my answer and none of your business."

"It is my business if you mysteriously don't come back."

Saul gave him a look. "Do you think we're savages and don't have even basic rules of hospitality?" Tommen felt his ears and cheeks grow red again. "If I were you, I'd worry more about myself mysteriously not coming back." He snorted indignantly. "Do you even understand what you're saying and implying?"

"Maybe not fully, but I'm guessing by your reaction that it's pretty racist."

"You think?"

Tommen swallowed. "Well, for what it's worth, I'm sorry. I mean, I don't try to be rude. I'm not racist, honest."

"No, you're just an idiot. *Nigila*, as my people would say."

"Stupid white man?"

"Something to that effect."

"Well, at the risk of being fed to your wolf, I'd like to point out that some of your remarks are pretty racist, too. Some of the things you say about me, I don't appreciate."

"That's against you, however, because you're an idiot. Not because you're white."

"Oh, I don't deny that I can certainly be an idiot. My girlfriend reminds me of that often enough. But I don't like being called 'chalk boy' behind my back."

Saul's expression changed, then, to something like surprise. "When have I called you that?"

"Um, just the other day when I asked for a hand with one of the classes, when it was rainy. You just came out of the bathroom, I asked for help, and then you muttered 'chalk boy' under your breath before helping me."

"I did no such thing."

"Um, yes, you did."

"No. I didn't. When I got out of the bathroom, you were already in class and doing very well, so I went off on my own into the woods for a bit."

The two of them stared at each other for a long minute, each trying to gauge the sincerity of the other. Saul was a dick; any doubt about that had left Tommen a long time ago. But he also wasn't a liar. The problem was, that only left one reasonable option for what had transpired. Well, it hardly sounded reasonable to the average person, but it was a very real possibility in Tommen's world. Someone had Disguised themselves as Saul and taken his place temporarily.

Come to think of it, maybe it wasn't just the one time. Saul's mood swings could be easily explained by some type of PTSD or other anxiety disorder, but what if someone was regularly taking his place? More to the point, what if it was Rifun checking up on him, Tommen?

"I can be anyone," Rifun had said. "I can be anyone, and I can go anywhere. I'm like Santa Claus. I see you when you're sleeping, and I know when you're awake. I know if you've been bad or good, so you better be good or else a lot more people are going to die."

"So, how much longer do we intend to stare at each other?"

Saul's irritable question brought Tommen back to reality and he shook his head to clear it. "Oh, sorry, just thinking of something."

"Uh-huh. Right." He stood, hunched over in the tent. "Well, maybe you ought to do more of it in the future in order to avoid unpleasant conversations like this, or anything else for that matter. And while you're at it, you may want to think long and hard about whether you want to come back for the next camp. As for me, I hear the lunch bell, so that's where I'm going."

A minute after he was gone, Tommen Banded and got out of the tent. Camp was a beehive of activity, all frozen as he moved Faster than any of them. Saul had found the boys, and they stood in the lunch line. Jonathon appeared no worse for wear, talking excitedly with another boy from his cabin. Pam was laughing about something.

Mr. Wilson sat a short distance away in his camping chair, spoonful of baked beans halfway to his mouth.

After giving the campsite another quick sweep, Tommen started off down the trail, going just a short distance until he was sure he would be alone under normal circumstances.

"Okay, Rifun. I'm here," he said out loud to the empty air.

Nothing happened. Rifun did not materialize from thin air or anywhere else for that matter. No one did, actually.

"Micaiah? Okay, funny prank, but it's over now." Playing pranks was certainly Micaiah's style, but this one was a little out of character. Still, it helped to cover his bases.

"Is anyone here?" Tommen wondered dumbly.

There was no answer but the wind. After a moment or two of standing there on the trail and shivering, Tommen felt like a fool. His paranoia finally got the better of him. Now here he was, standing on the side of the mountain shouting into the wind, certain there was a conspiracy out there somewhere. All he needed was the tin foil hat and a beard that reached his knees. And a cave; he needed one of those, too, if he was going to go full hermit.

He still gave it a good five minutes before returning to camp, ducking into the tent and releasing the Band. Outside, everything came to life with laughing and talking and a whole host of other noises he couldn't put a name to. Nothing sounded out of the ordinary. When he finally emerged from the tent, everything looked pretty normal, too. No one looked confused or out of place, no one was watching him with a sinister look; no one was watching him at all, actually. If anyone seemed out of place, it was him.

Feeling rather conspicuous, Tommen got in at the very end of the line, the last person to go through.

"I thought something might have happened to you," Pam said as she heaped food on his plate. "Thought maybe you got eaten by a bear or something."

"Nope. Just a wolf."

"Oh. Don't let him get to you. I mean, it's probably a little late in the game to be telling you that, but still, you can't let his surliness ruin your good time at camp."

"What's his problem, anyway?"

"I don't know. You want to hear my theory?"

Tommen shrugged. "Sure, might as well. Long as it won't make you mysteriously disappear."

"Ha! He'd have a hard time of that, I reckon."

In a war of wit, Pam won every time. But when it came to physical prowess, Tommen's money was still on Saul. Still, he listened as she presented her theory. "My theory is that it has to do with his tribe being so small, they're on the verge of extinction. They've kept to the old ways so rigidly that they've driven away all the young folks who want to be more modern."

"He did say something about there being a divide among his people."

Pam shrugged. "Yeah, he's vague like that, but I suppose it makes sense. Don't let the world smell your weakness. Honestly, I don't even know where he lives, where his tribe's land is, if that's any testament to how bad things must be. But that's just my perspective. Obviously, insider information is limited."

"Clearly."

"Well, eat your lunch before it gets cold. Then we'll see you in a couple of days. Suppose I'll have to cook a double batch of everything to put all the weight back on you that you're set to lose."

"I think you underestimate my trapping skills."

"And I think you underestimate just how much it's going to take to feed this little army. Deer and elk are great, but all you guys got are small game traps and a bunch of kids with short attention spans. Good luck."

Her words were decidedly less than comforting, but only because they were true. They weren't going to be out camping for very long, but in terms of food, it would be at least an eternity. If the kids even thought about the word hungry, suddenly they would be starving, and a handful of berries wasn't going to cut it. He meandered toward his group who had taken up residence on a circle of tree stumps a short distance from their tent.

"Are we going to have a campfire tonight?" Eric was asking when Tommen joined them.

"I imagine so," Saul answered. "It's the only way we'll be able to cook our fish and keep warm."

"We're having fish?" Peter asked, his eyes huge.

"Only if you catch some," Tommen told him. "Remember, we're providing for ourselves out here; Pam won't be around to save us if our stomachs are empty."

The thought was apparently enough to put the fear of God and starvation in the boys because they quickly began planning how to catch every fish in the river.

"We don't need to catch every fish in the river," Saul told them, sighing. "We take only what we need."

"But what if we only catch fish for breakfast, but then we don't have any for lunch?" Louis wondered.

"Then we have to find other sources of food. Those would be the traps or any number of edible plants in the area. Trust me, we won't starve."

Saul was a lot of things, the most prominent one being a dick. But he was also a survivor, a lethal combination of being Native and being a Marine. Somehow, Tommen found himself relaxing. Even if, somehow, they ended up stranded in the wilderness for weeks on end with no sign of rescue, he had little doubt that Saul would know what to do, how to take charge and keep them alive.

"So what are we doing after lunch then?" Tommen asked levelly, more for the boys' sake than any real curiosity seeing how he already knew.

"Well, I'll be going with a foraging group, looking for edible plants and setting some traps. You'll be going with the fishing group, hoping to catch some fish. Then we'll come back and cook up our catch for dinner and save the rest for breakfast. Then we repeat."

"That's all we're doing tomorrow?" Peter asked.

"Yes. We've been telling you guys this. It's survival camp. It's a lot of hard work, but it's a lot of fun, too. You catch your own food and reap the rewards of your own work."

When the boys still seemed uncertain, Tommen added, "Then you can go home and tell all your friends and family how you survived in the mountains with no food or water or backup. Believe me, girls really dig that sort of thing."

With older boys, they'd be all over it. Of course, they would have been all over the trip without the need for such reassurances. But the younger boys still thought girls had cooties and should be avoided at all costs, so the conversation turned in that direction. And an icy silence remained between Tommen and his counselor.

Chapter Eighteen
The Sign

For the evening, the groups were open choice, whether the kids wanted to go fishing, foraging, or trapping. Starting the next day, they would do rotations.

So it was that first day after lunch that Tommen ended up with a pretty good mixed group of boys and girls. The river was a short hike from the camp, and the kids were all good and hyped up from lunch, crashing through the woods and making enough noise to alert all the fish in the state of their arrival. Of course, he wasn't the only counselor there with the fishing; there were three others. But it was still a chore trying to get all the kids to pay attention long enough to get their fishing poles ready, never mind trying to get them all to be quiet and still and patiently wait for the fish to actually bite.

Patience was the virtue of few adults in the world, and even fewer children. Of the twenty-five to thirty kids they had there on the bank, only one seemed to have any inclination as to what they were supposed to be doing.

The noise and the jokes and the games were cute at first, until the kids started getting hungry again. Once Tommen and the other counselors reminded the kids that their dinner rested on them actually catching something—no, they weren't bluffing; no fish, no dinner—they started to get their act together and actually tried to do things right.

Suffice to say, dinner was a little sparse on the fish side of things. They did catch a few, but it was clearly far less than the bounty the kids had been expecting, as if they'd expected the fish to just leap out of the river onto the bank with little prodding. The foraging group, led unofficially by the vegetarian cabin, also appeared sorely disappointed, and Tommen found himself smirking. *That's right, honey, you're not going to find a health food store out here. Here, you have to work for your food.*

The trapping group managed to bring back a rather small raccoon, a young one that had gotten caught in a trap some time between when they set it and when they walked back past it. The counselor had dispatched it and showed the kids how to gut it. When they returned to camp, he showed everyone how to skin it, quarter it, prepare it, the whole nine yards.

As a side show, Saul took the raccoon pelt and did a mini-workshop on how to tan it Indian style, from the fleshing to the brains to the stretching.

Looking around at the expressions on the kids' faces, Tommen couldn't help but inwardly sigh. A lot of these kids, the ones who weren't Native or did this already at home, would be repulsed by it. Because they'd never seen it, because they'd never had to do it. They'd never truly had to survive. Sure, most of them would think they were dying if they didn't eat three or four times a day, but none of them truly understood survival, the need to go to any lengths to make it from sunrise to sunset, plus the skills it took to survive that bit from sunset to sunrise. These were children of the twenty-first century, who believed that milk and eggs came from the store, who never quite understood that a rack of ribs was literally meat on the ribcage of an animal. It wasn't just a fancy name, that's really what it was.

For a moment then, watching Saul entertain the last four kids who dared to watch his display of survival craftsmanship, Tommen could only feel pity for the man. His people and their traditions went back centuries, and they were dying just as readily as Tommen's heritage.

So dinner wasn't as grandiose as what everyone had become accustomed to with Pam's cooking. Tommen's stomach growled right along with everyone else's, but he figured that, in a way, it was good for them. Let their stomach grumble a little, let them feel a little hunger, then maybe they would pay a little more attention and try a little harder tomorrow to get things right.

Of course, it didn't help any when Mr. Wilson brought out s'mores supplies that he'd stashed away in his packs. Only enough for everyone to have one, but still. This was supposed to be survival. Not a gotcha moment. They were supposed to be teaching kids about hunger and trapping and foraging and catching their own dinner.

Well, when in Rome, do as the Romans. Eat s'mores. Which Tommen did.

The following morning before breakfast, he went out with the trapping group, looking to see if they'd gotten lucky in the night, which they had, snagging a couple coons, a possum, and a skunk. With exception of the skunk which he decided to free, Tommen dressed the critters with deft movements and handed off the skins to Saul when they got back. A small foraging group had also gone out, returning to some berry patches they'd marked, gathering some other wild edibles along the way.

Once again, mealtime was a pretty spartan affair. Tommen tried to tell himself that it was all for their good, but he found himself questioning the wisdom of it. Pam was right, a couple of deer would feed them. But as long as they were doing meager trapping and only going after small game, they were going to starve trying to feed eighty kids plus staff. Well, it was only for the rest of the day and breakfast tomorrow.

After breakfast, Tommen was chosen to help gather and chop some firewood, among other camp maintenance duties.

Truth be told, for as much as he liked to tout being a country boy and homestead raised, Tommen had never actually chopped firewood. As a child he'd set the smaller logs and then gathered the split pieces, but he'd never actually swung the ax. It wasn't exactly rocket science, sure, but he didn't have the natural lumberjack rhythm that his pa had, the strength and grace which his ma would swoon over when she paused to watch him work for a minute or two.

Usually Tommen thought she wanted something, so when he

caught her staring, he would point her out to his pa. Of course, his ma knew, like all of them, not to get close to an ax in motion. With his pa working, he wouldn't see her behind him. So naturally Tommen had to point her out. He thought it odd how, when his pa would turn to look at her, she would blush, giggle, and hurry off. Even more odd was that his pa would then smile, shake his head, and go right back to work. They hadn't said a word to each other. They just looked at each other and smiled. What just happened? Didn't they have to talk?

Tommen swung the ax hard and buried it in the stump, sending the two splits flying. It wasn't fair. His pa should be here to see this, to watch him work hard and try to teach these kids to do the same. His pa should be able to see that his son was alive and well, that his older brother had found him, that they'd been reunited. He should see that they were a family again. They should all be together right now, the entire Forbes household.

He let go of the ax and wiped his face, slick with sweat. Great, now he was getting sentimental. Fucking hell, he was a man grown. He should be over this by now.

Yeah, in the same way Walter is over his fear of the dark.

That comes from deep-rooted psychological and physical torture. That's understandable.

And a child being ripped from his home at a young age and transported a century and a half into a new world he knows nothing about?

A terrible thing, sure, but other kids recover. Jimmy will recover.

Not all of them do. Some break and lead only broken, messed up lives.

But I'm not one of those, Tommen resolved, wresting the ax from the stump. *I'm a survivor. I hunt, I trap, I fish, I chop wood, and I defend the universe from psycho cultists. It's all a part of me, and the most I can do is learn from each experience and use it to make myself better, faster, strong, tougher.*

That resolve lasted only a few more logs before he decided he'd had quite enough of the log splitting business, thank you very much. He sat down and wiped his face again. Mr. Wilson got him a cup of water from the hand pump at the edge of camp.

"You did some good chopping just now," he said.

"Thank you," Tommen breathed.

"You're a hard worker. Listen, why don't you head over to the river, do a little fishing, maybe a little swimming while you're at it and cool off a bit? Camp will still be here."

Tommen wasn't about to argue with the man, and he readily took the invitation, stripping off his shirt once he was out of sight of the camp heading for the river. There were precious few opportunities at camp for the counselors to have a little time to themselves, and Tommen wasn't about to pass up this chance. He wasn't like Saul who just wandered off on a whim because he was frustrated.

No, but you do quit your job when things get unfair. At the bakery, the government ousted you from your position. Here, Saul is a first-class jackass. Are you going to quit this job, too?

It was at that moment that Tommen decided no, he wasn't going to quit this job. He was going to come back for the second camp with the older kids. Regardless of their troubles, he was going to do his best to help them and have a good time at camp. Let Saul stew and groan and hum and haw all he wanted, Tommen couldn't be concerned with him at all hours of the day as if he were a camper, too. Or maybe he should treat Saul like a camper, just like one of their troubled kids. He just happened to be a troubled adult.

Fuck, was it that obvious his dad was a cop? Damn, he was even starting to think like one. This did not bode well for him. Maybe it was just as well that he'd taken this job and gotten out of the house. He needed some time away from his dad; they'd been cooped up together for too long.

His thoughts turned, unexpectedly, to his dad's girlfriend, Laura. His dad had confirmed, via text, that they were officially dating now. It still wasn't anything too serious, but Tommen knew it was only a matter of time. Older people didn't have the same luxuries as younger people when it came to partners and marriage. They had more experience telling them what was ideal and less than ideal in a mate, but less time to decide whether the person they were seeing fit the bill. After all, one or the other could keel over at any time. Not that his dad was in terrible health or anything, but even he was in a dangerous profession.

What if they decided to move in together, that meaning, Laura moved in with them? His dad had never really given a clear answer on his thoughts about cohabitation. He thought it was an idiotic idea for teenagers, non-roommate college students, and anyone who hadn't dated more than six months, but past that, he never really said much. Tommen had heard opinions varying from shacking up after the second date to waiting until the happy couple returned from the honeymoon.

But what if he went home and found perfume and lipstick and a hair dryer in the bathroom next to the sink? What if his dad had "cleared out a drawer for her" in his dresser? What if she brought over her cutlery set? Could he handle that? Could he handle the idea of a woman in the house? What if it wasn't the idea of a woman in the house so much as his dad's girlfriend? What if it was more than that? What if he was more repulsed by the thought of having some kind of stepmom?

He looked around from where he stood in the river, dressed only in his boxers, the water only about thigh-high. It moved swiftly down the mountainside, twisting and turning around rocks and reeds, disappearing into dense brush a little farther down. Overhead, a cloud passed over the sun, momentarily throwing everything into shadow. A couple birds took off from a branch, squawking angrily. A squirrel scurried up a tree trunk, chittering about this or that. Along the bank, a bush rustled, and a moment later...

A white rabbit poked its nose out.

Tommen's stunned silence quickly gave way to frantic movements as he raced back to the shore to grab his clothes. Even as he threw everything on—mixing up his shoes and putting his shirt on backwards the first time—he couldn't figure out why he was so eager to see the stupid thing, knowing that his sudden movements had probably frightened it off. But when he returned to the bank, it was still there, on the opposite bank, nosing around in the grass.

He squatted low and got as close as he could to look at it. It appeared to be an ordinary rabbit, merely stricken with some form of albinism. Maybe not even that as he couldn't tell whether the eyes were truly red. It paid no attention to him, just hopped along, minding its own business.

Well, what did you expect? Tommen scolded himself. *Did you think it was going to stand up, introduce itself, then lead you away to go down its rabbit hole? What are you, nine?*

As he stood and stretched, there was some other rustling noise and the rabbit took off, flying up the bank probably a hundred feet or so before turning and disappearing into another bush. Tommen walked along his side of the bank up to the point where the rabbit disappeared. There was the bush, but no rabbit. Nothing special at all.

Well, except the pair of flip-flops floating down the river. Just upstream, Tommen could hear the laughter and shouts of the fishing kids. With that racket, they wouldn't catch anything. At the same time, there was a good chance that the sandals belonged to one of the campers. Keeping an eye on the pair, he took his shoes and socks off and waded out into the water. It was deeper in this part of the river, and Tommen had to go out waist-deep to catch the flip-flops.

Just as he returned to shore, a couple of girls burst from the bushes. One had no shoes.

"I assume these are yours?" Tommen said, holding out the wet sandals.

"Yes!" the girl said, snatching them from his grasp. "Oh my gosh, thank you so much!"

"No problem," Tommen told her.

"We caught fish for lunch!" another girl told him proudly.

"Did you? A lot of fish?"

"More than yesterday."

"That's good." That really was good, and more than he had been expecting from them.

"We're going back now to cook them up." The girl twisted and dug in her purse. Because eight year olds need purses. For some reason. She handed him a box. "Saul said to give you this before you came to lunch."

Tommen raised a brow. "Did he? Did he say what it is?"

"Not really. He just said that it's a reminder and you would understand."

"Oh. Okay. Well, why don't you go back to the group and get going on that lunch? I'll be along."

The girls left then, laughing and giggling and carrying on about the girl who lost her flip-flops in the river. Tommen watched them go but did not move for a long time after they were gone. He stared at the box in his hands. It wasn't very big, maybe six-by-nine, about book size. Judging by the weight, he would guess about two or three pounds.

A reminder? What kind of reminder? Was this a book detailing all the atrocities white men had ever done to the Indians? Saul was a dick, but Tommen was forced to question his character, if not his sanity, if he carried around this kind of book for just this sort of occasion. Somehow it seemed unlikely.

Was there a chance that it could be harmful? A bomb, poison gas, something else? Tommen's paranoia was legendary, but even that was pushing it. If someone wanted to get rid of him, there were plenty of other, less messy opportunities to do so. Well, only one way to find out.

His pocket knife was waterlogged from the wade into the river, and Tommen kicked himself for being so careless. Still, it unfolded easily enough and sliced through the packing tape with ease.

It was, indeed, a book.

Time to Kill, he mused. *Brooke Shaffer. Book One of...* He blinked and shook his head, wondering if he was reading right. *Book One of the Chivalrous Welshman.*

"I thought it would be an appropriate gift, wouldn't you say?"

Tommen almost jumped out of his skin at Rifun's voice behind him. He whirled. The man sat on a rock probably fifteen feet from him. He wore no Disguise this time and walked just as he was, a little over six foot, long brown hair tied back to his waist, skin that was light enough to pass but still darker than most Caucasians, freckles, perpetual air of confidence and self-righteousness.

"So, you really are Saul, and you've been keeping tabs on me," Tommen stated.

Rifun shook his head. "No. Not quite. I have been watching you. And occasionally I have impersonated him in order to get close to you and assess you. But Saul is Saul. And I don't envy you for it."

"What about the kids saying—?"

"I support stranger danger protection as much as the next man. They wouldn't talk to me if I walked up to them as I am, so I had to be someone they knew. But I had to be someone that they didn't like very much or else I would just get bogged down in conversation. Saul afforded me just such an opportunity."

Tommen looked down at the book in his hands. "What is this?"

"It's your sign. I actually had it mailed to you in hopes that you would settle down one night and read it. But imagine my surprise when I learned that you had quit your job at the bakery and come here. Now, obviously your dad isn't just going to go rummaging through your stuff, so I thought it would be safe for a while and I could come see what was so interesting about this place that it had you running out of the bakery. Honestly, I don't know what you see in this place. But then, I'm not the best with kids.

"Anyway, after a short time, I had another idea. Why simply give you your sign anonymously—or not so anonymously—while you are in the comfort of your own home under the protection of those you know and love? It would be much better, and much more polite, to deliver the gift in person and have an in-person chat, give you your first lesson right here, right now. I won't even make you reimburse me for the postage."

Tommen flipped through the pages of the book, shaking his

head as he read a few sentences here and there. "What the fuck is this?"

"It's your Book. Judging by the title, I'd say the first of many." Rifun stood. "It's a gift from the Author."

"A gift?"

"Yes. See, everyone has a story. We lie and tell our own tales, but these are the stories the Author has written for us, the ones we cannot outrun. These are the stories that the Author has directed. One day, you could be reading about this encounter right here.

"I admit, I actually stole it from you in the first place. Once a Book is complete, it will randomly appear for you to find, but only if you are an Akari-bearer. It just happened to show up on your bookshelf one day. I took it for myself so I could read it, then I mailed it back to you to ensure that you saw it."

"Wait, you were in my room?" Tommen said.

"As I said, I keep tabs on everyone."

Rifun shifted his stance and looked ready to say more when Tommen cut him off. "Okay, ha ha. Funny prank. The copyright in this is 2017. It's only 2014."

"Never judge a book by its cover, and especially not by its copyright. Read the story, then tell me what you think."

Tommen paused a moment and drummed his fingers on the cover. Then he shoved the book back at Rifun. "Keep your pranks and your party tricks. I'm done."

He barely took one step back before he dropped to his knees, everything mid-chest and below going completely numb and disappearing as if he had no control over it whatsoever. He got up on his elbows, but Rifun merely turned him back over on his back with a boot.

"Does this look like a party trick?" Rifun wondered easily. "This is the Akari at work. The Akari is another gift from the Author, the absolute gift, the power to give and take away." He knelt beside Tommen. "You seem to enjoy having things taken away. Perhaps that is the only way you will listen.

"I realize that you aren't swayed by smooth words and party tricks. You believe what you see with your own eyes. Why do you still deny what you have seen? Whether it comes from me or Micaiah, you have seen the Akari at work. The Akarin deny him, but Richard was a great prophet. He wrote the book on the Akari, all the words straight from the Author. Now, I'm just trying to introduce you in baby steps, give you a little more each time, things you can touch and feel, something you can read and study. But if you want, I'll go straight into the flood of power, in which case, there is every possibility that you may drown."

Tommen shook his head incredulously. "What do you get out of this? What, do you, like, go and masturbate in the bushes every time you deliver a monologue or what?"

Rifun chuckled darkly. "Always quick with the tongue. If you're not careful, there's a few creative things I can think of to do with it."

Tommen shut up.

"Now then, I'm going to give you a little time to rethink your position. It's difficult to argue when your biography has already been written, wouldn't you say? I would highly suggest you read the Book before making any rash decisions. When you are done, we will speak again. We'll discuss what you've learned and determine whether you are ready to move on to lesson two. Is anything about this unclear?"

"What the fuck was lesson one supposed to be?"

"Ah, but that would give away the ending. And, really, if you haven't figured it out by now, perhaps you aren't as promising as I'd been led to believe. Such a pity. Now, I think I smell a pretty good fish fry going on back at camp. Better get back there and make sure they've left some for you, and let them know that nothing really bad has happened to you." Rifun stood. "I'll be waiting."

He started walking away but Tommen called after him. "Wait!" Rifun turned. Tommen inwardly sighed. "I don't know what you did, but...I can't walk."

Rifun dipped his head. "So it would seem. Are you asking for my help?"

Tommen bit his tongue and ground his teeth before answering, "Yes."

"I want to hear it."

"Will you help me?"

"Did your mother teach you no manners?"

"Will you help me, please?"

Feeling returned to Tommen's lower body in a rush of pins, needles, and boiling blood. He hated that man.

"Manners," Rifun goaded as he stood.

"Thank you," Tommen said grudgingly.

"You're most welcome. Not like Saul was going to help you. I really don't envy your lot in life, having to work with him. And don't forget your Book either. I would hate to think of someone else reading about your little escapades with your friends to go drink and smoke weed. They might end up putting you in the troubled kids cabin next time as a camper."

Tommen was still grinding his teeth as Rifun walked away, vanishing into the undergrowth. How he wanted to just run after him and beat him over the head. If he managed to get the jump on him and knock him out, he would be able to do anything he wanted, even kill him. Rid the universe of this psychopathic, genocidal murderer forever. No one could fault him for that, and if Earth-side cops found out, well, Rifun was still wanted for the murders of the two women and the fiasco at the warehouse. He would be doing everyone everywhere a huge service by killing him.

The problem, though, was getting the jump on him and subduing him. It was like going up against a firing squad with a bean shooter; he had no chance.

He stood on wobbly legs and looked at the book, sitting face-down in the dirt. He picked it up and read the back.

" 'What would you do if you could manipulate Time itself?' " he read, then flipped to the front inside cover. " 'Tommen Forbes is basically your average sixteen-year-old...' "

He shook his head and slammed the book shut. It had to be some kind of prank, Rifun patronizing him by detailing past events, past failures. Gingerly, he opened to the back inside cover. There was a picture of the supposed author, blond, pretty, early twenties. The bio said she lived in Michigan with her husband and five cats. A crazy cat lady, then, someone easily framed who would probably never find out that her name and likeness had been used to torment a teenager half a dozen states away. The picture had probably been ripped from her high school senior photos, assuming that was even her, assuming she was even real.

Well, if nothing else, his curiosity was going to get the better of him anyway, and he would need something to take his mind off the shit happening elsewhere, like back at camp. He would just have to hide the book really well in his bag and show it to his dad and the twins when he got home.

His trek back to camp only served to remind him how wet he was, and mostly because of his attempt at rescuing some girl's flip-flops. His only consolation came from the fact that it was warm enough that his clothes would dry quickly. Given the time of day, the sun would be right over the campsite. He could change out of his wet clothes and then hang them out to dry. And pray they didn't get stolen as some sort of prank. The last thing he needed was his boxers being run up the flagpole for all to see. Maybe he would just pack those away instead.

He Banded just before he walked into camp. Lunch was being served, and it looked a hell of a lot more promising than breakfast. The fishing group had been much more successful. They all had, really. The trapping group had half a dozen coons and a few other small mammals Tommen could not readily identify seeing how they were presently cooking. Even the foraging group boasted a good haul of berries, nuts, and other assorted plants. Hungry children were motivated children, and they did not disappoint.

Tommen crossed the open campsite and ducked into the tent. It was empty, so he elected to drop the Band even while he stepped over and around a terrible mess of things to get to his stuff to hide the book. He hesitated for just a moment, looking at the cover. It didn't seem terribly sinister, no more than a good book cover ought to, anyway, depending on the material. Inside, everything appeared to be in English, not the same gibberish as the journal. It really did look like any average book that might be found in any given bookstore.

He stuffed in it his bag anyway, burying it deep. He told himself that it was a safety measure so the boys wouldn't get into it, however unlikely that seemed. Really he was afraid that there might be some element of truth to this whole Author and Akari business.

"Well, there he is," Saul said as Tommen emerged from the tent. He went to the same stump he'd sat on at breakfast. "Taking a nap on us, were you?"

"Changing clothes," Tommen told him, indicating the ball of wet clothes in his arms. "Went swimming for sandals earlier. Water is wet."

"So I noticed."

Was that Saul watching him now, or Rifun? Had to be Saul. Otherwise there would be two Sauls in camp and that could get ugly. Or what if Rifun had been lying? What if he really was Saul and by saying that there was another Saul then it put Tommen into a false sense of security? Wait, no, Saul had been working at the camp for ten years, and Tommen highly doubted that Rifun had been working at a children's camp for ten years just on the off chance that someone he was stalking might just happen to work there one summer, all so he could keep a distant eye on him and hand him a mysterious package. Occasional impersonation was certainly believable, but this was no Cassius-Doug switcheroo. Although, if Cassius had been able to pull off Doug because Doug was a Narcissistic dick that no one bothered to read too far into, what if Rifun was impersonating Saul because he was a hostile dick whom no one wanted to get to know in the first place? Nuances be damned, all he needed was the surly disposition.

Paranoia was a bitch. But there was nothing he could do about it either way save get his share of lunch and join the rest of them at the stump ring.

"Looks like we're not going to starve after all," Tommen said, trying to sound cheerful and upbeat. After all, this was his kind of camping. Hunting, fishing, tents, campfires, it was all good. Right?

"I don't know," Saul mused. "Compared to how much you normally eat, you might still waste away on us."

"Not in two days I won't."

The boys then proceeded to detail their exploits so far. Eric and Louis had been on forage duty, while Peter had slipped off to go fishing again. He got a minor scolding for that, but it was only a minor offense, comparatively speaking.

"What are we doing after lunch?" Eric finally asked as they all finished up their meals. Tommen's stomach still grumbled.

"Well," Saul answered, "I believe Mr. Wilson is going to take you guys on a hike farther up the trail to show you something really cool."

"What is it?" Louis wondered.

"You'll have to go on the hike and find out. Meanwhile, most of us counselors will be staying behind to catch our dinner."

So there had been a little forethought given to this whole hiking business, Tommen thought, amused. Give the kids a chance to fish, forage, and trap, let them have a small taste of hunger in the wilderness, but in the interest of keeping everyone sane and not at each other's throats, let the experienced adults go out and catch a real, full meal.

Tommen asked Saul about it later as Mr. Wilson and a couple counselors gathered up all the kids to start out.

"Well, a couple of us will go out for some larger game," Saul explained. "Deer, elk, something substantial. A few will do some fishing, and the rest will be responsible for trapping and foraging."

"What if we get too much?" Tommen inquired.

"With this group? Unlikely. But if there does happen to be some leftover, we'll just keep it for breakfast."

Tommen almost didn't realize how quiet the camp had gotten

until someone across the site sneezed. He looked around and saw Mr. Wilson and the campers had gone off already. Turning back around, he saw Saul appear from the tent, bow in hand. It wasn't a high-tech bow either, but a recurve made from real wood. Knowing the man, the string was probably sinew and the whole thing was likely handmade. Maybe he was stereotyping. The feather fletching and copper tips on the wooden arrows looked real enough, though.

"Make it yourself?" he asked, indicating the weapon.

Saul nodded. "I did. With any luck, it will bring us good hunting."

It was the most upbeat he'd seemed in a week as he stalked off into the trees, completely unconcerned about anything else in the world, a man in his element.

It seemed to be a personal choice, which way he wanted to go. A few of the counselors grabbed poles and headed for the river. Well, he was dry now and sick of going fishing anyway. He joined the trapping and foraging group instead, jogging to catch up with them as they started off.

All the traps were empty, and Tommen suspected they would be later that night and probably the next morning as well. Too much death and too many human scents would start to frighten off the smaller creatures, and would give even larger animals cause to be wary, especially in this area where humans did not frequent. Their best bet now would be the foraging, the fishing, and the large game hunting.

The foraging was starting to get pretty slim, too. All the known, familiar patches were pretty well picked clean. Tommen had little doubt that the Natives, both modern and ancient, probably knew where all the best patches were and how to rotate between them so there was always a harvest, but they were just a bunch of intruders, here to camp for a few days. They didn't have the time or motivation to travel very far to look for food. Their survival didn't depend on it.

As for the fishing, well, it was pretty slim pickings. Better than breakfast, but less than lunch. A few of them were grilled just for the counselors, something to eat before the campers got back and devoured everything.

"Where's Saul?" someone asked suddenly, looking up from his fish.

"He's out with the hunting group," Tommen answered.

Another counselor snickered. "Saul is the hunting group. You might have noticed, he doesn't play nice with others. That goes for the hunting, too."

"Just as well, because any of you would have scared this thing off."

They looked up to see Saul just breaking through the trees into camp, a full-size buck deer across his shoulders, blood down his back. He was sweating bullets, but as proud as Tommen had ever seen him. He dropped off the deer and brought out a knife. "Don't worry, we won't starve tonight."

Once the skin was off, he left the meat to be cut, divided, and cooked by the other counselors while he himself took the pelt off to be fleshed. The man was a pro and had it clean in less than ten minutes.

"Shit, I wish I was that good," Tommen said, watching him.

"It takes time and practice," Saul told him, taking the pelt to a particular tree branch that he'd been using as a stretcher. He didn't sound sarcastic or bitter, and Tommen could not find any hateful, hidden double-meanings in his words. At the moment, Saul Wolf seemed like a normal, competent, content human being.

That only lasted until dinnertime when Mr. Wilson and the others returned with the kids. He ate dinner in sullen silence, endured the campfire in sullen silence, ate a s'more in sullen silence. The only thing he did not do in sullen silence was go to sleep.

"You sound like you're dying up there," Tommen hissed loudly, hoping he wasn't being too loud. Sometimes it was hard to tell without his hearing aids in.

"My back is killing me," Saul growled. "That damn deer was too heavy."

"Why didn't you get someone to help you? Either to go with

you, or just come back and take someone to where it was?"

"Because I'm not that helpless."

"Then stop whining about it."

He could practically feel Saul's glare through the darkness. He did his best to ignore it.

At some point, Tommen figured he must have slept, at least a little. When he woke, he could just barely see his hand in front of his face. Everyone else appeared to still be sleeping.

He couldn't remember any of his dreams, and that bothered him for some reason. When the sun finally got up enough that he could see somewhat well, he Banded and went rummaging through his bag until he found the box with the book.

It had to have gained ten pounds between yesterday and today. At the same time, though, it still did not appear to be anything sinister. There was nothing written in blood, no threats scrawled across pages, no huge chunks cut out in order to conceal a gun or a cassette tape or anything. The only thing that appeared unusual about it was the author's signature on the title page, scratched out in purple ink. Tommen wasn't much of a reader and didn't stalk any of his favorite authors, but he knew that a signed copy was a cool thing to have.

Cautiously, as if the book might grow teeth and start chomping away at him, he opened to the first page.

"Prologue, April 6, 1855," it read.

He paused right there. That was the day he went into the old salt cave, or so it had always been figured. Well, it wasn't like such information was hard to find; it was on the plaque in front of Forbes Cave, after all.

But as he read through the prologue, he felt his heart and gut twist and tighten. No one could have known all of this. He'd been alone in that cave. Rifun and Cassius' mad determination to find the journal and kill anyone who got in the way proved that no one else had been in there with him. And yet, reading about the way he ran down the slope, fighting for balance on an unknown trail and breaking out onto the rocky ledge, it was like he was transported back to that fateful day. Or night, whichever the case. The description of how he'd perceived the city with its firefly lights and growling bear sounds, and how he'd honestly thought he'd been attacked by a demon when he'd really been hit by a car, it was all spot-on. The information was too personal for it to have just been made up and happen to hit his exact feelings.

Objectively speaking, it was quite the hook for a science fiction fan.

Still, though, how could someone get this kind of information about him? Or, maybe it was a case of his emotional state lowered his defenses so he was being impressed upon by the book. It was effectively planting false memories and false feelings. At the same time, if that was the case, whoever this author was, she had a damn good way of messing with him. And how or why would an author from Michigan either get the story or care enough about it to write about it? Just another reason why Rifun was probably behind this little prank.

Even so, Rifun clearly meant for it to be "the sign" for him to begin his wacky Apprenticeship or whatever. Tommen wasn't going to go easily, but he and his dad and the twins had all agreed that if he went, he would be their mole to get information and relay it back to them. Following along those lines, he should report this as soon as possible.

He rummaged through his bag again until he found his phone, powered off to conserve battery life. Electronics normally didn't Band well, in the case of it reaching out to anything else, another phone, wi-fi, whatever. But his phone as an object could be Banded, so he could take a picture of the book without losing his Band. Once he got a decent picture, Tommen put the book away and dropped his Band so his phone could rejoin the outside world.

As expected, the signal was piss poor at best. He tried and failed several times to get the picture out. When he tried to send out a regular text, however, that managed to go through.

"Hello?" he ended up texting Micaiah.

"Can I help you?" Micaiah replied.

"I've been trying to send a picture all morning. The signal up here is shit."

"You can save your pictures until you get home. It's only a couple days."

"Rifun sent his sign. And he caught me alone."

"Fuck. What happened?"

Tommen tried to detail the incident, but the message wouldn't go through. He tried to cut it down, but soon discovered that he wasn't able to send more than three sentences at a time. He told Micaiah as much.

"Did Rifun hurt you?" Micaiah asked.

"Well, not really. I guess he did another Akari trick or something. Tell you later."

"Fair enough. What did he give you?"

"A book. He said it was a gift from the Author."

"Have you read it yet?"

"I only got through the prologue. I don't know, Cai. It's spooky how good it is."

There was a long pause, and Tommen grew worried. Either the signal had cut out completely, which was entirely possible, Micaiah was writing up a super long text which wouldn't get through anyway, or else he had no words to say. First two options aside, Tommen wasn't sure what to think. So far, whatever the Cult of the Akari believed or could do, the Akarin were like their equal and opposite reaction. Or maybe that worked vice versa. Which meant that if the Cult knew about the books, the Akarin did, too. Their opinions on them would be the difference.

Finally, Micaiah replied, "Read the Book if you get the chance. We'll talk about it when you get back. Easier than trying to send short texts."

Well, that much was the truth.

"Okay," Tommen said after a minute. "But I do have one

question."

"As long as it's short."

"It's a yes or no."

"Fire away."

"Do you have any books? Like this, I mean?"

Another long pause. This time, Tommen was almost positive Micaiah was hesitating. Yes and no were not long texts to write or get out. Then, "Yes."

"How many?"

"I thought you said you only had one question."

"Sorry. Two?"

"I have five books."

"How did you get them?"

"Tommen."

"Sorry."

"We'll talk about them when you get home. Easier than a bunch of short texts. All right?"

"What if something happens between now and then?"

"Then something happens. Aren't you supposed to be doing camp stuff?"

"Sleeping in today. Aren't you supposed to be doing bakery stuff?"

"Haven't left for work yet."

"Oh. I didn't interrupt anything, did I?"

"Only breakfast. Don't worry about it."

"Sorry. I'll see you guys when I get home. Can you tell my dad?"

"I'll try."

And that was the end of that. Tommen powered down his phone and lay back in his sleeping bag, trying to process it all. Read the book, Micaiah had said. Well, what harm was there in reading a book? That one was easy. Books contained ideas, and ideas could be a far more lethal weapon than any gun.

Throwing up a Band, he went back to his bag and pulled out

the book once more. It was a little dirty and worn already from being dropped in the dirt and shoved around in a bag, but it still hadn't burst into flames. If this thing was a gift from the Author, he figured it was a good sign that he still hadn't burst into flames either. It was just an ordinary book.

Just an ordinary book, he told himself, opening up past the prologue to chapter one, Birthday.

Chapter Nineteen
Vigilance

Holy shit, you look like death," Micah commented as his brother walked in the door.

"Good morning to you, too," Micaiah grumbled.

"Something happen? You and Kayla all right?"

"Huh? Yeah, she's fine." Micaiah flipped on the lights in the office. "We're good. She had to leave early for a consult this morning."

"Ah, so you didn't get any this morning is what you're mad about."

Micaiah went out and snapped a rubber band at Micah who swatted it away. His twin brother had deadly aim with those things, and Micah had learned decades ago to never get near him when he had a wet towel either.

"No, not that either," Micaiah informed him, retrieving the rubber band. He straightened and stretched. "Tommen got his first Book."

Micah frowned, mulled that over, then nodded as he went back to beating dough. "Well, it'll challenge his view of things, that's for sure."

"Rifun is the one who gave it to him."

"Fuck."

"That's what I said."

Micah floured his hands and turned the dough. "You mean to say that Rifun stalked Tommen all the way to camp? How did he get his hands on the Book anyway? Which copy was it?"

"I don't know and I don't know. But, if it just appeared while

Tommen was away, then it's more likely that it's only the second copy. I'll head to the fortress later to double-check."

"Good. God knows what would happen if Rifun managed to get his hands on both copies."

"Agreed. Copying services are in short supply these days. Everyone wants to split up and split off and merge with the like-minded, but they seem to forget the core of our existence."

Micah shrugged. "Maybe you should take them down to the print shop, get them printed up there. Make a couple thousand Xerox copies."

"Very funny, but we already went over that."

"I know, I know. Purple ink and all that." Micah dropped the dough in a bread pan and set it aside. Ripping off another chunk of dough, he went on, "So, what's next?"

Micaiah sighed. "I don't know. Rifun seems to be beating us at every turn, always getting to Tommen first."

"You think that maybe it's because you keep shoving him aside? Every time he asks about it, you tell him later, later, later. When you're ready, when we're ready, when such an event has happened. You're waiting for the storm to pass. Well, Rifun lives in that storm. He's sweeping up Tommen while we're all hunkered down safe and sound in our own shelters. Maybe it's time to go to him in the storm and teach him. Counteract Rifun, fight back. Stop playing defensive and go offensive."

"That would have been my next step, except that whole part about Tommen quitting and deciding to spend his summer two hundred miles away."

"Yes, but Rifun went to him. We're still here."

"We have day jobs."

Micah gave him a look. "We have the ability to fucking control Time and portal-jump anywhere we damn well please."

"The work load would be overwhelming."

"For Tommen? Or for you?" When Micaiah faltered, Micah continued, "Rifun is out there training him right now. Tommen is getting that workload dumped on him whether we're there or not. Difference is, Rifun is holding a gun to his head to make him do it."

"You seem to have this all figured out, so why don't you go?"

"Don't turn this back on me. Okay, I'm just as new as he is. Blind leading the blind and all that. Plus, you already said that you and Kayla were going to oversee his training. How would that look to him if I'm the one who showed up to the first day of school? Bad enough that Rifun seems to be the one at the front of the room right now."

"All right!" Micaiah snapped. "Fine." He sighed. "Tommen is coming home in a couple days. I told him to read the Book, and I'll give him the next couple days to do so. When he gets home, then we can talk about it a little more. After that, we can decide how to proceed since he has another half of summer camp to attend anyway. Does that make you happy?"

"At least it's a plan of action," Micah told him. "Something better than later, later, later, we'll see." He set aside another bread pan. "What about Walter?"

"What about him?"

"Has he gotten any Books? How are you going to explain all of this to him?"

"That I don't know. Probably the same way I explained it to you. At least he's already been to the fortress."

"True. Just making sure I'm covering all my bases and getting you thinking."

Micaiah sighed and shook his head. He was just turning to go back to the office when he paused. "And as for your comments about the blind leading the blind, that really only applies to learning the Akari abilities and the higher learning. Basic knowledge you can generally study together and be okay."

"So, what, you want me to be a teacher now?"

"Not yet, but you don't have to defer everything to me all the time."

Micah shook his head. "Whatever, man. I'm sending everyone

your way."

"What about after I'm gone?"

"I can still send them your way. Text, email, fortress, whenever and wherever."

"I think by that time, you'll know enough to take on some of the responsibility yourself."

Micaiah stepped back and headed into the office, firing up the computer and shuffling papers, musing over his work load for the day. Micah could almost count down to the exact second his routine. Eleven seconds of fussing with the computer, thirty-seven seconds of looking at papers, one minute and fifteen seconds of sorting some of those papers, six seconds of complaining about those papers, eight minutes and thirty-six seconds of printing off the daily reports and baking schedules, twelve seconds of doubting whether the numbers would suffice for the day, twenty-two seconds of running the numbers figuring out product and labor costs, four seconds of staring at the wall having his own thoughts, then five seconds to get back out to the kitchen with the daily sheets, ready to work.

"Right on time," Micah said, pulling out a large container of oatmeal.

"Huh?" Micaiah looked up from his papers as he set them out.

"I still don't know how I feel about you leaving, but at the very least, you need a vacation. You're becoming predictable."

"I'm not sure how I want to take that."

Micah just shook his head and rummaged around for the measuring cups. There was no real reason to get to the bakery so early. They could arrive half an hour before opening and still be on schedule to open. Part of it they did for show; their neighbors both at home and in the plaza were nosier than they let on, and they would realize that the bakers weren't exactly working baker's hours. But the other part of it was just having downtime. They could stagger their shifts and have some alone time to think and plan by themselves, or they could match the shifts and have a little bro time, something they didn't get a lot of despite working together. Somehow, with all that had gone on in the

Wheel and the Time Trial, now with Micaiah planning to leave, Micah found himself longing for more time with his brother. The little ironies of life.

"So, where are you planning on going?" Micah asked as Micaiah got an apron and washed his hands. "When you do finally take off?"

"Well, we'll probably spend a little time in the fortress, just making sure everything is taken care of. Kayla says the backlog for new lives is ridiculous right now. Depending on how that goes, we might do some traveling. Start in Ireland and go from there."

"Going to see what became of our home?"

"Something like that."

Their little village had been destroyed thanks to haphazard bombing during World War II, but supposedly it had been rebuilt in the decades since. Sure it would probably be bigger and as industrialized as ever, but home was home.

"I assume Kayla wants to head home to Alaska?" Micah wondered.

"Of course. And I assume we'll make it there eventually. She is adamant that our first child be born among her people. I have no real problem with it, except for that whole cold business."

"Top of the world, buddy. But you knew that when you married her, and she isn't one you want to cross."

"She gets her temperament as much from the cold and snowstorms as her name."

"Hey, I've asked before, does she have any sisters?"

"Please, you know they'd be long gone by now."

"Fine, how about grand-nieces or something?"

Micaiah just grinned and shook his head. After a minute of silence, he asked, "What will you do, once I leave?"

Micah paused in his work for just a moment. Then, "I don't know. I guess I should get my paperwork in for a new life. Ten-plus years, it's time to move on. I can't stay this young and good-looking forever."

"Yeah, but, what will you do? I mean, you have the opportunity to do anything you want without me looking over your shoulder."

"I don't know," Micah answered honestly. "I've always followed your lead." He sighed. "Maybe it's just as well we're going our separate ways."

"Aw, my wittle bruver is all gwown up."

Micah threw a small ball of dough at him that missed by half a mile at least.

When it came time to open, Micaiah took the counter and Micah stayed in the kitchen. Just a few minutes before the sign was officially turned from *Dúnta* to *Oscailte*, Kyle walked in.

"Morning," Micah greeted.

"Hey, so, busy day today you think?" Kyle wondered.

"Hard to tell. It's only Thursday and not a major holiday. Why?"

"Well, I kind of have a little business to take care of."

Micah raised a brow. "Mind if I ask what kind of business? Let me say it this way, is it Time business or personal business?"

Kyle squirmed. "Well, a little of both, actually."

Micah folded his arms. "This ought to be interesting."

"Okay, so, you know how I'm technically considered a Runner, right? Well—and believe me, I am so grateful to you guys for letting me kind of hunker down for a while, especially with all that shit in the Wheel, holy fuck—but my Master kind of figured out where I've been hiding."

"I see. Go on..."

"Well, I guess he's been in contact with Walter and they're going to be in today."

Micah nodded slowly while inwardly screaming. He should have known about all of this. He would have. They both would have, he and Cai, if they were still Lieutenants. But they weren't. They were just Lieutenant-trained Masters. They weren't officers and not privy to that kind of information anymore. They would have no knowledge of the goings-on in the District unless they wanted to go and hunt for it themselves the old-fashioned way.

As it was, business had been conducted, and Micah and Micaiah had not been informed of it or included in any way. It was both expected and yet still hurtful. He took an even breath. Maybe it was time to move on, get away from here, and start his own life.

Micaiah manned the counter for about an hour before handing it off to Kyle, but before he vanished into his dungeon that was the office, he popped back in the kitchen.

"Kyle said Walt and his Master are going to be coming in today," Micah told him.

Micaiah nodded. "Walt called about ten minutes ago, said they'd be over about two o'clock. He asked if we minded sitting in on it."

Micah took a pan of cinnamon rolls out of an oven. "Why? We're not his Lieutenants anymore."

Micaiah shrugged. "I don't know. I told him we were at his disposal. He said okay and hung up. I don't know what's going on. Just thought I'd let you know, but you seem to already be aware of it."

With that, he made for the office and Micah returned to his work. Micah mulled over the cryptic call and request. They were no longer Walter's Lieutenants. Given that they were both set to leave, even if they were offered their jobs back, it would make no practical sense at this point.

There were only a few reasons Walter would ask them to sit in on the meeting, in spite of their demotion. First, Kyle would need some sort of work reference. Not impossible, but hardly befitting such a cryptic call. Walter could just as easily spring that on them on the spot and it would be no big deal. Second, Kyle's Master wanted detailed accounts of his actions while in their jurisdiction, which would include the failed rescue attempt by Kyle and Jenna in the Wheel. That was very possible. Third, there was something far more sinister at work that involved them, the twins, that they needed to know about. Again, very possible. But what kind of sinister things would that be? Micah thought about it for a minute, then decided he didn't want to know.

The day wasn't an unusually busy day. People came in for breakfast, Walter came in for his pastry and did not disclose any details about his cryptic call, people came in for mid-morning snacks, people came in for lunch, all fairly usual. There was a retirement party. Micaiah delivered special order slips to the kitchen as they were called in.

Micah hardly looked up from his work until the back door opened and Jenna walked in around one-thirty. The way she'd been talking lately, she was getting ready to put in her two-week notice and head back home herself. If Kyle left, then she left, they would have no one to help until Tommen got back from camp. Jenna they might be able to persuade to stay a couple more weeks. Kyle, well, that depended on his Master.

Speaking of which, right on time, Walter and another gentleman walked into the bakery. The man was hardly what Micah might have expected of a Timekeeper Master. He was short, fat, balding in no graceful manner, and looked like he'd been sweating since the temperature climbed above sixty.

It was the middle of the afternoon, between lunch and late afternoon rush, so the bakery was empty.

"Jenna, can you man the kitchen for a minute?" Micah asked. "We have a visitor."

"Sure," she answered, not looking at him.

Kyle was told to man the front, which he did with what was, in Micah's opinion, a huge sigh of relief.

Then he, Micaiah, Walter, and the man ducked into the office.

"You must be Kyle's Master," Micaiah observed.

"I am. Terry Vaughn, Master Timekeeper, District Eight."

"Micaiah and Micah Durvin, Master Timekeepers, District Four."

"Mas—I thought you were the Lieutenants?"

"We were, until we were ousted by Her Majesty." Referring to

Regina. Regina DeBitch as she'd come to be called behind her back.

"I see. Well, be that as it may, seeing how you have been working with Kyle over the last few months, I expect that it would be more appropriate to speak with you anyway."

"Flattered. What can we do for you?"

So they spent probably half an hour discussing Kyle's work, both in the bakery and in Time, including the failed rescue attempt.

"If you don't mind my asking," Micah said finally, "why ask us about the rescue? Why not ask him?"

"I expect I will at some point, but it wasn't really about that. See, I don't know what he's told you about me, but I am concerned for him."

"So concerned you waited eight months to figure out where he'd run off to?"

"Information was unreliable, and I decided that in light of the events in the Wheel that it was best to lay low. If he was dead, then there was nothing I could do. If he was alive, I knew he had the cunning to keep himself alive and hidden, and I wasn't going to compromise that. Once things went back to normal, it took me a little time to track him down, yes, and be able to get out here to get him."

"I sense a 'but' coming," Micaiah said.

Terry sighed. "Kyle's introduction into Time...was poor judgment on my part. I work as a youth program coordinator designed to get kids off the streets, into homes, get them jobs, you know, help them out. Kyle was an outcast on the streets, none of the local gangs wanted him because he was unwilling to kill. In big cities like Los Angeles, that's a common initiation and he wouldn't do it. But he didn't have the resources to do much else, and—well, anyway, to make a long story short, I thought I could help him out by making him a Timekeeper." He shook his head. "He's not right for it. He doesn't want it. And I think we're in a time of peace, or enough peace, where he can be Suppressed or just allowed to go free without being threatened with clock-breaking and being turned into a vegetable.

"I ask you about his work both Earth-side and Time-side

because I want to judge his reactions and actions in both. In Time, he'll do as he's told, but only that. We both know how kids love party tricks, and he's just not that into it anymore. The ability to bend Time, and it's just not working for him. Having a steady job, steady income, having his own place? Watching him from outside, he was good at it and he enjoyed it."

"So what, exactly, are you asking of us?" Micah wondered.

Terry turned to Walter. "I'm asking that, if he wants it, that Kyle be Suppressed." He looked at the twins. "If you're willing, I would also ask that you keep him on in your employ here at the bakery. He's made something of himself and he's proud of it. I think he'll do just fine, just without Time."

Micaiah glanced at Walter who gave an almost imperceptible nod. Micah was the one who went to the office door and called Kyle into the office.

"Am I going home?" Kyle wondered meekly.

"Well, Kyle, that's your choice," Walter told him. "At this point, either here or California can be your home." He briefly explained the discussion. "You can go back to California with Terry and continue being a Timekeeper Apprentice, just as you were. Or you can stay here. I'll Suppress you, and you will have no further interactions with Time, save whatever Micah and Micaiah do with their Bands and the bakery and all that. You keep your job, keep your apartment, and all goes on as it was, just without Time."

"Really? Like, you'll let me? I don't have to have my clock broken or anything?"

"We're in a time of peace, Kyle," Terry told him. "Don't let the opportunity slip by if it's what you want."

"And, like, Suppression, I can still come back if I really did want to, right?"

"You can," Micaiah began slowly, "but it's not something you can treat as just an on or off switch. You are either here or you're not. There is no middle ground, kind of a Timekeeper or kind of not. You understand?"

Kyle nodded. "Yeah. Yeah, I get it. And I've been thinking about it a lot. Really, I have. I mean, I know I might regret it, but..." He looked at Terry. "I can't do it. It's really just not my thing."

Terry nodded. "I see that now. And I'm sorry I forced you into it. That was my error."

And just like that, Walter stood and Suppressed Kyle. After a few more minutes of small talk and pleasantries, he was dismissed to the front counter, and Terry was free to go. Walter, however, remained.

"Another happy ending," he mused sadly.

"Jealous?" Micaiah asked, semi-seriously.

"A little, but that's not the point. Point is, there's still work to be done."

"Walt, we're glad you like us, but we're not Lieutenants anymore," Micah reminded him. "And we're packing up here, Cai sooner than me."

"I know." Now Walter was all business again as he dug out a piece of paper from a pocket. It was laminated, so it folded weird. When it was unfolded, though, it gave Micah pause.

It was a message written out using the bodies of flies, from fruit flies to horseflies, like the stereotypical ransom message in old crime shows where the letters got cut out of magazines and newspapers.

"Dropping like flies, one by one. Who will be first?"

"Where did you get this?" Micaiah asked severely.

"It was taped to Tommen's bedroom door this morning," Walter told him, fire in his low voice. "Before you ask, I already texted him this morning and he says he's fine. Nothing in his room looked disturbed, nothing in my room looked disturbed, and other than that, everything has been so far normal."

"Have you alerted your new Lieutenants?" Micah inquired.

"I have. They say they'll keep an eye out, which I trust they will. But I think you have a better idea who this is from and what it's about."

"I expect so," Micaiah agreed grudgingly. "Problem is, until Tommen gets home, this is all we have to go on."

"You think Rifun will communicate further once Tommen is home?"

Micaiah and Micah glanced at each other. "I'm saying he already has. Tommen texted me this morning, too, saying Rifun had threatened him. His location made texting any more than short sentences impossible, and the subject matter is best covered in person. To answer your unspoken question, I expect he'll be safe until he gets home, yes."

Walter still seemed uncertain, and Micah really didn't blame him. The man had been through too much already; he needed to be cut a break. Micaiah seemed to sense his growing anxiety because he changed the subject. "Have you told Tommen about you and Laura yet?"

"Yes, I did. It's hard to judge his reaction through text though."

"I'll give you that."

"He hasn't said anything to you, has he?"

"Not a peep."

"You think she should come with me when I pick him up?"

Both Micaiah and Micah shook their heads, but it was Micaiah who answered, "No. He needs to be reassured that you and him are still tight. He'll want to talk to you, not you and her. When you come back, all three of you can go out to lunch, something informal so they can get a feel for each other without being cornered at home with no place to run."

Walter nodded. "Maybe you're right. I won't be you and just spring something on him."

Micaiah grinned and pointed at him. "But you were going to, if he hadn't guessed about it before going to camp."

Walter looked guilty. "Okay, I guess you have a point there." He stood. "And I suppose you have a business to run, too. Are you going to close up shop or sell this place?"

"Haven't decided," Micah said. "Officially, he's quitting, which leaves total ownership to me. I don't know if I want to go through the hassle of selling it, not the least because that would leave a legal paper trail back to me, and I need to disappear."

"That is true. Unless you sold it to another Time Agent looking for a new life as a baker."

"Well, if you find one, let me know."

Walter promised he would before he left, grabbing his pastry on the way out. On the counter, Kyle seemed both liberated and yet perplexed. He didn't have the burden of Timekeeping hanging over him anymore, and yet he also had to adjust to not having his abilities anymore either, from Banding and anything else he'd learned to a heightened perception of time. True, they'd all gotten some good practice in when they'd been Suppressed for six months, but it was still a strange sensation at first.

"How are you doing?" Micah asked him from the office door.

"Great," Kyle answered, and Micah found that he believed him.

He turned and closed the door to the office and faced Micaiah. "So."

"So," Micaiah echoed. "Six weeks into his defeat and Rifun is at it again. Looks like it's a mission of vengeance this time."

"Dropping like flies, one by one. Who will be first?" Micah folded his arms. "Question is, who all is on his hit list?"

"I think it would be safe the say the five of us are in the line of fire. Me, you, Kayla, Walter, and Tommen."

"The first four I could see, but I can't imagine he would hurt Tommen, especially after he just handed him his first Book. It doesn't make sense."

"What else doesn't make sense is that Rifun gave Tommen his Book while he is at camp. Rifun knows where he's at. But he still taped the message on his bedroom door at home where his dad would find it, and he would inevitably show us."

"Two different pieces to the same puzzle," Micah mused. "We're not out of the woods yet; Rifun wants us for something."

"Aye, and I don't think it's anything good."

"It never is."

Micaiah went and sat in his comfy office chair. "I'm going to call Kayla, make sure she's all right."

Micah nodded. "Without getting the full story, there isn't much we can do right now. We'll just have to wait until Tommen gets back from camp."

He left the office, but he doubted his brother noticed. Such were Micaiah's priorities these days. Micah didn't blame him or feel any anger toward him about it. His feelings were divided between jealousy and abandonment. Jealousy, because he wished he could find that same kind of love within Time or the Akari. Abandonment because all the changes seemed to just happen overnight. First they were two dudes living together, and one of them just happened to sneak off on Friday nights to go meet his secret wife. Suddenly that secret wife wasn't so secret anymore and she was moving in and living with them and suddenly, Micah was reduced to a mere roommate.

As he started on the next recipe in the queue, he almost had to laugh. Rifun had just delivered another threat against them, and Micah was fixated on his sister-in-law moving in with them. The threat of death seemed to be so perpetual these days that he hardly noticed the stink anymore. On the other hand, such complacency could be a dangerous thing, and their own ignorance of the danger could end up being their downfall.

Chapter Twenty
Vandalism

Tommen got partway through chapter five, Under the Bleachers, before deciding to call it quits. He told himself he needed to give his eyes a rest as the little inky letters squirmed on the page, but mostly he was unnerved by the accuracy and in-depth knowledge of the book. It was one thing to record events as they happened; it was another to record events no one else should know about as well as his private thoughts about those events. He stuffed the book back in his bag, then dropped the Band.

He carefully picked his way out of the tent, mindful of Saul sleeping near the entrance. Let sleeping Marines lie, he figured. The last thing he needed was a rabid wolf soldier chomping on his leg in a half-dazed psychotic episode.

But he made it out unmolested. The air was chillier than expected and he shivered. He thought about ducking back in to grab his jacket, then decided against it. Instead, he meandered his way over to one of the fires which Rick had managed to bring back to life.

"Good morning," Rick greeted.

"Morning," Tommen murmured. "Breakfast ready yet?"

"Just as soon as you go and catch it."

He was only half-joking, really. The plan for that day was one last massive haul — of fish, of small game, of forage — one last huge meal, then packing up and returning to the more modern camp, the base camp. Once they off-loaded everything from the buses and whatnot, then it would be open free time until campfire time, then to bed.

It was going to be a glorious thing to sleep on a mattress

again, Tommen thought. Here, the ground was hard and the company was decidedly less than desirable. At the very least, they hadn't had Randall with them to stink up the place. They all would have died from asphyxiation, Tommen was sure.

Taking care not to disturb the others, Tommen got back in the tent and changed his clothes. There would be no alarm today or tomorrow, both of them just days to relax. The only reason there would be an alarm Saturday morning was because parents started arriving at eight o'clock.

"I'm going to head to the river," Tommen said when he got back out.

Rick merely nodded and waved him off.

He wasn't sure why he wanted to go to the river. This early in the morning with no one around, there was every chance that Rifun would appear. He could do anything from kill him to merely threaten him or have one of his "friendly chats" as he "checked up on his students."

Instead, what Tommen found when he headed to the river and stood on its banks, were massive paw prints, wolf prints, the same kind that appeared outside Wolf Cabin each morning. It wasn't hard to think that wolves roamed all over West Virginia, but it was a little harder to think that they would all be so huge; the coincidence was too coincidental.

Tommen did not see any wolves, nor did Rifun surprise him with more Akari psycho-babble and mystical artifacts from some Author. He puttered around the river for a short time, and learned how to Band to catch fish with his bare hands. Water was one of those things that did not Band well seeing how it was an element in continuous motion that was fluid in itself and to attempt to Band a section of the river was to dam it. Instead, he had to Band the fish themselves. This was almost as difficult seeing how the sight difference fucked with trying to feel out where the fish were in order to Band them. But, once he got going and got the hang of it, he was able to catch half a dozen, which he took back to camp.

Saul was awake and stoking another fire back to life, and there was more rustling from the tent. Tommen took the fish and started to clean them.

"I didn't know we got delivery out here," Saul said sarcastically.

"Nature's little wonders," Tommen replied.

"Are we going back to camp today?" Louis asked as he stumbled out of the tent, still half asleep.

"Yes, we are," Saul told him. "Just as soon as we get a good, hearty meal and get everything packed up."

"Good, because I'm tired of being out here."

"I wanna go home," Eric agreed as he fought his way past the tent flap.

"Well, we've got the rest of today and tomorrow yet to go," Tommen said. "I think you'll survive."

"What are we doing tomorrow?"

"Free day," Saul answered. "Whatever you want to do."

The way it sounded, there was going to be a good dose of sleeping in followed by some relaxing and resting and loafing around, interspersed occasionally by eating. Personally, Tommen was cool with that. He also had the great suspicion that once the boys got up and got going, that they would be as energetic and active as ever.

"Did you intentionally wake them up?" Tommen wondered when the boys wandered off to brush their teeth away from the tent.

Saul shook his head. "Jerry came by and got us up."

"Well, if you want to go out hunting again, I'll stick around here and get the tent packed up and everything, make sure the boys get their stuff."

Saul eyed him suspiciously, but said, "That's all right. My back is just about shot from hauling that deer. If I take it easy for a while, I might be able to do it again next month. When we really need it. Teenagers eat a lot. Not that you would know anything about that."

"No, of course not."

Tommen finished cleaning the fish and stuck them on poles to cook over the fire which was burning nicely again. Saul excused himself and headed into the forest.

To say Tommen was a little suspicious of the man's mood swings was an understatement, and he still couldn't shake the feeling that not every encounter with Saul was with the real Saul. Still, there was nothing he could do about it until he got home and could talk to his dad and the twins. Bad enough that he had zero signal out here and couldn't do much better than an occasional three-sentence text.

Pretty soon, everyone in camp was up and around, slowly getting ready for the day. The girls' tents were busy packing up while the boys' tents were eager to get out there and get back fishing or trapping. Some had gotten used to catching their own food and were ready to learn more; others just wanted to get back to civilization. Tommen was always happy to do things on his own like this, catch his own food, fish in the river, hunt for berries and forage, but he couldn't deny that this particular experience was wearing on him. Having to watch out for eighty kids was exhausting, never mind trying to share food with them. Sharing food with a bunch of teenagers was going to be a small nightmare in itself.

Thankfully, the deer Saul had brought back still had enough left over that there wasn't a huge need to ravage the forest. Tommen's fish helped offset the food needs for his tent, and they were eating well by midmorning, eating quickly so they could pack up quickly so they could get back to camp quickly in time for dinner made by Pam.

But packing up a camp with a bunch of kids was nowhere near quick or easy. Things were lost, things were broken, and there were always accusations of things being stolen. Tommen just made sure that he got his hearing aid charger back, his phone was in his pocket, and his mystery book was still hidden away, and he considered himself good.

The hike back down the trail to the trailhead seemed to take only about half the time as it did going up, despite the fact that they were going primarily uphill on their trek back. Maybe it was all psychological. He wanted to get back to camp so he tricked himself into thinking that it didn't take as long. Or maybe it was one of those subtle things that average people were capable of, right up there with "time flies when you're having fun" and "a watched pot never boils." The collective desire of the kids to get home quicker translated into something of a subconscious Fast Band that carried them to the trailhead and deposited them on the bus half an hour earlier than expected.

Or maybe it was all psychological and Tommen was crazy, in which case he really needed to take a week off of camp.

Unlike the first ride, all the cabins got to the buses at the same time, and seating was determined solely by who could pile on the fastest and get their stuff stuffed in their seats first. Tommen watched as one girl tossed her bag four rows down so she could claim a seat before the girl in front of her. That led to complaints and accusations, but a word from Tommen and they kept moving. They were only going to be on the bus for a single ride that was only a couple hours. The fate of the world did not rest on which seat they sat in.

He hoped.

"Ready for camp to be over?" Saul asked, sitting by the window and shifting constantly, trying to find a comfortable position, flinching in pain.

"I'm ready to sleep in my own bed again," Tommen answered diplomatically. "One week, and then back to work." He mused over the timeline. "Then I go home, take my driver's test, and then it's back to school."

"You a senior?"

"Junior."

"Why did you decide to take twelve weeks off from driving right before your driver's test?"

"I've got time; I can make it up and get in some practice beforehand."

Saul studied him for a minute before reaching into his bag and bringing out his book. Tommen thought about the book hidden among his things. Truthfully, he hadn't stopped thinking about it, but seeing Saul now just brought it to the forefront of his mind.

What was he going to do with the book when he got home? Sure, sure, he'd show it to his dad and the twins and they'd do whatever they needed to do, but what then? He couldn't put it on his bookshelf with all the rest of his books. For one, it was just too weird. For two, chances were good that Becky would find it and want to read it. Who knew how she would react to it? She'd probably think it was pretty cool that someone wrote a story about him and his dad, but how would he feel about her dismissing it as fiction? Rejected, probably, told that it was all a nice little fantasy and he should live in the real world. Problem was, that fictional world was his real world. On top of that, there was something ominous about the words "Book One of the Chivalrous Welshman" implying that there were more books to come. What if Becky made an appearance in those books?

This was all way above his head. It was a mind-fuck. Honestly, he didn't even know if he could handle it. What he really wanted was to go back to the days when things were easy and the only thing he had to worry about was studying for his Apprentice review. The closest thing he was going to get to that right now was focusing on surviving the last two days of camp and trying to get enough rest in the next week to be ready for the second round of camp.

"What are you going to be doing for your week off?" Tommen asked conversationally.

"A lot of sleeping," Saul answered. He shifted positions and sucked in a breath at some pain in his back. "Probably have to go to a lot of meetings. Of the disciplinary type. Argue with my brother for a bit. Then I'll be back here."

"Why disciplinary meetings?"

"Reasons."

It was a dismissal, and Tommen knew enough to take the hint. Whatever stick had been up Saul's ass during the last couple days of camping, he appeared to have calmed down and they had a truce going again. If they had to work together for the next four weeks,

Tommen had little desire to make an enemy of him.

About twenty minutes into the ride, Mr. Wilson took the lead, standing in the front of the bus and calling everyone's attention, wanting to know what their favorite part of the three-day camp was, cool things they saw, things they learned, the whole nine yards. For some, the fishing was the best part. For others, the foraging and learning the edible plants was the highlight. For a few, it was the wildlife they saw—alive—walking and flying and rummaging and hiding, as curious about the humans as the humans were about them.

For one boy, not from Wolf Cabin, the best part had been cleaning and gutting the small animals they trapped and feeling all the organs in his hands. That grossed out most of the girls, but it was a practical thing to know. A liver was a liver, and pictures in textbooks could only go so far. For most people, a liver was simply an abstract concept, something that got ruined from too much drinking. But the seeing and the feeling, that could go a long way.

When called on for his answer, Tommen went the diplomatic route and said he enjoyed the whole thing, being able to get out and camp again. Needless to say, there weren't very many places to camp in the city of Charleston, and the backyard really didn't cut it.

Saul answered that he was happy to get out in nature, alone in his people's homeland, with the peace and tranquility of the woods, listening to the turn of the earth. He was happy to hunt the old way and do things as they used to do, bringing down the deer with his own skill and his own bow and his own arrows. Listening to him, Tommen could say it was probably the happiest and proudest Saul had ever sounded all throughout camp.

"What happens to all the furs when we get back to camp?" Tommen wondered once the last person had told of their favorite moment.

"They'll get used in arts and crafts in the older kids' camp," Saul replied, going back to his book. "They have the skill and patience to work with the furs, where the younger kids don't. The older kids do a lot of things the younger kids don't, including show respect and responsibility." His last words were filled with acidic sarcasm.

"Except Wolf Cabin, right?"

"Except Wolf Cabin."

Tommen did not say anything more after that; they were almost back to base camp anyway. It was strange to think that even once they got back, they still had one more day of camp left. It was like being in a race, getting to the top of a hill and seeing the finish line directly in front of you, only to realize that there's still another valley between the two hilltops. It was a slogging, exhausted sprint to the finish.

Well, maybe less of a sprint and more of a rutted, rocky, washed out dirt road that wound this way and that up the mountain. Those in the bus had to choose whether to keep hold of their things or find something to hold onto so they didn't go bouncing out of their seats.

The bus plugged its way up the hill, seeming to pause only once before giving a wheeze and crawling the last fifty feet and cresting the hill, pulling into the parking lot like an exhausted first-time marathon jogger. Anyone who had still been a little sleepy thus far quickly perked up, and all the kids were chatting away excitedly. Some were making plans for when they finally got home, others conspired to figure out a way to stay longer or sneak into the older kids' camp.

Only because the doors were still closed did the kids stay on the bus and not go rolling out like a tsunami, but no amount of yelling, threatening, or promising could keep them together in orderly groups until everyone had gotten off and gotten their stuff. Thankfully, the worst they did was run to the far reaches of the parking lot before turning back. Tommen could completely understand; his knees were sore and his legs were cramped from sitting in such a tight space for so long. Even the ride to school was less taxing.

Eventually, they found their three boys and corralled them to a slightly quieter area where they could talk.

"Okay, guys, we're going to head back to our cabin to get everything offloaded. Then we'll have a little bit of free time until Mr. Wilson calls us in for dinner. How does that sound?" Saul asked, trying to keep a cheery mood despite the gritted teeth.

"I wanna go to the fort!" Peter declared.

The others quickly picked up on his idea. Tommen could see that was the last thing Saul wanted to do, so he volunteered to take the boys to the fort so he could relax for a short time.

"But we still have to get all of this stuff put back," he reminded the boys. "So then, let's go. Faster we can get back to the cabin, faster we can get to the fort."

The boys tried to take off at a dead sprint, but they had only the energy for sprints, not endurance, and with their bags weighing them down, the best they managed to do was a fast walk. They crested the hill near the main hall where Tommen saw Mr. Wilson speaking with Pam and the kitchen crew in low voices, expressions dead serious. Their conversation seemed intense, as they appeared to have no awareness of anything going on around them. If they had, they might have been spared part of the mess than ensued.

Going downhill was a great asset when running, and as soon as the slope turned from up to down, the boys took off again. Unable to contain his own excitement, and desperate to stretch his legs, Tommen took off with them. He outpaced them two to one, but their head start made it a much closer race than it would probably normally be.

Tommen saw the broken window at about thirty yards.

"Hey! Hey, whoa! Whoa, whoa, whoa, stop! Hey! Stop!"

The boys did not pull up until probably ten feet from the cabin, but if their ungraceful, uncoordinated stop was any indication, they saw the broken window, too.

"Hold up, guys, hang on," Tommen said, coming in beside them, suddenly breathless. He herded them about ten yards away. "Let me take a look."

There were a few things to look for when examining a

breaking and entering, and the placement of the glass was not always a surefire indicator. Glass was stronger than it looked, and when it shattered, it didn't just fall inside or outside; all pieces went all directions. Tommen might have thought that the door was the point of entry based on the force and the broken handle, until he found blood on one of the broken window frames and a trail of blood leading into the cabin. He didn't actually go into the cabin, but he poked his head through one window and looked around. After that, he simply backed up and made sure to keep the boys away. A minute later, Saul painstakingly joined them.

"What the hell happened?" he demanded.

"I don't know," Tommen said. "But judging from the looks of things, we weren't the only ones."

Indeed, looking around, it seemed as though every cabin had been targeted, as well as some of the other buildings. He could see the girls' cabins all gathering together. Some were crying, some were shouting, but all were panicking. As for the other boys' cabins, a couple of the counselors were talking to each other while the counselor assistants tried to keep their campers occupied. At the very least, it did not appear as though any of the crime scenes had been disturbed too much.

Was it that obvious his dad was a cop?

"Well, there goes my nap," Saul sighed, sitting on his bag.

"I'd say he entered through that window," Tommen said, pointing. "Blood on the glass and inside, so he'd have to cut himself before he bled."

"I don't know, I've seen a few guys bleed before they ever broke skin, but I get your point. What about the door, then? Why not just unlock it from the inside? And how many guys are we talking here?"

Tommen folded his arms and let out a breath. "I don't know, I..." He started looking around in the dust. The wolf prints were long since swept away by time, wind, and rain. The bootprints, however, were fresh. Tommen did a quick check to make sure the prints weren't his, which they weren't. He looked around the cabin, trying not to get too close, and only saw one set of prints. He meandered over to Coon Cabin next door.

"Yours, too?" he wondered.

"Yup."

Again, he found only one set of prints. He headed over to Dragonfly Cabin and found the same. Then he returned to Wolf Cabin where the terror of the boys was quickly being replaced by novelty and curiosity, a very dangerous combination in children.

"Only one set of prints all the way around, everywhere," Tommen reported.

"I'm sure the police will be happy to note that when they arrive," Saul said, seemingly disinterested in the whole thing by now.

"The police?"

"There's a couple thousand dollars worth of damage here, if not more; you think Jerry isn't going to call the cops to at least get a report?"

Well, it made sense. Given that the cops showed up not two minutes later, Tommen was inclined to think the cops had been called even before they made it back on the buses. Probably Pam and the kitchen crew noticed it first when they returned and called it in. Was there damage in the main hall as well?

Only two officers showed up initially. Once they realized the scale of the vandalism, they quickly radioed for more help. Tommen watched from afar as they spoke with Mr. Wilson and the kitchen crew, then began a quick survey of the scene, starting with the main hall. By the time they got done there, two more officers had shown up. The first crew moved on to the office while the new crew went to the nurse's office and the camp store.

A few of the counselors and assistants had taken some of the kids up to the fort or on nature hikes in order to keep them busy and out of the officers' way, but most of the campers were more enthralled by the officers and evidence teams that began showing up in waves.

It put Tommen in mind of the night he, Eric, and Varad found the body of the nurse on the soccer field. Then his thoughts became torn between the incident itself, and the fact that he was reading about that same incident in the book Rifun had given him. It was uncanny. Worse, it was too coincidental.

Rifun had done this, of that much Tommen was almost certain.

Eventually, a team of officers and evidence gatherers made their way to Wolf Cabin. Eric, Peter, and Louis had gone with Crow Cabin on a nature hike, and Saul was currently napping under a tree, looking very uncomfortable on the hard ground.

"No one's gone inside," Tommen reported. "One set of bootprints outside. The door was forced, but there's blood on the glass around that window and inside the cabin; I'd say that's your point of entry."

One officer raised a brow. "How do you know there's blood inside the cabin if no one's been inside the cabin?"

Tommen felt his ears turn red. "Okay, I looked inside, but I didn't actually go in."

The officer nodded. "You find anything else, young sleuth?"

"No, but I can give you a pretty good guess as to who it was."

"Oh?"

"Rifun Ndolo."

"The Cutthroat Killer from Charleston?" one of the photographers interrupted, pausing in his work. "I find that hard to believe." He bent to take another picture.

"My dad is Homicide Detective Walter Forbes," Tommen said. "If you followed the story, you'd know who that makes me."

"His son," the first officer replied sarcastically. Then, "Yeah, we heard about the story. Some seriously f—messed up stuff down that way. But this is vandalism, not murder."

Tommen understood his logic, but that didn't mean he had to like it. He pressed harder. "Rifun Ndolo approached me while we were out camping."

"Did he? And what did he say or do?"

Problem was, there was no good way to explain their exchange without sounding like a lunatic. Everything they had talked about fell completely within the realm of Time. Tommen could probably make something up, but not only would that be dishonest, but...okay, it would just be dishonest. And probably largely unhelpful. Finally he answered, "Just...threats. Against me and my dad."

"And he somehow for some reason, leaves you alone in the woods without harming you, makes a two-hour drive back to your camp, vandalizes said camp, and then just disappears?"

When he put it that way, it did sound ridiculous. Rifun had killed women, killed a dozen officers, killed a man right in front of Tommen, and launched a coup that resulted in the deaths of billions. And he was going to trash a camp full of teeny-boppers? In the end, he was forced to relent and step back to let the officers do their job.

There was very little they could do, in the end. They took pictures, collected pertinent evidence like the bloody glass, but there were no bodies here, no witnesses, nothing to go on. That was the thing about the mountains; men could hide in them for years before they were found. Unlike the city where there were people around and cameras to catch every move, the mountains were wild and untamed, and they didn't care if the man traipsing through them was a saint or a terrorist.

Eventually, Mr. Wilson came around to each cabin, making his way to Wolf Cabin last. Tommen shook Saul awake, and the man came around less like a wolf and more like a grumpy grizzly just coming out of hibernation. He unsteadily got to his feet as Mr. Wilson approached.

"So, what's the plan?" Saul asked stiffly, though whether he was trying to hide the pain or stifle a yawn, Tommen couldn't tell.

"Well, the cops have finished up their assessment of the main hall, so we're going to get everyone there. We'll have dinner and try to reassure the kids that everything is fine and they're safe. Parents are being called. Some will be coming out tonight, others tomorrow. Most of the kids will be staying until Saturday, though. So if a parent shows up and wants to take their kid home, we're not going to stop them."

"Not that we could, really. Anything else?"

"All staff and counselors will have a short meeting tonight, enough to do a quick assessment and get the basics out of the way tonight. Tomorrow, once everyone has had a chance to sleep and calm down a little, we're going to have a larger meeting. Michelle, Dave, Andrew, and Pam and her crew will watch the kids so all counselors and assistants can attend." He sighed. "For right now, we're just going to round up the kids and get them to the main hall for dinner. I don't know about you, but I'm starving."

"I can agree to that," Tommen said.

"Are you ever not hungry?" Saul wondered, his tone difficult to judge. "All right. Well, our boys went out for a nature hike, so we'll have to do a little hunting for them."

Mr. Wilson simply nodded and left the task to the two of them. He looked like he'd aged ten years overnight.

"Has anything like this ever happened before?" Tommen wondered.

"Oh, sure," Saul answered. "But usually it's just some mischief done sometime between when the last camp ends and the first camp begins, those nine months when the camp isn't used. That's to be expected. And then there's the usual mischief that our boys typically cause. This, though, such brutal vandalism in the middle of camp while we're out camping?" He shook his head. "No, this is the first time that I recall seeing or hearing about. But I can't say it surprises me. The lengths some people will go to in order to get a thrill or steal a few bucks."

Tommen decided to not volunteer any information, such as how he'd once been an accomplice on similar breaking and entering runs. Difference was, they'd been looking for cash or small things to steal. This looked more like an act of rage, where the destruction itself was the point. Once they got in the cabins and started going through their things and got a better idea of whether anything was missing, then it would shed more light on the situation.

They found the boys just returning from their nature hike.

Whatever shock or fear they'd felt at the sight of the destruction, it seemed to have worn off on whatever adventure they'd been on.

"Okay, time for dinner!" Saul said, obviously struggling to remain upbeat. "Who's hungry?"

It was all they needed to hear. Dinner was almost an hour overdue, and everyone was starving.

The main hall wasn't in as bad a shape as Tommen might have imagined. The huge glass wall was still in tact, and he didn't see any evidence that tables and chairs had been manhandled and destroyed or anything.

Dinner turned out to be hot dogs, hamburgers, macaroni and cheese, and a number of other kid favorites, probably in an effort to keep the little campers happy and their minds off the event that had just occurred. Tommen grabbed two cheeseburgers, a hot dog, and a heaping scoop of mac and cheese.

"All this excitement probably isn't anything new to you," Pam said, her smile nervous and voice shaky. "Your dad being a cop and all."

"Nope, nothing new here," Tommen told her. "But still exciting. Everything okay in here? I mean, I haven't seen any windows smashed out or anything."

"No, nothing like that. Actually, the gas line was cut and this place was one cigarette away from becoming a huge bomb. Luckily Wallace smelled it before he lit up. The fire department left not ten minutes before you guys got back."

"Oh."

That certainly added a new perspective. Breaking windows and forcing doors was one thing. Cutting the gas like that so it filled a huge building and turned it into a ticking time bomb, that took malicious intent. There was no way to "accidentally" or "unwittingly" do that. That was just short of terrorism. And, hey, who knew terrorism better than Rifun, right? Tommen's suspicions were renewed.

"Anyway," Pam went on, "we're running the electric hot

plates so we could pan fry all of this; that's the real reason dinner took so long. Breakfast is going to be pretty sparse, too, but the gas company should be by sometime tomorrow morning to give us a fill. That way, we'll be all set for camp in a couple weeks."

"I'm not worried," Tommen tried to assure her. "You guys do a great job no matter what."

His words were true and sincere, but they still felt hollow as he knew that this was only the beginning. The question then became, what were Rifun's intentions here? Worse, since his gas bomb had been thwarted by sheer dumb luck on Wallace's part, what would he do the next time around to ensure that his plan succeeded?

"Am I taking your place at the meeting tonight?" Tommen asked as he sat down at the table.

"Are you insane?" Saul said, shifting and flinching at the pain in his back. "If you go to the meeting, that means I have to go to the campfire, which means hauling wood to put into the fire."

"I'm sure the others would understand if you didn't or couldn't."

"It also means campfire songs and dance."

"Well, you might have a point there. All right, fine, I'll go to the campfire."

"Good man." Saul sighed and shook his head. "I'm going to run off to the nurse's office for a minute before I have to suffer through a meeting like this. Don't eat my food."

"I make no promises," Tommen said, smirking.

Saul took longer than just a minute and returned long after his food had gotten cold. He ate it anyway.

"So, is Michelle part of your tribe, too?" Tommen ventured cautiously. "I mean, like, Saul Wolf. Michelle Trout. That sort of thing?"

Saul shook his head. "Shoshonee. Shawn, too."

He'd just finished up his food when Mr. Wilson made the silent sign for all counselors to follow him for the meeting. Seeing how dinner was almost wrapped up anyway, the counselor assistants,

Tommen included, took the opportunity to wrangle the kids and get them excited for a campfire with its ghost stories and s'mores.

It was obscenely late. The campfire got started at the time it was normally ending. Just as well that there was no alarm set for the next day. Even so, as the ghost stories began, Tommen's phone buzzed for a text. It was Becky.

"So, how was camping?"

He let out a breath. "It's been a really long day. Can it please wait until tomorrow?"

"Having too much fun without me, huh?"

"No more than I do with you."

"Very smooth."

"Please, Becky, I'm exhausted, and the campfire is still going."

"All right, if you insist."

She did not press the issue, which meant she'd probably been looking for conversation as an excuse to take a break from whatever project she was working on. Finding none, she didn't have time to complain about it, instead going right back to work. Tommen was never so relieved. He considered texting his dad or the twins, then figured that they would probably be asleep, and seeing how no one had been hurt and no explicit threats had been made, it could probably wait until morning.

Famous last words, he was sure.

Mr. Wilson and the counselors joined them just as the fire was wrapping up, the coals being spread so they could burn out safely, rousing tired campers to make it the last hundred feet to their cabins. When they arrived, Tommen was surprised to see that most of the mess had been modestly cleaned up. Gear and stuff had been sorted into vague piles, but the glass, blood, anything broken or dangerous was all cleaned up. The windows had even been covered in plastic sheets, like the kind used to winterize houses and keep cold air out.

"Part of the reason the meeting took so long," Saul reported grudgingly.

"Would you have rather gone to the meeting or the campfire?"

Tommen asked smartly.

"Meeting. Boring and dull, but nowhere near as strenuous as the campfire would have been."

"Michelle give you something?"

He nodded. "Yeah, but it only goes so far. What I really need is some good chiropractic work done, but that's not happening anytime soon."

"Why not?"

Saul gave him a look Tommen had come to know as the "fuck if I'm going to tell you" look.

Despite everyone wanting to just collapse into a good deep slumber for the next twenty hours, they still had to herd the kiddos up to the showers. They hadn't showered in three days. In kids, that was pushing it. In adults, that was most definitely crossing a line. Tommen could smell himself even above the smoky campfire smell, and he felt completely gross.

"No alarm tomorrow, right?" Tommen confirmed as he finally unrolled his sleeping bag.

"If it goes off, I'm beating it with a hammer," Saul said grouchily.

"Just checking."

And that was that. The boys had barely even made it into their sleeping bags before they were out.

Tommen had hoped that the excitement, combined with how long he'd been up, would make it easy to just drop out and sleep like a rock. It didn't. He woke up numerous times in the night, each time with a different feeling of impending doom. The first time had been a falling sensation, and he startled awake only to find that he was still safely where he needed to be in his sleeping bag on the bed. The second time, he'd been absolutely sure that something was hovering just over him, ready to spear him or shoot him or eat him or something else terrible. Again, he startled awake to find nothing of the sort.

The third time, he wasn't even sure at what point he was

awake and what point he was asleep, because both felt real to him. He could have sworn that someone had been calling his name. At first, he thought maybe someone was calling to him like they needed his help. In the darkness of some unknown dream, he was running in some unknown direction, looking for whoever it was calling for him. Then the voice changed, or maybe it hadn't changed at all, and suddenly it was mocking him, calling for him, taunting him. And he knew the voice, too. It could only belong to one person.

"Tommen...Tommen...Tommen...Tommen!"

Tommen jumped awake, flying out of his sleep and successfully thumping his forehead into the bar of the bed above him. He groaned, rubbed his forehead, and lay back down, looking up at Saul.

"What?" Tommen demanded. "There's no alarm today."

"Yeah, there's not supposed to be. But you are, apparently." Saul snorted. "You were yelling in your sleep."

"Oh." Tommen looked outside where the first streaks of dawn were lightening the sky. "Sorry."

Saul shook his head. "And I thought I was bad."

He stalked off back to his bed, leaving Tommen alone in the pre-dawn gloom. He may have slept a little more, he wasn't sure. But the next thing he knew, the sun was up and pouring in through the plastic over the broken window. It had to have been well past nine, but everything was quiet. Well, that was to say, everyone was still asleep. The beds squeaked something awful, and Saul snored lightly, to say nothing of all the new noises in the cabin via the broken window.

Outside, all seemed quiet, too. But Tommen's mind was awake and racing, and he knew he wasn't going to be getting back to sleep. He sat up, mindful of the bar over him. Just one more day, then he could go home to his own bed and sleep in for at least five straight days, maybe six if he got lucky.

Even though they'd just showered the night before, Tommen still headed off to the bathrooms for another one, just in case he'd missed anywhere in his fatigue. By the time he got back to the cabin, Saul and the boys were just starting to rouse and get out of bed, though none of them looked too thrilled about it.

"I wanna go home," Eric murmured.

"One more day," Tommen told him. "Then we can all go home."

"How long have you been up?" Saul asked.

"Not long."

"What are we doing today?" Peter asked, yawning.

"We're going to have breakfast, and then today is just kind of a relaxing day," Saul answered. "I think this morning you're going to be spending some time with Pam and the others in the main hall for a while."

"Are you going to have a meeting about all the broken windows and stuff?"

"Yes, we are. But don't worry; you'll have lots of fun while we're in there."

"You'll be having more fun than us," Tommen said honestly.

"Oh. Okay."

Getting up and around seemed to bring everyone out of their sleepy stupor enough to be functional. As far as anyone could tell, nothing had been stolen during the break-in. Sometimes it was hard to tell when something was stolen or just lost. Given the condition of some of the cabins, the line between the two was blurry at best.

"I'm going to head to the hall," Saul announced, pulling his boots on. "I need coffee."

"We're right behind you," Tommen promised.

Saul didn't seem to care one way or the other, as he grunted and left without another word, the door swinging awkwardly shut behind him. The windows could be covered, but the door was not so easily fixed, and it had to be held shut with a bungee cord.

Saul hadn't been gone more than ten seconds before there were screams and shouts and howls coming from the front porch. Tommen nearly went through the roof when he heard it, and he honestly wanted nothing more than to hide under the bed. As it was, he managed to Band long enough to get over the initial paralyzing fear. Then he told the kids to stay inside as he charged outside, certainly not the only one drawn to the spectacle.

Outside, he found Saul kneeling in the dirt just off the front of the porch. At first, Tommen thought he may have hurt himself somehow. Then he saw the blood. And guts. Then the fur.

It wasn't a white wolf, nor was it enormous. To his eyes, it looked like any common gray wolf that roamed the mountainside. Its throat had been cut, blood spattered all over on the ground. Then it had been cut open, entrails spilling out into the dirt.

Cautiously, Tommen approached and peeked over. He was entirely unprepared for Saul to rise up like a motherfucking grizzly and seize him.

"You did this!" he roared.

"No, I didn't," Tommen protested. "How could I have?"

"You were up early. You are the only one who has passed by our cabin. How did you not see this?!"

Around them, other counselors were slowly closing in, uncertain how to approach the situation.

"It wasn't here when I got back," Tommen said, wheezing in Saul's tightening grasp. "I swear to you, this wasn't me."

Saul's fury gave out and he let Tommen go, turning back to the wolf and dropping again to his knees. After a moment of silence, Tommen started to speak again, but Saul cut him off. "Shut—up." Another moment passed. Then, "I'm going to kill him. When I get my hands on him, he will know the pain that he caused this wolf, and he will know it ten times greater."

"If you catch him, I won't stand in your way."

"Smartest thing you've said all month." Saul stretched out one leg so he could reach his knife. "Go in and grab my leather bag. Should be at the end of the bed."

Tommen did as he was told. When he emerged, Saul and arguing with Mr. Wilson.

"Tell me to leave, and I'll leave," Saul was saying. "But either way, you are not getting between me and my duties."

Mr. Wilson hesitated, trying to choose his words carefully. "Believe me when I say I'm not trying to encroach on your religious beliefs, but your duties right now are to the kids."

"And I'm cleaning up a horrific mess so they don't have to see it. The two go hand in hand." He looked up at Tommen and motioned irritably for the bag which he surrendered. Then he knelt and cut out the remaining entrails, stuffing them all in the bag, ignoring the swarm of flies that had gathered.

Tommen could see the tremendous strain as Saul shouldered the bag and hefted the wolf on his back; he looked ready to collapse under the weight, and wolves weighed less than deer. He looked briefly at those who were still watching, his gaze settling on Mr. Wilson. "Don't follow me, or you'll be next."

Chapter Twenty-One
The Next Step

Breakfast was uneventful, a great relief considering the last twenty-four hours. After Saul had disappeared into the woods, Tommen had done his best to cover up the blood in the dirt before letting the boys out to head to the main hall. They asked what had happened, but rather than try to come up with some fudged story, he simply ignored them, hurrying them along to breakfast.

"Mini pancakes this morning, guys," Pam said, looking as harried as she had the night before. Behind her in the kitchen, Wallace was making tiny pancakes just as fast as he could in the little frying pans and it still wasn't fast enough. Meanwhile, Mark was having similar struggles with eggs and sausage.

"Just a couple more meals," Tommen told her, trying to sound cheerful.

"Yeah, that's what I keep telling myself."

She said it more to herself than as a reply, and Tommen left it at that. He led the boys to a table and they sat to eat; Saul still hadn't appeared.

"Did Saul die?" Peter asked.

"What?" Tommen looked at him. "No. What would give you that idea?"

"I saw the blood in the dirt."

Well, there went his brilliant idea to cover it up. Tommen shook his head. "No, Saul didn't die. Don't worry about it; he's taking care of it."

"Is he on his period?" Eric wondered.

"What? No, it's not that either." Tommen wanted to ask where he got that idea, then decided he didn't want to know.

"What's a period?" Louis inevitably asked.

"Something you'll learn about in the future," Tommen cut in. "We're not going to discuss that here. And we're not going to speculate what happened to Saul. We're going to eat breakfast and have a great last day together. What was you guys' favorite part of camp overall?"

That managed to steer the conversation more where he wanted it to go. About halfway through, Saul showed up, looking pissed and yet exhausted, and the day had only begun. Tommen was afraid of what the rest of the day had in store for them. Still, he tried to put on a good, if sympathetic face, as Saul sat down with a fairly meager breakfast, comparatively speaking.

"They run out of pancakes?" Tommen asked conversationally.

"No," Saul answered shortly.

"Did you die?" Peter wondered.

"Part of me."

"Are you on your period?" Eric cut in. "I saw the blood. My sister screams like that when she's on her period. Or that's what she said it was last time."

Saul's expression turned strange and unreadable. "What? No. Only girls do that."

"Oh."

Tommen managed to snag seconds before Mr. Wilson appeared and silently motioned for all the counselors and assistants to follow him to the office. Before, it had only ever been just the counselors—less Saul, plus Tommen. This time, though, with all counselors and assistants present, the room shrank very quickly, and there weren't enough seats for everyone. Saul got one on account of his back, but Tommen was made to stand.

"So what was that all about this morning, Saul?" one of the female counselors asked. "We could hear you howling from our cabin."

"Someone poached a wolf and left it out for him to see this

morning," Mr. Wilson answered when Saul would not. "We should therefore be respectful of his beliefs and do our best not to antagonize him during his mourning period." He said the words stiffly, grudgingly, like he would have much rathered deck Saul right there but was too cowardly or too smart to do so, at least with witnesses. Personally, Tommen's bet was on Saul, even with his injured back.

"Is that part of the thing, then?" Rick asked.

"What thing?"

"This whole thing. The vandalism and whatnot, is the wolf part of that do you think?"

"If it is, it certainly adds a whole new dynamic to the situation. Because then it goes from some random attack to something far more targeted. And whoever it was knew exactly who to target and how to do it effectively."

Saul just grunted.

"So what do we think happened?" someone else wondered. "Was this a gang of hoodlums out to cause mischief? Was it a targeted attack on the camp or on Saul? Could it have just been a bear and the wolf incident is separate?"

Oh, how Tommen wished he could have spilled everything right there. But, just like the police officer, there was no way to explain it where he didn't sound crazy. Okay, fine, so the perp was Rifun Ndolo. Why, though? What did he gain? More to the point, why was he targeting Saul instead of Tommen? Or was he trying to get to Tommen through Saul? Could he be after both of them for some reason? Was Saul an Akari-bearer as well, even if he didn't know it yet?

Or, maybe, Saul had once been one of Rifun's little minions. After the coup went south, Saul tried to desert, and this was Rifun's way of letting him know that he wasn't out of the woods yet. It would certainly explain his weird little statements about stories and lies. But then, why would Micaiah say he checked out?

This was all way over his head. Truthfully, he preferred the coup. Then there were more clearly defined lines, and the enemy was out in the open where he could see them. No hiding behind shadows and threats and lies and warnings, but right up front in the heat of battle. And when all else failed, just look out for yourself, maybe the guy next to you.

Saul had been right. If you don't know who the enemy is, don't go into the fight. Why, then, was it so hard to judge whether Saul was friend or foe?

"There were no bear tracks anywhere around camp," Mr. Wilson said. "Not around camp, not even anywhere on the property. It's a safe bet that this wasn't a bear."

"Then why wasn't anything taken?" someone asked. "I won't lie, I left a few things behind that could be considered valuable, but they weren't touched. I mean, windows were broken, doors forced, all that. Some of our stuff was moved and overturned to make it look like it had been rifled through, but no one actually lost anything valuable. Well, not that can be proved."

"That's the other hard part," another counselor agreed. "Up until the kids actually start packing up to leave, something could have been stolen, or maybe it's just hiding under the bed."

"Then it's a good thing that today is clean-up day," Mr. Wilson sighed. "When we get out of here, have your kids start getting their things together. I know a few of them will be leaving today, but just have them all get packed up. It'll save time tomorrow, anyway."

That much was the truth, and Tommen was grateful that they only had three campers. More to the point, he was glad they had three respectful campers. God only knew how things would have turned out if Randall and Carson would have still been around. That would have been a nightmare, and possibly a double homicide if Saul would have gotten hold of them had they commented on the wolf incident. That would have been a very bad day, and a hell of a mess to clean up.

"So, overall I'm hearing that nothing was definitely stolen," Mr. Wilson went on. "Of the few things I heard yesterday, most or all have been found, correct? Yeah, okay. Okay, good. That's good to hear. Other than the obvious windows, doors, were any personal items broken? I don't know what you guys all have with you, but in the chaos, was anything discovered to be broken? Ladies, hair dryers, other...hair...products? I don't know what you guys use."

"Nothing was found broken," Sarah reported, "but things got broken in the frenzy."

"Well, sorry to say, that's on you guys. I'm asking if anything was found broken, as in, you had nothing to do with it." He looked around. "All right, another good thing. And you guys did a marvelous job cleaning up last night, getting all the glass and whatnot swept up and disposed of. Did anyone find any new problems last night? Holes in the roof, screws loosened on the bunkbeds, or even broken frames, things like that?" Another scan of the room. "Excellent. So it seems as though anything that was going to be found has been found."

"Except the one who did this," Saul growled.

Mr. Wilson sighed. "Except the one who did this."

"I don't think it could have been just one," Jeremiah said. "I mean, one guy targets one, maybe two buildings, breaks a window, does a little graffiti. One guy cannot trash a whole camp like this."

"Why not?" Tommen wondered. "No one was here, so it's not like he didn't have the time. And something this big indicates quite a bit of rage. I'm no expert, but I know what I saw in that wolf." He ignored Saul's murderous gaze. "That was rage. That was targeted, passionate rage."

"As far as the wolf goes, I notified the Game Warden," Mr. Wilson said. "He'll be out today, and he'll probably want to talk to you, Saul. As for the rest of it, whether it's one guy or ten, we are not the police. The police were here, they did their search and collected their evidence. The investigation and the law is in their hands. Our job is to keep the kids safe. Now, we are officially ruling out a bear. But, in the interest of not scaring the kids, we'll still teach them about what to do if they encounter a bear. That will be our story to them. Remember, it's only today."

"Some of them have older brothers and sisters," Julie pointed out. "The story will spread."

"Stick to the story."

"So what are we going to tell the older kids?" someone asked. "And what about getting things fixed? Are we going to have a fix-it day, or are we coming back early or what?"

"I'm getting there." Mr. Wilson seemed a little frustrated, and Tommen could hardly blame him. He was working hard to bring the camp back from some terrible doom or bad reputation, and now this was happening. Plus, in the present moment, everyone wanted answers, assurances, and a plan of action, and it seemed as though he had nothing to give.

"What we're going to do," he said after a moment of tense silence, "is we're going to stick to the bear story for the younger kids. Let them talk to their older siblings, fine, whatever, but we stick to that story. They're going to know we're brushing them off, but we can't add fuel to a panic fire. If we're calm and collected about it, they have nothing to worry about."

They're teenagers, Tommen thought. *They can come up with a dozen more horrific stories to explain what happened here than you can. Telling them it was simple vandalism is going to bore them to death, not scare them.* Telling them the truth, however, that would get their hearts racing. It certainly did his.

"We're going to switch our calendar events, too. Instead of having the stay-at-camp week the first week with the soccer and basketball tournaments, that's going to be our camping week. In the time that we're gone, there will be contractors here working to repair windows, doors, and everything else. When we come back, everything will be good as new."

"Get the windows and doors replaced and the cabins themselves are likely to burn down spontaneously," someone chuckled.

"Hopefully not."

"Are we going to take any time to go over the plants, animals all of that stuff?" someone else asked.

"Yes. That will be Sunday night and Monday morning. After lunch is when we'll pack up and head to the campsite. I understand it will most likely be dark by the time we get there and get situated. Pam has been good enough to agree to send us with dinner so we don't starve that night. Then we'll be up and at 'em bright and early Tuesday morning. We'll be there until Saturday when we'll have breakfast, then pack up and get back here sometime before dinner. By then, everything will hopefully be put back to rights."

It sounded like a decent plan of action, actually. Get the kids out of the way for a little while so the contractors could work without interruption or interference. Plus, if they did the hardest, most exhausting week first, it might make everyone feel a little better about the remaining three weeks, especially since the easiest week, the tournament week, would be the last thing on the agenda.

"Are there any questions?" Mr. Wilson asked.

"What about the main hall?" Rick wondered.

"Ah, yes. For anyone who doesn't know, the gas line was cut—more appropriately, sawed off—and we lost all our gas, which as you may know, fuels the stoves and the ovens. Pam and them have therefore been using electric hot plates to get everything done. The gas guy should be here shortly to get that fixed and refill the tank, and lunch should be normal."

"Yeah, but, Jerry, that sort of thing goes beyond just breaking windows and smashing doors." *Here we go.* "I mean, that's a deliberate act of vandalism that not only costs a hell of a lot of money to fix, but it could have been lethal. I mean, that's a bomb waiting to happen. What if Wallace hadn't smelled it before he got his lighter out? No more Wallace. Worse, no more Pam."

Mr. Wilson shifted uncomfortably. "I know. Believe me, I understand what you're saying. The police made note of it, and now the investigation is handed off to them. Regardless of whether it was a deliberate attempt at, as you say, creating a bomb, or an idiot vandal who was too doped up to consider the consequences of his actions, there is nothing we can do about it now."

"Jerry," Saul said slowly from his spot where he'd been brooding the last half hour. "That wolf was not there yesterday when the police were here. It wasn't there this morning when Tommen got up to go do whatever. Whoever this fucker is, he's still around. He's watching us to see what we're doing, how we're handling all of this. I don't think it's anyone here, but whoever he is, he's not on the run. He's either too smart or too dumb for that."

"As I said, the Game Warden is coming out, too, and you can be the one to talk to him."

"But if that's true, are the kids at risk?" Julie asked. "I mean, how many games do we play where they have to run into the woods or something? A scavenger hunt, hide and seek, all of that."

"We have to assume he holds no fond feelings for the kids," Saul cut in before Mr. Wilson could speak. "He knew exactly how to hurt me, and that was by killing a wolf and leaving it for me to see. What would it take to hurt any of you?" He looked around. "Yes, I'd say the kids are at risk."

Mr. Wilson sighed. "I was going to simply say yes, but thank you, Saul, for the illustration. To that end, however, we're going to have to modify our game time a little bit. While I'm home, I'll grab some of my trail cameras and set them up around the property. To that end, no one is to go into the woods alone, if you must go at all. I'll work out how to change some of the games to be closer to camp, but that won't be today. For today, everyone stays in camp. Are there any more questions?"

Everyone had at least a thousand questions going through their minds, Tommen could see. No one liked the idea that something had happened that they couldn't control. No one liked the idea that they didn't even really know what happened at all. Was it just one or a couple stupid vandals looking to scare them? Had it been intentional, malicious destruction of property and an intentional gas bomb? Was the wolf connected in some way? Was it a one-time thing, or was this weirdo still hanging around, waiting for his moment to snatch one of the kids, too?

"What about canceling the camp?" someone suggested. "If it's really that dangerous just to leave the cabins, when do we call it quits? I don't feel like being part of a prison camp."

Saul shifted his position and snorted indignantly.

"If it does get dangerous, then we may have to send everyone home early," Mr. Wilson conceded slowly. "However, as far as anyone is concerned, a few windows got broken, a few doors were forced. No children were hurt. It's a few vandals and nothing more."

"So, we're just going to lie to them, to the parents, and say everything is fine?" Sarah wondered.

"We can't allow ourselves to be frightened by phantoms. If we start perpetuating a story about some terrorist threatening to blow up the camp, panic ensues. And we don't even know that for sure. We work with what we know and let the police handle the rest. We give no cause for panic. By rearranging the schedule and getting the contractors in here, everything returns to normal and all is well."

It wasn't the more reassuring thing, and certainly not what some of them wanted to hear, but Mr. Wilson did have the right of it. They couldn't just go off fighting every shadow and investigating every unknown sound; there were too many of both. They had to take their evidence and guard against that which they could see.

Was it that obvious his dad was a cop?

"Are there any more questions?" Mr. Wilson asked yet again. When there was silence, he nodded and gave a relieved sigh. "All right then. One more day. Then we can all go home." As people started to move and make their way out, he spoke again. "Saul, stay here a minute."

The man hadn't moved from his seat, and he still hadn't even as Tommen was one of the last to leave.

Pam and the others had effectively occupied the children with all manner of song, dance, board game, and arts and crafts in the various classrooms. Seeing this, Tommen and a few others took the opportunity to pilfer some snacks from the kitchen to make up for a rather skimpy breakfast. Even as they were doing this, the gas man showed up and Pam headed out to speak with him. Then the counselors were shooed out of the kitchen so work could begin. Following on the heels of that, the counselors gathered the kids and took them out of the main hall to find other things to do.

It was open free time. Some groups returned to their cabins, some headed for the basketball court or set up a makeshift soccer match. Per Mr. Wilson's instructions, no one went into the woods, though one group did skirt that rule by heading up to the fort on the south side.

"So, guys, what do you want to do?" Tommen asked, trying to sound nonthreatening and completely not shaken by the whole fiasco. "Mr. Wilson says we're not allowed to go into the woods just yet, so what else can you think of?"

They ended up joining the soccer match. About halfway through, out of the corner of his eye, Tommen saw Saul approach. He couldn't decide if the man looked ready to murder or ready to dance. He did neither as he stalked up beside Tommen and watched the game, not speaking for a long moment.

"Game Warden come by?" Tommen wondered.

"He did," Saul confirmed. "He was less than thrilled at what I'd done with the wolf, but he was even less eager to pursue an argument about it. No one likes getting tangled up in tribal law."

"Oh."

The kids took a short break for water and rest, but were quickly back on the field.

"What'd Mr. Wilson have to say, if you don't mind me asking?" Tommen inquired.

Saul smirked. "Well, the question of why the hell I keep coming back has finally been resolved." Pause. "I'm not."

"Wait, are you, like, fired? What's going on?"

"He said he'd like to fire me outright and dismiss me completely, but he doesn't feel comfortable having just you alone with the older kids. The older kids are decidedly more troubled than the younger kids. So I get to stay for the next camp, but after that, I'm out of here."

"Why?"

" 'An intolerable attitude' I believe were his exact words. He also told me that if I managed to get help while I was away, he'd consider letting me back." He shook his head. "Fuck that."

"You don't think you need help?" Tommen might have had a better idea than most of what to look for when someone needed some serious psychological help, but ten minutes with Saul and even the common man could see he needed help.

"Of course I need help; I'm not stupid. But at least this way, I'm finally free of my perceived obligations to this camp."

Tommen wasn't sure what to make of the whole thing. The only thing he could figure was that he had something to do with it, that his inexperience had been the tipping point of Saul's "intolerable attitude." Saul had been able to rely on Joe for years, pass things off as needed. Now, with Tommen, he'd had to shoulder everything and it had finally broken him.

But he also couldn't figure out when that turning point might have been. Saul had been bad-tempered the entire time at camp, but except for a short flareup at the hiking camp, it had all been pretty much the same mixture of grouchiness, surliness, sarcastic comments, and dry wit, regardless of whether Randall and Carson had been present. Or maybe it was a general increase in surliness over last year.

In the end, Tommen figured that he really couldn't be overly concerned with it. He'd already made up his mind to come back for the second camp, but not for next year. Once the older kids' camp was done with, he and Saul would part ways and have nothing to do with each other, which seemed to be how they both preferred it. He pitied Saul, to some extent, but the man had just admitted that he needed help, but seemed unwilling to do anything about it. Lead a horse to water and all that. If the man didn't want help, then he wasn't going to get it, no matter how great the counselor or religious leader.

Let his spirit wolf have him; no one else seems to want him.

The soccer match ended, but Tommen couldn't say who won

as the teams had been mixed. He figured it didn't matter; the boys didn't look either thrilled or dejected. Probably they hadn't even kept score, just played until everyone was tired of playing.

It wasn't time for lunch yet, though it appeared as though the gas guys had finished their work and left. They returned to the cabin and, as suggested, started packing up some of their things, leaving out only what was necessary to get them through the night and tomorrow morning.

"Are you guys ready to go home?" Tommen asked.

"I miss my dog," Peter said blankly. "He's gonna hate me because we haven't played in weeks."

"Oh, I'm sure he'll love you and be just as excited as ever to play."

"I'm excited to go home," Eric butted in. "My sister is going to come to the next camp, which means I get the house all to myself! That means the TV, the Xbox, all of it!"

"Cool. What about you, Louis?"

Louis shrugged. "I guess."

"You're not ready to go home?"

"I like being here."

What he said and what he meant were two different things in Tommen's mind, and Tommen could only guess that he liked being at camp because he didn't like being at home.

Throughout camp, both counselors and counselor assistants had had opportunities to talk to the kids one-on-one about their home life. As far as the troubled kids went, mostly it was absentee parents and older siblings who were hardly decent role models. The only thing Louis had ever mentioned was that his parents yelled a lot, at least, when they were both around. Sometimes his dad stayed out for days at a time, sometimes his mom. No, they never touched him.

If camp had taught Tommen anything—well, okay, it had taught him a few things. First, how to speak up and not be such a pushover. He'd never thought he had been until this camp. Second, how to pick his battles. Watching eight year olds get into the same fights that he and Tyler Freeman had, had been a bit of a wakeup call. Third, how to spot a liar. This may have been a moot point, however, because eight year olds were bad at it. And fourth, how to spot abuse. Again, this may have been moot because eight year olds didn't hide it well. For the most part, they still had the innocence to cry and show the signs. Their pride hadn't kicked in yet. Even Jimmy, who had basically been beaten into submission, hadn't been smart enough to try and cover up his wounds.

Tommen still wasn't sure about Louis. He never showed any wounds and remained adamant that his parents never hit him or did anything to him. Tommen was torn between true psychological abuse—his parents blaming him for all their woes and treating him like dirt—and the blame that a child takes on himself when divorce is not only inevitable, but imminent.

He wanted to tell himself he was overreacting and overthinking things, but even without Randall and Carson to make Wolf Cabin the prison cabin, this was still the troubled cabin, where everyone had a story.

"Are you ready to go home, Saul?" It was a courtesy question, meant to entertain the kids; Tommen already knew his real answer.

"I'll be happy to sleep in my own bed," was his courtesy answer, meant to entertain the kids; Saul probably didn't want to come back.

Tommen nodded. "I will, too. These bunks leave a lot to be desired."

"And you get to talk to your girlfriend, too," Eric said, evoking a chorus of "ooh" from the others. "You get to hug her and kiss her..." He grabbed Peter and pretended to spin him around, dipping him low for a kiss. He got a face full of fist instead, but it wasn't hard or malicious, and no real harm was done, except the part where he dropped Peter who landed hard on the floor. Still, it was all in good fun, and the boys were laughing.

"Ha ha, very funny," Tommen said.

Although, truthfully, he was looking forward to seeing Becky again and seeing about another kiss. He was still looking forward to getting more than that, but that was probably a little ways out, and there was no way he could entertain the idea here in front of the boys right now. They were both ignorant and extremely perceptive, and they'd notice his shame before he did. He could have Banded, but decided against it.

As they made their way to the main hall for lunch, Tommen saw that a few parents had arrived to take their kids home early. Had it been earlier in the week or the camp, he might have been a little more sympathetic, but now? With one day to go? Well, he supposed it really didn't matter. At least then they'd beat the rush in the morning of all the parents coming to get their kids.

The kitchen was still closed when they entered the hall. Judging by the looks on the other campers who were there, the wait would be a prolonged one.

"They're moving as fast as they can," Tim said. "But the gas guy took a while and they got started late and this, that, and the other thing." He shrugged. "It is what it is."

Some of the kids had gone into the classrooms to grab paper and colored pencils and other assorted crafting goodies. The only thing not allowed, per Pam, was glue. Glue was to stay inside the classrooms on the classroom tables so it didn't damage the dining room tables, you know, the ones they had to eat off of? It was the only time when Tommen had actually seen Pam be a stickler about anything.

But it was no matter; the kids simply made do. Thankfully, they didn't have to entertain themselves for long as more and more cabins trickled in. Eventually, the kitchen window opened and Pam started setting out the hot plates and food, but the line was not allowed to form until Wallace put out the plates and utensils. Then it was anybody's game.

Lunch turned out to be pigs in a blanket, grilled cheese sandwiches, and an assortment of snacking goodies, from salad to fruit to cheese sticks and the like.

"Sorry, Tommen," Pam said, still looking and sounding a little frazzled. "We were kind of short on time."

He shook his head. "I'm not worried. I take what I can get."

"Well, you'll have to come back a few times for that, I'm afraid. But then, that's nothing new for a starving teenager."

"With you around, Pam, I'm hardly starving."

"Let's hope the older kids feel the same way."

Tommen took his tray and sat down at the table. Everyone in the group seemed pretty dead out of it, trying to be happy and excited, but really just wanting to go home.

"Do we get breakfast tomorrow?" he asked.

Saul nodded. "Breakfast will be available, but parents start showing up at the crack of dawn, so be ready for anything. If your dad gets here and some of the boys are still left, you can go ahead and leave. It doesn't take me long to get home, so I can watch them."

Tommen nodded uncertainly. He wanted to say something to reassure Saul and make him sound committed and ready to stay until the end, but there were two problems with that. First, it would be dishonest. Tommen wanted to get home just as much as everyone else, and he would take the out if it was allowed. Second, regardless of whether he stayed or went, he suspected Saul wouldn't care either way. He'd just been handed the pink slip, so he didn't give a rat's ass about the job anymore. He'd put on a good face as long as it suited him, but short of him doing something illegal and being arrested, there was little worse that the camp could do to him now.

So he let it go, instead focusing on his food and going back two more times before considering himself full, or full enough to make it to dinner.

"So, what do we want to do until dinner?" he asked amiably, sitting down after returning his dishes.

Food had breathed some life back into the boys, but they really didn't want to do much more than go back to the cabin and read the comics they had brought. Saul had no objections as he had his book that wanted to read, too. Unfortunately, Tommen wasn't much of a reader, and he'd since outgrown comic books, at least the kind the boys were reading.

"I'm going to head out and take a walk around camp," he announced, three minutes and nineteen seconds into his boredom. Yes, he'd timed it. He'd been determined to find something to occupy his time, and puttering around on his phone just didn't feel very productive, or even very sneaky, in present company. He could have brought out the book that Rifun had given him, but he didn't need to have some sort of emotional or nervous breakdown because of the contents of the book. He would rather discover the story for himself, though he had a sneaking suspicion he already knew how it ended.

No one stopped him from leaving, and he quickly found himself crossing the open field, narrowly dodging children in the midst of a game of tag, heading for the office where Mr. Wilson was just walking out.

"Well, Tommen, I hope camp hasn't scared you too badly," he said, trying to sound cheerful. "Still got four weeks to go."

"Yeah, I noticed," Tommen said. "About that. Saul said you fired him."

Mr. Wilson sighed and his shoulders sagged a little, as if it was a topic he would rather not revisit right now. Tommen tried to save it by saying, "Well, not fired him per se, but, he's allowed to stay for the older kids' camp, but not allowed to come back next year. Said it had something to do with his attitude?"

"Tommen, I commend you for being able to work with him for four days, never mind four weeks. If Saul feels the need to disclose the transcript of our meeting, then he may do so. All I am going to say is that he has a number of personal problems. And, really, everyone does. But his problems are interfering with this camp, and I don't want it to jeopardize the safety of the kids."

"Is this about the wolf?"

"It's more than the wolf. As I said, if he wishes to disclose the matter to you, that is his choice. But I will not as I consider it a confidential matter between employer and employee."

It was a dismissal with no room for argument as Mr. Wilson brushed past Tommen to go do whatever it was he had his mind set to do. It made sense, really, but something about it still didn't feel very fair. Maybe he was just being sentimental. He'd been demoted at his job for bullshit reasons. Saul, well, he had some legitimate problems. The Chivalrous Welshman couldn't save everybody. Or, as further evidenced with his standoff over Jimmy, anybody. At least at camp. Maybe he really wasn't supposed to be here.

Tommen made a wide lap of the camp, skirting the tree line, looking for everything and nothing. Maybe he would see Rifun watching him from the trees. Maybe he would see a couple turkeys making their way through the brush. As it was, by the time he got back to the cabin, the most he'd found were enormous wolf tracks making the same loop, as if Saul's wolf spirit was also making protective laps of the perimeter. Maybe it was.

"So, did you get my job back?" Saul asked when he walked in the door.

Tommen stopped. "What?"

"I saw you talking to Mr. Wilson out there."

"Oh." He felt his ears flush red. "No. No, I didn't."

"You lost your job?" Eric said looking up from his comic book. "Are you fired? Do you have to go home?"

"Not yet," Saul told them, not looking up from his book. "But come next year, you won't have to deal with me anymore."

Tommen was forced to wonder whether the boys would be dealing with anyone at all, or if their spot in camp was dependent upon there being a "troubled kids" counselor available. Really, the three of them didn't seem too troubled. Louis probably had some pretty severe problems at home, but he wasn't a bad kid. None of them were, really. They were just boys being boys.

Eventually, boredom drove Tommen back into his book. He found it interesting how some of the chapters were from his dad's point of view. He was fascinated by his investigation into the murders, but even more fascinated by some of his thoughts about them. And, if he wanted to be honest, it kind of made him hate Lily a little more, too. Then he felt guilty about speaking ill of the dead, even if it was a death well-deserved.

By the time dinner came around, he'd just gotten to the part where he gave the twins the slip so he could walk home, thereby witnessing the break-in at the museum and the shenanigans that ensued. He told himself the book was only fiction, but it was kind of like reading his own obituary when he hadn't even died yet. Hm...maybe that wasn't the right analogy. Well, if the Author got anything right, it was his severe lack of English mastery.

Dinner was an all-American dinner, cheeseburgers, hot dogs, fries, chips, chicken wings, everything one might expect to find at a barbecue on the Fourth of July. Of course, the vegetarian cabin pitched a fit that the only thing they could have was the salad. Pam politely informed them that the only thing stopping them from gorging with the rest of them was their own sense of pride.

"Is there a vegetarian cabin in the next camp, too?" Tommen asked as the last of the girls went their way.

"There are vegetarians, but not a lot of them. Certainly not enough to warrant their own special club and cabin," Pam answered. She seemed to have recovered a little from the madness. "I'm all for healthy eating—"

"As you serve us hot dogs and fries."

"—but don't preach to me about not killing animals for food until the animals stop killing each other for food." She waved a hand dismissively. "Ah, but what do I know? I only grew up in poverty, after all. I didn't get to go to all these fancy health food stores that will cater to any imaginary dietary need a person can conjure up."

"You don't have to tell me that," Tommen said, moving away before his mind went too far down that path.

After dinner was the last campfire of the camp, where Mr. Wilson announced that everyone was allowed as many s'mores as they wanted just so they could get the supply used up. It sounded great to the kids until they came to realize that the supply had dwindled considerably, and the most everyone was able to have was two each. Then it turned into fighting and whining and complaining. Mr. Wilson decided to remedy the situation in a slightly cruel manner, taking all the s'mores supplies and redistributing them among the counselors, many of whom hadn't gotten any s'mores that night.

"When you start squabbling over your excess, maybe it's time to give to those who don't have that luxury," Saul told Eric when he started complaining about the unfairness of it all.

"But there's only so much and eventually it's all gone, so why does it matter who gets what?" Eric pouted.

"Well then maybe you should start working and asking nicely and making more and giving them out continuously," Tommen said.

Of course, it was no easy task trying to get a child to do work of any form, but then the songs and the dances and the campfire stories started up, and everyone moved on from that fight.

"So, kids come to camp where they get lessons in sportsmanship, following the rules, being responsible, learning plants and animals, learning how to fish and trap and forage," Saul said, "and as an added bonus, they get a little economics lesson, too."

"Marshmallows and chocolate, the new dollar," Tommen mused.

"Worst part is, it could be true. Once the world, or at least the country, collapses, paper is worth dirt. Food is where it's at. Anyone today who has a garden, chickens, cows, whatever, they're called idiots for not keeping up with the times. Eventually, they'll be called fools for not sharing with those who aren't smart enough to prepare."

Tommen raised a brow. "You're just Mr. Sunshine today, aren't you?" He shook his head. "I bet you're fun at parties."

"What are you talking about? I was the best wolf dancer the tribe had seen in thirty years." Saul shifted uncomfortably. "These days, I'd be lucky to even walk the Sacred Circle, never mind try to dance it. It's a wonder I didn't drop dead trying to carry that wolf."

Some people probably wish you had. "Michelle give you

something for it?"

"I'm here, aren't I?"

The campfire was intended to last late into the night, when in reality it ended earlier than some of the ones at the beginning of camp. Everyone was just too tired and too ready to go home and sleep in their own beds. Tommen was certainly ready to get back home and pick up a new hearing aid charger. His had managed to last for the duration of camp, but lately it had been pretty sketchy. Even now his hearing aids were running on fumes, and he hadn't been awake nearly as long today as he had been at other points.

"Are you still coming home tomorrow?" Becky texted just as he was starting to drift off.

"Why wouldn't I be?" he asked.

"I don't know. Fresh mountain air, camping, outdoorsy stuff that you always say you love to do. Plus getting paid for it. Why would you want to come back?"

"Because I want to sleep in my own bed again. Because I have to. Because I want to see you again and maybe get another kiss?"

"At least I made it in there somewhere."

"So...is that a no on the kiss?"

"Depends on how I'm feeling about it when you get back."

"I'm not sure how I'm supposed to react to that."

"That's okay. You'll figure it out."

He wasn't sure how he was supposed to react to that either, but he didn't say so.

"Oh, your dad got a new car by the way," she texted after a minute.

"Wait, what?" He got rid of the Cadillac? With its squealing brakes, questionable heater and even more questionable suspension? Damn, it was the best news he'd heard all day.

"Yup."

"What did he get?"

"I don't know make and model exactly; I've only just seen him drive by. The good news is that it's from this century at least. Maybe even this decade, but I'm not sure."

"Holy cow, he must be going all out to impress Laura."

He paused after he sent the text. The Cadillac had its problems, sure, and it was entirely possible that something had given out on it. On the other hand, what if it hadn't given out? What if his dad had just decided to get something newer and better in order to impress his girlfriend and show her that he wasn't an outdated slob? It was one thing to trade one crummy car for another crummy car—maybe a few years newer and fewer problems, but still crummy—but to make that kind of a leap...it smelled of both guilt and pride. Guilt that he was still driving a beat-up old Cadillac and hadn't gotten around to getting anything better because he was just set in his ways. Pride that he was a man and could fend for himself and darn it if he wasn't going to show it off in order to impress a woman. Was he overthinking things again? It was, after all, entirely possible that the Cadillac had just given out on him. Or worse, that he got the new car as a way of forcibly gifting Tommen the old car. For as much as he'd done to work on getting his license and saving up for a car, spending time at camp had seen him, in the end, with no car in his possession. And he still had to take his driver's test.

"Apparently," Becky replied. "She goes over for dinner probably twice a week, and he's out at least once a week."

Tommen sighed. "You're a good spy. How much do I owe you for your services?"

"Mm, a kiss or two ought to do it."

After a minute or two, they both conceded the need for sleep. Tommen put away his phone and lay there, staring in the darkness.

Chapter Twenty-Two
Wolf Tooth

The alarm the following morning saw everyone leaping out of bed in a frenzied, desperate attempt to get everything packed up and make sure nothing was left behind. Tommen was less worried about leaving something behind because he would be coming back in a week, and more worried about something getting misplaced and picked up by one of the boys on accident. Then he really wouldn't see his stuff ever again. All of this inevitably came on top of their usual morning routine, trying to get to the bathrooms and the showers in good order, even as parents were already pulling into the parking lot.

"For goodness' sake, it's only eight o'clock," Tommen commented.

"Hey, people got places to be and things to do," Saul said wryly. He'd been up even before the alarm and had his bags all packed and ready to go. Part of Tommen wondered if he would even show up to the older kids' camp. What were they going to do if he didn't, fire him?

Turned out that while there were a few parents more than impatient to get their kid and leave, not all were so sinister. Some wanted to have breakfast with their kids at the camp, and others wanted to take their kids out to breakfast somewhere else. Looking around, Tommen didn't see his dad anywhere, so his chances of going out to breakfast early appeared to be shot.

That wasn't to say he was complaining; Pam had spoiled them so hard it was beyond funny. Due to the rush and the constant flow of traffic, breakfast was lighter than it normally was — endless eggs, pancakes, and sausage — but Tommen more than made up for it by going up several times to refill his plate.

"Well, at least you've given me an idea of what I'm looking at for next camp," Pam teased as he made his third trip.

"I think you've been doing this long enough that you have a good idea," he told her. "Or else I would have starved after the first week."

"Very true. She who controls the food supply controls the camp."

"Oh boy, we're going to be in for it now, aren't we?"

Pam did her best evil cackle, and Tommen laughed. He returned to the table where Eric was busy gathering his things, leaving his plate almost untouched.

"Your parents here?" Tommen asked.

"My mom is," Eric replied. "So I guess it's time to go home."

"You can't even finish your breakfast?"

"She wants to get going. That's okay, we'll grab something from McDonald's or somewhere on the way."

In the time it would take them even to go through the drive thru, he could have finished off his breakfast in front of him, Tommen mused. But he didn't say this out loud. He simply greeted Eric's mom pleasantly when she came by, offered to help carry bags, got turned down, and returned to his own breakfast, taking both plates back to the kitchen when he was finished.

"Who are you guys expecting to pick you up?" Tommen asked of the two remaining boys.

Both answered that they were expecting their mom. By now, more parents were arriving and clogging up the parking lot. Anyone who wasn't currently eating breakfast headed out to the curb to look for parents. Saul made an excuse to go to the bathroom.

"Did you guys have fun this month at camp?" Tommen wondered conversationally. "What was your favorite part?"

"The bear attack was pretty cool," Peter said after a second of thought. "Even if it wasn't really a bear attack."

"It was a bear," Tommen said firmly. "And you're right, we

don't see that sort of thing every day. What about you, Louis? What was your favorite part?"

"The kayaking and canoeing and stuff."

"Oh, so you liked water week. Yeah, that was pretty fun, even if we got wet more from the rain than the lake."

To be honest, Tommen wasn't particularly interested in any of this, but he wasn't sure quite how to wrap this up. He kind of just wanted to send the kids on their way and go home himself, but that seemed cold and rude. They were supposed to be eager to go home and brag to all their friends about the great time they had at camp. This attitude of wanting nothing more than to go to bed and sleep wasn't supposed to kick in until they were at least fourteen and working.

"There's my mom," Peter said suddenly, gathering his things. "Looks like it's her and my grandma."

Tommen helped carry a few of his things over to the old Crown Vic where Peter's mom was just getting out. At least that seemed to be a family dynamic that was only poor and not poor and abusive. It was the small victories that counted, Tommen thought to himself as he helped throw the stuff in the trunk. He exchanged banal pleasantries with mom and grandma, then stepped back to watch them drive away, or, as circumstances demanded, putter around the parking lot amid a maze of illegally parked cars and inconsiderate pedestrians.

That just left Louis, who looked about as excited as Saul standing next to him. Given their grim expressions, Louis could easily be mistaken for Saul's son or nephew or some other relative.

Tommen did not ask Louis if he was excited or ready to go home; he already knew that answer. The boy would shrug, say something about being able to sleep in his own bed, and leave it at that. He probably didn't really want to go home to the fighting and the screaming. Maybe it would be a mercy if one of his parents did leave. Custody was a bitch, or so Tommen had heard, but there was also the relief of not listening to the arguing late at night and blaming himself for everything going wrong.

In the end, it was grandma and grandpa who picked him up. They were nice people, Tommen thought, though he saw how Louis seemed torn by their appearance. On the one hand, he was excited to see them and spend the day with them as they said—going out to eat and this and that as they helped get stuff loaded in the old pickup—but there was also the fear. What happened at home? Do I still have a mom and dad? Did one of them leave? Tommen hated to see that look on Louis' face as they pulled away from the curb, but if grandpa was any indication, they'd have him laughing by the time they hit the road out of the camp.

"So, that's all of them," Saul said when Tommen returned.

"All three," Tommen confirmed.

"Do you need me to hold your hand until your dad gets here?"

"No, I think I can wait by myself."

"Well, just don't talk to any strangers or accept candy from them or anything. Otherwise, I guess I'll see you in a week, barring catastrophe."

Tommen did not ask what he kind of catastrophe he was referring to. The man seemed to live in his own private hell, and Tommen had no desire to join him there. He also hadn't brought his things up with him, preferring to leave them locked in the cabin until all the boys had gone. He departed down the hill, leaving Tommen alone on the curb to watch people come and go.

"Are you on your way?" Tommen texted his dad, knowing that the man wouldn't reply if he was on the road. He'd probably check his phone to see what was up and who wanted him, but he wouldn't text and drive. Surprisingly, though, Tommen got a reply.

"Just getting gas. About half an hour out."

"It'll take you that long just to get through the parking lot."

"So you're saying I should have brought the lights and sirens."

"That would be funny."

"Too far away to turn back now. Sorry."

Tommen normally had mixed feelings about being picked up in a cop car. Back in the day—like, less than a year ago—when he was constantly getting into fights, it only served as a reminder of where his fighting would inevitably lead if he didn't get his act together. These days, since he'd stopped fighting, and because he was in a new place where people didn't automatically know him as the fighting kid, and the kids were easily impressed, he thought it might have been fun to get picked up in a cop car. But, as his dad said, he was too far away to go back now, and he'd never be able to pull it off. The camp was way out of his jurisdiction and he didn't have any other excuse to bring a car out this far.

After a minute or two, Tommen headed to the bathroom, figuring that he might as well go now before getting stuck in a car for two hours. As he thought about it, he wouldn't be able to just scan the crowd for the old Cadillac; his dad would actually have to come get him. There was something unnerving about that thought.

Seeing as he had the time, he paid one last visit to the cabin. Maybe he was hoping Saul would be there. Maybe he was hoping Saul wouldn't be there. When he pushed open the door, everything was quiet. Saul's stuff was gone. Nothing appeared to have been left behind, from anyone. They'd actually managed to get everything cleaned up and accounted-for. Holy shit. Well, it was probably a little easier for them, seeing how they'd only had three campers in the end.

That had been an unprecedented luxury, at least according to Saul. Next camp probably wouldn't be so easy. They'd be back to eight or ten boys, all of them hyped up on too much testosterone, all of them dying to fuck the girls and fight off any rivals and competition and prove their manhood.

Fuck, was that how he'd come across in school? Petty and shallow, desperate to prove himself in any stupid way he could? Fucking hell. The things you learn as an adult. Well, hindsight is 20/20 and all that. But still...

When he turned around to leave, his found a piece of paper taped to the door, as well as a leather thong with something on it.

Carefully, he approached and reached out. Then he shook his head and snatched the stuff off the door. What was he thinking, that it would be laced with some drug and he would pass out right here, or die? He paused and thought about it, then decided maybe he'd been a little hasty in taking the things.

But he hadn't died, and now he examined them. The leather thong might have been rather unassuming, except Tommen could tell by feel if not by look that it was genuine, brain-tanned leather. This was the real stuff. There were a few beads on it made of bone and, if he had to hazard a guess, shells as if from a walnut or almonds or something of the sort. The main pendant, however, was a tooth. It wasn't some shark tooth either. If his suspicions were correct, this was a wolf tooth, probably taken from the wolf that had been killed just the other day.

He looked at the note. It looked and moved easily like paper, but it didn't feel like printer or notebook paper. The closest he could figure was some old, thin, leafed papyrus.

"Watch your back," it read.

Above it was some more writing in some foreign script that Tommen couldn't read. There was no signature except a wolf print which looked like it came from a rubber stamp.

Tommen looked around, unsure if he would see Rifun or Saul standing behind him with a menacing grin. But he was alone, or so it seemed. He carefully folded the paper and put it in his pocket. The necklace he put around his neck, but tucked the wolf tooth in his shirt. Only then did he realize he hadn't gotten Saul's phone number, or else he would have called or texted and asked him about the cryptic note and strange gift.

Well, no matter. Tommen had had enough of Saul's thundercloud for the time being, and he was ready to go home.

By the time he got back to the curb, his dad was just walking up to grab his stuff.

"Holy cow, is that my son?" his dad said, looking at him. "No, couldn't be. He's way too tan. And he looks like he's put on some muscle. Who are you and what have you done to my boy?"

Tommen gave himself a once-over. He hadn't really given it much thought, but yeah, he looked like he'd gotten a little sun. Now that the burn had healed, he looked like he'd gotten a pretty good tan. The muscle he couldn't really speak for; he was still as tall and skinny as ever, no matter what Pam fed them or how much work they did.

"I don't think it's me," Tommen said. "I think your eyesight must be going bad."

"Well, there is that. All right, is this all your stuff? Are you allowed to leave yet or do you have to wait for something?"

"No, I'm good. All the boys are gone and Saul already left."

"If you say so."

Tommen grabbed a few things, and his dad grabbed a few things. "So, Becky tells me you got a new car."

Walter paused and looked at him. "Did you have her bug the house, too, or what?"

"Well, she's small enough that she could probably slip right by and you'd never notice."

His dad shook his head. "You're right about that. And yes, I did get a new car. I was hoping to surprise you, but I see my efforts were in vain."

"The Cadillac give out finally?"

"No, not yet. But I figured that with your birthday and your driving test coming up, and the fact that you haven't exactly had time to look for your own car, well, happy birthday."

"So you're using my birthday as an excuse to dump the Cadillac on me and get yourself a new car."

"Yes." His dad grinned when he groaned. "You're the one who decided to spend his summer stomping around in the woods instead of car shopping and preparing for his driver's test. At this point, you need a vehicle you're familiar with."

"I know, I know."

Walter's new car turned out to be a late 00's Ford. It wasn't a bad car, really, Tommen figured when he got in. It didn't smell funky, didn't seem like it was sagging, and it at least looked like it belonged in the 21st century. And it was clean. Yeah, his dad had kept the Cadillac clean, but this car was, like, actually clean, not just cleaned.

"Where'd you find this?" Tommen wondered.

His dad started the car, and it started right up. No coughing, wheezing, or hesitating. "I admit, I went to a dealership."

"Ah, so they upsold you."

"No, I've been looking at this car for a little while, but never had the nerve to go in and get beaten over the head with all their sales pitches. Finally I decided to just grit my teeth and do it."

"Uh-huh." Tommen shifted in his seat. "So what's the real reason you got this car? And not, like, this car specifically, but a new car in general. You've always talked about pawning off the Cadillac on me, but I don't buy the argument that you want me to have a car. You'd let me suffer if only to teach me a lesson and get me motivated to buy my own vehicle. Does this have something to do with the embarrassment factor and you wanting to impress Laura?"

His dad was silent as his ears and face flushed red with embarrassment. Then, "Do you have a problem with that?"

"No. No, not at all. At least it saves me the trouble of having to buy my own car right away."

"Tommen."

Tommen hesitated and shrugged. "I don't know. I mean, I haven't even met her."

"I know. Once again, you're the one who decided to leave for a month and be your own man."

"Yeah, and look how well that's turning out."

His dad raised a brow but said only, "Laura and I have lunch plans tomorrow, and I told her that if possible, I would bring you so you could meet."

Tommen shrugged. "Okay."

He could see from his dad's expression that this was not how he wanted the conversation to go. He'd probably expected the ride home to be some good father-son time for them so they could talk about camp and work and life without having to go through all the unpleasantness of the interruption that was his dad's girlfriend. All of this seemed to be happening at stunted, inconvenient intervals.

"Your knee seems like it's okay," Tommen observed after a few seconds of awkward silence.

"Yes, it is. Something about a speedy, almost miraculous healing," his dad confirmed with a glint of amusement in his eye. "Not that either of us would have any idea how something like that might happen."

"No, not at all. Miracles. Wonderful things, those, right?"

The new car even seemed to handle the rutted dirt road better than the Cadillac. They still felt the potholes, but it was less of a groin shot and more of a punch in the arm, as far as severity and pain tolerance went.

"Have you eaten?" Walter asked when they got back on pavement.

"I have..." Tommen began.

"But you can always eat more. I get it, I get it. What, did they starve you at camp or what?"

"No, the exact opposite."

They ended up going to the same diner they'd stopped at on their way up, and the whole ride there, Tommen spent explaining about Pam and the kitchen crew and how amazing the food had been. Well, except that part where they went camping in the wilderness and they almost starved, but whatever.

"Well, at least I don't have to worry about you wasting away to nothing," his dad said as he finished up his glorious exultation.

"Not at all. I have to worry about gaining weight."

"Tommen, you're too skinny to worry about gaining too much weight. All right, I have to worry about that sort of thing; you don't. And, really, you look better for it. I don't think you're going to blow away in the wind any time soon." His dad sighed as he sat down at a booth. "At the same time, I can feel my wallet getting lighter already."

Tommen grinned. "There goes the grocery bill."

"Exactly."

The diner wasn't extremely busy, but Tommen could see that ninety percent of the patronage were people from camp, both parents and kids as well as staff. The waiter came and took their drink order, handing out menus and going through the daily specials.

"So, I know for a fact that you talked to Becky ten times more than you talked to me," Walter said once the waiter had moved on. "So I want to know, how was camp? So far, I mean."

"Well...it was interesting," Tommen said evasively.

"Your charger still work?"

"Yeah, barely."

"Well, I went and picked up your new one; it's waiting for you at home. I want you to keep the old one just in case, as a backup. Do you think it can be fixed?"

"I'm sure it could if you could find someone who knows how to fix them. But that would probably be a question for Dr. Polski."

"Who I am sure you will see at some point this week when you go to visit his daughter." Walter smirked.

"Yeah, I imagine so."

"Anyway, back on track to my original question. How was camp?"

So Tommen gave him the highlights, or at least what would be appropriate in the public setting. Despite the diner being somewhat busy and everyone appearing occupied, Tommen had learned a long time ago to assume that everyone was watching and listening all the time. Maybe he was just being paranoid. After all, they were speaking in Welsh, and how many people here would just happen to know Welsh? Regardless, he didn't need to sound like a kook by talking about Time, the Akari, mysterious books, serial killers, or spirit wolves.

Instead, he talked about the basketball and soccer tournaments, the horseback riding, the ziplining, rock climbing, four-wheeling, going tubing for the first time, swimming one day and being poured on the next. He talked about the hiking and the camping, being able to fish and trap and forage and do all the things he knew how to do.

"Just think," his dad said as he was cut short by the waiter bringing their food, "you get to do all of this again next week, but with a group of kids your age."

"I know."

He was less than enthused by the thought just for the fact that he was still part of the troubled kids' cabin, and every one of their campers would be like mirrors of Tommen, or who he might have been if he hadn't shaped up and gotten his shit together. Was there any way he could inspire them to do the same, something that didn't involve being kidnapped by a genocidal terrorist and having loved ones die in their arms?

"I'm sure the older camp will be better than the younger camp," his dad was saying. "The younger kids you have to indulge and pretend to care about what they do. Teenagers can spot a liar a mile away, so you don't have to pretend to be impressed by every little thing they do and make."

There was a mildly sarcastic tone to his words, and a mocking glint in his eye. He was baiting Tommen, egging him on. Tommen didn't rise to the bait.

"So, were there any plans for today?" he asked instead.

"Getting home without any sort of disaster was first on the agenda," his dad said thoughtfully. "Getting to bed tonight without any sort of disaster was also on the agenda. As for anything in between, as long as it doesn't involve mischief, disaster, or catastrophe, no. Why?"

"Oh. Well, I kind of have to talk to the twins."

"I know. Micaiah told me. And..." He hesitated half a second. "Actually I got something, too. We all did."

"Books?"

"No. A warning. I was thinking we could put it off until tomorrow or the next day, but now that you've brought it up, I don't see why we couldn't all meet today to discuss it. After all, you're going back to camp in a week and you will need some information. Keeping you in the dark is doing no one any favors."

Tommen was stunned into silence. They were going to bring him in on something? Like, they were actually going to make him part of this...whatever this was? No more, let the grown-ups do their thing and stay in the corner. No more bullshit jobs to keep him busy while they went off and did all the heroics. They were actually going to bring him into their little circle of confidence? Was it too much to hope for that to be true? Fuck, life had changed since he'd been away.

"That's not to say that you're going to get a whole lot of information and training in the week that you're going to be home," his dad went on. "You still have to come back. But Micaiah said something about doing some remote training. I figure he means calling or texting you, but you'll have to ask him."

"Sweet."

Finally, things were moving again. It might be a little slow because of the distance, but he was back on track with his training. Even cooler would be if he got to continue his Apprentice training as well as whatever weird Akari training Micaiah had for him. Tommen was still immensely skeptical, but he'd take anything that let him get an edge over Rifun.

They finished their food and continued on their way, Walter having to redirect Tommen to the new car as he was still wandering around looking for the Cadillac.

"I don't know if I can get used to this," Tommen commented as they pulled back into traffic. "It's way too nice."

"Almost as scary as the renovation, huh?" Walter chuckled.

"You're having a mid-life crisis, aren't you?"

"No, I had that about ten years ago when I got you. It was that moment of, aw, damn, what have I gotten myself into?"

"I had a moment like that when I walked into that cave. Does that mean I'm about to die soon? Because if I was eight years old then..."

His dad shook his head severely. "Not if I have anything to

say about it."

He tried to make it light-hearted, but it was forced, and Tommen knew that it had probably been the wrong thing to say. They'd both almost lost each other too many fucking times to make stupid jokes about it.

"What do you think would have happened if I hadn't gone into that cave?" Tommen wondered after a minute or two. "If I'd been home when you came up the drive to see my pa?"

His dad let out a breath. "I'm sure I don't know. Your pa gave me that mission, I think, with the hopes of getting rid of me, or maybe testing my resolve. I either brought you back alive or didn't come back at all. So I don't know what would have happened if you hadn't disappeared. My best guess would be that he might have just run me off completely, but I don't know."

"Oh."

They rode in silence for about five minutes after that before some humorous event from camp popped into Tommen's mind that he just had to share. Then it all went downhill from there.

"Sounds like you had a good time," Walter said as they finally got within sight of Charleston. "Is this going to be a regular summer thing now?"

"Oh, God, I hope not," Tommen said. "All the activities are fun, but I'd rather be a camper than a counselor. Then I definitely don't have to care about what the campers say and think."

His dad shook his head and sighed dramatically.

A few minutes later, they pulled into the parking lot of the bakery. It wasn't terribly busy, and they went inside, the little bell over the door jingling lightly.

"Oh my God, he's joined the dark side," Micah said, walking up from the kitchen and stopping when he saw Tommen. "What were you doing up there, man, lifting weights and tanning? That shit's not good for you."

"Nope, just living the dream," Tommen told him.

Micaiah poked his head out of the office. "Well, look who

decided to come pay a visit to the meager bakery peasants."

"Peasants, yeah right. I've been to your house."

"Fair enough. You here to stay or just on leave?"

"No, I'm fully planning on going back for round two."

"Too bad."

"But I do have something that you said you wanted to see."

Micaiah nodded. "Oddly enough, we have some information as well. Step into our office."

It was like no time at all had passed. The baked goods, the mess in the kitchen, the bigger mess in the office, all of it exactly as Tommen remembered.

"So," Micaiah said, taking a seat. "First order of business. Saul."

"He's been fired," Tommen told him. "Not until the end of next camp, but—"

"I know. We've been in contact."

"You know him?"

Micaiah nodded. "Saul is part of the Akarin, as are his brothers and sister. There's a bit of a story to them, but I'll just give you the basic rundown.

"Saul probably told you that he is part of the Krydik tribe of Indians, right? Well, here's the thing, they don't exist anymore, if they ever did. Not here." He paused and shifted as if unsure how to say it. "Disease wiped out the Native Americans more than war and colonization ever did. The Spanish, the English, the French, all of them bringing smallpox, tuberculosis, yellow fever, you get the picture.

"The first round of deadly disease came through even before Columbus. Sorry to say, Columbus didn't discover shit, and certainly not America. But I digress. Anyway, diseases come through, wipe out a massive part of the Indian population. Those who die, die, and those who live, live. But they have little love for the white demons who brought the diseases to them.

"There is no record of a Krydik tribe anywhere on Earth

because they are, in fact, descendants of the Cherokee and other smaller tribes who were driven almost to extinction after the Seven Years—excuse me, French and Indian War, when the British made a hard push into their land.

"If you know your history, you'll know that some Europeans were the assholes that history makes them out to be, wanting to conquer the Natives and bring in slaves, establish the rule of the Monarchy of England, the whole deal. Saul's ancestors saw their villages burned, whole populations slaughtered. Not all of the Europeans were like that, but it's what sticks in the mind, these and other ideas.

"One of these ideas happens to be Time, specifically the Akari. Some of the colonists didn't appreciate what their brethren were attempting to do, subdue the Indians, so they thought to give them an advantage in their fight against the white demons. They exposed them to Time, taught them Time and the Akari.

"To make a long story short, it had its advantages and disadvantages. Some called it witchcraft. Others called it a blessing from their gods. It worked well in war, but as we all know, Time is not medicine, and it did nothing to stop the diseases which still spread like wildfire through the Indian communities, making them even easier pickings for the conquerors. Finally, the Time-wielding colonists had an idea."

Micaiah shifted again. "There are worlds out there that are either uninhabited, or have only small pockets of residents. We call them colony planets."

"The Akarin colonists moved the Indians to one of these worlds?" Tommen asked.

He nodded. "They did. They told them to capture as many of their hunting animals as possible—alive—and to bring everything they could with them, just as if they were migrating. And they were moved to a world they named Hlohi, somewhere in Quadrant Four."

"So then how did Saul get from there to here?" Walter wondered.

"The Wolf Clan was always charged with protecting the tribe. Traditionally, this was the warrior way, but it has since become more cultural, spiritual. I don't know, Saul tried to explain it. Anyway, the move was supposed to be temporary. They had full belief that the Indians would win the war against the white demons and they would be able to return home. The Wolf Clan was charged with keeping an eye on things here. They don't live here, but they drop in from time to time. For Saul, that means being a camp counselor for a couple months out of the year.

"Unfortunately, it's become pretty obvious that the Indians aren't going to win against the white man and get their land back. Recently there's been some turbulence in tribal politics. Some like using the Akari and Time and think it suits them well. Others think it's cheating and a disgraceful thing and they should go back to their old ways. Remember, most of them use Time to some extent, and some do remember living on Earth because of the slowed aging. You want to talk about old grudges, well, that's one way to do it."

"So Saul's older brother who is on the council and part of the Wolf Clan is trying to reconcile the two sides," Tommen guessed. "One side being those who want to return or keep things as they are, and those who want to make a clean break and do things the old way."

Micaiah nodded. "Ask him about it and he'll just give you a speech about tribal matters being tribal matters, but yes, that's the gist of it."

"But Saul is an Akari-bearer."

"Yes, he is. It's how he gets from place to place."

"Oh."

"Now then. About your book."

Tommen nodded and handed him the book. Micaiah looked it, flipped through it, and whistled. "Not bad. And I have to say, I love the series name. The Chivalrous Welshman." He grinned and shook his head. "It's so you."

"What is it, though?"

Micaiah handed the book back to him. "It's the words of the Author, written down for your benefit as well as Akari-bearers everywhere. When it's ready to be seen, one appears where you will see it—or the primary character for the series—and another appears in the Akarin Archives."

"The copyright date isn't until 2017, though."

"So? Think about it this way. Even if you went through and tried to edit it that, and maybe you even managed to somehow edit the one in the Archives, more copies will appear and be available to all. You will never be able to outsmart the Author and her own words."

"How do I know that this is from the Author, that it really is her words?"

Micaiah reached over and flipped a few pages. "Purple ink. She always signs that which is hers in purple ink because it makes it easy to spot a photocopy or a false document."

"So who gets a book exactly?" Walter wondered, folding his arms skeptically.

"No one knows why the Author picks one person and not another to document. But it will always show up on the shelf of the main character and the Akarin Archives. Then, once the copyright date is reached, everyone gets to see it."

"How do you know when the end is reached, though?" Tommen asked. "I mean, this says Book One. That means there's more to come."

Micaiah shrugged. "I have five myself. I haven't gotten a new one in quite some time. Could be that my unique story is over and I'm just supporting cast from here on out. I don't know."

Tommen leaned back in his seat until he was afraid he would fall over. "This is way too much to think about. This is just fucked up." He ignored his dad's look. "I mean, it's like...really? How does this sort of thing happen? Either it's a sick prank, or there just might be something out there. I mean, I'm reading about things from my own perspective that I never told anyone about. Not even you guys know about this, so how could anyone else? And I mean...come on..." He opened the back cover. "It says she's from Michigan. What good ever came from Michigan?"

"Maybe someday you can ask her."

He shook his head. "Anyway, that's not the only thing I've gotten lately." He reached into his pocket and pulled out the note. "I don't know if this is from Saul or Rifun pretending to be Saul."

They all looked at the paper.

"That's Saul all right," Micaiah determined. "That's the paper they use in the tribe, his handwriting, and his people's language there on top."

"He made me this, too." Tommen showed them the necklace.

"Wolf tooth," Micah stated. "His version of a good luck charm, I should think."

"That's not all, either." Tommen explained the vandalism and the mutilated wolf outside the cabin. When he was done, he noted his dad's particularly troubled expression. A moment later, Walter produced a laminated paper with a bunch of flies arranged in a message and handed it to him. "What's this?"

"It's the message Rifun left for us," his dad said gravely.

"So, Rifun steals Tommen's first Book and gives it to him, calls it his first lesson in the Akari and tells him that there's another one coming," Micah mused. "He leaves a cryptic message for you, Walter, which he knows will be shown to us. Then he kills a wolf as a direct message to Saul. Why?"

"Saul is an Akari-bearer and member of the Akarin," Micaiah went on. "He's the one I was going to have train Tommen a little while he's at the next camp. Seems pretty obvious to me. If Saul trains Tommen, he's going to die. Rifun wants to be the one to train him."

"Rifun is devolving," Walter stated. "As a criminal, he's starting to lose it and go rabid. He's lost everything, all the power and influence he once had. He has nothing to threaten us with except sheer force. He's powerless while we're becoming more powerful against him."

"What does that mean?" Tommen wondered.

"It means that he's volatile and could do anything. Even the smallest spark, the faintest slight could set him off. Means he's almost as dangerous now as he was when he was King of Time. Difference is, he'll kill you with his bare hands instead of just ordering an execution."

"Maybe so," Micaiah said thoughtfully, "but he does have plenty of supporters still, if Kayla's attacker proved anything."

"Kayla was attacked?" Tommen wondered.

"Then how do we proceed?" Micah asked. "Sounds like we're sending Tommen out to walk a field full of land mines."

"We do exactly what we were planning to do in the first place," Micaiah said calmly. "Tommen needs to get close to Rifun, even if that means going along with his crackpot plans a little, training and whatever else. We need to know if he's just got a small band of refugee fighters, or if he still has significant friends and forces standing behind him. But we also need to train him correctly in the Akari. Fight fire with fire and all that because Time will do you no good here."

"Speaking of which, you think we should tell him about the new rules?" Micah grumbled.

"New rules?" Tommen wondered.

Micaiah nodded and rolled his eyes. "The Hands have decreed that there is to be no mention of the Akari anywhere within Time. At all."

"Oh."

"Just means we have to be very careful. Think you can do it? Rifun's obviously dead-set on getting you under his wing. We want to show you how to actually beat him."

"Seems like I really don't have a choice."

Micaiah nodded. "Good. Then your first assignment is to finish your Book. When you go back to camp, Saul will instruct you from there, at least for the time being."

"Rifun will probably want me to report on you guys, too,"

Tommen pointed out.

"We know. And we'll tell you what to say." Micaiah went on before Tommen could say more. "It's a fine line, and a dangerous one, but as you said, we have no other options."

The four of them sat in silence for a minute or two. Walter spoke first.

"Where's Kayla?"

"Oh, she's doing a consult a little east of town. Supposedly a very high-paying client, but also a very finicky and very bitchy one. Can't please them—and by them, she means her, the wife—for anything. But hey, that's her gig."

They made a little small talk after that, the twins asking about the camp and how it went and so on and so forth. After a while, though, they all had to get a move on. Business was business. On their way out, Tommen grabbed a cinnamon roll and Walter got his pastry.

"What happened to your diet?" Tommen teased as they headed back out to the car.

"I can indulge every once in a while," his dad replied.

Driving through the city toward home, it was like no time had passed at all. Traffic was as congested as ever and city life never really changed. It made Tommen long for the safety and seclusion of the mountains even more.

"You want to go home, or do you want me to drop you off at your girlfriend's house?" his dad asked as they pulled onto their home street. His tone was teasing.

"No, I want to just go home and get everything unpacked and washed and whatever."

"And whatever. Very descriptive."

"Mostly I just want to sleep in my own bed."

"It's hardly noon."

"I haven't gotten more than six hours of sleep in almost a month."

"Aw, poor you."

Then they were home. Walter had barely turned off the car

before Tommen looked in the mirror and saw Becky walking up the driveway. She wasn't much of a runner because of her shoes, but she walked just as fast as she could so she could hug him. He managed to wiggle himself loose enough to kneel and return the hug, stealing a kiss when he knew his dad wasn't looking.

"Miss me?" he asked.

"Only a lot," she told him, eyes shining. "And by the way, you now have to take me out and we have to do all the things you've been bragging about doing. If a bratty little snot-nosed eight year old can do it, I can do it, too, whatever it is."

"Such a high opinion of young children you have."

"Let's just say I'm one convenient catastrophe away from never being asked to babysit again."

"Okay, this sounds like an interesting story. Why don't you tell me about it while I get my stuff in?"

Her ability to help was limited to his sleeping bag, pillow, and small backpack. The suitcase and large backpack he had to carry in himself, which he didn't mind. And she told him all about her mischievous exploits, having to watch her nieces and nephews. It sounded rather comical, actually, some of the things she did.

"So I figure the only thing I have left to do in order to get completely blacklisted from babysitting is something along the lines of finger paint, jell-o, and some crickets. I'm still working out the details."

Tommen had only been listening intermittently as he sorted his stuff and put things away, but with her last statement, he wasn't sure he wanted to know the full story behind that scheme. The last thing he did was Band so he could take the book and put it somewhere Becky hopefully wouldn't find it. It wasn't enough to put it somewhere high, because she had the ingenuity and the determination to get anywhere she needed to be, with or without someone's help. He would have to hide it, and hide it good.

Then he dropped the Band, moved his bags off onto the floor, and flopped back on his bed. Becky took her shoes off and crawled up onto the bed beside him, resting her head on his chest. Damn, he liked that. He hadn't realized how much he missed it.

"So, what are your plans for the week?" she asked.

"Well," Tommen sighed, "tomorrow my dad wants me to go to lunch with him so I can meet his girlfriend."

"Oh. That sounds nice. At least you'll finally meet her."

"Yeah. But, I don't know. I mean, I do but I don't want to meet her, you know? It's just..."

"Change?"

"I guess."

"You don't want your dad to be happy?"

"What? No, I want him to be happy. He's easier to live with when he's happy."

"You just don't want it to be a girlfriend that makes him happy."

"I don't know. Maybe."

"Because it's always been just you and him."

"Yeah."

She shifted position and sat up. "What's he going to do when it's not you and him anymore? What happens when you leave for college and he's left alone?"

Then he'll go dark and resurface somewhere else in another new life. "I don't know. I mean, you have a point, but still. Why not wait until after that point?"

"Tommen, your dad isn't getting any younger."

"Hey now, I resemble that statement," Walter said, appearing in the doorway. Tommen was forced to wonder how much he'd heard, but his voice and body language gave nothing away. "I know Tommen's been eating nonstop today, but are you hungry, Becky?"

"I could eat," she answered. "Actually, I probably should eat here pretty soon. I've been relying on candy to keep my sugar up more than I should."

"Well, I'll see what I can scrounge up. Maybe I can fill this black hole that's moved back into my house."

"Only for this week," Tommen said.

"And then you're gone for a month, but then you come back again. I don't think your stomach is going to shrink in that time, if your worshipful dissertation of camp food was any indication."

Okay, so he had a point.

Becky stayed for lunch which turned out to be simple sandwiches, Walter privately conveying to Tommen that the only thing he was spending more money on as far as groceries was the meat seeing how Tommen wasn't around to go poaching. Afterwards, they headed back to his room to play video games for a bit. Walter went out to the garage to do something or other.

"So..." Tommen said as he started up the game. "About that kiss..."

"What about it?" Becky wondered coyly.

"My dad's out in the garage right now, so obviously he's not watching."

"Uh-huh...And was a kiss the only thing you wanted?" She laughed when he burned red hot with embarrassment. "I know what you're looking for."

There was nothing he could say to that that wouldn't make him look like either an idiot or a player. Yes, he wanted to fuck her. He really, really wanted to fuck her. How did he convey this without sounding like an asshole who just wanted to use her and lose her? The other girls at school were usually as horny as he was. Becky wasn't like them, though. She was too difficult to read sometimes. What was she thinking right now?

She still managed to beat him royally at most every game he had. A few times he tried to Band himself and the controller to see if it would register faster reflexes or something, but the results were limited. He bested her a few times, but whether that came from Banding or sheer dumb luck was hard to tell.

After a while, he just lay back on the bed, conceding defeat. As he stretched out, Becky lay back beside him and poked him in the ribs.

"Hey, now, that tickles," he said, curling up.

"I know," Becky said. "But it's funny."

He relaxed and closed his eyes. He hadn't even done much today and he was tired. It was barely dinnertime. His dad was still out in the garage and they were sitting in his room playing video games.

Tommen barely knew what happened as Becky moved and kissed him on the lips. He opened his eyes and looked at her. Damn, still fully clothed.

"So is this a treat or a regular thing?" he asked, getting up on one elbow.

She kissed him again and he returned it. "It's our own regular treat." Translation: Our little secret. Then she took his hand and put it on her breast. Still outside the clothes, but it sent a familiar warmth through him as he felt her. "This is the rare treat."

Chapter Twenty-Three
Midway

Tommen was glad to sleep in his own bed again, and his dreams were filled with thoughts of Becky. Feeling her had naturally hardened him, and having her reach down to feel him, even outside his pants, had done little to help the situation. Only Banding had saved him then as his dad came back in the house. He walked Becky back home and they parted ways like nothing secret and sensual had happened.

It had only been light touching, true, but his dreams that night took it far beyond that, and he woke the next morning with wet on the front of his boxers.

"Sleep all right?" his dad asked when he emerged from his room in search of food.

"Yeah," he answered. "Slept real good." *God knows what I'll dream about if me and Becky ever do actually have sex.* "Glad to be back in my own bed."

"That's good."

His dad was in his recliner, reading the morning paper.

"So how did you get the weekend off, anyway?" Tommen wondered, grabbing a box of cereal and assorted necessities. "Are you still on leave because of your knee?"

"Light duty still, but I decided to use a couple vacation days. Summer is always ridiculously hectic. I decided to treat myself."

Tommen did not say anything to that. Summer was busy, true, but his dad never "treated himself," at least not like that. His idea of a treat was an extra pastry from the bakery, a new pair of boots when he didn't absolutely need them, things like that. Taking vacation days when he didn't have to? The only reason he would do that was because he was feeling good. And the only thing that had changed his mood that much lately was his girlfriend.

Sensing the silence, Walter asked, "So, do you want to come to lunch today?"

Tommen shrugged even though he was pretty sure his dad wasn't looking. "Sure. I mean, I guess I have to meet her eventually."

"I won't force you to go today. She'll be off Thursday night or Friday morning if you'd rather wait a few days."

"Not going to do me any good to wait. What time is lunch?"

"One-thirty." He said the name of the restaurant. It was more of a cafe, really, someplace to get a light meal to tide a person over until dinner.

Tommen still wasn't sure what to think and he ended up walking down to Becky's to pass the time. Her dad was working and her mom was still sleeping as she worked the night shift, but otherwise the house was empty. As usual, Becky was swamped with her sewing work.

"Come for more?" she teased as they headed upstairs to her room. "Don't worry, I won't make you answer that."

He had a snide remark, but was torn whether or not he should say it. He was finally starting to get the goods; he didn't want to jeopardize that.

"No, mostly I just came down to pass the time until lunch," he answered honestly, sitting on her little bed.

"Oh, when you meet your dad's girlfriend?"

"Yeah."

She got herself situated just so and started zipping away on her machine. "What are you most afraid of? That she'll be a total witch?"

"No. Actually..." He sighed. "I'm afraid I'm going to like her. Not, like, you know, like-her like-her, like I like you, but—"

"You're afraid that she'll be good for your dad and everything will be okay."

"Something like that."

"You don't like change. Few people do. And you're afraid that this change will be good because you would rather everything stay exactly the way it is."

"Are you a geneticist or a psychologist?"

"Please. I'm a woman. And by the way, you still owe me a happy birthday."

"What?"

"My birthday was three weeks ago."

"Oh. Sorry, I'm really not into birthdays."

"Yeah, that's what your dad said, too. He also told me when your birthday is."

"Too bad I'll be gone around that time."

"I know, it's terrible. How am I supposed to embarrass you on your birthday when you aren't even here?"

"I'm sure you'll find a way." He paused. "How old are you now? Nineteen?"

"I wish. Eighteen. I'm just older than you."

"Older than me and a grade ahead. Such a cougar."

"Yeah, well you didn't have a problem with that yesterday."

Heart thudding out of his chest, Tommen stood and went up behind her, sliding his arms around her until he could feel her again. "Is that an invitation?"

She paused in her work. "Depends. How much time you got?"

He glanced at the clock on her wall. "Oh, I'd say an hour or two."

"Good." She pointed. "You can start by sorting those for me. Big pieces in one pile, small pieces in another, and scraps go in the scraps bin."

His confusion effectively killed his mood long enough for him to mechanically begin his assigned task. He'd helped her before on small chores, and he didn't really have a problem with it, but...ouch. That was just cold. Well, maybe there would be more after he was done sorting. Get some stuff done for her, decrease her work load a little, help with the stress and the worry, and maybe she'd have time for other things, at least for a few minutes.

The way he figured it, there were only two more steps. Well, two and a half if he wanted to get technical. Clothes off touching was the first step, plus maybe half a step for handjobs and oral, and full-blown sex as the final step. They were almost there. The time between steps was long, but he was enjoying everything he got so far. He really didn't want to blow it now.

He finished sorting her fabric pieces and sat down on her bed again, ruffling Mr. Snuffles who was trying to sleep. Becky still worked away, zipping her fabric through her machine, turning, fixing, pinning, setting, and zipping it back through like nobody's business.

"How many times did you leave the house while I was gone?" he wondered.

Her head looked up, but her fingers still worked. "Um...not enough."

"Maybe I need to get you out of the house while I'm here."

"Well, that would be nice, but it's not going to be today or tomorrow. Today you have lunch and I have to get this work done because tomorrow I'm supposed to have a client come in for a fitting. That's assuming she shows up. It's about a fifty-fifty shot whether she does or not. It's irritating."

"Okay, so what about Thursday?"

"Thursday might work. Sure."

He stood and went to her, standing to the side and bending down so he could kiss her on the lips, surprising her as much as she'd surprised him. "I'll see you Thursday then."

She blinked and shook her head. "Yeah, Thursday. Yeah, sounds great." She kissed him again. "I'll see you then."

He let himself out and started back toward his house. Okay, so he hadn't gotten any, but the kiss was good, and, as she'd said before, the touching was a rare treat. And, just like the kiss had once been a rare treat, he would just have to wait this one out until they moved to the next step.

Until then, he now had the daunting task of accompanying his dad to lunch and meeting his girlfriend. Funny thing, over the last four weeks, he'd conjured up his own ideas of what Laura looked like, sounded like, acted like. What happened when she didn't meet any of those expectations? Worse, what if she exceeded them? Like Becky said, what if he ended up liking her? What if she really was a good fit for his dad?

His dad was just heading down to his bedroom when Tommen walked in the house. "I was beginning to think you'd changed your mind and weren't coming."

"No, no, I'm coming," Tommen said. "Not going to do me any good to wait."

"All right. I won't force you to come, but once you're in the car, you're committed."

"I know. Is there some special occasion?"

"You mean do you have to dress up? We're only going to lunch at a little cafe, Tommen. Just be presentable to the general public."

Clean shirt, clean pants, got it. His dad was a little more dressed up, but then, it was his girlfriend. Tommen was just along for the ride this time. He felt his palms break out in sweat. Fucking hell, but he was actually doing this. Why the hell was he so nervous again? Oh, right, new woman, potentially life-changing relationships, that sort of thing.

The cafe wasn't too far from the bakery, actually. As they pulled in, his dad looked around the lot.

"What's she drive?" Tommen wondered.

"Big truck, covered in bumper stickers, medic decal," he answered wistfully. "You can't miss it."

Well, it explained the new car a little better. Men liked big vehicles, powerful vehicles, loud vehicles, tough vehicles, fast vehicles, brand new vehicles. The Cadillac had been none of those. It had been an old, beat-up vehicle. Worse, his girlfriend had a bigger, more powerful, louder, tougher, faster, newer vehicle. Obviously he just couldn't let that slip by. That was an insult to his man card. Tommen said none of this out loud of course.

"Well, why don't we go in and grab a booth?" his dad suggested.

Tommen went along with it. There was no such thing as a large or filling meal at the cafe—seeing how it catered to petite little soccer moms and businesswomen who took their salads with extra kale and a small drizzle of olive oil as an indulgence—so he was left with a small sub sandwich and a bag of chips.

They'd just gotten their order at the end of the counter and were on their way to a booth by a window when the door opened and a woman in full paramedic uniform walked in.

She was taller and bigger than Tommen had imagined, easily five-foot-nine, a hundred and seventy pounds or so. Flat brown hair looked like it had been pulled back in a ponytail or a bun for quite a while but was now allowed to rest at her shoulders in an awkward flop. She saw Walter and Tommen and flashed a smile, silently indicating that she'd be there in just a second.

"You want the inside or the outside?" Walter asked, reaching the booth.

"Outside," Tommen answered.

"So you can run out the door screaming?"

"If necessary."

A couple minutes later, Laura joined them, her meal consisting of a sub sandwich, a bag of chips, a fruit cup, and a drink. Well, wasn't like there were too many options here anyway.

"Afternoon, Walter," she greeted.

"Laura, my son, Tommen," Walter introduced. "Tommen, my girlfriend, Laura."

Judging by his change in tone, his dad still wasn't comfortable introducing Laura as his girlfriend. Still, Tommen nodded, shook her hand politely, and returned to his sandwich.

"Your dad tells me you've been away at summer camp," she

said conversationally. "How was it?"

She tried to be friendly, but her voice was just naturally not friendly. It wasn't mean or rude or condescending, but she was clearly better suited for shouting commands in an emergency, like yelling at an underling to do better CPR, push this drug or that drug, or drive fucking faster because their patient was about to die.

"Could have been better, could have been worse," Tommen answered diplomatically. "We'll see how the next set of campers turns out."

"I had to do two weeks of clinicals at the children's hospital when I was in paramedic school. Sorry to say, that was a long two weeks."

"Don't like kids?"

"Kids are fine, generally speaking. Medically, however, there is a lot to know. You don't dare try to memorize it, though, because there's just too much. Med dosages, all that stuff. Plus we don't normally run kids, so the infrequency plays a terrible factor."

Her small speech was directed more at Walter, but Tommen jumped on it.

"We had a girl with a peanut allergy go down because she accidentally ate peanut butter."

"Is she all right? You guys had epi to give her, right? I mean, I imagine with a potential anaphylactic reaction she'd have her own epi at least."

"Yeah, she's fine."

So, the woman was more business than sentiment. Made sense in her line of work, and it was a little relieving. At least Tommen wouldn't have to worry about her getting all gushy and emotional about how she wasn't trying to replace his mom or butt in or anything. She was all business; give her the facts and none of the fluff.

Of course, that wasn't to say there wasn't a little light-hearted flirting between the adults, but Tommen was more intent on his sandwich. Why couldn't he and Becky flirt so openly? Why did they always have to be overshadowed by her dad or his dad or whoever?

Why couldn't they just be?

Maybe that was the reasoning behind the touch. She was just as tired of it as he was. Maybe she was looking for more, too, and this was her way of asking without asking. Well, she never was one for beating around the bush. Maybe instead of teasing and flirting, this was her way of mentally preparing herself, ramping up to what they both wanted. He wouldn't lie and say he wasn't nervous, but damn he wanted to fuck her so bad. At this point, he was even good with a kiss and a touch. Fuck, he wanted more, though. And letting his mind wander, especially with his dad literally sitting right next to him, was not helping things.

"Tommen?"

He looked up from his phone. "Huh?"

"I asked if you were ready to go back to school yet," Laura said.

"Um...no. Not really," he answered.

"Why not? Your dad says you're quite the whiz kid when it comes to science and physics."

"I guess so. In the same way you're good at being a paramedic. You enjoy it, you go to school for it, experience does the rest."

"Tommen," his dad began.

"No, it's all right," Laura cut in. "He's right. Passion is useless without intelligence, and experience certainly helps. Sounds like he's got at least two out of the three, estimating high."

Tommen met her gaze then, and they had an understanding, even as Walter tried to calm what he seemed to perceive as an impending war.

"True," Tommen went on, "but I also have something that you lack, speaking in such general terms."

"Oh, and what's that?"

"Youth."

"Tommen!" Walter barked.

But Laura just laughed. "So you do. And you also have the

tongue of a youth, quick and witty, but lacking the humor and refinement of age and wisdom, the ability to insult someone without them realizing it until they think it over an hour later."

"Oh, but that's just cheating. See, one should never engage in a battle of wits against one who is unarmed."

"Well, if that's a compliment, then thank you."

Tommen opened his mouth, but could only silently concede the point.

"I think I missed something," Walter said as Tommen went back to his phone, and Laura her drink.

"Don't worry about it," Laura told him. "I'm sure you can talk about it later."

Thus, Tommen resumed ignoring them.

"How's lunch?" Becky wondered when he texted her.

"Terribly unsatisfying. There's almost no food here," he replied.

"Very funny. How's it going, though?"

"Good, I guess. I mean, she's not a bitch or anything, so that's good."

"Usually is. Well, my client just showed up, so I have to go. Talk to you later, bye."

Even as he read the message, his dad was tapping him on the shoulder. Well, guess they were leaving. It would be kind of awkward to have an hour-long date while the kid of one of the parties involved was sitting right there. Fine for little kids, but not with bratty teenagers, he supposed.

"Why don't you get the car started?" Walter suggested, handing him the keys.

"You're trusting me with your brand new car?" Tommen wondered.

"Same as the last time, one chance."

"Got it." He looked back and forth between the two of them. "Just don't get weird or anything. I'm still watching."

They both blushed as he turned and headed out to the car. All right, so it hadn't been a total disaster. At least she wasn't a sentimental flake. His dad wasn't the hopeless romantic he'd feared he would be. It was a start.

A quick goodbye turned into a five or ten minute endeavor as they stood outside the cafe talking, Tommen waiting in the car, watching them. Strangely enough, he found himself thinking what he assumed his dad probably thought every time he went over to Becky's house. Becky had said that Laura had been over several times for dinner, and it wasn't unreasonable to think his dad had been to her place. Were they being good? Were they having sex in the usual manner of adult hypocrisy? Had they even kissed yet? Did older adults still do that? Neither of them was exactly a spring chicken. Maybe he had nothing to worry about.

His mind returned to Becky, how she'd felt in his hands. Fuck, he wanted to know more. He wanted to see more, feel more. He wanted to fuck her, dammit. He wasn't dumb enough to think he was going to get it before he left for camp, but he could hope, right? Damn it all, he wanted to do her so bad. Being stuck in a camp with a cabin full of horny teenage boys was not going to help the situation.

The lovebirds finally said their goodbyes. Damn, his dad was almost dancing to the car. Did women really have that effect on men? Tommen thought about Micaiah and his attitude change once Kayla had moved in with him. Apparently they did. Weird.

"Took you long enough," Tommen said as his dad got in the car.

"Got a hot date with Becky tonight?" his dad wondered.

"No, she's working with a client right now."

"So there you go." His dad shifted position. "So what exactly happened in there? I feel like I missed something."

"Nothing," Tommen answered. "Just wanted to see what she's like."

"And does she meet your approval, Dad? Can I date her?"

He shrugged. "You can date whoever you want; I don't have control of that."

"Do you think you two can get along if she comes over for dinner or something?"

"Yeah. I mean, she's not an evil witch or anything, at least she didn't seem like it."

"That's all I can ask."

"Now you guys are being good, right?" Tommen asked smartly.

His dad met him head-on. "Only as good as you and Becky."

He really wasn't sure how to take that. Did that mean his dad knew about the touching? Or did he suspect something and this was his way of fishing for answers without asking directly? That didn't seem like him; he was more apt to confront him directly if he thought they were having sex. Was this another example of him being in a good mood? It was too hard to tell.

"Well, in that case," Tommen said, "maybe since we're both dating, we should go out on a couples' night sometime."

His dad was supposed to recoil and refuse. He wasn't supposed to say, "Hey, I'm all for it. If it stops Becky from being your nosy little spy while you're gone."

"Hey, I didn't ask her; she does that sort of stuff on her own."

"I know. That's the problem."

Now if only she could nose her way into my — "Maybe after I get back from camp, that way we're not scrambling at the last minute."

"The only one scrambling here is you; you're the one going to camp. But if you want to wait until after camp, we can do that."

"She's not moving in, is she?"

"No. No plans of that."

They rode in silence the rest of the way home. Tommen glanced at Becky's house, but an unfamiliar car was still parked in the driveway. He pulled into the garage and they went inside.

"So," his dad said as he sat to take his shoes off. "What did you think of her? And I'm asking for your honest opinion."

Tommen shrugged. "I don't know. I mean, she's nice."

"If you have something to say, then say so."

"Not really."

"You weren't paying any attention, then."

"Dad, I've met her once. Literally, like, just now. Okay, I haven't interacted with her enough to say one way or the other except in extreme cases. I mean, she's nice. That's what I got. She's not a witch, not a psycho, not any of the extremes that I think you would be perceptive enough to pick up on and ditch."

His dad nodded. "All right. Fair enough."

"And, I mean, you don't have to ask my permission to date someone."

"Maybe. I know you're going to be gone in a few years, but you can't say it wouldn't have some impact on you. I just want you to know what's coming, or what's happening I should say."

Tommen hesitated. "I...appreciate it. But one date isn't going to sway me one way or the other. That's my opinion."

"All right. I asked for your opinion, and it looks like I got it. All I wanted to know. You can go back to whatever you were planning to do today."

Really, he didn't have any plans, but he turned and headed down to his room anyway and put on some music. His plans for the week between camps was to sleep in his own bed, raid the fridge any time he wanted, watch TV, and spend time with Becky.

Sleeping in his own bed, well, that was the easy part. As long as his daily shenanigans didn't land him in jail, he was free to sleep in his bed all he wanted. With no school and no work, he could sleep in as late as he wanted, too. With his dad gone to work, he didn't have to worry about getting woken up early for any other shenanigans either. What those shenanigans could be, he wasn't sure, and really didn't want to find out.

Raiding the fridge, well, that was kind of limited, actually. Either his dad hadn't gone shopping in quite a while, or the man really ate just that little thanks to the slowed aging of Time. Food selection was sorely limited to canned tuna, peanut butter, a small selection of deli meats, crackers and assorted snacks, a pizza, and pasta with a single jar of sauce. Tommen could eat that much in a day if he really wanted to. Given how much he'd been eating at camp, he really wanted to.

Oh well. His lack of activity during the day made up for it a little, he supposed. That was where watching TV came in. He managed to catch up on several shows he was following, plus watch a few movies he'd been waiting to become available.

As for Becky, well, he wasn't able to do much more than a few short texts during the middle of the week while she was busy working, but by Friday, she'd managed to clear several of her largest jobs and make time for him to visit. Problem was, with her dad being Jewish, he took Fridays and Saturdays off from work. For as much as he professed old bones, the man could still sneak up the stairs when he wanted to in order to check in on them.

Of course, he was only asking if they were hungry and wanted something to eat. He was busy preparing food for his Sabbath and figured he might as well whip something up for them too, if they wanted it. They accepted and waited until he was gone before talking again. They sat on her bed, Mr. Snuffles between them looking irritated but too enamored with the cat brush to want to leave.

"You honestly want to go on a couples date," Becky said, raising a brow.

"Not really," Tommen admitted. "I mean, it was kind of more of a joke. It would be cool, you know, I guess, if we were, like, serious and not in high school."

Her expression was unreadable. "So because we're in high school, a man-made institution, that means we can't be serious?"

"Um..."

"Are you saying you don't want to be serious?" She paused for just a moment, then lowered her voice a little. "Are you saying that touching isn't a little serious?"

"Well..."

"Considering where we're going with this, at what point does it become serious?"

"Ah..."

"Your dad and his girlfriend aren't in high school; does that automatically make their relationship serious?"

"No."

"We've been dating longer. Knowing your dad, we've probably been doing a little more."

"What, you think he has problems?"

Becky's expression turned amused. "I would be more worried as to how you would know if he did, or why he would impart such information to you." More seriously, "And I'm saying that he's older, probably has more reservations about it, and he seems to have a little more...morality about it."

"And you don't?" Tommen wondered. "Little Miss 'I'm a Catholic Jew' over here?"

She shrugged. "God designed sex as a measurement of a relationship."

"Well, at least you didn't say you wanted twenty kids."

"Oh, God, no. If I ever did want kids, I mean, it'd be, like, two max. But that's a big if."

"And what about your marriage prerequisite, hm? I seem to recall that's in the bylaws somewhere."

"Depends on who's writing them. I've seen unmarried couples who are more loyal and loving than some married couples out there."

Tommen let out a breath. "Amen to that." He stroked Mr. Snuffles and the cat rolled over to his other side, tail lashing. Slowly, he moved his hand over to Becky's thigh and worked his way up to her hip. "So...does that mean...?"

"Not now, idiot," she said, slapping his hand away. "For one, my dad is right downstairs. And for two, you let me decide when that time will be."

Tommen tried not to let his rejection show as much as his erection. He failed on both accounts, and it was made even worse when she moved to touch him, the thin fabric of his shorts doing him no favors.

"Someday," she told him.

"Even for a little bit?" he ventured, taking her hand and making a short motion.

She smiled coyly. "It'll give you something to look forward to when you're at camp. Make you want to come home."

"At this point, I don't want to leave."

"Well, you're going to have to do something because my dad is coming up the stairs."

He made a quick trip to the bathroom, avoiding Dr. Polski altogether. So close, and such a tease. Fucking hell, he wanted her. He wanted her now more than ever, now that he knew she wanted it, too. Oh, but she kept a tight lid on things. Everything was in her timing, and she was a master of suspense.

When he returned to her room, he found lunch to be a couple of sandwiches, two for him, one for her. He sat down to eat, turning his back to Mr. Snuffles who suddenly decided that he loved both of them and had to nose his way close to their food.

"I guess I should get going," Tommen sighed when he finished his last sandwich. "I still have to pack and be ready to go tomorrow morning."

"Aw..." Becky said, pouting. "You mean I won't see you for another four weeks?"

"Afraid so. Duty calls."

"Yeah, well, it calls to me, too." She indicated her sewing machine. "I'm sure I'll acquire more projects before the summer is over. Does the sun still exist or did I miss it?"

"No, it's still out there."

"Oh, okay. But before you go, I guess I might as well give you your birthday present now."

Tommen sighed. "I already said, I'm really not into birthdays or holidays or—Oh."

His words were cut short as she took his hands and put them under her shirt, saying, "Just mind the pump line."

It took a second before his mind caught up to his body and he knelt as he started moving, feeling. Soft, warm skin, firm breasts. His eyes met hers. Working so much and rarely leaving the house meant she usually couldn't be bothered to wear more than a T-shirt and sweatpants. Loose clothing. Being of such short stature proved to be an advantage as it provided all of the fun stuff with none of the extra space. He moved his hands down, always watching her, silently questioning what he could get away with. He touched her hips, her thighs, felt her butt. She stopped him when he moved to the front.

"We'll call that your Christmas present," she told him.

"Oh," he said. He kissed her. "So if this was my birthday present, does that mean I get to play with it whenever I want?"

"If you did that, you would almost certainly die. If not by my hand, then someone else's." She noted his dejected look. "But, if we happen to be alone sometime and you got an urge, well, we'll see."

"I have a little more than an urge right now."

"I know. As I said, we'll see."

"You are a terrible human being. And a really bad Catholic Jew."

"I've been called worse. Now then, you were saying something about packing?"

"Mm...the only thing I'm thinking about right now is unpacking. You." His voice was strained.

She kissed him. "Not now." *Not helpful.*

"Yeah, well, I really don't have much control over it at this point."

Even as he said the words, he spent himself. At one time, he might have found it amusing, even arousing, to ejaculate in front of a girl he liked and wanted to fuck. In real life, though, it was just humiliating, and he fully expected her to ridicule him, if not call for her dad and drive him out completely.

What was worse was her silence. His hands were still cupped around her buttocks and he rested his forehead on her chest. He wanted to die. He wanted to do it again. He wanted to melt into the floor and be anywhere else. He wanted to sweep her onto the bed and be inside her.

After a minute, she lifted his head, kissed him again and said, "Christmas."

He just put his forehead back down. "Did you tease your ex-boyfriend like this, too?"

"No." He looked up. "I never really wanted to do it with him. He was the ideal good little Catholic boy. Nice guy, but too good, and he never made me feel like I could be myself without reminding me of my shortcomings. You let me be how I am."

"That's a dangerous thing."

"Isn't it? And he moved away. Then I moved away." She paused a second, then shook her head. "So, provided you don't decide to just go off gallivanting across the country over Christmas break, you have something to look forward to."

"But five months is so long," Tommen whined.

"You've waited this long. And Christmas is only the endgame. There might be more for you when you get back from camp."

If he'd had anything more left in him, he really might have just taken her to bed right there. As it was, he was done for the time being. He was spent, both physically and, to an extent, emotionally. He wanted her. He wanted her right now. Just...enough with the teasing. Let him take her clothes off and feel her whole body, unrestrained. Let him see her, touch her, get inside her.

Slowly, he gathered himself and stood. Well, at least it didn't show against black shorts. One good thing about color-blindness, he supposed. Everything went with black.

He was still sure that Dr. Polski would know exactly what had happened and call him out on it as they headed to the kitchen first to return their plates. But the doctor seemed to have warmed up to him a little, wishing him a good day and telling him to enjoy his time at camp. Tommen politely returned the gesture and followed Becky out to the front porch.

"So, tell me honestly," Tommen said. "Is Christmas a promise or a tease?"

"Providing you don't go running across the country or piss me off, it's a promise," she told him. "I'll let you know more once we get closer."

"All right. You say it's a promise, that's how I'm taking it."

"Believe me. You're going to be so busy at camp this month you won't even have time to worry about it."

I'm not going to be thinking about anything but it. Still, he knelt to hug her, and he managed to steal a kiss, too. He'd learned a few things about the blind spots in the house, such as where they were standing, Dr. Polski couldn't see them from the kitchen.

"All right, Casanova, I'll see you when you get back," Becky told him. "Remember to text me."

"I never forget," he said, walking down the mosaic walkway to the sidewalk.

He walked in the house wanting nothing more than to collapse into his bed and sleep. Had all of that really just happened? Fuck, but he wanted her so bad. Why did she have to be such a tease? She was horny as hell, but still made him wait, as if her Catholic laws meant anything whether she was planning to break them in five months or five years. Did it matter if a guy was planning a robbery for five days or five weeks from now? Tommen was pretty sure his dad would arrest him all the same. Just so, he and Becky were doomed to one of the circles of Hell, he was sure.

Grudgingly he sat up and looked around. His suitcase was only half-packed. He'd had a plan at some point today, but Becky had kind of muddled his thoughts. Damn, she felt good. Soft and warm and beautiful. At one time, he'd thought that touching a girl who wasn't an hourglass model would be icky and repulsive. Actually, he found it rather attractive, just a little more to touch and caress and put his hands on. What fun was there when his hands could practically form a belt around a skinny girl?

Ugh, this was not helping him any. He was heading back to camp tomorrow and he was woefully unprepared. He managed to drag himself upright and mechanically start going through his dresser and closet, looking for the things he needed. If nothing else, he would pack the exact same thing he'd taken up the first time; it had suited him well enough, and no one would care if he wore the same shirt two camps in a row.

His dad got home sometime in the afternoon, poking his head in briefly to ask how the packing was going.

"Slow," Tommen told him.

"Just remember that the most important things are clean underwear, toothbrush, and toothpaste. Everything else is secondary."

"Dad..."

"I'm just trying to be helpful."

"You're such a dork when you're in love, you know that?"

"No more than you, and I've watched you date a lot more girls. Did you get over to see Becky today before you leave?"

"Yeah."

"She's going to let you go?"

She's going to let me fuck her come Christmastime. "She has a lot of work to do, so she wouldn't be much company anyway. Her words, not mine."

"Well, that's the way it is with a home business, I suppose. But at least she's working and making good money to go to college."

"Hey, I'm working, too."

"I know. I'm just saying, it helps to have a plan."

"I already have a plan. It might have to be tweaked a little here and there, but I do have a plan."

"Becoming a Scout?"

"Yeah."

Walter folded his arms. "And what will you tell Becky about your long absences?"

"I don't know. What are you going to tell Laura when it comes time for you to go dark?"

Tommen could see he'd struck a chord, and he instantly regretted his words. His dad sighed and said, "I don't know. I haven't figured that out yet."

"Yeah, well, I'm sure you'll come up with something," Tommen murmured.

"Keep packing."

His dad left the room.

Way to go, Tommen, he sighed.

He crept out of his room about an hour later. His dad was asleep in his recliner. It didn't appear that anything had been made for dinner yet, so he got out the pasta and the jar of sauce. He was just about ready to dish some out for himself, when he heard his dad in the living room.

"Is there enough for me?"

Tommen turned. "Yeah, do you want some?"

His dad got out of his recliner, still slightly favoring his knee. "I'll take a little."

"Why don't you Band your knee some more? Looks like it's still bothering you."

"Tommen, I'm fifty-two years old, give or take a century. Time does not heal all wounds. Some things are natural."

"I don't remember you ever favoring your knee before."

"And some things don't heal, not completely."

"Thought you said the injury wasn't that bad."

"And it's not." His dad sat at the tiny kitchen table. "But consider the difference between an injury that's 'not bad' for someone who's seventy years old, and an injury that's 'not bad' for someone who's sixteen. You probably wouldn't even notice a little fall and a little bump, but a seventy year old thinks he's dying. No different."

"Are you okay? Like, seriously, everything's all right? You're not holding out me, are you? I want to know before I leave. I can still text Mr. Wilson and tell him I'm not coming."

"For goodness' sake, Tommen, I'm not decrepit or in imminent danger. Hell, I was in imminent danger once and you still went cajoling across the universe."

Tommen had to snicker at that one. "Yeah, I guess you're right."

"But I thank you for the concern."

"Only injured, not helpless, right?"

"Exactly." His dad leaned back in his chair as much as he dared. "Ready for camp?"

"Almost done packing."

"That's your problem. But are you ready for camp? Four more weeks with Mr. Sunshine? From what you and Micaiah have told me, he doesn't seem like the easiest to get along with in general, never mind trying to train under him."

Tommen handed his dad a bowl of pasta while he ate his, leaning against the counter. "I'm not looking forward to that. I have no idea what to expect. But if we're going to have any chance at beating Rifun, I'm going to have to start doing something."

His dad nodded glumly. "Yes, and I know I've been neglecting your regular Apprentice training. Things have settled down now, and I need to get you back in or else you might be declared dead or out of service or who knows what else."

"Well, we can do that once I get back." He took a bite of food. "Why don't you do some Akari training? Then you can tell me what it's like, what I should expect. Heh, what I should actually be learning versus whatever hell Saul is going to put me through."

"I don't know, I'm still not totally convinced of it."

"Neither am I, but I'll take all the help I can get."

"Yeah, well, I'm also getting too old for this shit."

"Now, now, watch your language," Tommen teased.

"Very funny. Not your call."

Tommen grinned but it quickly faded as he said, "Can I ask you a question?"

"Sure." His dad took a bite of pasta and leaned back again.

"How do you know when a relationship is serious?"

"Are we talking about me and Laura, or you and Becky?"

"Either."

"Well, I'm going start off by saying that you and Becky are not serious, however much you think you are. You're still in high school and have no clue what real life is about, how to survive on your own. You still eat out of my refrigerator from food that I bought, and you still wait for your birthday and Christmas to come around because you know I end up buying you new clothes or equal gift cards because you want to spend your money on other things, or squirrel it away in the name of 'saving up.' The only bill you have is your cell phone. You haven't even gone with me to the DMV to register the Cadillac in your name yet. Therefore, you have basically zero transportation.

"As far as how this applies to your relationship, you have to be the pillar of the relationship. You have to learn to make sacrifices, which might mean giving up new music downloads in order to get her a gift for her birthday or Christmas, or, in a really serious relationship, maybe even lending her money for something she needs, like her insulin. Similarly, you should have at least similar goals, financial ideas. It's ideal that your spiritual or religious ideas line up, too. You have to be willing to accept that not everything is going to be sunshine and roses. She will never not be a dwarf. She will never not be diabetic. Those are things that are going to have to be dealt with for the rest of her life, which means time, money, hospital visits potentially—"

"Okay, I get it," Tommen cut in.

"No, I don't think you do," his dad said softly. "And that's the point. And one more thing, it also helps to have similar family goals. Kids, house, pets, daily life."

Tommen sighed. "Okay, fine, so we're a couple of stupid teenagers. What about you and Laura? You're not in high school. You're both self-sufficient. Why aren't you automatically serious?"

"Because it's also a matter of character and integrity. Is she loyal, honest, forthcoming, intelligent in what matters? Is she loving, devoted, a good mother to her own kids? Am I loyal, honest, forthcoming, intelligent, respectful? I'd like to think I was a good dad to you."

"Of course you are."

"Good to know. The point is, serious doesn't come into play until you are ready to make real sacrifices. Pretending that you're committed isn't commitment, because how can you pretend to give one hundred percent, knowing that you'll always be holding back that last one percent that it takes to back out? Commitment means never quitting. You can't pretend or simulate never quitting because quitting is always an option in a fantasy. In the case of Laura and myself, I wouldn't count it serious until I was ready for her to come and share my life completely." He sighed. "And even then, it would still only be ninety percent. And I've seen couples get divorced over less."

"Because of the Timekeeping."

He nodded. "Because of the Timekeeping."

"You're thinking about retiring."

"The thought has crossed my mind. I've still got a few decades left in me, though, so I have a lot of time to think about it."

"But you'd still have to leave Laura no matter what." Tommen ran his tongue over his teeth at his dad's dejected expression. "I'm really good at that today, it seems."

"What?"

"Killing your mood."

"Nothing you've done," his dad told him. "Only that which I've done to myself."

He got up and moved around the tiny table, trading spots with Tommen so he could wash his bowl.

"Why start dating her, then?" Tommen wondered.

For a long moment, Walter did not answer. He turned off the water and set his dishes on the drying rack. Then, "You're leaving in a couple years, and I have to go dark soon after that. Even knowing that makes it all the more unfair to Laura. But if you want the truth, I'm afraid to be alone. I've been alone far too many times in all the wrong circumstances. The best thing Time has done is bring you to me, but it's done little other good. I want to be the man my pa wished I would have been, the man your pa was. Maybe this is my chance to do just that."

With that, he headed back to his recliner and turned on the TV to the evening news. Tommen stared after him. His dad had never been so open or sentimental. It seemed as though the last year had worn him down, chipped away at his tough outer shell, revealing a lonely, broken man beneath the hard armor.

Chapter Twenty-Four
Restart

Tommen's phone buzzed again. And again. And again. He'd discovered after the first five texts to just let it buzz and wait until there had been five minutes of silence before checking it.

It was Micaiah who was texting him. He was probably sitting in the office at the bakery, slightly bored out of his mind, looking for any excuse to avoid a little work for a few minutes. Mostly he was texting him brief instructions about dealing with Saul, how the Akari differed from Time, what to expect, what he should be learning versus whatever hell Saul was going to put him through, that sort of thing.

Tommen still couldn't say that he was overly eager to be going back to camp, not in the same way he had been the first time around, but at least this time he felt a little more prepared and knew what to expect. Somehow, that didn't make him feel much better either.

The camp looked about the same as when he'd left, just with not as many kids running around. All the buildings still stood. As he carried his stuff off to Wolf Cabin, he saw that some of the broken windows had been boarded up. Only one looked like it had been replaced, but that was in Bear Cabin. Otherwise, everything looked pretty much the same.

To his surprise, Saul was already comfortably set up in the cabin. He picked the same bottom bunk by the door and kept his things in as pristine order as one would expect of a former Marine. And still he was reading his detective novel.

"So, you came back," he said, not looking up.

"Micaiah might have warned you," Tommen told him snidely, shouldering his way into the cabin. He dropped his stuff off at his same bunk, then faced Saul. "Why didn't you tell me?"

Still not looking up, Saul replied, "Micaiah asked me to keep an eye on you, so I did. There was no mention of me telling you who I was."

"Does that include the part where you living on a nearby reservation is bullshit?"

Now Saul looked up. "He told you, did he?"

"Yeah. So what's the story?"

"A simple one." And back in the book. "My people roamed these mountains freely since before anyone could remember. When the white men came, they brought their wars with them. They tried to persuade us to join this or that side, but no matter what, we were always betrayed. Hostages were taken and killed, villages were burned, and my people found themselves standing at less than ten thousand in number.

"A few of the white men, however, took pity on us. Not just us, but other near-extinct tribes as well. They taught us Time as well as the Akari. They hoped it would help us in our fight to retain our land rights, a polite way of putting it, to be sure. When that failed, they offered to move us to a new home where we could be free forever. Their words, not mine. When the larger tribes had beaten back the white man, then we could return. But if we stayed, we only risked extinction, and there was no honor to succumbing to fever and sickness. If you had to die, you died with blood on your hands.

"My grandfather was one of those Indian men who moved from Earth to Hlohi. He was the leader of the people. The Wolf Clan was charged with protecting the cultural integrity of the tribe, so once the tribe got settled into their new home, he was chosen to be the spy, or liaison if you will, to watch Earth and our sacred grounds, to let the tribe know when it was safe to return. So that is what my grandfather did. And my father. And my older brother. And now me. Even now, my younger brother is learning."

"But you said you remember when this camp was built," Tommen stated.

"I do. I was here. My father and brother were scouting and doing their usual intel gathering, and they brought me along since it was supposed to be an easy assignment. They had hope that this camp would begin to heal the rift, and maybe it would educate people and convince them to share the land once more. Because that was going to happen." Saul rolled his eyes.

"What about—?"

"That's all I'm going to tell you. You don't need to hear my story. You don't need to know all the dirty little secrets of tribe politics. Micaiah asked me to train you in the Akari, and that is what I will do. Listening to bullshit won't help you out any. And don't give me no shit about just being curious either."

Tommen blinked and turned away, rolling out his sleeping bag and getting all his stuff prepped and ready. The plastic over the windows vibrated against a breeze.

"So, we're going to be hitting the ground running, I guess," he said conversationally. "Starting out with the hike and all."

"Looks that way," Saul agreed.

Tommen could only pretend to be interested in his stuff for so long before he got bored and curious. He looked back at Saul. "So, when were we going to begin training?"

Saul looked up. "Oh, you wanted to start now?"

"Why not?"

"Because I'm going to kick your ass long before the campers do."

"Yeah? Try me. I'm no rookie."

Saul stood then. Even with his bad back, he seemed to grow a foot as he approached. "You're right. You're just a child."

Tommen figured he'd had enough exposure to the Akari by now that he could at least hazard a pretty good guess when an Akari-Band was used, such as now when Saul encased the whole cabin.

"Cabin's Banded," he said sinisterly. "No one can see what we're doing in here."

"Yeah, I can feel the Band. It's different than a Time Band.

Lighter, more...flexible," Tommen mused.

"Maybe. Does this feel any different?"

Years of fighting Tyler Freeman had developed Tommen's natural reflexes so that his body could react to a sudden fist before his mind knew what was going on. Problem was, he and Saul weren't fighting according to the basic laws of nature. They were bending the basic laws of nature. He was so sure he saw Saul's fist to his left, but suddenly it was coming up under him, clocking him in the jaw. It certainly wasn't a full-strength blow, but it still clacked his teeth and knocked him back a step. Saul's left hand hadn't moved.

"That's called Imprint," Saul told him. "Make a motion, then capture it in a small case of time, a small Band if you will, leave it as a flash for someone to see while you make your real move. Like setting spots before their eyes in a bright flash of light."

Tommen rubbed his chin and jaw. "Kayla did that once. So, it's like a modified Band, not just moving faster, but imprinting an image in the eye in order to distract."

"You're quick. But then, it's a pretty basic trick."

"I've done that before, but with my voice. Like a ventriloquist. I said something, then I somehow managed to manipulate it and—"

"Time cannot Band air," Saul said, ignoring him. "Sound is a manipulation of air waves. But the Akari can do things that Time cannot."

"Oh, fuck."

He moved again as he saw Saul's fist. In the instant between when he saw the fist and when it connected with his face, he remembered thinking, *Fool me twice, shame on me.*

"It's a bedsheet maneuver," Saul told him hotly, like he was just on the edge of turning into full-blown Marine combat instructor. "A magic trick. Do you believe in magic?"

"I don't know," Tommen admitted.

Again the fist, again a poor dodge, again a blow.

"Not good enough," Saul spat. "Stop falling for the ruse. Look for the truth."

But apparently that had to involve full combat as Saul ditched the single fist and went full commando on him, or maybe three-quarters commando. Tommen could see his movements were stiff, halting, limited in reach and function. Not that it did him much good, seeing how it was like trying to fight a ninja.

Even as he thought it, he saw it. The ruse was always given away, just slightly. It was like trying to spot white thread on a white dog laying on a white rug, but once he saw it, he couldn't not see it. And Saul stopped dead in his tracks once Tommen finally, deliberately blocked and countered one of his blows. He didn't make contact on the riposte, but he stopped the strike.

"Time always gives itself away," Saul said, "because it is deeply flawed."

"Is the Akari flawed too, then?" Tommen asked, bending over, putting his hands on his knees, and trying to catch his breath.

"The Akari is not flawed. But there are those who would misuse it. Therefore, the Author installed tiny markers in all the illusion tricks, that way an Akari-bearer will always be able to tell what is real and what is fake. There is always a way to tell." Saul straightened, sucking in a breath and putting a hand out on one of the bunks to steady himself. "That's the end of lesson one." Carefully he turned and started hobbling out. "I'm going to see Michelle for a minute. Get yourself cleaned up. You look like hell."

The only comfort Tommen got was that Saul had Banded him so that any bruising and swelling was gone, which left him just sweaty and exhausted. Fucking hell. Fucking Marine. Tommen grabbed his towel and wiped his face. Ten minutes into camp and Saul had already handed his ass to him. This did not bode well.

On the other hand, though, he'd finally gotten some real, hands-on training. No more of the "later" or "when it's safer" or "when you're older" or any of that. Shit just got real, and he was loving it.

The first day at camp was primarily small stuff, doing little things to get the cabins ready for the next set of campers, sweeping porches, washing windows, giving the bathrooms and showers a good scrub, that sort of thing. Despite his general disposition, Saul tended toward the lighter end of the labor spectrum that day.

"How's your back?" Tommen asked cautiously as they headed back to the cabin after dinner, the food as glorious as ever. It was late, and the counselors were encouraged to get as much sleep as possible before camp officially began.

"It was bad even before this morning," Saul said. If it had been his leg that was bad, he would have been limping, dragging, crawling along. As it was, he moved slowly and carefully. "This morning's little stunt certainly didn't help things."

They reached the cabin. Tommen was pleasantly surprised to not be assaulted upon walking in the door which, by the way, had been repaired so they no longer needed a bungee cord to hold it shut.

"Have you thought about getting it looked at?"

"I've had it looked at by several doctors. Part of the problem is that few are willing to attempt the surgery I need. Those that are, well, they don't do it out of the goodness of their hearts, if you know what I'm saying."

"What kind of surgery do you need?"

"I have shrapnel lodged in my spinal column. On the one hand, doing shit like we did earlier could push it into my spinal cord and paralyze me instantly. On the other hand, if they take a knife to me, they could do the same thing accidentally, or I could bleed out or any number of things that result in me dying."

For a moment, Tommen was more stunned that the man wasn't so depressed that he wouldn't be willing to undergo such a surgery and hope to die. But all he said out loud was, "Oh. What about the surgery it looked like you already had?" He thought about the scar running about half the length of his spine.

"That was to remove the big stuff. Shit I'm talking about is smaller than your pinkie nail, but no less sharp."

"Oh. So...does that mean that Akari training is going to be primarily lecture, then?"

"You thought this morning was a lecture?"

"I'll take that as a no."

"You think I learned how to be a Marine based only on lectures? You do the learning you need to do and let me worry about me."

"Okay, fine. Just trying to care. Sorry for taking an interest." Tommen crawled into his sleeping bag.

"Maybe next time I'll pit you against my wolf," Saul muttered.

"And about that. Without going into all the detail, I'll just ask outright. Are you the Chandler?"

"Chandler?" Saul questioned, looking genuinely confused. "I don't know who that is. Obviously I can't be him. Or her."

"Oh. Okay."

"Why do you ask?"

"It's just someone Micaiah mentioned, and there were other things. I don't know. Just thought I'd ask."

"Well, maybe you can ask him tomorrow, if you're willing."

"What do you mean?"

"If you want to be an Akarin, you should meet other Akarin, at least those who are better than the likes of me. There's a special meeting tomorrow night if you want to come."

"Sure, as long as they're not crackpots."

"Of course they are. We all are. But here's the stipulation. Unlike the Wheel of Time, where you can spend days in there and it's the same time out here, the Akarin fortress works on Base Time. It requires effort and sacrifice, which means losing a lot more sleep than you already are."

"No, I'll go. At least once. I have to see and start training and shit."

Saul nodded and maneuvered his way into his own sleeping bag, flipping off the light switch. "So be it. But if you thought the last camp was hard, this one is going to be even worse."

Saul was many things, Tommen knew, but he wasn't a liar. Given what he knew about the bad-tempered man and the camp and the role their prison cabin played, he found that he could find little reason to doubt that this time around was going to be much harder. Teenagers were terrible to try and control; they seemed to think they were people and had their own thoughts and ideas and lives. Of course, Tommen couldn't say too much considering he was one of them. Hell, just look at how he'd ended up here.

When the younger kids had arrived, it seemed like a proper summer camp welcome. Kids with suitcases, parents walking up to the registration to get them signed in before taking them to get checked for head lice and such, tears and emotional goodbyes on both sides, some friendly reunions, some new kids who were lost and cast out.

Watching the older kids arrive, Tommen might have thought this was Spring Break 1999 and the kids were here to party. Even though they ranged from twelve to fifteen years old, they ditched their parents just as soon as they could, running off to greet friends, hug, kiss, do whatever. Parents looked a little more willing to let the older kids go, and it took a little more effort to wrangle them into the nurse's office for lice checks.

Honestly, it kind of looked like the beginning of the school year at the middle school.

"Excited to be among your own kind?" Saul jeered as they watched all the cars pile into the parking lot and pull up to the curb. "Just like high school, right?"

"Worse. It's like middle school."

"Makes me glad I never went to public school."

It was a taunt, and Tommen knew it. There were any number of things he could have said, but he didn't need to start a fight right now and give Saul an excuse to beat him up even harder later on. Instead, he meandered his way into the main hall. There were decidedly fewer coloring books this time around. Rather, the occupation of choice was cell phones. Those would be confiscated upon cabin assignment, and Tommen loathed the inevitable reaction, the protests, the fights, even the crying.

The strange thing was, even though he was as addicted to his phone as everyone else, Tommen found that he had a less difficult time giving it up when circumstances demanded. Maybe because he hadn't gotten his first phone until he was twelve. Maybe because he'd never even heard of phones, especially cell phones, until he was eight. A lot of these kids had gotten their first phones when they started kindergarten or some shit. So they could text Mommy during nap time and complain about how Danny stole their goldfish crackers at lunch? He didn't know.

"That's Harry," Saul said, pointing to one particular camper. He looked about thirteen or fourteen, white, but with long black hair like Saul's. "He's a troublemaker, but he's also a bad liar. Once he's caught, he's caught. And that one—" Another camper at a different table. "—is Jacob. He usually goes by JJ or just Jay. He's a better liar, but a bad criminal. He could walk right out of a museum with a priceless piece of art but still convince security that the curator let him have it."

"He gets caught, but knows how to sweet talk his way out," Tommen said.

"Right. Don't let him. Always verify everything he says. The good and bad news of this is that Harry and JJ can't stand each other. So you don't have to worry about them teaming up, but you do have to worry about them fighting. And they'll fight over the dumbest things; no issue is too small."

"Why are they in the same cabin, then?"

"Why are they in our cabin at all?"

Right. Because they were troublemakers and no one else wanted to deal with them. Tommen was forced to wonder how much "dealing" Saul would be doing with his back the way it was.

"What about the others?" Tommen wondered.

Saul pointed out a few more boys as theirs, but their brand of trouble came more in the form of smoking, petty theft, and groping girls.

"And last but certainly not least, we have Zach. He's the one you really have to watch out for."

The kid he pointed to couldn't have been older than fourteen or fifteen, but he was built like a bear, big, tall, and thick with muscle, like what Micaiah might have looked like had he started bodybuilding at age twelve.

"Zach is here because a judge tells him he has to be here," Saul went on. "It's his last chance at avoiding prison, supposedly. I don't know the details. Last year it was as follow up to some community service he had to do. He's in our cabin, but he will rarely participate in camp events; he'll be working and doing volunteer sort of stuff—helping out in the camp store, the kitchen, running errands for Jerry or Michelle, that sort of thing."

"What do we do with him, or, like, do we have to serve as warden or what?"

"The only time we might is if Michelle asks for it. He's a little intimidating. Pam and her crew can keep him well enough, so can Jerry. Michelle is the only one who wouldn't fare well if he decided to try something."

"What'd he do, or what's his thing?"

"Breaking and entering. Assault. All the fun stuff."

"Oh. Wonderful."

Suddenly Randall and Carson looked like little angels. Tommen had thought the prison cabin was a bit of a scary overstatement used to keep kids in line. "Be good and you won't have to go over there to those people. Those are the bad kids." Now he was starting to see that maybe there was some merit to keeping these boys separate.

After a bit, Mr. Wilson walked in the room and began his welcome to camp speech, similar to the one he gave the little kids. The difference was, the speech and the camp welcome dance seemed more appropriate for the little kids. For Tommen, doing it in front of a bunch of teenagers felt on par with going up to the front of the class at school and reciting his favorite Dr. Seuss poem or something. Maybe it was just him, seeing how he was more of an age with them.

Once everyone was good and riled up, Mr. Wilson called for attention again and began giving cabin assignments.

"That's Jenny," Saul said, pointing to a girl who was heading to Dragonfly Cabin. "She's Harry's girlfriend, or she has been for as long as anyone knows. If they are still dating, expect there to be some attempts at late-night excursions."

Tommen just nodded. Somehow the only thing he could think was that these kids were, what, fourteen or fifteen? Fucking hell, he was almost seventeen and still a virgin. He wanted to fuck Becky more than ever. Christmas seemed so far away.

Then came the boys' assignments. Saul did not seem surprised in the least when the names were given for Wolf Cabin. Still, he put on a good face and waited patiently for the assignments to end and the kids to be dismissed. When the order came, it was much less chaotic for the older kids than the younger kids. The teenagers had a little better memory as to where they put things and knew how to at least do a preliminary search for missing items before shouting accusations of theft. On the whole, anyway. Some of them were only in the older kids' camp by default because of their age, not because they were any more mature.

"So, who's the new kid?" Harry asked, walking up, looking at Tommen.

"This is Tommen," Saul introduced. "He's taking Joe's place this year."

"How old are you?"

"Seventeen," Tommen informed him.

"Great, so we're still going to get bossed around by a senior."

Tommen elected not to correct him, and he was saved by his nemesis, JJ, cutting in, saying, "Because it's any different than your grandma telling you what to do?"

Saul stepped between them before either could say or doing anything. "Does everyone have all their stuff? Let's get going to the cabin."

He chose his words carefully and spoke levelly. He was in no mood to yell and in no condition to fight. He even let Tommen lead the way to the cabin.

"Holy shit, what happened here?" one camper, Tony, asked.

"Mr. Wilson will address that at dinner," was all Saul told him. "In short, there was a bear attack at the last camp, and some things have been changed around this time."

"According to Jenny's friend's little sister, it was vandalism, not a bear," Harry said.

"As I said, Mr. Wilson will be talking about it more at dinner. For now, just claim your bunks and get your stuff where and how you want it."

There were eleven campers starting off this time, which meant that a couple of them had to be on bottom bunks. Naturally, that led to some arguing. Saul eventually threatened that if they were going to argue, they could all sleep on bottom bunks and he and Tommen would move to top bunks. A few of the more mild-mannered boys eventually conceded to their more intimidating overlords and chose bottom bunks.

"What's that?" Dan wondered, pointing to Tommen's hearing aid charger on the windowsill.

"Ah, that's the charger for my hearing aids," Tommen said. His hair had grown out a little over the last month or so, and he pushed it back so the kids could see the aids.

"You deaf?"

"No, not completely."

"I got a niece who's deaf."

"I'm sorry."

He wasn't sure where Dan was going with this, but he appeared to have lost interest. Actually, Tommen was more curious as to how old his niece was, and then how old his brother or sister was who'd had the kid. There could be a significant difference in age, or not. Didn't really matter, and Tommen still found himself lamenting that he was almost seventeen and still a virgin. He and Becky had been dating for well over six months and they still hadn't had sex. He wasn't even going to be able to touch her again for another month, and he wasn't going to be able to play for another four months after that. Ugh, it was so frustrating.

A terrible thought entered his mind then. Becky had sworn off dances because she thought they were boring. What if he went to the Homecoming dance and found an easy date like Eric had with Michelle? At least then he could say that he had done it, finally.

The better part of him, though, knew that was a bad idea. Not only was it incredibly dishonest and went against almost everything he believed in about chivalry, but somehow, someway, he knew Becky would find out. Then there wouldn't be any kind of playtime. Plus there was that whole bit about Eric being accused of rape and whatnot. The last thing Tommen needed was some shit like that coming down on him. He already had enough problems to deal with.

"I don't think anyone here is new," Saul observed. "If anyone didn't hear, this is Tommen. He's taking Joe's place this year."

"Where's Joe?" JJ wondered.

"He had family problems to take care of and couldn't be here. He sends his love."

Based on the sarcasm in that statement, Tommen could only conclude that Joe was about as much fun as Saul. He could only imagine the shenanigans of years past.

"So, we're going to have a little open free time for a while," Saul went on. "Mr. Wilson wants it to be orientation and getting to know you games and such, but everyone here knows each other so we can skip all of that." Because Tommen could see it was breaking his heart to do that. "What do you guys want to do?"

The younger kids had been all about exploring and going out into the wilderness. The older kids, bereft of electronics and all technology, elected to congregate and share their woes. That is, they were more interested in basketball, soccer, volleyball, and whatever impromptu games they could come up with in the space and time allotted. Tommen was fine with that.

"The nice thing is that most of the kids are in sports," Saul explained as the boys went their separate ways to their chosen games. "Most of them will be too focused on the game to care much about mischief. By now, it's just habit. The only thing we have to watch out for is if Harry and JJ are in the same game. Doesn't matter if they're on the same team or not because they will be fighting the whole way."

Tommen just nodded and looked around to be sure the two were far away from each other. JJ was busy with soccer, and Harry had picked up a basketball and was looking for others to make a three-on-three game.

"So, where does their rivalry come from?" Tommen wondered. "Harry steal JJ's girlfriend or something?"

"Yes." Saul nodded. "It really is that simple. And that stupid. I mean, the boys are just starting high school. There will be other girls. But, whatever, not my problem. I just deal with the fallout."

"Yeah? And how are you holding up?"

"Fine."

He wasn't fine; that much Tommen could see. Everyone could probably see it, the way Saul favored his left side and moved worse than an old grandpa. Pain meds could only do so much, and it looked like they were covering only a small bit.

Still, Tommen knew better than to try to argue with him. Instead, he kept a general eye on the games as they happened. The younger kids were more likely to whine and cry about every little thing as a foul or some illegality. The older kids at least understood the rules of the game so they could correctly call out true fouls. Problem was, they were also more likely to get into fights over those fouls. Well, the Wolf Cabin kids were, anyway. The rest were generally pretty chill.

So far, just from a one-hour basic analysis and comparison, the older kids were easier and harder to work with. On the one hand, they were pretty self-governing. If they lost something, they looked for it and found it instead of whining to a counselor. On the other hand, everything was taken personally and as the gravest offense in the world. And it wasn't just the girls griping about who chose a bunk next to who; the boys were equally as petty, though it usually revolved around playing sports or impressing girls.

Was I that petty once? Tommen thought. *Am I still that petty? Is this how others see me, as some crass, vain, self-serving, loser teenager? It must be. Maybe that was why that bitch singled me out to get me fired from my job.*

Of course, judging by Micaiah and Micah's response to that incident, it was equally likely that the woman had just been a straight up bitch, and it had nothing to do with Tommen's attitude or anything that really mattered. Maybe he was overthinking things. Maybe he was being paranoid. At what point did standard, healthy paranoia turn into paranoid schizophrenia? Did he have to start wailing about conspiracies by the government to tap his phones and control his brain? What if that was true, but for the Wheel of Time, not any Earth-side government? Did that still make him crazy, even if it was true?

Dinner could not have come soon enough. Pam seemed back to her old self as she set the kitchen dance in motion, gathering this, cooking that, ordering this or that to be done; she was in her element.

"You gave me some good practice at the last camp," she said, grinning, as he approached the window. "I think I got a pretty good idea of how much to feed this hungry pack of wolves. Ha!" She lowered her voice. "Don't tell Saul I said that or he'd skin me."

"I think he has too much respect for you, Pam," Tommen told her. "He might be able to fend for himself, but I think he enjoys your cooking just as much as the rest of us."

"Of course he does. You men would be nothing without us women."

"Given that we wouldn't exist without you women, well, you may have a point."

She shooed him away and told him to go sit down at his table, which he did once he got himself something to drink.

"Do I have to call your girlfriend and tell her you're cheating on her with an older woman?" Saul asked. His expression was unreadable; he could have been serious or sarcastic.

"You don't know who my girlfriend is," Tommen said.

"No, but Micaiah does."

Damn. "Even so, I'm not cheating. Obviously."

"Yeah, but is your girl cheating on you?" JJ asked.

Tommen shook his head. "No. She's better than that."

"How do you know?"

"Because I know her."

"You think you do."

"No, I know her. I know her well enough."

"Ah, you know her 'in the Biblical sense' like my aunt says," another kid, Jason, said, grinning.

I wish. "No, we're not sleeping together either." *Yet.*

"The fuck are you?" Harry said. "A couple of Christians?"

I've seen, or at least heard of kids who claim to be Christians doing raunchier stuff than Becky and I do. "No. We just have respect for each other."

"Yeah, well, you can never really know," JJ concluded. "Like my da and my uncle says, you gotta keep 'em on a short leash. Keep the leash short and your dick long."

Saul took over from there, and once again Tommen was amazed at the things that were coming out of these kids' mouths. They weren't even eligible for driver's training yet and it sounded like they all went out to the club on Friday nights looking for open women. Tommen still really, really wanted to fuck Becky, but he wasn't that bad. He at least tried to have a little respect for women, and a woman who didn't respect herself wasn't worth his respect. But then, maybe these boys had no respect for women, only what they could get out of them.

Well, it was all too philosophical and political for his tastes anyway. This was camp and he was here to have fun. Go ziplining again, horseback riding, the works.

About halfway through dinner, Mr. Wilson finally went to the front of the room to address the camp at large. He told them a fudged story about the vandalism, ahem, bear attack, and gave them a short rundown of some of the damage.

"Some of the damage has already been repaired in the last week," he said. "However, it will be much easier for the contractors to do their job if we are not here to get in their way. Therefore, our schedule for this month has been changed up a little bit. Normally we do the hiking trip during the last week of camp, a last hurrah before sending you home. This time, however, we will be switching the hiking trip to the first week of camp."

He paused and let the kids murmur amongst themselves for a minute before continuing. "Tomorrow, we will have some brief class time to get you re-familiarized with the plants and animals in the area where we're going, as well as some of the basic skills you will be learning and using. After lunch, we will be heading to the trail head and hiking up to the campsite. Pam and her crew will be providing dinner for us that night so we don't starve, but everything after that is up to us.

"When we return from hiking on Friday, all the repairs should be finished so there will be no more broken windows, doors, or anything else; everything will be brand new. After that, our second week will still be outdoor adventure week with the horseback riding, ziplining, climbing, and so forth. The third week is water week. The last week will be a comparatively easier week, that being our sports tournaments.

"This isn't a huge change, but it is a sudden change. The good news is that we, your counselors, the staff, myself, have all prepared for this. If you have any questions or concerns about the changes, talk to one of us. Thank you."

"Wait, so we're leaving for the trail, like, tomorrow?" Dan asked.

"Yes," Saul told him. "Tomorrow after lunch. I would recommend that you not tear apart your suitcase between now and then."

It was a small slight seeing how Dan had already done just that, or near enough, strewing everything about looking for his favorite basketball tank top. You know, so he could impress the girls who would inevitably be watching him and want a good view. As far as Tommen knew, not one girl had approached him either before, during, or after the game.

"Are we still getting up super early?" Phillip groaned.

"Absolutely. In fact, I heard that we're not even going to sleep tonight because that's how early we have to be up."

It was Saul's sense of humor, and only Tommen seemed to get it at first. The boys did too, after a few seconds, but they could still only manage a nervous chuckle or two. Hey, they were becoming teenagers or were teenagers, and they all wanted to sleep in until noon. Tommen certainly felt like it.

This time around, Pam made enough to feed a starving army, and there was no shortage of food when Tommen and the others went up for seconds and even thirds. When he glanced farther in the kitchen, he saw the big kid, Zach, sitting in the corner with his own tray of food.

"Will Zach be hiking with us?" Tommen wondered when he sat down.

"He will," Saul confirmed. "He'll be hiking and camping with us, the same as the rest of them. He'll be doing most of the heavy lifting, chopping wood, gutting and carrying deer, that sort of thing."

If the kid is here in order to avoid going to prison for assault, why the hell are we giving him an ax and a knife? Tommen did not say this out loud. Maybe he would ask later when he and Saul were alone, after the boys had gone to sleep or something.

Due to the increase in food consumption in the older camp, dinner took longer, so the time between dinner and the campfire was shorter. An irony if there was one, but Tommen didn't dwell on it too long. They returned to the cabin after dinner and spent the time in equal parts bullshitting and keeping Harry and JJ from beating on each other. Problem was, only Tommen and Saul seemed to want to keep them apart; the rest of the boys looked eager for the fight. Only Saul's fearsome reputation seemed to keep the peace, but Tommen knew that if blows were traded, things would end badly. Saul would step in and easily stop the fight, but he would probably kill himself to do so.

By the time the call came to gather for the campfire, Saul was ready to just send both boys home and forget about the whole thing. He mentioned something about sending one of them to a different cabin, but the likelihood of that seemed pretty low. The younger troublemakers had been less bothersome and still no one had wanted them.

Older kids weren't as impressed by corny ghost stories as younger kids, Tommen observed, and he didn't blame them. Some of the stories that had made the younger kids almost piss themselves had barely fazed him at all. The older kids were more interested in funny stories, like the one about the time Mr. Wilson had tripped and fallen face-first in a pile of horse shit at the riding stables; or the time Pam had grabbed salt instead of sugar and made the most godawful cake anyone had ever tasted. But, it had been the winner's cake for the sports tournaments, the one that got smooshed in the faces of the winners. The actual cake served to everyone had been much better.

One good thing about the older kids, though, was that they knew how to form an orderly line and wait patiently for s'mores. More to the point, they were allowed to cook their own marshmallows and really only needed minimal supervision. There was still some complaining that person A was hogging the stick or person B had promised to give the stick to person C when they were finished but gave it to person D instead. Small things, petty things.

The campfire songs were considerably better, too. They were the same songs, but the older kids were more likely to get up and do the weird dances with them—or improvise their own dances—rather than just sit there on the logs and be entertained, pointing and laughing at the counselors. At least this time around, they were pointing and laughing at each other.

Okay, so the second time around didn't feel like as much of a nightmare as Tommen had feared. These kids were older, more mature, and could reasonably govern themselves in areas where the younger kids had required over-the-shoulder supervision. This could be okay. Yes, this one he might be able to do and survive. Some part of him told him that he would have to because Saul was not looking too well.

"Hey," Tommen said, elbowing him lightly in the ribs. "Are you okay?"

"I'm fine," he insisted. He let out a breath. "I'll have it checked out when we leave."

At first, Tommen didn't understand what he meant. Then he thought about their little excursion they were supposed to go on that night, meeting with other Akarin and stuff. Right, they still had to do that. And Saul had said that it took real time out of their day, which meant not a lot of sleep, and all this before having to get up early and hurry to get everything done and out of the way before going hiking. Maybe he could nap on the bus. Memories of the rutted road and bumpy ride quickly chased those fantasies from his mind. Well, he said he wanted to go, and he supposed he could suffer one night of little or no sleep. Not like he hadn't done it before.

Eventually, Mr. Wilson called for an end to the campfire, citing an early morning and a busy day. There was some grumbling and a last-second raid of the s'mores supplies. Tommen managed to grab a chocolate bar and half a package of graham crackers before herding the boys back to the cabin. He distributed the goods which were scarfed down quickly.

"Faster we get ready for bed, faster we get to sleep, the more sleep we get," Saul said, giving Tommen a look.

With the little kids, they could probably get away with just brushing teeth and other assorted nightly habits. With the older kids, though, showers were needed. Between the heat and smoke from the campfire and the sweaty nastiness from the sports tournaments, showers were definitely in order.

By the time they got back to the cabin and in bed, Tommen was sure they were only going to get about four hours of sleep, and he still had to go to some meeting or other. Once the boys were settled in, Tommen made an excuse to go back to the bathrooms and Saul cited taking a last look around the cabin. They stepped out onto the porch.

"So, you still want to go?" Saul asked. "You will get no sleep tonight and you look dead on your feet already."

"Is the walk through the portal as hard as it is in the Wheel?" Tommen wondered.

"It's harder. The Wheel and the Hands have a monopoly on interdimensional travel which makes it more difficult to go anywhere outside of the Wheel."

"Oh, lovely. Why are we going there again?"

"There's a special meeting about what to do about the Hands and their new rules. That means you will see a lot of high-profile stuff, assuming I can get you in. Mostly it's a chance for you to see the fortress, see who's in charge, and get a feel for how things work. It's not like the Wheel. Depending on how the meeting goes, how long it goes, I might be able to have one of them explain things, or I might just say fuck it and give you my own tour of the place. Wheel or Akarin, politics is politics."

"Well, you're not wrong there. How long are you planning on being gone?"

"We'll be back before the alarm goes off. I hope."

Tommen looked at his watch. On the surface, it appeared to be an ordinary watch. Actually, it was an advanced piece of Time technology, capable of displaying the time and date of anywhere in the universe, even showing it side-by-side to Earth so he always knew what time it was at home. Fuck, it was already one-thirty? They had to be up at seven. Damn.

"Like I said. You will get no sleep tonight," Saul repeated. "But if you're coming with me, I need to know now. Portals are hard to open and they don't stay open for very long."

Tommen hesitated. "The boys will be okay? Like, they won't mess with my hearing aid charger, right? Or anything like that?"

"I make no guarantees on their behalf, but I should think they're as tired as you are. Now, the next words out of your mouth are either yes, I'm going, or no, I'm not."

He nodded. "Yeah. Yeah, I'm going. I've got to see this place."

"Then stand back and hang on."

Watching his dad or the twins open a portal to the Wheel was like watching them try to lift and tow a car out of the ditch with their bare hands. Watch Saul open a portal to this "fortress" or whatever was like watching him trying to lift a tank out of sucking mud or quicksand with his bare hands, not to mention his bad back. Still, when Saul bade him go through, he did as he was told and stepped through.

Chapter Twenty-Five
Decisions and Declarations

Micaiah hated when meetings landed in the middle of the night. The fortress still passed in Base Time, which meant that he was losing some serious sleep. Sure, Kayla could Band him to get eight hours, but there was also the real life aspect of all of this. If the meeting went long and he had to leave for work, well, he was leaving a meeting. He didn't like doing that, and he really didn't want to do it now when everything was at its critical mass, or so it seemed.

Reports had already come in of Akari-bearers who had been arrested by the Grandfathers and charged with heresy. Well, it wasn't called heresy—propagandization was the term they used, and it wasn't even a real word—but everyone knew what it was. So far, all of those who had been arrested had simply been let go. Pushed around a little, terrorized a little, but otherwise unharmed. Supposedly, it was just to send a message to the rest of them. Right now, the Hands were being nice with their enforcement of the rules. Micaiah had little doubt that it wouldn't last long.

Only one of those arrested had been Akarin. The others had been from various factions, but that didn't make it any less unnerving or any more "right." Regardless of how the factions felt about each other, they couldn't afford division now. They had to stick together to fight off the common enemy, then worry about their own petty differences later.

Problem was, there already was division, and the lines were deepening, darkening more and more each day. The Cult of the Akari and their assorted groups, including the more freelance agents whom Kayla had already encountered, were grumbling once more, stirring pots here and there. Reports had already come from the Peaceful Akari-Bearers of attacks by such groups. Meanwhile, once-allied groups like the United Akari-bearers and the Free Akari-bearers were at each other's throats as their members were divided over fighting or remaining neutral.

Chaos had finally reached the Akari-bearers. Once the most powerful force in the universe, now reduced to a bunch of squabbling, powerless factions, like children in daycare. A Catholic daycare where the nuns would swat the children just for speaking.

So he wasn't sure if it was a good omen or a bad one when he spotted Saul across the cafeteria. On one side, his enormous wolf padded silently along like a killer ghost. On the other side, Tommen looked around, wide-eyed and open-mouthed. Grudgingly, Micaiah stood and went to them.

"You made it," he observed levelly.

"Holy shit," Tommen blurted. "How the fuck did you keep all of this a secret?"

"Well, to be honest, it's not hard to keep something a secret when it's routinely dismissed as crackpot nonsense."

The teenager opened his mouth again, thought a second, then closed it.

"What's the word?" Saul asked.

"Meeting is almost ready to begin. I was just about to head up there."

"Think they'll let him in?" He nodded to Tommen who had wandered off a short distance.

"Once their blood gets going, I don't think they'll even notice he's in the room, never mind care about what he's going to hear." Micaiah chuckled. "And if you're that worried, just have him hide behind Yawi there."

"Fair enough. Tommen!"

Tommen whirled around and rejoined them.

"So, is this like a secret underground bunker or what? I mean, it kind of looks like some old castle, actually, like the kind you see in the movies."

"Underground, sort of. Secret, yes. Or it was, before Cassius duped us and shared our secrets with the universe."

"What about Kayla's information?" Saul asked. "Was there any merit to that?"

Micaiah sighed. "Unfortunately, yes. A few were not as clever or sneaky as they thought they were, once we got to looking. But it's impossible to say if there are more and who they might be. The Hands are already paralyzed with fear and paranoia. We do not need to emulate them."

They made their way up the stairs, going ever slower as Saul faltered and eventually stopped, leaning against a wall and breathing hard as if to cover up pain. His wolf nosed him and he petted it absently.

"What's wrong?" Micaiah asked.

"It's his back," Tommen cut in before Saul could deny anything. "He did something to it at the last camp, and then this morning he decided my first Akari lesson had to involve combat training."

"I'm sure you did well," Micaiah told him, smirking. To Saul, "You need to get that looked at. I know you and you've never bowed to anything. It's a long walk to the next floor; I'll go and send someone down for you."

"And for what? They can't do anything for me. I'm already taking some pretty heavy drugs."

"Rest, at least."

"No," Saul insisted. "Maybe I can use a little Gravity to lighten the load."

Micaiah shook his head. "Gravity is too unstable. You'd make it ten steps before it failed and all that weight came crushing down on you."

"Go to your meeting," Saul hissed. "I'll be along."

It was only a short standoff, but only because Saul was so good at it and Micaiah was in a hurry. He motioned for Tommen to follow him and let the man stew in his pride and pain for a minute.

"What happened to him?" Tommen asked once they were a fair distance away.

"IED," Micaiah answered.

"Oh. So he was telling the truth."

"He was a Marine once, yes."

Tommen nodded. "So, what is all this? You guys look like you're gearing up for war or something."

"Problem is, we might be." Micaiah sighed. "True Akari-bearers are peaceful, fighting only for just causes. At one time, being an Akari-bearer and being Akarin were one and the same. Centuries ago, there was a split, as leadership began to decay and everyone had different ideas on how to save it. There was one divide. And then another. And then another. Now we don't seem to know how to do anything differently. Anytime there's a disagreement, there's another division. It's pathetic.

"What's worse is that in older times, despite our divisions, we were still Akarin. Everyone knew us and what we stood for. They may not have liked our power or believed where it came from, but they could not deny its existence. Now, some are trying to say that we somehow held out on Time Agents and kept the best Time abilities for ourselves, that we're some kind of cult, that we're the Hands' secret army. Some want us to teach everyone else and become just like everyone else. Others, like the Hands, want us wiped out completely."

"Well, no grudges there, eh?" Tommen mused.

"I'm just letting you know the broad state of things, that way you're not surprised."

By this time, they'd reached the third floor and were just approaching the meeting room. Micaiah could hear the arguing before he even walked in the door. As expected, they didn't even seem to notice Tommen as they were instantly upon him, Micaiah, like a pack of coyotes.

"There you are!"

"Where have you been?"

"You're late!"

"How long did you expect to keep us waiting?"

"I didn't realize I was the center figure of this meeting," Micaiah said finally, looking around and wondering just what had happened.

"It was a human who infiltrated our highest ranks," someone said. "Because your world is Unengaged, it must be a human who fixes things."

"Pray tell, how do we know that Cassius was the only one who infiltrated us? We have found others in the lower ranks as his planted recruits, true, but working with Rifun, do you think he was going to rely solely on a pack of untrained whelps? We have hard opposition coming from the Hands, but we also have rot from within. Which do you think is the more dangerous threat?"

"What does it matter if there is rot from within if we are wiped out?"

Micaiah shook his head. "We will never be wiped out. Not as long as the Author is writing. But there will be few of us left and we will have no power or credibility to speak of if these spies are allowed to walk among us and speak in our name and commit unspeakable atrocities."

"Then we will win them to our cause."

"All of them? Every last one of them? Because if even one turns out to be within our higher ranks, even among us here now, and does what Cassius did, it will be the end of the Akarin as we know it."

"Then what do you suggest?"

Micaiah hesitated, knowing that his suggestion would immediately paint him as the traitor he just suggested they look for. "I suggest that we go along with the Hands for now." He took a breath as murmurs and whispers broke out. "I suggest that, for now, we obey their rules and restrictions and we work internally to root out all possible traitors and spies. If we do it right, there will be no need for paranoia."

"Our recruiting numbers would plummet! Think of all the Time Agents out there who could be Akari-bearers!"

"Our numbers are suffering already because we are painted black! They would only fall more if we pushed harder and made no effort to right ourselves! What kind of sore hypocrisy is that? Yes, I realize that I am saying that we should shut our doors, but we cannot win a war on two fronts. We must purify ourselves internally if our weapon against external threats is to be effective. If we destroy the external threat but leave the rot, we risk that the traitors will slaughter us with our own weapons."

"If we ignore a threat we are aware of," someone said slowly, "it will be perceived as weakness by our enemies and folly by our members. No one will have a reason to stay with us if we do not care for ourselves. By the end, there will be no one left but the traitors."

"Exactly," Micaiah affirmed.

"Very well, so what is our next step?"

And this was where things all went to hell at the last meeting, because you people can't make up your minds what needs to be done. You need someone to tell you what to do, but you don't seem willing to consult with the one who makes the decisions. Then you get mad at her when things don't go the right way.

"In order to heal the world, you must first heal the person."

Micaiah turned to see Saul off to one side. His wolf was lying down, and he was leaning back against it. Slowly, he got to his feet. "The reason we can't identify a traitor is because we don't even know who walks among us. Masters and Apprentices train independently of anything you have to say, coming and going as they please with no accountability.

"Take your Core Akari-bearers, the ones who check out as genuine, the ones who are Captains or could be Captains, the ones who you would trust with your lives, the ones who connect well with others, and put them in charge of small groups of other Akari-bearers. Let the healing begin in each group. I expect many will be genuine Akari-bearers, and they will be grateful for the comradery. It will give them something to believe in. If there are traitors among them who do come to believe and turn to our side, so much the better, and we should not hold their past against them. How better to fight the enemy than with one of their own?

"As for the true traitors, they will make themselves known to those who know what to look for, who the Author will show."

"And what of the leadership?" someone inquired. "If there are indeed traitors among us here, who is to account for them?"

"Shine the light and the roaches will scatter," Saul said, grinning. "It doesn't matter whether the light comes from above or below."

There was some murmuring. Micaiah knew that while the idea certainly had merit and was probably their best approach, it was something that would just have to happen. It couldn't be voted on; it just had to be done. Probably from below, letting the people organize themselves instead of waiting for leadership to do it for them.

As expected, the subject changed abruptly.

"However, there is still the matter of Doug's absence," someone began. "His position remains unfilled. He oversaw those from Unengaged worlds with a particular, understandable interest in his home world which you, Micaiah, share. As Saul pointed out, there are Masters and Apprentices out there who are training with no one to oversee them. If we are to begin the rooting out of traitors at the lower levels, we need someone in the lower levels with them."

That was not how Saul worded it, and it certainly wasn't his intention, Micaiah thought grimly. "What are you saying?"

"You have been appointed to fill Doug's position. You will assume his responsibilities starting immediately."

"I'm sorry, but I already declined that role." He looked around. "Or is this the whole reason you summoned me to this meeting?"

"We do not have the luxury of numbers, Micaiah, we cannot simply send it on to the next man for his consideration."

"I think you can, seeing how Doug's position oversaw hundreds of worlds."

"No one wanted it, not after what Cassius did. You have been appointed because you are the same race as both the former occupant as well as his impostor. Consider this your opportunity to save your race's reputation."

"My race's reputation?!" Now his blood was boiling.

Someone slid something across the table. At first it appeared to be a nice tablet-sized slab of slate, but it proved to be an official declaration of some form. Saul came up on his shoulder.

"What's it say?" Tommen asked meekly from the corner.

" 'It is the decision of the Fifty-Third Council of Ancrath, Great Admirals of the Fleet, and Holy Men of War, to immediately pursue the capture, enslavement, imprisonment, and/or death of the race known as human or Earthling, originating from Quadrant One, Parsec Eleven, Sector Five, System Four, Planet Thirty-Eight, Earth, and including colonies on...' blah, blah, blah. 'Charges include but are not limited to treason of the highest order, including attempts to buy, sell, trade for, bribe for, or manufacture antidotes to the natural biochemical toxins of the Borelian race thereby inducing harm upon said Borelian race, this being of one count: first, Tommen Forbes willfully and intentionally bartering for, receiving, and distributing an antidote to Borelian biochemical toxins; interfering with and/or breaking a war contract, this being of two counts: first, Rivotra Andilan being unable to deliver upon his end of an established war contract, and second, Miach Dearbhfhine and MacEoghan Dearbhfhine interfering with a war contract between humans and Borelians such that said war contract could not be fulfilled; and interfering with and/or breaking a political contract, this being of one count, Miach Dearbhfhine and MacEoghan Dearbhfhinn interfering with a political contract between the Grandfathers of Time and the Borelians such that said political contract could not be fulfilled. Therefore, effective immediately, all humans are declared an enemy of the security and sovereignty of the planet Brelix and her allies, territories and conquests, and may be taken, captured, enslaved, imprisoned, tortured, or killed wherever they may be found throughout the universe at the discretion of the conqueror.' "

"What does that mean?"

Saul gave Tommen a look. "It means the Borelians have declared war on the human race."

"What the hell are these charges, though?" Micaiah wondered. "I mean, okay, yes, I understand the antidote one. But what about these other ones? What contracts are they referring to?"

"Rifun struck a deal with the Borelians," someone said. "In the war contract, if they helped him overthrow the Hands, he would give them access to any world they wanted to enslave, including Earth. In the political contract, he named them Grandfathers forever. They would be the eternal police force in the Wheel. And then there was the battle in which they are naming you as leader."

Micaiah pushed the tablet away. "Shit."

"That is why you have been named in Doug's position," another leader said. "Ignore the other Unengaged worlds if you choose, but you must prepare your people for war."

"My people are Unengaged. They won't know that any of this is happening until the Borelians are carting them off to slavery! There is no defense for this! How the hell did you get that, anyway?"

"A notice was sent to the Hands of Time as well as us and the other factions. Everyone knows."

"Fuck."

"You must figure out how to defend your people, whether that means doing it yourself with your fellow humans in Time and the Akari and keeping the majority of people in the dark, or bringing your people into the light."

Micaiah tapped his fingers on the table. "And there's nothing anyone can do about this? Do they have terms of how to un-declare war?"

"No one knows. The Borelians do not make peace; they make slaves."

"And you cannot look to us for help," someone said. "After all, you yourself have suggested that we close our doors and work from within."

Micaiah just about launched himself at the person. He might have if he'd been wearing his running leg and could get the springiness needed to propel himself up and over the table.

He shook his head. "I can't do it. My wife and I are set to go dark. Way dark."

"The backup is over two years; you can get much accomplished in that time."

"I would only be throwing myself into quicksand that I could never get out of, even once our turn came up."

"You have indicated that you wish to go dark, beyond even the reach of Time. With this new declaration of war from the Borelians, that could be a dangerous thing. You would have no power, no backup, nowhere to turn when they came for you."

He hated their logic. "There's just no way to win, is there? The Hands coming against us here, the spies from within, and now the Borelians threatening to enslave my entire race."

War is coming, Chandler had said. Fucker had been understating things. He should have said, *A shitload of bad stuff is coming, and you are probably going to lose a hell of a lot more than your leg this time around. Probably your life, but more likely your sanity, which is infinitely worse. Good luck.*

Micaiah pinched the bridge of his nose, then stormed out. He didn't go far, just far enough that he was out of sight from the door to the meeting room. A minute later, a big white muzzle appeared followed by a huge white head with large silver eyes. Yawi nosed him and whined, then looked back toward his master. Saul and Tommen appeared around the corner.

"He's quite the bloodhound," Micaiah observed dryly.

"So, boss, what do we do?" Saul asked.

"I...I don't know. I don't *fucking* know!" He closed his eyes and took a breath. "This wasn't supposed to happen."

"I'm sure a lot of things weren't 'supposed' to happen, but they are happening. Now we have to figure out what to do about them." Saul regarded him. "Close the doors of the Akarin, go along with the Hands for now. Okay, fine. That's one problem out of the way."

"You don't get it," Micaiah said slowly. "With the Borelians declaring war on humans, it means the Wheel is off-limits, too. The Hands won't dare step between a Borelian and his target; it's their little non-interference clause and whatever other bullshit they claim."

"So fucking what? Fuck the Wheel. Fuck the Hands. Fuck Time for all I care. I haven't been there in fucking years. Stop trying to marry Time and the Akari. They don't play nice with each other. Pick one and focus on it. Fuck the Akarin, too. Obviously they don't give a shit about shit. Focus on the Akari and what the Author is doing."

"This coming from the man who wants to heal the world one person at a time?"

"You bought that shit?" He shrugged. "Well, it's true. To an extent. In your case, fuck it."

"And when I'm done fucking everything, then what?" Micaiah asked.

"Then you start fucking working. Okay, the one thing the Hands are good at is letting people know when they're fucked. Borelians declaring war on humans? Yeah, we're royally fucked. So we can safely assume that all the human Time Agents are going to hear about it, which means you don't have to notify them. And it just goes up the chain from there, from probationary to officer to Gatekeeper or whatever planet-level officer there is."

"What do I do, though? I'm not a Lieutenant anymore, so I don't have that power. Regina hates my guts so she won't listen—"

"Then fuck her, too. You've just been appointed the Akari leader of Earth. Among others, but most importantly Earth."

"Which has been banned by the Hands of Time, and I just suggested that we go along with their declarations to stop using and talking about the Akari."

"Yes, but you're not using and talking about the Akari within Time trying to convert all their little wayward souls. You are talking about it as an alliance between the Time Agents of Earth and the Akari-bearers of Earth in order to defend the human race from the Borelians. And, quite frankly, what the fuck are the Grandfathers going to do to you that the Borelians wouldn't anyway if they captured you, hm? Break your clock? Newsflash, the Borelians were the ones who did that."

Micaiah blinked. "It's the same threat."

"Fuck yeah, it's the same threat. Difference is, if the Hands catch you, you go to prison. Well, you've already broken into and out of their prison at least once, if not twice. If the Borelians catch you, you go to the labor camps. Who do you fear more?"

"The Borelians."

"Right answer."

"What about you, though? You're human, but you don't live on Earth."

"And you think my people still use little spears and clubs? Fuck off. We have a higher percentage of Akari-bearers and Time Agents than Earth does. And, as a matter of fact, we're only considered Unengaged because we're human, and the lines are drawn by race and civilization. Really, with our unique situation, we're more like Engaged Privilege. So like I said, fuck you."

"I don't think that's going to help you any," Micaiah sighed. After a second, he chuckled. "At this rate, everyone's going to get laid tonight."

Saul folded his arms. "How is your wife by the way? I didn't see her."

"She's good. She's home sleeping because she has to be up early tomorrow." He broke into a yawn. "Speaking of which, so do I."

"How's life at the bakery?" Tommen wondered.

Micaiah gave him a look. "Please come back as soon as you can. I'm about ready to strangle Kyle and Jenna if they get into one more argument. The day you come back, they're gone. I can't take it anymore, Micah's sick of it, and the customers are starting to notice."

"I'll do my best, but I still got four weeks."

"Yeah, sure, wipe that smirk off your face." He shifted his stance. "As for your training, once your dad hears about the declaration of war, he won't be able to take you to the Arena for training. You can come here, if you want—we have our own version of the Arena—or you can try it 'wild' as it were, like you're doing with Saul and the Akari at camp."

"I'm cool anywhere," Tommen said, shrugging.

Micaiah looked at Saul. "I don't want you to hurt yourself. You can give him the lectures and stuff, but anything that's too physical, get a hold of me or someone else, and let us handle it. And seriously, see about surgery or chiropractic or something because it's not going to get any better."

"Yes, Dad," Saul said sarcastically.

"I'm serious. Now isn't the time to go beating up on yourself. The Borelians will do that well enough." He let out a breath and looked away at something down the corridor. "This is just way too fucking much to process right now. I need to go home and get some sleep. Wake me when this nightmare is over."

"I hear you. We better get back, too, so we might get a little sleep, too."

"Make him practice his Banding. It'll be good for him, and you'll both sleep a little better for it."

Saul did an imaginary tip of the tip as Micaiah moved past them, making for the portal room. Halfway down the corridor, he heard Tommen.

"Micaiah! Hey! Wait!"

Micaiah stopped and turned. "Yes?"

Tommen caught up to him and slowed. "I wanted to ask you something."

"And what's that?"

"Who's the Chandler?"

Micaiah stopped. "The Chandler? What do you know of the Chandler?"

"Nothing, that's why I'm asking you."

"He's..." He let out a breath. "Honestly, I don't know. I've only ever seen him half a dozen times. Honestly, I couldn't tell you if he's real or a hallucination. When did you see him?"

Tommen got a look on his face which Micaiah had taken to mean that he was about to say something which his scientific, atheistic brain would normally dismiss, but the unusualness and inexplicability of the situation demanded his attention anyway. "Well, I've kind of had dreams. At first, it was just about a white rabbit. In another dream, the white rabbit led me to a white wolf. In the latest dream, the white rabbit led me to the white wolf which led me to a man who called himself the Chandler, and he told me to seek him out. I don't know what the fuck is going on. I thought about just dismissing it, but then you mentioned him, and I just want to know who he is, if he's friend or foe."

Micaiah hesitated. Then, "I don't know who or what he is either. I've seen him in person, once, but then he just vanished. Other times, it's been dreams or hallucinations, visions, whatever you want to call them. I believe him to be friend, as he helped to defeat Rifun and the Bat in the Wheel. As for telling you to seek him out, I wouldn't know where to begin. But if you do figure it out, let me know because I want to have a few words with him myself."

"Oh. Okay. And...just...one more thing."

"What?"

"You don't...regret saving my dad, do you? Like, you don't regret that I went with Sifura to find a cure and—"

"What? No, never. No, just...Tommen, no. I don't regret it at all. Your dad is a good man and he is lucky to have you for a son. You make him very proud, and it makes me happy to see that you have a good relationship. No. I would never regret helping your dad. And if you're referencing the whole declaration of war, don't even worry about it. The Borelians don't restrain themselves because they don't have a declaration of war on someone; they'll enslave anyone they damn well please."

"Then why make one up?"

"Because they can't reach us from their solar system; they have achieved space travel, but not that sort of space travel. Which means they have to go through the Wheel or other interdimensional means, folding space. It's a way of letting everyone else—the Hands and so forth—know about it so they can stay out of the way. Similarly, by leveling such charges, it damages the reputations of humans by making us out to be foolish and warlike; by implicating both Rifun, who everyone knows led the coup, and myself, who led the revolution, it just lumps all humans into the same hostile, volatile, unpredictable basket. It would be more damaging if we were Engaged, but it doesn't affect us too much, really. And they also use the declaration as a type of psychological warfare, sending word ahead that you're all about to die, so form an orderly line and get your head on the stump."

"Oh." Tommen mulled this over for a minute. Then, "But, either way, we're pretty much fucked, right?"

Micaiah nodded. "Yeah. We're fucked. But if I have anything to say about it, we're going to keep it to a minimum. We still have time to prepare."

I hope.

He sent Tommen back to Saul and carried on his way to the portal room. Within minutes, he was sitting on the edge of his bed, removing his prosthetic. He rubbed his stump. Fuck, it was still so surreal how his leg just suddenly ended. Sometimes, in that state between waking and sleeping, he could swear that it was still there. Or when he sat at his desk and crunched numbers, his calf would cramp up and demand to be used, except it wasn't real. Phantom pains. Fucking hell.

"Babe?" Kayla murmured. "That you?"

"Yeah, just me," he sighed, laying down and pulling a light blanket over him.

"How was the meeting?"

"Well...can we talk about this in the morning?"

"It is the morning." She got up on her elbow. "Cai, what's

wrong?"

Micaiah let out a breath. "We are so fucked."

He explained the meeting, from his suggestion to isolate the Akarin in order to deal with the spies, to Saul's more nuclear approach, to his appointment as Doug's successor—

"But you declined," Kayla said. "They can't just force you into the position."

"I know. Believe me, I know. And I was prepared to walk away anyway...until they gave me their reasoning. I still can't decide if it's a blessing or a curse, as far as the appointment goes."

"Cai, you're not making sense. Actually, you're kind of scaring me."

There was no easy way to say it, so he might as well just get it out there. "The Borelians have declared war on humans." He described the tablet and tried to recite the declaration as best he could, at least getting the gist of the charges. "It's been sent to everyone everywhere, as far as Time and Akari-bearers are concerned. I expect we'll hear about it soon enough from Walt once he gets the news from Regina."

"Regina DeBitch?" Kayla said icily. "What does that have to do with you taking Doug's place?"

"Because then, even with the Akarin isolating themselves, I still have the power to unite human Akari-bearers and potentially form an 'alliance' with Mi Chin the Gatekeeper in order to try and defend Earth from the Borelians."

Kayla shook her head. "Fucking hell."

"That's what I said."

"And what about the Hands' threat about using the Akari wherever the Laws of Time prevail?"

"What are they going to do to us that the Borelians won't?"

"Mm...you do have a point there; I will give you that."

Micaiah rubbed his face. "I really just kind of want to sleep it off for a few hours. Maybe in the morning, things will look a little better and I'll be thinking a little clearer."

She nodded. "Okay. Roll over and I'll rub your back."

He did so, burying his face in his pillow as Kayla gently and less-than-gently rubbed his back.

"I've been thinking about our next life," she said after a minute.

"Oh? What about it?"

"I think I might be a masseuse."

"You want to rub people's ugly, sweaty, grimy backs all day?"

"People who go to spas are typically pretty clean."

"That they are, but I don't think there are too many spas in Alaska, not where you're talking."

"Then I'll open one, be the first one to break into a new market."

"Going full businesswoman again, huh?"

"Absolutely. Northern Lights Spa, the coldest hands you'll ever feel."

"I think your slogan needs a little work."

"You'd be surprised how effective an unexpected or unusual slogan can be."

She pushed back the blanket and started rubbing his thigh, his knee, even his stump. Circulation was important, and it kept the skin and muscles from feeling too tight or too stiff or too weird.

"You have a doctor's appointment next week," she reminded him.

"I know, I know. It's supposed to be the replacement for my running leg." *That got damaged in the thick of battle, but I told him that it had been a fall down the stairs. Ha!* "If I had been wearing that tonight, though, I'm sure I would have launched myself over that table to strangle them when they told me I was taking Doug's place."

"Then it's a good thing you weren't wearing it. Sounds like it might be advantageous, given this impending war."

"Why couldn't another human do it, though?"

"Because they wouldn't have the same respect and diplomatic status that you do. You are listed on the declaration of war, and you are the one leading the charge against the Borelians, or so it will seem. You have power, you have respect, you have admiration."

"I thought we decided not to do this because we're trying to go dark."

She hesitated for a minute. Then, "I know. But the backlog of work means we wouldn't be able to start over for a year or two anyway. In that time, I'm sure you could find some equally qualified human to take over your position. And if you recommend them personally, then you can have a change of leadership and politely step down."

"You make it sound so simple. Nothing we do is that simple."

"We can hope."

Micaiah rolled back over and Kayla moved so he didn't crush her hands. "I think we both need to get some sleep. We're becoming irrational."

She kissed him. "Good night, my love. See you on the battlefield in the morning."

Chapter Twenty-Six
Clean Slate

W ell, how's that for your first proper introduction into the Akari?" Saul asked as they grabbed a quick bite to eat from what qualified as a cafeteria. The food wasn't much, prepared more for nutrition than taste. Even Yawi seemed perplexed by the nutrition cube, and he simply nosed it around his plate on the ground.

"What the fuck have I gotten myself into this time?" Tommen sighed, wanting nothing more than to return to camp and get some sleep. At least now, though, he would be able to Band and be Banded in order to get more sleep. If Saul had been a little more forthcoming the first time around, the first camp might not have seemed so fucking long or hectic. Sleep deprivation inevitably made every problem twenty times worse.

"You haven't gotten yourself into anything," Saul told him. "You have been placed here, forced here, however you wish to say it."

"Yeah, well, I don't like being manipulated."

"Everyone is always being manipulated. They just call it different things. Your school schedule, for example. You go from Class A to Class B because someone has manipulated you into thinking that fire will rain from the sky if you don't. You don't think about it that way, of course, but that subtle fear of disobedience is there."

"In that case, though, everything is manipulation."

"Being free of manipulation isn't about breaking every rule that is set out for you. It's about examining those rules, understanding the conditions of them being set, understanding the impact of them being followed or broken, and generally being consciously aware of them. Certainly not all rules are good rules, but just because a rule is

533

set does not mean that it must inherently be broken, whatever someone tells you. That in itself is a form of manipulation, telling you that because you follow a rule that you are a loser."

"Manipulating you into following the rule that if there is a rule that it must be broken."

Saul nodded. "Circular logic. But here's the mind-bender: how do you break the rule that says that you must break rules? If you don't break a rule, you are following that rule. If you do break the rule, you are following the rule-breaking rule which is still a rule."

Tommen tried to wrap his brain around it, but only managed to give himself a headache. He rubbed his eyes. "Is there a point to this? You sound like my girlfriend."

"The Akari operates on a different set of rules than Time. Some rules you already know and so will have no trouble with. Other rules, you have never had to adhere to, so they will feel restrictive at first. Some Time Agents—and you yourself will feel this way from time to time; I know I still do—will say that you are being manipulated and bogged down by many rules. You must ask yourself then, why is it that I am being manipulated and they are not? Or is it possible that they are the ones being manipulated? Am I the one being bogged down by rules, or are they? To have rules is not enough; you must learn to understand them and even work with them."

"This sounds more philosophical than I was hoping for."

"Well, consider it your first lecture lesson. I'm too tired for another hands-on training, and especially too sore to attempt a combat training."

"I thought Akari-bearers were supposed to be peaceful."

"Do you think the Borelians are going to buy that argument?"

Tommen let out a breath. "No. How's your back?"

"Bearable." His tone was dismissive. "So, do you want to go back to camp and get sort of a stunted, half-normal, half-Banded sleep, or hang out here for a while and get a better feel for the place?"

"I think I've had enough excitement for one day. At least this place isn't as weird as the Wheel."

"There is no logic in the Wheel, however much they purport there to be. Everything is based on a whim and the musings of a select few; obey their convoluted logic or suffer the consequences. Here, at least, you know which way is up."

"Seven floors plus three sub-floors, correct?"

Saul nodded.

"That's a lot easier to remember. And navigate."

"Yes, it is." Saul set down his fork and stared at the half-eaten remains of his nutrition cube. Certainly, it left much to be desired. Finally he pushed it away. "I'm ready when you are. I could use some sleep myself."

Tommen had no problem leaving his cube, and he followed Saul out of the cafeteria, Yawi padding silently beside them.

"So, does Yawi wait for you here or how does he get from place to place?" Tommen wondered.

Saul glanced at him. "He does. He gets from place to place."

"But how? I didn't see him come through a portal or anything."

"He gets from place to place. That's all you need to know."

And they were back at it again, information on a need-to-know basis because he was just a dumb kid. He wouldn't have cared if Saul had given him a word salad of technical terms, even hokey mystical terms, but just any explanation would have been nice. Maybe it was more spirit world bullshit.

"Want to see one last trick before we leave?" Saul asked abruptly before they turned down the corridor leading to the portal room.

"Um...sure?" Tommen wasn't sure how to feel about this sudden offer. It wasn't that he didn't want to see it; it was that he questioned Saul's motives. His idea of fun wasn't the same as everyone else's, and things could get really bad, really fast.

As said before and easily observed, Saul was not in the best physical health. So it was a little comical and a little painful to watch him run. Tommen didn't get worried until he saw him head straight for the opening in the center of the large spiral staircase that led to all the different floors. He did not stop, slow down, or deviate in any way, just made a beeline for the gap.

Then he jumped. In the movies, it would have been an epic leap into open space, complete with choreographed slow motion. As it was, Saul went for the secondary, slightly less Hollywood heroic grabbing onto the wall and propelling himself over the edge in arthritic parcour. Tommen fully expected him to trip and fall and go splat three floors down. What he wasn't prepared for was Saul going up, seeming to fly through the open air until he could reach the wall on the second floor. Rather than pull himself over, he pushed off and made for the opposite side on the third floor. From there, he carefully maneuvered his way back to the first floor, floating in mid-air.

Tommen just stood there, completely dumbfounded.

"You flew," he stated stupidly.

"I did not fly," Saul told him. "I manipulated Gravity. The Akari is about more than Time; it encompasses all aspects of the physical world. And some aspects of worlds beyond this one."

"You fucking flew."

"Manipulated Gravity. There's a difference. Flying implies the overcoming of gravity by some biological means. This was changing gravity itself so I effectively became lighter than air. Problem is, Gravity has be manipulated along a track, otherwise I could have fallen to my death."

Tommen was ready to say more, but he just closed his mouth and shook his head.

They returned to the portal room. At some point, Yawi had disappeared, but Tommen could hardly care. Saul had just flown. Gravity or not, he had willfully moved through the air on his own.

"Didn't that kill your back?" he asked.

Saul shook his head. "Actually, it made my back feel pretty darn good, taking the pressure off."

"Why don't people just fly from floor to floor, then? Why walk up all those flights of stairs?"

"Because then things get complicated. The manipulative physics needed to lift a human—and even then, different humans are sometimes different—are different than what is needed to lift, say, a Warid. If two Gravity paths cross, well, nothing good happens, let's say it that way. And then there's the point that because it has to be strung on a path, they are not easily manipulated in mid-air to account for someone not paying attention. It's the logistics of it. Generally, flying is left to the flying creatures. The rest of us are doomed to walk."

Tommen shook his head again. "I don't even know what I just saw."

"Yes, you do. Your mind is just having a hard time accepting it. It's not always a matter of evidence, but a matter of will to accept it."

"So are your brothers and sister around here somewhere, too?"

"In the middle of the night, are you kidding?"

Tommen shrugged and waited patiently for Saul to open the portal. He may as well have been Atlas lifting the world, for the effort it cost him. But the portal got opened and they stepped through.

The forest was dark, and the cabins stood as grim shadows against a black sky dotted only with tiny stars and a sliver of a moon. Tommen managed to stumble his way to the porch of Wolf Cabin and sit on one of the steps, but Saul was not so fortunate as he was lucky to get to a tree and rest at its trunk. After a minute or two, Tommen approached. He was just about ready to poke the man when he spoke.

"I'm fine," he said grumpily. "Just give me a second."

"When are you finally going to admit defeat and actually get that looked at? I'm serious, you are not fine. You seem to barely register as tolerable. When will you go in?"

Saul stood painfully. "When I'm dead."

Tommen rolled his eyes but followed him silently back to the cabin.

"For tonight, just use whatever Band you feel most comfortable with," Saul explained, limping up the porch steps. "I'll teach you more about Akari Bands once we're out hiking in the woods. The Arena and the recreational areas are the best places for green skills, but a wild, empty environment is the next best thing. Mostly you just don't want to be around people."

"What about your little nature and woodland buddies?"

Saul stopped, and Tommen nearly ran into him. "Don't mock me."

They wouldn't know until morning whether anything had been messed with or stolen, but Tommen was too tired to care at the moment anyway. As long as his sleeping bag was still there and his hearing aid charger hadn't been turned into a drone charger. Actually, he was beyond exhaustion; he'd moved into total sleep-deprived delirium.

He felt the cool slip of the Akari Band as Saul spoke. "Band me first. Then I'll Band you. I can stay awake for a few extra hours this morning and get some stuff done."

Tommen shrugged and waited for Saul to get in his sleeping bag, something that seemed to take forever. Maybe he was just that tired, that every second felt like an hour. Once the man was finally situated and comfortable, he set up the Band. Even that was exhausting, it seemed like, and it wasn't anywhere near the best Band he knew he could muster. He could Band for a week in a blistering hot desert. He made it through his Apprentice review. There was no reason for him to be so worn out by this. Except fatigue.

He did not dream about the white rabbit or the white wolf, and he certainly did not dream about the Chandler person, but he would have preferred them over his nightmares about the warehouse and the things that followed. By now, the warehouse dream had become convoluted into something that in no way resembled the actual event; the only thing that really remained was the fear. Sometimes he dreamed that it was actually Micaiah under Rifun's gun. Sometimes he dreamed that Micah was the one holding the gun to his head. Sometimes he dreamed that Cassius had been there, lurking in the shadows. Other times, the changes were so strange, he couldn't even begin to describe them except as elements that had not existed there and should not have been part of the dream at all.

Only the fear remained constant. When the nightmares had first started, it had always ended with him being shot. This was, thankfully, not always the case in the dreams now, but the crushing darkness, the feeling of being alone and afraid and powerless to help the one who was fighting to free him, that all remained, as sharp and painful as ever.

He hated it, the feeling of being powerless. He hated not knowing, of being kept in the dark. Maybe that was why he'd gotten so emotional about finally being told that he was going to be trained in the Akari. Maybe it wasn't about the Akari at all, per se. Maybe it was about learning anything. Maybe it was about learning about this thing that Rifun claimed to wield, learn it so he could use Rifun's own weapon against him. Maybe it was about learning about the so-called "true" Akari, that way he had a weapon that might finally be useful against Rifun. Time had proved to be futile; it was time to move up to the bigger guns now.

At some point, Tommen had a dream about Becky. The two of them were walking on a trail through the forest. All around them, wildlife abounded, from squirrels and birds in the trees, to rabbits and chipmunks running across the trail, to moose and elk and bear coming out to the edge of the trail, simply watching them as if curious.

He didn't remember much more about the dream, if there was any significance to it. He remembered only that the light got brighter, maybe as the sun came up or went down and shone right in their faces. He put his hand up to shield his eyes. The light grew dim, and then it leveled out until he realized he was waking up.

He lay on top of his sleeping bag in his bunk. The first light of the morning meant he could look around the room and have a vague idea of where everyone and everything lay. Everyone appeared to still be asleep, except for Saul who was not in his bunk.

Tommen touched a hand to his ears. He wasn't wearing his hearing aids. They sat peacefully on an unmolested charger which was plugged into the wall. He didn't remember taking them out. He didn't remember getting into bed. He barely remembered Banding Saul so he could sleep.

Grudgingly, he pulled himself out of bed. He was awake now. The alarm was probably going to go off soon, but he needed some fresh air. Camping with older boys was a lot more, ahem, odorous than camping with younger boys.

Saul was on the porch, leaning on the rail, smoking something. It didn't smell like tobacco or weed, but Tommen wasn't about to ask.

"Well, Sleeping Beauty finally awake," Saul said, taking a drag and blowing out a huge puff of smoke that had a rather bitter smell.

"Indian pain medicine?" Tommen wondered casually, nodding at the roll.

"Hardly. Managed to grab a few while I was home. Normally I'm not allowed to have them. They say it makes me cranky."

"What is it?"

"We call it *nala*. It's about as close to tobacco as you can get on Hlohi, but without the addictive nicotine. Mostly it's just a pleasure smoke, something to do, something to pass around in friendly banter."

He took a last drag and flicked the butt away. "It's taboo to smoke it alone. Done together, it creates a bond of friendship and brotherhood. Warriors will do it before a raid or a battle in order to strengthen their bond as a party, make them more attuned to each other's movements. Hunters will do it before a hunt to get closer to each other as well as the animals, to think as their prey. Lovers will do it before, well, I'll leave that to your imagination. You get the idea."

"And smoking alone?"

"Makes you an asshole."

"Oh. How did I get in bed?"

Saul chuckled. "Well, you managed to Band me pretty well. I woke up about half an hour ago and found you on the floor, dead out exhausted. Couldn't wake you for nothing. So I carried you to bed,

Banded you for a good eight, nine hours. Then I let it go so you could either wake up on your own or wait for the alarm."

"You carried me?"

"With my back? Are you insane? No, I used Gravity."

Tommen nodded. "What else does the Akari manipulate?"

"Anything you want it to, as long as the Author allows it. The Akari isn't a tool, like a hammer, something you just pick up and start using. It's as much a living thing as you or I. You have to ask permission to use it."

"Ask permission? What about the way you can just jump off a cliff and hope that Gravity catches you?"

"Believe me, that could have ended very badly. But it suited a purpose, so it was allowed. Think of it like a horse. You can ride a horse, walk, run, go up and down trails, race, jump, do all sorts of things. If you and the horse have a good understanding, have trained hard, have a mutual respect, and know what is expected from each other, all goes well. But if at any time that horse doesn't want to move, it won't move. If at any time the horse gets spooked and bolts, well, you're just a thing on its back." Saul shrugged. "It's not a perfect analogy, but you get the picture."

"I think so." Tommen wasn't sure, but it would probably come to him later, once he actually started using the Akari. "Can you show me how to create an Akari Band?"

At that moment, the alarm went off inside the cabin. Saul turned around, pausing just long enough to look at him and say, "Nope."

Thus a new day had begun. A new camp had begun. This was a clean slate, full of possibilities of greatness and danger. Tommen stepped carefully through the sea of stuff that had migrated across the floor to get to his bunk. He was always a little reluctant to put them in first thing in the morning with all the moans and groans and other assorted noises of sleepy campers coming awake, so he flicked them to Quiet Mode before inserting them.

"Good morning, ladies," Saul said loudly. "Bright and

beautiful day out there. So let's get to it. Got breakfast to eat, coffee to drink, and mountains to climb. We are going nowhere faster right now."

All he really got in reply were grouchy moans and groans. This was a cabin full of teenagers after all, and up until today, they'd probably been allowed to sleep in pretty late. It was summer, which meant no school, and most of them were too young to have jobs. Of the ones who were old enough, well, Tommen was often the victim of lumped scrutiny, assuming that he was as lazy and ungrateful as his teenage peers. Most people did not take into account his frontier background, but then, most people would dismiss him as insane if they knew what really happened to him.

Or maybe it was just him. Maybe this was his competitive nature coming to the surface. Kids, well, kids were kids. So what? But these were, by most accounts, his peers to some extent. He wanted to prove to himself and everyone around him that he wasn't like them. He was better than them. To that end, while he was generally just as cranky and annoyed at having to get up early, he was committed to complaining the least and getting the most work done in the morning. He was sure his resolve wouldn't last more than a couple days, but he would take it while it lasted.

They headed to breakfast in the main hall, a bunch of sleepy teenagers rather than a bundle of energetic little kids. For that, Tommen was actually thankful. He was able to grab his tray and get his food in relative peace without having to keep an eye out for spontaneous games of tag or attempted food fights. This time around, everyone plodded along in the same line like a bunch of losers in the cafeteria. Or inmates in prison. After thinking about it, Tommen decided on the former analogy; the camp was way too awesome to be compared to prison, regardless of the reputation of Wolf Cabin.

"It's a good thing you guys are going camping first this time," Pam said as he walked by, grabbing biscuits and heaping on the gravy. "I think I may have severely underestimated my food stores. I'm going to have to get three times the amount of food that I got."

"How long have you been working here?" Tommen asked.

"Oh, about nine, ten years. Why?"

"Because I think you're full of it. I think you know exactly how much food you need; you're just giving us a hard time about it."

She shushed him. "Don't give away all my secrets. What do you think would happen if everyone knew this was an all-you-can-eat buffet?"

He laughed. "Everyone already does."

Only when she threatened to fling gravy at him did he scurry away and head back to the table.

"Your girlfriend's a good cook," Saul observed dryly.

"She's not my girlfriend," Tommen repeated, highly suspecting that this was going to be some sort of camp joke from now on. But then, who didn't joke with Pam in the lunch line? If they wanted good food, they had to make nice with the person who controlled the food. It was simple logic.

"So if we're supposed to be going hiking and stuff today, what are we doing?" Harry asked, yawning.

"Eating breakfast, dumb ass," JJ sneered.

Tommen let Saul handle that one. Then, "This morning will be outdoor survival classes; you are free to go to whichever ones you choose. There's fishing, foraging, trapping, hunting, dressing, tanning, cooking, all kinds of good stuff."

"Which one are you going to?" Nathan wondered.

"I will be teaching the hunting class," Saul informed him. "Everything from the weapons to the tracking to the art of the kill."

"You're not going to teach us some pagan ritual shit, are you?" JJ whined.

Tommen was almost sure Saul was going to launch himself at the boy. Surprisingly, Harry beat him to it, nearly biting his head off and chastising him for disrespecting ancient beliefs as well as the land they walked on and the animals that shared the land. JJ surrendered that argument out of surprise only. It wasn't difficult to imagine that Harry had Native blood in him, but to see him defend the beliefs so vehemently was a shock. But then, why did it come as a surprise that a teenager would feel deeply about something? Were they really too shallow and self-absorbed to feel passionately about anything but themselves? Tommen faced similar backlash frequently when he was taunted for his chivalrous nature.

As he thought about it, he considered whether he would have to surrender his chivalrous title when he and Becky started sleeping together, which he was still adamant would happen. Was it still wrong if she was the one who initiated it, if it was mutual? Well, he had time to consider it later; he still had to make it through four weeks of camp.

When breakfast was starting to wind down, Mr. Wilson got in front of the group and basically restated what Saul had just said. Yes, it was kind of short notice, but they would make this work. He thanked everyone for being patient and flexible and willing to go with the flow. Then he started listing all the different classes that would be going on, including the instructor and where it would be held. Each one was about forty-five minutes long, and there would be three of them. The kids and counselors were free to go to any class they wanted. Once the classes were all wrapped up, they would reconvene for a quick lunch, then it was time to grab their stuff and pile onto the buses.

"Did you volunteer to teach the hunting class or what?" Tommen wondered as the mass of people began moving to throw away garbage and get to where they needed to be.

Saul shrugged. "I've taught the hunting class for the last eight years. Personally, I think they were desperate. Then it just kind of stuck. Same with the cabin."

"Do I dare ask what happened to the last guy?"

Saul snickered. "He was injured in a hunting accident and couldn't work." He shrugged again. "I shouldn't laugh. Accidents happen all the time. It's part of the risk, part of the thrill."

Out of sheer curiosity, Tommen tagged along to Saul's class for the first round. He waited a few minutes for everyone to get situated in the uncomfortable plastic chairs, setting up his only prop, a hunting decoy of a deer. When all was said and done, there were about twenty in the room.

"Oh, wow, people actually want to hear me speak," Saul said. It was difficult to judge his level of sarcasm. "Well, this is the hunting class. Our weapon of choice is the bow. I have my own personal bow that I will be using. If you have your own, by all means, be comfortable. Otherwise, we have five compound bows here that we will be using out there if you so desire. Now then, this is not an exhaustive class, but I suspect that most if not all of you here are hunters already and have some familiarity with the basics of hunting.

"Out on the trails, we will either be doing a group game drive or going out no more than two at a time on solo hunts. This is to reduce the number of potential accidents as well as be able to actually get something. Too many people out traipsing around will only scare game. Now then, what is this, can anyone tell me?"

Saul went to a desk and picked up a shiny stone. He held it up for all to see.

"Copper ore?" someone ventured.

He sighed and rolled his eyes. "Okay, fine, get technical. This is a rock. Who here is a rock? No one? At least you're that intelligent. Rocks are quiet. That's why they make good pets and even better neighbors. The best hunters are quieter than even this rock. Sorry to say, I don't know that any of you would qualify. So the next best thing is being swift and sure, taking a shot and making it count as soon as you have your target.

"Ideally, you want a heart-lung shot or a head shot, most often through the eye. Failing that, if you can hit any major artery, you have a chance at tracking their escape as they bleed out."

Tommen had shot a bow half a dozen times; he was more proficient with a gun by far. While he certainly preferred trapping overall, he could plink a squirrel or a raccoon out of a tree, or shoot a turkey in the brush. The one time he had tried to get a deer, he'd missed anything lethal or even serious, merely wounding it and watching it run away, his pride wounded more than the deer.

So he was less than confident when the practical portion of class rolled around, and Saul took them all outside for a little target practice.

Up close, Saul's bow was certainly impressive. He'd bragged about it being handmade, though one would never guess it, given how perfect the lines were, how polished the wood was, and how smooth the draw seemed to be. Saul was able to launch three arrows in rapid succession straight into the bullseye he had set up, and the string, which he'd said was actual sinew from a moose's hind leg, barely gave any audible twang. Except for the *thud!* into the styrofoam target, the man was a ghost. Or, as he'd described it, quieter than a rock. Though the one thing that was not quiet was his expression, one of sheer pain.

"Now then, we only have five bows and twenty students," he said, keeping his voice soft so it did not crack or strain against the evident pain in his back. "Five of you grab a bow, and you only get three arrows each until you have all gone through at least once. Begin."

Tommen was less than prepared for Saul tossing one of the bows to him, saying, "Maybe the deaf one among us will teach us a thing or two about being quiet."

Tommen couldn't decide if it was meant as a slight, a challenge, or an encouragement. Regardless, it was an embarrassment, and so was he. He counted himself lucky that he managed to hit the target all three times, never mind that one of them somehow landed within two inches of the bullseye. Once everyone had shot their three arrows, Saul went down to inspect the damage.

"Jenine, you missed two shots and the third one is running away into the woods on your deer. Brian, you've got some tracking to do, but it might come down. Aaron, good job, you managed to bring it down. Tanya, good job, you're bringing home dinner tonight. Tommen, well, you might have hit an artery, so it could come down. Get ready to get tracking."

Then they rotated the bows while Saul grabbed the arrows and inspected them. These were only blunt-tips, but that didn't mean they didn't see a lot of abuse.

The end of class could not have come too soon, and Tommen drifted away in the crowd of people, looking for his next class. Trapping and dressing he knew enough about that he could teach those classes. So, in an effort to perhaps broaden his skill set, he elected for the fishing class next.

Fishing wasn't exactly rocket science, and it wasn't so much different from hunting either. Patience was key, being mostly quiet when in the river, not splashing around or stirring up the bed too much. They learned about the fish, their habits, their food, their river. They learned how to tie bait and lures, how to navigate the fishing pole and use it properly. There was no decent practical portion of it because the creek was seasonal and currently dried up, but they did go out into the yard to practice some casting and reeling. For the more advanced fishermen among them, the last five minutes were spent going over the basics of fly fishing. There was no guarantee that they would have the time or ability to do fly fishing, but if they had the chance, they would.

Tommen knew his dad enjoyed fishing. On multiple occasions, he talked about how, when he lived and worked in Detroit, he would go out on fishing charters into Lake Huron or Lake Erie and catch him some good fish. Strangely, they'd never gone fishing together. They'd been camping and hiking together, even hunting together once, but never fishing. It was weird considering there was a river flowing literally right through Charleston. Well, maybe he'd keep it as an idea for his dad's birthday or something, just as a nice gesture.

Overall, though, his casting was better than his shooting, and he didn't leave the fishing class feeling quite as dejected and inadequate. With Time, he could feasibly "hunt" anything he wanted, but there was still that source of pride in fulfilling the traditional hunt, picking a target, skillfully tracking it through the trees to a successful kill.

He did not hold such reservations about trapping.

For his third class, Tommen chose the foraging, learning about all the edible fruits, nuts, berries, and leaves hidden in the hills. He wanted to learn all the ways he could flavor and sweeten his meat, add a little kick or a subtle tang. Half of his reasoning behind trapping, even illegally, was so he could do his little bit to contribute to the household and take some of the pressure off his dad. Hey, meat was expensive. The other half of his reasoning was that he didn't want to forget. In a world that was desperate to get away from the past and move into the glorious, technological future, he wanted to always hold onto his frontier roots. Trapping and dressing was only part of that equation. There was also the quieter, more delicate work of truly preparing a meal, the way his ma used to do. He'd long since mastered his pa's work. He wanted to know his ma's work, too.

The class was pretty much a nature walk through the forest surrounding the camp. Not all of the edibles they were studying would be found around the camp, and not all of the edibles found around the camp would be out there on the trails around the campsite. Still, they were good to know and memorize. Equally as important were the poisonous plants. The severity of the poison ranged from harmless until ingested, to so poisonous you almost couldn't look at them or else be stricken down.

Tommen tried to take in everything and memorize it the best he could, even Banding to buy himself more time to study and memorize certain plants. He knew he wouldn't remember everything, but something had to stick, right?

Then the class ended and the group meandered back to the main hall. He found a couple of the boys at their usual table, and they waited for the rest of their cabin to show up.

"So, what did you all learn while you were out and about, learning in all your different classes?" Tommen asked conversationally.

"I learned that fish are dumb," Nathan chuckled.

"I learned that it's really hard to clean out a chest cavity when dressing an animal," Dan said.

JJ snorted. "I learned that Saul's a dick for a teacher."

"You're just mad that I shot better than you," Harry said pompously.

"Yeah, well, you and him have been shooting your whole lives in your little war parties. The rest of us civilized men are just beginners. Why the hell are we doing this, anyway?"

Tommen got between them before fists could be thrown, but the fight did not really end until Saul appeared out of nowhere and dragged JJ off one way while Tommen got Harry moved several feet away.

"You call our people primitive," Saul hissed, "but when I look around, I see very little here that makes me hopeful about your modern civilization. And when we go out there to the campsite and have to rely only on ourselves and our skills to eat and survive, I suggest you take notice of who is bringing back the meat each night. I suspect it won't be you."

He released JJ and grouchily took a seat. After a moment, Tommen let Harry return to his seat before sitting down himself.

"Wait, are you two from the same tribe?" Tommen wondered, looking back and forth between Saul and Harry.

"No," Saul answered irritably.

"Shawnee," Harry replied. He glared at JJ. "That's right, we're going into the land of my people. Better hope one of our little 'war parties' doesn't catch you out in the woods alone."

Saul intervened again, though Tommen could tell he did it only out of formality; he not-so-secretly agreed with Harry. The rest of the kids just looked on, some afraid of what might happen if a fight did break out, the rest secretly hoping it would so they could find out.

The last of the loose kids and counselors were rounded up and the window to the kitchen opened for business. A throng of starving teenagers swarmed Pam and her crew, but were soon moving through with the same efficient ease that she had perfected over the last decade. Tommen grabbed a heaping helping of everything, fully aware that everyone was allowed only one plate at this meal just so they could hurry up, get packed up, get on the buses, and get going. This was supposed to be a quick meal with little time for dillydallying or lollygagging. Well, they would see how that turned out.

As expected, lunch was not quite as speedy as Mr. Wilson had hoped. The older kids were faster than the younger kids, true, and were more easily rounded up, but they were not yet adults who were ingrained with deadlines and could scarf down three sandwiches, two slices of pizza, a helping of mac and cheese, a salad, and two rolls in under ten minutes. Even Tommen, who was doing his best to make it quick, still came in behind the others just for the fact that he had taken a lot of food. He had to survive for the next five hours somehow.

Eventually, a sense of urgency overtook them and they hurried to finish their meals, all but running out the door back to the cabin. Dan still had all his stuff strewn about, and the rest were apparently not as prepared as they thought they'd been. Problems ranged from being unable to find certain shirts and underwear to missing deodorant and sandals. There was even a pretty lengthy discussion over whether they should bring razors and shave while at camp. Tommen had shaved during the first camp, mostly just from habit. This lot, though, apparently wanted to have a beard growing competition. And, despite repeating warnings about how fast they were supposed to be moving, a couple of the boys ended up running off to the other boys' cabins and challenging them to a beard growing competition. The humor came from the fact that eighty percent of them couldn't even grow peach fuzz yet.

"What about you, Tommen?" Jason wondered when they returned with multiple agreements to their challenge. "Are you going to join the beard growing competition?"

Tommen grinned. "I think I would end up shaming you all. I can grow a pretty impressive beard."

"Yeah? Prove it."

"I don't have to."

"Baby face."

Well, it wasn't calling him chicken, but it was pretty darn close. He raised a brow and studied the group, five sets of eyes all watching him, daring him to back down. Finally he nodded. "All right. I'll do it. I'll grow my beard out. Then at the end, when I win, I'll cut it off so you can wipe your tears with it."

Well, that apparently cemented him as the cool counselor, the awesome one of the group. He was one of the homies now. Or something. It earned him an eye roll from Saul, but nothing more. No harsh words or cold warnings or anything of that nature. They just kept packing up, rummaging through stuff left out, complaining of things that mysteriously went missing.

"What about you, Saul?" Tommen asked when they were finally almost possibly ready to get started making for the buses. "Can you grow a beard?"

"I don't have the genes for it." Saul already had everything packed and was simply sitting on his bed, reading. He did not look up.

"No beard growing challenge for you, then?"

"A man's braid is his beard. In that case, I've got you all beat."

"Oh, come on, join the fun. See what happens."

"I think I'll sit this one out."

There was little point in trying to argue with him or convince him otherwise.

"Good book?" Tommen wondered.

"It's all right." Still he didn't look up. If Tommen didn't know better, he might have said Saul was completely oblivious.

"Is it the same one you've been reading for the last month or so?"

"Don't have a lot of time to read at camp."

"Oh, please, we both know that's not true."

Saul gave him an irritated look. "And I'm dyslexic. I have a hard time reading. That make you happy?"

Tommen shrugged. "Why would it? I'm color-blind. I'm half-deaf. What do I care that you can't hardly read? You seemed to write your little note well enough. What did that top part say, anyway?"

"It is a prayer of protection, not that I would expect you to care."

"Then why leave me this?" He brought out the wolf tooth necklace. "If you just thought I would discard it, why bother in the first place?"

"Call it force of habit."

"Habit of what?"

"Something to discuss later."

It was frustrating, but at least it was something. Maybe Saul would explain it at their next Akari training session. When that would be, however, remained a mystery. Tommen didn't want to ask about it now, because asking about anything involving a secret, late-night meeting would probably be misconstrued by present company as them being gay and going out for a little bum-fun in the bushes. That was the last rumor he needed, and he had little doubt that Saul wouldn't take too kindly to it either. He had his suspicions that if anyone was going to accuse Saul of being gay, that they were going to get a full, forceful education on what that meant, and it wouldn't be pleasant or soon-forgotten.

Once everyone was as packed up and prepared as they would confidently be, they headed out to the buses. They were not the first ones there, but neither were they the last. Given that they had a full crew compliment this time, Tommen thought they were doing pretty well. They claimed their seats on the bus, then headed back out to help load the rest of the stuff, the tents, the fishing poles, the bows, and so on. Saul kept his bow close to hand, or rather, around his body, just as Native peoples of old would have done.

"Did you make your bow?" one girl asked, walking up to him. Tommen recognized her as a special needs girl who had virtually no fear of anyone or anything, from spiders to grizzly bears to Saul.

"Yes, I did," Saul replied simply.

"How?"

"First I had to prove myself worthy of it, worthy of being a man of the tribe. When I had done that, I had to find the wood that spoke to me and asked to be used and made into a bow to help find food for my people. The first string I made from woven reed fibers. They are good only for a couple shots. The first animal that is killed, that is the sinew used to make the string."

"And you killed a moose the first time?!"

"I did. Such is the trueness of my aim, and the relationship I have with the bow."

"Cool!" The girl smiled a toothy grin. "I'm going to make a bow when we get to the campsite."

She wandered off then, apparently taking Saul's rendition a little too literally as she began talking to various trees and asking them if they would like to become bow wood for her. Tommen found it amusing, but Saul seemed to regard her with an unusual sort of curiosity.

"She has more respect and a better sense of things than most learned men do," he observed. "Sometimes our thoughts get in the way of our knowledge, our intuition, our connection to everything around us. We think our way out of where we need to be and declare ourselves better off for it."

Tommen raised a brow as he started off. "You must be fun at parties."

"My grandfather once said that I was never a child. I was born an old man and so I shall stay an old man. There is nowhere for me to go."

"I've known old men who are a lot more fun than you." *Even Dr. Polski is looking pretty good right now.*

"Perhaps. But I am your counselor and your instructor. Therefore, you're stuck with me. At least for a little while longer. Then you can go back to Micaiah."

At least Micaiah has a sense of humor.

But there was little time to dwell on this as final preparations were finished up and everyone began piling onto the buses, looking for their stuff and claiming their seats. Some complained that their stuff had been moved and rearranged. A couple of the boys got into a fight over it, mostly because all five of them wanted to sit close to a girl they all liked. Saul merely threatened that if they couldn't figure it out on their own like well-behaved men, he was going to separate them like little boys and none of them would get to sit close to the girl. That shut them up pretty quickly; there were few forces in the universe as powerful as the male sex drive and the female's ability to set it off at a wink. As soon as the girl got on the bus and took her seat, that's exactly what she did, and she did it with full knowledge of what she was doing.

"Wake me when we get to college," Saul grumbled. He watched them for a moment longer, rolled his eyes, then settled in for a bumpy nap.

Chapter Twenty-Seven
Full Circle

Tommen understood why the Powers That Be had elected to take away the phones and electronics of all the campers. This was camp, where they should be learning about nature and enjoying the myriad of activities that were laid out for them, without getting hung up on texting or posting or whatever else they did on the their phones or the Internet. But when it came to long car rides, Tommen was forced to wonder if it really would have been so bad to let them have their electronics. Let them listen to their music and play their games; it would help to pass the time, anyway. More to the point, it would help them pass the time quietly.

Seeing how this was a group of teenagers or almost teenagers, image was everything, and that ranged from clothes and appearances to whom one associated with. Most of the kids already had their circle of friends, their own version of "cool" to hang around with. For many, that meant not clinging to the counselors like a frightened child. Counselors were generally only included in the general conversation if they were deemed "cool" also.

This seemed to be an easier task for the female counselors, but maybe Tommen was imagining things. Girls seemed to bond as they talked about clothes, boys, home life, hobbies, anything at all. Boys, well, they were all trying to be their own man. That meant standing apart, standing tall, being the alpha male, and impressing girls. Getting too close to one of the counselors either made them a little boy or gay. Even among the male friends, there was still that air of competition.

So it was that Tommen was by and large excluded from

conversation. It wouldn't have bothered him except it was almost impossible to escape; there was no good way he could tune it out because his hearing aids delivered everything directly to him. He was loathe to switch to Quiet Mode in the event that someone needed him. Although, about half an hour into the right, he decided that was highly unlikely, and he changed modes, settling into a comfortable, cottony silence.

Saul had somehow, miraculously, gone to sleep. Even amid the bumps and ruts, the man did not appear fazed. Tommen found it slightly suspicious, given that he'd Banded him so he could get better sleep. Maybe he hadn't Banded well enough or long enough before passing out himself. Maybe his *nala* was also a sleeping agent of some form. Or maybe...

Saul jerked awake as Tommen broke his Akari Band, as easy as snapping a rubber band. He probably hadn't even been sleeping. Grudgingly, the wolf got into a more comfortable position.

"So, you figured out my little secret," he said.

"I didn't buy that you were tired. And regardless of how bad these roads are and how much you've been trained to sleep on anything at any time, I didn't think your back would let you, not that well," Tommen said.

"Then why did you interrupt me?"

"I wanted to see what the difference was."

"Ah. And what did you discover?"

"It's invisible and harder to feel out, but I don't know for sure considering you may have made it weak on purpose just to test me."

"Interesting theory."

"Am I close?"

"Half-right on the intentions part. You think I want to sit for two hours bored out of my mind?"

"What about your book?"

"Can only read so much at once. Are you quite done?"

Tommen gave him a look, but let him go back into his Band. He kind of envied the man, actually, and thought about slipping into a Slow Band of his own. It would certainly make things easier, but with the way their kids were, he didn't want to leave them unattended for so long. It wasn't that there weren't other counselors on the bus, but he and Saul were the only ones willing to deal with a fight if it got to that point.

It never got to that point, thankfully. Harry and JJ had their arguments, and it got loud at one point, but that was easily solved by moving them to opposite ends of the bus. Otherwise, it was just a long, boring bus ride, and Tommen had to listen to every piece of gossip from every cabin. One of the girls from Butterfly Cabin had reportedly come out as bisexual or some such thing and was hitting on another girl who really didn't appreciate it. Another girl from Caterpillar Cabin was accused of cutting and burning and a whole host of other self-destructive behaviors which she denied. One boy from Beaver Cabin supposedly had a stash of steroids for anyone who wanted an edge in the basketball or soccer tournaments. A Crow Cabin boy was rumored to be a eunuch and challenged to prove that he wasn't.

When it came down to it, Tommen didn't see a huge difference between Wolf Cabin and any other cabin, other than the bitter, bloody rivalry between Harry and JJ. As far as he was concerned, all the cabins had their problem kids, all the cabins had their rumors and their fights and their drama. It just came in different forms under different names with different kids. But hey, what did he know? He was only in high school, the drama capital of the universe.

Maybe that was the reason he'd been hired for this position, they'd been looking for someone who was part of yet not part of the kids' world, who understood what was going on and could tell the difference between petty bullshit and a real threat. Several times, Tommen had seen or heard things which he knew Saul would have jumped on, but they turned out to be idle mischief only. That wasn't to say something couldn't develop out of it, but not everything could be taken as gospel truth.

Still, Tommen was more than happy to see the trail head come into view, the tiny parking lot that could somehow fit all the vehicles and still have enough room for a quick snack for all of them. He moved up to Saul's seat and snapped his Band again.

"What?" Saul asked irritably.

"We're here," Tommen informed him.

Even as he said it, the bus came to a halt. Mr. Wilson was not on their bus this time, so they didn't have to listen to him give any sort of speech before getting off. Instead, Rick went to the front and started giving instructions about how to disembark in the most orderly manner possible.

Needless to say, this did not happen, at least not in the way he was hoping. There was chaos and rummaging and bumping and pushing and shoving and all manner of roughhousing as everyone tried to get off at once, desperate for some fresh air and to stretch cramped legs. Even Tommen stumbled a bit when he hit solid ground. When he turned around, he found Saul kneeling in the dirt about three feet from the bus door, one hand on the side of the bus.

"Hey, are you okay?" Tommen asked, approaching Saul like he was approaching a trapped bobcat.

"I'm fine," Saul hissed. "Just have to get my bearings."

Tommen said nothing after that, just backed up slowly and turned away, making sure he had all his things in order. By the time he got the boys rounded up, Saul had joined their little gang. He was straining something fierce, however. Tommen had his doubts whether he was going to last the week, never mind the rest of the month.

But he'd learned to keep quiet, though he did still cast worried glances in Saul's direction from time to time as Mr. Wilson joined them and took charge of the group. He gave a similar speech as the one he gave the little kids, telling them to eat their snacks quickly because they had to book it down the trail in order to get to the campsite before total darkness to set up their tents. As he spoke, Pam and her crew were busy setting up tables and getting out the snacks for everyone. It wasn't much, really. Cheese and crackers, a bit of fruit, some trail mix, jerky, things to keep them going until they got up to the campsite.

The group swarmed the table once Mr. Wilson was done talking, and soon everyone was scarfing down their food. Hardly the last little paper plate of snacks had been taken before the kitchen crew was moving again. They had to get to the campsite first so they could prepare dinner, too. Probably not the relaxing camping vacation Pam had envisioned, Tommen mused.

"Are you sure you can make it?" Tommen asked Saul as everyone finished up their snacks and gathered their things, preparing to hike.

"Ask me again, and you won't make it," Saul growled, though his threat sounded empty, another indication that something was wrong. "I'll be fine after a good night's sleep."

"Fine. I'm just asking."

With Mr. Wilson at the head, the group started moving down the trail. It was slow going as everyone grabbed their things, dropped their things, found that things were missing. In the chaos, Tommen dropped back a short distance to send a quick text to Micaiah.

"Saul's not doing so hot. And I mean he's seriously hurt but he won't acknowledge it or get help."

A minute later, Micaiah replied, "And what would you like me to do about it? He should be called Saul Bull, because of how stubborn he is and most of what comes out of his mouth."

"Is there any way in Time or the Akari to relieve pain?"

"If there were, you think he's not already doing it? You can't help someone who doesn't want to be helped."

"I just don't want something to happen to him while we're way back out camping. I'd rather send him out now while we're next to a road."

"Some people only learn through hard experience. You can't do anything for him, Tommen."

"All right. Just thought I'd ask since it seems like you know him pretty well."

"Ha! Hardly."

That was the end of that. Tommen grabbed his things and elected to play the role of pig board, herding the slackers along the trail until they were within reasonable distance of the main body of the group.

They actually moved at a pretty good clip, or maybe it seemed that way since teenagers were a little more focused than a bunch of little kids. They weren't asking about this bug or that leaf, wanting to know how many bears they would see. They didn't distract themselves by—okay, yes, they did stop to make stupid animal sounds and see if anything would answer them. Nothing ever did. Tommen would have been surprised if there were any animals within a thousand feet of their group. Fast they were, quiet they were not.

Up ahead, Tommen could see Saul staying with the boys from their cabin. He seemed to be doing all right, all things considering. He had fastened his bow to his backpack and did not appear to be limping or lagging.

But the hike itself was cause for mischief, especially between rivals. Along the way, Harry and JJ seemed to have picked up supporters for their respective teams, and it wasn't just boys from Wolf Cabin either. There were a few from all the cabins it seemed, even the girls' cabins.

The fight started out as typical trail mischief. JJ trips on a root, Harry laughs. Well then JJ tries to trip Harry intentionally, but Harry dodges and gets in a counterstrike, tripping JJ again. Everyone on Team Harry thinks this is hilarious and congratulates him for some perceived victory. Team JJ is less than thrilled and so encourages revenge. JJ tries again to trip Harry; this time, Harry doesn't trip so much as he actually falls to his knees.

Well, that doesn't go over well with Harry or his posse. So he tries to outright kick JJ, aiming for the back of the knees, and brings him down as well. JJ goes down, but comes up swinging. He gets in a glancing blow, but Harry responds by all out falling on top of him. Then, what started out as an innocent trip and a few snickers quickly devolves into a true fistfight. A few on the sidelines try to get in on the action, too.

None of the other counselors were particularly enthused about trying to get in the middle, but the boys' backpacks allowed for some good handholds. A couple counselors managed to get the two main brawlers separated enough that Saul came out of nowhere with a long, slender stick, slapping them both hard across the arms and backs of the hands with an audible snap! As soon as the boys let go, the counselors pulled them apart.

"Now that's enough!" Saul snarled, every bit as fearsome as he had been on day one of camp. "You are not little boys and you are not a couple of street thugs. You are mature young men, so start acting like it! If we were in a real survival situation, you two would be the deaths of us all. As it is, you are probably the most worthless members here. Food, water, shelter, those are our goals this week. We have a village chief, and that is Mr. Wilson. We have tent chiefs, and they are your counselors. You listen to them." He looked at JJ. "You can drop your tough guy act because it will do you no good out here." He merely gave Harry a hard regard. "And you..." He shook his head. "You're a disgrace to the ancestral land you walk on. Picking a fight with him." He spat at Harry's feet. *"Nikig."*

Harry looked rebuked well enough, but JJ stood brewing in silent anger. Tommen could already see that if Saul hadn't been an enemy before, then he most certainly was now. The key then became making sure that JJ never knew just how weakened Saul had become.

"Well, let's go!" Saul barked impatiently. "Burning daylight here!"

It was a second or two before they actually started moving. The whispers began even before they'd even left the area. Some said the fight should have been allowed to continue; Harry and JJ were only going to fight again later, so why not let them duke it out and see who really was better and stronger? Others debated whether one or the other had cheated.

Meanwhile, Saul made sure to keep the two boys far apart

from each other, placing JJ at the front of the group near Mr. Wilson, and Harry at the back of the group with Tommen and his slackers.

"So," Tommen said. "What happened?"

Harry shrugged. "He tripped and then I tripped and then we both went down...I don't know."

"What got all this started between you two anyway? Saul seems to think it's about a girl."

"Well, it is, kinda. I'm actually dating JJ's sister. Well, let me rephrase, she's his adopted sister. Now, I don't know the details, but I guess they kind of had a fling going on. They figured that since they're not blood relatives, then it was okay. Whatever. I guess they had some kind of fight over it, and then we started dating, me and her. JJ's been all bent out of shape ever since."

"Wait, so, he's got a thing for his sister?"

"Yeah. I mean, I think it's pretty creepy. Most people who hear about it think it's pretty creepy. But I guess they had a thing. Anyway, he's hated me ever since we started dating."

"And what have you done about it?"

"What do you mean?"

"Have you talked to him about it, talked to her about it?"

"Why would I? I mean, she dumped him, or so she said. She has a right to choose who she dates, doesn't she? He just has to learn to deal with it."

"You think there might be some resentment in there?"

Harry raised a brow. "You're a couple's counselor now? I didn't start the fight."

"But you didn't stop it either."

"What would you have me do? Walk away? We kind of share a cabin."

Holy fuck, this was all starting to sound familiar. But instead of being on the receiving end of this advice, now Tommen was doling it out. "Maybe it's time to be the bigger man and not engage unless you absolutely have to. Force him to throw the first punch. Force him to be the petulant child and goad you into a fight. And even then, yes, walk away if you can. You don't gain anything by fighting. You don't gain any friends, and you certainly don't gain any respect." He went on as Harry rolled his eyes. "Hey. You see these two teeth?" Tommen pointed to them. "They're not real. They're porcelain replacements. I used to get in a lot of fights, we're talking an average of three times a week. But I don't anymore, because I have bigger things to worry about, and I don't let every little thing get to me."

Never mind that whole part about his Banding saving his life on more than one occasion. Or that bit about how his "bigger things to worry about" involved interplanetary war. Or how his fighting was reduced the most by the fact that Tyler Freeman had first been expelled and then graduated, meaning he wasn't around anymore. Harry didn't need to know any of that.

"But I can't just go crying to the counselors," Harry was saying. "I have to be a man and stand up for myself, you know?"

"Standing up for yourself is a good thing," Tommen acknowledged. "Now, I'm not Native at all, and I mean no disrespect, but isn't part of being Native being part of a village or community or a clan or something of that nature?"

"Yeah..." Harry eyed him suspiciously.

"What would happen if you treated this like that? If JJ is just going to be a child who throws temper tantrums because you looked at him wrong, why not be a man, take your place among the adults, and all work together to curb his anger? Everyone against him, instead of everyone on one team or the other cheering you on?"

It was probably a poor analogy, all things considering, and Tommen hoped he hadn't offended Harry trying to make his point. But the kid mulled it over for a minute, then shrugged. "I guess. I don't know."

"Listen, would you rather have Saul's wrath on your head, or on his head?"

Harry barked a laugh. "Now that's a fight I would pay to see." He grew serious. "For as tough as Saul is, he better watch his back. JJ may be small, but he knows how to hold a grudge. Well, you've probably already figured that out."

He had, but Tommen didn't say anything to that. Actually, he found himself at an existential crossroads, the realization that he'd come full circle. He was no longer getting into fights, but breaking them up. He was the one in control. And these kids were just about his age, only a few years younger. It was like looking at himself from his own days in middle school. It was uncanny. It was weird. It was terrifying. Was this how others had looked at him? A boy to be pitied? Someone who would hear the advice thrown his way but never listen? Had the teachers had similar misgivings about the situation, day in and day out, week after week as he made the familiar walk of shame to the office to explain himself? Had they ever held out hope that he would change, or had they given up on him and simply acknowledged him as the perpetual ticking time bomb?

Tommen was grateful for the dim light so the others didn't have to see his dismayed expression. The good news was, he had two years left of school. Without Tyler Freeman, he had a chance to set everything right.

By the time they arrived at the campsite, it was near dark, and they had to pitch the tents by the light of flashlights and any of a dozen small fires which Pam and her crew had managed to get going in between their normal cooking duties. Dinner consisted of hot dogs, hamburgers, and the same snacks they'd munched on before starting the hike. To lighten everyone's mood, Mr. Wilson had also packed some s'mores supplies which he broke out once dinner was over and all the tents had been set up.

"You two are going to sleep on opposite sides of the tent this week," Saul said severely, pointing at Harry and JJ while they cooked marshmallows. "If possible, you're going to be doing separate activities during the day, too."

Harry agreed shyly, but JJ still looked like a simmering pot of murderous rage. Tommen couldn't even say who the target of his rage was. One minute, he looked ready to throw himself over the fire to get to Harry, the next, he looked ready to go after Saul and take him unawares.

"So what are we doing about breakfast since we haven't gone out to set up traps and stuff?" Nathan wondered, hoping to ease the tension crackling louder than the fire.

"Well, the fastest and easiest way is going to be foraging, and probably some fishing, too. Most of us can do that, and then Tommen and a couple others can go out and start setting traps. Hopefully we'll have something by lunch. If not, well, I'm sure a few adept hunters can head out after breakfast, too."

Tommen wasn't sure if he should feel confident or suspicious that Saul had told him to lead a trapping party. On the one hand, it could be a show of confidence in his abilities. On the other hand, it was more likely a way to just get rid of him and keep him out of Saul's hair for a little while. Well, he wasn't bitter about it; he wasn't too keen on working with the grouchy old wolf anyway, and he got to do what he was best at. He was even going to show a couple others how to do it, too, passing on knowledge to the next generation. Problem was, he was still part of that generation. Hm...

From the chaos of trying to hoof it to camp and set up in the dark, everyone was pretty well exhausted. There were no campfire songs or anything of the sort. The boys disappeared one by one from the fire, getting ready for bed, rummaging for bottled water to brush teeth and so on. After a time, Tommen got up and headed across the site to Mr. Wilson's tent. He had the generator which powered all the chargers and an assortment of other potential emergency supplies.

"Got your hearing aid charger, do you?" Mr. Wilson said, relaxing in his foldup chair. "All right, you can plug it in just like last time." As Tommen knelt to plug in the charger and take his hearing aids out, he continued speaking. "So, is everything all right in your cabin?"

Tommen looked up. Even though it was dark, he did his best to give Mr. Wilson his, "Are you fucking with me right now?" look, even as he said, "Well, we have two boys locked in a blood feud. The rest of them seem to be pretty run-of-the-mill mischief makers. And

Saul looks ready to go down for the count even if he denies it."

"Did he tell you why he has such back problems?"

"IED, shrapnel in his spine."

Mr. Wilson nodded, his head only a vague outline against weak firelight. "Between me and you, I don't think he's going to last the month. I'm actually surprised that he came back. His stubborn pride is going to be the death of him one day." Tommen elected to stay silent. "If that does happen—not him dying, but if he does end up leaving for one reason or another, do you think you can handle Wolf Cabin alone? You saw the fight that happened earlier."

"I've been in fights like that."

"This I can imagine, but that's not what these kids need. They need someone, like Saul, who can break up a fight with all authority without getting involved himself."

Tommen hesitated. "I don't know."

Mr. Wilson nodded. "I understand. And I appreciate your honesty."

"If Saul did leave, would you send the kids home?"

"No. It wouldn't be fair to them, especially if they haven't done anything really wrong. No, I figure I would have to take his place for the duration of camp."

"Oh. Okay."

"But nothing is set in stone yet. Saul is still here, and for the moment, all fights have been quelled. Maybe we'll get lucky and it'll stay that way, hm?"

Tommen had his doubts, but he tried to remain optimistic. He returned to the tent where Dan had just flicked on the lantern, casting eerie shadows over everything. He grabbed his toothbrush and toothpaste and headed a short distance away to brush his teeth.

There was no possible way that they were going to make it through the week without having another altercation of some kind. But Saul had the right idea, keeping the boys as far apart as possible. Though Tommen was forced to wonder, if the feud was so bad, why they'd been placed in the same cabin in the first place. Well, didn't matter, he supposed. They were together now, and they just had to make do with what they had.

"Come on, someone has to have a good ghost story," Jason was saying when Tommen returned to the tent. "Just one before bed."

"Your mama still sing you to sleep, too?" JJ taunted.

"I'm just sayin'. What's camping without a good ghost story?"

"Quiet," Saul muttered in his usual position by the entrance.

"Come on, Saul, you probably know a good ghost story," Tommen chimed in, sliding into his sleeping bag.

"I'm not telling any more stories, I am going to sleep. The rest of you should, too. We have to be up early to go catch our breakfast from scratch."

"Party pooper!" Dan said.

They argued about it for a short time until they decided that no one apparently knew any ghost stories, or else they weren't giving them up that night. Eventually, the lantern was turned off, and there was the rustling and shuffling of campers trying to get comfortable in sleeping bags on hard ground. They didn't have the same spot as last time, the nice high ground above everyone else, but it was a decent spot, all things considering.

Tommen did not go to sleep right away. He stayed awake, listening, only slightly paranoid about what could be out there. About who could be out there. He heard the crickets and the owls in the immediate vicinity. In the distance, he thought he could hear coyotes screaming at the moon. Otherwise, everything was peaceful.

His heart leapt into his throat when he heard footsteps, but calmed when he heard the giggling of a couple girls, both trying to shush the other and tell them to be quiet. Well, safety in numbers, Tommen figured, about the only instance when he figured he could justify two or more girls going to the bathroom at the same time.

He was just dozing off when there was rustling in the tent. It was too dark to see who it was exactly, but if Tommen had to hazard a guess, he'd probably say it was Harry. Going off to meet his girlfriend.

Tommen knew he should probably investigate, maybe stop

him. But for one, the last thing he needed was for it to be anyone just on a simple bathroom run. He wasn't gay, and he really didn't need to seem like some creepy stalker out to rape his campers in the middle of the night. Besides, how could he chastise his campers for going out and doing something he desperately wanted to do for himself? He had only to close his eyes and he could feel Becky's smooth, warm skin, cup her breasts and her butt, all of it beautiful and perfect to touch and feel and just to look at. God, he wanted her. He wanted to see her naked, see her beneath him, feel her on him, over him.

A short time later, the missing camper returned, settling back into his sleeping bag and going still. Not five minutes later, the group of girls also returned, giggling and whispering and shushing. Threesome? Damn. How the hell could a fourteen year old get it better than he could? It wasn't fair.

Tommen fell asleep feeling rotten, slept pretty rotten, and he woke up feeling rotten. The only thing he could think about was that he wanted to get laid. Had he woken up really early, he might have texted Becky and complained to her a little. Was she in as much agony as him, or was it all a game to her? He liked to think she was hurting and aching as much as he was just by the sheer fact that she was the one leading this whole thing. She was horny, too, she was just having to mentally overcome all the traditions ingrained in her since birth that told her no. Had he woken up early, he could have texted her to find out.

But he hadn't woken up early. He'd woken up at the sound of the alarm like everyone else. He jumped awake, fought to find his way out of his twisted sleeping bag so he could grab his rifle and head out to the frontlines with the other soldiers, then realized that he was only camping. After a minute or two, he relaxed and waited for Saul to shut the alarm off, which he did grudgingly.

"All right," the old wolf said, "up and at 'em. Gotta go catch your own breakfast this morning, kiddos, because Mama ain't cookin' for you."

Saul was at the front of the tent, but Tommen was at the back, and he was forced to wait for the campers to scramble out ahead of him. It was certainly different having to manage eleven campers instead of just three. For one, everything took at least ten times longer, from wrangling them for meals at the main hall to just getting out of the dang tent. Or tents. Tommen took the opportunity to change clothes, but still...hurry up.

To his surprise, Saul was not the first one out of the tent. In fact, it looked like he'd hardly begun to wriggle out of his sleeping bag.

"You okay?" Tommen wondered.

"I've just been trampled by eleven teenage boys, about to be twelve," Saul answered grumpily. "How would you feel?"

Tommen shrugged. "Sorry for asking."

He headed out and made for Mr. Wilson's tent to grab his hearing aids before returning and really getting ready for the day. He arrived just as Saul drunkenly limped out of the tent. When he went to help, he was swatted away.

"Just slept wrong is all. My left side is numb. I'll be fine once I start getting around."

"Saul, you are not fine," Tommen told him forcefully. He looked at the campers. "One of you get Michelle."

By the time Michelle arrived, Saul was up walking around and griping about having to find something for breakfast because hunger was not going to make him any more pleasant to work with. Michelle still made him sit for an examination while Tommen divided the campers into groups for their tasks.

He took care to keep Harry and JJ far from each other. Foraging and trapping were too likely to run into each other. He decided to keep JJ around camp. Mostly he would be chopping firewood, but he would also be setting up the fleshing boards and stretching rings once they started getting some pelts in with the meat. Harry he sent off fishing. Hopefully that would be far enough for the two of them. He himself, as directed, led the trapping party. He took Charlie and Jason as his cohorts, and he divided the rest between fishing and foraging, sending them off with the respective counselors.

Even before they had set out, Tommen knew the pickings would be slim this time around, comparatively speaking. One week wasn't enough to restore an area, to fool the animals into thinking all humans had gone and it was safe to return. The only thing that would save them was going to be some strong bait for the first round of trapping, that way they would have enough entrails to lure in larger predators which they could now hunt thanks to the hunting teams with their bows. Tommen was liking the older kids' camp more and more.

Still, he did his best to convey his knowledge without conveying his fear. He showed the two boys how to tell if a location was good for setting a trap, and what kind of trap to set based on the location and what they wanted to catch. It was a longer, more detailed explanation than what they'd gotten in the crash course before their departure, and he was surprised when the boys actually thanked him for it.

When they finally made their way back around to camp, Harry and the others had a decent catch of fish which they were cooking over the fire. The foraging team had also returned with a small salad of edible greens. Saul did not appear to have moved from his spot, but Tommen knew better than to approach.

"So, how'd it go?" he asked instead, taking a seat by the fire.

"Had a good run of fish," Harry reported proudly. "I don't think we'll starve for breakfast."

"Good to hear. How about the foraging?"

"You can see where the little kids really cleaned a lot of stuff out," Dan said. "Some of it's coming back, but not quickly."

"Yes, that does happen. But consider this: you don't have to pick every plant every day. Pick one plant one day, then a different plant the next day. It not only keeps the flavors different each time, but it gives the foliage a chance to recover, even a little bit." He looked at JJ. "How were things here at camp?"

JJ shrugged. He mostly stared at the ground, but Tommen

didn't miss the glares he cast at Harry and Saul. "Okay. We have wood for the week. The skinning stuff got set up if you guys manage to trap or hunt anything."

"Well, that brings me to my next question: who wants to do what after breakfast? I totally understand if you guys don't want to do the same thing day in and day out, or even in the same day. For now, unless something comes up, I'll leave it up to you. We might have to adjust as needed, but go for it. Hit me. What do you guys want to do?"

Charlie and Jason wanted to continue trapping, just so they could see if their labors paid off. Harry elected to stay in camp and Jason chose fishing. The rest moved and shuffled and did whatever their friends wanted to do. It was a decent arrangement. Once the other cabins decided what they wanted to do, a few people had to be switched around just to balance out the teams, but otherwise it worked out well.

Only once the teams were dismissed to go do their thing did Saul finally move from his spot, standing stiffly and heading for the tent to grab his bow.

"You need someone to go with you?" Tommen wondered, hoping he sounded friendly and nonthreatening.

Saul looked ready with a sharp reply, but at the last moment, he appeared to bite it back. Finally he relented. "Probably," he grumbled. "Grab a bow, but know that's it more for your own protection than hunting, in case something sneaks up on us. I'll bring it down and dress it out if you want to haul it."

"Works for me." Tommen bounded away to grab a bow and some arrows. He returned and caught up to Saul just within the treeline. "What are you hoping to get?"

Saul shrugged. "A deer. A bear. Whatever is unlucky enough to get within range."

Their unlucky victim turned out to be a deer, about a two year old doe. Saul took it down with a single arrow, piercing heart and lung. Tommen followed him down the slope and watched as he dug his arrow out, then began working on dressing it, muttering something in his native tongue as he did so, probably thanking the deer's spirit or something.

Just as they were ready to leave—Tommen faced with the daunting task of having to carry it back—they were happened upon by one of the foraging groups.

"Aw, poor deer," one of the girls said.

"This is dinner," Saul told them. "Not a deer."

"Hey, could one of you guys help me carry this back?" Tommen wondered.

The foraging group was pretty self-sufficient, and Jeremiah agreed to help. He shouldered most of the weight while Tommen weakly brought up the rear, both literally and, well, literally. They'd fastened the deer to a pole, and Tommen got the butt end. They followed Saul back to the camp where he began skinning and butchering the deer.

Saul never did do much heavy lifting at that camp, Tommen noticed. He would go out and hunt. He would dress and butcher an animal, but he never hauled it back unless it was one of the small game animals in a trap. Whether this was because he recognized his own physical limitations or because he'd been ordered to hold back, Tommen did not know.

Tommen told himself not to care, not to bother with it, let the man stew, but it was hard, especially when the others started catching on to his weakness. Harry had been pretty good about not letting every little thing provoke him, but there were still times when he and JJ got into a small pushing match or a tussle. And when Harry couldn't be provoked, JJ knew how to bully others into a fight. It wasn't just the other boys from Wolf Cabin either; he could provoke anyone, even some of the girls.

Tommen did his best to keep JJ busy and out of everyone's way, but he couldn't just keep him in camp chopping wood all week. He'd let him go out hunting a few times, hoping that might do something to calm the storm. It worked, but only when he got something. More often than not, he returned frustrated because he hadn't found anything or it had gotten away or any number of things that had gone wrong.

Breakfast was always the hardest part of the day. They were pretty okay if there was something leftover from dinner, even a bit of jerky to nibble on. It was the mornings when there was nothing on the plate that got everyone up tight. Tommen couldn't really chastise anyone about it because he was right there with them.

But once the food started coming in and filling everyone's bellies, tempers settled, and life resumed. The older kids' camp was a little easier to handle, Tommen thought. For one, they were bigger, stronger, could do more, and had the patience and willingness to learn that the little kids didn't. For two, the little kids' camp had only really been one full day, hardly enough time to really learn anything and put new skills to use. And, if anyone was feeling lazy or stubborn, they could suffer a day and a half without food and suffer few consequences. With the older kids' camp, it was four full days plus half a day on Saturday, which meant multiple opportunities to try new things, hone skills, and explore camp life. And it was a little harder to go four days without food.

It wasn't like they were lacking for food, either; it was just a lot harder to feed eighty teenagers versus eighty kids. They needed the deer to sustain them. Once, on Wednesday, someone did actually manage to bring down a bear. It wasn't a particularly large bear, probably last year's cub, but it was enough that everyone was called back with whatever they had and the entire camp was able to completely stuff themselves at lunch and dinner.

Tommen had only had bear a handful of times. In his old life, they were tough to take down, dangerous for a man alone. His pa and Teo had gone out bear hunting only once, and it was supposedly a pretty close call. In his modern life, bear was not something Tommen hunted or trapped. His trapping was illegal, and it was a little harder to conceal a bear trap or a trapped bear. On the off chance he did manage to keep such things hidden, he still had to get the bear off the mountain and back home, no easy feat for him, even with a Band to give him all the time he needed. Then he would need a place to store five hundred pounds of meat, and the chest freezer in the garage was not equipped to handle that. Nor did he have a space large enough to properly tan a large bear pelt.

Maybe one day he would get a legal license to do such things, but that was not today. As he licked the grease from his fingers, Tommen looked around and found Saul carefully stretching the bear hide, securing it to some low tree limbs and stretching it down to the ground. He took a knife and started cutting away at the chunky fat, waving away a cloud of flies as he worked.

"So, who wants a new fut coat?" one of the female counselors asked. "I bet that thing would be warm."

"You'd roast in that if it was anywhere above ten degrees," Tommen said.

"Who teaches the fur crafting class, do you know?"

"I don't know. It's not as hard as it seems, or so says my girlfriend."

"You've never made anything out of your pelts? I thought you said you did professional tanning."

"I tan the pelts and then I sell them. I don't make hats or mittens out of them."

After a short time, Tommen took pity on Saul who was working alone and fighting the flies more than he was fleshing the hide. He did not presume to take up a blade beside him on the pelt. Rather, he found a decent bundle of leaves and tried waving the flies away. Saul gave him a look but did not say anything for a long minute.

"Taking pity on the cripple, are you?" he said finally.

"Taking pity on the man being assaulted by flies while he works," Tommen answered.

Saul grunted. "Well, you have that right at least. Are our campers behaving themselves?"

"They're still eating."

"Have you noticed if any of them are particularly decent at

tanning?"

"Um, I think Harry was pretty good. Jason is getting the hang of it. Maybe—"

"Well, whoever they are, when they're done eating, they can help me. They might learn a thing or two."

Tommen nodded. "And when were we going to get back to training?"

"Once we get back to camp and aren't cooped up in such tight quarters. Once I have a chance to sleep on a real bed again."

"Your back still bothering you?"

Saul did not reply to that, just kept fleshing. In the modern world, the weight of the bear pelt itself would be enough to keep it in place while a power washer could take the fat and extra layers of skin right off. But they didn't have a power washer, and they had to make due with knives and rocks. Still, for a skilled tanner like Saul, fleshing the bear hide didn't take more than an hour. By then, everyone had finished eating, and the Wolf Cabin boys got wrangled into helping him with the next steps of tanning, taking it to the river to wash it a second and third time, then hanging it and waiting for it to dry a little before smearing bear brains all over it. Tommen stood back and watched.

"What are we going to do with the bear pelt once its all tanned and ready?" Nathan asked as they sat around the campfire.

"Take it back to camp," Saul answered, gnawing on a bit of leftover meat. He sighed. "I imagine it will get used in one of the crafting classes later on. Show you guys how to make hats and mittens and scarves and such, same as the rest of the pelts."

Between the two camps, they'd amassed quite a collection of furs, everything from rabbit and coon, to deer and now bear. One of the hunters had even gotten lucky one day and managed to bring in two turkeys, so they also had a nice collection of feathers for crafting purposes.

"So, what do you guys think of camp so far?" Tommen asked genially. "We've got a day and a half left; what are you guys thinking?"

Some were cool with it, enjoyed it, but were ready to get back to civilization. Others believed they had found their new calling in life and didn't want to leave. Tommen estimated that their feelings would last up until they got on the bus, maybe until they got back to camp and could sleep on a mattress again under a roof.

He texted Becky about it later when he found a few minutes and a little signal to work with.

"The joys and temptations of modern life," she told him. "Bathrooms, for instance."

"Yes, those are very important," Tommen agreed. "Soap and hot water, too."

"Exactly, which is why I could never do any kind of extended camping. I'll go out for a weekend, but please let me come back."

"I'll let you come back, if you insist."

"I do insist. And you better come back, too."

"Every intention."

But you know what they say about the road to Hell.

Chapter Twenty-Eight
Wilderness Survival

Morning came too soon, but Tommen took comfort in the fact that this would be the last full day of camping. That meant one more evening, one more morning, and four more meals. Count them off one by one, and he would be checking one meal off his list within the hour. That didn't make the early wakeup much easier, though, as he and everyone else in the tent rose slowly, tiredly, yawning and complaining. As usual, he was the last one out of the tent, blindly clutching his toothbrush and toothpaste.

As he brushed, he felt his cheeks, tried to judge how well his beard was growing in. Well, it wasn't exactly long and luscious, but it had only been a couple days after all. It was just starting to get past the knife's edge stubble and into the annoyingly prickly stubble phase.

"You can stop caressing your beard," Saul told him when he returned. "Kevin from Crow Cabin has already got everyone beat."

Tommen shrugged. "So? I'll still grow it out. Who knows? Maybe I'll even keep it for the whole month, just to see what my dad and my girlfriend think when I get home."

"What you really mean is that you want to show it off to your girlfriend. You're including your dad so you don't sound like a hopeless sap."

"Is it that obvious?"

"Afraid so."

Saul was in one of his good moods, that being sarcastic, rude, and constantly smirking. He also appeared to be feeling better because he wasn't limping or minding every move he made.

Tommen's attention was distracted then by a commotion from

the tent. Not three seconds later, he and Saul were forced to intervene as Jason and JJ very nearly got into a fistfight.

"What's the problem here?!" Saul demanded hotly.

As usual, Wolf Cabin was the center of attention and attracted a crowd.

"Motherfucker stole my shit!" Jason shouted, pointing a finger menacingly at JJ who glared at him and looked tense and ready to go again.

"Watch your tongue!" Saul snapped. "And speak like a real man. What happened?"

"My knife went missing the other day. This morning I found it in his bag."

"You lie!" JJ snarled. "And you went through my stuff without my permission!"

"Where is the knife in question?" Saul demanded.

"Here," Charlie said, meekly holding it out to him. It was a decent knife, really, solid handle, sharp blade. Tommen had seen it multiple times, but never knew it was Jason's knife specifically, or so he claimed.

"Is this the knife?" Saul asked, looking at both Jason and JJ.

"Yeah, that's my knife," Jason said even as JJ nodded grudgingly.

"I didn't ask if it was your knife, I asked if this is the knife you're fighting over."

The boys nodded again. "Yeah, it is."

Saul examined it, looking it over thoroughly like a collector looking to buy. He tested its balance and its sharpness, making a real show out of it. Finally, "JJ, is this Jason's knife?"

"He went through my bag without my permission," JJ growled.

"That's not what I asked."

"So, what, he gets off scot-free?"

"Answer the question. Is this Jason's knife? Yes or no?"

"I don't know."

"But it's not yours."

"I was borrowing it."

"Borrowing it."

"Yeah. I used it yesterday when I brought in a couple fish."

"This knife is too big for fish. Have you learned nothing, or are you lying?"

"It's my knife," Jason cut in. "Give it back."

"Well, we've established that it's not JJ's knife, but we haven't established that it's yours either. Mr. Wilson brought plenty of knives to use at camp. Is he missing any?"

Mr. Wilson, who had been silent thus far, shook his head. "No, sir. All of my knives are accounted for."

"Anyone else wish to lay claim?" Saul asked, holding up the knife. "No?" He held it out to Jason. "I guess today is your lucky day. Either you just recovered stolen property that rightfully belongs to you, or you're a better liar than he is."

Tommen could see that Jason was less than thrilled with the exchange, but glad to have his knife back. JJ, however, was a different story as Saul spoke quietly to him.

"Remember what I said about surviving out here? It's a group effort, and we don't have time for this shit. We move individually, but we function as a unit. The worst thing you can do is make enemies of everyone around you."

JJ scoffed. "Yeah, and you can talk. Why don't we go, just me and you? Then we'll see how alone you are."

For a second, Tommen thought Saul was actually going to go for the challenge. He lowered his voice and said something more that Tommen couldn't catch, then moved off to find what leftovers he could for breakfast. Meanwhile, Tommen went over in his mind what teams were needed and where he was going to send the boys. Now he had to keep JJ and Jason apart, in addition to JJ and Harry. What was it about the kid that he just had to make enemies of everyone? Or was it just a personality thing, like Saul?

Breakfast was a silent affair, and Tommen did his best to try and read body language, not that the boys didn't know how to project so loudly the girls across camp could probably tell what they were thinking. JJ hated everyone. Harry found the whole thing exhausting and despicable, but he would find no subtle support from Jason who just wanted to get on with the day and his duties, and maybe just get back to camp and sleep it all off like a bad dream.

"JJ, I'm going to send you out foraging," Tommen said.

"What?" JJ whined. "Haven't I been punished enough already?"

"It's the only thing you haven't done yet this week. Do it this morning, and then you can go back hunting or trapping this afternoon. You have to exercise all your skills. Foraging is as much about knowing the poisonous plants as the edible ones." Tommen continued before the boy could complain further. "Jason, you'll go out fishing. Harry, you can go either fishing or trapping."

"I'll do some trapping," Harry decided. "I've done fishing more than anything else I think."

"I'll come with you, then."

Tommen continued handing out the assignments. Other than JJ, no one gave any argument. The boys seemed to be catching on that every duty was important. With exception of the one who brought down a very unlikely bear, there was no more glory in fishing than there was chopping wood, or trapping versus foraging. Too bad it was only the last full day and they wouldn't get to really put that to the test. One week was great. How about a month? Or a year? Or a lifetime?

"What about you, Saul?" Tommen asked once all the boys had been assigned.

Saul gave him a look seeing how he was still chewing his food.

"Well," he said when he was done, "I figure I'll check on the pelt and see how its doing. Then I'll head out hunting one last time. The more food we get today, the less hunting we have to do tomorrow, and the less time we'll waste packing up."

"Do you need someone to go with you?"

"No, I think I'll be all right. I'm not intending on going after any deer or anything big. A couple turkeys ought to do it for us, plus whatever they bring in from fishing."

He said it calmly, generally a good indication that he was in an agreeable mood and open to acknowledging the existence of other human beings. Tommen jumped at the chance and took it in stride before he could change his mind.

The other tents finished up breakfast and the camp assembled into the various teams. Typically, each tent hunted for themselves first, but they tried to keep the teams balanced that way there weren't too many people splashing around the river or stripping all the edible plants bare, or any number of things. It also kept the hunting accidents to a minimum as only a couple hunters were allowed out at a time and only with three arrows. If a hunter couldn't bring something down in three, he was probably an idiot and the prey had gotten away, or the prey turned out to be a predator in which case he was going to need his knife because a long-range weapon was only good for so much. Or that was the theory, anyway.

"All right, here we go again," Tommen said as he and Harry started out on the trail. Ahead of them, Saul moved off the trail, slinking through the trees, bow in hand.

Each cabin used different colored ribbon to mark their traps, and it was considered as dishonest as theft to mess with another cabin's trap or take an animal in their trap. Wolf Cabin used blue ribbon. The first trap they came to was empty, but the bait had been scattered.

"How did this not trip?" Harry wondered, lightly fingering the line.

"Probably a turkey," Tommen mused. "They can peck the bait off the top without triggering the weight release."

"Maybe we should make a secondary trap for those stupid turkeys."

Tommen laughed. "Maybe we should."

They triggered the trap using a stick, then reset it. They tried to keep quiet as they worked so as not to alert or disturb the wildlife too much, but conversation was inevitable.

"So, you've been staying out of fights," Tommen observed. "That's good."

Harry shrugged. "Yeah, I guess. Don't take this personally, but Saul had more to do with it than you did."

Tommen raised a brow. "I'm not offended, but I am curious."

Harry laughed. "Yeah, I guess that is kind of a weird thing to say. No, he was right. I should know better than to get into such fights."

"Fights with white boys?"

"Mm...something like that. I mean, it doesn't reflect very well on me or the tribe; we face enough discrimination as it is. Fighting doesn't help. I mean, fighting with another tribal member, that's one thing. It's like bro fighting, you know? Everyone knows it's not serious. Or if it is a serious fight, then it's an honor thing. Any other kind of fight, though, and I'm just some loser teenager who's going to grow up to be a drunk like my dad."

"I'm sorry to hear that."

"I want to be better than him, I do. But I hate JJ."

"Why? He seems to be the one with the problem, not you. Don't let his jealousy influence your life. Defend yourself when necessary, but otherwise, if he's going to self-destruct, get out of the blast zone." Tommen spit a laugh. "Sorry, my dad's a cop. I kind of picked up a few things."

Harry shrugged. "Well, at least they're good things. My dad never taught me anything. He just drinks. Literally everything I know comes from my mom or my uncles."

"Then keep learning." Tommen got a step ahead of Harry and stopped. "Hey. Eventually you come to a point where you have to decide where you are going. Your dad can't dictate that to you. Your mom can't force you. You have to choose for yourself whether you are going to be intelligent and upstanding, or a loser. For a long time, I thought that the bullies at school were forcing me to stay a loser. Then I realized that regardless of whether I was an idiot or a super genius, they were going to harass me no matter what. Idiot or genius, single, dating, loser, jock, didn't matter. I was never going to be good enough for them. And I don't have to be. Neither do you."

Harry nodded. "You're pretty good at the pep talk thing. At least you seem to have a basic idea of what my life is like, or you say you do. Heh, Saul keeps me in line with my people and you keep me in line with myself."

They headed to the next trap.

Actually, that little exchange had Tommen feeling pretty good. He was able to use his past experience to help other kids who were going through it in their present. It made him feel special, and a little useful. He'd been a loser once, then risen above all that to become a super awesome physics nerd with a hot girlfriend. That was awesome and all, but there had, admittedly, been a lot of selfish pride involved. Reaching out to others, well, that felt pretty good. Did that still make him selfish? Was he self-seeking for wanting to use his experience to help others and make himself feel better in the process? He mulled it over but couldn't decide.

"This one's empty, too," Harry reported. He was ten steps ahead of Tommen looking at the trap.

This trap had not only been cleaned of bait, but it had been triggered as well, though with nothing to show for it.

"What could do that?" Harry lamented.

"Well, two things," Tommen said, squatting down to check the area around the trap. "Either it wasn't set correctly and triggered before anything got caught, or else whatever got caught was too big for it. A coon would walk in and get trapped, but a coyote for example would be able to slip its paw right out. Judging by the tracks, I'm going to say that's about what happened, too. Either way, it's not the end of the world."

They reset the trap and triggered it with a stick to be sure it was working correctly. Then they reset it again, added new bait, and did their best to hide their tracks and scent. Once they were satisfied with the setup and the covering, they started off north, making for the next trap. Wolf Cabin had five in all. Each cabin had been issued three traps, but between Tommen and Saul, they managed to pull off a couple more.

The third trap, one of Tommen's making, was also empty of any prey, and the bait didn't look disturbed either.

"Why would an animal pass this up?" Harry wondered.

"Maybe the right animal didn't come by. Maybe it wasn't hungry at the time. Maybe the human scent wasn't covered enough." Tommen shrugged. "There are any number of reasons why a trap doesn't work right. Best you can do is try to figure out the why, reset, and move on."

So that's what they did. They tested the trap to ensure it worked before resetting it, replacing the bait, and covering their scent as well as they could.

"How many uncles do you have?" Tommen asked casually.

"Oh, well, I use the term loosely," Harry explained. "Generally, in native tribes, everyone's an aunt or an uncle or a cousin or something of the sort. There's not a whole lot of distinction between blood relative and non-blood relative, at least within a clan."

"So when you say you learn from your uncles…"

"I learn from the other men of my clan. And sometimes outside the clan, too. The only time it really matters is for weddings. Then, I mean, suddenly everyone knows the exact family bloodlines. It's a little spooky. Like, when my cousin—my actual cousin—got engaged, my mom and her mom and his mom all got together and, like, just started spewing family trees out of nowhere."

"Weird."

"It's cool stuff, though. And these days, I mean, I can trace my family tree back a long ways and actually keep it recorded, written down, you know?"

Tommen nodded. "I know back about to my great-grandparents, but that's it. Maybe my great-great grandparents, assuming my dad has his names straight. A lot of seniors and juniors and everything else."

They were rewarded at the fourth trap, one of Saul's making no less, with a fox. It was a beautiful thing with a nice thick orange coat and bushy tail. As they approached, it bared its teeth and growled, but mostly it just tried to run away.

"Oh, shit, what do we do with that?" Harry asked, stopping dead in his tracks.

"Just like this."

Tommen went to a small tree and hacked off a branch with a V at one end. He Banded only a little bit, enough to jump out of the way if it became necessary. The fox watched him, baring its teeth and trying to circle back, keeping him in sight at all times. Scooping up another stick, Tommen poked at the fox from one direction. While the fox snapped at the stick, he took the V stick and drove it hard into the back of the fox's neck into the soft ground. It wasn't a very strong stick, and the fox could easily overpower it, but while he had one and a half seconds of surprise advantage, Tommen moved in for the kill. Just as the fox was about to break free, he sat on its neck instead, took his knife, and cut the fox's throat.

He jumped off as the blood began pulsing from the artery and the fox began thrashing like, well, a dying animal. It got in one last snap at his ankles before succumbing to the sudden blood loss, but it took a good two or three minutes for the twitching to stop and the blood to stop flowing so freely.

"That's how you do that," Tommen said. He held the knife out to Harry. "You get to do the other honors."

"Right." Harry numbly took the knife and approached the dead fox.

"Think you can handle it?"

"Yeah. No, I can do it. I've just never seen anyone dispatch an animal quite that way before."

"All right. Well, if you can do that and get it back to camp, I'll check the last trap."

Harry waved him on, and Tommen moved off. He'd never dispatched an animal quite that way before either. If it was too big to just quickly snap its neck, he would usually Band and either cut the throat or strangle it. This time, he really hadn't been able to Band except to give him an edge on his reflexes. That had all been entirely him that time. No cheating of any kind. He felt pretty proud of himself, actually.

The fifth trap was empty. Seeing how this one was the farthest from the camp, Tommen dismantled it and cleaned up the area. They wouldn't need all their traps to catch a little bit of breakfast. As he headed back, he checked the fox trap again, too, since Harry had already gone back to camp. It had been reset, but Tommen dismantled that one, too. The other three would have to do, or else they would be feasting on fish and wild salad for breakfast, and whatever Saul brought back from hunting.

His trek down the mountain was uneventful, but still his mind was whirling. This morning, he'd been more than ready to go back to the base camp and sleep in a bed again. Now that he thought about it, he really kind of liked being out on the mountain again. At least this time it had been more than a day. Maybe it was the pioneer in his blood that told him this was home.

He found a rocky outcrop and looked out across the valley. This was home. These peaks and these valleys. He was born and raised here. He was meant to be here.

Then his sentimental moment passed and he continued on his way, occasionally tripping over an invisible rock or root, all the while trying to find his way back to the trail that would take him to the campsite. That was the thing about these wild lands. There were no trails. No markers to tell him which way to go, or if he was even heading in the right direction. It was both glorious and infuriating.

But he figured he must have done something right as he found the trail and walked right back into camp. Harry had passed the fox carcass off to Charlie who handed the cut strips to Jason who was already grilling several fish.

"Looking good," Tommen commented, looking over the fox pelt. "I'd say you picked up a few things during your time here."

"Well, I've had a good teacher," Harry told him, still scraping off the fat. "Speaking of which, where is Saul?"

Trying not to let his dejection show, Tommen shrugged. "I don't know. I expect he'll be back soon. Or later. Saul does what Saul does."

With that, he made a quick trip to the river to wash his hands and arms of the fox blood. His clothes had gotten a little bloody, too, he saw. He rinsed what he could in the river, but changed once he returned to the camp and could get in the tent. Outside, some of the boys were already stripping the fish that were cooked and ready to be eaten.

"Save some for me," Tommen said, grabbing one and juggling it onto a plate. "Were the foragers able to find anything to flavor these with?"

"Foragers aren't back yet," Jason reported.

"Well, they better get back soon or else lunch is going to be pretty plain," Harry mused, grabbing a fish for himself and taking a quick break from the pelt.

Tommen hadn't even finished his fish before a party of foragers returned. JJ was not among them. When asked about his whereabouts, the others only shrugged.

"We saw him out there," one of the girls said, "but we didn't really keep tabs on him or anything."

"Where do you think he could have gotten off to?" Nathan wondered aloud.

"Maybe he fell off a cliff," Dan murmured.

"We'll give him another five, ten minutes," Tommen decided. "Maybe he just got mixed up on the trails or something." He shifted his seat. "How did things go otherwise? Looks like fishing was pretty successful."

So the boys launched into a few classic fish tales. First it was a competition of who had actually caught the most fish. Then it turned into one boy didn't catch the most, but he had caught the biggest. Another shouted him down, bragging about how he'd almost caught a fish and "it was this big!" But, of course, it got away. The others called him a liar and full of shit, and it was all downhill from there, though not in a bad way, but a sort of bro bonding way. They were stuck with each other in the cabin for the next three weeks, and Tommen had a feeling that they would be just fine.

"JJ still isn't back yet," Dan observed after a short time. "And it's been longer than ten minutes."

"Saul hasn't returned either," Harry said.

"Think they finally had their fight?" Charlie chuckled.

"That's what I'm afraid of," Tommen murmured, half to himself. He set his plate down. "I'm going to—"

He nearly went sky high and the whole camp came to a screeching halt as a single gunshot rang out through the air. For a full thirty seconds, everyone remained exactly where they were, no matter what they were doing. Sitting, standing, eating, everyone became a statue.

The stillness was broken by the rustling of leaves and stomping feet as JJ finally came off the trail back into the campsite.

"Where is he?!" Harry demanded, jumping to his feet.

"Who?" JJ stopped and stared.

"Who do you think? Saul!"

"How would I know where he is?"

"Didn't you hear the gunshot?"

"Yeah, so? What, you think I had something to do with that? I don't even have a gun!"

"Yeah, like you didn't have my knife?" Jason challenged.

"What the fuck?" JJ took a step back. "I don't know what you guys are talking about."

Before either side could say more, Tommen got between them. "Enough. We don't know what happened. It could be that there is a poacher out there somewhere and it's not related to us at all."

"Guns aren't allowed on Shawnee land," Harry stated flatly.

"As I said, it may not be related to us at all. We're in the mountains and sound carries. Who knows where that shot came from?"

It managed to smooth some ruffled feathers, but JJ was still skeptical about taking his spot at the campfire.

"Now then," Tommen said, "I think we should—"

He was stopped again as a long, lonely wolf howl echoed through the valley. In the distance, a few others took it up. Now Tommen's stomach twisted in real fear.

"Yawi," he hissed, staring up at the trail and the mountain beyond. He shook his head and grabbed a chunk of meat from the fire. "I'm going to look for Saul."

"Tommen, it's a mountain out there," Mr. Wilson said, approaching, looking just as concerned. "It's total wilderness. We can't lose you, too."

"I have to find him. I'll be all right."

"You don't even know that he's really missing," Jason pointed out.

Tommen hesitated, but nodded. "I do know. That was Yawi."

"Yawi is a myth. And even if he was a real wolf, how do you know it was him?"

"I just know. Please, you've got to trust me on this. I have a gut feeling that something is very, very wrong. I know how to track, I know how to leave a trail, and I know how to survive. I'm going."

He turned and started up the trail before anyone could protest further. He couldn't decide if it was intuition or paranoia that drove him out into the woods, but he figured that whichever it was, it was mixed with an equal portion of stupidity. First, he had no clue where Saul had gone, and if the man didn't want to be found, Tommen was sure that he had ways of making sure he wasn't found. Second, yeah, he knew a few things about survival and stuff, but that didn't mean he wanted to be stuck outside overnight with the lions and tigers and bears because of his own stubbornness. He cared for people and didn't want to see Saul wounded or worse, but sometimes his compassion overrode his better judgment.

Third, and most important, there was always the chance that the gunshot was related to the situation. If he had to hazard a guess, he might even say that the gun probably belonged to Rifun, a nice, big, shiny revolver with wood grips, freshly oiled. He could be running right into a trap of some form.

Tommen paused briefly and looked back the way he had come. He wasn't actually all that far from the camp. If Mr. Wilson had managed to conjure up even a small search party, he didn't have much of a lead on them. He tried to come up with reasons why he wouldn't want to be with them. There was safety in numbers and they could canvas a wider area more thoroughly and professionally. But then, if Rifun was involved, Tommen had no desire to see more people die. If they could talk alone, maybe he could save the need for bloodshed.

It was a stupid reason, anyway. That sort of shit spawned bad novels and movies. The hero foolishly tries to do everything himself, pushing friends and family away both physically and emotionally in the name of protecting them. Walter had done that, and it had nearly cost him his life. Of course, he'd also attempted a rescue operation with two fully armed police teams and still almost died. Was there no way to win?

Another howl split the air. This time, Tommen was able to get a better sense of direction. Northeast. He started plodding along. *Come on, Yawi, take me to your master.*

It also occurred to Tommen that he had brought only a knife as a weapon. He hadn't even thought to grab a bow or something. Rifun was the most dangerous thing on the mountain right now, but he was by no means the only dangerous thing. What if a bear decided to try a little human with his berries? What if a mountain lion managed to sneak up on him? He'd be cat chow in no time.

Way to go, Tommen, you've done it again, he sighed to himself. *You let your feelings escape before your brain could wrangle them in.*

Okay, so the analogy was pretty bad, but he knew what he

meant. One thing was for sure, though. No matter how much camping or hiking he did, he never seemed to build up the strength and endurance for when it really mattered.

Yawi howled a third time, this time louder, or maybe Tommen was getting close. He paused and listened, trying to assess any other threats in the vicinity. He didn't expect to hear anything, and he pressed on, homing in on the source of the howls. There were no trails here. If there were, he might have been able to cover the same distance in half the time. As it was, it had been probably forty-five minutes to an hour and he'd covered a mile, max. Probably more like three quarters of a mile.

Tommen jumped as something moved in the bushes, but it was only a deer, startled by his presence and bounding away, white flag bouncing along until it disappeared into the brush. Collecting his nerves, Tommen kept going in the same direction, but he couldn't just keep waiting for Yawi.

He stopped, then. Feeling the fool, he cupped his hands around his mouth and did his best to howl. If Yawi was as intelligent as Saul seemed to think, maybe the wolf would understand.

For a long minute, there was no answer.

And then there was. It was frighteningly close, and Tommen half-expected to see the enormous white wolf crouching behind a bush that was presently within arm's reach. Still, he turned in the direction of the howl.

The search took him up what almost amounted to a sheer drop in the hillside. Several more deer bounded away as he was climbing, and he could understand why Saul had chosen this spot to hunt. It was plentiful in game, and, once Tommen climbed up to a less steep slope, afforded an excellent view of the area.

A flash of white and a rustle in the bushes alerted Tommen to the presence of something big. Pushing through a small patch of brambles and low-hanging branches, he stumbled into a forest clearing. The first thing he saw was Yawi, but the white wolf was not as big and bushy and brilliant as he had been in times past. Rather, he was covered in blood and limping, looking like he'd just come out of a fight.

The big wolf watched Tommen for half a second before swinging its huge head around, as if pointing. Then Tommen saw.

Saul lay face-down in the dirt with five arrows sticking out of his back, hand still clutched around his own bow. Sliding in beside him, Tommen saw that there was a sixth hole in his back, a bullet hole.

"Shit," he hissed. "Oh, fuck. Oh, fuck. Fucking...fuck."

He put two fingers to Saul's neck, surprised to find a pulse, though it was slow and weak. Honestly, Tommen wasn't even sure if he felt a pulse in Saul's neck or just the one pounding through his own shaking body.

"Saul?" Tommen asked, shaking him gently. "Saul, can you hear me?"

Yawi nosed Saul's head and licked his face, but the man did not respond.

"Oh shit." Tommen sat back on his heels. "Fuck."

His mind went into panic mode then, but sometimes he had good ideas in panic mode. Such as his whistle. Good for buddy checks during swim week and for getting the attention of just about anyone in the mountains, assuming Mr. Wilson had dispatched a search party and they were anywhere close to the area to be able to hear the whistle and respond. Still, he had to try.

He went back to the edge of the sheer drop, put the whistle between his lips and blew as hard as he could. He did this several times, hoping someone would hear him. Behind him, Yawi howled again.

"Come on, guys, get the hint," Tommen whispered as he took up the whistle again.

After his third blow, he was rewarded with a response of someone else blowing their whistle in reply. Tommen returned to the clearing where Yawi was curled up around Saul as best he could.

"They're coming," Tommen said, unsure who he was talking

to. "They're almost here."

He put his fingers to Saul's neck again, but this time, he couldn't even feel his own pulse, if that was indeed what it was.

The whistle came again. Tommen stood and went a short distance to reply and hope to draw in the search party.

Some semblance of order came back to his mind, then. They couldn't just carry Saul willy-nilly back down the mountain. He would have to be carried on a stretcher or something. He barely had time to consider support poles before he heard shouting at the bottom of the steep slope.

"Tommen! Are you up there?!" Mr. Wilson shouted.

Tommen burst through the trees and looked down. "I'm here! Saul's wounded!"

"Is he conscious and breathing?" Michelle asked, stepping up beside Mr. Wilson.

"No. I can't get a pulse. He's been shot."

That put a little more fire under them. As they scaled the slope, Tommen saw there were ten in the group, and about half of them were boys from Wolf Cabin.

Tommen returned to the clearing. Yawi had gone. He put fingers to Saul's neck again. Barely a pulse. Maybe. Assuming that wasn't his fear acting up on him again. He looked back as the search party finally entered the clearing.

"Oh, shit," Michelle said, breaking into a run.

She all but pushed Tommen aside, but he was more than happy to get out of the way and let her work.

"Call 9-1-1 if you can," she ordered. "See if there isn't some way, somewhere we can get a rescue chopper. Otherwise, at least get them on the way to the trail head."

"Is he alive?" Dan asked. He and all the Wolf Cabin boys hid behind Mr. Wilson like frightened children.

"He has a pulse," Michelle reported, "but it's very weak. He's going to die if we don't get him out of here fast."

"What do you need?" Mr. Wilson asked. He tried to remain

calm, but Tommen could see the sweating and the fear.

"These arrows need to be secured." Michelle studied them for a moment, then slipped a slender hand under Saul's chest. "They're all the way through, so we need to secure both ends. Help me roll him onto his side."

"He's got a bullet wound, too," Tommen chimed in, moving to show Michelle the mysterious sixth hole.

She nodded and took a moment to address that. Then she and a couple others rolled Saul onto his side. She ordered them to hold him there while she did her best to secure the arrows.

"If they're all the way through, why not just cut the heads off with something and remove them?" Nathan asked.

Michelle did not look at him. "Because he could bleed out. If any of the arrows hit an artery, they're also acting as a plug."

"What if it hit his heart?" Charlie wondered.

"Then he would have died instantly and would not still have a pulse." She said it very matter-of-factly, but her expression betrayed the stress she was under. "What's the word?"

Mr. Wilson approached and knelt to be of help. "They said they can't send a chopper because of impending weather, but they're going to send an ambulance to the trail head with a wilderness rescue team; they'll meet us wherever we are on the trail or in the woods."

"How are we going to get him back to the campsite?" Charlie asked fearfully.

"Very carefully," Michelle told him. "But it's going to require some ingenuity and a lot of teamwork."

"That's why we're here," Dan said.

While she tended to Saul's wounds, Michelle began instructing them in how to build an emergency wilderness stretcher. It had to be modified slightly, given the terrain and the nature of the injuries, but it would have to work. They hadn't brought any kind of backboard with them, but they had rope and clips and other useful amenities. By the time they were finished and had tested its capacity by loading Mr. Wilson into it, Saul was ready to go, or as ready as he could be.

"Make sure his head fits in and around this hole," Michelle instructed. "Load him slowly, because I'm going to have to adjust these straps so the arrows don't get pushed back into his chest."

By this time, it had been probably two hours if not longer since the first gunshot was heard. Mr. Wilson and some of the stronger boys got into position to lift and move Saul. Tommen went around and took the bow from Saul's hand; his only comfort came from the fact that his fingers were still pliable, which meant there was a chance he was still alive. And if he was still alive now, there was every chance he would be able to make it to the ambulance and the hospital thereafter. He slipped Saul into a Slow Band, knowing it would scare Michelle because it would appear that he had no pulse, but it might be his only chance of survival.

Still, he took nothing for granted. Tommen elected to serve as a watchful eye as Saul was maneuvered onto the stretcher, Michelle moving the straps as much as she dared in order to accommodate the arrows. Viewed just from above, Saul resembled something like a porcupine. To see him from the side and how the arrows went right through his body, churned Tommen's stomach. He thought he might be sick. To cover it up, he went to the edge of the clearing and to the edge of the slope, as if to scout a gentler path down.

"Tommen, if you could be our guide, that would be golden," Mr. Wilson said, coming up behind him.

Tommen nodded uncertainly even as he spotted a slightly nicer path a short distance away. He notified the others of it and led the way, always making sure to keep an eye out behind him to be sure they didn't slip and fall into him.

"How is he?" he asked once they were on more friendly ground.

"His pulse is gone, and I can't do CPR with these arrows," Michelle said hoarsely, walking beside Saul, always checking the bandages and his pulse.

In a split-second decision, Tommen Banded and looked

around at the gathered team. Mr. Wilson had a look that was divided between sheer determination and sheer terror. This wasn't supposed to happen, not in his camp, not on his watch. Maybe Saul had it coming, maybe not, but for as much of an asshole as the man was, he didn't deserve to die like this.

Michelle's expression was about eighty percent professional, twenty percent panic. She had the training to treat and the experience to do it well, but sometimes there was no getting over the pants-pissing fear accompanied by such an emergency, that someone she knew and worked with was injured and had a pretty good chance of dying on her watch.

Rick and Shawn, the counselors, they were sweating something fierce, but they had the attitude of just getting something done and think about the details later. In contrast, the boys looked straight-up terrified, like they wanted to burst into tears, curl up into a ball, and cry. They had probably never seen anything like this before in their lives, however tough they professed to be.

Tommen released the Band and kept moving. He had a pretty good idea of where he was going, but every so often, Mr. Wilson redirected him.

"Do we have to go through the campsite?" Shawn asked. "I know the rescue team said they'd meet us wherever we were, but we can't just parade Saul through the camp in front of the rest of the campers."

"No, but once we get close enough not to get lost, we'll go around and Tommen will go ahead to the campsite," Mr. Wilson said. "If the rescuers are there, he can show them where to go." Without looking back, he asked, "How's he doing, Michelle?"

There was a pause, then, "Still no pulse, but he's warm. If he has any activity in his heart, it's minimal."

"Is there anything that can be done?" Charlie asked, looking about ready to sob. "Like an ice pack or something?"

Tommen did not hear Michelle's answer, if she gave one at all.

Getting down a mountain was infinitely easier than trying to get up, and it was the only reason that the trek back was about the same length of time as the trek out. Tommen figured the initial journey had been about an hour, and the return seemed about as long. Eventually, he began recognizing trees and landmarks, and he caught sight of a pink ribbon for another cabin's trap.

"Tommen, go ahead to the campsite," Mr. Wilson ordered. "We'll take a slightly different route. Direct the rescuers back down the trail to the road. We'll meet you."

Tommen nodded and bounded off, running down the slope, acutely aware that he could trip and fall and go careening into a tree at any moment. He did stumble, once, but managed to catch himself before he went headlong into the dirt. Once his feet found the main trail, he pushed himself even harder.

He slowed only once he got to the camp itself. As he looked around, he spotted the team in the red suits, speaking to one of the counselors.

"We got him," Tommen said breathlessly, approaching them on legs that apparently thought he was still running full steam.

"I'm sorry?" one of the men asked.

"Saul. We got him. They're heading for the trail now, around the campsite, so they don't have to come straight through and scare the kids. Come on."

He didn't check to see if the rescue team followed, just headed for the exit trail. After a minute, one of the men, the leader he assumed, caught up to him.

"What exactly happened? We were dispatched for a hunting accident."

"He's got five arrows in his back," Tommen reported. "And one bullet."

"Guns aren't allowed on Shawnee land," one rescuer growled. To look at him, Tommen suspected the man was Shawnee himself.

"It is what it is."

"Did you find him?" the leader asked.

"Yeah. He didn't respond to anything, and the last I knew..."

He didn't get a chance to finish as they rounded a corner and intercepted the search party.

"Five arrows, one bullet," Michelle reported, exhausted from the hike. "His pulse is gone, but he's still warm."

"Time to hoof it, then," the leader said as he and his team gave Saul a quick assessment. "Who's got the AED?"

Tommen folded his arms. "An AED only corrects the heart; it won't restart it." He knew that much from looking in his dad's medical books.

"True," a rescuer said, "but if he's still warm after all this time and in this weather, his heart might still be functioning just enough for this to work."

"What about the arrows?" Rick asked. "These are metal arrows."

It was hell trying to get Saul in a position where the pads could be stuck on, but the rescue team managed to do it while moving him to their own rescue basket. Tommen dropped the Band. One of the rescuers answered, "No one should be touching him anyway, so it shouldn't transfer to anyone. The worst it will do is burn him a little, but it might help to cauterize the wounds internally. And at this point, we don't have a choice. Everyone clear?"

As predicted, one shock managed to get a pulse moving through him again. Mr. Wilson and the others were more than happy to surrender Saul to them to carry. As the team started off down the trail, Mr. Wilson hung back for just a second, instructing Rick and Shawn to take the kids back to camp and keep them quiet until the rest of them got back.

Tommen would claim he was too busy trying to keep up with the team to have heard Mr. Wilson say he wanted him back at camp, too. He couldn't just abandon Saul. He had to see this through to the end. So he ended up accompanying them down the trail, Banding Saul whenever he could.

They stopped again when his pulse faded out, shocking it back to life after three tries. Five minutes later, it was gone again.

Running down the trail with a team of rescuers didn't take nearly as much time as walking up the trail with a bunch of campers, and the ambulance came into view, crew ready with a cot.

"Five arrows, one bullet," the rescue team reported. "We keep losing his pulse, and it doesn't come back easy."

"We need to cut these shafts down," one medic said as they transferred Saul to the cot.

One of the rescuers had heavy-duty snippers which were able to cut the shafts down to a more manageable size. While he did that, the other medic started an IV.

"Anyone got information and a history on him?" the first medic inquired.

"I know a little," Tommen said. "His name is Saul Wolf."

"He's got a prior back injury," Michelle jumped in. "Prior military, IED screwed up his back. He still has shrapnel embedded in his spine which has been causing some severe problems lately. Other than that, if there was anything wrong, he'd never admit to it."

The medics seemed less than thrilled with the scant information, but once the well ran dry, they had to move on and get packing. They gave all the rescuers and the search team brief thanks, took down Mr. Wilson's contact information, then packed it up and blew out onto the road, lights flashing, sirens wailing.

The rescue team got some more information after that. It was a combined team made up of Indians and non-Indians. Needless to say, the Indians were less than thrilled about a gun being brought onto their land, especially since it had resulted in such an injury. Still, Mr. Wilson and Tommen and the others did their best to report everything they had seen, heard, and done. When all was said and done, the head rescuer simply shook their hands, wished them well, then the team packed up their gear and drove away, leaving the three of them standing there in the dirt lot, looking down the empty road.

Chapter Twenty-Nine
One Less

Tommen couldn't remember what story Mr. Wilson told the campers once they got back. Certainly it wasn't anything about a mysterious murder, though those rumors would probably circulate once the Wolf Cabin boys who had been there found their tongues again, buried somewhere beneath their fear.

In the meantime, he had meandered his way toward the river, sitting on a large boulder with Saul's bow and quiver on his lap. The quiver and arrows had blood on them, but the bow was as pristine as ever.

There was only one way Saul could have taken five arrows and one bullet and have no defensive wounds to show for it, and that was because it had happened just that fast. The only one who could do such a thing would be Rifun, the same way he'd helped Cassius murder those women and make it look like they'd just stood there and asked for their deaths. Probably he'd shot Saul first, then went up and stuck five arrows in him. Tommen was no expert, but for the arrows to go straight through Saul, they would have had to have been close range, and Saul was no rookie when it came to tracking and being aware of his surroundings.

No one came to get him, assuming they knew where he was, and the sky quickly went dark. In a way, Tommen almost expected Yawi to come sniffing around, maybe looking for his master, or even just to the river to drink and wash his wounds. Had Yawi tried to defend Saul? Had he attacked Rifun and tried to drive him off? Had he killed Rifun? Or had he just been a figment of Saul's—and Tommen's—imagination?

A rustle in the bushes alerted him to the presence of someone else, and he half-expected Rifun to appear, grinning nonchalantly and making threats. Instead, it was Mr. Wilson. He took a seat on a smaller rock about five feet away.

"I just got off the phone with the hospital," he said quietly, studying his folded hands. He looked up. "Saul never made it off the table. Unofficially, he never made it to the ER in the first place."

Tommen did not look at him, instead choosing to look at the bow, barely visible in the starlight. He hated to admit it, but while he did feel saddened, he also didn't really feel anything. He'd only known the man for six weeks and working with him had been half a nightmare in itself. But he had no desire for him to die this way, whether by Rifun's hand or not.

Finally he asked, "What do we do now?"

Mr. Wilson shifted position. "Well, the Shawnee are less than pleased that someone brought a firearm onto their land, so they're going to be conducting an investigation. Once we're back at camp, I'll go through his file and get a hold of his next of kin, or emergency contact, whoever."

"I can do that," Tommen said. "I know who to call."

"I won't ask you to, and I'll be doing it anyway. Don't beat yourself up." He shifted again. "It's too late and too dark to start packing up and head back to camp, but we're going to skip all the trapping et cetera tomorrow. It's just going to be a pack and go from first light."

"What about the kids? What have you told them?"

"I haven't told them yet. All they know right now is that Saul's in the hospital."

"What are you going to tell them?"

"The truth. It's only right. Saul Wolf died in a hunting accident. That's all they need to know."

"So the hospital acknowledges that it was murder."

"Well, he didn't shoot himself in the back. And it's pretty hard to dismiss one bullet and five arrows as just an 'accident.' But the investigation we're going to leave to the Shawnee. You may be contacted to give some kind of witness testimony."

Tommen nodded. "I know. How is it going to go over, since Saul wasn't Shawnee?"

"Damned if I know. That's tribal politics, and I'm not even going to touch it."

"Fair enough."

"What about the kids, though? Who's going to be the counselor now?"

"As I said before, I'll step in and help. And if need be, I'll take over." He studied Tommen. "If you need to talk, I'm here. Or if you just want to pack up and go home, I completely understand. All the kids, especially the ones who were there, they'll all have that option."

Tommen let out a breath. "No, I'm going to stay."

"Don't make a decision now. You need to get some sleep tonight and think it over, and we still have to get back to camp." Mr. Wilson paused. "I'm putting you in charge of his things, making sure everything gets back to camp and packed up so his family can retrieve them."

"Okay."

Mr. Wilson shifted position. "Is there anything you'd like to say or talk about?"

Tommen shrugged. "Like what? I didn't know him well or anything, and he was a pain in the ass to work with."

"Maybe, but you were also the one who found him, and that can be traumatizing."

Tommen chuckled stupidly and looked at him. "Last fall, me and a couple buddies found a dead body under the bleachers at our school soccer fields. First one I'd ever really seen, you know, for real, up close. My dad got in a shootout with the person responsible and he was shot in front of me. I held my dad in my arms while he bled to death, or close enough." Tommen shrugged. "He lived. One of my friends got hit by a truck, had a piece of rebar go through his leg; he ended up losing the leg." He looked away and searched for words. "I don't know if it's just me that's bad luck or what."

"Tommen, you can't blame yourself," Mr. Wilson told him.

"The thing is, though...I don't. I don't blame myself necessarily, but I also don't really feel anything. There's nothing there to feel."

"I think there is. You just don't know how to express it in words. But keep talking."

"There's nothing left to say. We've got three weeks of camp left, and I'll be doing it without Saul. I mean, it's almost a relief, until you consider why he won't be there." He shook his head. "I don't know." He took the bow and quiver and got off his boulder. "Guess I should get some of his things packed up."

Mr. Wilson also stood. "I'll tell the other counselors and they can tell their tents. You can tell your boys. All right?"

"Sure, I guess."

They returned to the campsite where it appeared that most of the campers had been herded into their tents while the counselors waited around impatiently. Mr. Wilson took them aside to talk while Tommen made for his tent. He looked back only once to see the dim expressions of the other counselors as Mr. Wilson broke the news: Saul was dead.

Dan had the lantern turned on in the tent, but none of the boys looked particularly eager for ghost stories this night. They watched Tommen with wide eyes as he dropped off the bow and quiver, then sat on Saul's sleeping bag. Immediately, he was barraged with questions.

"What happened?"

"Where were you?"

"Is it true he was attacked by a moose?"

"Is Saul okay?"

Tommen took a breath, feeling his whole body start to shake as he answered, "Saul is dead."

Silence.

"He was out hunting, and someone shot him in the back. That was the gunshot we heard. Then whoever it was also put five arrows in his back. He never made it to the hospital."

More silence.

"If anyone needs to talk, I'm here, or Mr. Wilson is available, too. Come tomorrow morning, we're just packing up and leaving to head back to camp. We're not doing morning trapping or fishing or anything like that. Similarly, if anyone here—" He looked at Dan and Charlie and the others who had be on the search party. "—wants to go home, Mr. Wilson said he'll arrange it."

Still there was silence. The boys looked around at each other.

Finally, after a minute or two, Charlie asked, "Does that make you the counselor now?"

Tommen shrugged. "I suppose, in a sense. Mr. Wilson said he would also step in."

"Are you leaving us?" Harry wondered.

"I don't expect so, but I haven't made up my mind yet. We'll see how tomorrow goes. Until then, I suggest we all get some sleep, but I'm going to be just a minute."

The boys wordlessly slipped into their sleeping bags and Dan turned off the lantern while Tommen stepped outside and brought out his phone. He didn't have the best signal, but it managed to get through, though he still had to wait a few seconds before anyone picked up.

"Hello?" Micaiah answered grudgingly.

"Cai, it's Tommen."

"Yes, that's what the Caller ID said. What is it?"

Tommen took a breath. "Saul is dead."

"What?" He could imagine Micaiah sitting up, and he heard Kayla's muffled voice in the background. "What do you mean he's dead?"

Tommen wandered off as far as he dared before giving Micaiah the story, everything from Saul going off hunting, to his not returning, to the gunshot and the wolf howl, to the search party and the rescue attempt. He described everything as vividly as possible, which wasn't difficult since the images were seared into his mind's eye anyway.

"Fuck," Micaiah sighed.

"I think it was Rifun," Tommen said.

"I imagine so."

"Mr. Wilson said he wouldn't be able to notify his family until we get back to camp tomorrow. I was kind of hoping you'd be able to get through to them tonight."

"Yeah, I can do that." He sighed. "Fuck. Oh, they're not going to be happy about this. But one thing is for sure, Rifun will never get any allies or apprentices out of the Krydik. He's just made them sworn blood enemies for life."

"That's...good? Isn't it?"

"Well, doesn't matter right now, I suppose. Yeah, I'll see if we can't contact his brothers and get them here to claim his body."

"Okay." Tommen let out a breath.

"Hey," Micaiah said.

"What?"

"How are you doing?"

"Okay. I mean, not my first body, and it's not like I knew him that well."

"I don't care. How are you doing?"

"Fine, I guess. I don't know. Right now I just want to get some sleep and worry about all of this tomorrow."

"All right. Fair enough. But if you need to talk or anything, you can call me or Micah or your dad. I'm sure you could call Kayla, too, if you really wanted."

"No, I'll be okay. Listen, I have to go. I'm just exhausted."

"I imagine you are. Take it easy, all right?"

"Sure."

Tommen hung up and closed his eyes, tried to breathe. It was going to be all right. He just had to sleep on it and wake up with a clear head. When he opened his eyes, however, he almost expected to see Rifun standing there, waiting for him. Was he really that paranoid?

He made his way back to the tent and picked his way over the boys until he got to his sleeping bag. In the dark, it was almost surreal. He could almost pretend Saul was in his usual spot by the entrance.

By morning, though, the fantasy was over. As promised, Mr. Wilson had woken everyone up at the crack of dawn to get them moving and packing and ready to go. They'd probably arrive back at camp in time for a late breakfast or early lunch.

Gradually, the boys filed out of the tent with toothbrushes and toothpaste, but Tommen stayed behind to pack up Saul's things. The good news was that the man had traveled light, requiring only the barest essentials. All of his things managed to fit in one backpack, less the sleeping bag, pillow, bow, and quiver.

By the time Tommen emerged from the tent, having packed up his things, too, it looked like most everyone was just about ready to leave. Mr. Wilson approached him.

"How was last night?" he asked.

Tommen shrugged. "Night was fine. Day brings the reality."

"And the philosophy. How are you doing?"

"Fine, I guess. Did we really have to tell the kids that Saul died? Why not just say he was wounded and would be in the hospital for a while and wouldn't be coming back to camp?"

"Because that would be dishonest to them and disrespectful to the dead. These aren't the little kids who have never seen death. They're older, and they can handle it. It will be difficult; the boys who were there will probably have to talk to someone about it, but they'll recover. Just like you will, in time."

Tommen shrugged. "Doesn't bother me that much."

"Don't play the tough guy. Talk to someone if you need it. Otherwise, how are things coming?"

"Just need to get the boys' things out of the tent and pack that up. Then we're good to go."

"Sounds good."

When he returned to the tent, however, he found that the boys were already in the middle of taking it down. Tommen offered them a few pointers as he put the last of his things away, but otherwise left it in their hands. For once, even Harry and JJ weren't bickering over every little thing. Actually, all the boys appeared to be pretty docile this morning. They did things well, but they also seemed to move in slow motion, and they ended up being the last ones to pack up and be ready.

"The buses are almost to the trail head," Mr. Wilson announced, not anywhere near as cheerful and upbeat as he normally was. "If we make good time, we'll get back to camp that much sooner, which means breakfast that much sooner."

Truth was, though, there was still some meat and forage left, at least enough for most everyone to have a light snack. Tommen declined, passing his off to one of the boys. He wasn't really hungry. Maybe he would be by the time they got back to camp, but he didn't want to tease his stomach right before going hiking. It would cause cramps, or that's what he told himself.

As they started down the trail, Tommen could only recall how hurried they'd been just yesterday. All eleven of them, racing just as fast as they could, stretcher in hand. Faster, faster, hurry, hurry. Meet up with the professional rescue team and hand off to them. Saul's pulse had gone, but they were able to revive it, if just barely. Keep going, faster, faster, had to make it to the ambulance. Saul lying there with five arrows in his back, on his way to death faster than the hospital.

One of the campers tripped then and cried out in pain. Tommen's heart jumped out of his chest, but his body did not move. After a brief assessment from Michelle, the camper's ankle was wrapped and she continued limping between a couple of her friends. Nothing life-threatening or even moderately serious here. Just an ankle.

The girls were markedly less affected by Saul's death, but that may have just been because they rarely interacted with him. Anything they did hear from him or about him pegged him as a cranky old man with a bad attitude. That wasn't to say none of them were affected, or that any of them were unaffected. It was difficult to comprehend that one day a person was here, and the next day they had died, riddled with arrows on the side of a mountain.

"Who is going to claim him?" Harry asked, walking up beside Tommen.

"Well, I hear he has two brothers and a sister, and they're probably going to be the ones to come down and get him," Tommen answered.

"That's good. He'll probably get a full tribal burial with military honors. That's pretty high honors, if you didn't know."

"I don't know how he'll be buried or treated. Rest in peace is the most I think anyone can hope for."

Everything still felt like it was moving in slow motion as they continued their trek down the mountain. Eventually, Tommen started feeling the effects of his empty stomach as he got light-headed and his limbs turned to jelly. He stopped once to chug some water, but it did little to help.

"You all right?" JJ wondered.

"I'm fine," Tommen told him. "Just ready to get back to camp."

JJ nodded. After a moment, he said, "I hated him. Honestly, I thought he was a first-rate asshole. Now I feel guilty about it."

Tommen hesitated, trying to choose his words carefully. "Saul had a lot of problems which we can't appreciate. His time in the Marines certainly wasn't good to him. But he tried to do good, same as the rest of us. He just had a little harder time than most."

"I think he hated me, too."

"Well, as he himself said, he was equal opportunity. He hated everyone equally. And that's not so much a reflection of you as it is a reflection on himself and his struggles."

Tommen felt like he was spewing pithy quotes from long-dead thinkers and psychologists, and he could see it wasn't having the best effect on JJ either. Regardless of how intolerable the man could be — could have been, no one had wanted it to come to this, not really.

When they reached the buses, Tommen was one of the last ones on, lugging his stuff and Saul's stuff, too. He sighed as he realized he still had to pack up Saul's stuff in the cabin, too. There wasn't much, but it still felt like a heavy chore. But still, one thing at a time.

Mr. Wilson gave some kind of speech to the kids, trying to reassure them, trying to get them excited for the rest of camp, congratulating them on everything they'd accomplished so far. Most of them reacted, but Wolf Cabin was noticeably absent from the whole thing, each person lost in his own thoughts. When they started rolling out of the little dirt lot, Mr. Wilson moved to sit beside Tommen.

"So, how are things on the home front?" he asked.

"Good," Tommen answered, shrugging. "Just thinking about the stuff I have to do when we get back to camp. His family's been notified, by the way. His brothers are going to come and get him."

"You're sure about this?"

"Sure as I can be."

"Well, I'll give them a call anyway when we get back, make sure they know that they have the sympathies of the camp and the Powers That Be."

Tommen shrugged again. "Whatever you need to do."

"You called your dad yet?"

"No, not yet. Figured I'd wait until we got back and I had better reception. And it's during the day."

"Well, there is that. Have you considered whether you're going to stay or go home?"

"Right now, I'm still planning on staying. I mean, the shock is wearing off I guess. Once I get Saul's stuff picked up and sent off, I'll probably be okay."

"Well, I admit that it may not be as awful as losing a close friend you've known for years or a family member, but you worked with him nonstop for six weeks, got to know him somewhat decently, and you found his body. It's a lot to take in. Are you sure you're all right?"

No. "I'll be fine. Time and distance, all I need."

"If you say so. I won't force you to stay or go right now, but if you're going to leave, I'd like to know by tomorrow evening, maybe Sunday morning, just so I can get some things rearranged and whatnot."

"Understood."

Mr. Wilson put a hand on his shoulder. "You're a good kid, Tommen, and I'm sorry this had to happen to you at all, never mind that it's your first year. Trust me, this isn't a regular thing."

"It is if you hang around me for too long."

Mr. Wilson's expression was unreadable, but he did not say anything more as he stood and moved on to sit and speak with each of the boys in turn. Tommen's phone jingled. It was Micaiah.

"Saul's family have been notified. They'll be on their way soon."

"We're still on the road back to camp," Tommen informed him.

"Just letting you know. They're going to claim his body first, then retrieve his stuff, so make sure you get everything around and packed up."

"Will do."

"I also told your dad about it."

"Fuck. Why?"

"Because I didn't know if you were going to, and he needs to know. Mostly he just needs to know you're safe."

"For now. God knows what's waiting for us at camp. Maybe Rifun vandalized it again. Maybe he burned it down completely."

"Even so, your dad knows now. I told him to lay off for today in order to give you a chance to call him and tell him, but he'll probably contact you tomorrow or the next day if you don't."

"Why are you doing this to me? You, Mr. Wilson, everyone it seems like."

"Because you're not the tough guy you think you are. I'm sorry. You've seen more death and destruction in the last year than most people do in a decade or even a lifetime. It will wear on you."

"I'm fine. I didn't even know him that well. And he was an asshole."

"Don't harden yourself, Tommen."

And that was the last of it. Tommen stared at the message for a long minute before shoving his phone back in his pocket. Everyone seemed to think he was frail-minded and thin-skinned. Yes, it was tragic. No, he wasn't going to go weeping and wailing off a cliff or anything. And he certainly wasn't going to call his dad and start bawling like a child. He was a man, and he could handle this like a man. He'd wait until dinner or something to call his dad, once he got Saul's things packed up and a good meal in his stomach. Once those two things were done, he'd been fine. And maybe a good night's sleep on a good mattress; that was probably in order, too.

Perhaps the strangest thing about the whole ride home was that he managed to somehow sleep on the bus. It wasn't particularly restful sleep, mind you. When he wasn't being jolted awake by one pothole or another, he was having fitful nightmares, all of them stacking on top of one another.

First it was the warehouse nightmare, where Rifun shot his dad then turned the gun on him. Then it was finding Saul face-down in the forest, arrows sticking out of his back. But there weren't just five arrows in the dream; now there were ten, fifty, a hundred, all of them sticking out every which way. Then the nightmares rushed together as he was suddenly back in the warehouse, except this time Rifun was shooting Saul in the back. The nightmare restarted and Rifun was shooting Saul execution-style in the back of the head. Then it was his dad lying in the dirt. All the dreams and nightmares meshing and twisting and convoluting into something that could only be traced back to a single element of fear.

Somewhere in there, he had a dream about a white rabbit. Or maybe it was Yawi or some other white wolf. And there were candles involved. And fire, lots of fire. Or maybe it was just a campfire, a memory of when Saul told his people's creation story. It was so hard to tell one thing from another; they just kept running together in an endless carousel of terror and confusion and memory. It made it impossible to sleep, yet Tommen found that he could not wake up.

He thought he might have had a dream about Becky, too, but by the time his mind registered her in the dream, she was gone. When he tried to run after her and bring her back, he discovered that he was on a rocky, rutted path, climbing ever upward. He kept climbing, determined to find whatever was at the top of this mountain, be it Becky or Rifun or something else entirely. As the path turned east, he found only fire. He put his hand up to shield it, but not in time to avoid the hole that had opened up under him.

He tripped and fell and landed face-first in the seat in front of him. Tommen jolted awake, momentarily unsure of where he was. Then the bus hit another pothole. Then another. Then it got off the pavement onto the dirt road and it all went to hell from there. Tommen rubbed his eyes and looked around; they were very nearly back at camp. All around him, anyone who had managed to sleep was just waking up, looking equally confused. Otherwise, any conversation was quiet and polite. Mr. Wilson was walking down the aisle, making sure everyone was awake and ready to disembark.

The camp still stood when they pulled into the parking lot. It hadn't burned down while they were away. All the new windows and doors had been installed, making the cabins look almost new. The buses squealed to a stop and the doors opened.

Some people had appeared to have recovered quite well from the events of the morning and previous evening. They flew off the bus, talking excitedly, ready to get back in the swing of things. Even some people on their bus seemed to have mellowed out, accepted the fate of their comrade and prepared to move on calmly, mourning the death and contemplating mortality in their own spiritual way.

Wolf Cabin descended the steps like a pack of whipped puppies who'd just been orphaned. Again, Tommen was the last one to move, hauling his stuff and Saul's stuff. He gathered the boys and spoke to them.

"Why don't you leave your stuff here or in the main hall?" he said. "Get some seats for breakfast or lunch or whatever it is. I'm going to gather the rest of Saul's things, and it'll be easier if everyone's stuff isn't in the way."

The boy's agreed wordlessly and made for the main hall. Tommen dropped his stuff off there, but took Saul's pack and effects with him down to Wolf Cabin. He was, however, surprised to find the door not only open, but a stranger inside.

"Can I help you?" Tommen asked.

The man turned. He had dark skin, though his black hair was buzz cut on both sides, with the middle just long enough to be slicked forward. He wore an unassuming T-shirt and cargo shorts with socks and tennis shoes. But it was the wolf tooth necklace that gave him away.

"Oh, sorry," the man said, extending a hand. "Blake Wolf. Saul was my brother."

"Yeah, that's kind of what I figured." Tommen showed him the necklace Saul had made for him. He indicated the backpack and other items. "I believe these belong to you."

"Well, these things do." Blake nudged the pack and sleeping bag with his foot. He picked up the bow. "This, though, this still belongs to him. It'll be buried with him. So he can hunt in the spirit lands." He managed a lopsided smile. "Not that I think he would have any problem with beating the animals to death, but it'll give him the option, at least."

"Is there anything I can do to help?"

"Um...if you know where his stuff is, if he's hiding anything. He didn't carry a whole lot with him."

Tommen went in the cabin to look anyway.

"You're Tommen, aren't you?" Blake wondered.

"That's me."

"He told us about you." Blake grinned. "Called you *Nigila*."

"Stupid white man. I know."

"Yes, but he also said that you were very determined and very stubborn."

"If that's intended as high praise, it's a little late to say thank you." Tommen straightened from where he'd been checking under a bed. "You already got his body, then?"

"Logan and Natalie—our brother and sister—they're on their way to claim him. We'll meet together again at home and begin the burial preparations tonight."

"Is night on Hlohi the same as night here, or what's your timetable?"

Blake gave him a look, then went back to packing. "He told you?"

"A mutual friend."

"Micaiah?"

"Yeah." Tommen sighed. "Saul gave me my first Akari lesson when we got back for the second camp. We were supposed to train together again when we got back from hiking."

"I'm sorry. I would volunteer myself, but I can do no work during the time of the burial ceremonies."

"You know the Akari, too?"

"All the Wolf Clan does. All the Wolf Clan speaks English, too. Or did you think that there are a lot of Europeans where we live?"

"Oh. Guess I never considered that."

"Perhaps once my brother is buried and has crossed into the spirit lands, then I can continue your training, at least for a short time while you are here."

"I do have one question, though. Why didn't Yawi protect him? If Yawi is supposed to be your great protector and defender, why didn't he anticipate the threat?"

Blake paused and studied him. "Saul also mentioned that you enjoy belittling other people's beliefs."

"Answer the question."

For a moment, Tommen thought he was going to refuse. Then, "The spirits are either good or evil, and within those, there are ranks. Some good spirits are more powerful than other good spirits, and some evil spirits are more powerful than other evil spirits. Yawi did defend Saul. But the evil spirit that rose against them was too great for him to handle."

Tommen scoffed and shook his head, murmuring, "Clever way of saying he wasn't faster than a speeding bullet."

Blake said nothing to that, though Tommen could feel the irritation coming off him in waves. Before either could say more, however, Mr. Wilson walked in the door.

"Oh, you must be —"

"Blake. Saul's younger brother."

"I see."

"Logan and Natalie are on their way to claim his body. Then we'll be out of your way and you can carry on as normal."

Mr. Wilson shook his head. "There is nothing normal about this. And I'm sorry for your loss."

"My brother has simply shed his physical body and stepped into the spirit lands. There is no loss here, though we still mourn his passing. He was a jerk, no one can deny, but he was still a good man and a good brother."

"Indeed. And he was a good counselor to these kids." Mr. Wilson shifted his stance. "Is there anything we can do? I can do? If you've got the time, we're just about ready to have lunch; you could join us."

Blake looked ready to refuse, then paused and reconsidered. Finally he nodded. "That would be greatly appreciated, *giwad*. At least until I get a call from Logan. Then we have to leave to prepare."

"I understand. It's ready whenever you are."

Mr. Wilson left then, and Blake began hauling things outside. "If you want, you can help me take these up to my car."

Tommen grabbed a couple bags. "Do you have cars in Hlohi? Or phones? Or any of that?"

"Wolf Clan operates partly on Hlohi, partly on Earth. We have resources available to us when necessary."

"I remember hearing something about Wolf Clan being charged with keeping an eye on things here to let those back home know when it's safe to return. Why do you keep waiting when it's obvious the glory days aren't going to return?"

Blake gave him a look that was impossible to read. "Tribal politics are complex, and the desire to change is as great as the desire to remain in the old ways."

So, basically, the only reason Wolf Clan still operated was because some group of people wanted to come back and assimilate into the land of technology and convenience. Or maybe take technology and convenience to the people back home. Tommen didn't find anything terribly complex about that, but maybe it was different for them, suspended between two worlds and unable to call either one home. And if some of them were truly as old as they said, old enough to remember five hundred years back when they roamed Earth's mountains, well, that was, as Micaiah said, a good way to keep a grudge alive and well.

They dropped off the stuff in Blake's car. Still Tommen felt nothing, or less than he thought he should. Saul had been brutally murdered, yet he was just packing away his things like he'd been fired by Mr. Wilson and told to leave and never come back. It felt cold, heartless, and Tommen felt nothing for it.

Blake looked out over the camp. "Saul told me stories about this place. He told me all about how he helped our dad and Logan build Wolf Cabin itself."

"You mean this is the first time you've been here?" Tommen wondered.

Blake nodded. "It is. I never cared for this sort of thing, though they all tried to get me into it. My assignments tend to be more on the side of the DNR and the Game Warden."

"Watching the game and the movements of the herds."

"Now you're catching on."

"What does the rest of your family do?"

"Logan doesn't come to Earth very much anymore seeing how he's married. Mostly he's dealing with politics back home. Natalie also tended to work with the DNR, Game Warden, and some government agencies as a...liaison, you might say. Between the Europeans and the tribes, whether Krydik, Shawnee, whoever."

"Hate to say it, but we're not exactly Europeans."

"You will always be Europeans to us. As long as you intend to conquer, you will be Europeans. Until you learn to share, you will never be Americans, whatever the lines on your maps say."

So it was a cultural thing, Tommen decided. He mulled it over for a second before deciding to let it go. Instead he said, "Well, main hall is this way, if you're joining us for lunch."

Blake followed him wordlessly to the main hall, appearing almost stunned when he saw just how many kids and staff were running around. The food smelled wonderful, though, and Tommen got in line eagerly. Should he be so eager? Shouldn't he be sick to his stomach and have no appetite? Was he that heartless, or was that just how it was? He couldn't decide.

"Are you new?" Pam asked amiably when Blake stepped up to the window behind Tommen.

"No, just passing through," he answered. "Saul was my brother."

"Oh, sweetie, I'm so sorry to hear what happened. We all are. If there's anything we can do for you, just let us know, all right?"

"*Giwad.*" (Thank you.)

They made it through the line and Tommen headed toward his campers, all huddled around one table. Half of them seemed to be recovering, talking and laughing nervously. The other half still looked pale as death.

"Eat up," he told them, taking a seat. "It's going to be a few hours until dinner."

"Who's that?" JJ asked, nodding toward Blake who still looked lost.

Sighing, Tommen waved Blake over.

"You're not comfortable around people, are you?" Tommen asked.

"People are fine, as long as I know them and I know what's expected of me," Blake said.

"Who are you?" JJ repeated.

"Blake. Saul was my brother."

"Oh."

That shut up conversation for a few minutes.

"How are your parents taking the news?" Tommen ventured cautiously.

"Our father's been dead for nearly twenty years," Blake said, shrugging. "It was one reason Saul became a Marine. Our mother, well, she's grieving. Most mourning is reserved for the burial ceremonies."

"Ah. No wife or kids?"

Blake shook his head. Then, surprisingly, he Banded. Tommen had become accustomed to the Akari Bands by now, how different they were from Time Bands.

"No, he wasn't married, though he did have an on-again off-again lover."

"Oh. Guess that's a good reason to Band and not say it in front of the kiddos." Tommen blinked. "Wait, so, he has a lover but no kids?"

Blake shrugged. "In the tribe, a woman may take as many lovers as she pleases. All children are hers by rights automatically, and her husband is considered the father whether true or not. Saul may have genetically fathered some children, yes, but according to social custom, they belong to her first and her husband second. If anyone knows Saul was a helper, well, it doesn't really matter because he has no say."

"Fuck. Is that why he came to work here?"

"Who knows? When Saul started working here, he wasn't in the best standing with the tribe and wasn't home all that often." Blake sighed and dropped the Band. "Saul was always troubled. If anyone got through to him, if he loved anyone, it was Natalie."

"Your sister."

"That's right. When she became engaged, she chose him as her blood-taker."

"Blood-taker?"

"Let's just say that it is a very high honor, and when there is more than one brother, competition can be fierce."

"Jealous?"

"A little, especially since we only have one sister."

"But, if she's only still engaged, and he's gone, wouldn't that honor, whatever it is, go to you or your other brother?"

Blake shook his head. "No. It is a ceremony done at the time of the engagement." He rubbed his eyes. "Natalie's taken it the hardest out of all of us."

"I'm sorry."

"She's the one who...I guess you could say she cared for him when he finally made it home after the Marines, when he was injured." He rubbed his eyes again. "I'm sorry, I don't mean to unload on you. You should be enjoying your time at camp, not listening to me ramble on."

"No, it's all right. Did you and Saul get along?"

"Yeah, I suppose. I learned to avoid him when he got in one of his moods. But when he was in a good mood, especially when he was teaching something, he was easily the best brother you could ever ask for. I think what really got him was that he was a traditionalist, but being part of Wolf Clan meant he had to also be a bit of a modernist. Ideally, he should have gotten married, because then he could have joined his wife's clan and forsaken everything else, all of this. But, life happens, and nothing else did."

Tommen nodded, even though most of it went way over his head. Tribal politics, tribal social customs, tribal this, tribal that, all of it a world and a galaxy away. He opened his mouth to say more when Blake's phone went off. He brought it out and studied the caller ID before answering.

"*Siya.* Uh-huh. Uh-huh. *Eyun.* Uh-huh, *giwad. Dami-jeno.*"

Blake hung up and stood. Tommen followed suit though he wasn't sure why.

"They got him?" Tommen asked.

Blake nodded. "Yeah. We're going to meet up and head home."

"You can finish your lunch at least, right?"

"No. Fasting begins now and will last until the end of the ceremonies. But I thank you for the kindness." He Banded. "When this is all over and he has been committed, if you are interested, I will come back and train you myself."

Tommen let out a breath. "I haven't even decided if I want to stay or just go home. If you are able to, contact Micaiah, and he'll get a hold of me. Then maybe I'll have a better idea. How long are your ceremonies?"

"Three days."

"More than enough time, then."

Blake dropped the Band. "I expect I will see you again soon, then." He nodded graciously to the boys, then turned and left.

After a minute, Tommen finished his own food, plus whatever Blake had left, then returned both trays and dinnerware to the kitchen.

"How much younger was he?" Pam asked.

"What?" Tommen looked up.

"Saul's brother. What was the age difference, do you know?"

"I don't know."

"Such a shame. It's got to be hard on him. All of them."

"He said that their sister is taking it the hardest."

"Yes, I would imagine so. Are you sure you're still all right? From what I've heard, you were the one to find him. Honey, if you want to talk, I'll make up some tea or whatever you want to eat, and we can sit down and chat. All right?"

Her offer sounded the most enticing because it involved food.

Still, he just nodded and thanked her before heading out to round up the boys.

"So, what do you guys want to do this afternoon?" he asked, trying to sound calm even if he couldn't quite muster up cheerful or upbeat.

"Some of the pelts need to be finished," Harry said. "I figure I could do that. Or if someone wants to come and help, I don't know."

"All right. You can do that if you want. Anyone else?"

A couple wanted to see if they could start a pick-up game of basketball. A couple wanted to kick a soccer ball around a bit. A couple wanted to get in a nap since sleep had been cut short that morning. Tommen simply told them that as long as they could be honest and police themselves, he would let them do what they wanted, but as soon as any bad reports got back to him, their free time would be decidedly less free.

The boys agreed and went their separate ways. Most of them were starting to come around, with a few notable exceptions. Well, give them a day to process it and think it over. He would ask after them in the morning. That would give him time to relax and process everything, too. He headed back to the cabin with a couple boys who wanted to nap. As they settled in and drifted off, Tommen dug in his bag and brought out his book. Even the past seemed more inviting than the present, and certainly more inviting than the future.

Chapter Thirty
Liaison

The Akarin had certainly seen better days, Kayla thought as she roamed the corridors of the fortress. By Micaiah's suggestion, they'd closed off their recruiting until they could determine who was trustworthy and who was untrustworthy. It seemed a cruel thing to do, and opponents noted that if promising new recruits were denied, then they could end up in the hands of the Cult or another heretical group. But, as the proponents had pointed out, the Akarin could be considered just as heretical if the leadership was corrupt. Where the leaders go, so do the followers. If the leaders were heading for a cliff, the recruits who didn't know any better would go right over with them. They needed to reaffirm their doctrine and have a stable leadership before they could start chastising anyone else about being heretical.

It was kind of refreshing, though, in a way. They'd plodded along in a mundane routine for too long; they needed to take a fresh look at things. Maybe if they re-figured out what the hell they believed and stood for, it would begin to heal the rift that had been forming in all the factions.

Some placed the blame for the rifts squarely on Rifun's and Cassius' shoulders. And it was true that they were responsible for most if not all of the physical aspect of their impending demise. But Kayla had another theory, and she thought it was proven correct when a new Book had appeared in the Archives. The Author was speaking again, trying to move them in a certain direction, giving them just enough of a hint that, if they listened, they might be able to avoid disaster.

But then, there were always the snooty ones who saw heresy in every word that didn't come from their own mouths. They didn't think it was right that the Book was about Tommen. Yes, he might be an Akari-bearer in the future, but he wasn't one yet, and he certainly wasn't one in the Books. What good did it do to read about someone who wasn't one of them? It would only encourage others to stray and perhaps embrace the other factions. Trying to explain to them the merit of seeing the bigger picture was like trying to explain the merits of fine art to a wall in the museum where said art was housed.

Kayla looked at the book, sitting on the shelf. *Time to Kill, Book One of the Chivalrous Welshman.* It sat right up there between *The Hand Holding the Knife* and *Wolf Pack.* The former was the presumed final book about the rise of Rifun and Cassius, and the latter was the first book about the Wolf Clan of the Krydik people. Saul's people.

She sighed and turned away. She still couldn't shake the image from her mind, watching Micaiah grouchily answer his phone in the middle of the night. Suddenly, he sat up, saying, "What do you mean he's dead?"

When she finally got him to tell her what was going on, he explained that Saul Wolf had been found high up in the mountains, dead, riddled with arrows. Rifun was suspected to be behind it. Micaiah had left, then, to go and inform the family. The camp director could have done so easily, but Micaiah wanted to waste no time, especially given the lengths the family would have to go to in order to get his body back home to be buried.

All of Wolf Clan were Time Agents in some fashion, but many were also Akari-bearers. Saul and his siblings were among the Akari-bearers, as evidenced by Micaiah asking Saul to train Tommen while he was at camp. Maybe that was what had gotten Saul killed; Rifun didn't want Tommen to be trained in the true Akari, and certainly not by the likes of Saul. Or maybe there was no reason at all except sheer opportunity. It was already proven that Rifun was insane, and with the loss of his power, he could very well be losing his grip on reality and so going on a crime spree of any opportunity. And nothing was above or beneath him.

Kayla left the Archives on the fifth floor and headed to the third floor. The staff had come to know her as she checked on her paperwork at least two or three times a week, if not more. She didn't think that it helped any, but she was eager to get going. They had five months left, but the paperwork was said to take at least a year or more. Wasn't there anything she could do to speed it up?

"Kayla, if you keep coming here, we will have no choice but to put you to work," the attendant said. It was not human, so its expression, body language, and tone were impossible to read to know if it was being serious or sarcastic. She hoped sarcastic. "Your paperwork is the same as it was a couple days ago. It's being processed. As you say, take a number and sit down and wait to be called."

The only reason it was funny and not infuriating was because the attendant had no idea how to correctly use the phrase, nor any clue as to what it was referencing. It was like watching a child try to quote a line from a movie but in a situation that wasn't quite appropriate. Darmok and Jalad with no backstory.

She was pretty sure the attendant was equally confused when she snickered at his attempts. Mostly she was just nervous and had it up to here with all the shit going on around her. Why was it too much to ask for a speedy registration so they could leave as soon as they were ready?

Just the other day, Micaiah had mentioned that a customer had walked into the bakery and made some comment about how the twins hadn't changed in ten years and how good they looked for it. Micaiah had brushed it off as all the healthy foods they baked and some other bullshit. But it was coming. It was here. The twins had been in their mid-twenties when they opened the bakery, and they still looked pretty darn good for being in their mid-thirties. Sure, some people didn't change a whole lot in that time, between twenty-five and thirty-five, but twenty-five and forty? Twenty-five and forty-five? Longer? They had to get out.

Some days, Kayla almost felt like beating her head against a wall, for as much good as it would do her. God, she was sick of interior design, dealing with snobby clients, the ever-changing design fads, and, God help her, but she was sick of Charleston, West Virginia. Fucking hell, but she had to get out of the city. She hadn't even been there that long, really. She'd lived on the outskirts for nearly a decade, making excursions into town to meet Micaiah or to meet a client. But moving into town with the twins, that was a whole new drag, and not one she cared for.

She considered heading down to the recreation area, then decided that she really wasn't in any sort of mood where seeing her home again would be helpful; probably it would only depress her more. She could probably doing one of her training regimens, but the last time she'd tried to do that, she'd been attacked. What she really wanted was to sit down and have a nice cup of tea and a nice conversation, one that didn't involve politics, religion, or death threats.

So she headed to the cafeteria. The nutritional cubes left much to be desired as far as comfort food went, but at least it kept her from gorging on snacks she knew she shouldn't have. She could do that just fine on her own at home. As she took her tray and looked around for a spot to sit, someone caught her eye. Getting closer, she saw it was almost exactly who she wanted to sit with.

"You look like you could use some company," she said.

"I'm not really in the mood," Natalie murmured. She looked like she'd been crying.

"I know. Which is why I'm going to sit here anyway."

So Kayla did, sliding into the seat across from her and picking away at the nutritional cube, wanting to look and gauge Natalie's thoughts without staring and being thought rude. Finally, Natalie spoke.

"Have you lost siblings?"

"I've lost all four sisters, yes," Kayla answered.

"How did that go? Because you were the only one exposed to

Time, weren't you?"

"I was. My youngest sister was abandoned in the snow as a baby, as was custom during harsh winters. The clan could not feed her. Perhaps someone else would find her or else a wild animal would. It sounds cruel, but there just wasn't enough food to go around."

"And the rest?"

"Two were slaughtered by the Russians. I and one sister and a few others managed to escape to a distant village that took us in for a time. Between the massacre and a prophecy I'd heard, I decided to continue on. Then I became exposed to Time and the Akari, and I never saw my sister again."

Natalie wiped away a couple tears. "Do you know what it's like for all of your siblings, your whole clan, to be part of Time? It's infuriating to see the same people day in and day out for decades, but it's also the most wonderful thing you can imagine. Time is something everyone wishes they had. I mourned for Saul when he left for the Marines because I thought for sure I would lose him. I was overjoyed when he returned home. But...I don't know that he ever really did."

"He probably saw things you and I can't imagine," Kayla said softly.

"Yes, he said as much. And I believed him. He told me a few stories, and I can honestly say I don't know how he did it, getting up every morning after that. He said that sometimes he didn't think he could. But the sun would rise, and there he was, right along with it." She sniffed. "I remember taking care of him when he came home. He was always in such pain because of his back. He still had shrapnel embedded in his spine because of the IED. It was so close to his spinal cord that no doctor would touch it. He had to live with that slicing into his back at all hours of the day for over ten years."

"That sounds awful."

She nodded dramatically. "I can't even imagine it."

Kayla did not say anything as she took another reluctant bite of the cube and waited for Natalie to continue. There was silence for a long moment.

Natalie sniffed and wiped her nose on her sleeve. "He was my blood-taker, you know." She managed a snotty grin. "Actually, he was my blood-taker even before I got engaged. I thought it would help him, give him a sense of purpose and remind him of his duties and his place in the clan. Then, when I did get engaged, well, no one would have to know; I'd just name him again."

Kayla shook her head. "I'm sorry, I don't know what a blood-taker is."

"Well, unlike what some of the other clans would have you think, it's not an ancient tradition going back to the dawn of time. It was actually invented after the Great Migration, when all the different tribes were learning to live together as one, forsaking old ties and becoming one Krydik tribe. It started out as a way of protecting the women of the tribe from rape. But as time passed and we maintained our matrilineal roots, it turned into a rite of passage."

"Do I get the details or just the history lesson?" Kayla leaned back and crossed her legs.

Natalie shook her head. "It's not important now. It's done, and he's gone. And I'm supposed to get married in three weeks."

"You can't postpone it?"

"At this point, it would be unwise."

Kayla studied her but elected not to push the issue. Instead she asked, "When are you burying him?"

"Um, we just brought his body home this morning. Or this afternoon. Whatever time it was. The men are having their time of mourning now and it will last until dawn. Tomorrow the women will have the time of mourning. On the third morning, we'll bury him and commit him to the spirit lands. We, as his family, will observe the final ceremony until evening when there will be a feast in his honor. And then it's over."

"Sounds nice."

Natalie shrugged. "Sun comes up and all is as it was. Worst part is, Saul was never a big part of clan life, or even a small part.

When he was home, he kept to himself in his little reclusive house up on the ridge. Did his own hunting and trapping, did his own housework. It started out as a form of spite and punishment, being isolated up there, but it only got worse as the years went on. Months would go by when no one would see him but me, and that only because I made the trek up there every day or every other day." She sighed. "Honestly, after the ceremonies, I don't think anyone will actually notice that he's gone."

"You will. And that's all that matters."

When she didn't reply, Kayla asked, "So, if you don't mind my asking, why come here? You don't come here to be alone, however much you claimed earlier."

Natalie shrugged again and looked around. "Have you seen this place? Not exactly a hopping establishment."

"Well, that much is for sure."

"After we delivered his body and the men began their time of mourning, I went up to his house to start cleaning it out. And I just couldn't do it. He didn't have a lot, but I couldn't just pretend like I was cleaning his house like any ordinary day. Okay, he was—is *never* going to return."

"Do you want help?"

"Huh?"

"Do you want help cleaning out his house and sorting his things?"

Natalie sighed. "Maybe later, once he's been committed. Then maybe I'll feel better knowing he's gone to spread his joy across the spirit lands." She snorted a laugh and even Kayla had to grin. "Oh, Aklaq, thank you so much for coming."

Kayla stood and went around the table to hug her as she cried anew. "I know, sweetie. I'm so sorry for what happened."

Natalie sniffed and pulled away. "If I ever get my hands on that motherfucker who killed him, he's going to wish he were dead. And then I'm going to send him to the spirit lands so Saul can kill him, too."

"I'm sure you will. And I think Saul would appreciate that, too." Kayla returned to her seat. "How are your other brothers?"

Natalie waved a hand. "Oh, Logan will be dealing with the political fallout once the men's time of mourning has passed. Some want a full-blown retaliation. Others are citing it as a reason to give up on returning. Let those who want to return, return, and seal off those who wish to remain. End the argument, I say. But the clans have already been divided once, during the Great Migration; the last thing Logan wants to happen is to see them divided again."

"And your other brother?"

"Blake? He's taking it harder than he lets on. It's the first death in the family since our dad. He and Saul never really saw eye-to-eye—well, Saul never really saw anyone eye-to-eye—but Blake was closer than most. On his good days, Saul was awesome, a good brother, good teacher, everything he could have been."

"How about your mom?"

"It's her son. He was murdered on foreign soil. How do you think she's taking it? She's the one who wants to retaliate."

Kayla just nodded coolly. "Of course. Hell hath no fury."

"I hate doing this. I hate all of this."

"I know."

Natalie sighed and stood. "I should be going. It's probably close to dawn by now, and I have to prepare for the time of mourning. As if I haven't been doing enough of that already."

Kayla nodded sympathetically. "I understand." She stood and hugged Natalie again. "And you'll let me know if you need anything, right? You can just ask and I'll come over to help clean or do whatever."

Natalie nodded. "I know. And I thank you. It means a lot. But I have to get going."

"Of course."

Kayla watched her leave, and she could only feel pity. She'd only ever met Saul a handful of times, but he was certainly a handful each time, crass, rude, sarcastic, grouchy, always ready with a sharp remark or insult. And yet she'd also heard from multiple sources that if you were able to catch him in the right mood, there was no one in the world you would rather be with. He was smart, funny, extremely competent, religiously observant of the ways of his people, practically a walking encyclopedia of every custom, tradition, and story. He was meant to be a storyteller, some said, not a warrior. But the grudges of the past, carried down from his ancestors since the Great Migration had turned him wrong. And look what had become of him.

She managed to choke down the rest of her nutrition cube and returned the tray and utensils. Other than going up to bother the paperwork attendant again, there was no reason for her to stay any longer. As she was heading to the portal room, however, she nearly ran into Micaiah who motioned for her to follow.

"Didn't expect to see you here," she observed. "Are you off early or have I lost track of time?"

"Um...I don't know." Distracted. Never a good sign. "I think I got off early. Doesn't matter. We have bigger things to worry about."

"Do I dare ask what?"

Kayla followed him back up to the fifth floor to the Archives where he began rummaging through some of the maps. The Akarin Archives were nowhere near as extensive as the Archives in the Wheel. If they did have something, it was easier to find, but there was no guarantee that they would have the item one was looking for.

"Cai, what are you looking for?" Kayla repeated.

"We got word of the first potential attack by the Borelians," he said, apparently finding the map he was looking for, spreading it out across a table. The Akarin Archives were also decidedly more old-school than the Wheel.

She looked at the map. "Where is this?"

"Quadrant Two...Parsec Thirteen..." He tried to make out the faded lettering. "It's a colony planet, I know that."

"Why not look up the information in the Wheel?"

"Because that's how it happened. A couple of humans from that colony planet opened up a portal to the Wheel to do whatever their business was, and a small legion of Borelians entered back through that portal and decimated the colony. Estimates are between two and four thousand dead, another ten thousand missing, presumed captured and enslaved. As of right now, all human travel to the Wheel is considered at your own risk and a general warning has been issued."

Kayla collapsed into a chair. "Shit. What are we going to do? We can't not go to the Wheel. Humans still have business in the Time industry."

"I don't know. I don't fucking know." He found a chair and sat down heavily, rubbing his eyes. "They expect me to be able to do something, but I don't know what or how. I don't know how to defend against the Borelians except to shoot their asses dead. But in order to get that out there, I need to be able to go to those places or send word. I can do that with the Akari. But, because of my other brilliant idea to seal off the Akarin, I can't train anyone new."

Kayla ran her tongue over her teeth. "Maybe you can."

Micaiah did not look at her, just stared at the faded map on the table. "I don't see how. There are nine human colony planets out there. And even if I do get those fortified, how the hell am I supposed to get Earth prepared? I go out there yammering on about alien attacks, abductions and whatnot, and they'll lock me up in the loony bin for sure."

"What about instead of coming up with something new, you work with what you already have?"

"Kayla, I have nothing left. Every time I come up with an idea, it backfires. I can't just bring them all here to hunker down until the Borelians lose interest."

"Then don't bring them here. Go to them. Train them there. You sealed off the Akarin because of the infiltration and suggested the small group theory in order to more intimately assess everyone. Take that beyond these walls. Send those small group leaders out. If they can be trusted here to evaluate those here, then they probably know a thing or two and can train the defenseless people out there. Even better, reach out to the splintering factions. Call in those who left because they wanted to fight. If they want to fight, well, there's some helpless colonies out there that need defending. Cai, this might be exactly what saves the Akarin."

"And what about the Hands who have forbidden the Akari wherever Time prevails?"

"Well then they can send in their own forces to fight the Borelians. You said it yourself, they can't do any worse than the Borelians can; it's why they were the go-to Grandfathers since the Dispersal."

Micaiah leaned back and rubbed his eyes. "Why did I agree to this?"

Kayla walked over to him and kissed him. "You didn't agree to it, but you did it anyway."

He sighed and leaned forward, elbows on his knees. "The Akarin have been too complacent for too long. Look at this shit. We're reading off of, what, papyrus maps? While the Wheel and everyone else in the fucking universe has moved on to at least twentieth or twenty-first century technology. It's not just the colonies we need to defend, it's everything. And it starts right here."

"What are you proposing?"

"How much time do you have?"

"As much as you need, I guess. I'm done for the day and don't really have much going on tomorrow. Why?"

"I need to do some research. Actually, a lot of research. I need everything, about the Akari, its history, Akarin history. I need to research those Books—" He nodded to the Authored books. "—and everything in them. I need a history on the other factions, even the Cult."

Kayla was scanning the shelves, looking for anything and everything available, which wasn't much. "What are you looking for?"

"Hindsight is 20/20," Micaiah said, clearing the table and replacing the map. "I'm looking for everything. And then I'm going to show it to everyone."

She still had no idea what he was really talking about, but he got sexy when he got dramatic, so she obliged the best she could, pulling out books and scrolls—scrolls!—as he asked for them. At first, they appeared to be random, as scattered as his thought pattern. After a couple hours, though, she started noticing a pattern, and she paused so she could read his sloppy notes.

"You're trying to start a Crusade," she stated.

"Not a Crusade," Micaiah said, scrawling something on a sheet of paper. "A Renaissance. I'm trying to unify all the Akari-bearers by reminding them what we stand for. And rather than have different factions and divisions based on the stupidest shit, we have different roles within the singular Akarin system. Instead of having a bunch of little chiefs ruling their own little factions, we have one body, one leadership. Together, we become a real force of might that can defend the colony planets, beat back Rifun and his Cultists, and meet the Hands of Time head-on in their tyrannical, communist regime."

"Nothing like a lofty goal," Kayla chuckled. "But seriously, what are you trying to do? You just got done preaching about how we needed smaller groups that could be intimate and trusted because larger groups—"

"Yes, I know. That's in this, too. It starts with the individual, but as a whole, we are unstoppable."

Kayla folded her arms. "Sounds like a Crusade to me."

He put down his pen. "Then what would you have me do?"

"I don't know. Maybe instead of rushing headlong into this, telling everyone else what to do, maybe you should do the research for yourself first. Figure out what the Author suggests."

"And lock myself in a library while another colony gets obliterated, its citizens hauled off to the most inhumane tortures known in the universe?"

"I don't want to see anything get destroyed, least of all the Akarin because you decided to play the pope." She paused and closed her eyes, tried to breathe. "You're using the Akarin to fight a different war. Okay, it's like Italy contracting the Vatican to go fight its wars. It's a bad idea and can only end in disaster. I get it. We, as humans, have two wars going on. The Hands have come against the Akari-bearers which are in the middle of our own civil war, and the Borelians have declared war on humans. You already went over this. But you can't mix the two like that."

"I don't know how to keep them separate. I see them as the same. The Borelians were the Grandfathers and if the Hands of Time were the right hand of the Time industry, the Grandfathers were the left. I don't see a difference."

"Then you have to adjust your thinking. Okay, you started the Akarin on the right path, I think. Getting everything cleaned up here is a good start. Let that work in its own time. I know you want everything fixed right now, but it's not going to happen. But while that's working, use your position as the...leader, ambassador, liaison, I don't know. But use your position over the Unengaged Civilizations to figure out a way to defend Earth and the human colonies from the Borelians. Have you talked to Mi Chin?"

Micaiah pinched the bridge of his nose. "No, I haven't."

Kayla started rolling up the scrolls and closing the books on the table. "Save the Crusade for later. Right now, you have politics to deal with."

"That sounds even worse."

As Kayla started putting things away, she heard Micaiah sigh and start talking. "You're right. I did go over this. With Saul no less."

"Yes, you told me."

He shook his head. "Cranky fucker, but he was right."

"Right about what?"

"Fuck everything. Fuck the Hands and the Wheel, Time itself. Fuck the Akarin because they're too busy bickering. Take the Akari and run."

Kayla nodded slowly. "Now it sounds like we have a better plan going here. Keep going."

"Everyone already knows about the declaration of war, so I

don't have to tell them. What I do need is to find trustworthy leaders, both Time and Akari, to either send to the colony planets or put in charge of them if they're already there. If possible, they are to train up their peoples to fight. Don't worry about what the Hands have to say because they can't do worse than the Borelians. And if the Hands do pitch a fit, well, they can send their own forces to fight the Borelians."

"And on Earth?"

"I need to meet with Mi Chin and explain the situation in a similar manner. We have to send word to all Time Agents and Akari-bearers and figure out who is willing to fight. Then we have to keep some line of communication open to the Wheel or anywhere else, via non-humans, to see if we can't track the Borelians' movements and patterns."

"There you go. Now then, take a deep breath. And breathe."

As he did so, she went up behind him and rubbed his shoulders. "See what happens when a plan falls into place?"

"That's the second time you've saved me from making a shitty mistake with my plans."

She raised a brow. "Only the second?"

"Okay, I've lost count, but the second time in the last year. I don't know where I'd be if you hadn't taken charge of my Time Trial plan."

"Well, that one might be a special case because of Doug and Cassius."

"But still, the first time around I definitely would have died. And Micah. And everyone else."

Kayla smiled and kissed him. "If that's your way of saying thank you, then you're welcome."

"How did I manage to live without you?"

"Now you're pushing it. What do you want?"

Micaiah groaned and leaned forward, dropping his head so she could rub his neck. "I want a way out of this. I want to go back to simpler days when everyone was who they were supposed to be and shit like this didn't happen."

"I know. I wish for that, too."

After a few minutes, Micaiah stood and faced her. "I guess I need to go speak to Mi Chin. If you're willing, I have a special task for you, because I think I know exactly where to start to get forces rallied and ready for war."

So it was that after a little research and a few failed portals, Kayla stood on an alien world. It wasn't too freakishly alien with four moons of all different colors and mountains that looked like swiss cheese and oceans with red, slimy water. Viewed from above, it might have looked mostly like any hardwood forest found in North America. Up close, differences could be seen in the trees and the undergrowth. While the migrants had brought over several species from Earth during the migration, there were some truly alien life forms mixed in as well.

It was about mid-morning, Kayla judged, moving through the forest in what she hoped was the right direction. From what she'd read, the Wolf Clan of the Krydik had made the mountains their home, just as they had lived back on Earth. The mountains here were not so different, though they were larger than the Appalachians, more like the Rockies. They consisted primarily of some form of red rock, though it was red only at its core. As the sun beat down on it, it turned a chalky white and would eventually break off in massive rockslides.

She walked about at the top of the treeline, just before vegetation gave way to bare rock. In the higher elevations, it was impossible to tell if the peaks were white from bleached rock or snow.

It was just past midday when she saw the smoke. She followed it until evening when she finally found the Krydik settlement, tucked neatly in the side of a mountain where the bleached rock had tumbled away. A river ran into the bowl valley, then down through the pass. Looking around, there was only one easy way in and one easy way out. As she tried to get close and walk through the pass, she was stopped by a couple of large warriors.

They said something she did not understand, but, judging by

their bows, meant something along the lines of, "No outsiders allowed."

"I need to speak to Natalie Wolf," she said, hoping the name would spark some recognition. If it did, the warriors gave no indication of it and repeated their warning.

Kayla sighed and searched for an idea. Finally she took a step back, cupped her hands around her mouth, and attempted a howl. She barely got two seconds into it before one of the warriors hit her in the stomach with his bow. She coughed and curled up to protect the injury.

They said something else this time and took a menacing step forward. Still recovering from the blow, Kayla took a few steps away, unsure quite what to do. Eventually she retreated a short distance down the path and looked around for another way in. Of course, it was entirely reasonable to expect that there were sentries posted all along the ridge. But then...

It took some doing, but Kayla was able to find a well-worn trail along the southern end of the ridge that eventually ducked below the treeline. Most would dismiss it as a deer path. Even she might have, if not for her earlier conversation.

Saul's house was a quaint thing, almost invisible between the trees and the bleached rock. Kayla did not dare enter out of respect for the dead, but she peeked in the windows out of sheer curiosity. It was one room only, with half of it appearing to be common living space, decorated with all manner of Native artifacts and weaponry. A bed sat in one corner, unmade. There was what appeared to be a tiny kitchen with rustic, handmade cabinetry. A wash basin sat empty on the counter. A tiny table with two chairs sat between the bed and the kitchen.

Immediately, Kayla knew she should not have come, not now. She should have waited a couple days, until after they'd buried Saul. She sat against one wall of the house, wondering if she should return to her own home or wait it out.

Eventually she did return home, explaining to Micaiah what

had transpired. He agreed that she made a wise choice.

"If you would have told me that was what they were doing and that it took so long, I would have told you to wait in the first place," he said matter-of-factly.

"I know," Kayla sighed. "I suppose I just got excited."

"Guess we're both a little flawed then, huh? A little eager to get this show on the road and get this war over with."

"Guess so. How was your meeting with Mi Chin?"

"Ah..." He ran his hand through his hair. "Less than what I was hoping for. She was already implicated once during the Dispersal, and she's not eager to get on the Hands' bad side again. I made the point that the Borelians are going to do much worse than the Hands, but no go. She might come around, but until she does, I might have to go to the Managers individually."

Kayla frowned. "What if there was another way? Some way we could pull rank and pull a favor?"

"How is that? Neither of us is trained."

"Not us. Assim Foyez."

"He's the District One Captain."

"But he was the Gatekeeper of Earth at one time."

"During the Dispersal."

"Yes, yes. Forget the Dispersal. He has the training. He has the experience dealing with Rifun. He probably has some experience with the Borelians, too; I can't imagine he doesn't have some knowledge after helping Tommen escape the Wheel."

Kayla folded her arms. "Okay, you have a point. What are you proposing? He can't just override Mi Chin; she's in charge."

"I'm not talking about going above her. I'm talking about going behind her. Behind her back."

"Using his training and experience as a rallying point for all the Time Agents willing to help us."

"If a Time Agent isn't willing to help, he or she can follow standard protocol under Mi Chin. If he or she is willing to help, he gets his orders from Foyez."

"You're talking about a secret underground network."

"Something like that. My point is, we can't do nothing. There are Time Agents and Akari-bearers willing to help, but we need some sort of structure of communication and accountability. Foyez can act as the Time Agent medium, and I can be the Akari-bearer medium. And because Foyez is Gatekeeper trained, Mi Chin can't accuse him of being inexperienced or unqualified, and acting on his own, he isn't in any danger from Regina, or no more than usual. Once again, Hands can't do much that the Borelians can't multiply." Micaiah shrugged.

"Foyez is an Akari-bearer as well, or he was," Kayla mused. "So he'll have a good idea of what's going on for both sides, same as you will."

"Exactly."

"Who do we have for the middle leaders? We're going to need, as you said, structure. Hierarchy."

"We'll have to see who we have first." He chuckled. "There, is that a good enough plan to pass your inspection?"

Kayla nodded coyly. "It is a good plan. But I'm going to take your plan and raise you to almost foolproof."

"Oh?" Micaiah raised a brow and folded his arms.

"District Nine. I don't think any of them are Gatekeeper-trained, so we might still need Foyez to lead, but use District Nine as your leading force."

"District Nine doesn't exist."

"Not officially, which means Regina has no jurisdiction. They govern themselves. We govern ourselves, and it runs across international borders. Put us in the higher positions and everyone else is just a grunt. What's the worst that's going to happen to them?"

Micaiah put his arms around her waist. "You're sexy when you scheme; do you know that?"

She shrugged. "I try."

"Then you can be the liaison between them and, possibly, the colony planets. The Krydik won't listen to me, but they will listen to you. Get District Nine involved, and it should form a pretty solid alliance. Once Hlohi gets in the fold, assuming they aren't obliterated in one fell swoop, then the other colonies should fall right in."

"You become the head of the Akari-bearer forces, and the package should just button up nicely."

He kissed her. "What did I ever do to deserve you?"

"You can be such a sap sometimes," she told him, but kissed him again anyway. She pulled away. "Okay, we have work to do. You call Foyez and tell him what's up. See if he wants to join. I'll run through my contacts in District Nine and figure out what kind of support we can expect from them. Then, in a couple days, I'll see if I can get in touch with Natalie again and talk to the Krydik."

Even as she spoke, she fished out her contact book and started flipping through the pages. District Nine was kind of like Fight Club, in a way. No one admitted to it out in the open. But when one was in trouble, the rest would flock to their aid. It was a nice sentiment when the problems were simple. She hoped this wasn't too far of a reach. So she started with the basics and the familiar stuff.

"*Nayaŋŋaq*," came the voice on the other end of the line. (Hello.)

"*Nayaŋŋaq, Putuu. Aklaq una itchuq.*" (Hello, Putu. This is Aklaq.)

"*Aklaq. Akkuni. Takupqaŋaruŋa.*" (Aklaq. Been a long time. Good to hear from you.)

"*Aagaluaq.*" (Certainly.)

"*Amiami, suliaqpich?*" (So, to what do I owe the pleasure?)

"I need to ask a favor. And it's a big one."

"Do you do anything small?"

Kayla laughed. "*Naumi*, I suppose not." (No.)

"*Sua-li?*" (What is it?)

So Kayla explained the situation, most of which Putu already knew. He was not an Akai-bearer and had no desire to be, but he wouldn't turn them away, the same as if they were any other human being, or, well, Time Agent she supposed.

When she was done, Putu was silent for a long time. Kayla

had to check several times to make sure she hadn't lost signal. When Putu did finally speak, every word was deliberate.

"The Borelians do not back down. They do not surrender. And they do not change their minds. If they have declared war on humans, it must be all or nothing."

"Unfortunately, you have the right of it," Kayla sighed.

"Are you expecting our help in your Akarin community as well?"

"No, not at this time. We believe we have that under control. We're asking help only for the Borelians at large right now."

Putu grunted. "And what do we get out of it?"

"You get to live."

"Oh, yes, of course, we all do. But what do we get from it?"

Kayla sighed. "Putu, I can't make any promises."

"Of course not. But if we have a standing agreement, then it not only motivates us, but it provides a certain...understanding."

"What do you want? Recognition as District Nine?"

"And live under Regina DeBitch? Of course not. We want to be our own Region. If we must surrender to Mi Chin or Assim Foyez, so be it. We have little desire to engage in Time politics if we don't have to. But for those times we have to, we would govern ourselves."

Kayla nodded even though he couldn't see. "Okay. Sounds fair. I make no promises, but I will do what I can. I would like to see that as well."

"Good to know you haven't left us completely."

"Of course not. I'll be home soon. Don't worry about that."

"With your husband."

"Naturally."

He grunted again. "I will speak to others in District Nine, and we will be in touch."

Chapter Thirty-One
The Elephant

Tommen must have fallen asleep at some point while he was reading because the next thing he knew, he was being shaken awake. He almost expected to see Saul and get a sarcastic comment. But it was only Harry, letting him know that it was almost time for dinner. Grudgingly, he pulled himself to a sitting position and looked around, trying to get his bearings.

Nothing appeared to have changed, not that he expected it to. Harry woke up the other boys who were napping, but otherwise, everything appeared calm and orderly. There was no screaming, and nothing seemed to be burning down outside. The world had continued to turn while he had slept. Which was good, considering the boys could have caused any amount of mischief and he would have just snoozed away.

Slowly, he got upright and managed to stand, stuffing his book, which had fallen to the floor, into his sleeping bag. He managed a stretch and looked around.

"Okay, who do we have?" he wondered, doing a quick inventory of the boys.

"Mr. Wilson got the others from basketball and soccer and whatever," Harry said. "The rest of us are here. We're ready when you are."

Tommen nodded. "Okay. Well then, if dinner is ready, let's get up there and get our seats."

It was strange. For as surly as Saul was, and as often as he sneaked away to do his own thing, he still kept everyone on track. Granted, he kept everyone on a tightrope when a single-file footpath was more appropriate, but he got everyone where they needed to be. Now Tommen was stuck with the job, and not only did he feel inadequate and unprepared, but being of an age with the campers, he would have much rathered been one of them and have someone else tell him what to do.

Still, they made it to the main hall without complication and carried on like normal. They waited patiently until the window opened and the line formed.

"Where's Blake?" Pam asked as Tommen went through.

"He had to leave," Tommen answered. "Funeral arrangements."

"Aw. I feel so awful."

"Why? You didn't have anything to do with it. You couldn't have stopped it."

"Well no, but still. I mean, it's terrible to lose a brother, especially in that way. I wish I could do something. How are the kids taking it? Most of them seem pretty okay, but have you talked to them about it at all?"

"That's going to be our after dinner conversation tonight. Now that it's been a day and they've had a chance to process it a little more."

Up until that point, Tommen had no clue what he was going to do. But it seemed like the logical thing to do. They would have dinner, go back to the cabin and talk a little, head to the campfire and have a good time and finally return to the cabin to get ready for bed. In the morning, they would start getting ready for the outdoor adventure week. After that was water week. Finally, the easy week came last this time, basketball and soccer tournaments. Supposedly there would even be a volleyball tournament, too, if they could get enough kids on the teams.

"So, how was everyone's free time this afternoon?" Tommen asked amiably as he sat down.

Seeing how he hadn't woken up to an angry lynch mob at the door to the cabin, Tommen figured it couldn't have been too bad, and the boys said as much. The pelts were nearly finished, but there was no way to hurry those anyway. A couple had started a basketball game. The teams were mixed, but otherwise it went well. Same with the soccer game. Supposedly, a group of them had gone up to the north fort and tried to clear out old storm debris to see if they couldn't resurrect the old fort—some of the kids were old enough to remember when that was the only fort at camp, and they wanted to restore it for nostalgia reasons.

As for the kids who had been napping, well, they slept pretty good, or they said they did. A few hadn't been able to sleep, so they read quietly, borrowing a few books from the camp store.

"What are we doing after dinner?" Charlie wondered.

Tommen shifted in his seat. "Well, we're going to go back to the cabin for a bit. Then we'll go to the campfire tonight, have s'mores, tell stories. When that's over with, we'll get ready for bed and...go to sleep."

It wasn't the best explanation, and it certainly wasn't anything cheery or hopeful. He couldn't make himself sound enthusiastic and upbeat. He might have been able to, for the younger kids. But as Micaiah or someone had pointed out, teenagers could smell a phony from a mile away. They didn't need the bullshit and they didn't want him to speak to them like a bunch of little kids.

Maybe that was why they were being so good now. Maybe that was why they were willing to listen. He was one of them; he was a peer. Peers and bros banded together. If something happened to one, everyone rallied around him. All for one and one for all sort of thing. Similarly, he was just older than them, which meant they were looking to him for guidance. Some of the boys had been there, had helped carry Saul off the mountain, and they needed to know how to deal with that. All of them, though, Tommen included, had been under his thumb, enduring the same sarcastic remarks and dry wit. He wasn't the beloved grandfather whom everyone adored, but he was still a familiar, and suddenly he was gone, murdered. They needed to know how to deal with that, too. So this would be a learning experience for all of them.

This was going to turn into group therapy, wasn't it? Tommen hoped not. While he was all for the idea of learning and talking together and figuring out what exactly happened and how to proceed going forward, he was not too interested in getting all mushy and emotional. There would be a time throughout camp when he would talk to each of them individually about their lives, but this was not that conversation.

"What are we doing tomorrow?" Dan asked.

"Tomorrow, we are beginning the outdoor adventure week," Tommen answered. "So we'll be doing horseback riding, ziplining, rock climbing, ropes course, all sorts of fun stuff. Just don't forget to be safe."

JJ scoffed. "Please. They worry so much about keeping us safe and rig us up in so much equipment, there isn't any room left for fun."

"When we go horseback riding, can I bring my own horse?" Harry asked, grinning.

"You ride?" Tommen wondered.

"Well, I'm on the equestrian team at school, so I do jumping and barrel racing, but I go out riding with my brothers. We use the horses in our game drives sometimes. It depends on where it is; sometimes the trees or undergrowth is too thick."

"Sweet. Should have brought the whole family, could have had a ball up out there camping, bringing in the big game to feed everyone."

Harry just shrugged and said, "Yeah, and maybe Saul would still be alive then." He shook his head and stared at his food as he ate.

Before Tommen could say more, Mr. Wilson got up to address everyone, basically reiterating everything Tommen had just explained about the schedule of events for the night and the following week. He appeared to be cheerful and managed to sound upbeat and excited for the rest of camp, but Tommen could see he was still pale and shaking.

Maybe the man was expecting the tribe to sue him or sue the camp or something for wrongful death. Tommen couldn't speak as to the disposition of the Krydik at large, but he was fairly certain there was no lawsuit coming. Or maybe the man really was just that shaken. Did he blame himself? Was he thinking that if he hadn't "fired" Saul, that he might still be alive? Would it have made a difference? Saul had gone out hunting alone, tracking game that was unpredictable. Saul knew the risks. Rifun knew the risks, and he took advantage of that to corner Saul and murder him.

"All right," Tommen said finally. "Is everyone here done with their food?"

Most plates were empty. The boys who still had food on their plates abandoned it as they stood, dropped off their stuff to the kitchen, and returned to the cabin.

"So, what are we doing?" JJ asked as they all found seats on bunks around the room.

Tommen let out a breath. "Well, I want to talk. About Saul, about what happened."

"This isn't group therapy, is it?" Nathan wondered.

"It's not meant to be. If you don't want to say anything, then don't. If you want to talk privately later, then by all means. Mostly..." He paused, looking for the right words. "I just want you guys to know what happened. What really happened. I know some of you were there, and if you want or need to speak, then feel free."

Tommen shifted position and waited a second before speaking. "Saul went up hunting alone. He was an experienced hunter, as you know, and he had his bow and a couple knives with him. While he was out, he must have been tracking some sort of game, when someone cornered him. And by cornered, know that I use the term loosely; they found him in a position where he could not see them and could not run easily if he had.

"He was shot six times. I believe they shot him with the gun first, in order to take him down and subdue him, then went up and shot five arrows into him at close range to ensure that he was dead."

"But he wasn't dead," Charlie said, his face pale as he remembered the incident. "He had a pulse; Michelle said so. I thought she did."

Tommen nodded. "He did have a pulse, but because of the arrows and the way we had to evacuate him down to the trail, it was impossible to do CPR or anything like that." And it would have been sketchy anyway if that bullet had severed any arteries or anything. "In the end, obviously, he did die. I don't know if it was from sheer blood loss, shock, the arrows themselves, the bullet, something we didn't even see up there on the hillside, I really couldn't tell you. Believe me when I say there was nothing more that we could have done to help him. It was just his time."

"He was an idiot," JJ said, staring at the ground. "Why the hell would he tell us to always buddy up, but then he goes off on his own?"

"Because you are inexperienced, for one. For two..." Tommen sighed. "Saul had a lot of problems, most of them personal. Sometimes, when things got too overwhelming, whether at home or here in camp, he just needed to get out and be alone, do something he knew how to do and do well."

"If he had so many problems, why did he come to work at camp in the first place?" Jason asked. "He never looked excited to be here, or even that he wanted to be here in spite of any problems he was having."

"Well, I can't say for sure, but I think he considered himself a watcher, a keeper of the land. This area he considers important or sacred, and he felt he had to oversee it. To that end, I think he did enjoy being here to an extent, in that he could teach you guys about the land, how to enjoy it but also how to care for it, which was why the camping was his favorite part."

Interestingly enough, Tommen couldn't decide how much was true and how much was bullshit. Saul had never shown anything but disdain for the camp and the kids, but something kept bringing him back. Yes, he was part of Wolf Clan, watchers and defenders of Earth and whatever, but Tommen figured he knew him well enough to know that if he didn't want to come to camp, he would have found a way to tell his commanding officer, his tribe, whoever, to fuck off and leave him alone. Blake had mentioned that because of the matrilineal structure of the tribe, he could have gotten married, joined his wife's clan, and left it all behind to stay permanently on Hlohi. But he hadn't. Extenuating circumstances aside, there had to be a deeper reason behind why he kept coming back.

But that was neither here nor there, and Saul was dead. Any motivations, intentions, wishes, dreams, accomplishments, failures, desires, and secrets he had left, he took to his grave.

"If that's true, then why didn't he just say so?" Dan wondered.

"I don't know," Tommen repeated. "I didn't know him very well, but I knew him well enough to say that he had problems. I think you guys are smart enough to have seen that. And maybe you can take it as a teaching moment, too, to look at yourselves and make sure you don't end up like him."

It felt a terrible thing to say, like pointing at a heroin addict on the street and using him as an object lesson, laughing at a freak show at the circus and warning kids never to run away and become a carny. At the same time, it was also very true. Saul's problems may have been a little different than any of the boys' in the cabin, but he had not handled them in a very productive or healthy way. Tommen hated to think about it, but if Rifun hadn't killed Saul, Saul probably would have killed himself.

"I thought you said this wasn't group therapy," Nathan pointed out, though his words were hardly malicious.

"It's not. Or it's not meant to be. But this way, everything has been said and now you all know what really happened; it's all out in the open. Does anyone else have something to say? Something to say, question to ask, anything like that?" When there was nothing, Tommen nodded and shifted position. "All right. Like I said, if you want to talk, I'm here or Mr. Wilson is available. Don't be shy. Otherwise, we've still got a few minutes until the start of the campfire."

A few boys headed to the bathroom while Tommen and the

others stayed in the cabin. After a few minutes, Tommen decided to head up to the bathroom as well. He was barely ten feet from the cabin when he heard Charlie behind him.

"Tommen, hold on! Wait!"

Tommen stopped and turned.

Charlie was about as white as white could get with orange hair and orange freckles. He was thirteen, overweight, just hit puberty and still struggling with the concept of daily showering and deodorant use. He was already huffing and puffing just hurrying after Tommen, and it was a second before he could speak.

"Um, so, Mr. Wilson said that any of us who...wanted to go home...you know, after that...would...could go home," he began unsteadily.

"Do you want to go home, Charlie?" Tommen asked.

The kid nodded guiltily. "Yeah. I just can't get that image out of my head, when we all picked him up to put him on the stretcher, and to see the arrows going through him...I don't know. It scares me. I had nightmares about it last night."

"I understand. But believe me when I say the nightmares won't go away just because you leave camp."

"I know. But...I just want to go home. I mean, it's nothing against you, but, I have this one uncle who's really awesome and he's a veteran and he saw things and anytime someone goes through something difficult, he's the one to talk to."

Tommen nodded. "I'm glad you have someone like that. Have you told Mr. Wilson yet?"

"No, not yet."

"All right. When do you think someone could pick you up? Tonight or tomorrow?"

"Probably tomorrow morning, but I'd rather go tonight."

"Okay. Well, why don't you start getting your stuff packed up? Leave out enough that you can get by for tonight if you have to, but that you can pack if quickly if you need to. I'll talk to Mr. Wilson."

Charlie breathed a sigh of relief and returned to the cabin.

Tommen still made a quick stop at the bathroom before wandering off to find Mr. Wilson who was just heading down to the fire pit to get the campfire started.

"Tommen, something I can do for you?" he asked, apparently harried but trying to sound polite.

"Well, not for me. Charlie says he wants to go home. It's just been too much for him."

Mr. Wilson nodded and slowed in his steps before eventually turning back to the office. "I understand. He was one of the ones who was there, right? Yeah, I imagine it's tough."

"I told him I was available to talk or you were, but he just wants to go home. I guess he's got a family member he would rather talk to."

"Well, that's good that he does. All right, I'll call his dad and let him know."

Tommen kept pace with him back to the office, saying, "He says that, if possible, he'd like to go tonight. Otherwise he can wait until morning."

"Fair enough. I make no promises."

"Understood."

He waited patiently for Mr. Wilson to make the call and make arrangements before returning to the cabin.

"What did my dad say?" Charlie asked when Tommen returned.

"He says he'll be here early tomorrow morning and to be ready to go."

"When is the campfire?" Harry wondered.

"I think I saw Mr. White Cloud and Zach heading down there to start it. We can probably go now and help feed it."

The mention of playing with fire was all the boys needed to get them motivated as they hurried down the slope to the fire pit. They were the first ones there. As expected, Shawn White Cloud and Zach were busy trying to get kindling and old newspaper to catch so they could add the larger logs. With the boys of Wolf Cabin now joining the party, the fire was rip roaring in record time, enough that Mr. Wilson had to shoo them away so it didn't get too big.

"Enthusiasm is great," he told them. "Not burning the camp down is better."

"We wouldn't let it burn down," Dan said. "At least not all the way."

"My confidence is renewed, I'm sure."

With the fire flickering in the dim light, the other cabins appeared like a swarm of moths, and soon enough, the line for s'mores was growing. Tommen did his best to help Deborah and Jeremiah hand out marshmallows. It wasn't so much that the counselors were worried that the kids would hurt themselves—which they inevitably did anyway—but it was mostly to control the flow of goods. Some kids wanted six marshmallows dripping off their crackers, while others would sooner take a whole chocolate bar as the little bits they were given. Personally, Tommen would have preferred graham crackers and milk.

"All right, guys, how are we all doing tonight?" Mr. Wilson asked once most of the kids and staff had settled down with their s'mores. There was a muffled cheer. "Excellent. Glad to hear it. Coming up we have our outdoor adventure week. The weather forecast looks promising, but as always, we ask you to be a little flexible if things don't quite turn out the way we hoped. All right? Awesome. In the meantime, though, while we're here, who knows a good story?"

He held up the Story-mallow, and immediately at least half the campers jumped to their feet, waving and yelling and spitting cracker crumbs, all vying for the right to speak.

"Just remember," Mr. Wilson said, waving the Story-mallow back and forth and watching the kids move with it like a dog intent on bacon, "these are supposed to be camp stories, ghost stories, things like that. We don't want to hear about the time you and your friends went to the movies or about you and your girlfriend or boyfriend holding hands. Okay? Save that stuff for your cabin. Not here. Got it?

All right, here goes!"

He drew back as if to throw it all the way to the back of the group. A couple of the boys who were probably in football took the hint and went long, only to be disappointed when the Story-Mallow simply got tossed to someone close by. It was one of the girls from Butterfly Cabin. Her ghost story was actually pretty good, and that was saying something for a group that couldn't normally be swayed by ghost stories.

The rule was that the Story-Mallow had to travel at least three people away, in order to keep friends from just handing it off to one another. It was a nice concept, but some groups still figured out how to get around it, and Tommen was about ready to claw his eyes out by the time six out of the nine Butterfly girls was done telling stories and had handed it off to another group. With exception of the first girl, they were terrible storytellers. They had no concept of plot or suspense or anything at all. Most of them said they'd heard the story from someone or got it somewhere, but Tommen figured that either they all had shitty memory to be able to retell something, or else they thought they were cooler than they were as they tried to make something up on the fly.

Still, Tommen waited patiently, munching nonchalantly on graham crackers. He hadn't gotten the Story-mallow at all during either camp, and he was fine with that. He didn't know too many ghost stories—none that he was willing to share, anyway—and even if he did, he didn't fancy himself much of a storyteller.

The fire burned low into perfect marshmallow coals, and another couple bags were opened up. The sticks were handed out again, and storytime was put on hold for a short time.

"Okay, everyone," Mr. Wilson said, "I think we've got time for two more stories, maybe three if they're short." He shrugged at the groans and protests. "I know, I know. I enjoy them, too. But there's always tomorrow. All right, who has the Story-mallow?"

The first story came from one of the boys in Bear Cabin. It wasn't half bad up until the end, then it was like a bad joke with a bad punchline that just makes everyone groan and beg for it to end. It was more difficult to judge whether the storyteller knew his story was bad and intended it to be bad, or whether he honestly thought it was halfway decent. When he was done, the Story-mallow wasn't so much tossed to the next person as it was forcibly removed from his possession.

The second story actually came from Andrew, one of the guys who ran the camp store. They didn't always stick around for the campfire, but once in a while they made an appearance.

His story was actually pretty good. It started out as weird things happening around the camp store, things being moved or randomly falling off shelves or the desk. Turned out it was the ghost of the last store runner. The previous store runner had also been the first runner as he'd helped to build the camp store some years ago. Supposedly during the construction, he'd lost his wedding ring. Well, life went on and the guy died. As the story went, it wasn't Saint Peter denying him access to the Pearly Gates, it was his wife who had commanded him not to return until he'd found his wedding ring. So he haunted the camp store, sometimes moving things or knocking things over, looking for his ring.

Or, as Andrew confessed to a few of the counselors, it could also be a rather pesky and highly intelligent mouse that had managed to evade all the mousetraps yet still leave little droppings of evidence of his existence. Ah, but the ghost story made it much more fun for the kids, or so he reasoned.

After much begging and pleading, Mr. Wilson allowed for the third story, despite the first two having been pretty long and the chorus of yawns that had already begun sweeping through the group. And to think they still had to shower and actually get ready for bed, plus there was an alarm in the morning.

And Saul isn't here to Band me to get more sleep, Tommen mused sullenly. *I wonder if I could get Micaiah to come here to do it.*

He decided against it in the end. It had been a nice convenience, but he also needed to do things the hard way, too, from time to time. Or, in his case, most of the time. He had to be a man, suck it up, and deal with it.

Mr. Wilson himself was the third storyteller. He preferred to tell funny camp stories, and his chosen tale this night was the time Wallace's pink striped underwear got run up the flagpole—by Wolf Cabin boys no less. When everyone turned to look at the middle-aged cook, he blushed, shrugged, and confirmed that it had actually happened. He'd gone outside to smoke, leaving his laundry in the dryer, and Wolf Cabin boys had gone searching for gold. Well, the gold they found came with pink stripes. They had been a satirical gift from his wife, or that was his excuse.

"Okay, I think that's all the stories we can stand for one night," Mr. Wilson concluded. "Time to head back to your cabins and get ready for bed. We have a big day tomorrow!"

Tommen was more than happy to get up and head back to the cabin, though it was still strange to walk in and not see Saul's stuff laid out meticulously on his bunk. These were his campers now. His alone. Mr. Wilson would step in from time to time, but for most of the major stuff, they were his to oversee.

Thankfully, with exception of Charlie and Sam, the boys were well-versed in daily showers. A few even preferred them at night because they couldn't stand the thought of a dirty bed. That thought spread quickly among the Wolf Cabin boys. It was true, their cabin was a mess, but they were not dirty. The boys knew that they had to keep clean and fresh if they wanted to ever have a chance at talking to girls. Unless, of course, sports were involved, in which case, they had to play harder, be faster, stronger, all the good stuff in order to attract attention.

Tommen showered in the first group, but there were four showers and about fifty boys total. While he waited for his campers to filter through the line, he texted Becky, including the part about Saul's death.

"Oh my gosh, are you okay? Like, are you seriously okay? That's so terrible! Oh my gosh, you're not, like, all depressed are you?

I will come up there if you need me to. I'm so sorry to hear that," she replied.

"No, no, I'm okay. It's the boys I'm more worried about. They didn't like him much, but I think he had a bigger impact than they first realized. One kid is going home tomorrow. He was there, too."

"I can't even imagine seeing something like that, especially when it's someone you know. Especially so young. I'm referring to both you and your campers, by the way."

"I know."

"But you're okay, right? Oh my gosh, I wish there was something I could do, like come up or something."

"No, just stay where you are. At this point, I'm just telling you about it. I'll let you know if there's anything else or something."

"Like what? Needing a shoulder to cry on?"

"I don't need that. I don't know. I'll let you know. Right now, I'm just telling you."

"Okay. If you're sure."

"Absolutely. Anyway, I have to go. My boys are almost out of the showers and we have an early day tomorrow."

She still texted him half a dozen times between the bathrooms and the cabin. A couple were commands to let her know if he needed anything, if he wanted to call or wanted her to make the trip so he could cry on her shoulder. He politely declined, at least the shoulder-crying. He really wasn't that torn up. A couple texts were little prayers for him in case he wanted to talk to God and wasn't sure where to begin. He politely mentioned that he spoke to God quite a bit, and it wasn't about Saul's death. Then she sent him a couple Bible verses, one about loss and one about heaven. He politely informed her that, by her standards, Saul would be a pagan and, according to her own beliefs, he would be burning in Hell, not walking his spirit lands.

"The living can't help the dead," she told him. "And the verses weren't meant for him."

Tommen did not reply as he removed his hearing aids and set everything on their appropriate chargers. Then he looked around at the boys, his gaze resting on Charlie.

"Still want to go home?" he asked.

Charlie hesitated, but nodded. "Yeah. I mean, tonight was fun and all, but it was just a distraction. I just kind of want to go home and talk to my uncle. I mean, I know I could probably ask Mr. Wilson and he'd let me call, but..."

"You just want to go home and get away from it before you talk about it."

"Yeah. Something like that."

"Nothing wrong with that. And you know what? It means you're smart enough to know yourself and understand your limits. Makes you emotionally intelligent." *Something I lack*, though he did not say this out loud. "I'm just making sure, though. I'd hate to see you get halfway home and have second thoughts."

Charlie shook his head. "No, I don't think that's going to happen."

Tommen nodded and looked around at the rest of the boys. Some of them wore true pajamas, others their clothes from the day, a few just their undershirts and boxers. "Does anyone else want to go home at all, while we're talking about it?"

The boys shook their heads no. What Tommen was more impressed with, however, was how not one of them ridiculed Charlie or called him weak or a crybaby or anything of the sort. If any of them thought it, they were smart enough to keep it to themselves. Otherwise, they seemed to be mature enough to understand the gravity of the situation, that they couldn't just walk away from every explosion and be the tough guy. Some things got to you. Saul's death had gotten to Charlie.

He didn't dwell on it too long as he told the boys to hurry up and get in their sleeping bags. He half-expected Saul to give them a swift kick in the ass by reaching up and flicking the lights off whether they were ready or not. It never came. It fell to Tommen to ensure everyone was in bed, then cross the cabin to flick out the lights, then pick his way back to his bunk and climb in without stubbing his toe or tripping over anything. This he failed miserably at as he stubbed his toe more than once and, when he got to his bunk, found that one of his toenails had cracked or split or done something. He gritted his teeth as he peeled off the loose nail. Well, he'd just have to wait and examine it in the morning.

He was just about to settle in when his phone buzzed again. Grudgingly, he checked it. It was from Micaiah.

"How are you holding up?"

Tommen sighed inwardly as he replied, "Cranky. Trying to get to sleep, but everyone seems intent on giving me their shoulder to cry on. I don't need it."

"Yeah, well, there's a difference between your dad offering, your girlfriend offering, and me offering."

"Yeah. You're my boss. That makes it even weirder."

"Ha ha, very funny. Hey, if you say you're fine, then I can only take you at your word at this point. You've got three more weeks, though, until you come home. Just checking up on you."

"I know. I appreciate it. Can I go to sleep now?"

"Oh, I suppose. If you must."

Tommen put away his phone, then stared up at the bottom of the top bunk. Now that he thought about it, his dad hadn't actually texted or called him about it at all, and he was the first one Tommen would expect to get all emotional about it, or about him, anyway. Had no one told him? Well, he'd call him tomorrow maybe. He certainly wasn't going to do it tonight, not with his sleep ticking away on the clock. Rubbing his eyes, he rolled over and tried to sleep.

Chapter Thirty-Two
Final Warning

The one called Man and the one called Woman were fighting. They were fighting so that birds and beasts could settle their age-old war over who dominated the land. The birds had fashioned their warrior, Woman, so she moved with the land, worked with it to defend herself against Man. But she was not strong enough to defeat him completely. The beasts had fashioned Man to be above the animals, above the land, bending it to his will. But perhaps they had made him too strong and powerful. He took the land and manipulated, but he also harmed it, broke it so he could use it as he would, rather than how it was meant to be used.

Suddenly, Man caught Woman in a trap. The fight was supposed to be over. But Man moved ever closer to Woman, with that look in his eye when hunter has caught prey. But this was not even that look. When hunter catches prey, he gives thanks, because prey is his sustenance. Without prey, hunter would be nothing. Woman was not Man's prey. He did not rely on her for sustenance. Indeed, such a thing was a dreadful thing. There were only two of them. Without one or the other, there would soon be no more.

As Man raised his arm to deliver the killing strike, Wolf burst forth from the ring of spectators. He caught Man squarely in the chest and drove him to the ground. But when the dust settled, he saw it was not Man at all.

It was Rifun.

"So. You found me," he said, smirking.

In that moment of confusion, Tommen felt himself being lifted and thrown off into the bushes. When he got to his feet, he saw Rifun crossing the clearing. It was the same clearing where Saul had been murdered. All the birds and beasts and all evidence of the fight had gone.

"If I didn't know better," Rifun went on, "I'd say someone else was training you besides me. I already killed Saul. So who is it?"

Tommen looked at his hands, at himself. "I don't know. I don't even know what this is. It's a dream, but...dreams aren't real."

Rifun brandished something that resembled a bowstaff. "It's as real as anything else. Does this feel real?"

He swung the staff at Tommen and clocked him over the head. Tommen stumbled to the side. "What the fuck?" He righted himself and dodged another blow. "I don't understand. Dreams aren't real. They're images and sequences conjured up in our own brains, the interactions of neurons in REM sleep. Nothing more. They're not messages or anything. And they certainly can't be manipulated by someone who's hundreds of miles away. Or even in the next bunk."

Rifun paused in his advance and lowered the staff. He studied Tommen. "So it is possible that you don't know. Would you like to learn?"

Tommen coughed as he felt his eyebrows shoot up in surprise. "Are you fucking insane?! You beat me over the head with a stick, kill one mentor, threaten another, plus everything else that you've fucking done in the last year, and you still think I'm going to just waltz after you like an eager puppy?" *Even though I told the others I would try to get close to you, you're just too fucking insane to try that now.* "I don't care what fucking deal we made. Which, by the way, you forced me to agree to, which is called duress. I'm not doing it."

Rifun shifted his stance. "Last time I was here, in your dreams, you seemed very pleased with yourself that you had somehow figured out that I wasn't really here."

"I don't know. Maybe. Which means you can't be here now."

"Your reasoning last time was that you couldn't defeat me, but you could defeat yourself any day. Why don't we put that to the test once more, hm?"

"How about you go the fuck away and let me rest in peace?"

Rifun grinned. "Oh, that much I will do once I'm through with you."

Tommen jumped and ungracefully rolled out of the way as Rifun made another swipe at him with the staff. When he stood, Rifun swung again, but this time he managed to anticipate the strike, ignore the Imprint, and even caught the staff. But Rifun was ready and waiting. As Tommen jerked on the staff, trying to wrench it from his grasp, he moved with it, crashing into Tommen and driving him to the ground, pressing the staff against his neck until he choked.

"If I am you, throw me off," Rifun hissed.

Tommen opened his mouth, but could not find the breath. He wiggled and thrashed under Rifun's weight, but could not throw the big man off. He tried to remember back to his karate lessons, see if he could apply anything. He searched for some sort of leverage under Rifun's arms, in his elbows, but no matter what, the man was just bigger and heavier, and he was currently squeezing the air from Tommen's body.

Then the pressure released. Tommen lay on the ground, coughing violently, vision swimming. He blindly accepted the hand that was offered to him, getting up on unsteady legs and feet.

"You are weak because your mentors are weak," Rifun growled. "They teach you party tricks, and they expect that it will be enough. Did they never teach you anything like this?"

Tommen was still bent over, hands on his knees, coughing and fighting to catch his breath, but he shook his head no, whispering hoarsely, "I don't even know what this is."

"I thought as much." Rifun took a few steps back. "When you wake up, meet me where the stony guardians protect a wooden throne."

Tommen looked up, but the clearing was empty. He looked around. The trees seemed taller than he remembered, the shadows longer. Even the mountains seemed to have grown a few thousand feet. As he turned to look out over the valley, the shadows grew longer and the mountains blotted out the sun. Darkness came down upon him like a gavel, cracking hard.

He jolted awake to find that the cracking gavel was actually his forehead cracking against the bar of the upper bunk bed. He cursed silently as he lay back down, rubbing the sore spot. He had to tie a T-shirt or a sock to that bar or something, because this was getting ridiculous. He was going to have a bruise there sooner or later.

Groaning, he slipped out of his sleeping bag and swung his legs over the edge of the bed, ducking until he could sit up more comfortably without hitting his head on any other part of the bed frame.

His dreams were getting way too fucked up. Maybe he did need to go home so he could get counseling. Start out with the regular Earth-side counselor, talk about the shit from the warehouse, Saul's death, all the obvious, easy stuff. Once that had been sorted out as best it could be, then he might ask his dad about a Time-side counselor. Barring that, he should at least look into anti-anxiety medication, anti-depressants, and possibly some sort of sleeping pill. He just couldn't keep doing this. Whether the dreams were more than dreams or not, they were kicking his ass.

All around him, the campers slept soundly. JJ and Charlie had kicked their sleeping bags and blankets to the ends of their respective beds while Jason and Dan had pulled theirs up around them just as tight as they could. In the darkness, Tommen was pretty sure he could hear a mouse or something scuttling to and fro in the darkness, looking for crumbs from the snacks each camper had packed.

Otherwise, everything was quiet and peaceful. Looking at the clock, he'd only slept a couple hours, though it felt like less than that. He rubbed his eyes and yawned hugely.

He tried to tell himself it had all been a dream, but what if it hadn't? What if Rifun really was waiting for him out there at the hollow stump? Would he just figure that Tommen had dismissed it as a dream and gone back to sleep? What kind of horrendous retribution would he wreak if that was the case? His dad was right; as a criminal,

Rifun was devolving. He craved power and control and attention. If he felt powerless, out of control, and ignored, there was no telling what he could do. Saul had been better trained than Tommen and look at him. Tommen was a comparative weakling, plus he had the campers to think about. What would happen if Rifun started threatening them?

Well, it probably wouldn't hurt to go out and take a look around anyway. His mind was too active to let him just go back to sleep. He'd get up, look around a bit, get some fresh air, then he'd come back. Yes, that sounded like a very good, reasonable plan.

He got out of bed slowly and tried to sneak across the cabin. He stubbed his already injured toe and bit his tongue until it bled to keep from crying out. In the morning, he was going to find out what the hell he kept tripping over and murder it. But until then, he kept his silence as he reached the door, found the handle, and slipped outside.

His first thought was that he probably should have grabbed a jacket. His second thought was that if he stubbed his toe too many more times, it was liable to fall off, the whole thing, not just the nail. And anyway, he was only out for a quick stroll. The chill and the fresh air would do him some good.

He told himself to head up to the bathroom or maybe scour the main hall for a midnight snack. More importantly, he told himself not to go into the woods to meet Rifun, if indeed that had all actually happened and that was what he was supposed to do. He couldn't allow himself to give in to the demands of a terrorist. Problem was, even his dad had succumbed to that. It was a damned if he did, damned if he didn't scenario. Fuck, why did Rifun have to be so good at this?

Answer: because the man had no emotions and no restraint. He didn't hold back on anything because of some sense of morality. He had no sense of morality. The only thing that would stop him was death; otherwise, he just couldn't be stopped or reasoned with. What chance did Tommen have against him, really?

As he got off the porch, he paused and surveyed the surrounding area in the dim moonlight. Paw prints. Massive ones. Yawi was still around. Tommen let out a breath. Before he could say or do anything, a flash of white caught his eye, and the great white wolf emerged from the trees. It looked better than it had before, covered in blood and limping. Now it appeared whole and sound, fur fluffed out and shining white, eyes glittering in the dim moonlight.

Tommen's heart stopped for a moment as the wolf approached him. But it did not eat him. Rather, it simply nosed his hand. Carefully, Tommen reached out and gave it a little scratch between the ears.

"Hate to break it to you, Yawi, but your master's dead," he said sadly. "Better go find one of his siblings or some other member of Wolf Clan, because this one has checked out."

Yawi nosed Tommen's hand again and whined, looking at the cabin. Tommen shook his head. "No. Saul's gone. He's not coming back."

The wolf snorted and shook its head. Now it nosed him in the ribs and looked at the cabin. Tommen took a step back. "No, Yawi. I don't have anything for you. Why are you coming to me, anyway?"

If wolves were capable of human expression, or even if there was some truth to reincarnation, Tommen suddenly knew he was either looking at someone who'd spent way too much time with Saul or else was Saul in a different form, as the look on the wolf's face was unmistakable. It was an expression that read, "Are you fucking kidding me? Am I speaking gibberish to you? Listen to me!"

"I'm sorry, Yawi," Tommen said finally. "Saul's gone. There's nothing for you here."

He thought about just returning to his bunk. In hindsight, that probably would have been the smarter idea. But he didn't. Instead, he went to the north end of camp and ducked into the trees, making for the hollow stump. If Yawi was tagging along with him for some reason, well, he could tag along to the stump. If not, well, he could make a few more worried laps of the cabin.

The woods were hard enough to get through during the day, and it was even worse at night with all the invisible branches and brambles snagging his clothes and scraping his skin.

"I'm insane," Tommen muttered to himself. "I'm hallucinating spirit wolves and following the commands of a psycho in a dream. All I need now is the tin foil hat and the white coat that lets you hug yourself. This is fucking unbelievable."

Still, he made it to the stump with the three rocks around it. This was a popular spot for scavenger hunt clues, but now it sat alone and deserted, except for the crazy teenager standing there in its midst. He looked around and didn't see anything. He strained to hear, but that much was utterly useless.

"Okay. I'm here. No one else is. And if anyone finds me here, it better be a hot girl because that's about the only thing that's going to—"

"Hm...so much for chivalry."

Tommen almost jumped out of his skin at Rifun's voice. He whirled to see the man leaning against a tree, eating an apple, looking like even more of an asshole.

"Honestly, Tommen, why do you still tout your flag of chivalry?" Rifun asked, not moving. "I mean, I think it's fairly obvious to everyone that you really want to sleep with your girlfriend, if you aren't already. Where's the chivalry in that? Given that chivalry was developed by Christian knights and the fact that your girlfriend is Catholic—or proclaims to be something of the sort—then either you should have your eyes gouged out for lust, or the two of you should get married so as not to burn with desire." He shrugged and tossed the apple core away. "Not that it matters to me; I'm simply pointing it out for your sake. After all, I would hate to think of the fate that awaits you if you are indeed wrong in your assessment of the afterlife."

Tommen blinked. "So, you dragged me out here in the middle of the night, interrupted my sleep, so you can lecture me on morality and religion?"

"Hm...in a sense I suppose." Now Rifun approached, steps as uncaring and unconcerned as ever. "See, you want everything to operate in a universe of logic, facts, mathematics, things that make universal sense. But there's one element that you are forgetting, something that is as universal as mathematics."

"And what is that?"

"Faith. I'm not talking about hokey beliefs and rain dances of some Pango Pango tribe running around naked on the African savanna. I'm talking about sheer, unadulterated faith."

"What are you talking about? The only kind of faith is hokey beliefs and everything else. It comes in a lot of different varieties around the world, but they're all the same thing."

"No. There is more. It's the kind of faith that can move mountains."

"Yeah?" Tommen pointed to a nearby peak. "Tell it to move."

Rifun grinned. "Cute. I will, however, point out that if I did so, it would cause a minor earthquake. Who knows what would happen to the camp then? And you running around out here doing who knows what?"

Tommen grunted and Rifun went on. "It's the kind of faith that can reach inside a person and manipulate their body to do whatever I want them to do."

Even as he spoke, Tommen felt his lungs get heavy, as if from a cold or the flu. Then the thick, slimy phlegm turned into water, and he began coughing and sputtering, trying to suck in air and expel water, doing neither action successfully. As he went down, remaining on the teetering edge between living and drowning, Rifun knelt in front of him. "It is the manipulation of atoms, of DNA, of the very fabric of the universe. It's not something you can do just by thinking about it. You have to believe you can do it. This is the secret of the Akari."

He released Tommen from his invisible drowning. Tommen dropped to all fours and spit up water for several minutes before finding enough air and enough strength to stand and breathe.

"Here's an analogy you may appreciate," Rifun said as Tommen found his feet. "Think of the Akari like your dick. It's part of you, it can do great things, wonderful things, and sometimes it has a mind of its own. But until you start entertaining it, pouring your whole heart and soul and mind into your work and pumping away, it is almost completely useless except to get rid of waste."

"That's...actually kind of a sick analogy," Tommen decided. "I honestly don't want to know how you came up with that."

Rifun waved a hand dismissively. "Well, it doesn't matter anyway. What does matter is that your days of being an untrained whelp are over."

"Saul already gave me my first lesson," Tommen informed him. "He was starting to teach me about Imprinting and combat."

"Excellent. Then that is where we shall begin."

"What?"

To say Tommen was unprepared for Rifun's attack was an understatement. Before he even had time to process Rifun's presence, he'd already taken a blow to the face and a blow to the stomach, then had his feet kicked out from under him so he landed hard on his back on the ground, the wind driven from his lungs. Again.

Coughing, he unsteadily got to his feet, looking around, waiting to see the tiny markers just a split second before the actual blow. None came. Rifun stood in front of him.

"Try to do the same to me," he ordered.

Tommen merely looked at him for a second, trying to judge how serious he was being. There was no way he was going to be able to touch him. And even so, why should he fight him in the first place? This was a game, not a lesson. The only thing being accomplished here was Rifun ensuring that Tommen never forgot how feeble he was compared to him.

"I won't do it," Tommen said. "I can't."

"I know you can't," Rifun chuckled. "That's why I am here to teach you."

Tommen shook his head. "You're smarter than that. You won't

teach me how to beat you. You might teach me some techniques and try to have me beat up on others, but you'll always save the best cards for yourself, and you'll use those to beat up on me and keep me in line and remind me how weak I am. And of all that remains, there is nothing you can teach me that Micaiah can't also."

Rifun raised a brow. "You know, you're shaping up to be quite the actor yourself with your little monologues. And you are quite the detective with all your deductions. You're right, of course. Micaiah could teach you many things, I'm sure. Even his brother might show you a magic trick or two. Any one of the Akarin could probably get you trained within reason. But they lack the final piece of the puzzle, the one that unlocks that final level of power."

And the cuckoo comes out, right on time. "Okay. I'll bite. What is that?"

"The journal. Richard's journal. While the Akarin squabbled and feuded over old teachings, he wrote the manual on the Akari. All the information in one spot, straight from the Author. Start to finish, it details everything."

"Then what about the books? You yourself gave me one."

Rifun shrugged. "Oh, they're interesting tales, to be sure. Good to read, good to study, but limited and incomplete in their usefulness. And they're not even fully correct. Nor are they originals, but just copies! We'll go over that part at a later date. The point is, I can teach you the Akari from start to finish, with none of these...substitute teachers or reluctant teachers or any of that."

Tommen blinked and shook his head. "You think that after everything you've done to me so far that I'm going to just drop everything and sit at your feet because you make a pretty speech?"

"Fine. Don't ask me. There are plenty of other groups out there who have been delighted to have Richard's journal found and brought to them. But, as I've said before, we have a deal. You owe me."

"I don't owe you anything."

"Don't you? And what makes you think that? Actually, no, skip that. I know what you're going to say. You're just going to cite duress or some such thing. Maybe I'll rephrase the question: what is stopping me from turning you over to the Hands or the Grandfathers? After all, you said it yourself, you're training in the Akari. All I have to do is get someone to claim that you were trying to get them to 'convert' from Time to the Akari as it were, and there you go. Instant prison time, if not worse. Or, there is that whole bit about the Borelians declaring war on humans. I know you were personally listed on the declaration of war, and I bet your name is still running around in some circles. I'm sure I could find someone to take you in."

Tommen ground his teeth. Everything he said was true, and he had the power and the friends to back up everything he threatened. Were any of his friends actually friends, or were they all just shanghaied lackeys? Finally he took a calming breath and said, "All right. I'll see your deal and raise you one more."

Rifun raised a brow, intrigued. "Very well. Let's hear your offer."

"You want to teach me and have me as your student? Then cut the shit. Teach me something right here, right now. Something useful. Something I can take home with me, or back to the cabin as it were."

"I tried that already. You refused."

"Teach me something that doesn't involve getting my ass kicked. I can't go back to my cabin looking like I've been out wrestling bears all night."

Rifun nodded. "Baby steps then. All right. Why don't we start with something your daddy would be teaching you had you stayed home this summer? Pinpoint Banding for example. Your face looks simply awful."

"No thanks to you."

"And perhaps there will be a lesson in gratitude while we're at it."

Tommen cringed, afraid of what the man was going to do to him, but nothing happened. Instead, Rifun continued, "All right. Show me your best Band. Let's go with a Fast Band."

Tommen did so, telling himself it was just like his review.

He'd barely begun before Rifun stopped him. "No. No, no, no. Not Time. Akari."

"Um...I haven't...really been shown that yet."

Rifun ran his tongue over his teeth. "Hm. Of course you haven't."

There was no way in hell that Tommen would ever sympathize with Rifun, but he knew well the frustration of admitting that he hadn't actually been taught anything. After all the shit that had happened, even giving a little leeway for the months of Suppression, and he was still no better than a glorified probie. Although, there was still that little annoying fact that he'd effectively run away from home. Metaphorically speaking. So part of this was on him, too. He would grudgingly admit that.

"Perhaps we should start even smaller, then," Rifun was saying. "Teaching you how to wield the Akari will do you no good if you can't even tell the difference between the Akari and Time."

"I'm listening," Tommen said irritably.

"Tell me, Tommen, do you believe that mountain right there exists?" He pointed to the same peak Tommen had.

"Um...duh."

"Why? Because you can see it, correct?"

"Yeah."

"Do you believe atoms exist?"

"Yeah. Those can be observed, too, through a microscope."

"Do you believe in the wind?"

"Yes."

"Why? You can't see it."

"No, but you can feel it."

"The same goes for the Akari. Metaphorically speaking, Time can be seen and manipulated. The Akari is much more subtle. You can only feel it."

"So we're talking about the Force. Right." Tommen chuckled. "Well, at least it's a better metaphor."

"Put up your Fast Band again," Rifun ordered. "Regular

Time."

Tommen did so, struggling to suppress a sigh. This was like that time in middle school when one of the girls was inviting a whole bunch of people to a seance where she was guaranteeing contact with a spirit. No one could see the spirit, but they might be able to feel it, and she would be able to communicate with it.

"Now then, strip away all that is visible Time," Rifun continued. "If Saul showed you what an Akari Band feels like, you ought to get down to that same level."

Tommen wanted to whine and ask how he was supposed to "strip away" the "visible" Time, then decided to just keep his mouth shut. If it was something he could do, he'd figure it out. If the whole thing was bullshit, well, that would quickly become apparent, too.

Still, he did try. He remembered how Saul's Akari Band felt, and he tried to see if he could somehow split his Band, get down to that same light, flexible feeling.

"It's not enough to just see it and try to force it, the same way you do with Time," Rifun told him. "You have to feel it. As I said, treat it like your dick. You're not going to force it to be hard; you have to entertain it and make it happy."

"Your analogy is not helping things," Tommen informed him. "And I still think it's pretty disgusting."

"Why, because I'm not your girlfriend? If she was here instead of me saying that, you'd be all over her."

Tommen dropped the Band. "Leave her out of this."

"I made no threats. Try again."

"You don't have to be explicit to make threats."

Rifun rolled his eyes. "All I said was that if she were here and I wasn't, you two would probably already be getting it on, at least two or three times seeing how you're both virgins and dumb teenagers." He flicked his hand. "Again."

So Tommen did, throwing up the Fast Band and working to erase all Time from it. He was still pretty convinced that Rifun was bullshitting him, until he found the peeling corner. He couldn't say how he found it or how he knew what it was, but once he did, it was like his Band became riddled with cracks. Separating the Bands suddenly became easy, like stripping bark off a dead tree.

The difference between the two Bands was like night and day. The Time Band was like a coat made of hard leather that hadn't been properly softened and so remains stiff and bulky. The Akari Band was like that same coat made of properly tanned and softened leather. The Time Band had been like wearing dark sunglasses indoors. The Akari Band was like wearing expensive polarized sunglasses outdoors where everything that had once been blinding now came into crystal clear, full color focus. And yet, it did nothing to help him come up with better analogies.

"Good," Rifun remarked. "Now you're starting to get it. Anything you can do with a Time Band you can do with an Akari Band. Practice with it for a few minutes, work with it a little."

Tommen did so, making it go Fast and Slow, bending it and pulling it tighter, making it looser, adding more space and drawing it close. He was doing nothing different from what he had with his Time Bands, but it felt so much better and easier. After a short time, Rifun stopped him.

"Now, was that so hard?"

"No, it wasn't," Tommen said, hardly looking at him. Rather, he was still intent on studying the Band itself. Time Bands were colored. Fast was orange—or red, in some instances, not that he could see. Slow Bands were blue. But Akari Bands were almost completely invisible except for a faint touch of blurriness or fuzz around its perimeter, just enough to see where it was.

"Shame no one taught you that little trick," Rifun commented, picking at some dirt under his fingernails. "It's very easy, as you've just admitted. Would have been nothing for Micaiah to teach you before you left."

Tommen dropped the Band. "I know what you're doing. You can cut the crap."

Rifun shrugged, unconcerned. "I'm only saying—"

"I know what you're saying. What's next?"

Whether Akari or Time, Tommen had pretty much already reached the limit of what he knew about either. Predict didn't seem special to either side, and his one incidental Imprint he still wasn't sure how to replicate. As far as Pinpoint Banding, double Banding or any of that, he didn't know diddly squat.

But Rifun taught him. True to his word, Rifun taught him how to do both. His primary focus was the Akari, but he let Tommen practice a bit in Time, just so he could see the colors of the Bands and understand how to manipulate them.

"Time isn't bad," Rifun said. "It has its limited uses. But mostly it's just for practice. You can see the difference in the colors, can't you?"

Tommen gave him a look. "I'm red-green color-blind, not monochromatic. Yes, I can tell the difference. One is blue, the other is yellow." He paused. "That thing you did before. To fix my color-blindness. Can you show me how to do that?"

Rifun chuckled. "In time. Baby steps."

"What about that water trick you seem so fond of?"

"Oh, the drowning? That's a little more advanced, sorry to say."

"You know, your sales pitch for new converts isn't very good. If it's not threats, it's too advanced."

"Ha! Still with the sense of humor, even under duress. It must run in the family."

Tommen dropped his Bands and faced Rifun. "Tell me something, though. In the warehouse. If my dad had confessed. To being my uncle, to being a murderer locked up in prison, all of that. Would you have spared him?"

Rifun did a sweeping bow. "I am a man of my word, child. If I say I will spare someone, then I will spare him. If I say I will kill someone, rest assured, death is coming."

"So then who was the note intended for? The one with the flies on my bedroom door?"

"Who indeed?"

"That's not an answer."

Rifun grinned. "Call it a warning. And as you have seen, one has already fallen. Saul is dead."

"And the others? Would that be my dad, the twins, someone else?"

"Tell me, Tommen, is that what you want to know? Because I think you already know that answer. What's really on your mind?"

Tommen searched his face, looking for anything, but the man was a brick wall. Finally he relented. "What would it take to get you to spare them?"

"Ah, so the truth comes out. He wants to be the protector, the hero, the real man. What must he do to ensure the safety of his family and friends? Concealing the truth and withdrawing to become a hermit is very Hollywood, I will give you that. But, it is a multi-billion dollar industry. In real life, however, it is as simple as this: If you continue to train under me and be my student, I will let your father et al live. I make no guarantees as to their safety concerning the war with the Borelians and anything else that may arise, but I assure you that they will not die by my hand or on my order."

"As long as I train under you," Tommen sighed.

"Exactly."

"Is there an end date on this contract?"

"Of course not. As I said before, pretty soon, you won't want to leave."

"I have my doubts."

Still, Rifun made him practice a little more. Mostly it was Fast Bands, that way they could train longer without cutting it close on time before the alarm went off. Even when Tommen finally made his first double Band, it was a Slow Band inside a Fast Band, that way he could trick his brain into perceiving Time normally even as he quickly healed a cut on his foot.

By the time they called it quits, Tommen was exhausted and ready to crawl back into his sleeping bag. Rifun still looked as fresh as a spring rooster and about as arrogant as one, too, about ready to go up on the barn and start crowing for all to hear.

"One more thing before you go," Rifun said, stalking up behind Tommen as he headed for the cabin. He leaned in close and whispered, "I'm almost certain that you intend to report on this to your little friends. Whether this was a predetermined plan to get close to me and learn my movements, or just something you intend to do on your own, I don't care. You are not to report any of this. Not what I have taught you, not even that we have met. Nothing. I'm adding that as the fine print to our agreement."

"Let me guess. You want me to report their movements to you, though."

"I have enough moles without having to worry about a turncoat like you. I wouldn't trust you with something like that, not at this point. You're too questionable. Given time, maybe. But not now. And if you break our agreement, and you do tell your little friends, well, there are always more flies, aren't there?"

Tommen grunted. He made to leave, but once more, Rifun held him back, saying, "And just something to keep in mind. You're one of those flies, too."

"What happened to keeping your word and sparing those you say you will spare?"

"It only means I won't kill you. But Borelian slavery is still a very viable option. Something to consider."

Tommen tried to just walk away from it, keep his back straight and shoulders square. He told himself that his hunched creep was due to fatigue and the low-hanging branches. It was a lie.

If he wanted to be honest, he was frustrated. He was sick of putting up with Rifun's bullshit, trying to make sense of his weird threats and crackpot religion. He was tired of everything being a moving target, whether it was his mood swings, his seemingly ever-changing contracts and deals and whatever the fuck else he came up with, or anything at all. Once upon a time, back during the murders and shit, Rifun had seemed to be a pretty predictable, reliable, even if frightening as fuck, bad guy. He tried and failed to kill Lily Guile. Open and shut, well, at first. He tried and failed to be King of Time. Open and shut. Now everything about him seemed super dodgy, his plans, his motivations. He really didn't seem to have either. That was what made him dangerous.

And if Tommen wanted to be even more honest, even though he'd never admit it out loud, he was afraid. Rifun had tremendous power that he could invoke at will. What was worse, where most men spent only a short time on death ground before either being shot or taken into custody with evaluation and treatment, Rifun seemed to have not only set up camp, but was working on building himself a permanent residence, or maybe an apartment complex so his weirdo cronies could join him.

When he emerged into the camp clearing, all was as it had been. Nothing was burning down, the gas tank hadn't exploded, and no one was lying dead in the open. That wasn't to say Tommen was eager to find out if anyone was lying dead in their bunks, but for the moment, everything appeared normal.

He made a quick trip to the bathroom, telling himself to just breathe and remain calm. He also reminded himself that while Rifun was powerful, he was not God. He could not see all and know all. All Tommen had to do was wait until the camp was busy enough that he could fire off a quick warning text to his dad or Micaiah so they knew what was going on. Unless Rifun was standing there looking over his shoulder, he wouldn't know if Tommen was texting his dad or Becky. And even then, he wouldn't know if Tommen was texting his dad a warning or simply a pleasant good morning and inquiring after his knee and how things were going with Laura.

But damn did he feel like he was walking a tightrope. There had to be a way to get the jump on this guy, disable him long enough to shoot him or strangle him or do something.

Tommen zipped up and stumbled back to the cabin, fatigue dragging at his heels and his eyelids. Checking the time, he was only going to get a few hours of sleep, and that was assuming he got to sleep right away. More likely, he was going to be laying there for a while, staring into the darkness, his mind torn between trying to figure out what the fuck just happened and how to ignore whatever the fuck just happened so he could try and get some sleep.

He paused outside the cabin and looked around. Yawi's tracks still circled the cabin and seemed to make a perimeter loop, but the wolf was nowhere to be seen. Well, maybe he'd realized that his master was gone and decided to move on. Either way, it wasn't hanging around, looking for scratches and treats, or whatever Saul did with it. Maybe they went hunting together or something. Great, something else for his mind to dwell on while he tried to sleep.

He slipped inside the cabin. The new door didn't squeak and the new handle didn't rattle, so he was almost silent except for a few squeaky floorboards. If anyone noticed the boards, though, they gave no indication of it. All around him, the boys slept soundly. He did notice that, compared to the younger kids' camp, the cabin was decidedly warmer thanks to the increase in body heat. In August, this was not a welcome change.

His sleeping bag was long since cold, and he came almost fully awake as he slipped into it. Wonderful, just one more thing for his mind to think about while he tried to sleep. He sighed. There would be no sleep for him tonight, no matter how tired he got.

After a few minutes, he rolled over and checked his phone, squinting against the blinding light. Almost quarter to four. Fucking hell. Had he really been out that long? Well, no matter. He racked his brain, trying to think. If he waited just a few more minutes, his dad would be getting up to get ready for work. Wait a few more minutes, and the twins, or at least Micah would be doing the same. He could text any of them, really. He certainly didn't have to force himself to stay awake for another fifteen, twenty minutes. There were any number of things his mind could mull over while he waited, like the things Rifun had taught him, whether or not Saul went hunting with his wolf, how far he could push his luck with Rifun as far as the reporting went, whether any of the boys had noticed him missing.

He jerked awake at a squeak in the floorboards. Not moving his body, Tommen looked over. One of the boys was climbing carefully out of bed and heading outside. No crazy psycho killer come to murder them all.

He looked at the time. Five o'clock. So he'd gotten a nap in. Probably all he was going to get at this point. He opened a text, electing to send it to Micaiah. His dad and Micah would be up and ready for a conversation. Micaiah, seeing it wasn't urgent, would grumble and growl, turn his phone off, roll over, and go back to bed. Then he would respond later, once he and Tommen were more rested and in a better mood.

"Met with Rifun tonight. Did some training. Your life and others dependent on me training with him. Says telling you is forbidden. Threats ensued. Just thought you should know."

Tommen stared at the text. Just thought you should know? That was like writing a quick note and sticking it on the fridge. Hey, I ate the rest of the macaroni salad that I knew you wanted to take for your lunch. Just thought you should know. Or, Laura is coming by for dinner on Tuesday so don't make any big plans. Just thought you should know. Since when did threats from Rifun qualify for something as mundane as "Just thought you should know"?

Shaking his head, Tommen sent the text. He set his phone aside and rubbed his eyes, tried to tell himself he had to get some sleep before he went insane. But then, maybe it was too late for that.

Chapter Thirty-Three
Smoke on the Water

Tommen wasn't even sure he got more sleep between the time he sent the text and when the alarm went off. He'd no sooner woken up than he remembered Charlie was going to be leaving soon because his dad was supposed to be arriving at about the same time as the alarm going off. Fuck. Because he really needed this kind of stress right off the bat. Maybe he should just go home and forget all of this. It was like a bad dream or something.

Thankfully, Charlie was completely prepared. By the time Tommen was ready to slog off to the bathroom and make himself basically presentable, he was already packed up and ready to go, though he hardly looked enthusiastic.

"Do you not want to go home now?" Tommen asked.

"It's not that," Charlie said. "But, I mean, my dad is going to want to know why I want to go home, which I get. But then I have to tell him what happened. It's not always easy telling my dad stuff. My dad's a veteran, too, but he's more of the...suck it up, take it like a man. Here, let me tell you about some of the things that I had to see and do."

"Twenty miles, barefoot, uphill both ways?"

"Basically."

"Maybe you could try telling him enough to get through the conversation on the way home, then when you talk to your uncle, maybe have your uncle talk to your dad and try to explain things a little better."

Charlie mulled it over for a second, then shrugged. "I guess."

Before either could say more, a large blue pickup pulled into the parking lot. Bags were loaded, kid was loaded, then it was over to the office to sign a few papers. Then he was gone. Just like that, all evidence of Charlie ever having been at camp that summer was wiped clean.

Few of the other boys seemed to notice or acknowledge his absence as they went about their morning routine.

"Is it supposed to be hot today?" JJ asked.

Harry gave him a look. "It's eight in the morning and it's almost seventy with humidity so high we're practically underwater. I'd say it's going to be hot."

He was exaggerating a little on the humidity part, but he was right that it was quite warm already and only going to get warmer. That could make the outdoor adventure week miserable, but if it kept up for another week, it would make water week awesome. Unlike the younger kids' camp where it seemed like it had rained every other day, the older kids' camp was mostly hot and dry. The only reason they kept the campfires going at night was because there were four garden hoses ready and waiting at any given moment if anything escaped.

As the group headed to the main hall for breakfast, Tommen's phone chirped. As expected, it was Micaiah.

" 'Just thought you should know.' How quaint."

"Well, it wasn't really anything unusual or unexpected, which is both weird and annoying," Tommen replied. "And I didn't think you were going to rush out here at a moment's notice anyway."

"You do have a point. What did he teach you, or supposedly teach you?"

Tommen did his best to detail the training from the previous evening, but fatigue muddled his memory, and he was sure he missed a few things.

"What do you mean by 'supposedly' teach?" he asked at the end. "Isn't the Akari just the Akari?"

He could imagine Micaiah shaking his head as he answered, "Not necessarily. Not all who call themselves Akarin wield the Akari, and there are more forces in the universe that just the Akari and Time. Similarly, some groups would claim to wield the Akari, yet do not consider themselves Akarin."

"Why can't all the groups just get along? Or maybe make their lines in the sandbox a little neater and easier to distinguish?"

"Believe me, you are not the only one asking that question. All right, I'll take your report and send it along. The more people with the information the better."

"Now what? I mean, what do I do? I don't want to train under him. Micaiah, he's freaking me out. It's like he's officially gone insane."

"He went insane a long time ago. All that's left is for his facade to fail, which it is. I would recommend that you carry on like normal. Enjoy camp. But don't make any unnecessary midnight excursions."

"I'll try."

"That's all I can ask."

"Hey, so, does my dad know? About Saul, I mean?"

"Yes, I told him. Would you like me to tell him to call you when he comes in, or can you find time to call?"

"If I call, then I have to explain, and I don't have the time. If you can just tell him, I'll see if I can call him later after dinner or something."

"All right. Hang tight. We'll get you out of there soon."

Tommen almost texted back, "If you had started training me in the first place, this rescue mission probably could have been avoided altogether!"

But he didn't. Because he was half the reason he needed to be rescued. And he knew it. So he just got his breakfast and sat down at the table with the rest of the boys.

It was adventure week. And it was hot. The horseback riding was done in the shade, and that made it bearable. The rock climbing was not done in the shade, and multiple jokes were made about them being baked alive on a real stone hearth, and about what pizza toppings would go good with each camper. Apparently, Tommen came across as a chicken parmesan sort of pizza. Maybe it was because of how white he was, though you'd never know it, seeing how both burned and tanned he'd become.

He finally found ten minutes to call his dad and tell him what happened. As expected, Walter offered to pick him up, but Tommen refused. He still had his obligation to the boys, and he was fine. It was fading. He could last a couple more weeks. His dad relented, but gave him the speech about "if he needed to talk."

Meanwhile, Tommen did as Micaiah suggested, sticking to the camp routine and not going out on any late night walks. Rifun did not come calling, nor did Micaiah say whether any further threats had been made or if there had been any attempts on anyone's life. He did mention that there had been more attacks on human colony planets by the Borelians, but the rest of the colonies were beginning to organize and ally themselves. Supposedly, Earth's strongest alliance came from, no surprise, Hlohi, thanks to Kayla's efforts to unify them through District Nine. He did not go into detail, but both he and Tommen figured that was something of a trade secret.

As far as the Akarin, well, things were sort of straightening out. Now that the initial hype and fury over the ban had died down, most of the leaders were more willing to talk. Micaiah had his doubts over whether their talking was producing any results. But that was all politics anyway, something Tommen didn't need to concern himself with.

Although, whether or not he had information to process, Tommen's mind was determined to concern itself with anything and everything. Three nights of little or poor sleep was wearing on him. Eventually, it had to break, get to a point where he was just so exhausted that he would conk out and sleep a hard eight to ten, regardless of any alarm. Maybe it was the heat getting to him, making him dehydrated. Mr. Wilson had finally called off the campfires until further notice because of the lack of rain.

"When is it supposed to rain?" JJ complained. "I want to have a campfire."

"I want this humidity to break," Jason said. "Holy crap."

"Yeah, but with our luck, it's going to rain all during water week so we don't get to do anything," Nathan grumbled. Tommen did not say that he secretly agreed with him. Instead, he spoke up and calmly said, "I'm sure it will break eventually. And if it does rain a little during water week, so what? We've got plenty to do around here. And I don't think it would rain the entire week, so we would probably still get in a few days."

The response was less than encouraging, so Tommen decided to suggest they get some sleep. It was more for his benefit than theirs, but they took the hint, slipping into sleeping bags and flicking off the light.

Tommen couldn't decide whether he was dreaming, or if he actually woke up several times that night. The first time, he thought he might have heard Yawi stalking around outside. Through bleary eyes, he might have caught a glimpse of white fur, but he really couldn't be certain. The second time, he thought he heard one or a couple of the boys getting up and heading out on a midnight bathroom run. He was pretty sure he was awake at that point because he considered joining them. In the end, fatigue must have won out.

The third time he woke wasn't too long after that as the boys returned, whispering and tiptoeing and slipping back into sleeping bags, or on top of sleeping bags as weather demanded. The temperature and humidity wasn't unbearable at night, but packing eleven sweaty teenagers into a single cabin was quite toasty.

The fourth time Tommen came awake, he almost came out of his skin, too, as Saul looked down at him in the gloom.

"Oh, shit!"

In his bid to escape, the most he did was fall out of bed. His antics did not wake the boys, but as he looked around, he saw the cabin was empty. When he looked at Saul, he found it wasn't Saul, but Chandler.

"Oh, fuck," Tommen breathed, putting a hand to his chest. "Don't fucking scare me like that." He sighed. "Are you and Saul related? Like, ancient ancestor or something?"

Well, for one thing, at least Chandler knew how to smile instead of smirk, like the rest of the Wolf Clan apparently. He shook his head. "Would it matter?"

"I guess not, but... Oh my...holy crap. What are you doing here?"

Now Chandler smirked. "Oh, so now you believe I am actually here and this isn't just some dream conjured up by the neurons in your brain as your subconscious tries to give you information."

Tommen shook his head. "I don't know, man."

"Why does it take a trick of evil in order to make you believe what good has been trying to tell you all along? There is more to the universe than what can simply be seen or tested in a laboratory."

"Great, so you're an angel. Are you here to comfort me in my woe and despair of Saul's death?"

Chandler raised a brow. "You know what I've always wondered?"

"No. What?"

"Why in the world humans are always such mouthy, back-talking brats."

"That's kind of a harsh judgment, don't you think?"

"Depends. When have we ever conversed where you didn't say something snarky and sarcastic and try to somehow prove my nonexistence?"

Tommen opened his mouth but had no answer. Finally he just shrugged.

"Anyway," Chandler went on, "that's not why I'm here. I am here to warn you of dangers to come."

"Well, I hate to say it, but you're about a year too late on that one."

"I'm not talking about Rifun, or not only about him."

"Oh, wonderful. You mean there's more?"

Chandler nodded gravely. "I am speaking of the power that controls Rifun. You and it are on a collision course."

Tommen rubbed his eyes. "Fantastic. Is there any more to this or are we going to play the pronoun game? Do I get any details of this doomsday prophecy or is it going to be just vague enough that I can blame every bad thing on it?"

"See, there you go again with the mouthy back-talking. I really don't understand it."

"Are you going to answer my question? What is this power, how are we going to meet, and what can I do to stop it? Or at the very least, escape it? Run away from it?"

"It is a deceptive power, one you cannot defeat on your own. You may run from it, but you cannot escape it."

Tommen rolled his eyes. "God, I love prophets."

Chandler dipped his head. "But if you wish to have a chance against it, search me out."

"Excellent. I love a course of action. Where are you? Or how can I find you?"

"Let the wolf guide your way."

Tommen gently knocked his head against the upper bunk a couple times. "Why are these things never clear? Is it too much to ask for just a straight answer, a—"

"Are you quite done complaining?" Chandler interrupted.

"No!" Tommen barked. "I want a straight fucking answer! I want to know who or what this power is. I want to know when and how we're going to meet. If I can't stop it alone, fine. Who or what do I need to find in order to defeat it? Because I am sick of this shit with Rifun, the threats and the training and the people dying; I want it all to be over! I want things to go back to the way they were before."

For a long moment, Chandler did not speak and the cabin was silent. After a minute or two, Chandler made a motion, saying. "Come here. A little closer." Tommen took a step forward. "Little closer." He leaned in. "Little closer, little more."

Tommen leaned in close so Chandler could get right up next to him and whisper in his ear. For a moment, there was nothing but soft breathing. Then, finally, "No."

Suddenly it was like Tommen was hit with a battering ram straight in the chest as he went flying across the cabin which had inexplicably grown larger. Then he was falling, falling, into a black chasm with no foreseeable bottom. He heard echoes of voices and laughter, but could not make out individual words or voices. The air was sucked from his lungs as he tried to breathe. The voices gradually stopped echoing, and that could only mean one thing—

Tommen came awake suddenly, sitting up in his bunk and only narrowly missing the bar of the upper bunk above his head. He was slick with sweat and breathing heavily. All around him, the boys slept soundly, if noisily, between the snoring, the shuffling, the scratching, the farting, and other assorted bodily noises. Outside, it appeared as though the first colors of dawn were just streaking through the sky as clouds made the light waver.

He lay back in bed. His dreams had gone beyond weird; they were practically uncontrollably insane. He needed therapy or something. Maybe Saul's death had affected him more than he realized. Maybe he really should talk to a shrink. Oh, this was just fucking unbelievable.

Well, either way, nature was calling. He hadn't gotten up earlier, and with his adrenaline pumping, he really needed to go now. Grudgingly, he swung his legs over the edge of the bed and stood, stretching and yawning and feeling like he hadn't slept well at all. He narrowly avoided the foot of the one bed that had been the cause of his stubbed toe misery lately as he made it to the cabin door. Moving around, he felt nauseous and sick to his stomach, and his lungs felt heavy, as if from Rifun's little drowning trick. Maybe he'd found out that Tommen had texted Micaiah about the meeting. Maybe this was some subtle sign that he wanted to meet and have some sort of chat about rules or discipline.

First things first, though, Tommen had to pee. Regardless of Rifun's wrath, things would not go well if he ended up pissing down his leg. There was no good way to explain that away in the laundry. Even among the younger kids, it was a sign of shame. One kid from

Beaver Cabin had actually peed his pants or wet the bed or some such thing, and he ended up going home crying because of the ridicule of the other boys. How much worse would it be for a counselor to do that in a cabin full of teenage boys?

But that was neither here nor there. Tommen made it out of the cabin without disturbing any of the sleeping campers, and he even got to the bathrooms without pissing down his leg. The fresh air had relieved his nausea some, but he still ended up coughing and hacking, almost sure that he was coming down with something. Well, camp full of campers all traipsing around the woods and various places, someone was bound to pick up something somewhere.

Typically when that happened, the sick camper was sent to spend a day or two with Michelle, just to make sure it wasn't the flu or anything really harmful. If Tommen got sick, though, would Mr. Wilson have to step in as counselor entirely? How would that go over?

Tommen washed his hands and stepped outside. But now that he was a little more awake, he was also a little more confused. He'd thought that it was almost dawn because of the light, but, looking around, the sky was still pretty dark. More than that, though, it was hard to see. It was way too humid to be foggy, and the temperature variance from the cabin up to the bathrooms was too great. Furthermore, fog settled in low places. As he descended the hill toward the cabin, the fog got thinner. Therefore, it wasn't fog...but smoke.

Carefully, he picked his way down the hill in the wavering darkness, past the cabins to toward the campfire site. He didn't even make it to the site before he knew exactly what he saw, exactly what he feared. The fire ring itself was filled only with coals, but at some point, embers had gotten kicked up and ignited the leaves and brush a short distance away. Anything small and used for kindling, like leaves and small twigs, those had already burned away. Now the larger sticks and logs were burning steadily, following the path from stick to stick to stick to log to tree.

Breath catching in his lungs, Tommen made a dash for the water faucet, cranking it wide open and following the hose down to the pit, scooping up the end and blasting the hell out of anything that glowed red.

The problem was, hitting hot stuff with cold water produced more smoke and steam which made it hard to see. Once Tommen stopped spraying and waited for the fog to clear, he found the problem was a lot bigger than originally anticipated. The fire had already left the confines of the campsite and surrounding area. Only the wind direction kept the flames moving down the valley, away from the camp, but even an idiot knew that it could change in an instant and put them all in danger. One little garden hose, even all four little garden hoses would have little effect on the fire now.

Heart thudding wildly in his chest, Tommen made a mad dash for the nearest cabin, Coon Cabin, pounding wildly on the door. For a long moment, there was no answer, but he persisted, using one fist, then both fists, yelling for all he was worth. With the noise, he might even rouse some of the other cabins.

Suddenly, the door flung wide open.

"What?" Gary demanded.

"There's a forest fire. We have to evacuate!" Tommen said pointing in the general direction of the fire before nearly falling off the porch in his attempt to reach the next cabin. Even as he crossed the open ground, he heard general commotion behind him.

Bear Cabin was next. Apparently, his ruckus at Coon Cabin had woken someone up, because he didn't have to pound on the door long before it opened. He relayed the warning again and moved on to Beaver Cabin. In his peripheral vision, Tommen saw someone run across the field to start waking up the girls. It came none too soon as the wind shifted and started blowing parallel to the camp. If it shifted again and started blowing it back toward camp, well, fire traveled upward and the entire camp was situated on a hill; it would be nothing for one cabin to catch fire, then another and another.

By the time he made it back to Wolf Cabin, a couple of the

boys were blearily coming awake, blinking sleepily and drunkenly trying to sit up. A couple of them were coughing and hacking, and JJ was looking pretty green. The cabins were by no means air tight, and smoke had begun to filter in. Probably their only saving grace was that the new windows and doors were sealed a little better than the old ones.

Tommen's eyes were watering as he flung open all the windows and started shouting at the boys to hurry up and get out of bed.

"What's the big deal?" Jason asked sleepily even as he rummaged around for a pair of pants.

"The camp is on fire!" Tommen snapped, maybe a little more harshly than necessary. "Grab only what you can carry! Don't worry about anything material because your life is worth more!"

Even so, he took a minute to grab his hearing aids and put them in, then stuff the charger in his jacket. Other than being immensely helpful in an emergency situation, there was no way he would be able to face his dad and tell him—again—that he needed new hearing aids and a new charger. He'd probably understand, true, but why go through the hassle?

He Banded and looked around at his things. Other than his hearing aids, his phone, and his wallet, he couldn't say that he had a whole lot that he might consider valuable. He hadn't brought any other electronics, and clothes were clothes. They could be replaced easily. Same with any of the other small things he'd packed. This was only camp, not his bedroom.

Tommen dropped the Band and looked around at the boys. "As soon as you are ready, grab a buddy and go up to the parking lot! Stick together! If Mr. Wilson has instructions for you, follow them immediately! Don't wait for me, and now is not the time to get smart and talk back!"

A couple of the boys had already gone, but he really hadn't been giving instructions for their benefit. Speaking the procedure aloud did wonders for his sanity. Yes, the camp was burning down.

Yes, the entire mountain would have to be evacuated. In fact, crews were likely already on their way, if not already here. But there were crews, and there was a plan, and if they all stuck to the plan, then no one would get hurt. Well, rephrase that. People were less likely to get hurt. He had a pretty good feeling that most firefighting plans went something like, "Put the damn fire out," and yet firefighters still got hurt.

He shook his head, trying to clear it. Fire moved quickly, but smoke moved even quicker. The cabin was full of it now, and it was almost impossible to see. Tommen couldn't breathe for shit, and he was pretty sure he was going to be sick as soon as he hit open air. He pushed the boys along, telling them to move it or lose it. They had their chance to grab whatever they needed, and now they had to go. On a normal day, they would probably be protesting and complaining. Now, though, the best they could manage was a wheezing cough.

Looking down the hill, Tommen could see that Coon Cabin was already engulfed, the old pine logs acting like gasoline as the flames shot twenty feet in the air, licking at the dry leaves of the overshadowing trees. Across the way, fire had just started creeping up to the girls' cabins, testing the foundation, the porch, the lower logs. Once it found purchase, it was like lighting a matchstick statue.

The whole camp was old, almost half a century old. And it was dry from several weeks of no rain and scorching sun. In the five seconds it took Tommen to look around and come to this obvious conclusion, the first flames were tearing into Bear Cabin. The only thing between Bear Cabin and Wolf Cabin was Beaver Cabin, and that was no kind of comfort.

Seeing how he appeared to be the only one standing around like an idiot instead of running for his life, Tommen finally got his feet moving and stumbled up the hill. With the open air, the smoke was less dense, but the canopy of the trees still kept some of it down near the ground. Having to go up the hill to the parking lot was exhausting enough without the added difficulty breathing. He went to his knees once and threw up, his stomach roiling, his head felt full of cotton, but he forced himself to stand and make a last mad dash for the parking lot.

He'd no sooner touched asphalt than someone grabbed his arm and hurried him along. He had no clue where he was going, but anywhere away from the fire was all right with him. Before he knew quite what was happening, he was pushed into a seat. Before anyone could say or do anything for him, he got sick again, relinquishing the last of his dinner. Strangely, he found himself lamenting the fact that this fire was going to cause him to miss breakfast. Fuck.

"Hey, are you all right?" someone asked.

Tommen looked up to see Brian staring down at him. "What? No, yeah, I'm fine. I'm good. Just the smoke made me a little dizzy is all."

"Here." Brian thrust a water bottle into his hands. "Drink this and count your kids. Jerry's getting the buses and everything all fired up so we can get the hell out of here."

Tommen nodded blankly and opened the water bottle, chugging its contents until he thought he would throw that up, too. He looked around for a minute, just trying to get his bearings, even as he coughed and hacked along with the rest of them. After a moment or two, it occurred to him that he probably should get his boys together and make sure they were all present and accounted for. He was pretty sure they'd all been in the cabin when he first sounded the alarm, but he had to be sure none of them had gotten all turned around in the bid to run up the hill to the parking lot and escape the flames.

He found Jason and JJ first. To think that a week ago they'd been ready to tear each other apart over some stupid knife. Now they'd worked together to be sure both of them made it out safely. They'd even gone out on their own little side quest to make sure the girls got out safely, too.

Of course, safe was a relative term. The fire wouldn't stop at the parking lot because it thought there was some invisible force field there. There were still trees all around the parking lot and all down the other side of the mountain — and up the side of the next mountain. And every single tree was just as dry as every one that had burned so far.

Tommen gathered his scattered campers like a mother hen gathering her chicks, constantly counting them and absently rattling off their names just to be sure, constantly reminding himself that Charlie had gone home earlier that morning. Lucky bastard. He should have done the same thing. Well, that was neither here nor there.

As he went about his business, getting all of his campers together to a safe location in the parking lot, his head cleared up a little, enough that he could think straight and form coherent sentences without sounding like a babbling idiot. His throat and sinuses burned like hell, his stomach still bubbled discontentedly, and his head sort of felt like he had a hangover, but he was on the mend, he figured. He even managed to breathe a sigh of relief as the wind changed again and started blowing back down the mountain, taking the smoke away from them for the time being.

"Oh my God," Nathan said, rubbing his face. "Oh my God."

"We'll be all right now," Tommen told them. "Mr. Wilson is going to bring the buses around, and then we'll all head down the mountain. You can call your parents, and we'll all go home."

"Oh my God," Nathan repeated. "I can't believe this."

"It's been dry. Dry lightning is very possible." He elected not to mention his suspicions that someone had intentionally started a fire in the fire pit and it had gotten out of control.

Dan shook his head. "It wasn't dry lightning." He studied the ground guiltily. "We did this."

Tommen raised a brow. "Oh? Care to explain?"

"We wanted a campfire," Harry confessed surprisingly. "And we wanted to be able to tell 'ghost' stories that we normally couldn't share at the group campfires. We had all the hoses and it never got very big, just enough to see each other, you know? When we were done, we hosed it down and thought it was good."

Tommen rubbed his eyes. Of course Wolf Cabin boys would be behind it.

"It wasn't just us," Nathan said quickly. "A couple of boys from other cabins and a couple girls came out, too." He shrugged. "Sorry to say, but after a few days, you counselors sleep like rocks, so we knew we could get away with it. Unless, you know, this happened." He gestured to the fire.

Tommen shifted in his seat. "You boys do understand why Mr. Wilson called off the campfires, right?"

"We thought the hoses would be enough. And we did spray it out."

"That doesn't mean that it was completely out. With the ground as dry as it is, the water probably got soaked right up. The embers probably reignited, a wind carried them out of the ring where they settled onto dry leaves or whatever, and whoosh! Instant wildfire."

He did not mention that he'd done the same thing once. He'd been about their age, just starting out on his illegal trapping, and getting more of a feel for Time and how to use it, manipulate it, and strengthen his paltry abilities. He'd just finished checking his traps, finding that most of them had been discovered and/or confiscated, and settled down to pout about how he hadn't gotten anything. So he did what all good thirteen year old boys did at such times, he decided to play with fire. It hadn't been quite as dry as it was now at camp, but he didn't have the benefit of a garden hose at that time. He thought the fire had burned low enough that he could leave it, and so he did, heading for home with nothing to show for his efforts. But where the DNR had discovered his traps, they did not discover his fire so quickly, at least, not until it was a much bigger problem. Thankfully, only about thirty acres had been burned by the time it was completely put out.

Looking at the fire now, Tommen knew that there would be a lot more than thirty acres burned. Right now, it was still moving with the wind, but eventually, it would get big enough where it would move anywhere it wanted to, wind or no wind. Peering through the smoke down into the valley, it was like a gas line heading all the way down to wherever the valley went. The fire would catch and take off.

"Oh my God," Nathan said, looking ready to cry. "I can't believe we did this. Camp is ruined forever because of us."

"The camp is burning to the ground, true, but it can be rebuilt," Tommen told him, hoping to sound encouraging. "Who here wouldn't like to sleep in a cabin where the mice haven't made nests in the walls next to the electrical outlets and drafts don't come at you from every angle?" He sighed when no one reacted. "It will be okay, guys. Really, it will. But you know that once we get down to safety, you will have to tell Mr. Wilson about what happened."

"We know," Dan sighed.

Harry shook his head. "I am going to be in so much fucking trouble."

There was nothing Tommen could say to make them feel any better, he knew. They knew very well that they had done something they shouldn't have. Not only that, but it had caused a much bigger problem, a much bigger fire than any of them had wanted. Not only that, but they'd also successfully burned down the camp. Maybe now they would understand what it meant to be a Wolf Cabin camper. Sure, they knew it meant that they were troubled or troublemakers in some fashion, but this would follow them, maybe for the rest of their lives. They weren't arsonists, but they would probably be treated like it if any of the other campers ever found out, which they inevitably would.

He almost wished he could conjure up enough sympathy to say that he wasn't going to make them tell about what they did, but he knew them too well. He was one of them, after all. One of them would blab, and word would spread. Mr. Wilson might find out or he might not, and he may or may not suspect Tommen's involvement or at least his knowledge. But it was all moot. If the boys manned up and told the truth now, it would be easier for them in the long run. If only he could give that advice to himself five years ago. When had he become so philosophical and an expert on such matters?

He heard sirens in the distance, but knew that it would be a few minutes before the fire crews actually arrived. Mountain roads were a bitch. It was like the driveway to the Durvins' house. Less than a quarter mile from top to bottom, but with the way the drive had to be constructed, it was easily three quarters of a mile or more.

The fire trucks pulled in just as the wind shifted again. Shawn White Cloud went to meet them, pointing here, pointing there, making gestures and screwed up faces. More trucks pulled into the lot, scattering counselors and campers. Most of the rigs were fire trucks, but the ambulances came in behind them, staying to the far edge of the lot. Lights were everywhere. Flashing lights, spotlights, scene lights, flashlights, and somewhere in the sky, the sun was just starting to peek over the edge of the horizon. Michelle herded a few select campers into an ambulance; Tommen did not see any obvious injury, though he thought he recalled that one of them had epilepsy.

He turned his attention back to Shawn who was now speaking to a couple firemen, both with fancier helmets, one reading "Chief" and another reading "Captain." There were more gestures and pointing, now around the lot at the different counselors and campers, huddled in various groups around the lot. After a minute, the conversation wrapped up and Shawn headed around the lot, speaking to the different groups.

Meanwhile, the firemen were busy offloading gear and equipment, shouldering air packs and tightening chin straps on helmets. They all had tags which they handed off, attaching them to this truck or that truck before taking the plunge down the hill. Tommen found himself smiling wryly. Going down was the easy part; it was the climb back up that was the bitch, and they had to do it in heavy ass gear.

Soon Tommen discovered the plan, as Shawn spoke to each counselor. Mr. Wilson, wherever he was, was taking too damn long. The counselors were to pack their vehicles full of campers and get the fuck away from camp. They were going to meet up at the park in the town where pretty much everyone stopped to eat before and after camp.

"We don't have enough vehicles for everyone to go at once," Shawn explained once he got to Tommen. "We're taking the girls out first. The ambulances will be taking any injured campers, as you might have guessed. We'll be back for a second trip. If something happens and you guys are forced to leave before we get back, call me. Someone here has my number."

"I know," Tommen said. "I do. How long do you think it will take?"

"Damned if I know. Half an hour, maybe more. Each way. It could be a wait. That's why I said to call me if anything changes."

"Got it. Where's Mr. Wilson?"

"Honestly, I don't know. Maybe the buses wouldn't start again or something. But we don't have time to wait for him. This is the plan, and we're sticking to it for the foreseeable future. Any questions?"

"No sir. We'll be here."

"Good man. We'll see you boys in a bit."

With that, he turned and stalked off. Already some of the counselors were pulling out of their parking spots and leaving, cars and vans and trucks stuffed full of campers. Tommen could tell that there would be more than two trips needed to get everyone out. If they were taking just the girls out first, they were already leaving some behind.

It was probably an hour before they returned, and another group of campers was taken away. Wolf Cabin was not among them. By this time, dawn had broken. The roaring flames stood out against thick black smoke, but the firefighters were not giving an inch when it came to the camp side of the fire. Tommen could not speak for whatever was going on in the valley, but they appeared to be safe there at the top of the hill.

Mr. Wilson still had not returned.

Fear lodged itself in Tommen's gut, though he remained stoic and impassive on the outside. What if something had happened to him? The garage should not have been affected by the fire yet, so what was going on? Okay, so maybe the buses weren't starting. He highly doubted that the man would just sit there in the garage, tinkering with mechanics for an hour while his camp was burning down and his campers were in danger. He'd try a few quick fixes, then return and come up with a plan B.

"Stay here," Tommen told his boys, standing and approaching the fire trucks, looking for an officer. Or anyone at all, really.

"Stay back, man," one firefighter told him as he got close. "It's hot and dangerous and you don't want to be breathing this stuff."

"I know that, but..." He searched for words. "Someone's gone missing."

The firefighter looked uncertain, but motioned for him to wait. A few minutes later, another firefighter, his helmet reading "Lieutenant," appeared.

"What's this about someone going missing?" he asked. "As I understand it, you guys are evacuating."

"I know, but he's been gone too long. Well, okay, so, he was supposed to be going to the garage to get the buses to haul everyone out of here at once. That was when this whole thing started. That was an hour ago, or more."

"Where's the garage?"

"Not in the line of fire." He turned and pointed back across the parking lot. "I mean, it's just down there—"

"Wendy! Carl!" the lieutenant barked. Two more firefighters approached. Their helmets and heavy outer jackets were off, sweat had plastered their hair to their scalps, and they each had a cold bottle of water and a chocolate bar of some form. Still, they appeared alert and ready for anything. The lieutenant addressed them. "You feeling up to a small mission?"

"Sure, what's up?" the woman, Wendy, inquired, looking first at her officer, then at Tommen.

"This young man here says one of their guys has gone

missing. Says he went to a garage somewhere over that way, was supposed to get a couple of buses started, never returned." The lieutenant turned back to Tommen. "You know exactly where this garage is?"

No. "Yes."

Back to the two grunts. "You two go with him. Make sure the garage is safe, look for the guy." Back to Tommen. "Is it terribly far?"

"Not really, but I mean, everything's up and down hill."

Back to the grunts. "Grab one of the ambulance crews, too. Save time trying to haul him back up here if there is some emergency involved."

"Yes sir," Carl said, chugging his water and tossing the empty bottle away. He looked at Tommen. "Lead the way."

Wendy went off to grab an ambulance crew, while Tommen started nervously across the parking lot.

"What's your name?" Carl asked.

"Tommen. Tommen Forbes," Tommen replied nervously.

"Well, Tommen, you ever seen anything like this before?"

Tommen's breath caught in his throat and he managed a small, "Well...yeah. I've seen worse, actually."

"Ever wanted to become a firefighter?"

"No. And even if I did, I don't think I could. See, my dad's a cop."

Carl just laughed. They met up with Wendy and the ambulance crew. All of them were very serious and mission-oriented, to be sure, but none of them had the fear that Tommen had, that a really bad day was only just the beginning, and a very modest description of things to come.

Chapter Thirty-Four
Fire in the Sky

No, Tommen did not actually know where the bus garage was, not exactly. He knew it was down a short distance from the camp because it was the only spot level enough for such a large garage to be built. Mostly, though, it was just Mr. Wilson or a couple of the other counselors and staff who were licensed to drive the buses who went down and brought them up to the parking lot in order to get all the campers loaded and whisk them away to whatever adventure they were on that day. Then, at the end of the day, they would be brought back, dropped off in the parking lot, and the buses crept quietly away, back to their little hidey-hole.

The only saving grace came from the fact that it was supposed to still be visible from the road, and Tommen thought he had seen it on occasion when they drove by. Plus the fact that it couldn't be too far away, considering how little time it took the buses to get up to the camp, and it would probably be the only other drive this far up the mountain; the camp didn't exactly have a ton of neighbors.

"So, tell us about this guy we're looking for," Wendy said, all business.

"Um, his name is Jerry Wilson. Little shorter than me, maybe two hundred pounds, max," Tommen told them. "I mean, theoretically, he should be the only one in the garage. Or I would think so. If something happened to him and someone else was there, they should report it. Right?"

Wendy said nothing and Carl merely grunted.

Tommen almost wanted to Band and call out to see if Rifun was watching. The boys had admitted to being the cause of the blaze, but there was no reason not to think Rifun would take advantage of the situation, attempt to trap the campers and counselors just to make a point to Tommen about his power, as if there had ever been any doubt.

They found the dirt drive more by chance than intent. It went up a gentle slope and curved around the hill to the garage which was almost out of sight. Mr. Wilson had once explained that the garage and the buses were the most recent addition to the camp, and it showed in the landscape around the garage. Excavation was still very much in evidence as the plants and land hadn't settled and regrown, as if around an older structure. To that end, the ground was still quite soft and even sandy, that is, where it wasn't rutted and washed out from the last time it had rained, however long ago that had been.

The good news, though, was that the building was not on fire, or not yet anyway. At the moment, there were no guarantees about anything.

The garage itself was quite massive, able to house three buses and half a dozen smaller vans and vehicles. As Tommen approached, his mind involuntarily went to the warehouse, how big it had been, how stuffed with stuff, how dark, how frightening. His throat closed and his heart seized as he reached for the door handle on the man door with shaking hands. He forced his fear to the back of his mind, telling himself to be a man and not let the fear control him. It was almost a year since that event; he should be over this by now. But his thoughts felt hollow, and as the door squeaked open to reveal a flickering light within, every sense in his body told him to turn and flee as far and as fast as he could. It didn't help that his unwanted subconscious subtly reminded him that his dad wasn't here to save him this time if something went wrong.

But three steps into the garage and his mind registered something else, one which the firefighters picked up on as well when they stepped inside. Carl took a step forward and put an arm out to stop him.

"Do you smell that?" he asked quietly, as if speaking too loud might make the garage spontaneously combust.

"Electrical burn," Tommen answered. Earlier in the year, the cafeteria at school had caught fire because of an electrical fire in one of the ovens, and the smell had permeated the entire cafeteria for a week. This smelled similar to that, but with the added tinge of automotive, which was not a comfort.

"I'm going to call for a few extra guys," Wendy said, stepping back outside.

Carl nodded absently and looked at Tommen. "Do you know where the extinguishers are in here?"

"No, not really. I mean, the buses should have them though, right?"

"Should." He looked around, examining the room in the dim light, looking at all windows, doors, vehicles, assessing the situation while he could still see. In the event of fire, he would be making his way blind.

They stood near two of the buses. One was situated over a mechanic's hole, oil pan set off to one side. The third bus was at the far side of the building, its hood up. In the middle were the vans and cars. One van was up on a jack, one tire removed. Heavy mechanical work was done by professionals, but basic maintenance could be accomplished right in the garage. All around the garage on the walls were enough tools and parts to open up a small parts store. Overhead, only half of the industrial lights were on, and most of them were dim or flickering menacingly.

Tommen let out a breath. Why did the lights always have to flicker? Did they somehow know what a high stakes, tense situation this was? Wasn't that like some sort of cliché to have them all flicker? Wasn't that along the same lines as it always rains at a funeral in the movies?

"Mr. Wilson?!" Tommen yelled.

His voice echoed, but there was no reply. Wendy stepped back inside.

"Mini-pumper is coming down just in case," she reported.

"They're going to circle around and hose down the area a little so the wildfire doesn't sneak around and bite us in the ass while we're still in here."

"All right then," Carl said. "We'll do a quick check in here, see if we can't find our guy. Be on the lookout for any extinguishers while you're at it. I don't see anything, but nothing smolders forever, especially in a fuel-rich environment like this."

The two of them seemed to have a system they liked to follow, but Tommen didn't quite know what that was. He supposed that an ordinary person would take heart at their courage and determination, their cool attitude and serious demeanor, and so head back outside to let them do their job. An ordinary person might do that. A logical and intelligent person would do that.

Tommen did not do that, and there were several reasons he used in order to try to justify remaining in such an obviously dangerous situation. First, there was no immediate danger that he could see, no fire or anything, and a small electrical fire could be put out by anyone with an extinguisher. An ordinary person with an extinguisher was far more effective than a firefighter without one. Second, there was still the lurking danger of Rifun, that he could be around. Tommen couldn't bring himself to leave the two firefighters alone knowing that the wacko could be waiting for them. To that end, he also wanted to conquer the fear that had swollen inside him, one that compared it to the warehouse and told him to run away as fast as he could before the big, bad wolf got him. Third, Tommen was comparatively smaller than either Carl or Wendy, so he could go places they couldn't easily, such as looking in the mechanic holes. Fourth, even though he wasn't trained in jack shit, if for some reason they had to carry Mr. Wilson out of the garage, an extra set of hands was an extra set of hands, right?

He knew his reasoning was probably flawed. In all reality, he was probably caught either way. If he stayed, shit could happen. If he left, shit could still happen. There was just no way to win. But if that was the case, it made the decision pretty easy. If shit was going to happen, he was at least determined to be around to see it and try to figure out what the hell was going on, versus trying to piece together bits of information from the outside. He'd done quite enough of that already, thank you. He was done sitting on the sidelines; he wanted in.

Although, trying to get in on the action had seen him almost drown and then almost get murdered, losing his hearing at the very least. But staying out of the action had put him at a distinct disadvantage when Micaiah launched his revolution.

There was just no way to win, it seemed.

At one point, Carl announced that he'd found and acquired a fire extinguisher, in the event they determined where the burning was originating from. As Tommen crossed the garage to the far side of where they'd entered, he noted that the smell got stronger. If he had to hazard a guess, it was probably coming from the bus with its hood up. It, too, was situated over a mechanic's hole.

Tommen got down on all fours and peered into the gloom in the hole. It was difficult to see, but at the last minute, he caught sight of red plaid Mickey Mouse pajamas.

"I found him!" Tommen shouted, standing suddenly, knocking his head on the back bumper of the bus. He cursed quietly as Carl and Wendy's heavy footsteps came from the corners of the garage and converged on his location.

Carl brought out a flashlight and flicked it on, shining it around the hole. It was bigger than expected. Rather than just a straight hole, it was like a small room with a workbench and a few tools scattered here and there. A metal ladder descended into the darkness, about twelve feet down. In the middle, about five or six feet from the top was a rolling platform so the underbody could be easily accessible, but without knocking the head of someone below in the workshop.

Mr. Wilson lay the bottom of the ladder, unconscious, bleeding from his head.

"Judging by the blood, I'd say he tried to step off the platform onto the ladder and lost his footing," Carl said. He turned and looked at Tommen. "Go out and grab the EMS guys. If any of our crew are available, get them, too, and tell them what we have. We're going to have to hoist him up." He hiked up his bunker pants. "I'm going to go down and get a better look at things. Is this bus running?"

"I wouldn't think so," Tommen said. "He was going to bring it up to us. No reason to come down here if it was running."

He did not hear what the two of them started talking about after that as he ran outside to meet the ambulance crew as well as a couple more firefighters, presently on watch for either wildfire or other catastrophe. He did as he was told, informing those gathered of the situation. They listened intently, occasionally nodding.

When he was done, it was like pulling the zip strip on a bunch of toy cars, the way they suddenly moved, grabbing this and that, shouting orders, suggesting things, all of it like some sort of perfectly dysfunctional clockwork. They bumped into each other, snapped at each other, and occasionally forgot what they were doing, but they did it all with a fluid grace that, had Tommen not been exposed to some of the missteps of first responders, he might have mistaken it all as intentional.

He followed meekly behind them, noting how the crew paused once they got inside and smelled the electrical burn. A few made hushed comments about it, but Wendy met them and guided them over the hole, at the bottom of which Mr. Wilson still lay. Tommen stood back to let them work, but stayed close enough to hear generally what they were saying.

"Carl, what's the situation?" one paramedic inquired.

Carl relayed his patient findings.

"Do we know where the burning is coming from?" another firefighter asked.

"No, we haven't determined that yet. If you can kill the power and get some scene lights to set up so we can see what the hell we're doing down here, that would be excellent."

"I know where the box is," Tommen volunteered. "I can cut

power when you're ready."

Another firefighter regarded him, then nodded as he stood and headed outside.

Actually, Tommen had no clue where the power box was, but he figured the garage was only so big, and he could always Band if he had to. He moved out of sight of the workers and looked around until he saw the heavy line running down one wall. When he got close, he saw that it was, in fact, the power box.

He opened it up, marveling at all the switches. Most of the labels were worn and peeling, but there was no mistaking the red master switch. When in doubt, kill it all. Worst he was going to do was kill the A/C. A generator fired up noisily.

"Cut power!" someone shouted.

Tommen flipped the switch, but the ironic part was that it almost got brighter. The scene lights the firefighters brought in were brighter than the overhead lights had been. Except for the vehicles being in the way, once Tommen got back to the scene, it was like broad daylight.

"How's the patient, Kevin?" someone asked.

"Breathing and he has a strong pulse," the medic responded from the hole. "The head wound has stopped bleeding for the most part, but his pupils are unequal and very slow to react. Responding only to pain. He's got some possible broken ribs, maybe a broken shoulder, but otherwise, no other noticeable injuries at this time."

A radio chirped and the information was relayed to someone outside the garage.

"How's the ropes coming?" someone else wondered.

"Last rope is secure," Carl reported. A second later, there were heavy boots on the ladder and Carl's head appeared. He handed off four ropes, saying, "I'll stay below and make sure everything goes smoothly from there."

"Is there no way we can move this bus?" another firefighter complained.

"Winch it out with the mini-pumper," someone suggested.

"Hurry up!" Carl snapped irritably. "Should have thought about this before!"

The firefighters scattered. One dashed outside while two more made for the large garage door, using flashlights to look for the manual open chains. A minute later, the large bay door opened, one foot at a time.

"It doesn't need to go all the way up!" Carl said. "Just until the bus can get out of the way! Secure the lines and get back in position!"

Tommen could understand how he might be frustrated about the whole thing. They needed a lot more guys to do a lot more things in a lot less time. Head injuries were nothing to sneeze at, and Mr. Wilson had already been out for at least an hour. Waiting was doing him no favors.

Even as the bus was being secured and winched off the mechanic's hole, a couple of firefighters were carefully raising Mr. Wilson out of the hole. A few more firefighters joined them, and they lifted the basket up and got it onto solid ground. The cot from the ambulance was brought in and lowered, and Mr. Wilson was effortlessly transferred from the basket to the bed, then whisked away. The medic who had been down in the hole with Mr. Wilson hauled himself up and chased after them, shouting orders to his counterpart on the other end.

"Will he be all right?" Tommen asked as Carl stepped over the lip of the hole and stood beside him.

"I can't say for sure, but I definitely think there's a chance," Carl replied honestly. "Head wounds are serious things, but I've certainly seen them a lot worse." He looked at Tommen. "And good job, following your instinct."

"What do you mean?"

"You knew something wasn't right, and you acted on it. Honestly, you could have saved his life. Good job. You ever thought about becoming a firefighter?"

Tommen shrugged. "Not really. And anyway, my dad's a cop, so I don't think he'd take too kindly to that."

"Well, to each their own." Carl shrugged and patted him briefly on the shoulder. "At any rate, now that he's been taken care of, why don't you step outside for a minute? I think we all smelled that burning electrical, so now we're going to get a good look around and make sure this place isn't about to suddenly go up."

Tommen nodded. "Yeah, I think that's about the last thing we need right now, that on top of what's going on over on the other side of the hill."

Carl headed out ahead of him, moving purposefully even as the firefighters outside were gathering various gear and gadgets. Power wand, thermal camera, all the fun toys, going to track down the source of the initial electrical fire, if there was one to be found.

Four of them had no sooner walked in, and Tommen had no sooner gotten within five feet of the door when there was a sound like a wobbly cable, shaking chains, and groaning metal. Half a second later, they all looked up as one of the door chains snapped, falling to the ground and snapping like a whip, chipping the concrete floor and sending shards everywhere. Tommen jumped back instinctively as the door shifted, twisted, strained on the second chain which gave way with hardly any resistance. The door came crashing down, burying itself in the floor. The second chain struck the bus which had been winched forward, sparking against the metal. It might not have been so bad, except some of the sparks hit the battery cables which then caught on fire.

"Aw, shit," Carl said. He looked around. "Where'd that fire extinguisher go?"

The guys looked around dumbly for a second in the near-dark, none of them entirely sure. It did them no favors. The buses were new to the camp, but as far as vehicles went, they were old. When the road conditions were factored in and the strain it put on the buses, they were even older. Not only was the fire electrical, but there were any number of fluids and other fuels readily available to feed it.

"All right, everyone out!" Carl ordered finally. "Man door, that way! Move it!"

The guys still took half a second to grab their lights before heading in the general direction of the man door. Tommen did his best to keep up, but he was not well-versed in escaping from large dark rooms while trying to escape a fire. He was saved only by the light from the fire, but it wasn't much to be thankful for. In just a couple minutes, the entire bus had caught and was now a huge fireball on the far side of the garage. Worse, it was spreading, catching on the work benches, papers and packaging scattered about. Tommen could feel the heat on his back.

He jumped when he felt a gloved hand on his arm. He tried to pull away, but relaxed when he saw it was only Carl.

"Hey, hey, that way!" Carl said, pointing in a different direction. Tommen realized that he'd gotten a little mixed up as the smoke began to thicken. "Keep your head low and follow the light from outside. I'm right behind you."

Right. Keep his head low. Trying to suppress a cough, he got down on all fours, hoping he was facing the right direction. The ground was warm, but he made only small movements, suddenly unsure of what could be on the floor, despite knowing that all his footsteps had been more or less unhindered on the way in. Except for the occasional stack of papers or cardboard box, which were now igniting as readily as the leaves outside.

"Ah!" Tommen jerked his hand back as it touched hot metal, the outside wall of the garage.

"Are you hurt?" Carl asked behind him.

"No, no. Just surprised."

"All right. Keep going. Door is just up ahead."

Tommen wondered how he could know that, given that he'd only been in the room for half an hour total. But maybe it was something learned in fire school, how to commit a room to memory almost instantly. Tommen bumped his head on a hot front bumper, keeping his thoughts to himself, and turned the corner. He was rewarded with the sight of the man door, dim sunlight hazy in the smoke. But he also saw the fire had skated around the outside wall, jumping from workbench to tool rack to posters and everything else. Bits of burning paper and embers floated through the air in front of the door.

"Just jump right through it; then you'll be out," Carl said. "I'm right here with you. You'll be fine."

Tommen nodded uncertainly, gathering his nerve as he faced the fire. It was hardly a fire, really. Just a few embers, he told himself. Floating harmlessly through the air, just like any ordinary campfire. All he had to do was jump through it, like a dog jumping through a hoop at the circus or something. A flaming hoop. But this was less than a flaming hoop.

Just as he was prepared to make a mad, drunken four-legged dash through the door, he was distracted by a fireball that suddenly appeared to his right as the oil pan under the first bus ignited. Instinctively, he tried to move out of the way, but there was nowhere he could go. The sudden ignition saw a sudden intake of oxygen through the man door. The fire carried from the pan into the bus where it spread even faster. At the same time, the door slammed against the wall, causing it to shudder and send several layers of flaming paper and cardboard down in front of Tommen. The garbage next to the door was full. A few pieces on top of the pile fell off, igniting, melting the plastic container until the entire garbage bag went up. Then, as the fire went to take a breath before sucking in more oxygen, the man door suddenly slammed shut. Frantically, Tommen lunged for it, jerking back at the touch of hot metal.

"Stand back," Carl ordered.

Right. Let the man with fire gloves touch the hot doorknob. Tommen managed to stay low, feeling the heat of the fire practically melt his face.

Then the door was open and he shot out like a bullet, stumbling forward until another firefighter caught him, coughing and wheezing. He was quickly handed off to a medic who got a mask over his face, blasting sweet oxygen. He took several huge gulps of air, but could still only cough for a minute or two.

"Okay, okay. You're okay," the medic said. "Breathe. Just breathe. In and out. In. Out."

Tommen did so, trying not to let the dizziness drag him to the ground. He was still made to at least sit on the back bumper of the ambulance which was parked a fair distance from the garage.

"Okay," the medic said, kneeling in front of him with a clipboard and a bag. "How are you feeling? What's your name, by the way?"

"Tommen Forbes," Tommen answered, rubbing his eyes. His skin felt tight and he was hot and cold at the same time.

"All right, Thomas—"

"Tommen."

"Tommy? Okay, we'll go with—"

"No. Tom—" Tommen lifted the mask. "Tommen. Tommen Forbes."

The medic's ear turned bright red as he erased his notes again and did some corrections. "All right then, Tommen, how are you feeling right now? Nauseous, dizzy, confused, anything like that? Did you hit your head?"

Tommen shook his head. "No, I'm good."

"You're a bad liar, you know that?"

He shrugged. "A little dizzy, but it's better. Can I go now?"

The medic still subjected him to a small interrogation. Tommen ground his teeth irritably, knowing that he was probably going to be carted off to the hospital against his will for the sheer fact that he wasn't eighteen and therefore couldn't legally sign a refusal.

He looked over at the garage. It was fully engulfed by now, and one little mini-pumper wasn't going to be able to handle it. What was worse, it was starting to spread to the surrounding landscape, regardless of any hosing that had been done earlier. If everything caught, the firefighters and any remaining campers would be trapped at the top of the mountain. Tommen removed his mask and got off the bumper, unheeding of the medic's questions.

"Tommen, please sit down," the medic said firmly.

Tommen pointed at the fire. "If that goes, everyone up top is going to be trapped. I need to go up and gather my boys if they haven't already been gotten."

"I will radio them and let them know, if the guys down here haven't done so already. They will come down. There is no reason for you to go back up."

"I have to get them and make sure they are all there."

"Someone will do that. Now sit down."

Tommen studied the medic for a second or two. He'd already played the hero once today. Twice, even. The first time, he'd woken everyone up. The second time, he'd helped to get Mr. Wilson out of danger. How much did he want to bet that he could pull off a third time and come out unscathed? As it was, he'd breathed in a pretty good amount of smoke, and had been dangerously close to fire.

He sat.

He put the mask to his face and endured the questioning of the medic once the warning had been called in. No reason to go and play hero this time. About five minutes later, big red trucks started pulling into the dirt drive, too many for them all to fit. More hoses were run and primary consideration seemed to be given to the garage fire. Listening to the conversation, Tommen learned why.

The remaining counselors and campers were on their way, walking and running down as fast as they could. The firefighters were buying them time to get down to the garage drive where the counselors who were shuttling them to town could pick them up. Then, once all the campers had been evacuated, the firefighters would shift and adjust and regroup and, with no civilians to worry about, attack the fire full steam ahead.

It was a nice plan, Tommen thought. Given that it should only take maybe ten more minutes for Shawn and the group to get back to retrieve them—assuming he had his clock straight—they should all be well on their way to safety in no time. That was assuming all went according to plan. Regardless if there was only one minute or ten minutes that they had to wait, until he was standing on solid ground in the park with no fire around him, Tommen wasn't counting anything out.

A minute or two later, the remaining campers arrived, huddling around the ambulance like a bunch of frightened chicks. Even the Wolf Cabin boys seemed pretty docile.

"Hey, are you all okay?" Tommen asked, giving each of them a quick glance.

The boys nodded in turn, all pretty glum.

"Did you find Mr. Wilson? Is he going to be all right?" Dan wondered.

"He should be," Tommen answered, willing it to be true. "Just took a little bump on the head."

"Are you all right?" Harry inquired.

"Yeah, I'm good. Just breathed in a little smoke is all."

"And burned off your eyebrows," Nathan chuckled.

Tommen's hand shot to his face. Well, he still had eyebrows, or so it felt like, but they were probably singed pretty good. His beard felt singed and prickly, too. Well, there went his hopes of impressing Becky. Oh well. He could try again some other time, he supposed. When he wasn't competing—and losing—against fourteen year old boys. There was just something not right about that.

"Well, one thing is for sure," JJ said. "This has definitely been the most exciting year of camp."

"Yeah, I don't think you're going to forget about it easily," Tommen laughed.

"Maybe next year, instead of learning hunting and trapping and stuff, we can learn about building and construction," Harry suggested. "We can rebuild the camp. Cut the logs, saw them down, the whole bit. I think that would be pretty neat."

"Yeah, have our camp first so we can do the heavy lifting, then have the little kids' camp second so they can paint and do the decorating and whatever," Jason continued.

"Maybe you should take your ideas to Mr. Wilson once he's out of the hospital," Tommen said. "Or even while he's still there, assuming he can see you. I think that would be a lot of fun, too."

And it did sound like fun. Hunting and trapping was great and all, but the other half of pioneer life was the home life. For the men, it was about building the house, making sure it was snug and warm and didn't leak or let in mice easily. For the women, it was about cooking and crafting and taking care of the household. That also included livestock, but Tommen wasn't sure how well that would go over. The older kids might be able to handle the responsibility, but the younger kids, well, who knew? It might prove just the kind of exciting challenge they needed. Chickens, rabbits, goats, sheep, horses, the works. Turn the kids loose and see what happened. Maybe they'd get their very own kibbutz going.

Well, fuck. Becky. He was going to have to tell her all about this. He could hear the fretting and the questioning already. Are you okay? Are you hurt? Did you save any kittens from burning buildings? Are you the one who started it? Why didn't you tell me camp was going to be so exciting?

He put his phone away. Maybe he would just surprise her. At least then they could have an in-person conversation about it instead of listening to his phone blow up.

As he did that, the first of the cars, Shawn no less, pulled into the drive as far as he could. The others pulled off onto the shoulder behind him. He got out of his car and went to one of the firefighters. He got redirected to an officer who explained what was going on. They had to evacuate the campers, like, yesterday, and get to safety. The fire was becoming too large for them to handle, and having civilians in such close proximity was not helping. Already it was starting to creep around and they were on the verge of having to evacuate farther down the mountain themselves. If they needed an extra vehicle, the ambulance could take probably a dozen kids if they all packed in there.

"Okay, who do we have left?" Shawn wondered, looking around.

There weren't many. The few girls who were left got loaded

first. After that, it was a matter of campers first, counselors second. Tommen did a final headcount of his boys, the same one he'd been doing for the last ten minutes, then divided them specifically among the vehicles. Everyone had a buddy, and they were to be fully responsible for their buddy until such time as parents came and took them home.

"Hey," Harry said, turning to face Tommen before ducking into Rick's truck. "If I end up leaving before you get down there and stuff, I just wanted to say thank you."

"For what?"

He shrugged. "Everything. I definitely feel like this year has been different, and I'm not just talking about the murder or, you know, this." He gestured to the fire. "I wish Saul were here so I could thank him, too."

Tommen managed a lopsided smile. "Maybe one day you'll meet in your spirit lands and you can thank him yourself."

"Maybe."

Then Harry got in the truck, closed the door, and they were off, pulling a slow U-turn, then gunning it down the mountain.

Well, to say that was unexpected would have been an understatement. It was certainly awkward; Tommen thought that kind of sentimental shit only happened in books and movies. Yeah, thanks for everything, you really made me a better person. People actually said that out loud? And meant it? Weird. Even weirder was that he was the one being thanked.

"Okay, JJ and Dan," Tommen said. He looked around, but could only find Dan. "Hey, where'd JJ go?"

"Said he had to take a piss first," Dan said, rolling his eyes.

"When I said you had to be fully responsible for your buddy, I do mean fully."

"I'm not going to watch him!"

"No, but you could have told someone." Tommen shook his head. "Which way did he go?"

Dan pointed. "Up the road a little ways on the other side."

Tommen sighed. He really didn't want to go after him, but hadn't he just said Dan should have done the same thing? Grudgingly, he got Jason and Nathan loaded up, then went off to look for JJ. The middle of a fire evacuation and he had to wander off to pee. He couldn't wait just a few more minutes until they were down at the park, or even just down at the base of the mountain. Just not right in the middle of the fucking fire. Well, every little bit helps, Tommen figured.

He startled as he came around a tree and almost ran right into JJ.

"Oh, shit!" JJ hissed. "Don't scare me like that!"

"I could say the same to you, wandering off without telling anyone," Tommen said.

"I did tell someone. I told Dan. Which you obviously know or else you wouldn't have known where to look for me. So everyone is fine. I'm fine. I'm away from the fire. And I'm coming back."

In another life, Tommen might have pursued the argument. But he didn't have the time or energy right now. Maybe once they were safely off the mountain, they could have a talk. For the moment, though, he let it go and let JJ pass. The teenager irritably pushed past him and headed back toward the group.

Well, no time like the present. And, now that he thought about it, he kind of had to go, too. He waited until JJ had disappeared from view, just to be certain. Even then, he Banded first before fussing with his belt.

He had to call his dad, too. Fuck. His dad would be working today. Would he be off yet? Not likely. Would his commanding officer understand if he had to skip out a little early so he could save his son from a burning wildfire? Probably.

Still, once he zipped up, he dug out his phone and dialed his dad.

"Hello?" his dad answered.

"Dad, it's me."

"Yes, I gathered this. What's up?"

"Um...flames? About fifty feet in the air?"

"What are you talking about?"

"Well...my campers kind of set the camp on fire and now it's a raging wildfire. We're evacuating down to the park in Wellspring."

"Jeez, Tommen. Just can't leave you alone for ten minutes."

"So...can you come get me?"

His dad sighed. "It's a busy day today, kiddo. I'll see what I can do. It's going to be a couple hours anyway because of the drive."

"Because that's stopped you before."

"If I can't come, I'll see if Micah or Micaiah can't get you. How does that sound?"

"Sounds better than walking."

"You have the right of it there. All right, I'll either see you in a couple hours or when you get home."

"Thanks, Dad. Bye."

He shoved his phone in his pocket and trudged up the hill to the road where he started back down the mountain. As he neared the drive, though, he noticed something was off. Once he got within five hundred feet, he knew instantly what it was.

Everything had stopped. The cars had stopped, the people had stopped. The water spraying out of the fire hoses at a bazillion psi stood frozen in midair. Only Tommen was moving. Him, and one other person. He looked around until he saw Rifun walking casually down the road, straight out of the fiery inferno at the top of the hill.

"I suppose you're going to claim all of this was your plan, your execution, the whole works," Tommen said.

Rifun shook his head. "No. Your boys did this all on their own. And I will say, they did a pretty good job of it."

"So what are you here to do? Taunt me? Make threats? Remind me of our deal?"

"Well, there is that. Since you seem to understand the procedure, we can skip right to the end part. As you can no doubt conclude, you'll be going home tonight, since, clearly, your workplace just burned down. And that's fine. I wish you well. But I decided that, before you go, this affords an excellent training opportunity. You yourself said that you wanted your training to be meaningful. Something you can take home with you."

"Yes...?"

"You also said that nothing I teach you is of any significance since I seem to keep all the best things for myself."

"That's right."

"Would you like to learn one of those things now?"

Tommen's breath caught in his lungs. He didn't want to answer yes. He didn't want to give in. But the things he'd accused Rifun of earlier, he was now sidestepping. He was willing to show him something advanced, something he could use right away. Rifun grinned as he sensed Tommen's reluctance to resist.

"Come with me."

Chapter Thirty-Five
Hell on Earth

Tommen followed Rifun up the mountain toward the camp. The heat was blistering, and Tommen was pretty sure his face was going to melt off if they stayed there too long. The firefighters had abandoned the camp, and the fire had spread until it encircled the parking lot. It didn't look all that bad, really. Once a fuel source had been consumed, fire moved on, so the hillside of the camp was pretty well burned out by now as the fire moved out in all directions, anywhere it could find fuel. The buildings were still smoldering pretty well, but the grass had all given way to black ash.

Rifun paused in the middle of the parking lot and looked at Tommen. "Before we begin, let's see how much you remember from the other night. Show me an Akari Band."

So Tommen went through a dozen different drills over the things he'd learned so far, from simple Bands to double Bands, pinpoint Banding, all of it. Rifun did not say whether he did well or not, merely gave commands to start and stop the various exercises. He did all of this while standing in Rifun's Fast Band.

"Very good," the mass murderer said finally. "It seems you aren't a complete waste of my time."

"Excuse me?" Tommen hissed.

"With all the trouble I've gone through to finally get you here, training, I was afraid you would turn out to be an idiot who wouldn't remember anything he was taught. Turns out you have an excellent memory."

Tommen closed his eyes. *He's toying with you, Tommen. He's trying to get under your skin and manipulate you into submitting to him.*

Don't let him. Keep your head on, stay focused, and find a way out of this. You have to get home tonight.

"When you've quite found your zen...?" Rifun said.

Tommen opened his eyes and followed Rifun as he approached the hillside where the camp used to be. As if the heat wasn't already bad enough, now they were getting even closer to it.

"Where are we going?" he asked nervously when their path did not appear to deviate.

"Did you know," Rifun began studiously, "that wood does not burn?"

Tommen laughed and poorly tried to cover it up with a cough. "Oh, good, I'm sure Mr. Wilson will be glad to hear that. And the firefighters. And I'm sure that anyone with a wood stove is going to be devastated. Think of the logging industry. It's going to suffer."

"Wood does not burn." As he said it, one of the decorative trees which lay in a heap on the curb, which still had some flames on it, suddenly went dry. The fire completely disappeared.

"What happened?" Tommen asked. "You can't Band fire."

"No, but it can be manipulated. Fire requires ignition, fuel, heat, and oxygen. Take away the fuel, and the fire cannot be sustained." Rifun began pacing like an excited professor at the lectern. "Wood does not burn; the gases coming from the wood are what burn. If wood was the substance that burned, it would be considerably easier to burn wet wood and green wood as it lay. But it must be dried first. Have you ever watched the sap boil out of a log as it burns? Once the wood is dry, all that remains is the gas. Add in some oxygen to that mixture, a little ignition, and you have fire."

"What—exactly—did you do?"

"Patience, my young apprentice. This is a very advanced lesson, and I don't want to see you get hurt. See, it is entirely possible for me to stop this fire, or greatly reduce it into something manageable that the firefighters down there can put out before nightfall."

"I would ask what's stopping you, but I think I know the

answer."

"That I'm a heartless bastard? Honestly, Tommen, I'm starting to think you don't like me. If I was that heartless, I would have helped your boys with their fire. More than that, I would have started it myself. Not only that, but I could have barricaded all the doors and windows to each cabin so you all would have perished. After all, what's a hundred more after the slaughter in the Wheel? The only one whose loss would be significant is you, as you are the only Time Agent or Akari-bearer in camp, now that Saul is gone." He ran his tongue over his teeth and sighed. "Perhaps I should have done it that way. You might be a little more motivated to learn, then, if you thought you were saving little kids from certain death."

"You promised to show me something worthwhile. I want to learn it."

The words were out before he could call them back, and he found himself torn by them. Yes, finally, this was something he wanted to learn. It was cool and exciting and advanced and, in this sort of situation, extremely helpful. The camp was toast, true, but the kind of abilities demonstrated here were far more than anything his dad or Micaiah had ever even hinted at. He was tired of feeling like a useless, glorified probie. He wanted to learn.

Rifun could sense the desire and the divide as he grinned. To make a silent point of it, the main hall which was still burning pretty good, suddenly stopped burning. Well, the tree stopped burning suddenly. For such a large structure, it actually took about three seconds for the burning to stop completely.

"This is where that element of faith comes in," Rifun continued. "It's not enough to know that you must get between that which is solid wood and the gas coming off it. You must believe in it, feel even the smallest particles, touch them, manipulate them. If you wish to Band air, you must learn to have faith and be fluid in your use of the Akari. Time is so rigid with so many rules; the Akari frees you from those rules, but only if you let it."

"What do I use?" Tommen asked. "A Fast Band or a Slow

Band? I would think a Fast Band, right?"

"Now we see why I don't start with the advanced lessons. You won't be using a Band for this because it's not about Time. The Akari opens you up to so much more, the vastness of the universe, the very chemistry and physics that make the world go round. The same way I could drown you, even here. Or fix your eyesight, if I so chose."

"So really you just brought me up here so you could gloat and show me that you know something I don't. We've established that already."

Rifun shook his head. "Oh no. I have said that I will show you this, and this I will show you. I am a man of my word, after all. But before we can get to the grand finale, we must first wade through all the boring preliminaries. All of which you are free to use at your leisure as you learn them and practice them on your own, which I am sure you will do since you have expressed such a desire."

The man was too good at this. He knew exactly what to say and how to say it, how to reach into Tommen's psyche and pull out his dreams and fears. He knew how to twist those dreams and fears, playing off them, manipulating situations until all dreams had been met and fears quelled, until Tommen had nothing left to fight with. The only thing he had now was his own experience at Rifun's hand, the warehouse and everything else, but on the psychological plane, Rifun knew how to play this game.

"In times gone by, Akari-bearers were seen as sorcerers as they manipulated the very fabric of space and time," Rifun began. "They were the original alchemists, turning lead into gold, or trying to, anyway. As such, they were imprisoned, tortured, and burned for heresy and witchcraft. Many chose to become reclusive hermits, learning the ways of the earth. It was Akari-bearers such as these who first approached the Native Americans with Time and the Akari. They hoped that by helping the Indians against the white man, they would learn more about the ways of the earth from those who lived most closely with it.

"It was during such times when there was a sort of Akari

Renaissance. Akari-bearers were finally able to perfect their craft, which led to Richard composing his journal."

"Fascinating history lesson," Tommen interrupted irritably. "Get on with it. Give me the goods."

Rifun gave him a hard regard. "We really must have a lesson in gratitude. And perhaps another in patience." Nevertheless, he went on, "In old vernacular, it was said that these pagan Akari-bearers had learned the 'names' of things. They were said to be so in tune with the earth that they could, as you once challenged me, tell a mountain to move, and it would do so. Again, more imprisonment, torture, and burning ensued.

"What they had really done was simply Feel. Take an object and Feel its individual components and manipulate them. To put this in perspective, it would be like taking a tub of ice cream with cookie pieces or some candy in it, and being able to not only feel each individual piece—where ice cream ended and cookie began—but separate them completely."

Tommen let out a breath. "Well, I guess it's better than your dick analogy."

"A human, when he walks into a pizza shop, will smell a pizza in the oven, baking. A dog will smell the crust, the sauce, the ingredients in the sauce, the cheese, and each individual topping. For our purposes, Time is merely human. An Akari-bearer is the dog."

"You've gotten better with your analogies."

Rifun barked a laugh. "Yes, I believe the Author wishes to make a point about the subject." Beat. "Time is but one aspect of the universe. Matter is another aspect."

Tommen nodded. "Okay, so we're going into Doctor Strange territory. Got it. And to add to that line of thought, Energy is probably the third aspect, right?"

Rifun dipped his head. "You are intelligent. Fire would fall into the Energy category. Our concern today is only with Matter."

He turned and started down the hill into the burned out camp. The cabins were still burning pretty well, but the open field was just black ash and a few smoldering embers. It was also very hot, and Tommen hopped anxiously from one foot to the other as he followed Rifun. At one point, Rifun looked back, saw his discomfort, and grinned.

"That would be an Energy lesson. Controlling the transfer of heat so it does not transfer, so you don't burn your feet. Basic Thermodynamics."

Even as he spoke, Tommen's feet no longer burned with each step. They still hurt from any burns he'd suffered already, but there was no new heat transfer. He paused for a moment to look at the bottom of his shoes where the rubber soles had begun to melt. They were cool to the touch.

"Where are we going?" Tommen wondered. "There's enough stuff burning on the other side of the hill, I'm sure. And I still have to walk back so I can get in a vehicle and evacuate so I can go home. Any of this ringing a bell?"

"I am looking for an area where we can be undisturbed and have as few complications as possible," Rifun answered coolly. "As any firefighter will tell you, house fires are becoming far more dangerous because of all the synthetics and plastics used in construction nowadays. I seek a simple lesson where what you see is what is actually there. If it looks like wood, it is wood, not some carbon plastic composite."

Well, it made sense, but did they really have to come all the way down here just to prove that point? There were burning trees around the garage, too.

Eventually, they ended up back in the small clearing where the hollow stump used to be. It had since burned away, but the three stone guardians remained.

"Now, because playing with fire is inherently dangerous, we're going to start with a much simpler object lesson," Rifun said. He gestured to one of the rocks. "All rocks have water in them. When they dry out, they crumble. You may have noticed that in previous campfires."

Not really, but now that he said it, Tommen supposed it made sense.

"I want you to take the water out of the rock," Rifun ordered. "Since the fire is already gone from here, there won't be a lot left."

Tommen stared at the rock for a second. "So, do I just, like, will the water out of the rock or touch it or speak to it or hit it with a stick or what?"

"It may help to put a hand on it at first, much like I had you making Time Bands before Akari Bands, for the visual reference. Then, just as you learn Time, you must also learn how to feel Matter."

"The fuck is that supposed to mean?"

"How do you create a Band?"

"Um...I don't know, I just do. I mean, I can perceive Time and—"

"So perceive Matter."

Tommen looked at the rock a moment longer before putting his hand on it. This was ridiculous. Was he supposed to be fucking Moses right now, calling water out of a stupid rock? It felt like a rock. Imagine that. It was a rock.

At the same time, though, most people would call him weird for his Time abilities. Why shouldn't he be able to manipulate Matter, too? If he could perceive Time—something that could barely be quantified scientifically—why should he have such a hard time with Matter, something he could see and feel?

He stood there, trying to throw himself into the rock. He tried to tell himself about the rock, how smooth it felt, how it looked. He tried to envision the moisture that was still within it, tried to meld the two feelings together, tried to imagine the moisture being sucked out of it as the fire raged on.

After a good sixty seconds, he took his hand off and faced Rifun. "I feel ridiculous."

Rifun shrugged. Somehow he had procured an apple. "You look ridiculous. Try again."

Tommen grunted, but did as he was bade. If he wanted to

control fire and Energy and whatnot, he was going to have to get the water out of this rock.

He looked at Rifun. "The portals that get opened to the Wheel, the Akarin hideout, or anywhere else...that's all Energy manipulation, isn't it?"

Rifun nodded. "It is."

"Why doesn't the study of Time include more about that? Or this? Or any of it?"

"Oh, that's an easy answer. Power. Each aspect of the universe is representative of a flaw. Time is the flaw of fear. The fear of death, as is the case in the Time industry. Control the fear of death and manipulate everyone into doing whatever is necessary to stave off that fear. But consider all the other fears Time is used against. The fear of failing a test, in your case, perhaps? You Band so you can cheat and pass your infinitely important exam.

"Energy is the flaw of power. The Hands of Time have the monopoly on interdimensional travel. And as you know, it is a very unpleasant experience to go through those portals. Make everyone dread that energy and let it remain in the hands of those who have the power to control it."

Tommen raised a brow. "And what is Matter's 'flaw'?" This was starting to sound New Age-y again.

"Desire. Lust, greed, it comes in a variety of forms, just as matter does. Why manipulate matter at all except to change it? Why change lead into gold except for money? Why correct color-blindness except for the desire to fit in and see things as they were meant to be seen?"

"Not all desire is evil. Is it wrong for me to want to see normally? Or...or for a paralytic to walk again? If Saul had known about this, could he have healed his back?"

Rifun shrugged. "I don't know. Maybe, maybe not. But now I've got you thinking. And while we're on this bandwagon, do you know what ties the three of them together?"

Tommen nodded. "Faith. That little bit of Something that

keeps it all moving."

"There you go. Now then, about that rock."

Tommen faced the rock again and put his hand on it. Honestly, it still sounded like hokey New Age bullshit. At the same time, stripping it down to Time, Energy, and Matter, the Akari was starting to make a little more sense. The Akari wasn't really some artifact or mystical ninja Force power; it was the name of the culmination of those three things and those who could perceive and manipulate them. But because of the power that its bearers appeared to have, it was given a name and some fucked up, forbidden history and mythology in order to keep people from snooping too far into it and taking power away from the Hands of Time.

Even as he thought it, his palm felt moist. When he took his hand off the rock, he watched it crack and split into several large pieces.

"Not bad for a beginner," Rifun commented, his tone suggesting he was mildly impressed. "Now do the other two."

Tommen wasn't even sure how he'd done the first one. Maybe it had been his revelation about the Akari, what it was. But as he put his hand on the second rock, he could almost feel it exactly as Rifun had said. It was like he could feel the very atoms that made up the rock, the different deposits and impurities. But he could feel the moisture in it as the thing that still held it in one piece, that filled all the miniscule cracks and pores. He took the moisture and, this time, pressed it into the ground until the rock cracked and split apart.

"Now you're getting it," Rifun said. "And the last one."

Yeah, now he was getting the hang of it. He could do this. He was getting the feel for it. It was like Time. Once he knew something, he felt like an idiot for not realizing it before. This was totally cool. This was way more than his dad could ever teach him in the Arena. Two whole new aspects of the universe were up for grabs.

He stared at the rock, confused, when nothing happened. He tried to feel it. Maybe it was a different kind of rock. He was expecting granite and he was encountering slate, something like that.

"Knowledge isn't enough, Tommen," Rifun told him, finishing off his apple. "It's that little bit of faith that makes the world go round."

"Why don't you need faith to use Time? Why only the Akari?" Tommen asked, not looking at him.

"Such is the way of the Author, I suppose. To keep men from growing too conceited in their power."

"Yeah? Then how do you use it?"

"I have great faith. Greater than most, I believe."

"And that's not conceited?"

"It's a statement of fact. Try again."

This was ridiculous. Rifun was using the faith bit as a controlling force. Pick the one thing, religion, which he, Tommen, appeared to lack, and turn it into a weapon. It was just one more way in which Rifun was trying to subdue him and make him his slave. Well, Tommen had no intentions of being Rifun's slave, apprentice, or anything else. He was going to figure out this Akari thing with or without him.

The rock cracked, and moisture dribbled from Tommen's palm, down his arm. Now what kind of faith had he been demonstrating there? Rebellious faith? The faith of stepping out on his own? Ha! That had been faith in himself, not in Rifun's hokey religion.

"Very good," Rifun said.

Tommen gave him a hard regard. "Thanks. Now can we get to the fire thing?"

Rifun grinned. "The fire thing. How quaint. Such a glorious demonstration of power and you name it like a child. If you are referring to dividing the Matter and Energy of a burning stick, then, yes, we can move on to the 'fire thing.' " He used bunny ear quotes, an awkward motion with his right hand, using his ring and pinkie fingers, seeing how his index and middle fingers were gone. "We will start out with something small. After all, fire is a dangerous thing to play with, and we don't need you to turn up mysteriously injured when you were so close to going home."

He led the way out of the small clearing, back toward the camp. He stopped a short distance from the campfire pit, at a tree that had burned and fallen and was still burning. There were no flames, but it was still glowing bright and hot.

"This ought to be moderately safe," Rifun mused. "Not enough left so it shouldn't ignite and flash over, but still enough Matter and Energy to be manipulated so you can see the effects."

"So, what do I do?" Tommen asked.

"What do we have here?"

"Um...a smoldering log?"

"What forces are at work?"

"Uh...Matter, the log. Energy, the heat and the burning process. Matter again as the chemical makeup of the wood is changed."

"Very good. All those science classes are doing you well. How would you put out the fire?"

"I could take away the heat."

"You could. That would involve manipulating the Energy. What if you didn't want to do that?"

"Then I could...stop the wood from burning?"

"Scientifically, please."

Tommen shook his head. "I would literally have to prevent the wood from chemically changing in the burning process, and I would have to cut off the gas from the heat and the burning."

"Like shutting off the gas to a stove burner."

Well, when he put it like that, it seemed pretty simple, really. Tommen studied the log, wondering if it was safe to touch, or if he should just try to wing it this time. Hand gestures were the things of magic, a sleight of hand, a trick that street magicians used. Going hands-free was where it was at. That's how you really wowed the audience.

But then, maybe he didn't have a choice. Time was something he inherently perceived. Energy was all around him. Matter was something that had to be seen, touched, or observed in some way. Even gases could be observed.

He blinked. Gases could be observed. Heat, as an energy, could be felt. Getting as close as he dared, Tommen knelt beside the log, fixing his gaze on a particular spot that was burning and hoping it would work for the whole thing. Even though Rifun said to focus on the Matter aspect of it, he decided to dabble a little in the Energy side of it, too. He chose something that was easily felt, the heat. He stretched his hand out and let it get as close as he could, feeling the heat as the log burned. It was still pretty hot, too, there was no doubt about that.

He felt the heat, and he felt the gas being given off. He couldn't harness the gas, couldn't catch it, but if he let it go and traced it back, like following a river, he could feel it. He could feel the chemical reaction, the point at which the wood changed chemical composition. It was a nerdy, scientific orgasm if there ever was one, feeling the fulcrum of material change on a microscopic level, feeling both the Matter and the Energy at the same time.

He moved past the fulcrum, past the balancing point, until he felt the wood, or what was left of it. Then, it was just as Rifun said, like turning the valve on a gas line.

The balance tipped, then shattered. The heat dissipated, and the log went cold. The chemical composition went wild for a second, then stabilized until the remains of the tree were just a chunk of burned wood, charcoal at this point. Tommen lifted his hands away from the log and stood.

"I did it."

"Hm, for a second, I thought you meant that literally."

Tommen checked himself suddenly, but he was clean. He gave Rifun a look, but the man only smirked.

"Now then, tell me what else you learned in your little revelation there," Rifun said.

"Disguise is a Matter ability. Gravity is Energy," Tommen told him. "The Akarin have known all along."

"Well of course they have. They are Akari-bearers, or they'd like to be. But then the question becomes, why were they so reluctant to teach you this? Any of this? Even just the smaller great mysteries, like the other aspects of the universe, would have been a good start. It would have given you something to think about while at camp. And as you can see, they don't take much to learn. An afternoon is all. Instead, they try to reteach you things you already know and give you baby food. Clearly, you are not a baby."

Tommen stared at the burned log. Why hadn't Micaiah or Saul or anyone told him about this? He wasn't a child. And this was all so simply explained. He was a science geek, so it wasn't like the terms would be foreign to him. Hell, even some of the worst science kids understood things like "time" and "energy" and "matter," so why hold out on him? Was it because they thought he would be irresponsible? If he'd known some of this shit before, he might have been able to prevent the fire from getting this bad! Just walk up, touch, feel, whoosh, boom, fire out. All is well, time to go back to bed.

"Why don't you try it out on a few more things around camp?" Rifun suggested. "I think the firemen would appreciate all the help they could get."

Tommen nodded. "I do have a question, though."

"I was beginning to worry; you clearly haven't asked enough of them."

"We're doing all of this in a Band. What happens when you drop the Band? What happens when you add Time?"

Rifun grinned, and it wasn't a comforting thing to behold. Tommen almost expected him to say, "And that is the right question." Instead he simply said, "We are in a Band only so you don't mysteriously go missing. Try out your new abilities on other things."

Tommen didn't like it when he got mysterious and evasive, but he knew better than to try and push the issue, not unless he wanted a face full of dirt and ash. Still, he did as Rifun said, turning and going around to various burning objects. Some of them were almost out anyway, and he had a harder time pinpointing the fulcrum of change. Others were still burning steadily, and he had no problem finding the fulcrum, but it took more effort to wrangle the "shut off valve" closed.

He started out on small things like logs and small trees. Once he figured he got a pretty good feel for those, he walked up to one of the cabins, now little more than a burned out shell ready to collapse. Rifun walked up behind him.

"Well now, this is a challenge," he mused. "There's more than one thing burning here. You've got wood, plastic, metal, plus whatever the little campers brought with them which will be made out of who knows what kind of materials. The flames have largely gone, but don't be fooled; everything is still burning."

"Then I'll just go one at a time," Tommen decided.

It was harder than expected, though, because so many of the materials just in the building alone ran together. The logs, the insulating pitch, the melted asphalt shingles. It wasn't just about the chemical composition of the wood, because some of the materials had melted together in a whole new composite material. And it wasn't just about throwing a few things together like particleboard and calling it composite, but these things were a composite at the molecular level.

He backed off from the cabin at large, and instead tried to focus on the smaller things, what little had survived on the inside. He tried to do the floors, but the fabric and plastic of suitcases and clothing made that difficult. The mattresses he didn't even bother to touch since those had become gooey with melted sleeping bags and pillows. The best he managed to do was feel out the heat energy and clumsily dissipate a little of it, get rid of some of the heat, even if he couldn't do anything about the fuel and oxygen.

"A little tougher, wasn't it?" Rifun said when he finally admitted defeat.

"Yeah, a little," Tommen grumbled.

He moved off before his big mouth could get him in trouble again. This time he made for the fort. At least that was all wood, or he hoped so. But then, once he started getting into it and feeling its structure, he felt the fool for not considering all the nails and screws involved. Of course, it was the same thing at the cabins; why had he expected anything different?

But he was determined to get this one right. There were no plastics or anything like that to melt and screw things up; there was just the wood and the metal fasteners. Once he learned to differentiate the two, he was able to slowly reduce the heat and the flames until he could find the fulcrum and move past it to put out the fire.

"You're a quick study," Rifun commented. "Sure you don't want to give that cabin one last shot before you go?"

"Wait, that's it?" Tommen asked.

"What do you mean, 'that's it'? My goodness, boy, I think I've taught you quite a bit today. I wasn't even sure you were ready to learn it, or that you'd make it this far. I was thinking maybe you'd get the rock thing down, get frustrated with everything else, whine, complain, want to go home, we'd fight, I'd threaten you, you'd brush me off, and then go home. But here we are, manipulating Matter to put out fire. What do you mean, 'that's it'?"

Tommen felt his ears turn red. He had actually considered giving up at one point, but he had been more determined to learn something and not get his ass kicked. Finally he nodded. "Yeah, I'll give the cabin one more shot. If I can do one, then I might try the others."

"So very noble of you."

They returned to the camp, to the same cabin where he'd failed before. This time, he was more prepared for the funk of chemicals that were burning, the parts of the walls there were pure, and the parts that were melted and imbued with other materials. He spent a little time just getting a feel for them, what they felt like, how they differed from their "pure" forms, if that was what they could be called. Then he started in on the manipulation, the energy, finding the fulcrum of chemical change.

It wasn't easy, because there were multiple changes and multiple fulcrums. Plastic melting into wood was a chemical fulcrum just the same as pure wood that was burning. He would have to stop each and every individual chemical process in order to put out the fire completely. But that was on the Matter side of things. On the Energy side, he just had to get rid of the heat. Then the plastic would stop melting, and the wood would stop burning.

Dissipating the heat wasn't any easier the second time around, regardless of how much better he understood the chemical processes. Still, he figured that dissipating a little heat was better than nothing. One cabin might not make a difference, but cool off all of them, and it could help things a little. Maybe he was being unrealistic.

So he went from cabin to cabin, dissipating the heat energy as best he could. The fire had gone from the area, so he might as well do what he could. He would do more of this on his way back down the mountain to the vehicles, making it just a little safer for them to get away. The firefighters could do the rest.

"I think you've made a lot of progress today," Rifun said firmly once Tommen had finished up in the last cabin. "You've certainly learned more in just this one day than you have in the last eight months. Such a pity, too."

"You were responsible for the first six months," Tommen reminded him.

"Be that as it may, eight months or two months, you have certainly learned a lot. I'm impressed."

"So that's it? No monologues, evil schemes, threats, anything like that?"

"Here I thought we were past all that. And I was fairly certain that I already made my point the last time we spoke. If you like, I would be happy to remind you."

Tommen took a step back. "No, no, that won't be necessary."

Rifun studied him. "Such a shame. Although, I'm surprised at you. Normally you're a pest for questions, but you haven't pressed on the only one I haven't answered today."

"Which one is that? There are so many."

He smiled again, and Tommen's stomach twisted in fear.

"What happens when you introduce Time to Matter and Energy?"

Suddenly there was an explosion of fire as Rifun dropped his Band. Tommen dropped to the ground and put his arms over his head as he looked around. Rifun remained standing, grinning like a lunatic. "Flash over." He looked down at Tommen. "They're like the magical automatic re-lighting candles. You can blow them out for just a moment, but give them half a second and they'll be right back to what they were." The cabins were like small infernos, blazing high into the sky. "Dissipating the heat isn't enough. You had the right idea when it came to the easy stuff like the logs. But with the cabins, well, you really should have gone all the way or just left them."

Tommen stood. "You knew this would happen. That's why you wanted me to try out the cabins one last time."

Rifun shrugged. "I admit, I had ulterior motives. Consider this a learning experience and a lesson learned."

"How do you dissipate the energy?"

"Now, now, I'm not going to overwhelm you with too much information. Think about everything you've learned, including what you've learned from your failures. We'll talk about them at our next training. Now then, I believe you have a van waiting for you to take you to safety so you can go home."

Rifun moved past him to start walking down the hill. Tommen looked after him for just a second before shaking his head and saying, "No."

Rifun stopped and turned. "No?"

"That's right. No. Teach me. You caused this, now show me how to fix it."

"You already know how to fix it. That's part of learning from your failures."

And he turned and walked away. A second later, he was gone, leaving Tommen amid the inferno. Well, inferno was a strong term. The initial blaze had been startling, but it had calmed down now.

Well, he didn't have a whole lot of time, enough for a quick experiment before returning to the rescue vehicles. He walked over to one of the cabins. In all irony, it was Wolf Cabin; he knew it only by its position relative to the other burning cabins.

So, Matter was out of the question. The chemical processes were too varied and complex. He would have to try that another time. But Energy, the fire, that was pretty straightforward. Fire was fire. He found a relatively cool spot to place his right hand. He wasn't going to manipulate the Matter, but he still wanted to know where it was. Then he reached out and tried to feel the Energy, the heat, the fire, all of it. That, at least, was consistent, or it should have been. Now he just had to end it. Without Time getting in the way, maybe it would be easier to dissipate the heat and kill the fire that way.

But fire was a dodgy thing, and trying to manipulate it in that way was like trying to catch smoke. Well then, maybe it wasn't about going at it from the outside in, but from the inside out. Instead of using Matter as a gateway or a tunnel, just go straight for the heart of the Energy.

As soon as he hit the fulcrum, he knew it was a bad idea. Before, he'd been manipulating the Matter on either end of the balance. This time, he went straight for the balance itself, the Energy that was fire, the chemical process of burning and changing. As soon as he hit it, it hit back, releasing all the energy in an outward force that picked him up clean off the ground and threw him through the air. He reached out, looking for something, anything. He felt like the air was being sucked from his lungs, the strength from his limbs, and every fiber of his being felt like it was being compressed and stretched into shapes it was not meant to go. He saw something white and he reached for it. It might have been a rabbit. It might have been a wolf. Or it might have been the light at the end of the tunnel, in which case, he was fucked.

Chapter Thirty-Six
Ashes to Ashes

Retirement was looking better and better every time the alarm went off, Walter thought. He pulled himself out of bed and into the bathroom. He was getting way too old for this shit. Forget being in his fifties, he was in his hundred and fifties. He needed to retire. At the very least, he needed to look for a job that didn't involve getting up at four in the morning. Sometimes, when he was especially sleepy, he even considered retiring from the field to go teach at the Academy. Sure, classes started at eight, but he still wouldn't have to be up at four.

Then his better judgment got the better of him. There was no way he could teach at the Academy. He just didn't have the patience, or the organization. He knew what had to be taught, but he neither had the ability to organize the lesson plans effectively, nor the patience to deal with idiots and whiners. And maybe that last part was a good thing. Well, he was still going to use it as an excuse not to pursue that career. He would finish out this life in the field and go dark with dignity.

Instinctively, he pushed open the door to Tommen's room, but it was empty. Still off to camp, and apparently having a hell of a time, and he didn't mean that in a good way. Walter had never met Saul, but anyone who knew him said he was a first-class dick. Tommen had confirmed that on many occasions when he texted to complain. But then to see him murdered? Walter sighed. How much more could his son take? Walter wasn't even experiencing some of the things he described, and already he was exhausted just from thinking about it.

Was there any way to talk him into going dark together? One

735

more life together. Tommen could go to college, and Walter could move to a nearby city or town. Maybe he would be retired and just work part-time somewhere, enough to keep himself busy, but still being within reasonable distance of his son.

As he headed out to the car, he knew that wasn't going to happen. It was certainly feasible, but Tommen was intent on other things, and they just happened to not involve his dad, or involve him as much. It certainly didn't entail them living together anymore, but would holidays and some weekends really kill him?

"Well, there's Mr. Sunshine himself," Standish said as Walter joined him in the break room to grab a cup of coffee. "How are you and Laura doing?"

"She hasn't killed me yet," Walter sighed.

"Obviously. And how are you this morning?"

"Exhausted. Too old to be getting up this early."

"I hear you there, buddy."

"Why are you so cheerful, anyway?" He groaned as Jim's smile got wider. "Oh, don't tell me..."

"We got a live one," Standish said. "Or, you know, a dead one. It's a figure of speech."

"I know that. What are we looking at?"

"Not quite sure. Steggmann just handed me the file this morning."

"Greg's here already? He's not normally in until six at the earliest."

"Well, our workload is doubled because of the short staff. His is quadrupled, or worse. Guess the city is on his tail and everything else. I don't know the details, only that he's going to be doing the sunrise to sunset and pitch a tent in his office routine for a while."

Walter grunted. "All right, so where's the file? What have we got?"

It turned out to be an elderly couple shot dead in their home, found by their son. Right from the beginning, Walter smelled murder-suicide. No evidence of a break-in, and the doors and windows had been locked according to the son. No signs that anything had been stolen or rifled through, though the son mentioned that his dad had been trying to give more of their stuff away; he'd thought it was just him trying to pass on as much as he could before he died and the state got hold of it. And as far as the crime scene itself, there was no sign of struggle, and both shots had been clean and precise. The wife probably wouldn't have noticed anything, and there were just certain patterns to look for in a suicide shot.

Still, everything had to be investigated thoroughly. Right off the bat, there was no reason to think that the son couldn't have potentially done it and tried to claim break-in or murder-suicide or something else. Fifty years ago, such a thought would have been horrendous, even unspeakable, but modern crime dictated that Walter treat even kids and other family members as suspects.

It was late when Walter finally got around to the bakery to get his pastry and give his brain a rest from everything that had happened.

"You look deep in thought," Micah commented. "Anything you need to get off your chest? Anything you need investigated off the books?"

Walter shook his head. "No. I need a vacation and then retirement."

"You know, you keep talking about it, so why don't you do it? I mean, it's not like it'll be for that long and you can't do it again later."

Translation: You can take retirement now and live it up for a couple years until you go dark. Then, if you want, you can spend your next life in retirement, and make sure to give yourself a very generous pension so you can live it up again and do what you want.

It wasn't a bad idea, really, except there was just something awful about retiring before his son was out of high school. It made him feel old. He liked it when his son bragged about him being a police officer, a homicide detective at that. Telling his friends that his dad was retired...that just wasn't cool. It might be cool if they were rich and it could seem like the early retirement of a successful businessman, but too many people knew Walter. They knew he wasn't rich. He was just old.

"Well, at the very least, maybe you can take a short vacation before Tommen goes back to school," Micah suggested. "He's been out camping for the last month and a half, going to be gone for another few weeks. Maybe the two of you can do something when he gets home."

"Oh, please, he took the job so he could get away from all us old guys."

"Who are you calling old?"

"You, old man."

Micah grinned and wished him well for the day. Walter wished he could feel so optimistic. Didn't help that Micaiah was going to be leaving soon, and Micah was still a little dubious on whether he was going to stick around for too long after that. What would he do without them? What would he do without their pastries?

"So, you got your happy cake this morning and now you're ready to rock 'n' roll, right?" Standish said when he returned to the precinct.

"I don't know about that, but if you're asking if I'm ready to get back to business, then I guess the only acceptable answer here is yes."

"You sound like you've done this before."

"Only a few times."

It wasn't any kind of back-breaking labor, really, when it came to this type of scene. A lot of phone calls, note-taking, timeline-making, cross-referencing, and so on. Mostly, it was just tedious. It was made a little easier when four out of the six children and most of the other living relatives didn't even live in the area. As for the rest of them, it was pretty much the same story. They were home sleeping. All night. With spouses, kids, whoever. No, they weren't sure what was in the will or if there was any life insurance. No, there weren't any heated family feuds, just the usual bullshit, but nothing major and heated that could turn into this.

Walter took a break around noon or one o'clock to grab lunch, egg salad sandwich with a regular leafy green salad plus a dinner roll leftover from dinner with Laura few nights ago.

"Salad again?" Percy asked, sitting across from him. "Man, you're going to waste away on us."

"I don't know about that," Walter told him, "but if I manage to lose a few pounds, I'll be better for it."

"Are you still trying to impress Laura?" Standish teased, joining them. "Come on, Walt, if she was going to run out the door screaming, I think she would have done it by now. As it is, you got the new car, trimmed up your mustache a little, now with the weight. She's not going to recognize you. And if that happens, she'll leave you high and dry."

"I highly doubt that. And besides, it's good to eat healthy every once in a while."

Standish and Percy murmured their sarcastic agreement, egging him on some more to no avail. Walter was ready to say more when his phone rang.

"Ooh, there she is," Percy laughed.

"No, it's my son," Walter informed him. "Hello?"

"Dad, it's me," Tommen said. He sounded oddly distraught and badly trying to hide it.

Walter shifted in his seat. "Yes, I gathered this. What's up?"

"Um...flames? About fifty feet in the air?"

"What are you talking about?"

"Well...my campers kind of set the camp on fire and now it's a raging wildfire. We're evacuating down to the park in Wellspring."

Walter sighed and rolled his eyes. "Jeez, Tommen. Just can't leave you alone for ten minutes."

"So...can you come get me?"

He sighed again. "It's a busy day today, kiddo. I'll see what I can do. It's going to be a couple hours anyway because of the drive."

"Because that's stopped you before."

"If I can't come, I'll see if Micah or Micaiah can't get you. How does that sound?"

"Sounds better than walking."

Walter grinned. "You have the right of it there. All right, I'll either see you in a couple hours or when you get home."

"Thanks, Dad. Bye."

Click.

Walter set his phone down on the table, the dropped his head into his hands, blew out some air, and rubbed his face. "Oh, I just can't leave him alone for anything."

"What happened?" Standish wondered. "He lose his hearing aids again?"

"No." He looked up. "The camp is burning down. He needs a ride home."

"Oh. Damn," Percy snickered.

"Is he okay?" Standish asked, concerned.

Walter nodded. "He's fine. Says it was his campers who started the fire. It hasn't rained in a couple weeks it seems like, so it's dry as a tinder box up there."

"Shit, no kidding. So, are you going to do it?"

"What?"

"Go get him."

"We're in the middle of an investigation."

"He's your son."

"He's not hurt. It's not an emergency thing. He just needs a ride home."

"From Wellspring. Not like he can just crash at a friend's house for a while or anything waiting for you to get up there later tonight."

Walter rubbed his eyes. "All right. I'll see if I can get out of here."

"We'll cover for you," Standish promised.

"We got the perfect alibi," Percy told him.

Walter gave him a look. "Are you going to tell me what that is so we're all on the same page?"

"Yeah, some EMS unit headed by this really hot chick was calling for law enforcement on a scene, but she didn't want just any law enforcement—"

"Okay, that's enough out of you." Walter shook his head. "What are we, in high school?"

Standish laughed. "Some days I wonder."

Walter hurried to finish his lunch, but did not hurry to get to Steggmann's office. The man would either be so busy, he wouldn't care what Walter wanted to do. Or he would be so busy and so grouchy that no hair could be out of place or else it was an automatic writeup with threatening suspension. He knocked on the door and entered.

"Ah, Walter, good morning. Or afternoon. Whichever it is, I've lost track." He certainly looked harried. "You have something for me on the Karcher case?"

"Only my suspicions at this point, but that's not why I'm here," Walter told him. "Actually, I was wondering if I could duck out a little early today."

"A little early meaning...?"

"Like right now."

"Is this an emergency of some form?"

Walter shifted his stance. "Well...I told you my son is away at summer camp, correct?"

"Yeah, he's the counselor or something. What of it?"

"The camp is burning down as we speak. He needs a ride home."

Steggmann's eyebrows went sky high. "Oh. I see. Dry lightning?"

"Ill-advised campfire."

"Ah. Is he all right?"

"Yes, he's fine. Sounded exhausted, but I don't blame him."

Steggmann grunted. "Well, in all honestly, Walter, I'm inclined to say no because of your case. At the same time, you've been working like a dog lately, and the city is snapping at my heels about hours and overtime. I really don't know what they expect from me. At any rate, it's fortunate for you. Yes, you can go. Get out of here, go pick up your son. Just can't leave him alone for five minutes, can you?"

"Apparently not," Walter said, relieved. "I may just have to keep him home forever."

"Good luck with that one. I'll see you in the morning."

It was a brusque dismissal, and Walter took it before Steggmann could change his mind. He grabbed a last cup of coffee before heading to his cubicle to log out of his computer and grab his things.

"What's the word?" Standish asked.

"I'm heading up to Wellspring," Walter said. "I will see you tomorrow morning."

"Let me know how it goes. I want details, Walter."

Walter did not reply as he punched out and headed out to his car. As he pulled out of the lot, he considered calling the twins, then decided against it. There was no reason for them to know. There was no apparent Time interference or investigation going on. Even if there were, unless it had to do with Rifun, he should be calling his Lieutenants anyway, not the twins. As it was, though, this was a freak accident caused by a lot of dry weather and a bunch of teenage boys anxious to play with fire. He tried calling Tommen back, but couldn't get through. No surprise there; the signal in the sticks could be sketchy at times.

He thought about Banding the drive, but decided against that, too. Aside from how suspicious it would be if he showed up five minutes after being called, Walter knew that there was always work to be done during and after a fire. The firemen would probably want to get a few statements; if Tommen's boys were the ones who started the blaze, then they would probably have to question him a little, too, make sure he wasn't in on it. For Tommen's sake, Walter hoped he hadn't been in on it. That sort of thing could actually land him in jail for all the damage it caused.

So he would just take the drive as it came. It was kind of nice, really, peaceful and relaxing. The drive itself was, not the idiots he had to share the road with. What he wouldn't give some days to have lights and a siren when he needed it most. But that was neither here nor there, and he zoomed along with everyone else on their way to everywhere else.

Say one thing for the new car, it got good gas mileage. Walter wasn't having to stop every twenty exits to get gas or do this, that, or the other thing to make sure the car was going to hold together going at such high rates of speed. When he did stop to get gas, about three-quarters of the way there, he tried calling Tommen again. Again, it didn't go through, even to leave a message. Well, if they were evacuating down to the park in Wellspring, someone would probably have some clue what was going on.

He got back on the highway and set the cruise. Dangerous thing to do that. He hadn't slept well the last couple nights, and without all the bumps, squeaks, and rattles of the Cadillac, he was liable to just nod right off. Where were those self-driving cars when you needed them? Oh well. They wouldn't last one winter in these mountains anyway.

Eventually, once he found his exit, he started seeing signs for Wellspring. Podunk as the town was, it was still one of the only ones out here. In an effort to make West Virginia not seem as deserted as it was, it included even the little podunk towns on the road signs. But about the only thing they included as far as information was mileage. If Walter hadn't been there multiple times before, most recently a week and a half ago, he wouldn't have any clue how to get there. They'd gotten lost on their first trip up.

As he pulled off the ramp and headed north, he had only to look up to see the smoke rising from the mountain. Well, there was a pretty good bet that there was the fire Tommen had been talking about. There goes the camp, up in flames.

Wellspring was a one-road town with only a couple dozen permanent residents, but it had come alive that afternoon. It was impossible to tell who was there as a summer tourist, checking out all three shops in the downtown strip, and who was there for the spectacle, whether to watch the fire and get the gossip or pick up a kid. He found the park easily enough, overrun by kids, adults, firemen, policemen, EMS, the whole crew. Walter ended up having to park a couple blocks away and walk back to the park.

He barely got two steps into the park, when someone called a "Hey, you!" and motioned him over once they got his attention. Only then did it occur to him that, still being in uniform, there was every chance they'd mistaken him as one of theirs. Well, that would change as soon as they saw the patches on the sleeves.

"All right, so, now that you're here, we can—huh?" the officer said, almost launching into full-scale battle plan before the recognition, or lack thereof, dawned on his face. "Who are you?"

"Captain Walter Forbes, Charleston PD," Walter introduced. "My son is part of this camp, and I'd like to know where he is."

The officer, only a road patrol officer, opened his mouth, but had no words except a nod. Then, "Yes. Of course. The head counselor I guess you could call him is Shawn White Cloud. That's him there."

He pointed to a tall man with tan skin and black hair. Walter thanked the officer and approached the man who was speaking with another man and a woman.

"Mr. White Cloud?" Walter asked.

The man turned. "Yes, what can I do for you, sir?"

"I'm looking for my son. Tommen Forbes."

Now the man turned pale. "Tommen is your son?"

"That's what I said. He called me and said you were evacuating to this park. Is he here?"

"Well..." He glanced uneasily at the man and woman, then back at Walter. "No."

"No? What do you mean, no?"

"I mean, he went to round up one of the campers who had wandered off, but then he disappeared."

"What do you mean, disappeared?"

Mr. White Cloud opened his mouth to say more, then turned and called for one of the boys. "JJ! Come here!"

The kid jogged over quickly. He kept his gaze firmly fixed on White Cloud, though it darted nervously toward Walter.

"JJ, this is Officer Forbes. This is Tommen's dad."

The kid, JJ, turned stiffly to look at Walter.

"Tell him what happened," White Cloud said.

"I didn't do anything!" JJ blurted.

"I'm not interested in what you didn't do," Walter told him. "I'm interested in what you did do. What happened?"

JJ shuffled his feet guiltily. "Okay, so we all got our buddies for evacuation. I was with Dan. We were one of the last ones to leave. We'd been up there forever, and I had to take a piss. So I kind of wandered off a little ways so I could, you know? After a few minutes, Tommen came after me and told me I shouldn't go off on my own. Then he told me to hurry up and get back to the car because we have to go like right now. Or then. Whatever. We had to go. I said okay, and that's what I did. I went straight back to the car. I swear, I thought he was right behind me. Counselors were the last to leave, so I thought he just got in a different car or something, you know? I promise you, I don't know what happened to him after that."

"Did he say anything about forgetting something or where he might have gone?"

"No. I mean, he was just super serious that we—had—to—leave. Now. No more talking until we got to the park."

Walter brooded on that for a moment before deciding the kid was telling the truth. He thanked him and sent him on his way, then looked back at White Cloud. "Could he still be up there? I don't know how you guys did it, but what if he got left behind by accident, didn't catch a car or something?"

White Cloud shook his head. "Nope. A couple cars had open seats. No one reported seeing him after that. We called up there to the fire crews, but no one has seen him."

"What's the terrain like up there? Could he have fallen and

hurt himself, maybe he's unable to get out?"

"A few crews have gone looking, but, I mean, there is still a fire up there that they have to fight."

"How is that going?"

"Well, from what I've heard. The winds are still fussy, but there should be some rain coming in soon. Clouds have come in and the temperature has certainly dropped."

"How long until—?"

"I don't know. I really don't. Believe me, I wish I had answers for you. Are you able to call him?"

"No, I can't get thr—"

He stopped and thought a second. He turned and headed back to the officer who'd first met him.

"Something I can do for you, sir?" he asked formally, with all the nervousness of a new recruit fresh from the Academy.

Walter dug out his phone. "What's the non-emergent number for your dispatch here?" The officer gave it to him and he dialed. It took a minute, but someone picked up. "Randolph County Dispatch, how can I help you?"

"This is Captain Walter Forbes from Charleston Police Department."

"Good afternoon, Captain, how can I help you?" Even as he spoke, Walter could hear the dispatcher entering his information, checking his credentials. This would probably get back to Steggmann before the end of the day.

"Can you ping a phone for me, please? Are you able to do that?"

"I expect so. I'll need the number, and if you have a rough idea of where it could be, that would be helpful."

He gave him Tommen's number. "And if you've been getting calls about the summer camp burning down, well, that would be the area."

The line went dead quiet for a moment. Then, "All right, running the number now."

Walter could hear the clicking of the keyboard and little grunts and nonverbal noises of the dispatcher as he worked. After a moment, Walter asked, "Anything?"

The dispatcher hesitated for half a second. The number had probably come up as Tommen Forbes in the system and he'd made the connection between the caller and the phone being traced. "I can't seem to ping his phone, sir, I'm sorry."

"You can't ping it anywhere?"

"No, sir. Not in the county, not in the surrounding counties. It could be that the battery or the GPS has been damaged in some way; that would prevent us from pinging it."

Walter let out a slow breath. "All right. Thank you for trying."

He hung up and looked around. He'd wandered off a short distance where there was less noise and commotion. A few kids were running to embrace parents as they pulled up. One was crying. Counselors were talking to kids or whispering amongst themselves. After a minute or two, Walter returned to the group and found White Cloud again.

"Where's the director of the camp? Mr. Wilson, wasn't it?"

White Cloud let out a breath. "Ah, Jerry was injured in his attempt to get everyone out of the camp and down the mountain. He's been taken to the hospital."

"Bad?"

"Head injury. We don't know how bad."

Walter grunted. "No one else was hurt, I hope?"

"Scrapes, bruises, a few minor burns and some smoke inhalation. Nothing too serious."

"Is there any chance he was able to make it and maybe he got...I don't know, picked up by some emergency personnel? Maybe he was confused, so they just handed him off to an ambulance and kept going?"

White Cloud looked uncertain, but shrugged. "I mean, it's not impossible, I guess. I don't know how likely, but I guess I wouldn't rule it out."

"Where would they take him?"

"Nearest hospital is forty miles away."

"If they're still fighting the fire, I won't be able to get close enough to do a search anyway," Walter informed him. "Where is the hospital?"

He still seemed reluctant, but he gave Walter directions as best he could. Walter thanked him and was soon again on the highway.

Oh, what he wouldn't give to have Tommen in the hospital right now. God only knew what would happen if he'd gotten trapped on that mountain and...

Walter shook his head and forced himself to think of anything else. In the hour it took him to find the hospital, he wasn't even sure what he did manage to think about. Maybe nothing. Maybe that was for the best.

The hospital was small compared to the ones in Charleston, but parking was decent. He headed in the emergency room exit.

"Good afternoon, how can I help you?" the receptionist inquired.

"I need to know if my son came in recently, with the camp fire in Wellspring," Walter said, trying not to sound desperate or pleading.

"Okay, well, we had several kids come in from there."

"His name is Tommen Forbes. He's seventeen and has hearing aids. Tall, skinny, looks like he's going to blow over in a strong breeze, pale as death with dark hair."

The receptionist looked uncertain. "Okay. I don't know of anyone by that description, but I'll look to see if he came in recently. Sometimes we don't get the updated lists right away, especially if multiple patients come in at once. If you'd like, you can have a seat; we have coffee and water for you."

Walter didn't need the coffee, but the water helped calm his nerves a little while the receptionist disappeared into the depths of the ER. He did not need this today. He didn't need this any day, actually. Tommen stays home, he gets into trouble. Tommen goes out into the world, he gets into trouble. Was there nowhere he could go where he wouldn't get into trouble?

After about ten minutes, the receptionist returned. Walter stood eagerly.

"We do have one potential patient. He's a John Doe, came in unconscious with no ID, still hasn't woken up; they're getting ready to move him upstairs. No hearing aids either, but if you want..."

She seemed uncertain about it as Walter agreed and followed her back.

"Official police business," he told her. "If it's not him."

She nodded absently and led him to one of twelve emergency rooms. When she opened the door, Walter's heart sank. It wasn't Tommen. By a basic description, it might have been him, but that wasn't his boy. He sighed, shook his head, and took a step back. She nodded and closed the door.

"I'm sorry," she said. "I wish I could help."

He nodded. "You've done all you can. Is there anywhere he might have been taken?"

"I don't think so. It depends on his injuries. Anything really severe would probably go to Charleston to one of their trauma centers."

Walter let out a breath. Well, there was nothing more he could do here, then. He thanked the receptionist and saw himself out. He sat in his car for a minute or two, trying to decide if there was any other possible explanation for Tommen's disappearance. Besides, well, that. After a minute, he decided there really wasn't any, unless he'd been so severely injured that he'd been flown to Charleston. But if that was the case, one would think the rescue effort needed would stir up some news among the firemen which might get passed along to the counselors that, hey, one of your guys might be hurt, just FYI.

On his return to Wellspring, he stopped for a quick fast food dinner. Well, so much for the salad at lunch, but he needed some food to clear his head and give him energy because he had a feeling it was going to be a long night one way or the other.

By the time he returned to the park, it was getting dark. All the kids had been picked up, and most of the counselors had gone home. Even the police, fire, and EMS has dispersed, all but one or two, probably jotting down final statements and contact information. White Cloud saw him before he got too close.

"Anything?" he asked, looking concerned.

Walter sighed and shook his head. "No, he's not in the hospital. Anything more than a minor wound I think would generate enough buzz that someone would have heard and or seen something."

White Cloud nodded. "True. But listen, I heard over the radios that the south side of the fire is out, and the north side crew is just about wrapping up. They're going to be starting on overhaul, if they haven't already. You could probably go up there and see if you can't snoop around a little."

Walter nodded. "Maybe I will. Thank you."

It was a minute or two before he actually got the nerve to walk back to his car. Could he go up there? Should he go up there? Could he really face it if his son had died on that mountain? He couldn't do it. He had to. He wanted to run away and pretend it was all a bad dream. He had to know one way or another.

And anyway, he told himself, there was no guarantee that he was dead. Maybe he'd hit his head, gotten a little turned around, and was wandering around the mountain somewhere, lost and confused, but otherwise safe. That was entirely possible, too. Maybe he'd just gotten a little turned around anyway, trying to get back to their pickup location. If that was the case, then Walter had little doubt that his son would be able to not only survive, but find a way to either get back to civilization or bring search and rescue to his location. Tommen was a smart kid; he would find a way to survive one way or the other.

It was a meager hope that Walter clung to as he made the turn and headed up the winding mountain road toward the burned out camp.

Command had been set up at some husk of a garage or pole barn. Walter parked just off the road and walked into the post where it appeared that a fire officer was marking things on a map and handing out various team assignments. Walter waited until the majority of the people had been scattered before approaching.

"Can I help you, Captain?" the fireman, his helmet reading Deputy Chief, inquired as he looked at Walter's chevrons.

"My son was a counselor at this camp," Walter told him. "He's not at the hospital and no one else saw him come down off this mountain."

The firefighter nodded slowly. "Yup. We've heard. We have orders to either search and rescue or search and recover. I've got guys searching his last known location and the whole burn site. Once that's been cleared, we'll start on everywhere else."

"Thank you. With your permission, I'd like to join them."

"As you wish. I can tell you that it won't be very long; we try to limit our night ops. We don't need any of our guys wandering off in the middle of the night, if you know what I mean."

"I understand. From what I've gathered, the burn was only difficult, not large."

"That would be a modest assessment."

"Point is, searching the burn site shouldn't take long. And I'm less worried about him if he isn't here. If you know what I mean."

The man dipped his head once. "Of course. If you'll follow me, I'll point you in the right direction."

Walter joined up with one of the burn site groups. While he was shocked at how different the camp looked with all its burned out husks, he was also remarkably surprised at how well the buildings had held up overall. It was hot and dry and the logs not much better, but they were still heavy log cabins. They could burn forever, but they wouldn't burn down easily.

They started on the west side and methodically made their way east, scanning the ground, turning over rocks and logs and unidentified burned objects of all shapes and sizes. They did not go inside any of the cabins or buildings; a separate team did that.

Perhaps the only comfort that evening came from the fact that no one called out to report a body. As far as the search crews were concerned, everyone had at least made it out of camp and escaped the fire. Still, it was a meager comfort, and Walter was too grateful for the coffee that was given to him when they finally returned to the command post.

The Deputy Chief went over notes and observations from the teams. He introduced Walter and made sure everyone knew his face and how he was related to the search and rescue operation. Then he handed out assignments for the next day so that way the teams could come in and get right to work. Since the burn site had been cleared, they had a lot more ground they needed to cover.

"Are you going to be out tomorrow?" he asked as Walter refilled his coffee before leaving.

Walter hesitated. "I'd love to. I really would. I don't know that I can. I've got a case I'm working on and I was lucky to come out today when my son called and said he needed a ride home." He took a drink. "But if he's out there, I know he's alive, and he'll find a way to survive. It's just what he does."

"Well, we'll let you know as soon as anything comes up. Do you have a business card or something? Sorry, I tend to lose things in these loose notes."

Walter fished out a business card and handed it to him. "Any time, day or night. Chances are, I won't be sleeping tonight anyway."

"I understand. Until tomorrow, then, Captain."

Walter thanked him, got in his car, and maneuvered carefully around until he was facing the right direction. Once he was safely on his way, he fished out his phone. He hesitated for a moment, wondered if he should. Maybe he was just overreacting. No body had been found. That meant that Tommen was still alive out there somewhere. They just had to find him.

At the same time, if he hadn't been able to make his way back to the road—or any road—and his phone had been broken so it couldn't be pinged, that meant that he was probably injured, likely a head injury. What if it was serious? What if he was lying unconscious somewhere in the leaves, unable to call for help or assist search and rescue in any way? What if he was alive now but wouldn't be come morning? They should have kept searching. He should go back and keep looking. He shouldn't give up.

But he just plodded along, making the turn to head back through Wellspring to get to the highway. All was quiet in the dinky town once more. When he'd gotten on the highway and set his cruise, he fished for his phone again.

"Yeah, Walt," Micaiah answered.

"Cai, I need your help," Walter sighed.

"This doesn't sound good."

So he relayed the tale, from getting the call to his conversations with the counselors, his trip to the hospital, and finally the unfruitful search and rescue.

"Shit," Micaiah sighed. "Can't leave that boy alone for ten minutes. Well, Walt, what would you like me to do?"

"I don't know. I know that you and anyone you can rally up are only as good as the search and rescue teams. But I do have one idea, and I'm not sure how much you're going to like it."

"At least you're honest. What do you got?"

Walter explained his idea. He could almost feel the frown on Micaiah's face, feel it deepening with each layer he added onto the plan.

"Well, it would certainly put them to work doing what they do best," Micaiah said finally when Walter had finished. "And we did use them once as common animals. I don't know that we still could, though. It's been a long time."

"It's all I got. I understand if it wouldn't work."

"I'm not going to discount it just yet. Who knows? In this war with the Borelians we got going on, it might be helpful to have them around anyway. I'll give it a shot and let you know what I come up with."

"Thanks, Cai."

"All right. Take it easy, Walt. Get some sleep tonight."

"I make no promises."

He hung up before Micaiah could protest. After a few more miles and a few more debates, he picked up his phone again.

"Hello?" a female voice wondered sleepily.

"Laura, it's me. Did I wake you?"

"Only a little. What's up?"

"You're not working tonight, right?"

"Nope. Not sleeping either, apparently."

"Do you mind if I come by?"

"Now?"

"Well, I'm about an hour and a half out."

She groaned. "What's this about, Walter?"

He hesitated. Then, "Tommen's missing."

"Missing? What do you mean, missing?"

He told her the story, the same one he told Micaiah. When he was finished, Laura was silent for a long moment, and he was afraid she'd fallen back asleep. When she did speak, her words were slow and deliberate.

"Walt, if you need to come over tonight, by all means, I'm here. But I would really recommend you go home and get some sleep. Sleep on it, get some rest, get some food, and clear your head. I'm not working tomorrow, so we can have lunch or something, whatever you want to do. All right?"

He reluctantly agreed and hung up.

It was a long drive back home, and the house never felt more empty. Actually, he knew this empty feeling; it was the same one he'd gotten when Rifun had kidnapped Tommen last fall.

Walter slogged through his nightly routine, exhausted, but, once he actually got in bed, unable to sleep. His alarm was going to come way too soon. Then he would have to go to work on a case he didn't care about while his son was still missing in the wilderness. After probably half an hour of batting the idea back and forth, he rolled over and rummaged in his night stand drawer, bringing out a plastic bag of pills. He tapped a couple out, chased them down with water, then lay back and tried to sleep.

Epilogue

Tommen's first sensation was searing pain, burning agony racing through his left arm. His mouth opened in a silent scream even as dusky gray light hit his eyelids. He opened his eyes just in time for rain drops to hit him square in the face. He squeezed his eyes shut and turned his head. His body was awash in confusing, simultaneous feelings of extreme hot and extreme cold. One minute he wanted to strip off every layer of clothing he had; the next, he couldn't get warm enough.

But through it all was the pain. He couldn't find anything to block it out as it tore through him. Tears streamed down his cheeks and his breath came in ragged gasps. Each rain drop on his left arm may as well have been a bullet tearing through him.

Come on, Tommen. Get up. You can't just lay like this. Get up!

Taking a breath—okay, multiple ragged, wheezing gasps, he forced himself to sit up, gritting his teeth and biting his tongue, telling himself to take in his surroundings and calm down before assessing the pain and any injuries.

He was alone in the forest, a short distance from the cabins. Everything around him was burned and dead, but the fire was out. Overhead, gray clouds finally dumped much-needed rain on the parched land, about twenty-four hours too late.

He shivered again. Halfway through the shiver, a heatwave rolled through him. Then another shudder of cold. What was wrong with him? Had he caught a cold or something in this rain?

He groaned as he tried to twist and get a feel for himself, something other than the pain. As long as he wasn't moving, it was bearable, almost forgettable. But every little move was agony. Finally, he dared to look at himself, and he didn't like what he saw.

His left arm where he'd touched the fulcrum of energy in the fire was burned. And it wasn't just a little accidental touch on a hot stove. His hand was white and blistered atrociously, everything from wrist to fingertip swollen grossly and barely able to move at all. Worse than that, though, was the rest of his arm. He didn't imagine that it was in much better shape, though it was hard to tell as his jacket had melted to his skin, from his wrist all the way to his shoulder and just under his arm. His collar was still somewhat loose, though his neck, ear, and ribs felt more than a little tender

What the hell happened? He couldn't remember. Well, either way, he had to get off this mountain and get some help.

As he stood, nausea washed over him and he was driven to his knees, throwing up anything he had in his stomach, which wasn't much. The motion made every muscle tense and soon he was crying, from the pain of throwing up to the pain in his arm. He shivered and sweat and shivered and sweat again. He was dizzy and nauseous and extremely thirsty, actually.

Come on, Tommen. You have to find a road, find a town, find some kind of civilization. But you can't stay here.

After a few minutes of recovering from the pain and another few minutes of gathering his nerve, Tommen stood. He was unsteady and still quite sick, but he had to find help. Survival instincts were kicking in, slowly but surely. Stumbling forward, he made his way up the hill to the parking lot, then followed the road down the mountain.

Author's Note

I'd like to think that *Free Time* demonstrates a huge shift in the plot and the way The Chivalrous Welshman is presented, if not the whole of The Timekeeper Chronicles. For the first time, we're seeing Tommen out in the wild without backup and without much guidance, and he has to navigate by himself everything from keeping track of bratty children, to dealing with new bosses and coworkers, to saving lives and keeping calm in an emergency, or multiple emergencies.

I admit that Saul was a lot of fun to write, and he is one of my favorite characters. He's not modeled after anyone I know, though he does come across as the personification of what goes on in my mind when I'm interacting with people. There are the things I do, and there are the things I would like to do. Or say.

The good news is that you are able to dive deeper into the story of, not only Saul, but the Krydik people as well. *Wolf Pack* is the first of three books following three generations of the Wolf family, starting with Saul's grandfather, as they move from Earth and everything they've ever known, to Hlohi, desperate for an escape and peace for themselves and their tribe.

Free Time was very enjoyable to write because it opened up so many new possibilities outside of Charleston and outside the usual cast of characters. It was almost like writing the start of a whole new series. I got even more excited when I started to loop things back on itself, introducing the Books.

For any author, writing yourself or your works into your own books is terribly risky. Some consider it author suicide if it's any more than a passing mention, an Easter egg. As you will see, however, as you dig into The Timekeeper Chronicles—not only The Chivalrous Welshman—you will find that they can happen no other way, and I do hope it provokes some serious critical thinking and even makes your brain hurt a little.

Leap Second is going to be a lot like *Tick Tock*, in that, it only spans an incredibly short period of time. But it will introduce several characters we've only been introduced to in passing, and it is going to set up everything that happens in the following three books of TCW. The stakes are getting higher and sides must be chosen.